A Suitable Concealment - J.J.Roberts

Chapter 1

Six and a half years ago

Amanda

Now is not the time to realise that if she'd been more inclined the night before, then she wouldn't be in such a rush now. Distinctly, Amanda Davies remembers looking at the contents of the fridge: the wedge of cheese, the ham, yogurt and fruit, everything she needed to make her seven year old son's lunch in readiness for the morning, and she recalls firmly closing the door, reassuring herself that making Oliver's lunch was a two minute job at most. So she returned to the bottle of wine and the new ITV drama.

In the cold light of the next morning, it's taking a lot bloody longer to make a simple lunch because everything is conspiring against her. Oliver's sandwich box isn't in its usual place, the ham isn't ham but garlic sausage, and the yogurt is out of date because Oliver didn't stay last weekend and neither she nor David like eating kids' yogurt.

She has so much to do and must be at the salon before 9 when her first client is due. And the builder…. Shit! What time is he starting?

She reaches for the jar of sandwich pickle at the back of the fridge, but her fist clips the bottles of home-brewed beer arranged like a triangle of ten-pin bowling pins.

'For God's sake, David,' she hisses angrily to herself, straightening the bottles. 'Must you keep this piss water in the fridge?'

On the radio in the corner of the work surface, the *Take That* song finishes and the presenter helpfully informs his listeners that it's eight o'clock and time for "news and weather where you are".

She slaps another slice of bread on the sandwich, slices it in half even though Oliver prefers quarters and, with an apple and a carton of blackcurrant juice, locks the lot inside his *Thomas the Tank Engine* lunchbox.

Her hand hovers over the packet of Penguin biscuits by the bread bin but, after yesterday's little find, Amanda is limiting Oliver's treats. She suspects that it's not Declan who is making their son's lunches, even though he assured her otherwise, but that it's that fat cow he lives with, and she loads Oliver up with crisps, sweets and chocolate because that's how she makes her own brats' lunches. Amanda found far too many empty wrappers tucked inside the lunchbox and schoolbag to ignore so later she'll be having words with Declan again about this and, if it continues, then she knows exactly the threat to issue.

'Roadworks on the A5689 are still causing problems with reports that drivers can expect up to a 15 minute delay to their journey,' Tara the Traffic Tart cheerily informs Amanda.

She glares at the radio and reaches over to turn it off, but a loud squeal from the back garden makes her jump with fright.

Through the kitchen window, she watches Oliver, duffle coat around his upper arms, race around the damp lawn, arms outstretched like an aeroplane, whooping with joy. Standing in goal, the crossbar level with his waist, is David, Amanda's husband, his hands out as if to catch the ball in a stooped stance, an amazed smile on his face as if to say how-did-that-happen?

Amanda dismisses the rapidly disappearing time and the fact that they all have more important places to be. She is very conscious that this opportunity cannot be wasted. Another may not present itself for several days; it's already been nearly a week since she last looked.

She checks they're still outside, embroiled in their kick-about, before walking to the end of the work surface where David's mobile phone is on charge.

She picks it up and quickly presses a button on the side of the device, waking it up. The screen illuminates, warning that the phone is 86% charged. She presses the button at the bottom and the screen changes, revealing the phone's icons. Firstly, she checks the texts. There are no unopened messages. Her eyes scan the list of read text messages, fear rising in her throat, but it's soon quashed when she sees that the only people to have contacted David are her, his mum, that awful mate of his; there are certainly no female names unless Paul is really Paula, but she has no time to check the content of the message. David could barge through that door at any moment. She checks emails next, but nothing there either apart from ones trying to flog yet more brewing equipment. She taps the icon for photos, wondering if perhaps on one of his nights out he decided to take a selfie with a girl, but there's nothing untoward. Finally, she checks his browser history.

And is surprised to see that last night he visited a porn site.

She feels a spark of anger. Porn for God's sake. What does he need porn for? Is that what he's looking at when I'm out or asleep? How long has he been doing this?

4

Her finger hovers over the button; she's intrigued to see what type of porn because she can't gauge from the website's name what it might be. What if it's women younger than her?

A sudden screech outside reminds her of the danger if she's caught so, with annoyance, she moves on, scrolling through the list of subjects in the search box: more brewing equipment, lock-ups to rent. She rolls her eyes. He's still on about getting a bigger premises. As if the shed isn't big enough. Adidas trainers...like he doesn't have plenty already.

Suddenly the kitchen door opens, crashing into the wall behind and, at the top of his voice, Oliver shouts out, 'Mummy! Did you see my goal?'

Amanda jumps with fright, emitting a tiny screech of her own. Why didn't she hear them coming? The phone falls from her hand, but the attached charging cable stops it from landing on the tiled floor. The weighty phone is suspended in front of the closed washing machine door and swings guiltily to and fro.

'Shit,' Amanda mutters, scrabbling to put it back in its place. She's aware David is standing behind her son, his view unobscured, his eyes watching her.

'Mummy,' Oliver says in an accusing tone. 'You swore.'

'Is that my phone?' David asks, easing himself around the child and further into the kitchen.

Her hands don't appear to be working. She has never been caught handling his phone like this before.

'I'm sorry...I...' Finally she grabs the device and heavily puts it back down on the work surface, whilst the excuse she had in readiness for an event such as this comes back to her.

'I thought your phone was ringing,' she lies, 'but it must have been mine. Right young man,' and she turns to Oliver, ignoring the questioning look on David's face. 'Have you brushed your teeth?'

'Yes, Mum,' Oliver replies. 'David helped me.' And he looks up at him.

David ruffles the boy's blond spiked hair, a style similar to his own.

'Me too,' David replies cheekily, making Oliver giggle. 'Have you, Amanda?'

Her eyes blaze with embarrassment. Of course, she has. Hasn't she? Her hand reaches up to her long amber-coloured hair. It's loose around her shoulders and Amanda never goes to work with it like this. She would have done her make-up, hair and teeth at the same time, so no she hasn't brushed her teeth. Shit. She is going to be so very late. She could honestly do without these last-minute sleepovers. What exactly is this important reason of Declan's that Oliver had to stay over last night when it's not one of their arranged nights? It has thrown her off kilter.

'I have, yes,' she informs him haughtily and mutters, 'Idiot.'

'There's no need for name calling. Not in front of,' and he points to the top of Oliver's head. 'Sets a bad example.'

His grin annoys her all the more and she stomps upstairs.

Minutes later, as she descends the stairs, her teeth glistening, hair up and make-up fully on, she finds Oliver patiently waiting by the front door, coat on properly and buttoned up, schoolbag slung across his shoulder. David is kneeling in front of the boy, clipping the lunchbox shut, the cuff of his black t-shirt hiked up revealing the Celtic band tattoo and his multi-coloured sleeve. She spots the area of bare skin on his forearm where he promises to get her name inscribed as soon as he's got the money.

'Not a word, mate,' David is whispering with a wink and suddenly Amanda is horrified. Her reaction is instant. She pushes him aside, nearly toppling him onto the hard floor, and snatches the lunchbox from tiny fingers. As she yanks the lid off, a chocolate roll and a bag of jellied caterpillar-shaped sweets fall out. She holds them out in front of David accusingly.

'He's not allowed sweets.'

'Why not? You haven't been naughty, have you, mate?' David asks Oliver who vigorously shakes his head.

'Declan and that…' she struggles to find an alternative word for that fat cow which can't be construed as name calling.

'Kerry,' David offers helpfully.

'Oliver's been eating too many sweets lately. I don't want his teeth rotting.'

'Which is why we clean them, isn't it, mate?' David winks at Oliver who grins and nods.

'Stop calling my son "mate",' Amanda snaps, voice rising. 'He has a name.'

'Amanda,' David begins calmly, glancing at the child, 'at least let Oliver have the sweets. He can share them with his ma- his friends.'

'No. He's my son. I decide what he eats. Not you.'

Offended, David backs away, hands up. 'Yeah, you're right. It's nothing to do with me.' He smiles at the boy and cheerily says, 'See you later, mate, have a good day at school.' He retreats to the kitchen, closing the door behind him.

Amanda snorts with humiliation. Yet again, David has made her look the bad guy.

Oliver stares up at her, a tiny frown between his eyebrows. 'Mum, why do you always—'

But she cuts him down.

'Let's go. Now, Oliver.'

*

Amanda looks across at Oliver sat in the passenger seat. His face is turned to the glass though there's nothing interesting to see, just other kids making their way to school albeit at a faster speed than they are. They've been stationary for several minutes and Amanda is too far down the queue of traffic to see what the holdup is. Oliver emits a small cough and it amuses her that he even does that in a sulking tone. Sulks just like his father, she thinks. Another child.

It's because she wouldn't relent on the sweets, but that's David's fault. He's always doing things behind her back. She tells Oliver five more minutes and David gives him twenty; she tells him it's mashed potatoes and David gives him chips; she says homework and David gives him telly. It's a constant battle and she's always the villain.

'Where's my list?' she suddenly asks aloud and Oliver turns to her. Amanda looks around the car, the compartment by the gears, in the door pockets, in the footwell. It's her to-do list, scribbled yesterday evening in between glasses of wine and whatever crap was on the TV. Without it, she has no idea who she's supposed to call today, what she's meant to order, and…what was that other thing? She scratches her head, tries to retrace her thoughts. What was she scribbling on?

'Ollie, are you sitting on Mummy's list?' He shakes his head moodily. 'Please don't sulk—'

'It's Oliver,' he corrects her. 'That's my proper name.'

She mashes her lips together to stop laughing at his smart retort, something he gets from her.

'Okay, you're right. And I'm wrong about the sweets.'

'I like David being my stepdad. He's fun. And I like being his mate.'

'I know you do. Can you just lift your bottom up, please? I need to see if you're sitting on…'

With a sigh, Oliver unclips his seatbelt and lifts himself off the seat.

'Thank you. Put your belt back on.' Amanda thinks. Shit, it could be anywhere. What was I even writing on? Oh, yes. It was the receipt from Tesco's petrol station. She found it in David's black fleece pocket.

'Oh, oh!' Oliver says, pointing with excitement at two small girls wearing pink coats and carrying pink rucksacks with sequinned unicorns on the back, strolling unaccompanied down the street. 'There's Lola and Scarlett. Can I walk with them?'

Amanda peers through the windscreen at Kerry's daughters. 'Where's their mother?'

'Don't know. Mum, can I?'

Unable to miss the opportunity to find out what's going on in Declan's life, Amanda makes her own suggestion. She'll drive all three of them to school. The girls need little persuasion. Turning up at school in a posh black car is exactly the sort of enticement they need. They climb into Amanda's 4x4 and run their hands over the leather interior in amazement.

'Where's your mum, girls?' Amanda asks, peering at the children in the rearview mirror.

'She's sick,' Lola, the older girl, replies. 'I heard her throwing up in the bathroom. Declan is looking after her.'

'We missed you yesterday, Ollie,' Scarlett quietly says to him. 'We went to Nan's. We had pizza for tea.'

So the impromptu sleepover affected Kerry's daughters too, Amanda thinks. Wonder what's going on.

'Did Declan take your mummy out for a surprise meal last night, girls?' Amanda asks, careful of her tone of voice. Not that Declan can afford meals out. But if it was somewhere cheap, Kerry may have a bout of food poisoning. Amanda sniggers at the thought. 'Is that why the three of you couldn't stay home?'

'Mummy went to the hospital,' Lola explains.

Maybe she's got appendicitis, Amanda wonders bitchily.

'She came back with a photo,' Scarlett announces. 'I found it in her handbag.'

'What was it?' Oliver asks.

Maybe she had a camera shoved up that big arse of hers, Amanda thinks, turning up the air-con.

Scarlett shrugs. 'Mummy said they didn't want to know. Declan said it would ruin the surprise.'

Amanda's eyes widen and she stares ahead, oblivious to the gap increasing between her and the car in front.

8

You've got to be kidding me, she thinks. Two adults, three kids and a newborn in *that* tiny house. What the hell is Declan thinking, getting that fat cow pregnant? He can barely afford one child. Did he do it on purpose? Or was it like with her, too much alcohol and failing to think with his head?

Even the sharp honking from the driver behind fails to snap Amanda out of her thoughts.

'Mummy!' Oliver shouts, making the sisters giggle. 'You're holding everybody up.'

Amanda shakes herself from her thoughtful trance and engages first gear. She will not have her little boy pushed further aside and neglected because Declan insists on producing a second family.

Chapter 2

Tamsin

Tamsin pauses mid-flick through the appointments' book to examine her nail varnish. The candy pink colour complimented the sparkly dress she wore on Saturday night in *The Solo* nightclub, but now her nails remind her of Barbie dolls and rainbow stickers.

She flicks a flake of pink off her thumbnail and onto the white lined page. She blows and it disappears. She looks back at the diary to see who her ten o'clock is, her heart falling at the name.

Fucking hell, Tamsin thinks miserably, I could do without that old bag. All she goes on about are her grandkids and how well they're doing. Like I give a shit that what's-his-name is on for a First in maths.

Tamsin doesn't know how she can summon the energy to listen to this client. It's not even as if she can switch her ears off. The woman will study Tamsin's reflection in the mirror and Tamsin will have to put on her mask and nod and smile. After all, some clients treat their stylist like a confidante.

Not that I get paid enough to listen to their shitty drivel, she thinks.

She can't believe the hangover she's had since Sunday morning is still lingering 48 hours later. Fucking hell, she must have been knocking the vodka and cokes back. Not enough to let her standards slip though. The nameless man she got to know on the dance floor was easy on the eye; she can't recall his name now. Maybe the music was too loud but, she couldn't care less what it was. They weren't going to make an everlasting couple.

When she woke up in his bed the next morning, she carefully grabbed her clothes and descended the stairs as quiet as a mouse, dressing in the cold kitchen before leaving the house, her strappy pink stilettos rubbing her bare heels painfully.

Her thoughts wander back to that night, not the nameless man; she only went home with him in the hope it would temporarily fill the void left when *he* walked out of her life. Did the one-night stand help? Has it gone some way to easing the pain and loneliness?

No, it has not, she sadly concludes. They never help.

My life is shit, she concludes. It wasn't meant to be like this.

She looks around at the salon. The pastel-green walls, the pale pink-framed mirrors, the vases of fake flowers and those annoying little wooden signs Amanda loves to hang on door

10

handles, off the corner of mirrors. They're meant to brighten up your day, boasting their little inscribed words of wisdom: "Be the reason someone smiles today"; "Laugh a lot, love a lot"; and Tamsin's favourite: "Smile! It could be a lot worse".

I seriously fucking doubt it, she mutters to herself each time she walks past it.

She's sick and tired looking at the same decor, hearing that same annoyed ringtone from the salon phone. She hates the clients, all of them. Which is why, come the weekend, Tamsin enjoys herself. Except she doesn't. She drinks to forget what she doesn't have any more and she sleeps around to numb the pain. Pain which has got worse over the last few months.

Why can't she get over her ex-boyfriend? Their two year relationship was intense and ended because their careers were headed in different directions. When he walked back into her life, she hadn't seen him for 3 years, and during that hiatus, Tamsin had hardly given any thought to him. Now, he's always on her mind.

Suddenly the door to the back room opens and Amanda escorts her client, an overweight woman in her mid-forties, across the wooden floor to the pink fake-leather chair waiting in front of the pink ornate mirror.

'So I said to her,' the client says in a gossipy tone, '"you can't do that here; it's private property." Do you want to know what the cheeky mare said back?'

Tamsin will readily admit that the one skill she admires in Amanda is her ability to throw dirty looks at her staff whilst maintaining a contradictory tone of voice with her clients. Tamsin has no such skill. *He* always said he could read her like a book. Which meant he knew exactly what she wanted.

Tamsin pushes back the chair, ignoring Amanda's glare, and walks across the salon floor in her heeled boots. God only knows what misdemeanour she has committed now. Perhaps Amanda can detect that Tamsin is slightly hungover or that she's been spending too long on her mobile, but Tamsin has neither the energy nor the inclination to care.

Tamsin enters the staffroom, desperate for a wake-up coffee before her next client arrives. The room is about the size of her kitchen at home with worktops down one side, a squashy sofa down the other, separated by a washing machine and a tumble dryer. Jenny the Junior looks up from where she's folding hot towels straight out of the tumble dryer to meet Tamsin's hard stare.

'When my ten o'clock client gets here, take her straight through to have her hair washed.'

Jenny raises her eyebrows as if to question Tamsin's order but quickly resumes her towel-folding. Holly, the other stylist, turns from where she's stirring powdered cappuccino in a mug to smile at Tamsin. The tinkling spoon irritates Tamsin and stirs up the nagging hangover again.

Tamsin digs her mobile from the front pocket of her plum-coloured tunic. With quick fingers, she taps out a message to her friend asking if she's finished with the bottle of nail varnish remover.

'Amanda's written the advert for the new stylist,' Holly tells Tamsin. 'I saw it on the side earlier before she whisked it away.'

'Oh, what does it say? Can I have that drink?' Tamsin asks, pointing at the cup.

Holly pushes it closer and reaches for another mug and sachet. 'She wants a senior stylist and get this…someone with managerial experience.'

'What?' Tamsin says angrily. 'Managerial experience? Oh, fucking great. So despite promising me more responsibility and a pay rise, she's going to appoint someone new and expect us to answer to them so she can have another day off. Fucking bitch.'

'I know.' Holly nods. 'Exactly what I thought. I don't know why she doesn't increase Jenny's training and move you up to being in charge in her absence. It's a right fucking snub after all the years you've given her.'

Tamsin sips the drink but it's hot and burns her tongue. She puts the cup down heavily and creamy froth slops over the side and onto the work surface. Holly smiles sympathetically and wipes it up with a cloth which she chucks into the sink.

'I can't believe it, Hol. When is she going to give me a break? It's so unfair.'

'I know, hun. I agree. But what I want to know is, when is she going to do something about all those grey hairs? How can she promote the salon and the "wonderful things we can do with your curls" when her hair is essentially a cross between a bird's nest and an orang-utan?'

Tamsin laughs hard though it isn't that funny a joke. It feels good to be laughing behind Amanda's back; it's the only weapon she has.

'What's with her staring daggers at me all morning?' Tamsin asks.

Holly stops laughing, wipes a laughter tear from her eye and says. 'The builder has postponed. She's got to take it out on someone. He's starting tomorrow now. Some family drama, I think. But tomorrow, we can look forward to her never-ending complaints about the noise of drilling and the dust.'

The faint tinkling of a bell coming from the front of the shop heralds the arrival of a client.

Tamsin looks at Jenny. 'Go on then,' she tells her bossily.

Without a word, Jenny does as she's told. Holly is looking at Tamsin, shaking her head slightly.

'What?' Tamsin says but she knows it isn't fair to treat Jenny the way Amanda treats her. They must stick together. 'I'll apologise.'

Holly steps closer, her face concerned. 'Is everything okay? Has something happened?'

Nothing's happened, she wants to confide, just that my life is shit. I hate my job but love hairdressing. My boss is an absolute bitch and we used to be friends until she got married and changed. Oh and the lad I love is not with me and I can't stop looking at his pictures, reading the birthday and Valentine's day cards he sent, and thinking about all the good times we had because we only ever had good times, and it wouldn't be that painful if only I could stop torturing myself with alcohol, occasional drugs and casual sex.

Tamsin feels one of the tiny tears in her heart split wide open and as emotion wells up. It feels like pint after pint of blood is draining into her chest, restricting her breathing.

'Okay, if you're sure,' Holly replies. 'I'd best take this through or Bitch Features will have a go at me.' Holly winks at Tamsin but as she turns for the door tray in hand, the door opens and Amanda stands there, hands on her hip, a pair of scissors gleaming in her fist.

'Tamsin,' she snaps. 'Why haven't you given your client a consultation before she had her hair washed?'

Tamsin's eyes drop to the scissors and she pictures herself snatching them from Amanda's hand. Tired, she shrugs insolently. 'What's the point? I colour and cut her hair the same *every* time.'

'The point, Tamsin,' Amanda states condescendingly, her expression stern, 'is, *I'm* paying you to give every client a consultation.'

'Amanda,' Holly begins, 'it was my fault. I asked—'

In her mind's eye, Tamsin raises the scissors, their sharp points together, high in the air.

Amanda glares at Holly. 'That drink will be going cold.'

Holly nods in acquiescence and carries it from the room.

With a war cry, Tamsin plunges the scissors deep into Amanda's chest, piercing a hole in her heart the size of her fist. She keeps stabbing until the heart is a torn mass of mush. Amanda collapses to the tiled floor and, with satisfaction, Tamsin watches the blood pool around her boss's lifeless body as Holly puts the kettle back on to make them all a celebratory cup of tea, and Jenny begins to mop the mess up. Triumph swells in Tamsin's chest.

'Are you listening to me, Tamsin?' Amanda demands loudly.

Tamsin blinks, snapping out of her thoughts. She nods at the person she once referred to as a good friend, muttering, 'Yes.'

Amanda narrows her eyes, points the scissors at her. 'I don't believe you. But maybe you'll hear this. You're on your last warning. Any more disobedience, slovenly attitude, tardiness or anything else I deem to be well below my high standards, and you can look for another job. Understand?' she threatens.

Defeated, Tamsin nods. She has got to make changes in her life or she may as well be dead.

Chapter 3

David

David Bywater opens the fridge door, grabs two bottles off the shelf and kicks the door shut with his booted foot. He holds a beer out to his best friend, Jake Bunby, who sits at the bench on a high stool, clapping his hands like a performing seal.

'I've been looking forward to this all day, mate,' Jake enthuses, excitedly. 'The juniper will cause a taste revolution.'

David smiles and slides the bottle opener across to Jake who grabs it and prises the cap off.

'Cheers, mate,' Jake says, holding his bottle out. The glass clinks together and each man takes a large gulp of beer.

David washes the liquid around his mouth, over his gums, his tongue and the roof of his mouth. He even squirts the liquid between his teeth like it's mouthwash. He swallows. Not bad, he concludes. Reminds me of cold winter nights by a roaring fire. He takes another gulp, looks at Jake who is grinning and nodding at him.

'Very fucking nice, mate.' He points a nicotine-stained finger at David. 'I told you it'd be good. Juniper has long been used in brewing; I've done my research.' He takes a longer gulp, rinsing it around his mouth before swallowing it noisily. 'You are a talented man, my friend.'

David blushes, hides his proud expression behind the bottle which he raises back to his mouth. It has both a refreshing and warming quality, perfect for the winter months ahead.

'I'm serious, Dave,' Jake says, 'you're a talented brewer. Even that shit you used to make at school is better than the stuff you get in pubs. And now you've mastered the art, time after time, you brew fantastic beer. We definitely need to do this on a bigger scale.'

David sighs, rubs a hand over his forehead. 'It's not gonna happen, Jay, until I can get some serious money. This little experiment has cost me enough as it is. I need bigger equipment, more time, a bigger shed,' and he waves his free hand around the four walls. The shed is large, but his brewing equipment shares space with the lawn mower and other gardening equipment. In the summer when Amanda took Oliver to her parents' house for the weekend to celebrate their fortieth wedding anniversary, David invited Jake around and they sorted through the entire contents of the shed, chucking stuff into David's van to take to the local recycling centre. They cleared enough room to expand the brewing empire by several metres. They installed a proper workbench, plumbed in a sink and a draining board, fitted a small

15

fridge and a stove, and filled the shelves with as much brewing equipment as David could afford.

But just a few months later and David is finding conditions seriously cramped and that the few metres gained still aren't enough. He regularly visits home brewing websites and punishes himself with the equipment he wants and needs but cannot afford; stuff that would seriously help him grow his home brewing to the point it could become a second income. This is more than his hobby. This is his love and his passion. To Jake too who has been his assistant and chief taster since the days of making beer in the cupboard under the stairs in his mum's house.

'I've said it before,' Jake begins in that tone that both saddens and annoys David, 'your missus needs to quit throwing money into her business and invest in yours. Hairdressers are fucking ten a penny these days.'

David smirks.

'I'm serious. How much is she spending on this refurbishment?'

David shrugs. He's glimpsed the quote from the builder but, if he reveals the amount to Jake, he will literally blow his top.

Jake points the bottle at him. 'I know you fucking know. Don't keep shit from me. Thousands, I bet. Thousands could rent us a property.' He stops, frowns. 'In fact, we don't need to rent somewhere. I know a perfect place that's sitting empty…'

'Not this again,' David says tiredly.

'Hear me out,' Jake insists. 'It has everything we need,' and he lists its advantages, ticking them off on his fingers. 'A large kitchen to brew in, catering-sized fridges, a cellar, a fucking bar, living quarters, ex-patrons who will fucking flock back in their droves when the place reopens, selling your beer! It's there for the taking, Dave.'

'I'm not squatting in a closed down pub,' David responds. 'I've told you before.'

'It's called Squatters Rights and technically we're not breaking the law. I've looked into it.' Jake grabs David's arm imploringly. 'Let's go and have a look now. Drink your beer.'

'Mate, the place is surrounded by steel fencing, it's sealed to the roof with chains and padlocks, CCTV is in operation…'

But Jake is shaking his head, grinning. 'The CCTV cameras are fake. I can get us in without breaking and entering.'

16

David already feels himself responding to his friend's persuasive powers. The old pub, which is a Grade II listed building is perfect for more than the advantages Jake has listed. Back in its heyday, it was a popular place. It was Jake's local and, when it closed, he genuinely mourned its passing.

David has had this conversation several times and it's getting harder and harder to say no to Jake. He's being worn down and needs to steer the subject onto a less painful subject. David glances at the large white envelope on the windowsill containing forms and information. Now is not the time to admit that he's enquired about a bank loan. The situation doesn't need further inflaming. Jake would not approve of a loan when David's wife has the money but she just won't give him any despite her promises. So he reaches into the back pocket of his black workman trousers for a folded sheet of paper. This is perfect.

'I've been thinking of names to call the company. You know, for when we go big.'

Jake adjusts his seating position on the stool, wincing with pain in spite of the grin on his face. He's been sitting on the stool since he arrived half an hour ago and even though he knows he needs to move around to ease the pain and stiffness in his back, he's a lazy sod, preferring to rest his bones on any available surface.

David unfolds the paper. 'Paying homage to our love of bacon and sausage sarnies, but mostly to the porcine who caused your life-limiting injury,' he pauses as Jake, with good-nature, raises the middle finger of his left hand. 'Now, I know when you were struck by the carcass, your first words included a swear word but I thought it wise to omit that and keep the rest. To…The Filthy Pig.'

Jake laughs.'You don't know how much this means to me, mate. Here,' and he reaches for the rest of his beer to clink bottles with David. 'To The Filthy Pig.'

Suddenly, David hears something, a noise from the garden, a word shouted on the wind and he freezes, his eyes glancing at the clock on the wall above the door: 8.10pm.

Shit. She's back. How long have we been talking?

David curses himself because he meant to send Jake home ages ago, well before Amanda was due back, and now he feels guilty like he's been caught with a woman in the house rather than a friend. In the last few weeks, Amanda has had a real issue with him spending time with his friends, rolling her eyes and muttering to herself which has escalated to complaining loudly and sulking.

He hears his name again, louder this time and ignores the pitying look Jake gives him. He steps outside, closing the door behind him and gazes past the goalposts, the dark shapeless shrubbery, the folded-down rotary washing line and the collection of wheelie bins.

The kitchen blind is up and Amanda stands in front of the illuminated kitchen window. The outside security light needs a new bulb; something he still hasn't got around to replacing.

His heart is thumping wildly; he can feel it in his throat. It's stupid to feel afraid, but he can't bear another confrontation. This morning's was nasty and completely unjustified. He doesn't want a repeat of it but, judging by Amanda's stance and her harsh expression, that's what's in store for him. He doesn't know how much more he can take, but equally he's loath to throw in the towel and admit defeat. He knows exactly what he'd be returning to.

He walks over. He has only a few metres to decide how to be: apologetic, easy-going, nonchalant, confrontational, defensive. He's tried all the tactics. They have the same result.

The apology leaves his lips with a mind of their own.

'I'm sorry,' he says, holding out his hands, 'I meant to get rid of Jake before you got back but I lost track of the time. We were talking about...It doesn't matter...Have you had a good day at work?'

His attempt at deflection doesn't work. Her green eyes don't lose any of their hardness, her jaw is clenched and her arms remain tightly folded.

'I've had a busy day at work,' she tells him in that tone he despises so much. 'I've barely had time to eat my lunch, my feet are aching and I'm starving. I was going to suggest a Chinese takeaway but I can see from the empty pizza box in the utility room that you've dined with your friend.'

He doesn't like her tone. He hates the way she always suggests there's more to their friendship, but he tells himself it's because she has no friends of her own.

'What's for my tea, David? What slap-up meal have you made for your hard-working wife? Steak and chips, or perhaps Thai green curry with jasmine rice?'

'I asked this morning what you wanted to do for tea but—'

'You obviously didn't notice that I had a lot on this morning, running around after you and Oliver. Why can't you use your damn initiative for once and make a decision?'

Taking another deep breath to calm his nerves, he knows it's easier to acquiesce, offer to put the oven on or collect a takeaway. He studies her. The anger ages her, wrinkles her skin, narrows her pretty green eyes. The snarl on her lips ruins her mouth, that mouth he found so kissable. And suddenly he wonders: when was the last time we had sex? Got to have been three weeks ago. He wrongly assumed that a thirty seven year old woman would be experienced in the bedroom department. It's a situation men joke about. But it wasn't like that with Amanda. She didn't seem to know what she liked and so let him lead, a role he was only too pleased to take on. He thought at the time she was playing him somehow and, eventually, she'd throw off her coy act and become that adventurous demanding older woman.

A month later nothing had changed and he knew why. She had little experience. Yes, she ran her own business and had a child, but before he was two years old, she had sent Oliver to live with his dad, another man who can do nothing right, because she couldn't cope.

It shocked David to discover that Amanda had never been in a long-term relationship before. He's starting to see why.

He considers shocking her with an unexpected reaction, grabbing her, wrapping her messy ponytail around his fist and kissing her hard. Perhaps that's what she needs - a good seeing to. God knows it's been too long for him. Porn isn't doing it for him and he feels a strange guilt when he watches the videos online.

David laughs at the ridiculousness of her suggestion. 'I'd love to make a decision if I knew it had a chance of being right.'

'Don't be so childish, David.'

'I'm not being childish,' he complains, sounding whiney. 'I can't do anything right. I can't give sweets to *your* son, I'm not allowed to pop into the salon to say hello or bring you a Cadbury's Flake, and what about that stack of post-it-notes I bought to stop you from making your lists on *my* paperwork? You threw them back in my face in front of your staff and customers. You have a way of making me feel,' and he pauses, holding his thumb and first finger millimetres apart, 'this big.'

Amanda smirks. 'You're imagining things, David. You're starting to sound neurotic.'

He knows there's a word for this thing she does, how she turns the tables and calls him paranoid. Jake told him what it was but what's the point of saying it when he can't recall the term.

'If I'm neurotic, what are you?' he replies. 'You blow hot and cold. One day you can be distant and frigid, the next snappy and sarcastic, and the day after that amorous and flirty. You have me walking on eggshells. And you actually seem to get off on seeing me struggle.'

Amanda stares wide-eyed and he worries that he's gone too far, but so what if he has? If she kicked him out, then at least he would know where he stood. It might shock her into reassessing the way she treats him.

'Do you love me, Amanda?' he asks, his words barely audible. ''cause if you don't, what's the point?'

Her expression doesn't soften and he fears her answer. How can an eight-month marriage have turned so sour?

Suddenly a noise from over the fence startles him: the sound of glass hitting the inside of a wheelie bin followed by the lid being dropped down. David glances and he sees the next-door's back door is open, light illuminating the brickwork above.

Shit. Now the neighbours know they're having marital problems.

'Get rid of him.' Amanda is saying, nodding at the shed where David can see Jake's outline through the frosted glass window. He can't tell from her tone of voice if it's an order or a suggestion.

He nods, defeated.

'I'm going to get changed. I'm covered in hair and dye. You'll find me upstairs. Bring a bottle of wine.'

He knows how red wine affects her. It'll have double the impact on an empty stomach.

She smiles at him. A smile he hasn't recognised in a while.

Now she's blowing hotter than a desert wind.

Chapter 4

Lawrence

Lawrence Hayden assesses the ten foot long studded wall so far. He's removed the coving and skirting board, disconnected and made safe the electrics - there was only one light switch to worry about. Using a claw hammer, he has made a hole in the plasterboard so he could start pulling the boards off the wooden studs. They came away with brute force.

He's making excellent progress, but it's definitely dusty work. The elastic from the mask is digging into his stubble and he wishes he'd had a shave this morning, but there wasn't time; he had to get the kids to school because Rachel had been on a night-shift.

He spent the first hour at the salon moving stuff out of the storeroom so he could put up the plastic sheeting. He did advise Amanda to clear the room herself, pointing out that'd it save her some money and time but she didn't seem keen. He clocked her wedding ring, almost suggested she rope her husband into helping, but maybe he isn't the practical type. She could've asked her staff to do it, paid them overtime to work a Sunday, but then he supposes they don't want to ruin their nails and hair. Appearances are important to a hairdresser. He's glad his Rachel isn't like them but, as a nurse on a geriatric ward, she doesn't mind getting her hands dirty with hard graft.

Still at the end of the day, it's easy money for Lawrence and he needs this job. Eight months ago, he took his family and business, and upped sticks from their home town. He could've stayed, weathered the backlash, reassured his family that the hostility and hatred would die down, but when his eldest child was assaulted and his van torched, Lawrence knew they had no choice. People wouldn't forget and they certainly wouldn't forgive the things he had said. And he refused to retract or apologise.

Instantly, things looked brighter in Lexington. Rachel got a job, the kids settled quickly into their new schools, and he found, to his amazement, that there wasn't much competition for one-man band builder-cum-handyman in the town. Lawrence picked up small, quick jobs the way a hoover picks up bits off the carpet.

But he needed that big job to put him and his business back on the map

And renovating the Colour and Curls Hair Studio is the one to do it.

Lawrence finishes bagging the debris up into black bin liners. He piles them in a corner to put into the back of his van and take to the recycling centre on his way home.

21

Back in the salon, behind the dust curtain, he can hear the mundane chatter of women talking about how the country is in for a hard winter, how earlier and earlier Christmas seems to be appearing in shops, and when the local firework displays are taking place. He contemplates turning up the volume on his handy little stereo but he saw the frown on Amanda's face when he took it out of his bag and plugged it in. He couldn't tell if it was an objection to him using her electricity or whether she doesn't want his music drowning out the chatter of her customers.

Probably both, and it doesn't look as if she's going to offer him a cup of tea anytime soon. Maybe she's punishing him for postponing the start date, but what could he do? Nathan had another crisis. Lawrence can't just leave him. Lawrence is all his brother has.

So, it's just as well Lawrence bought a flask and noted a café a few doors down the street. Someone should tell her every tradesman works harder and better on copious amounts of tea. But then she'd probably object to him using her toilet. Lawrence keeps a mobile toilet in his van - a two litre empty *Sprite* bottle.

He lifts the mask off his face and rests it on top of his head like a little bowler hat whilst he assesses the wooden framework from the top plate to the sole plate. He notes that the noggins or horizontal bars have been placed between the vertical studs at staggered heights. Behind him, the sheeting rustles. Lawrence turns to see the plastic being prised apart by awkward fingers.

Amanda smiles at him, but her eyes flick to the wall and widen at the progress he's made so far. This is the closest he's ever been to her and he notes how green her eyes are, like pond algae, which typically accompanies a freckled complexion and long amber-coloured hair.

But she isn't his type. Far too haughty and bossy for him.

He wonders if she has a temper to go with her hair and if her husband has a job handling her.

'It's coming on well, isn't it?' she says in awe, stating the obvious. 'You just never give a thought to what's inside walls, do you?'

He forces a laugh at her stupid remark, hopes it sounds genuine. 'Only if you're a builder.'

'Quite. I'm just putting the kettle on for a client, would you like a drink? Looks like you've earned one,' she offers.

Oh, so she *did* want progress first, he thinks.

'I'd love a brew. It's thirsty work. Two sugars, please.' He wonders if he's done enough for one of those small cakes he's glimpsed accompanying the customers' drinks. One wouldn't be enough.

'Shall I put your bag in the staffroom, Lawrence?' Amanda asks, picking up the battered black duffel bag off the floor. 'It's covered in dust.' She slaps a hand on the side, sending a small puff of dust outwards.

He doesn't really want his lunch in another room, especially if he isn't going to be offered a cake. But he might be able to sneak a toilet break in a bit via the kitchen when he's after a bit of grub.

'Yeah, thanks. I'm just gonna pop to the van for my reciprocating saw and wrecking bar.' He loves flummoxing people with technical names for his tools. Rachel jokes that it makes him sound sexy.

At the van, Lawrence gets waylaid by a call to his mobile from a potential customer asking if he can give a quote for installing new fence panels and clearing gutters. There's also the promise of more work in the new year: redecorating bedrooms, re-roof a shed and build a raised bed. Lawrence makes an appointment to call by in a couple of days' time.

With a spring in his step and a buoyant feeling in his chest that things are looking up, Lawrence reenters the salon with the tools, itching to text Rachel but remembering that she'll be fast asleep.

He places the items down, looks for the drink, which should have been made by now, but isn't anywhere to be found.

'Should have guessed she'd leave it in the staffroom in case I break the precious cup,' he mutters, pulling apart the sheeting to go on the hunt. He strolls past the trio of empty backwash units, the shower heads on their chrome pipes coiled inside the porcelain bowls like resting snakes, past the shelving unit housing neatly folded towels and the large pump-action bottles of shampoo and conditioner.

He finds the staffroom just past the toilet. The frosted glass door is ajar and Amanda is leaning against the work-surface reading from a sheet of paper. The kettle is silent and two cups, one flowered presumably for the client, and one with faded writing on the side, his, are waiting for hot water.

His knuckle raps against the door and Amanda looks up, her earlier smile gone.

'I'll take my tea if it's ready,' Lawrence says.

She stands up straight and her fingers hold up the letter, not for him to take. He can't see what it is, but his eyes move to the squashy settee where his bag is, the zip undone, the way it always is because it's broken and often it spills its contents all over the floor of the van. This morning, it spewed the lunchbox containing Lawrence's two ham rolls into the passenger footwell. He found the letter to his brother crumpled underneath the bag of cheese and onion crisps. He should have posted it on the way to the school. Then she wouldn't be reading it.

'I wasn't prying,' she explains, unapologetically. 'The handle gave way and the envelope fluttered out.'

Rachel is forever resewing the handle back onto the canvas. She keeps nagging him to get a new one.

Lawrence hadn't sealed the envelope because he was going to put some money inside. But it wouldn't have mattered. His brother's name and location are clearly written on the envelope and Lawrence has such nice neat penmanship.

Amanda looks back at the letter, a snarl forming on her lips.

He wants to tell her that his private life is none of her business, but clearly she has made it so and has an opinion on it.

'Nathan Killingworth is *your* brother,' she states with contempt, glaring with hard and unforgiving eyes. 'You don't look like him.'

Lawrence silently disagrees. They have the same colour eyes and hair, but styled differently. Nathan is taller, Lawrence is broader across the chest.

'I've just googled you,' Amanda continues. 'I've watched the news report after the verdict was delivered. I remember it, of course. Who could forget what a...' she pauses, trying to find the right word. Her lips twist. 'Sickening and unforgivable thing you said.'

Lawrence's guts twist and coil, and his legs drain of blood. This can't be happening. He should have posted the fucking letter. He should have let Rachel buy him another bag or use one of the carrier bags she's got stuffed in the cupboard under the sink. He shouldn't have let Amanda take his bag away. He should have said no to a cup of tea. He should tell her that it's none of her fucking business.

She thinks the same as them.

That he should have been bundled into a cell with Nathan and the key thrown away.

She stretches her arm over the bag and releases the letter. It zigzags down through the air, landing on top of the bag. 'Gather your belongings, your tools and get off my premises. I'll pay you for the time you've spent—'

'What? You're sacking me?' Lawrence waves a hand back in the direction of the half-finished wall. 'I'm halfway through a job. The place is a mess—'

'That *is* my problem, Mr Killingworth. I no longer require your services.'

'My surname,' he states forcibly, 'is Hayden.'

Amanda shakes her head. 'I don't care what you're calling yourself now; I know who you really are. I will not employ a man,' she says, hatefully as if man is the last thing he is, 'who could publicly place blame on the doorstep of a mother in grief. You have five minutes.'

'Then what? You'll call the police?'

'Yes, I will. We might live in a democracy where *people* like you have the right to say what they feel, but it is still my choice who I employ.'

Now Lawrence shakes his head, realises the mask is still perched on his head. It feels stupid so he pulls at it, but the elastic twangs his neck smarting his skin and bringing tears to his eyes, which he knows is nothing to do with the mask. He feels exposed and humiliated. His cover has been blown and he's been sacked.

'Look,' he begins pleadingly, wondering if he can salvage anything from this, 'I need this job. I have a family. Let me finish the job. Pay me half of what I've quoted. You're getting a bargain.'

'Mr Killingworth, I would rather have an unfinished wall than have you here a second longer. You have four minutes left.'

It's useless. She will not be budged. Stuck-up fucking bitch. What right does she have to treat me like this?

He glares at her, but hears movement behind him. He glances over his shoulder, sees the mixed race girl with the frizzy hair leading a woman wearing a black cloak around her shoulders to the backwash units.

'Holly,' Amanda calls, 'would you phone the police, please? This man is refusing to leave the premises.'

Holly frowns, the customer looks worried. 'You want me to do what, Amanda?'

'It's a simple instruction, Holly.' She turns to Lawrence, lowers her voice. 'Or would you rather I tell everyone in the salon who you are?'

It's enough of a threat. With a burning red face, Lawrence swipes up his bag, stuffing the letter inside and gathers his tools. He leaves the bags of plasterboard behind and walks quickly across the salon floor, much to the consternation of Amanda's staff and customers.

Parked between two buildings, with the van windows up, Lawrence releases his frustration and pounds the steering wheel, silently screaming. Minutes later, he breathes deeply as he tries to desperately pull himself together. What can he tell Rachel? She will go up the bloody wall.

He has no one else to sound off to…apart from Nathan.

But even Lawrence can't help think that his situation is far worse. After all, how difficult can it be to serve a life sentence?

Well, he thinks, serving six of them must be harder.

No, he suddenly disagrees, I have it worse. Inside, Nathan is away from it all. Out here, I have to deal with people.

Chapter 5

Amanda

'They're hoping to get married next Christmas. Perhaps they think it'll be cheaper but it'll certainly be a lot colder. December is such a damp month. They could do what you and David did. Go to the Caribbean.' Jean pauses for a response, but Amanda doesn't know what to say. She can't even remember who the betrothed couple are, so she murmurs, 'Hmm,' thoughtfully.

'It's the only place to go for a honeymoon at *that* time of the year,' Jean continues.

Amanda can tell from the tone of her mother's voice that it'll be a long time before she'll be forgiven for marrying the way she did. She'd only been seeing David for 6 weeks; she'd never even introduced him to her parents. In fact, David had only met Oliver a few times. But marrying that way felt right. Get on a plane to Barbados, stand on a golden beach wearing a floaty white dress, the hot sand burning her toes, a yellow flower tucked in her hair, holding hands and looking up into the eyes of the man she had fallen head over heels for.

It had taken literally only a few minutes to get married before they headed back to the hotel for chilled champagne.

She waited until they landed back in England to tell her parents what she had done. And even then, it was another month before she sat down with them to chat it through.

It was another couple of weeks until they met David.

They liked him but, in their eyes, Amanda saw them question the twelve year age difference. And they wondered when the twenty-five year old David would start to notice that his wife was much older than him.

'Amanda, are you still there?' Jean asks.

'Yes, Mum. Sorry, I was just negotiating a difficult island,' she lies.

'You really shouldn't talk whilst driving.'

'*You* rang me.'

'I know, but you should have said you were on the road. How is everything, anyway? Has the builder started? How is the work progressing? Have you advertised for a new stylist yet?'

Amanda rolls her eyes. She doesn't really want to talk about what happened, who she stupidly employed, the mess that's been left, and what on earth she's going to do now. But it's easier to lie on the phone, so she tells her mum everything is going smoothly and she should be in a position to put the advert out next week.

'Is David supporting you?' Jean asks.

Suddenly, the white Audi in the inside lane cuts in front of Amanda and applies its brakes to avoid hitting the truck in front. Amanda hits the brakes too and the heavy catalogue of hair colours slides off the passenger seat, landing on the bag of grocery shopping she had placed in the footwell. She should have put the shopping in the boot. She should have left the catalogue at the salon. She shouldn't have hired Lawrence.

'Fuck's sake,' she shouts.

'Amanda!' Jean scolds. 'Must you swear? I hope Ollie isn't in the car with you.'

'Of course he's not. I don't see him on Tuesdays.'

'You sound very stressed. I do hope you haven't taken too much on again.'

'Mum,' Amanda begins, after taking a deep breath did nothing to calm her down, 'the idea of refurbishing the salon was to hire another person, so I can relax and maybe have another day off in the week. Unfortunately, stress cannot be—'

'There is no need to make yourself ill.'

'I'm not making my—'

But Jean interrupts her. 'Darling, we've been here before, and it wasn't all that long ago. David is a good man; he clearly loves you very much and is there for you to lean on. And, if there is anything your dad and I can do, then please ask.'

She should have asked for help five years ago when the salon was getting too much and trying to raise a toddler was becoming too demanding. But rather than do that, Amanda made a different cry for help. Or at least that's what they thought it was. To her, it was an exit. If it wasn't for the fact she had left her mobile in the hotel reception and a helpful maid had brought it to her room, Amanda wouldn't have been found until the morning when it all would have been over.

When she was discharged from hospital, changes had been made in her absence: Oliver was living full-time with his dad, Holly was temporarily running the business, and her parents had paid a fortune for builders to finish the work.

'There won't be a repeat of it,' Amanda assures Jean. 'Now I really must go. The traffic is building up and clearly everyone on the road is in a hurry to get home.'

She says "bye", with a promise to ring if she needs anything and pulls onto her drive, relieved to find that Jake's red mobility car is nowhere to be seen.

Amanda kicks the front door closed with her foot, the catalogue sliding out from under her arm and the handles of the heavy carrier bags threatening to snap. She chucks the heavy book onto the bottom stair and carries the shopping into the kitchen. The house sounds eerily quiet but she knows David is home because his battered van is on the drive.

'Don't tell me you're in that bloody shed again,' she mutters angrily, parting the vertical slats on the blind and peering out into the garden, but the shed is in complete darkness. Surprised that he's heeded her request that he spend less time out there and more time in here with her, she begins to put the food away, wondering what to do with the raw chicken she has bought. Red Thai curry, a stir-fry, or perhaps…her thoughts are interrupted by the sound of the upstairs shower being turned on.

Amanda glances at the ceiling. This could be the opportunity to tell David about the salon, not that it's his business really, but he might have a solution. He certainly has a mate who's a builder. Perhaps David can give him a call for her, plead that Amanda has an emergency.

The bedroom door is open and she can hear the water roaring from the en-suite. His work clothes of black trousers, t-shirt, socks and screwed-up underwear lie on the floor. She steps over them. One rule she made right at the start was that she expected him to clear up after himself; she was not his mother.

The door is ajar and she can feel steam exuding through the crack. She raps her knuckle on the door and opens it further. A large blue bath sheet is folded over the radiator and all the surfaces are covered in steam. She pulls the cord on the extractor fan and it begins to whirr.

David wipes his hand over the inside of the shower door, clearing away rivulets of water to grin at her. His blond hair is dark with wet and lies flat on his head. In his other hand is the shower gel Amanda bought him for his birthday. He squeezes a generous amount onto a flannel and watches her as he starts rubbing it onto his skin.

The scents of peppercorns and vetiver fill her nostrils and she sits on the closed-down lid of the toilet. Her heart rate begins to increase and she starts to feel heady. She wants to blatantly watch him shower. He has a great physique. She will never tire of watching him in different poses, whether it's showering, mowing the lawn or lying in tangled bedsheets with her.

But Amanda feels surprisingly shy.

She wasn't shy last night. A large glass of red wine on an empty stomach had the desired effect. It went straight to her head and she was able to shake off several of her inhibitions and relax. Their night together put them back on track. For now. She must be more careful. One day David may tire of her attitude and behaviour.

David faces the powerful stream of water, swaying his chest from side to side to wash the soap away. He speaks but, over the roar of the water, she doesn't hear.

'What?' she says, leaning closer.

He opens the shower door a few centimetres and puts his face to the gap. The scent of his shower gel causes a yearning inside her and she's glad she's sitting down. Her eyes stray downwards from his handsome face, past the defined muscles of his chest and lower still...

'What happened at the salon?'

Her eyes flick sharply upwards, narrowing with annoyance. 'What do you mean? Who told you anything happened?'

He answers but still she can't hear. He turns the shower off, slides open the door and grabs the towel. He rubs it over his head first, making his hair spike up.

'I bumped into Holly outside the Red Lion.'

'What were you doing at the pub?'

'Dropping some beer off.'

'How do you know her?'

'She works for you, Amanda,' he reminds her.

'Yes, but I didn't know you knew each other well enough to gossip behind my back.'

David smiles. 'She's a woman. They like to gossip. She said you kicked the builder out. Why?' David wraps the towel around his waist and turns on the basin's hot water tap. The basin begins to fill.

Amanda's eyes roam over his shoulders and down the pictures on his tattooed arm: the pocket watch, the handles telling the time he was born - 11.20; the serpent winding its way up the inside of his forearm, its forked tongue protruding over the top of the skull. She stares at the details of the skull: the hollow eye sockets, the pear-shaped hole of the nasal cavity, the indentations of the bones. She sees tiny letters and numbers in the suture lines and wonders what they might refer to. Her index finger reaches to touch two letters. Is that a J or a T?

David moves as he cups his hand over the nozzle of shaving cream and sprays a generous amount into his hand. He smears it carefully onto the lower half of his face.

Why is he having a shave? she wonders. Is he going out tonight?

'Amanda, why did you sack the builder?'

'I don't really want to get into the why,' she replies defensively.

David sighs, swishes the razor through the water and leans close to the mirror, positioning the blade against the bottom edge of his sideburn. 'You mean, it's none of my business.'

'I mean,' she replies in a firm tone, 'that I made the decision based on my principles.'

'Holly said the salon is a right mess. Bags of plasterboard all piled up, inches of dust everywhere, and a big frame of wood stuck in the middle of—'

'Holly should keep her bloody nose out if she wants to keep her job.'

David glances, a frown creasing his forehead.

'I don't pay her for her opinion. I made a mistake hiring him.'

'You made a mistake firing him too,' David adds. 'What are you going to do now? Who are you going to get to finish the job, because I recall you refused to pay a proper builder. You said, and I quote, "It's just a wall. How hard can it be to knock down?" Me and a couple of mates could've done it. Now, you're back to square one. No, you're further back than that. You've got to find someone who, at short notice, will finish the job a perfectly capable bloke started! Good luck with that,' he laughs.

Amanda glares at him, hoping that the sharp blade cuts his skin. 'Can't you ask that builder mate of yours?'

'I can, yes.' David agrees. 'He might be able to fit you in, say around July.'

'July! I can't put up with that until July. It's October now. He can't be that busy.'

David looks at her in the mirror, half his face covered with lime-scented foam. 'Amanda, he's fully booked. When he put his quote in, he said he wouldn't be able to do it until May. Now, you've moved further down the queue. But, I tell you what…'

Her eyes narrow. She doesn't like that tone of his voice. It's sly, mocking. She has never heard him sound like this before.

'Pay me what you were going to pay this Lawrence bloke and I'll do the job. After all, it's only a wall. How hard can it be?' and he laughs.

'Sod off, David,' she snipes.

He laughs. 'Oh, come on, Amanda. I'm only teasing,' and he dabs a blob of shaving cream on her nose. 'But I am offering my services.'

Amanda lifts the corner of his towel to wipe the cream off. It's an option. There are plenty of YouTube videos out there to explain the stages of removing a wall and making it good. David's practical and he's strong. She could even get away with paying him less. He doesn't have to do the decorating. She's sure she could find someone to do that.

'I've had my eye on some new brewing equipment for a bit, plus I can finally get your name engraved on my arm. We'll both get what we want.'

Amanda cares little for the tattoo, but the addition of more brewing equipment means he will be spending more time in that precious shed, that shed she wishes she could set fire to and burn to the ground. He'll spend more time with his crippled friend, the one who looks at her like she's shit on his shoe. She'll be elbowed further out by hops and barley and beer and then, when he's happier and drunk because he's selling his stupid home-brew to local pubs, he'll want to go bigger still and expand and she'll be relegated. And women will throw themselves at him, wanting to drink in his success, younger women like that fucking poisonous Tamsin. And finally, David will see Amanda for what she is: a bitter and selfish wife, and then that 12 years age gap will feel as wide a hundred years.

He will leave her and she'll be on her own again.

And it'll all be because she paid him to fix a stupid wall.

She can't give him money for his stupid hobby.

The sound of water gurgling down the plughole startles Amanda out of her frightening glimpse into the future. David is patting his face dry with the bath towel.

'Come on then,' he's saying, 'get your kit off.'

She blinks at him, confused. Is he offering to take her back into the shower? The first time she ever had sex in the shower was with him and it was the most sensual experience she'd ever had. Since then, Amanda has been doing a lot of research online and found a few positions in the shower they could try.

David puts his hands on her waist but instead of helping her undress like he had done last night, he moves her aside to leave the room. He tugs out a drawer and searches for clean underwear. She's still staring at him several moments later when he stares at her, a sock half-pulled onto his left foot.

'You've forgotten, haven't you?'

He doesn't mean the shower, at least not the two of them. Shit. Suddenly, she feels embarrassed for misinterpreting him.

'We're going out for a meal…you asked me to book a table at The Oak and Cedar, which I have for seven o'clock.'

She doesn't remember suggesting this, but then she was pretty tipsy. She could have suggested anything last night, not giving him money though - she wouldn't have done that.

'Are we going or not?' David asks. 'Otherwise I'll just put my scruffs on. There's a couple of things I need to check on in the shed…'

Bloody beer again, she thinks angrily and, though she has bought shopping and it means showering and putting on make-up, the alternative doesn't bear thinking about. David will retire to that damn shed for the evening and she'll be left on the settee to drink alone.

'Yes, we'll go,' she agrees.

He grins and yanks his sock on.

Amanda unbuttons her tunic and eases it down her shoulders, her thoughts wandering back to the salon and the mess that lies in wait for her.

'There is an alternative,' David says.

It's the tone of his voice that snaps her out of her thoughts, but the wicked glint in his eyes tells her that it's not the suggestion she's hoping for. Perhaps he does mean the shower after all.

'You could always apologise to the bloke and rehire him.'

Her shoulders sag.

'Over my dead body,' she answers.

Chapter 6

Declan

Declan Page is on edge. He races around the downstairs of his house but his hands can't keep up with his brain and, instead of tidying up, Declan is making more mess. The stack of clothes topples like a felled tree and they scatter over the living room floor messily; the hoover sucks up the fringes of the rug until they get stuck in the beater bar; there's no washing-up liquid and nowhere to hide the toys since all available surfaces are taken up with pages of homework, remote controls, magazines and toys.

He warned Kerry yesterday that he'd arranged for Amanda to come after school today to discuss his "urgent matter". He knows she's struggling with this pregnancy, crippled with morning sickness and bone-aching tiredness but, really, she could have made a start on the housework. And God help them if Amanda wants to see Oliver's room. The ironing board and the stepladder have been parked behind his door for weeks. There's no room in the garage. The place is rammed with kids' bikes, Declan's weights and boxes and boxes of Kerry and her daughters' belongings, yet to be unpacked. It's obvious they need a bigger house, but that will mean paying more rent, and things are stretched as they are. Declan works full-time; he gets in as much overtime as he can but competition is strong amongst the other factory operatives. They all have bills to pay. And he keeps meaning to look for another job. The disappointment in Amanda's eyes is very evident when he admits he still hasn't uploaded his CV to the job sites. Or is it disgust?

Kerry only works part-time, which means she's around to take the kids to school and pick them up after her shift at the supermarket has finished but, in a few months' time, she will be on maternity leave.

He won't admit it, but this pregnancy couldn't have come at a worse time. Christmas isn't far away and Kerry is already encouraging the kids to think about their letters to Santa Claus. He doesn't know how he's going to afford to give the kids the Christmas Kerry wants them to have. It's not even as if she is demanding of her own ex-partner to cough up for his daughters. He gets away with giving her a pittance. At least Declan receives a rather generous payment from Amanda, but with his own child due, he is the only one who can pay for it.

Kerry always said that a baby will bridge their two families, bind them forever.

Bind them in debt more like, Declan thinks.

'Arghhh!!" The sudden scream makes him jump and the bottle of shower gel slips from his fingers into the bowl of water, splashing the front of his white t-shirt.

'Shit,' Declan mutters, assessing the damage. He cannot open the door to Amanda looking like a contestant in a wet t-shirt competition.

'I'm telling Mum. MUM!' Lola screams, barging her way into the living room and straight into the hoover.

'Watch where you're going,' Declan says as he watches the hoover fall backwards towards the TV stand. But the little girl takes no notice.

'Where's Mum, Declan?' she demands. In her hands, she holds a naked decapitated *Barbie* doll who appears to be sporting extra drawn on make-up.

He doesn't ask.

'She's gone to *Asda*,' he tells her.

Knowing that Amanda can't stand Kerry, he made the sensible decision to send Kerry out to do the food shopping, with the promise that he'll pick her up when she's done.

Lola frowns and steps closer. There's chocolate on her chin. Where's she got that from? Shit. I hope Oliver's got a clean face.

'Are you washing the plates with Mummy's *Dove*?'

'We've run out of washing-up liquid,' he explains.

'You're funny.'

'Do me a favour, please, Lola. Run upstairs and tell Ollie to wash his hands and face.'

The eight-year old pulls a face. 'It's not time for tea yet. What are we having? Not nuggets again. Sammy Pearce says they're not made of chicken but rat meat,' she announces dramatically. 'Sammy is vegetarian. Can I go veggie? Mummy says I can.'

Bloody hell, Declan thinks. Vegetarian food costs an absolute fortune, which doesn't make sense considering it's only vegetables.

A tapping on the front door makes Declan jump again, but this time his heart rate increases because he knows who this visitor is.

'Shit,' he mutters, shoving the *Dove* out of sight and checking his reflection in the small mirror glued to the back of the cupboard door, something he put up for just these occasions.

He opens the front door and lets Amanda in. She stands on the tatty hall rug, her eyes moving over the black scuff marks on the walls, the untidy collection of shoes and boots at the foot of the stairs, and her nose wrinkles at the smell of fried food which Declan can never rid the house of.

He admires the way she dresses: knee-high black boots, smart black coat and an emerald green scarf wound around her neck. She looks good, but it's been a long time since he fancied her.

Noisily jumping down the stairs two at a time, Oliver races to greet his mum, throwing his arms around her waist and crumpling her clothes. Amanda laughs, kisses the top of his head and asks why he's still dressed in his school uniform, but her eyes flick to Declan for the answer.

He thinks about lying but, if he announces that Oliver has been to an after-school club, Amanda will want to know why she wasn't consulted. Lying won't help his case either. He should have made sure Oliver had changed and washed his face.

'Hello again Ollie's mum,' Lola says with a grin, squeezing past them on her way back up the stairs.

Amanda smiles. 'Hello again, Lola.'

Again? Declan thinks with a frown. Have they met recently? Kerry has never said. Oh… they've probably all met outside the school gates when Amanda has taken Oliver to school.

'Have you bought me something nice, Mum?' Oliver asks, trying to pull apart the carrier bag in her hand to see inside.

'I don't know,' she says. 'I think you're getting too many "nice" things at home, young man. Far too many biscuits and sweets, and not enough fruit and veg.' Her sharp eyes glare at Declan who steps back. Why does she always make him feel that he's doing things wrong? Five years he's being bringing their son up. So far, he thinks he's been doing a bloody good job. Where would Oliver be if he'd been left in Amanda's shaky grasp?

'Actually, Mum,' the little boy begins, 'I was thinking of going vegetarian. Lola—'

'That's a brilliant idea. You can start with this,' and she thrusts the bag at him.

Declan steps closer to see inside. Punnets of grapes and plums, a bunch of small bananas, a net full of satsumas and a bag of small apples.

'Thanks, Mum,' Oliver politely says, reaching inside the bag to pluck a grape off the bunch. He pops it in his mouth. 'I only ever eat fruit at your house. Kerry says it costs an arm and foot.'

'You mean an arm and a leg, Oliver,' Amanda corrects.

Declan makes a fist so tight that his short fingernails dig into his fleshy palm. Out of the mouth of bloody kids.

'You pop upstairs and share your fruit with the girls whilst I have a word with your dad. Apparently he wants to talk about something serious.'

Oliver winds the bag handles around his wrist and makes his way upstairs, being careful not to bruise the fruit against the wall.

The fruit gift has given Declan just the opening he needs.

'Let's go into the lounge,' Amanda suggests, walking around him, her heeled boots sounding like a Nazi's jackboots on the hard floor.

Declan nods nervously. She always puts him on edge. How did they ever get together and have a child? Well, he thinks, they didn't *actually* get together. They met in a nightclub. Amanda was celebrating a colleague's 21st, and Declan was out with a few mates. They shared a few drinks and dances; a drunken fumble in the taxi led to a one-night stand back at her flat and the next morning they decided it was fun, but not to be repeated. He was surprised to hear from her a couple of months later with the news that she was pregnant and no, she assured him, no-one else could be the father. They decided not to attempt at being a couple, but Declan promised to support their child.

Amanda doesn't wait for the invite to sit down, but makes a point of moving aside the glossy magazines containing photos and stories of celebrities' lives. He knows what she's thinking. It's exactly the same thing he sees on her face every time she comes to his house. If he found Amanda attractive enough to go home with, then why has he allowed his standards to sink low enough that Kerry is now his partner? She is the polar opposite of Amanda. An overweight mouthy woman, who argues with strangers in a car park; a woman who thinks her legs are perfect for leggings, that her three tattoos should be on full display in the summer. But Kerry is always laughing; she's fiercely loyal, loves his son to death, is great in bed and has a kind word for everyone.

Apart from Amanda, of course.

Declan perches on the edge of the armchair, puts his hands together but realises that makes him look nervous so rests them on his thighs.

'This is about money, isn't it?' Amanda tuts when Declan shakes his head. 'Declan, we only ever discuss two matters: Oliver's schooling and money. And since I spoke to his teacher yesterday, it can only be about the latter.' Amanda crosses one knee over the other and loosens her coat buttons. She waits.

Suddenly, the fruit idea sounds lame. She will not increase her monthly payments so Oliver can go vegetarian. She knows he will never give up sausages and she will gladly buy him enough fruit to feed a troop of chimpanzees.

'Does Oliver need new clothes?' Amanda suggests helpfully. 'There's a long way to go yet before he's fully grown. If he needs new shoes, longer trousers, then let me know and I can take him shopping.'

But Declan is aware that Amanda bought Oliver all new stuff for the new school term. So pleas for pretend clothing won't work either. He really should have given his game plan careful consideration. He also knows he's got to say something. He asked her to take time out of her busy day to talk.

'Well, it's…it's been twelve months since you increased the monthly payments to two hundred a month. Can we…would you…perhaps, revise it?'

Amanda's expression remains completely unreadable. She doesn't reply for several moments and it makes Declan feel very uncomfortable.

'You want less? Is it too much?' she asks.

'No,' he replies quickly. Shit. 'I mean, I..would you increase it? Please.'

'The amount I provide is calculated according to lots of different factors: how much I earn, how many nights Oliver spends with me,' she explains.

'I know this—' but Amanda raises her hand and Declan shuts up.

'I pay more than the government recommends because I want my son to have the best. It's what I choose to do because he doesn't live with me. However, if Oliver were to spend more nights at my house, then this might alleviate any financial hardship you might be experiencing.'

'Oliver can spend as many nights with you and Dave as he wants,' Declan says, his tone argumentative. 'That's never been an issue.'

'Then what is? Have your circumstances changed, Declan? I hope there hasn't been a repeat of what happened four years ago.'

Four years ago, Declan was forced to ask Amanda for money to pay off his credit card bill after he fell behind with payments. Amanda then took a pair of scissors to the plastic.

'Or six months later.'

Six months after that, whilst dropping Oliver off, she found Declan in the house with the door wide open, crying in pain with a broken finger. She paid off his payday loan before the lender took the matter further. She left him with her own threat. If there were any more similar incidents, she would take Oliver back.

'It's nothing like that, Amanda. I promise you.'

'Declan, if you're going to insist on wasting your time and mine, then I'll spit it out for you. Kerry is pregnant and you don't know how you're going to pay for it. Do you?'

Declan's breath catches in his throat and he thinks about denying it, but what's the point? In a couple of months, it will be blindingly obvious that Kerry is expecting.

But how does she know? Has Oliver told...no, he doesn't know. They haven't told the kids yet.

'There is the obvious option,' Amanda is saying and he doesn't like her tone. 'I don't know how much a termination costs but it can't be more than a couple of hundred—'

'Jesus! We're not getting rid of it,' he replies defensively. 'I never asked you to get rid of Ollie.'

'No, but I could've afforded Oliver on my own. You don't even have the luxury of affording *this* child with two wages coming in. You must be practical.'

'Practical! Fucking hell, Amanda. How can you...the idea of getting rid of a...no way.'

'Stop swearing, Declan. There are three children in the house. It's an option. Plenty of women use the service for different reasons. I had no idea you were planning on having another child.'

Declan laughs and shakes his head. 'Why would I discuss *our* business with you? We're a family, Amanda. We've been together over a year. Why wouldn't we have a child together? You and David must have talked about having a baby. Surely he wants kids.'

Amanda doesn't reply, just stares at Declan, giving him his answer.

'I see...It's none of my business. Well, neither is this any business of yours.'

'It is when you're trying to con money out of me to pay for *your* child.'

'I am not trying to...fucking hell...I asked for an increase to—'

39

'I know exactly where the money will go. On nappies and nipple cream,' she states. 'Well, I have an option, which will alleviate the financial burden our son has placed on your new family.' Amanda reaches for her handbag off the floor and gets to her feet. Her face is serene. A slight smile is on her lips but her eyes dance with mirth. 'You've had him five years; Oliver can live with me.'

'No!' Declan shouts, leaping to his feet. 'This is his home. He's settled with me—'

'Declan,' Amanda says, her voice calm and non-negotiable, 'Oliver can stay with you as many nights as he likes. It'll be good for him to have a younger half-sibling. You won't have to worry about money for your baby; it will have everything it needs. Besides, Oliver has a budding relationship with David. It'll be good for him to have his stepfather's undivided attention.'

'We had an agreement,' Declan reminds her.

'It's not a court agreement though, is it?'

He resists the urge to call her a bitch. Everything has always been amicable between them. They're always able to talk about matters concerning Oliver. He will never, in a million years, afford to battle Amanda if she takes this to court.

'How are you going to cope with Oliver being at home?' he fires back. 'It wasn't so easy five years ago, was it?'

Amanda smiles coldly. 'It wasn't, no. But things are different now. I'm married, I'm making changes at the salon so I'll be home more. I'm more relaxed and I have a good support network.'

Declan's shoulders sink. He's run out of ammunition. But playing dirty was never his style.

'I won't let you do this to me, to my son.'

'You forget, he's my son too.'

'I fucking wish he wasn't.'

'Without me,' she points a finger in his face, 'you wouldn't have him.'

Declan snorts. 'Without *you*, I'd have him.'

Amanda tuts. 'Is there anything else? Only I must go. Let me know if Ollie needs anything. I can drop some fruit off on Friday when I pick him up. For the girls too. Let me know what they like. It's important they watch their weight. They're battling against their genes there.'

Powerless to stop her, Declan watches as Amanda strides across the floor and opens the front door.

'Oh, hello Kerry. How are you?' she asks, her voice sing-song.

Declan rushes to the door, but stubs his toe on the chair leg. He hobbles the rest of the way. Amanda has deliberately positioned herself so that Kerry can only enter the house by stepping sideways over the threshold. Her hands are carrying several bulging carrier bags and there's a box of washing powder tucked under her elbow.

'I said I'd pick you up,' he tells Kerry.

'Barry over the road gave me a lift,' Kerry grunts breathlessly, shoving a handful of bags at Declan who struggles to disentangle the handles from her chubby fingers.

'I must say, Kerry,' Amanda begins in that tone, 'you look positively radiant.'

'What?' she huffs, blowing out her fat cheeks.

'Bye bye Ollie.' Amanda shouts up the stairs, her mouth right by Kerry's ear. Kerry flinches, throws a dirty look at Declan.

'Bye Mum!' the little boy yells.

Kerry slams the door shut with the flat of her hand and drops the remaining carrier bags on the floor, the contents spilling out. Declan looks at all the naughty things she's bought: crisps, sweets, biscuits. Many are crushed and broken now. For fuck's sake. There's nothing here he can make a meal out of.

'I take it the stuck-up bitch said "no"?' Kerry tugs her tatty pink waterproof off her shoulders and hangs it on the stair post.

He hesitates. He can't tell Kerry about Amanda's two options or risk her storming around to Amanda's salon and pounding her head in.

'She knows you're pregnant. Don't ask me how, but she was prepared for me.'

'Decide what action you're going to take. Is there a bank that needs robbing? I'm going to the loo. My bladder's fit to burst.' Her thumbs hook over the waistband of her grey leggings and she starts to pull the waistband down as she heaves herself upstairs.

Declan squats to gather the shopping up and put it away. He opens the cupboard doors and stacks the cheap tins of beans and spaghetti away, the three-for-two pizzas go in the freezer with the boxes of other frozen food. Looks like chicken nuggets, instant mash and baked beans for tea. Again.

41

Amanda was never going to go for it, he consoles himself, stuffing the sack of Asda's own flavoured crisps into the cupboard. She's not stupid. She's an astute businesswoman. No matter how I dressed it up, she was always going to see through anything I said.

He balls the carrier bags up and shoves them in the cupboard.

'No washing-up liquid then.'

Declan stares out of the window at the garden that needs mowing, trimming, weeding and landscaping. They should move into a house with a concrete garden. Oliver's cheap plastic goalposts have gone green from the slimy stuff that usually grows on paving slabs. The crossbar snapped in two when Lola swung on it. Kerry promised an upset Oliver that she'd buy him another but she never did, and now Declan understands that Amanda bought Oliver a proper sturdy goalpost to use at her house.

Declan cannot compete.

But he won't stop trying.

He considers Kerry's idea. Rob a bank, he silently laughs. When was the last time someone did that? It's all stolen credit cards and online fraud nowadays. His thoughts wander down winding paths, thinking about who now has the cash and the balls to fund a bank robbery - or any crime for that matter?

Declan frowns as his mind stops on a name. Robbery isn't *his* thing, but *he* pays reasonably well. And the work is…how to describe it? A bit of driving, a lot of keeping your mouth shut. Declan can do that. He used to do it a lot back in the day when money was short. He should have gone back to it instead of letting Amanda bail him out.

The man's number might've changed, but he knows exactly where to find *him.*

He passes Hock's paper shop every day on his way to work.

Chapter 7

Amanda

'Pick your feet up, Martyn,' Amanda says, nudging his *New Balance* trainers with her broom. 'Come on! I'd like to get home sometime tonight.'

'Alright, alright, Mandy. Keep your wig on.' Martyn Hepworth lifts his feet off the floor and swivels himself away from the styling unit with a push of one hand.

Amanda raises the broom like it's a fighting staff but Martyn reaches out a lazy hand and presses the broom head down to the floor. He winks and she sniffs haughtily at him.

He's the only one that can get away with shortening her name. Even then, it's confined to his visits to the salon after hours.

Amanda manoeuvres the broom under his feet gathering the fallen hair into a small pile. She glances at the large clock on the wall. 8.20pm. For the last two hours, Amanda has been stuck in the salon dyeing and cutting the hair of a late-night client and she's found it's sapped all of her strength. She's had to pretend to listen and show an interest in what the client said, nothing of which she can now remember. Twice she caught the vacant look on her own face in the mirror and had to hurriedly alter her expression.

She sweeps the same spot under Martyn's feet over and over, her mind returning to the earlier conversation with Declan.

How utterly irresponsible of them to have a baby they cannot afford, she thinks angrily, and then expect *me* to pay for it. If Declan curbed Kerry's spending, because the fat cow clearly overeats, they'd have ample enough money to raise their child. Mind, he's shit with money. The times I've sorted his finances out.

You absolute idiot, Declan, getting that lazy, common trollop pregnant.

'Can I put my feet down now?' Martyn asks.

Amanda looks up, notices how tight her grip is on the handle and that she's made no progress during her daydream.

'Oh, sorry, yes, of course.'

Martyn smiles with concern. 'Stop dwelling on it. You've made your decision. It's exactly what I would've said. You've been very helpful, given them a couple of options.' He touches her arm. 'Come on. Don't spoil my visit. I haven't come to keep you company to see you mope around the place.'

'I'm not moping. And you,' she points a finger at him, 'haven't come to keep me company. You've come for a free coffee whilst you wait for your darling daughter to finish her shift.'

Martyn makes no attempt to hide his grin and laughs loudly.

Amanda and Martyn go back to when she was 15 and he was a newly qualified PE teacher. Amanda lost touch with him for several years as each moved away to learn their trade before returning to their home town, pulled back by their family roots.

Martyn is head of PE at Lexington Secondary but, more than that, Amanda believes that he deserves to be recognised for his services to sports in the community. Martyn and a fellow teacher from another school set up a company offering their expert coaching to promising swimmers. He strongly believes that sports is essential to promote young minds and bodies, and if he finds a rising star during his tutoring, Martyn has the contacts to put them on the right path to reach their full potential.

Amanda sweeps the pile of hair into the dustpan and starts polishing the styling units and each accompanying mirror.

'Young Dave warming the bed and chilling the wine for you, is he?' Martyn says, looking up from his mobile and leaning back in the swivel seating. He gives her a cheeky grin.

'He certainly is. I have him extremely well-trained.'

'That boy will do anything to get a few quid for his brewing business. Actually, I tried a bottle of his recent creation in the Red Lion the other night. My wife and I had a date night. Her idea. I thought it was stupid but I'd thought it wise to go along with it. It was very nice. The beer that is. The date was okay. You must be very proud of Dave. He's becoming quite the master brewer.'

'I am,' Amanda agrees, making Martyn burst out laughing. He knows she hates beer, hates David's passion for brewing even more.

'The more you restrain him, the harder he'll pull. A bit like a naughty disobedient puppy.'

'Very profound, Martyn,' she replies disdainfully.

'You should give him some money, Mandy. You always promised to. Even if it was just a hundred nicker. If you don't,' Martyn wags a warning finger at her, 'he'll leave you. And then, you'll be back on that shelf collecting dust.'

'Oh, thank you very much, my best friend. I don't think I want to discuss the state of my marriage with you—'

'So, it *is* in a state then?'

'Piss off,' she laughs, aiming the screwed-up yellow duster at his head. Or maybe the can of *Pledge* would do more damage if she lobbed that at his skull. 'How's the family?'

Martyn plucks a pair of thinning scissors from a ceramic pot on the styling unit and snips at the air. 'The wife is busy complaining that her budget has been slashed again. Bloody council cuts. The boys are arguing over the tiniest thing; it was cereals yesterday. Sarah floats around the house, dreaming of her new boyfriend instead of studying for her exams.'

'How is her job going?' Amanda asks, referring to his 17 year old daughter and the reason why he's camped out in the salon after eight pm.

'She's really enjoying cutting cheese with a wire and counting out slices of salami. Every penny earned goes towards driving lessons and that all important little runaround. Then I can retire Dad's Taxi until the next child gets a part-time job. Have you and Dec considered sending little Oliver out to work? I'm sure there are little buttons he can sew on, or perhaps chimneys he can sweep.'

'I have, yes.'

'Nipple cream?' Martyn suddenly laughs. 'You really said that?' Amanda nods and he smiles proudly. 'I will never understand what you saw in Dec the Speck.'

'I was drunk,' Amanda reminds him. 'Blame the cheap alcopops.'

'Oh, I do, believe me. Now, you and Dave the Brave will have beautiful children. But you better get cracking. Time is ticking. You're no longer that nubile fifteen year old with those innocent green eyes, slender firm thighs and perky little—'

'Enough!' Amanda shouts, and this time she throws the duster. It plummets to the ground, several metres away from its target. It still embarrasses her all these years later to hear him say these things about her. She can feel the hot blush spreading through her hair, where it prickles her scalp.

Martyn laughs and swivels back in the chair to face the huge mirror. He stares at his reflection. From her position at the reception desk, Amanda studies him too, seeing the young man she fancied. He was so athletic. Broad-shouldered, narrow waist, muscular arms and legs. He had the physique of a male gymnast.

One touch of his hand on her bare skin or his mouth on hers and she would melt like snow on a hot August day.

The lies she told to keep him.

The lies he told to keep her.

They were as bad as each other. Sneaking around behind people's backs to meet up and drive forty odd miles out of town to conduct their illicit relationship without fear of being seen.

You have no conscience when you're a precocious teenager with nothing to lose and everything to gain, Amanda thinks. And absolutely no thought of the consequences.

'Do you think I should start dyeing my hair?' Martyn asks, running his fingers through the front of his hair and making it stick up. 'If I do, I run the risk of the pupils taking the piss.' He smooths his hair down, turns his face to the side, touches the hair at his temple. 'Kids can be fucking ruthless. I have to be their mate *and* their teacher. It's such a hard balance.'

'Dye your hair,' she encourages, pretending to be serious. Personally, she never recommends men colour their hair. Only women can get away with it because it's expected of them to try to look younger. Men age better. 'Go for it. I can show you some swatches and do it next time you're killing time waiting for Sarah. I think a delicious chocolate brown or maybe a rich auburn would suit you.'

Martyn stares at her in the mirror. 'I'm blond.'

'Really? Are you sure?'

'Cheeky cow. Don't you remember my gorgeous blond locks?'

Amanda mashes her lips together and frowns thoughtfully. 'No. I thought under all that white and grey you were once dark. Are you sure? What colour is your chest hair?'

Martyn tugs down the front of his fleece to check. 'It's blond, I think,' he mutters quizzically. 'There's only one way to be sure. Let me just,' and he gets to his feet, his fingers pulling at the ties at the front of his jogging bottoms, 'see what's down here…'

'Jesus, Martyn, no!' Amanda yells, leaping to her feet and looking at the huge shop window. 'The lights are on. Somebody will see. For God's sake, put it away. No one wants to see your tiny member.'

Martyn stares at her, pretend insult on his face. 'My tiny what? I don't seem to remember you complaining about its size on the backseat of my Escort. I can still hear the cries of "More, more, Martyn, harder, faster."'

Amanda retrieves the duster, shudders at the memory of how she was with him: nervous and terrified at first, but slowly he began to unravel her until she became compliant and often brazen and slutty. A sharp contrast to how she is now with David. Why is that? she asks herself. Why am I so shy? Why do I always need alcohol to relax and let go?

She wonders if it's worth asking Martyn but knows she won't get a serious answer. He is the only person she can discuss these matters with. Opening up that box now, twenty years later and with them both being married with children, doesn't seem right.

Martyn is scrutinising his reflection closely in the mirror. 'There's still some blond strands left. Here, you can see them at my temples. I suppose they could be silver.'

Amanda shakes her head and turns her attention to the client list for the next day. 'I'm sure I have a very detailed description of your physical attributes in my diary.'

It's several seconds before he replies. 'What diary?'

Amanda looks up, his harsh tone surprising her.

Martyn has swivelled away from the mirror and is staring very seriously at her. 'What diary? From when?'

'From when I was fifteen, Martyn. Every girl keeps a diary at that age. We wrote down the boys and pop stars we fancied, practised signing our names with our boyfriends' surname. I must've filled pages and pages with different styles of Amanda Hepworth.' She laughs. 'Along with—'

'Are you telling me you kept a diary of our time together?'

'Yes. I was fifteen, Martyn. It was something I wanted to remember.'

Martyn gets to his feet and walks to the desk, his trainers squeaking on the floor. 'No,' he says in a tone she can't recognise. 'Have you *kept* it? Do you still have it?'

Amanda hasn't seen any of her diaries for many years. But they're definitely at home. When her parents downsized and moved into their bungalow, they insisted Amanda take or throw away the belongings she'd left. There's no way she would have thrown them out.

'They're in the loft.'

'How sure are you? When was the last time you saw them? Who has access to the loft?' he demands, placing his palms on the chest-high reception desk. He leans over her.

Amanda leans away. His hot breath touches her face; her nose detects coffee. She looks for an exit route. Behind her is the wall. There's only one way out from behind the desk - to her left, but he only needs to take two or three steps to the right and he will have closed the exit off and penned her in.

She can't understand why he's making a big deal out of a 22 year old diary. Who would want to read it? Or maybe he's toying with her. Sometimes, his jokes go too far and she has to ask him to stop. Is this one of those occasions?

'Okay, okay. I did send it off to a publisher's and they were very interested in serialising it for ITV. They were quite prepared to change the names of those involved to hide their identities.' She laughs, hoping he'll snap out of this mood he's suddenly in.

But his face remains stern. 'It's not a laughing matter, Amanda,' he informs her forcibly.

She stands, but the movement pushes the chair into the wall and she can't squeeze through the narrow gap easily. Why's he being like this? Why does she feel scared of him?

'Answer my question,' he demands. 'Who has access—'

'David has,' she shouts, shoving the chair out from behind the desk and stepping into the floorspace. Martyn doesn't come any closer. 'But he never goes up there. He has no reason to. There's some of Oliver's baby stuff up there,' she hurriedly says listing the items, which makes her think of Kerry's impending pregnancy. 'My hairdressing crap, a Christmas tree…'

'Get rid of it,' Martyn orders viciously.

'What?'

'The fucking diary! Get rid of it, burn it if you have to. You can't keep it, Amanda. Surely you can see that.'

'No, I can't. Who would be interested in a teenage girl's diary?'

Martyn laughs sardonically. 'You've mentioned me by name, signed your name with my surname, given a very detailed description of my looks and what we did. Amanda, our relationship wasn't exactly…well, you know what I mean. I'm a teacher. If it got out, can you imagine the damage it would do?'

'Why would it get out?'

'Because your fucking husband has access to the loft! One day, he might decide to have a nosy around up there, find out about his new wife's past and, before he knows it, he's fully enlightened as to what kind of child she was!'

Martyn stops shouting. His chest is rising quickly as he breathes hard. His face is red and, if he wasn't such a fit and healthy bloke, Amanda would be more concerned about him having a heart attack.

'What *kind* of child?' she demands. 'What's that supposed to mean? If I was the child, you were the adult. And you would definitely be the one to blame.'

'I seem to remember that you were well up for it,' Martyn reminds her, his voice sharp.

It feels like a hard slap across her face. Certainly the insinuation that she was a slag stings like an assault.

'I want you to leave,' she orders. But he ignores her.

'Amanda, there are very few people who would understand what we had,' he begins, his voice softer, more pleading. A change of tack. 'And there was nothing wrong with it. We both knew who we were and what we wanted. All I'm saying is that we are both well-thought of figures in the community. In order to protect my position as a teacher, and both our reputations, then I am asking you to safeguard that by destroying your diary.'

A sharp rapping on the glass startles them and they jump. Amanda looks at the front door, her heart pounding. Martyn's daughter is waving and grinning.

'You'd best go,' Amanda tells him, coldly.

He walks towards the door, pauses before he leaves, and looks at her.

'Please Amanda. It's one tiny thing I'm asking for. Destroy it.'

Amanda reaches around him, unlocks and opens the door, allowing a cold gust of wind to blow into the shop. She feels it around her legs.

'Your daughter's getting cold. Take her home.'

'I'll see you next week,' he mutters.

'Bye Martyn.'

'Hi love, he says brightly to his daughter. 'How was work?'

Amanda shuts the door and locks it. Martyn's shoulders tighten at the abruptness of her action. Quickly, she retreats into the salon, flicking the light switches off and plunging the place into darkness. Only the lights from the lampposts and passing cars illuminate her path back to the staffroom where she collects her bags and keys and locks up.

She exits the shop via the back door, has her car keys ready in case he wants to plead or threaten her once more.

'Destroy my diary…' she mutters, punching in the five-digit code. The alarm starts beeping and she hurries away, down the well-lit passageway towards her car. 'I am sick of men thinking they can get away with bullying and conning me. Well, Martyn Hepworth, you can go fuck yourself too.'

Chapter 8

Martyn

Martyn Hepworth grabs the rugby-shaped stress ball from his desk drawer. His daughter bought it for him last Christmas as a joke but rugby has never been his game. And, up until last night, he had no use for it. Martyn doesn't usually get stressed.

A diary, he thinks, squeezing his fist. His skin stretches taut over his knuckles until he can see the outline of his bones. What the fuck was Amanda thinking, cataloguing their relationship in extensive detail? Was she mad? Why has she completely failed to understand how serious this is? It only needs her husband or son to go rooting through the boxes in the loft on some kind of innocent quest, stumble across a sticker-covered diary, have a bit of a flick through the pages, and before you know it, the police are knocking on his door asking questions about sex with an underage girl. Not that Martyn knew that at the time. Amanda looked 17; she *told* him she was 17, so why wouldn't he believe her? But then he realises, it's what came later that would convict him. He'd have no defence.

The feeling of dread sits heavily in Martyn's chest, and he asks himself: is the game over? Perhaps this is a warning, the writing on the wall before his name is splashed all over the papers.

He leans back in the swivel chair, ignoring the paperwork on his desk, aware he has a deadline to meet. How the hell can he be expected to concentrate and grade the little shits when his mind is firmly elsewhere?

He can perhaps understand, at a push, why she wrote it? But why keep it? Is it to reminisce about her first romance, the night she lost her virginity, the sneaking around and the lies she told her family, the pregnancy scare, their break-up and their promise to each other. Does she need written words to remember all that?

Martyn can instantly recall every detail about her. He can pluck it from the depths of his mind and relive it easily. And that surprises him considering the relationships he had either side of the one he had with her.

He remembers how naive and enthusiastic she was. He took complete advantage of that and her desire to please him, but he would also argue that she was willing. He never forced her. He just introduced her to sex and how best to please a man. The man being him.

There's something wonderfully endearing and sexy about a teenage girl and the way they'll *do* anything for an older man, provided you choose the right girl.

Some of the comments Martyn hears from the girls at this school as they stroll up and down the corridors beggars belief. It's enough to make his eyes water. He can't believe how promiscuous and experienced they are. But rather illogically perhaps, these girls do nothing for him. He doesn't want a girl who knows as much or more than he does. He gets such a thrill from teaching them what he likes.

Besides, getting involved with a girl of this type is a road to disaster.

But Amanda…

He thinks about the first time they had sex in the back of his car. No easy task. But he couldn't very well take her back to his flat. That would have given the game away. She'd have found out he wasn't a university student like he claimed. It was safe after she knew the truth. He could get adventurous then.

The first time was out of this world. He'd waited three weeks to get his hands on her. Three long weeks of charming and complimenting her.

And fuck, did it pay dividends.

'Jesus,' Martyn whispers, glancing down at his lap and seeing the effects his own reminiscing is having. 'I've got to stop this.'

It occurred to him at 3.20am during his sleepless night, that it's possible Amanda has kept the diary as insurance to use against him. He doesn't know for what purpose. They've always remained friends, although they conduct large parts of it in the salon after hours. He's supportive of everything she does, he offers advice and is frequently a shoulder to cry on and an ear to moan at. But her reaction to his suggestion of destroying it has unnerved him and sent his mind hurtling down this track of worry.

They've been friends for 22 years, surely that must mean something to her?

Exasperated with his thoughts and Amanda's stubbornness, he squeezes the stress ball once more before throwing it across the room. It bounces off the notice board where the wall calendar and various important notes are pinned, lands on the floor and rolls back under his desk.

'Great,' he mutters and swivels around in the chair to face the window. Through the vertical blinds, he can see the black all-weather pitch where the pupils play tennis, hockey and netball. It's a sunny dry morning. He wonders what classes are doing PE now. He glances at the wall chart, squinting at the small words.

'Oh,' he says, his interest piquing. '11A. Miss Evans is taking the girls for football.'

Isn't Lucy James in 11A?

Martyn reaches for the short pole hanging to the side of the blind and twists it, turning the slats to the right, which allows light to enter the office and increases his view. He knows the football pitch behind the hedge where they normally play is too muddy. Yesterday one of the boys twisted his ankle whilst going in for a tackle and had to be taken to A&E by his mother. So the girls will be confined to the all-weather pitch.

His ears detect the unmistakable chorus of girlish shouting and chatting and, from around the corner of the sports' hall, a group of teenage girls appear. All of them are dressed in black leggings and short-sleeved polo shirts.

Miss Evans is carrying a net of football balls over her shoulder the way Father Christmas carries a sack of presents. When she reaches the centre of the pitch, she flings it to the ground, pulling off the netting and scattering the footballs. The girls scrabble around, stopping the balls with their feet or hands.

That's when he spots Lucy. She's got an armful of coloured bibs, which she chucks on top of the empty netting.

She's a tall girl, close to five eight and slim. Martyn reckons about size 8, with a bust size of 32 inches, which is good going for a 15 year old.

Lucy has long blonde hair which is so straight and soft, Martyn knows that, if he had the chance to run his fingers through it, her locks would feel like silk.

Today her hair is woven into a single plait, which hangs between her slim shoulders.

But Lucy isn't the slightest bit sporty. He's studied her. Seen the way she stoops at the back of groups, hoping to be picked last. And when she's supposed to be warming-up with all the other substitutes, she stands around gossiping to the other girls who don't want to take part.

The school is big on sport, in particular swimming. It boasts a six lane, 25 metre pool. Martyn believes that sport is the elixir of life, that swimming is important in young lives. In the same way that boxing can save the lives of young men and stop them entering a life of gangs and crime, swimming can do something similar.

Provided you can swim.

Lucy cannot swim and shows no interest in learning.

Martyn is gutted. He was British junior 100 metre front crawl champion in his younger years. And he would kill to see this gorgeous girl in a swimming costume. Though he's not supposed to ever be in the water with a pupil, unless it's warranted and witnessed by a third person, he would risk it because he'd love to get his hands on her young flesh. And he'd assure her that yes, with the right technique and complete dedication to the sport, she could be a junior champion too.

And she'd lap it up, enticed by his encouragement, the promise of medals and podium positions, fame and money. And once he'd groomed her to that point, the rest would fall into place easily. Like it had so many times before.

But she's no water baby.

And so, he resigns himself to stealing glances from his office window, fantasising about her.

He lifts the waistband off his jogging bottoms, glances at the door; should he risk a quick tug?

Best not. His mind is running away with him. It is not wise to eye up, let alone get involved with, a girl from *his* school.

He's always refrained from it. He has no need. There are plenty of young women out there who *want* to make it big in the swimming world, and whether they have the talent or not, Martyn is more than willing to coach them.

He has a girl on the go at the moment and this one is very involved with Martyn. He's been grooming her for weeks and now it's paying off. It'll last as long as it's meant to but, when it ends, they'll part on good terms. Martyn will make sure of that. It's his security. The last thing he needs is a scorned ex or a tell-all diary coming to light.

'That fucking diary,' he says aloud.

If he can't make Amanda see sense and destroy it, what can he do? Trust her word that she'll find a better hiding place? He could offer to have it and then accidentally 'lose' it. She'd never go for that. Can he break into the house and steal it? Or will their earlier conversation have forced her to move it to a safer location? Perhaps she could redact it?

He must make her understand the consequences of the diary being seen by someone else. He must lay it on a bit more about how people will judge her. After all, she lied too. Even after

54

she discovered he was older and already a PE teacher, she continued to lie because she wanted to continue their relationship.

Will she want people knowing what a promiscuous teenager she was? That Oliver wasn't her only pregnancy. Amanda is far from being the angel she perceives herself to be.

Chapter 9

Amanda

'Come on, Oliver, take your coat off,' Amanda tells him, her arms laden with his PE kit bag and satchel. The little boy shrugs the anorak off his shoulders and down his upper arms, leaving it on the floor.

Amanda picks it up and hooks it over the stair post, tutting loudly, but Oliver pays no attention and heads straight for the lounge and the television, settling himself in the over-sized armchair with the remote control.

'Don't get too comfortable, Oliver. I want you changed before your dinner.' She waits by the door for his acknowledgement. 'Did you hear me?' she asks loudly.

'Yes, Mum,' he replies, turning the volume up on the cartoon.

She heads to the kitchen, switching on the light. It buzzes and flickers into life, casting a bright whiteness over the surfaces. Amanda drops his bags on the floor to sort out whilst she cooks tea, but first decides to peer through the blind into the back garden. The light is on in the shed but this time, Amanda's heart doesn't sink with disappointment. There was no sign of Jake's car in the street so for once David must be alone. She smiles and glances back through the open door. Oliver's cartoon is on loud but she doesn't tell him to turn it down. It'll keep him busy for those few minutes she needs.

Amanda switches the oven on to warm up, sliding a baking tray onto the top shelf. She looks back through the window to make sure the shed light is still on. Seeing that it is and David is snug inside, she steps back into the hall on silent feet, arm outstretched, fingers reaching for the curved handle on the top of David's battered *Nike* rucksack. The weight of it pulls her arm unexpectedly down and she has to grab it with the other hand to catch it.

What's he got in here? she asks, tiptoeing back into the empty kitchen. She places it on the kitchen table, pushing the fruit bowl and the pile of post aside, and quickly unzips the bag. The contents smell of David: his zesty deodorant, the cheap aftershave that he bought himself, the wax he runs through his hair, which he doesn't wash off his hands afterwards.

They're all familiar scents for Amanda and they cause a longing in her. He's her husband. He said "Yes" to her when she proposed. He didn't have to. He could have said, 'No, it's too soon. We barely know each other,' or, 'I'm too young to get married; I want to play the field.'

56

David suggested a long engagement, to give them time to get to know each other, but Amanda was adamant that she wanted them to marry soon.

'I'm 37,' she had told him. 'And I have never felt this way about someone before. You're absolutely the one I want.'

So why is she tiptoeing around, going through his phone, his wardrobe and drawers, and his van when she gets the chance? What is she looking for? She has never even seen David so much as glance at another woman. He doesn't talk about any of the women whose houses he goes to when he lays carpets and floorings. She has never found anything untoward in his belongings. No piece of lost jewellery, a different coloured hair, or the smell of an alien perfume.

Absolutely nothing.

But it doesn't soothe her doubts. David is a handsome young man.

She must be vigilant at all times.

Women can be predatory. Men can be weak.

She pulls the zip down all the way, opening the mouth of the bag wider, and removes the cumbersome sandwich box, empty except for an apple core, a chocolate bar wrapper and a piece of kitchen towel he lines the bottom of the box with. She removes two empty water bottles, his tea-stained travel mug and the empty flask he puts hot water in. David tells her frequently his customers don't offer him a cup of tea, so he takes his own.

There's a bundle of papers lying creased against the back of the rucksack. Amanda pulls them out and flicks through them. One is a stapled booklet explaining the terms and conditions of a bank loan and the other is an application form several pages long, a paperclip in one corner. The first couple of boxes are filled in with details of his full name, address. Tucked inside the stapled booklet is a torn-out piece of note paper. On it are hand-written numerical workings out. If David borrows £1000, he'll repay x amount each month, but if he borrows £2000, he'll pay y amount.

'A loan,' she mutters. It's the last thing she wants him to have, but she should have seen this coming. She should have bloody known that *this* is the only legitimate option for him… unless that friend of his lends him money. He has in the past. But Jake only got wealthy because he was injured in an industrial accident and received a huge payout.

She briefly toys with the idea of giving David what she sort of promised him at the beginning of their relationship. Would a couple of hundred be enough to appease him? Or would he want more? She puts the papers to one side and carries on rummaging through the bag. She flicks through the pages of his hard-backed diary which lists the names, addresses and job details of the customers he's got lined up. There's no hand-scribbled mobile phone numbers on scraps of paper. But she scans the names and addresses of the last couple of weeks to see if David has paid the homeowner a return visit, because what better way to hide a fling than to write it blatantly in a diary and later claim it was a genuine job.

A clicking sound makes her jump and she quickly looks around, expecting to see David standing in the doorway watching her, but it's just the oven reaching temperature.

She sighs with relief; she's nearly done. The tabletop is covered in David's belongings, which must be replaced and the bag must be returned to the hall before he walks through the door. The last item in the bag is David's tablet.

Is there stuff on here not found on his phone? Pictures, or messages, websites he's visited, videos he's been streaming. Because surely watching porn on a screen of this size is more pleasurable than a phone screen.

Amanda lifts the tablet cover and the screen illuminates, but the battery icon says there's only 12% of juice left. It's enough for a quick look. She presses the button but, rather than unlocking the device, it asks for a four-digit code.

'Shit.' What is it? David had this device before they met so it can't be their anniversary or her date of birth or Oliver's. Is it his own? She types in his year of birth. No joy. She types in his day and month of birth. No joy. Will 1234 unlock it? Might Oliver know what it is?

Amanda only manages to type in 1 before there's a sound at the back door. Her head jerks to the door, her heart suddenly pounding in alarm. She sees it open and still she stands there, frozen to the spot. A laughing male voice; cold air enters the kitchen and wafts across her bare arms. David steps over the threshold, his work boot landing heavily on the doormat, his handsome face sweeping around to look in the direction he's going, and his gaze lands on her. He stops, drinks in the scene.

Amanda closes the cover on the tablet, her arms dropping, lowering the device behind the wide open rucksack. David steps closer and behind his left shoulder, Jake's smug face appears.

'What are you doing, Amanda?' David asks.

She cannot say she thought the device was ringing because would there be any need to rummage through the entire contents of his bag? She cannot lie that Oliver wanted to play with it because he has the latest tablet, far superior to this slow clunky device. She cannot say she wanted to borrow it to google something because her mobile is quicker.

'It looks to me, mate,' Jake quips, 'that the missus is going through your stuff. Again.'

David's head turns to him. 'Yes, it does, doesn't it?'

Amanda's eyes blaze. How dare David involve Jake in this?

David steps closer and looks at the items on the table. The diary is closed but a corner of one page has folded over. The bank loan documents are untidy and the paperclip that was holding the papers together hangs guiltily off one corner.

'Amanda, what are you looking for? Oh, you don't know the code for the tablet. It's 0783. The first four digits of my mobile. Let me put it in for you. Then you can have a good look around that too.' He snatches the tablet from her grasp and the sharp action snaps her fingertips together.

She winces.

'Here,' and he shoves the device back at her. Its screen is lit up, showing a photo of the two of them on their wedding day, their happy faces against a backdrop of a Caribbean shoreline. Across the bottom of the screen where the golden sand meets the turquoise sea, she glimpses the icons and sees that he has 27 unread email messages.

'Go on,' and he pushes the tablet further at her. But she doesn't take it though she desperately wants to. Twenty-seven unread messages scream at her.

'Oh, you're not interested now. If you tell me what you're looking for maybe I can find it.'

She glances at Jake who has settled himself against the sink, arms folded, an amused smirk on his face.

David snaps the cover back over the screen, the sharp noise making her jump. He shoves the device back into the bag and turns to the other items spread out on the table. 'Have you gone through every page of the diary? What about the side pockets? Checked those too, have you? No? Let me,' and he turns the rucksack around, unzipping the hidden pockets. 'Nothing but a couple of used tissues.' He extracts a screwed-up tissue, unfolds it. 'This is snot by the way, not cum.'

Amanda flinches. Jake laughs.

David drops the tissue onto the table. 'Because that's what this is about, isn't it?' He glares at her. She barely recognises him: his hard blue eyes, his clenched jaw, the tone of his voice. She has never seen him like this before. It worries her.

'You think I'm fucking women behind your back. Because I'm young and good-looking, I mustn't have an ounce of decency in me. I must be chatting up every woman I meet and fucking them in the back of my van or on the carpet I've just laid in their house. This is what you're after, isn't it? Evidence of my adultery?'

'I…I'm sorry. David…can we talk about this when we're alone?' she asks in a small voice.

'No,' he announces to the room. 'Why should we? To save you from further embarrassment?'

Amanda lowers her burning face. She should walk out of the kitchen, go upstairs to the bathroom and refuse to come out until Jake has gone, but her humiliation appears to have rooted her to the floor. Why didn't she hear them coming? Why didn't she take the rucksack upstairs to the sanctuary of the locked bathroom?

'Mummy, when's tea?' a little voice complains. 'I'm starving.'

Amanda reacts first, turning to her son. This is just the interruption she needs. 'It's in the oven, Oliver,' she lies. 'Come on. Let's get you changed. You can't eat in your school uniform,' and she reaches for his hand to lead him upstairs, but the little boy shirks away, hiding his hand behind his back.

'I want David to take me,' Oliver demands, grinning at David.

'Be with you in a sec, mate,' he tells Oliver before turning to Jake and saying, 'Give me five minutes with Oliver and I'll drop you off at home.'

'Take as long as you like, mate. Amanda will keep me company.' Jake smirks at her and she cringes. 'Car's off the road. New exhaust.'

David walks past her. Out of the side of his mouth, he mutters, 'I'm not letting this drop, Amanda.' Then to Oliver: 'Come on, mate! Race you to the landing. Ready…GO!'

Oliver squeals with mock terror and, with socked feet sliding on the hall floor, he races to the bottom stair and upwards. David gives chase with a war cry, leaving Amanda in the kitchen with Jake.

She feels Jake's penetrating gaze and, needing to hide from him, she opens the door to the freezer.

She hears him straighten. The soles of his trainers squeak on the floor and he emits a little groan because his back is playing up. Her shoulders tense in response, bracing themselves against what she knows he'll say. He won't miss the opportunity he's longed for, now she's alone, to tell her *exactly* what he thinks of her. And it's odd how she is always on edge when Jake is there. Whenever they've been left together, because David has gone to put his trainers on or he's forgotten something upstairs, Amanda can't even make mindless small talk with Jake. She makes an excuse too, citing a window that needs closing or an appliance that needs switching on.

She knows she is jealous of their friendship, their closeness. She wants that with David. She wants to be the only one he comes to.

Jake always looks straight at her, as if he knows every lie she has ever told, every bad word she's said behind someone's back, and every evil thought that's lurked in her mind.

Jake knows *exactly* what kind of bitch Amanda is.

'David's a good bloke,' Jake tells her, stepping closer.

Out of the corner of her eye, she can see the red toes of his trainers but busies herself sliding out the bottom drawer and rummaging through the boxes for the frozen cod even though it is on the top.

'He's had some cracking girlfriends in the past. Really good-looking women who have been generous and caring and funny. Women you'd give your right arm to have one date with.' Jake sighs.

Is that all he has to say, Amanda wonders.

'I don't get it,' Jake ponders with puzzlement.

Brace yourself, she thinks.

'I just don't fucking get what he sees in a bitch like you.'

Chapter 10

Lawrence

'The trouble is, well, you can see here, Mr Hayden—'

'Call me, Lawrence,' Lawrence tells Mrs Newman for the fourth time.

She smiles. 'The fence panel is wrecked and, what with the strong wind we had last week, it's hanging by a thread.'

'They're over ten years old,' Mr Newman tells Lawrence, grabbing the top of the fence panel and rattling it vigorously. Lawrence notes that it's literally only being held in place by lots of garden twine.

Lawrence steps off the patio and onto the stepping stones sunk into the lawn. As he walks along the stone path, he inspects the rest of the fence. Well-established bushes and shrubs crowd the border, hiding the fence from view. He reaches around the plants, moving aside branches to check the condition of the other posts and panels. Many are covered with ivy, buckled under the weight of the foliage and its clinging shoots. He can see that Mr Newman, over the years, has tried to repair each one with garden twine and small wedges of wood lodged into gaps between the posts and panels.

Lawrence returns to where the retired couple wait. Mrs Newman is shivering in her long cardigan.

'Go back in the house, love,' her husband tells her, 'and stick the kettle on.'

She nods and heads back to the house.

'Mr Newman, it's up to you, but I recommend you replace all the fence panels. Some of them,' and Lawrence waves his pencil along the panels, 'are quite rotten. I can see you've bandaged them up as much as you can, but the storm due next week could bring the whole lot down. And I'm sure you don't want one of the panels flying into your greenhouse.' He waves the pencil at the glass structure standing a few metres away. 'They have a way of taking flight.'

Mr Newman nods his understanding. 'You might as well quote for the whole lot. Is there any chance you can paint them before they go in? It'd save me a job.'

'The wood is already treated but, yeah, I can do that. No problem, Mr Newman.'

'And the wife's asked you about the gutters?' Lawrence nods. 'I don't think there's anything else at the moment. In the spring, I want a raised bed building. I used to do all this myself, but I've got osteoarthritis in my back. Some days, I can't even pick up a bag of sugar.' Mr Newman chuckles with sadness. 'Never mind my aches and pains. Old age comes to us all. Come inside for a cuppa.'

He leads the way down the side of the house and into the warm kitchen. Mrs Newman is pouring boiling water into three cups.

'Do you take sugar?' she asks Lawrence.

'Two, thanks,' he replies, wiping his feet on the mat.

'How soon can you get us the quote?' Mr Newman asks.

'I can do it straightaway.'

Mrs Newman settles Lawrence at the dining room table with his tea and a plate of chocolate digestives, and leaves him alone. Lawrence gets straight onto his mobile and rings up a couple of fencing supply firms for costs of eleven featheredge fence panels measuring 6 by 6 feet and concrete posts and gravel boards to boot.

He jots down the costing, adds his labour, including the painting of each panel, both sides and one side in case Mr Newman's neighbour objects to the chosen colour. He does two quotes, one including disposal of the old panels, and the other excluding in case Mr Newman knows someone who can get rid of the old wood. He creates another quote for the cleaning of the guttering.

He sips his tea, picks up a second biscuit and relaxes back into the seat. He gazes through the dining room window into the autumn garden.

It's not a big job. It'll take maybe two and a half days, weather permitting. And the couple seem nice; they even mentioned that a lot of their friends were looking for a trustworthy handyman to do jobs they can't do anymore. It all helps. And this job will put him back on track after last week's humiliation.

That fucking bitch Amanda Davies.

He puts the end of the pencil in his mouth and bites down on it. Back in his hometown, after Nathan's conviction and after that news reporter shoved the microphone and camera in his face as he was leaving the house to take his kids to school, and he said what he said, Lawrence felt everyone turned their back on him. People in his local supermarket gave him stern sideways glances. They stepped away when he reached to take groceries off the shelves in case he had something that was catching. Neighbours out cleaning their cars or tending their front gardens whispered to each other. Customers cancelled jobs citing money or time pressures. Mates stopped asking him out for a drink. His daughter was dropped from the school hockey team.

Amanda has been the only one who has told him to his face exactly what kind of scum he is. He supposes he should admire her for that. Everybody is entitled to their own opinion but only when they have the full facts, and the full facts did not come out in court.

No one told the jury how long Nathan's partner was cheating on him, that it was literally mere weeks after the death of their little girl that she had sex with another man. They didn't call for the expert opinion of the psychologist to tell the courtroom the depth of the grief Nathan was experiencing. They kept quiet about the sly things *she* had said about Nathan, how she blamed his "bad" chromosomes for Millie's death. They weren't silent about how his drinking had spiralled out of control, but they didn't mention that he *only* drank because she had deserted him. They told the jury how Nathan had been barred from his local, the only place he could find solace after the unimaginable had happened, but not that he kicked off after trying to play Millie's favourite song for the fifth time that evening.

It was so unfair; Nathan was a loving father.

Someone had to put them all straight.

So Lawrence had. He told the reporters congregating outside his house who exactly was to blame. Her. The dead child's mother. That cheating, neglectful bitch, too busy opening her legs for another man rather than support her grieving husband.

'How are you getting on?' The voice makes him jump and Mrs Newman apologises profusely. 'I'm so sorry, Mr Hayden.'

'It's alright,' he assures her, 'I was just admiring your garden. Got lost watching the birds feeding,' and as if on cue, a blue tit lands on a metal arm of the feeder and pecks at a suet log. Lawrence tears the page off his notepad and hands it to Mrs Newman. He gathers his stuff up and stands.

'My numbers are on the top. Give me a call if you want to discuss the quote or anything.'

'Thank you, Lawrence. We'll let you know.' She smiles pleasantly and shows him to the front door, but Mr Newman emerges from the lounge asking if Lawrence can spare a quick second.

'Yes, of course,' he replies, following the man outside onto the path. A few steps down, Mr Newman stops and turns back to the house, pointing up at the eaves.

64

'Have you got a decent ladder?' Lawrence nods. 'That'll reach up there?' Lawrence nods again. 'Can you put something up under the eaves to scare the swallows off? They come back every year to nest. Bloke next door,' and Mr Newman jerks his thumb at the house on his right, 'says a couple of CDs will do the trick. I can't put up with the mess. Bird crap all over the windows. Every house in the street has got a bloody nest.'

Lawrence nods. 'Yeah, no problem, Mr Newman.'

'Good lad.'

Lawrence hears the muffled sound of loud music being played behind the windows of a vehicle and turns to see a black 4x4 driving too fast down the leafy road. The driver swings the vehicle wide, its offside wheels breaching the central white line, so it can swing left onto the driveway. The Newman's neighbour.

The driver turns the engine off but lets the music continue to play for several seconds before removing the key and silencing the noise.

Lawrence makes no comment about the neighbour's lack of consideration for others. But he knows it'd bother him if he had to put up with that racket.

'Hi George,' a female voice shouts cheerfully from over the box hedge separating the two properties.

Lawrence fishes out his car key out of his pocket as the driver's door slams shut.

'Hi Amanda, love,' Mr Newman replies, raising a large hand.

Lawrence can feel his eyes widening and his breath catching in his throat. He shuffles backwards, partly obscuring himself behind the tall conifer tree.

You've got to be fucking joking me. *She* lives next door.

But Amanda has turned her gaze back to Mr Newman and is smiling pleasantly at him. And Lawrence wonders if she's seen him. It might be that she can't place his face, or better still, that what happened meant so little to her that she's forgotten she sacked him.

Either way, Lawrence has to leave now before Mr Newman calls him by his name.

Keeping his voice at a volume only Mr Newman can hear, Lawrence bids his goodbye and hurries down the drive to his van. Without putting on his seatbelt, he executes the speediest and untidiest three-point turn ever and accelerates away.

*

65

Lawrence grabs a plate from the draining rack, shakes the excess water off and wipes it dry with a tea towel. He stacks the clean plates and bowls back in the cupboard.

'When do you think you might hear from them?' Rachel asks, sliding the rectangular lasagne dish into the bowl of soapy water. It causes a small tsunami to break across the surface, sloshing water over the rim of the bowl.

'They said they were getting a couple of quotes, so maybe by the end of the week. I think I've got a good chance. I hope I have anyway,' Lawrence says.

'I hope so too.' Rachel turns from the sink, but leaves her hands in the water which is turning orange from the lasagne sauce. Her tone changes. 'Sam brought a letter home from school. There's a trip next April to Paris. She really wants to go.'

'I bet she does.'

'But they need to know by the end of November. It's a lot of money, but it'd be a lot more expensive if we took her.'

We wouldn't take her, Lawrence thinks. Because all five of us would have to go. And the kids would want to go to Disney World or whatever it's called. And I lost that bloody job because of that bitch.

'Lawrence,' Rachel says sharply, snapping him out of his thoughts. 'I can speak to my mum and dad.'

Lawrence looks confused. What were they talking about? Paris.

'No.' Then firmer, 'No. I'll sort something out.' But Rachel doesn't look reassured, and he's reminded that she didn't want to move. She wanted them to stick it out, ride out the hostility. Soon people would find something else to gossip about. He knows she'd have preferred it if he'd retracted his criticism of his sister-in-law, but that was never going to happen.

What would Nathan have said?

'Dad! Dad!' shouts a voice from the hallway. Lawrence tosses the sodden tea towel on the work surface and finds his daughter standing in the hall, holding out his mobile.

'Your phone's ringing.'

He snatches it with a thank you and looks at the screen. It's Mr Newman.

Lawrence clears his throat and steps into the downstairs toilet, closing the door behind him to drown out whatever noisy drivel the kids are watching on the telly.

'Evening Mr Newman,' he says, politely.

'…hello Mr Hayden…'

Back to the formal greeting, Lawrence notes. This doesn't sound good.

'Erm, I just want to say thank you for your quote, which my wife and I have considered… along with the others we received…erm, but our son has offered to pay for the replacement fence panels. He knows someone and, even though your quote is cheaper, we feel we have to go with his suggestion.'

'Oh, okay, Mr Newman.'

Shit. Shit.

'He's also going to get this man to clean the gutters out too.'

Of course he is, Lawrence thinks.

'Don't forget to ask him to hang some CDs up in your eaves.'

'What?' Mr Newman asks.

'To frighten the swallows away.'

'Yes. I will. Yes, thanks. I'm sorry, Mr Hayden,' he says sincerely.

And he does sound sorry. He also sounds unhappy with the decision, but that'll be his wife's influence.

'Don't worry about it, Mr Newman. I'm getting used to it. Goodbye.'

And Lawrence ends the call. He wants to smash the mobile phone into his reflection in the mirror, but what's the point? It'll scare the kids and Rachel will make him clean it up and replace the mirror, complaining that he's inflicted seven years of bad luck on the family and haven't they had enough in the last year?

He opens the door and returns to the kitchen to find Rachel filling the kettle and removing a box of *Mr Kipling's French Fancies* from the cupboard.

She looks at him, her eyes full of hope. 'Well? Did you get it?'

He thinks about lying, about telling her that Mr Newman chose one of his competitors. He considers telling her what the old man said, that his generous son is paying for the work so has the right to choose the tradesman. But why cover up Mr Newman's lie with one of his own? She'll find out.

'I didn't get the job,' he mutters.

She frowns with concern. 'Were you too expensive?'

He shakes his head. 'I tried to be cheap without looking like I was cheap. No. It was her again. He probably couldn't have cared less, but his wife...women care more about appearances than men.'

'Lawrence,' Rachel says, putting a hand on his arm, 'who are you talking about? Who's her? Mrs Newman?'

He looks at her, angry tears springing into his eyes. 'She fucking lives next door to them. She went round their house and put her fucking poison down.'

Rachel shushes him and firmly shuts the door.

'Why the fuck does she care so strongly about what I said? What difference does it make to her miserable existence?' Lawrence implores his wife. 'Is she soulmates with Nathan's ex?'

Rachel steps in front of him, catches his eye, grabs hold of his upper arms in an attempt to calm him down. 'Stop, Lawrence,' she orders. 'Who are you talking about? I don't—'

'Amanda fucking Davies!' Lawrence bellows, flecks of spit landing on his chin. The force of his words releases Rachel's hold and she steps away. 'She's on some kind of fucking crusade to ruin me.'

'Lawrence, calm down,' Rachel urges. 'You don't know—'

'And she won't stop either...not until she sends me packing or sends me down. I am not leaving again, Rachel. No way!' His hand swipes through the air. 'This is our home, our town...that fucking bitch...I will snap her scrawny little neck first.'

Chapter 11

Amanda

Amanda sits at the reception desk with the appointment book opened in front of her trying to find a slot in couple of weeks' time to fit in her client's next appointment. Mrs X wants half-term week but that's when Amanda is having Oliver. How can she work late to accommodate her client's shift pattern if she's looking after her son? It might mean she has to ask David to mind Oliver that evening - a scenario Declan won't like. She doesn't have to tell him. But she will have to ask David and sooner rather than later. They're barely speaking to one another after he caught her snooping through his belongings.

Her attention is snagged on what happened after he raced Oliver upstairs, which was even more unpleasant than being caught red-handed. Without a word, David left the house with Jake. Amanda cooked tea, put it out and waited for him to return. Dreaded him returning. With her appetite gone, she picked at her food, moved it around the plate. She couldn't even make conversation with Oliver and allowed him to eat in front of the television. She spent the time desperately trying to conjure up explanations for her behaviour that he would believe but all the time she felt that she had gone too far.

An hour later, David texted to say he would be late home and not to wait up.

Now, it was his turn to punish her. She drove herself crazy for the rest of the evening, worrying that he was doing what she was accusing him of.

By 1am, he still wasn't home.

At 7am, he texted again to tell her he'd spent the night at Jake's as he was over the limit but he'd see her later. That sounded promising and Amanda's hopes rose that they would talk, she'd apologise and they'd make up. She entered the kitchen to find David cooking tea. He asked her how her day had gone but he kept his eyes on the cooking and she could tell he wasn't listening. She skirted the issue of her snooping through his stuff. Desperately, she wanted to raise the subject but couldn't find the words, and it didn't help that he didn't seem to want to talk about it either. They ate in near silence and when Amanda could stand it no longer, she offered to stack the dishwasher, allowing David to seek the sanctuary of the shed where he stayed until after eleven.

He came to bed at midnight, snuck into the bedroom, got under the covers and kept to his side of the bed. She slid her hand across the cool mattress, wanting to touch him, hoping that would be enough, that he'd grab her hand and pull him into his arms, but instead she pretended to be asleep.

Amanda has no idea how to make things right between them. He can barely look at her. His eyes only glance towards her when he's speaking to make sure she's still there. It feels like he's looking right through her.

He has never done that before.

And it hurts. It worries her that this time her marriage is irreparable.

Even worse, she has no one to ask for advice.

'How about Friday teatime?' the client suggests.

Amanda blinks suddenly, her head snapping abruptly out of her daydreaming.

'I can be here by 5.45.'

Working late on a Friday night, Amanda thinks miserably. I should be getting ready to go out for a romantic meal or going for drinks with the friends I haven't got, not stuck in here for two hours cutting and colouring hair. Is this my life?

'Yes, ok,' she agrees, scribbling the client's name in the book and instantly regretting how easily she has accepted the date.

She says goodbye to the client with what she hopes sounds like genuine niceness and, as the door closes, she sits back in the chair, feeling exhausted with the pretence. She gazes around the salon. Her eyes move over the fixtures, and the horrible mess left by the builder. She watches Holly chatting easily to an old lady whose grey curls lie against her skull like rats' tails.

'I have just the style for you,' Holly promises. 'By the time I'm finished, you'll look a million dollars.'

The old lady grins with glee.

Amanda watches Tamsin expertly run styling wax through her client's short hair but the young woman is oblivious to how her hairstyle is coming on; she's preoccupied with her mobile phone. Several minutes later, after Amanda has made her staff's afternoon drinks, she wanders back into the salon.

Amanda watches Tamsin sweep up the fallen hair. These days she only has one expression: sullen. She rarely smiles, never laughs. She speaks sharply to the clients as if the effort is too much. Her work is still to a high standard but her customer service is well below. Amanda knows what it's like when you can't be bothered to chat to people who you encounter once every four to six weeks. You try to remember what's going on in their lives so it looks like you care, but really you don't. But Amanda has a foolproof plan - she makes little notes on her clients after they've left: such as Mrs so-and-so's son will have sat his GCSEs by the time her next appointment is here, Miss X's sister will have had the baby, or Ms What's-it is going to Venice.

Granted, she often makes these notes on random pieces of paper, usually receipts and copies of invoices she finds in the pockets of David's fleece and work trousers, or torn scraps from the corner of a newspaper or a blank page from one of Oliver's exercise books, but it works.

Tamsin has stopped making the effort and Amanda doesn't know why.

She wonders again what has happened to the young woman she once called a friend.

When did it start to sour between them? Was it around the time Amanda got married? Could Tamsin be jealous? Surely not, Amanda concludes. Tamsin is a good-time girl, likes clubbing and drinking with her mates, getting off with different blokes. She's too young to be tied down; there's too much she wants to do with her life before that time comes.

Amanda tried to reach out to Tamsin a couple of weeks after she first noticed the change and nearly got her head bitten off. Since then Amanda has become Tamsin's boss, correcting her mistakes, reminding her of what is expected of her, micromanaging her subordinate.

Should she try and reach out to Tamsin one last time? Should she try and find out what has changed between them, and why Tamsin is so unhappy?

Tamsin is standing by the door, one hand in her tunic pocket, the outline of her mobile pressing against the fabric. Any second now the temptation will become too much and she will reach for her mobile and Amanda's chance will be gone. Amanda joins Tamsin at the window.

'Anything interesting going on?' Amanda asks.

'Nothing much. Kids are coming out of school,' Tamsin replies.

'Ahh, the happiest days of our lives. I loved school,' she enthuses. 'My favourite lessons were maths and biology.'

Tamsin slightly turns to her. 'Maths? Really? I didn't think anyone enjoyed maths.'

'I was good at it,' Amanda explains. 'If I hadn't turned to hairdressing, I fancied being an accountant. If I could go back, I'd definitely do that. What about you, Tamsin? Did you like school?'

Tamsin shrugs as if she's never given it any thought. 'Not much, no. I only went into hairdressing because my friend was and she didn't want to do it on her own. She works in television now. Gets to rub shoulders with celebrities and make loads of money. Lucky cow.'

Amanda thinks about encouraging Tamsin to do the same if that's what she wants. She's young, she should be ambitious. There's a world outside Lexington. But she doesn't. Baby steps first. This is the start of the nicest conversation they've had for a long time. Best not to ruin it with Amanda's ideas on how Tamsin can improve her life.

She turns back to the high street outside.

The mass exodus of pupils has thinned out to just a handful of stragglers dawdling down the pavements, their shoulders weighed down by heavy-looking bags. Outside the White Lion pub, opposite the salon, is a lay-by two-cars in length. It's the perfect place to pull into if you have an emergency prescription to collect from the nearby pharmacy, but people frequently use it to pick up takeaways from the Chinese. Amanda watches as a sleek black BMW pulls into the lay-by. The driver's door swings open, nearly clipping a white transit van as it passes by. A woman in her mid-fifties, well-dressed in grey trouser suit climbs out.

Amanda recognises her. She's one of Holly's clients but she can't be here for an appointment. You can only park in that spot for a maximum of twenty minutes. Besides which, Holly is tied up with the old lady having her hair washed.

The woman is looking back down the street, a smile on her well made-up face. Intrigued, both Amanda and Tamsin keep watching. After all, neither have clients for a while yet.

A few moments later, the well-dressed woman is joined by a tall and athletic teenage girl, wearing jogging bottoms and a hoodie. Her hair looks damp and, over one shoulder, she carries a sports bag. They have the same dark hair and Amanda concludes they must be mother and daughter. The woman opens the boot of the BMW and the girl drops her bag inside, but rather than get into the vehicle, they wait to be joined by a third person. A man wearing jogging bottoms, a fleece and trainers.

It's Martyn. Amanda hasn't heard from him since last week when they had that…what would you call it? It wasn't a falling out but it was unpleasant. His demands were outrageous and unfair. In fact, with the upset caused by David and Declan, she'd forgotten about Martyn.

The girl stands between the adults as Martyn talks animatedly, using lots of hand gestures in his usual way. They must be talking about swimming. It's the only subject Amanda knows he gets passionate about.

He must be coaching her.

She glances at Tamsin and is surprised to see that she's watching them with interest too. A little frown has appeared between her perfect eyebrows. Did Tamsin go to Martyn's school? He wouldn't have taught her since male teachers don't take girls for PE, but she would've known him.

The suited mother fishes a mobile out of her large handbag and strolls away to take the call, leaving Martyn and the girl. Interestingly, they stop talking and watch as the mother continues walking down the street further away.

When it feels safe, the girl turns to Martyn and suddenly she's closer to him then she was before and doesn't seem like just his pupil anymore. It's the way she looks up at him: intently, her head slightly tilted to one side. And coldness rushes through Amanda because she recognises it. She looked at him like that too when she was this girl's age. She hung on his every word.

They're talking. Martyn is less animated, but his right hand is very close to the girl's left hand as if he dares to reach out and touch her.

'Mr Hepworth coached my friend Jess for a while,' Tamsin is saying. 'He told her she was a natural at…erm…backstroke, I think it was. I can't remember. It was six years ago.'

'Did she make it?'

Tamsin looks at Amanda. Her eyes narrow. 'How do you mean?'

'Did she go on to compete professionally?'

Tamsin laughs as if the idea is ludicrous. 'No. Jess was a big girl. I don't mean like eighteen stone, but she wasn't an athlete. She was okay at swimming. Better than me. But she liked food too much.'

Amanda is frowning. What has this got to do with anything?

'Her parents were alcoholics,' Tamsin helpfully explains. 'They didn't care much about what Jess got up to so she skipped lessons, went down the park, dossed about. Anyway, the school recommended that Jess take up something, you know like a hobby or sport to get her off the streets and back into school so she took swimming up.' Tamsin nods at the window. 'He coached her.'

Amanda watches Martyn and the girl. They're standing too close for Amanda's comfort.

'Did your friend go to the same school as you, Tam?' she asks.

'No. A few weeks later, Jess dumped her boyfriend. She told me she was seeing an older man.' Tamsin smiles, nods at the window again. 'Him.'

'Martyn Hepworth?' Amanda gasps.

'Yeah. None of us believed her. She was always fantasising, telling us these stupid far-fetched stories. Stuff like she was adopted, that her real parents would come back for her. She told me the year before she had ovarian cancer. It was all bollocks. But him,' and Tamsin points at the glass. 'Jess said he was lovely to her. They'd meet in secret and have sex in his car. We asked for proof and she told us he had this tattoo.'

Amanda's blood runs cold and she sways on her feet. She grabs the door jamb, steadies herself.

'On his upper chest. An eagle, I think. Well, it was some kind of bird of prey.'

It's an eagle owl, Amanda wants to say. The detail in the tattoo is incredible; it's a work of art. She liked to trace its orange eyes with her fingertip, lightly scratching his skin until he begged her to stop. And she wouldn't stop until he grabbed her and kissed her.

Oh, God, she thinks. I feel sick. Is he doing to other girls what…we…she would only know he had a tattoo if she'd seen…oh, God, no.

'We had to take her word for it,' Tamsin continues. 'How would we know if he had a tattoo? Male teachers don't take girls for PE and swimming coaches aren't allowed to get in the water with pupils unless they're covered up. To protect them from accusations of indecency. The irony of it. There was always something about him that made me feel uncomfortable. He used to watch us play netball from his office.' She looks at Amanda. 'It overlooks the netball court.'

Amanda looks back through the window. The mother is on her way back. Martyn and the girl are back to standing a respectful distance apart. They chat for a few more moments before the mother thanks Martyn with a handshake and opens the passenger door of the BMW. Martyn raises a hand in goodbye and strolls away.

Tamsin sighs, straightens her back out of her slouch. 'Well, I must get back to it.'

'Yes,' Amanda mutters thoughtfully, still staring out of the window at an empty street.

First there was me, she thinks. I thought I was the only one. I never considered there'd be others. But why wouldn't there be? Why would a twenty-three year old man with a thing for teenage girls stop at one? And when they get older, surely they're not the same anymore. You don't fancy them and you have to find someone younger? And so it starts again.

After me, there must've have been another girl.

After Jess, he would've have moved onto the next teenager.

And this girl here, she's his current victim.

It's no wonder he wants me to destroy my diary.

That book is enough to ruin his career and reputation and put him in prison for a very long time.

Chapter 12

Declan

Declan pulls up outside the newsagents and decides that he could do with a drink. He has a dry mouth. He can't believe how nervous he feels. His hands feel shaky and he could hardly eat his breakfast, throwing the soggy cornflakes in the bin.

The fiery nerves bite into his stomach threatening to upheave what little is inside. He knows this, coming to Hock is the only thing he could do. He has no ammunition against Amanda, no other way to take her on. And yet, yesterday, it felt right. He was on a high as he drove away from Hock. He smiled all the way through his normally miserable shift. It really did feel like a weight had lifted from his shoulders.

But now, in the cold light of the next morning, Declan is suddenly apprehensive about what this job is.

I'm only driving him somewhere, he thinks. That's all I *ever* did. I'm not a heavy so he won't be expecting me to rough someone up. Besides, he has blokes to do that. There's no way Hock would risk dishing violence out himself. There's nothing to worry about.

Declan unclips his seatbelt and gets out of the vehicle. A *Mars* bar and water is just what he needs.

He enters the shop. A young woman is kneeling beside a toddler in a pink coat and helping her choose a comic from the shelf. Little fists grab at the free toys attached in plastic bags and the mother tells her daughter to stop snatching.

I've got all this to come again, Declan thinks with a smile.

He takes his drink and chocolate to the counter but Hock isn't there. The till is being manned by a woman in her late teens. A silver ring adorns her left nostril and there are green streaks in her short blonde hair. He wonders if this is one of Hock's kids. He's sure Hock's eldest are twins.

Her mobile is out on the counter. She pauses the YouTube video playing on the screen but doesn't make conversation as she rings the total up on the till.

Declan hands over the money and asks if Hock is about.

'Who wants to know?' she replies casually, sliding the coinage from the till tray and placing it on the counter so Declan has to pick them up one by one.

Her defensive tone throws him and he steps back. Anyone wanting to get to Hock has a hell of a job defeating her first.

'I'm meeting him here at eleven,' Declan explains, wishing his voice sounded more confident.

She glances up at the wall above the top shelf. 'You're early. It's only five to.'

'Mr Hock appreciates punctuality.'

She smiles coldly. 'He also appreciates people following his direct orders.'

Declan frowns. 'What?'

She stares at him for several moments before her eyes brighten and her snarl straightens and curls into a grin. She laughs. 'I'm just messing with you, Declan. Hock's in the back with an associate. Go on through,' and, with one hand, she lifts the hatch in the counter and to let him pass by.

He doesn't ask how she knows who he is. Hock will have filled her in.

Declan has never experienced the other side of the counter before. Hock has always preferred to do business with him on the customer side. He glimpses lots of boxes of crisps, plastic-wrapped packs of water and soft drinks, piles of magazines and papers tied with string.

Through the doorway, Declan can hear two voices. One he identifies as Hock who is louder and more brash. The other is a male voice.

'It's time to clean up,' Hock is saying. 'Place is getting scruffy. You put these people in place and they take the piss.'

Declan steps closer and Hock comes into view. He's perched on the edge of a very strong desk with sturdy legs. His arms are folded across his broad chest and he wears a black waterproof. A laptop is open on the desk. The screen shows a photo of Hock's family behind a sprinkling of at least two dozen icons. Hock's wife, he quickly notices, is a bit of a looker: good-looking and fit, with a big smile and a pair of sunglasses pushed through her blonde hair.

How the hell has a guy like Hock got a woman like that?

Sensing a new presence, Hock turns, a big grin breaking out onto his face. 'Declan! Alright, mate? As punctual as ever. Excellent.'

'Hello Hock.'

Hock gestures to the owner of the other voice who Declan can't see behind a stack of magazines.

Declan steps forward and sitting in the desk chair, a huge black leather thing with chrome arms a bit like the chair off *Mastermind*, is a bloke somewhere in his twenties wearing a black jeans, a red puffa jacket and big white trainers. His shaven dark hair is starting to grow back and Declan can see that he's suffering from premature balding. His small eyes are dark and his lips are thin and colourless.

Declan vaguely recognises him from somewhere.

'How are you, Dec?' the man says, lifting himself out of the chair just enough to hold out his hand for Declan to shake.

Declan accepts the hand but it's clammy and the handshake is limp. His touch makes Declan want to immediately wash his hands. 'I'm alright. You?' he says awkwardly.

'Yeah, I'm good, mate. Me back's been playing up, but it's the weather, you know. The cold gets into my fucking bones.'

Hock laughs at him. 'For fuck's sake. You sound eighty five, not twenty-five.'

'I feel eighty five,' the man insists with a laugh.

Hock laughs louder.

Declan looks between the two men. Where does he know him from? It's not work and it's not from his street. Why does he have a vague recollection that it's something to do with Amanda?

The younger man looks at Declan. 'You've forgotten who I am, haven't you?' He shakes his head in pretend insult. 'It's been a while since you saw me. April, I think. Oliver's birthday. Amanda threw a party. Beautiful sunny day. You bought your missus and her kids.' He waits but still Declan doesn't know. He glances at Hock but he's smiling with amusement and Declan gets his first thought that he's been set up.

'David's mate - Jake.'

Declan's jaw clenches. Shit. Shit. Amanda's husband's friend. And he remembers that Jake is around Amanda's house a lot because he's *best* fucking friends with her husband. She can never get him out of the house.

Now he recalls Jake from Oliver's birthday. He sat talking to Kerry for ages because they knew the same people, and afterwards Kerry told Declan how much she thought Jake was a good bloke, a really great mate to David. And Declan can't understand why David, who is such a decent bloke, has friends like Jake. Because, like Amanda, Declan thinks there's something creepy and nasty about Jake.

Jake is exactly the kind of man who will not casually, but very deliberately, tell David who he has encountered today and what they did. And then David will say to Amanda over their Marks and Spencer's dinner, 'I didn't know Declan had a new job.' And Amanda will be enlightened. She might not know who Hock is. They don't mix in the same circles but she only has to google the surname and she will know the kind of stock Hock comes from. That his brother was convicted of violent crime, his cousin is a serial arsonist, and his sister was done for assaulting a teacher last year.

What the fuck is Declan doing resurrecting an employment with Hock? A business relationship that was dead and buried. If she finds out about this, it will literally fuck everything up.

I need my fucking head examining, Declan thinks.

He snaps out of his thoughts to find that Hock and Jake are looking at him quizzically.

'Nice to meet you again,' he manages to squeeze out to Jake. Jake nods slightly and turns to Hock, tapping the back of his wrist with a nicotine-stained finger as if to indicate the late hour.

'It's time we got going, Hock. It's quarter past eleven. He should be awake soon.'

'Right then. Declan, fire up your motor,' Hock says, slapping his massive hands on his muscular thighs and heaving himself upright with a grunt.

Declan leads the way back through the shop, putting the water bottle into his pocket and quickly unwrapping the *Mars* bar to bite off the end. He feels sick but hopes the chocolate will stop him from shaking. The sweetness fills his mouth, dribbling a strand of caramel over his chin. He licks it away and unlocks the car. Hock uses the upper edge of the door frame to ease himself into the passenger seat. Jake opens the offside rear door and shoves aside the collection of toys left by the kids.

'Where we off to?' Declan asks, engaging first gear and flicking the right indicator on. He stares into the wing mirror, waiting for a gap in the traffic.

'Head to Kelsall,' Hock orders, pointing a finger at the windscreen. 'And change the radio station.'

Declan's eyes flick to the left at Hock whose demeanour has suddenly changed. Is this how he gets into character before he does whatever it is they're going to do? And what's Jake come along for?

'Put Lexington FM on,' Jake orders. 'They do a cracking quiz at 11 o'clock.'

Hock has no suggestions of his own so Declan changes the station and pulls into the traffic, heading for the dual carriageway, the quickest way to the neighbouring town of Kelsall. Kerry thinks he's spending the morning sorting out the junk in the garage and taking the unwanted crap down to the recycling centre. He still has to go back and do the job, or at least start to make it look like he was doing it.

Everyone settles into the journey, the only sound being from the radio and its endless drivel of pop tunes which sound exactly like the one before, spliced with high-energy adverts for replacement windows, second-hand cars and discount furniture sales. Every so often, Hock gives Declan a direction to take.

Declan finishes his breakfast, glancing occasionally at Hock. But he stares out of the window watching the scenery whizz by, whilst Jake sits in the back, tapping away on his phone.

Suddenly, Jake's weasel-like face appears in the rear view mirror making Declan jump. 'Sorry, mate, didn't mean to scare the shit out of you,' he laughs. 'How long have you been working for Hock?'

Declan's grip tightens on the wheel. 'This is my first day.'

'Your first day back, yeah? How long you been away for?'

'A couple of years,' he replies, keeping it vague. 'How about you?'

'Turn here.'

Declan looks around to see where Jake is pointing. He isn't but his head is turned to the left. Declan brakes hard to avoid missing the turning. They enter a housing estate. Terraced houses built from pale yellow bricks stand opposite identical houses across a wide road. Several large square patches of recently Tarmacked areas adorn the bumpy surface.

'Second on the right after the postbox,' Jake orders, his bossy tone irritating Declan. Declan does as he told, eventually pulling up outside number 17 Carmichael Drive. Without a word, Hock releases his seatbelt. Jake puts away his phone, zipping it into his pocket, and climbs out of the car. Declan doesn't know if he's supposed to get out too.

'Declan,' Hock barks, rapping the inside of the glass with his knuckle. 'You're with us.'

Ignoring the bad feeling in his guts, Declan gets out of the car, locking it securely. 'Who lives here then?' he asks but no one pays him any attention and it's Hock that leads them up the short path to the front door. A child's bike lies on the tiny patch of lawn, which is more weeds than grass. The pink paint has rusted and both tyres are flat.

Hock and Jake look at each other across the threadbare doormat. Neither speak but their eyes seem to communicate instructions. Declan hangs back until Hock glares at him and he automatically steps closer, interpreting the look as *you're coming in with us.*

Jake knocks the door, hard and fast. They wait a couple of seconds but Declan can't hear any movement from within so Jake bangs the door again with the side of his fist.

Hock holds a hand up, confirming a sound from within. The hinges squeak as the door opens a few centimetres. Hock doesn't wait for an invite as he lays a hand flat on the door and pushes it open, forcing the person on the other side to squeal and step back.

'John! How's it going?'

As quick as flash, Hock steps over the threshold and, like the rodent that he is, Jake darts inside, hissing at Declan to follow. Declan closes the door behind him. The hall is tiny and the air stinks of cannabis and unwashed bodies. Black scuff marks adorn the walls. A wooden-framed mirror hangs at a weird angle, its surface covered with dust. Scattered on the floor are unopened envelopes, plastic charity bags and flyers advertising cheap takeaways and local supermarket offers. A black bin liner lies on its side, several crushed beer cans and empty spirit bottles spewing out from it as if the person lacked the energy to do the job properly.

Declan trails after Hock before he's told off again.

'Sit down, John, and let me tell you what's gonna happen,' Hock says as Declan appears in the doorway to the lounge. A huge hand pushes a frail-looking thirty year old man with longish unkempt hair back onto a sagging settee. A television is on in the corner of the room, its volume muted. On the untidy coffee table is a collection of drug paraphernalia: lighters, spoons, screwed up balls of tinfoil. There are more empty bottles on the laminated floor. Jake goes over to the curtains and draws them, plunging the room into a dark yellow.

'Can…can I just explain?' John pleads, adjusting the contents of his pants with one hand whilst scrabbling about on the table for something.

'We're past explanations and apologies now, John.'

'It wasn't my fault! I haven't been well,' John explains. His fingers fumble at the packet of cigarettes but the box is empty and, in frustration, he throws it back onto the cluttered table. 'I've been diagnosed with alcoholic hepatitis.'

'Hepatitis, my friend, will be the least of your worries,' and Hock leans close to John who backs away until his head touches the back of the settee, 'if I rip your fucking liver out. Won't it? Eh?' Hock's index finger stabs at John's forehead.

Declan feels sick. The *Mars* bar lies like sludge in his stomach.

'But,' and Hock straightens up, smiling menacingly, 'I have a solution to *your* problem, which has become *my* problem. Jake here,' and his hand gestures to Jake who is opening the various drawers and doors of the wall unit.

Jake looks up and waves at John. 'Hi John.'

'Will be taking over your patch.'

John's eyes widen and he grabs Hock's hand. 'No,' he shouts. 'You can't. I need the income, Hock. I've got kids. You can't take it from me. I've always been loyal to you.'

Hock violently shakes John's hand off.

'Loyal?' laughs Hock. 'The definition of loyalty means unswerving in allegiance, devoted, faithful. When was the last time you paid me what you owed? When was the last time you left this shit tip and sold your goods? When was the last time you had a fucking shower, John? Who in their right fucking mind would buy dope from you? No one, John. And meanwhile, you're costing me money. So no, you don't know the meaning of the word loyalty. However, you do know how to take the piss. But it stops now, today. You found it yet, Jake?'

Out of a cupboard, Jake holds up a slim rectangular object the way someone holds a trophy. 'Got it.' He jabs a finger at it. 'Battery's dead,' he mutters. 'Fuck's sake, John. How can you do any business if your mobile's dead? You stupid bastard.'

Hock tuts at John. 'Give it to me.' And Jake throws the object to Hock who catches it in one hand. Declan peers closer. It's a mobile, outdated with a scuffed screen.

'If I didn't need this so badly, I'd wrap it around your fucking head, John.'

'I'm sorry, Hock,' John cries before breaking down into a sobbing and snivelling wreck. 'Please Hock. Give me another chance. I'm on meds now.'

Declan looks at the druggie tools on the table.

'Yeah, I can see that,' Hock says, reaching down to sift through the debris carefully. 'It's a very poor dealer who smokes and shoots more than he sells.'

Jake has found another object in the cupboard which he turns over several times in his hands. It looks like an ornament. An ugly figurine about nine inches high. Hock turns to Jake who holds up the item. Hock nods.

'Yeah, that'll do.'

Jake throws it to him.

The chocolate threatens to make a reappearance. Sensing imminent violence, Declan slides his feet backwards, but his trainers squeak on the laminate flooring alerting Hock.

'You,' Hock says, pointing at him. 'Come here.'

Too scared to move or breathe, Declan remains fixed to the spot, his chest in mid-inhalation.

'"Come here" I said. Or did you think I was paying you just to ferry us here?'

Over his shoulder, Declan sees that Jake is grinning with amusement. Nasty little shit, he thinks. He walks closer, his arms limp by his sides. John stops crying, pleading with wet eyes. Hock grabs Declan's right hand, his fingers digging into his flesh, and slaps the ornament into his palm.

It is a figurine of an old lady wearing a bonnet and carrying a basket of apples in the crook of an elbow. Declan tests its weight. It's not made from delicate bone china but a heavy kind of ceramic with a solid base.

Declan looks at Hock, confused.

'Hit him with it,' Hock orders.

'What?' Declan gasps, glancing at John who scoots along the settee, shaking his head, terrified.

'You stupid moron, Declan. I'm not giving you a hundred quid to drive me here. It's cheaper to come on the bus. It's a lesson you need to learn. You can't just drop me like a hot stone when you've had enough and waltz back in when you want something. So, if you want the best for that new baby of yours, you'd best do as you're told.'

Jake sniggers. Declan tries to ignore him, turning to the task in hand. All he has to do is hit the guy with an object. He doesn't know him. What does he care if the snivelling junkie gets hurt? Sounds like John deserves it, that he's been trying Hock's patience for a long time, something that anyone involved with Hock knows is a very unwise thing to do.

The figurine is cold in Declan's hand. He assesses the best place to hit John. Top of the head is the thickest part of the skull isn't it? A blow to the temple will surely break his skull and cause brain damage or kill him.

'You're stalling,' Hock accuses. 'Get the fuck on with it.'

Declan wants to throw up. These two, Hock and Jake, are like peas in a pod. Who'd have thought that a monster like Hock would pair up with a cripple like Jake and become the scariest double-act Declan would ever know?

John is curled up against the arm of the settee, his hands protecting his head, emitting great sobs of terror.

Finally Declan regrets resurrecting his involvement with Hock. This time he may never get out. He swallows his sickening nerves and raises the ornament above John's head.

Chapter 13

Tamsin

Tamsin throws her head back and whirls around. The 90s dance track is loud and pulsates in her ears. The baseline is beating to the rhythm of her fast heart. The black stiletto is rubbing against her right heel and the hem of her silver dress has ridden up so high it is surely showing her knickers, but she barely notices. The fifth vodka and coke is numbing the soreness nicely and the surrounding throng of fellow dancers is hiding her modesty, but Tamsin couldn't care less. Over the heads of her friends, she spies Gina being served at the bar, so the next drink will see her definitely on the road to drunken oblivion.

It's boiling in the middle of the dance floor, sweat has pooled in the small of her back and the skin on her arms and legs feels damp. She should really sit down, rehydrate and take a breather, allow her heart rate to get down to a semi-normal level but Tamsin is enjoying herself too much. She's had a particularly shit day today and needs to let off some steam. What better way than getting pissed in a nightclub?

Amanda was the worst she's ever been. It's not as if Tamsin wasn't on time. She strolled in at half eight exactly as Amanda demanded. She helped Holly get the salon ready whilst the boss from hell continued her ringing around various builders, even as far afield as Liliton, to get someone to fix the mess left by the other guy. Tamsin can't believe the builder walked out without a word to Amanda. There wasn't even an over-the-shoulder mutter of "Fucking bitch" from him. Talk about a missed opportunity. Tamsin made up her mind that the day she receives her marching orders from Amanda, she will literally let rip with everything. And she doesn't care who in the salon hears. It'll be a hair appointment for them all to remember.

As the morning progressed, Amanda took her frustrations out on them all: barking at Holly to bollock Jenny who had failed to put that in the bin, sweep that up, do this, do that. She glared at Tamsin every time she walked past, argued with her over the appointments' diary which culminated in Tamsin having to ring each one of her clients to move their appointments backward by a mere ten minutes. She didn't dare question Amanda, just got on with it, but then she wasn't doing it quickly and had to stay behind half an hour to get it done. Then it was a rush to get home, have her tea and get ready to go out on the tiles. She opened a cheap bottle of white wine and drank from it as she showered, shaved her legs, did her hair and make-up. Her hair seemed to conspire against her. She couldn't get it to go where she wanted and her anger was growing to the point she wanted to pull all of it out. Another glass of wine calmed her down though.

A hand touches her on the shoulder and Tamsin turns, her head swaying a little. It's Gina, smiling tipsily. 'Drink?' she mouths, lifting her hand up and making the universal sign for drink.

Tamsin nods, accepts Gina's hand and allows herself to be led out of the labyrinth of dancers and to the edge of the dance floor, but as Tamsin steps into space, a figure on her left steps backwards, loud laughter ringing in her ears. His foot stomps on hers and she yelps. Her hand slips from Gina's clammy one.

'For fuck's sake,' a male voice says. 'You should really watch where you're going, you drunk cow.'

'What?' she fires back, ready to give the perpetrator a mouthful until she looks up into the smirking face of Jake Bunby and her anger dissolves. She feels a smile grow on her face. 'You wanker.'

'Nice to see you too, Tam,' he grins, leaning forward to give her a quick kiss on the cheek. 'You look good. How have you been?'

'Mostly shit. How about you?'

'Mostly good.'

Jake was three years above her in secondary school. He's friends with one of her exes and of course, his best mate David is married to her boss. Another reminder of something she's come here to forget.

'Dance clubs aren't normally your scene,' she says as Gina thrusts a plastic cup containing her drink at her. 'Thanks, hun.' She turns back to Jake. 'I thought you only liked working men's clubs and dusty old boozers these days.'

'Yeah, I do normally, but I'm here on business,' he says, tapping the side of his nose. 'Even a cripple has to make a living.'

'You haven't spent all your six-figure payout, have you?' Jake laughs. 'What sort of business would you have in a club? Do they sell pork chops and sausages?'

'I'd forgotten you're quite witty, Tam. I've taken over someone's patch,' and he reaches into the pocket of his jacket and takes out something small. Keeping his hand between their two bodies, Jake opens his palm and Tamsin gasps when she sees the tiny white ball.

'Vodka,' Jake says, tapping the side of her drink, 'and coke.' He grins and puts his hand back in his pocket.

'Does David know?' she asks, and then questions why she said that. What business is it of David's what Jake does? David's set up now with a wealthy older woman. Stop it, she tells herself. Don't go there. This is your time.

'None of his business. You should meet up with us one night for a drink? I'm sure Dave would love to see you.'

'No thanks. I have enough of Amanda at work; I don't need to hear all about her in my own time.' Tamsin feels a warm hand on her waist as someone moves behind her. She turns and looks up into the face of a man with blond hair and, for a split second, her heart leaps and her eyes widen. Is it him? Has he come—? but just as quickly, her hopes plummet and crash. He leans towards Jake, cups his hand around his mouth as he talks into Jake's ear. Jake listens, his face serious, and nods towards the back wall where the gents' toilets are.

Suddenly the man looks at Tamsin, eyes her up and down appreciatively and smiles slowly. She turns to him, allowing his gaze to pass over all of her and she eyes him back. He's better looking than some of the blokes in here, better looking than most of the blokes she's had. Her head is level with his chin. His hair is dark blond and he's overdone the product in it but who can blame him if he comes to a nightclub? There's an inch of hairspray on her own locks. He's unshaven and has a tattoo on the inside of each forearm. As Gina would say, he looks "a nice bit of rough". If she passes this chance by, she'll be going home empty-handed.

She smiles sweetly and he leans forwards, speaking into her ear. His breath is hot on her neck and it sends a shiver through her. 'You with him?' His thumb jerks subtly at Jake and she shakes her head firmly. 'Will you be here when I get back?'

'I can come along with you, if you like.'

'Yes,' he replies, grabbing her hand and pulling her through the crowd as he follows Jake to the gents. Her drink spills and she raises the cup to her mouth to lick the vodka off her hand. Her feet stick to the tacky floor. The black door to the gents is flung open and suddenly the sound of the music is pleasantly muffled and her senses start to relax. It's peaceful in here. The stranger releases her hand, leaving her to sway on her heels. Weirdly there is only one man visible - a young man wiping his hands dry on his trousers. He doesn't give her a second look. A couple of cubicle doors are closed but there are no noises coming from within.

Jake nods to the buyer and they make their way down the row of hand basins to the wall where the hand dryer is. Tamsin leaves them to their deal and looks in the large mirror, plonking her drink down. She rubs a finger under her eye where her foundation has smudged, and tightens the clip in her hair. Something catches her eye and she leans forward, nearly head butting the glass. Her lipstick has smudged. Where's my bag? she thinks, patting her hip, but remembers she left it with the friend who doesn't dance. She pulls a face and glances slyly at the deal. She only had coke once before. Within five minutes, she felt euphoric, in love with everyone. Her heart had raced and she'd desperately wanted sex, searching for her then boyfriend, dragging him off into a quiet corner. This stranger might offer her some and of course, she'll take it. Why turn down a chance to blot out some of the misery?

She knows what Gina will say, but she's heard it so many times that words like "reckless", "unsafe", "reputation", "promiscuous" fall like water off a duck's back. What's the problem with casual no-strings sex? Where else is she supposed to meet men? Nightclubs and bars are a lot safer than dating sites. Besides, Gina knows the attraction these liaisons have for Tamsin. They are her escapism and much quicker fixes than trying to get out of a job she hates, working for the worst person in the world whilst pining for the man she can never have back.

Tamsin leans back against the hand basin, a square of toilet paper stuck to the bottom of her shoe. She uses her other foot to get it off as Jake strolls past, winking at her and saying, 'Have a good time, Tam. I'll tell your ex you said hi.'

'Fuck off, Bunby.'

Jake laughs and throws the door open, letting in the music. The stranger is grinning at Tamsin and nodding his head at the furthest cubicle, whose door is wide open. 'You coming?'

Tamsin nods enthusiastically and totters towards him, stepping over the debris on the floor, torn open condom wrappers, toilet paper, empty plastic cups, puddles of liquid which could be drink or piss.

The man locks the door behind them. She can feel heat and strength radiating from his broad chest and strong arms. She wonders if he's a good kisser, if he's so good she can forget about her job and Amanda. She leans against the side of the cubicle, feels the toilet roll holder press into her bottom. The man puts the toilet lid down, holds the coke in his rough hand. She reaches out a finger and touches the embedded ink pattern on his arm. She adores tattoos.

'You had coke before?' he whispers.

'A while ago.'

'Ever had sex after coke?'

'No,' she lies, 'any good?'

He's weighing her up. He won't offer her any coke if he's not going to get anything out of it and he'll fling open that door and kick her out quicker than you can say, 'Rolled-up note.'

Swiftly, Tamsin assesses the risks. Drugs, stranger sex, nightclub…this is an improvement on last week: virtually paralytic, broken shoe heel, body odour, oral sex behind a kebab shop, the smell of fried food in her nostrils and hair.

The man smiles. His eyes are blue like her ex-boyfriend's, friendly and familiarly trustworthy. 'Pretty good. Wanna try?'

'Let's have a before and after test,' she tells him, running her hand up his bare arm, pausing to circle one tattoo with her thumb; she reaches up and his arm snakes around her waist, holding her up. She kisses him deeply, imagining the man is someone else, and he presses her against the cubicle wall.

He buries his hand in her hair, roughly pulling her head to the side so he can kiss her neck. Christ, she thinks, shuddering from the way he yanks her dress up. He has a touch and a half. If he's this good without, bring on the cocaine. It could be another route out of here.

Chapter 14

Amanda

Amanda ties the belt of her spotted dressing gown tighter as she descends the stairs in her slippers. She contemplates finishing off the last dregs of the Sauvignon Blanc that's in the fridge. It'd be a shame if it went to waste. She glances at the wall clock in the hallway: 8.20pm. David will be late home again. Last night he was out until nearly eleven and spent another 30 minutes in his shed. She couldn't rest until he came to bed. Once under the duvet, he confined himself to his side of the bed as if clinging to the edge of a cliff. It took her another hour to get to sleep and she wishes she'd slept in the spare room. Not that that would've helped the situation.

'Sod it,' she thinks, padding down the hall to the kitchen where she pours the wine into a glass and breaks off a couple of squares of Cadbury's chocolate. She switches the light off and heads back to the lounge, curling up on the sofa with her treats and flicking through the channels. She settles on a film she's seen before, but one that'll hold her interest. Anything to stop her from thinking about the shit state her life is in.

But just a few minutes later, her thoughts stray off the film and onto Martyn's text message. He wants to see her to apologise for his behaviour, admitting that it was out of order, he's stressed at work, his wife's stressed, the kids are stressed. But his excuses and pathetic attempts at light-hearted jokes have fallen far short of the mark as far as Amanda is concerned. She can't get her head around what Tamsin said about her friend being groomed by Martyn and also what she saw in the street with her own eyes. Touching a teenage girl in broad daylight and deceiving her mother that his coaching is honourable when the truth is that is Martyn is a paedophile and he's using his position as a swimming coach to groom young girls. The thought sickens Amanda to her stomach. And there's no one she can talk to. People won't understand how she can be friends with Martyn after what he did, but she didn't know until recently that it was abuse.

And now Martyn wants to destroy evidence of his wrongdoing, cover it up. How can she live with herself if she does that? How can she reconcile herself to her part in all this? Why couldn't she see what he was all those years ago? Was she that naive, that stupid and clueless? She wasn't so clueless that she didn't know how to lie to her parents about where she was going, lie to her friends that she was busy with other friends, so no-one had the tiniest inkling that she was sneaking off to see a man eight years older. She wasn't so naive that she didn't know how to terminate her pregnancy.

And even when she discovered the truth about him, did it make any difference? That moment when she stood on the hockey pitch at Kelsall Girls' High school waiting for the team from Lexington Secondary to show up for their match and who gets off the school bus as stand-in teacher, but Martyn Hepworth, her boyfriend.

She couldn't stop staring at him. How can this be? she wondered. He's supposed to be at uni, studying to be a PE teacher. He's not supposed to already be one. He lied to me.

But then she lied too.

She told Martyn that she was training to be a hair stylist. That she was 17 years old.

They met up the following evening, both shamefaced. They listened to their reasons for the lies and deceit, concluding they were as bad as each other. And they agreed to carry on with their relationship. It lasted a couple more months until Martyn got a job up north. Too far for a teenager to visit without her parents asking some serious questions.

Now Amanda wonders if Martyn knew all along she was telling lies about her age, but he pretended to buy it so he could get his hands on her.

This is fucked up, Amanda thinks, reaching for the wine. I have to do something. Should I go to the police, show them the diary, tell them what he did, what we did, what Martyn did to Tamsin's friend, what I saw in the street? She finishes the wine, puts the glass down, but it's left an unpleasant acidic taste in her mouth and she wants a glass of water.

She uncurls her legs but stops when she hears a key in the lock. David's back early. Perhaps he'll go in the shed or straight upstairs, maybe opting for the spare room, which suits her too, because she might get a better night's sleep.

He drops his key into the glass bowl on the hall table. She expects to hear his footsteps pass by the lounge door which is slightly ajar, and head into the kitchen, but there's silence. The door to the cupboard where coats and shoes are kept opens and closes.

I'm not getting a drink until he's gone, she thinks childishly and turns back to the film.

'Amanda,' a quiet voice says and her shoulders tense. She stares at the screen, pretending she hasn't heard him.

David comes into the room, stepping into her peripheral vision. 'What you watching?'

She shrugs. 'Some film.' He remains standing, waiting for more. I sound hostile, she thinks, glancing up at him. She notices how sad and worn out he looks.

'I've seen it before,' she explains, 'but there's not much else on.' She attempts a welcoming smile. David returns it and sits on the arm of the sofa, fidgeting with his coat zip.

'You're back early,' she comments, muting the volume and shifting position on the settee so she can see him clearly. 'I didn't expect you till later.'

'I wasn't enjoying sitting in the pub with Jake.'

I wouldn't enjoy a drink with that nasty shit either, she thinks, trying to keep her face expressionless.

'Well, I'm glad you've come home early. Do you want a cup of tea?'

'I'll make it,' he offers obligingly and gets up. He places his mobile on the coffee table, less than a metre from her reach. 'Biscuit as well?'

'Yeah, thanks. There's some chocolate chip cookies on the side.'

He leaves the room and suddenly his mobile buzzes quietly, the dark screen illuminating brightly. Typical, she thinks. Just as we're making slow progress there's an interruption. Who's messaging him now? She leans over the table, her arm stretching out. She could call out that he has a message, but he'll find that out when he returns. She could press the button and light up the screen and decide for herself if it's urgent and requires his attention. Then she'd know who the person messaging him is.

Her outstretched fingers curl into a fist and she retracts her arm. Perhaps he's set a trap. He could be waiting behind the door, to see if she has the temptation to snoop, and then he'd know for sure that she isn't to be trusted.

The screen lights up for a second time because David has altered the settings to remind him that the message is unread. All she needs to do is lean over and press that button. But what if she sees something, a name she doesn't recognise. It'll torment her.

No. She must resist. Start as she means to go on. She picks up the nearby nail file but quickly replaces it when she realises that he might assume she used it to extend her reach to his phone without moving from her seat. She increases the volume on the TV, tries to dive back into the nonsense film.

92

He returns with their drinks, the packet of biscuits lodged under his arm. He moves his phone over to make room for his cup; his finger touches the screen and it lights up. He frowns at the device, glances at Amanda who is smiling at him.

'Thanks for the tea,' she says.

'It's just Jake,' he explains. 'Wants to know why I left without a word.'

She wonders, hopes they've had words, that a row has spoiled their friendship, that it might push David back in the right direction towards her. Wives should be more important than friends.

She sips the tea but it's hot and burns her tongue. She replaces it on the coaster, spilling liquid over the rim. Her hands are shaking. She looks at him. 'I'm sorry for going through your stuff, David,' she says desperately. 'But I'm glad you caught me. I don't think I could have stopped if you hadn't. I've never been so humiliated. I've thought of nothing else but why I do it.' She looks up at him. The sadness on his face only moments earlier is softening.

'How long have you been doing it?' he asks. 'What do you go through? My wardrobe, the van…'

'I started about four months ago. There was a song on the radio in the salon. It's way before your time. It's by a band called Dr Hook. It's called *When you're in love with a beautiful woman*. Do you know it?' David shakes his head. 'Well, it's basically about a man who's in love with a beautiful woman and he's on edge all the time, watching her and all his friends for any signs that she's cheating.'

A smile appears on David's face but, rather than get irritated, Amanda smiles too. 'My client said it was her mum's favourite band and they don't make music like this anymore. Anyway, she looks at me and says something like, "I suppose it's the same for you, isn't it?" I asked what she meant. She said, "Handsome young man like your husband. I bet you watch him like a hawk, don't you? All these young women who work here must be eyeing him up. His female customers, his friends' girlfriends. It must be such a worry for you." I told her it wasn't, that I had no reason not to trust you, but her words got in my head, and I started looking for women who were looking at you. They were your age and it made me feel old, inadequate, poor in comparison. One day, your phone beeped in the kitchen when it was on charge. You were in the shed. I picked it up. I had a good look through it.'

'What did you find?'

'Nothing to give me any concern. But I am my own worst enemy. And I thought, if you did have something to hide, then you wouldn't leave your phone lying around. So I started looking through your rucksack, your coat pockets, your bedside table. Still found nothing. I was doing this two or three times a week.'

David shakes his head. 'I had no idea. None of my stuff ever looked out of place.'

'I was careful,' she admits. 'Until I got caught that is.'

David dips a cookie into his tea and asks, 'What if I am cheating on you? What if I have a second phone? What if the evidence is hidden in a place you haven't looked?'

Amanda watches him.

'What if it wasn't Jake I was with tonight, but another woman?'

Her heart quickens at the possibility he's lied to her, at the thought of him being with another woman.

Calm down, she tells herself. It's just a suggestion.

'Apart from following you, I'd never know.'

'No. If you want to continue looking through my stuff, even the shed and the van, that's fine. But I can only put up with it for so long.' David sits forward. 'You have to trust me. Because we won't last if you can't.'

Amanda listens to her husband. *We won't last if you can't.* She nearly lost him; she could still lose him if she doesn't change her behaviour.

'If a woman should wink, make a pass, give me her mobile number, just remember something, will you, Amanda?' David continues, his tone serious. 'I have a say in this. I can't stop people looking at me, but that doesn't mean I look back. I know Jake's not your favourite person, but he will vouch for my good behaviour, and not because he's my best mate. Do you know what his advice tonight was?'

'Tell me to fuck off?' she suggests.

He chuckles. 'Go through your stuff, see how you like it. He told me to search the house from top to bottom. Starting with the loft.'

'There's nothing in the loft,' she replies, suddenly thinking about her childhood diaries and the incriminating evidence the pages contain.

'Amanda,' David begins, amused. 'Your loft is full of stuff. I might have only been up there once but I'm not blind. Look, I'm not searching your house. I'm making a point. What do you want to do? How can we fix this? Do you want to?'

'I do, yes. Of course I do,' she implores, reaching for him. 'These last couple of days have made me thoroughly miserable. I hate being apart from you. I love you.' She sighs, knowing it'll take more than these words to repair their marriage. 'I promise I won't go through your things ever again, and I'll stop looking to see who might be eyeing you up. I have no reason not to trust you.'

David's smile broadens.

'And to apologise for my appalling behaviour, I want to give you some money for your brewing.'

David's expression freezes, only his eyes widen and brighten with joy. 'You don't have—'

'I should've done it before. It was selfish and wrong of me not to. I can see how much it means to you, but I want you to do something too.'

'Okay.'

'Involve me in it. I know Jake helps you, but I want to as well. We don't spend enough time together. Brewing beer together could be the making of us.'

David smiles and moves nearer. He takes her hands in his. His touch is warm and welcome, and she feels herself leaning towards him, desperate for his comforting embrace.

'Thank you, Amanda. I don't know what to say. This is great. There's some new equipment I want, which is gonna help us expand the scale of the brewing. Local pubs are starting to show an interest in the beers I've already created. I'm onto something.'

Amanda tries to push her concerns aside about where her money will take David and how fast that journey will take him. She needs to get onboard, however boring she finds the process of brewing, or she'll lose David for good.

'Come here,' he whispers, pulling her closer and wrapping his arms around her. She heaves a deep sigh and buries her face in his chest, breathing in the scent of his aftershave, feeling the warmth of his body.

'I don't deserve you,' she whispers.

'Yes, you do,' he replies.

Chapter 15

Martyn

Martyn arrives at the salon at his usual time. He sees Amanda sat at the desk, her face partly obscured by the vase of flowers on the counter. Eventually, having made him wait two days for a reply, she texted to say yes, he could come to the salon because they needed to talk. The tone of the text felt cold, businesslike, and he expects to have to make a heart-felt apology first to get on her right side. There was no kiss at the end of her words. He thought about bringing her flowers, chocolates, but realised sensibly that a gift was not going to rectify this situation.

He raises a knuckle and raps on the glass. Amanda looks up. There's no smile or greeting from her. She gets up and crosses the floor to unlock the door.

Martyn smiles but it feels fixed and false on his face. All he can think about is what could he do if she refuses to destroy her precious diary.

'Evening Amanda,' he says pleasantly, as she opens the door allowing him to step inside the salon.

'Hello,' she replies, her voice formal. She closes the door but doesn't lock it. She turns to face him, arms folded across her chest, barely able to meet his eyes.

'Can we talk?' he asks, keeping his stance open, friendly, not hostile.

She nods, holds a hand out to a nearby chair. He remains standing. Sitting down and having to kook up at her will make him feel at a disadvantage. He notices that the salon is tidy. She's already swept the floor and completed all the other tasks. Usually when he arrives, she's in the throes of bundling wet towels into the washing machine, tidying hairdryers and scissors away, polishing surfaces.

'How's everything?' he begins, nervously.

'What's the real reason you want me to destroy my diary, Martyn?' she asks.

He stares at her, taken aback by the force of her hostile tone.

'You must know why. What's in it that is so harmful? It's been in my loft for twenty odd years…'

'I didn't know you wrote a diary when you were fifteen,' he argues. He pauses, takes a deep breath to calm down. 'You never mentioned it at the time. I certainly didn't know you'd kept it.'

96

'You're not answering my question.'

He stares, his mind racing for an explanation. 'I don't want anyone else to read it,' he says weakly.

She scoffs. 'Why would anyone else read it after all these years? I'm the only one who knows of its existence. Why do you want me to destroy it? That's the question I'd like an—'

He interrupts. 'I'm concerned that *if* anyone should read it, such as David or your son, then they would realise that we were in a relationship when perhaps we shouldn't have been,' he explains.

'I think it's more likely that they would question if it was a *relationship*.'

'That's what it was,' he argues. 'You were my girlfriend. We were in love. Amanda, we were involved for months and months.' His hand reaches out but she steps away from. 'I wasn't seeing anyone else. Only you.'

'And why was that?' He opens his mouth to interrupt but she continues. 'Why were you involved with me?'

'What do you mean? I don't under—'

'What was so special about me, Martyn?'

'You were gorgeous. Fiery, sexy. I had heart palpitations just thinking about you.'

'I was also only fifteen years old.'

'I didn't know that.'

'You didn't know that?' she mocks. 'I think you did.' He frowns with confusion. 'You coach teenage girls and young women in swimming. I know you're not allowed to get in the water with them, but you must see them in their swimming costumes. There are big differences between a girl of 15 and a young woman of 18. Their bodies are different. Young women are more developed. Their hips and breasts for example. Their voices and behaviour too. Do you agree?'

The question throws him. 'I don't know…I haven't given it any thought…'

'Consider it now. What is the difference between me as a child and your own daughter?'

Martyn frowns. Is she asking him to think about his daughter's naked body? For fuck's sake.

'Or is the thought too disgusting?'

'I don't see the point, Amanda. What is this all about?'

'I was, at the time, a childish fifteen-year old. Still getting told off in class, refusing to tidy up after myself, putting up pictures of pop stars on my bedroom walls, cheeking my parents. I documented my behaviour in extensive detail in my diary, particularly my sneaking out to see you. I was childish until I was at least eighteen. Are you sure you don't want to sit down?'

Martyn's head is swimming. For the last couple of days, he's had a blinding headache and, when his wife insisted she take his blood pressure, to his shock he found it was raised. This, he found difficult to understand. He's a fit man. It should be normal. But this fucking situation and this silly bitch with her games is playing havoc with his health.

He pulls the chair out from under the dressing unit and sits, swivelling around to face her.

'I don't understand why you didn't see how silly I was,' Amanda continues. 'Maybe you did but you preferred to ignore it. Do you remember our first kiss? You asked if you could kiss me and I explained that I'd never been kissed before.'

Martyn smiles at the memory. Her hand was shaking; he could feel the tremor travelling up his arm, across his chest, warming his groin. He couldn't wait to touch her. He'd held off for as long as he could.

'You never questioned why I'd never been kissed before.'

'That's what you told me,' he explains. 'Why wouldn't I believe you?'

'Didn't you think it odd that a 17 year old hadn't been kissed before?'

He shakes his head. 'Not really. Some 17 year olds are inexperienced. And it's polite to ask first. Where are you going with this, Amanda? Why are you bringing all this up now?'

'I've been reading my diary.'

His heart leaps. Has she bought it with her? If so, he might be able to wrangle it from her. She might be about to hand it over…if he says the right thing.

'It's a very interesting read. And I realise that things back then were perhaps not as innocent as they appeared to be. After our first kiss, I wrote down your words to me. You said, "I don't want kissing to distract you from your homework". It never occurred to me at the time what you meant. I told you I was training to be a hairdresser, attending college one day a week. You don't refer to college work as homework. You slipped up, Martyn. You knew I went to school, you knew I was a child.'

Martyn shakes his head. 'I didn't. I…what's that evidence of? I slipped up. Maybe I was thinking about my own job. That I had homework...' Martyn's voice trails off as he realises what he's said. What kind of homework would a PE teacher set?

She shakes her head. She doesn't believe him.

'Was I the first teenager you had sex with? Or were there others before? I know I haven't been the last.'

'What? What is this? I thought this would be a chat, a reconciliation of sorts. But it's turning into a rather unpleasant interrogation…' He tries a smile, hopes for one back but her expression is serious and stoney.

'Abuse is unpleasant,' Amanda points out.

He stares. 'Abuse? Don't call it that. You were a willing participant in a relationship. I loved you. I have always cared about you.'

'You were very careful to make sure our break-up was amicable. Anything else and I might have gone running to my parents. It was abuse, Martyn. I realise that now. It's taken time for me to see that.'

'Is there any hint of abuse in your diary? Can I see the diary? I'd like to see what you wrote about us because I doubt you've used that word.'

'Admittedly, I never wrote that word. But after reading what I'd written after some of the sex we had, it now makes me feel uncomfortable. For example, you pressured me into giving you oral sex. Three times I told you I didn't want to do it.'

Martyn shifts uncomfortably in the chair. 'Do we have to—'

'In response, you told me how much you enjoyed it and that it would please you if I did it.'

'I returned the favour. You got off on it as I seem to recall. Couldn't get enough of it. Did you write that in your diary? Here's a question for you: does David do it as good as me?' he demands. He watches for her response. 'Or are you still so shy you can't even undress in front of him?'

Amanda's eyes harden. She switches her weight to the other leg, refolds her arms, her face reddens. 'There's no need to be crude. My sex life is none of your business.'

'Oh!' Martyn says, his eyes wide. 'Now it's none of my business.' She shakes her head but he ignores it. The truth is he finds her reluctance to talk about married life amusing. 'You were never so prudish when I was screwing you. I got the distinct feeling that during our conversations you were trying to get advice or guidance from me. Stuff you could use with David. Maybe you need to get back some of that confidence; remember how to lose your inhibitions.' He smiles. Her humiliation and annoyance starts to thrill him. There's more than one way to get his hands on that diary. She can't be at home all the time and David works late. He'll tear her house apart if he has to. But he must destroy it. And if she is home when he calls by, well, that's her problem.

Martyn slaps his hands on his thighs and stands. 'Right, well, I'm guessing you're not going to hand the diary over or destroy it, unless you want me to pay for it. Is there is a price? Money, a quick fumble in the back of the salon for old time's sake? No? There's no need to continue this conversation, is there?'

He turns to the door, his trainers squeak on the hard floor.

Her voice stops him dead.

'I know there have been others.'

He turns back to her, stares. 'Other what?'

'Victims of your abuse. There was a girl about 6 years ago. Let's call her Jane. Her friend told me all about how you groomed Jane. At first I didn't believe her. Even the friend admitted how Jane liked to fantasise, but Jane told my friend that you had a tattoo of a bird. Which I know you do. Now, if you're not allowed to enter a swimming pool with a pupil, how did she see it?'

'What?' Martyn smirks. 'She could have seen it at any time. She could have walked past my house whilst I was mowing the lawn bare-chested! Lots of kids have probably glimpsed me changing my sweaty sports tops. It means nothing.'

'I think it does. Especially after what I saw last week. In full view of my salon, in that lay-by just out there, a BMW pulled up. Shortly afterwards, you arrived with a tall girl with wet hair. Do you remember it?'

Fuck, Martyn thinks, keeping his face expressionless. He can feel his heart rate increasing. How the hell has he let this happen? Bloody Heather and her sly little touches...he knew one day she'd get him into trouble. Should he lie that she's the daughter of a friend? Or will that sound worse? Should he tell Amanda that the girl has a crush on him? She's screwed in the head?

Martyn shakes his head. 'This is bollocks. I'm her swimming coach.'

'Looks to me that that's not all you're coaching her in.'

'That's a disgusting accusation and not true,' he argues defensively.

'The girl touched you in a way that is wholly inappropriate for a pupil to touch her coach. I could tell that you were struggling to keep your hands off her…'

Martyn laughs. 'You're fucking deluded, Amanda.'

'It's evidence, Martyn.'

'Did you film it? Then it doesn't exist. It's all in your head and we both know how screwed in the head you are. It was not abuse, but if you want to reveal your diary to Lexington, so they all know what a slutty teenage tease you were, then go right ahead. Humiliate yourself and David and Oliver. His school mates are going to get such a thrill bullying him about his slut of a mother.'

'You bastard.'

'It's your decision, Amanda. Bury the diary and save yourself and your loved ones the humiliation.'

'Or I could go the police and reveal what kind of prolific paedophile you are.'

'You'll ruin yourself in the process. Your only option then, will be to take another overdose.'

'Get out of my shop,' she shouts, pointing at the door.

'With pleasure.' Martyn walks to the door. Amanda keeps a few metres behind herding him the right way. He reaches for the latch and opens the door. One more thing occurs to him and he turns back, but the movement has him colliding with a person walking past the shop.

'Shit. Sorry, mate,' Martyn says automatically, looking around.

'Alright sir!' says a young man with dark hair. 'You don't recognise me, do you? Jake Bunby, sir.'

Oh, Martyn thinks, isn't he friends with Amanda's husband?

'Hi Jake. How's it going?'

'Oh, you know, sir, could be better. Did you hear about my—oh, alright Amanda?' Jake grins at her. 'What's going on here then? Giving sir a late night trim of the bush, were you? Or has he asked you to put on your short pleated PE skirt and show him how to toss his javelin?' Jake's smug laughter makes Martin flinch and turn his head away. 'No wonder your marriage is on the rocks if you're fucking this old bastard.'

'You nasty little shit,' Martyn hisses at Jake.

'What?' shouts Amanda at Jake. 'How dare—?'

'I've waited a long time to say this to you but, fuck you, Hepworth. And you,' Jake says venomously to Amanda, jabbing a finger at her, 'you've got some face accusing Dave of adultery. Wait till he hears about this.' Jake walks away, laughter trailing behind him.

Martyn turns to Amanda, thinking he can salvage something here if he can reassure her that he'll tackle David and Jake if she wants.

'Do you want me...?'

'Fuck off Martyn!' Amanda shouts, slamming the door.

Through the glass, Martyn watches her stomp across the floor. She's never going to speak to him again. His options are limited. Break into her house and find the diary or shut her up for good.

Chapter 16

Amanda

Amanda carries the large mug of cappuccino to a table by the window, readjusting the glossy magazine under her arm. She sits down, pushing away the dirty plate and coffee-stained mug left by a previous customer. Seconds later, as if by magic, a member of the cafe staff collects the crockery and wipes the table of spilt sugar and crumbs. Amanda mutters a thank you, sips her drink and stares thoughtfully through the window at the bustling passersby; some drag wheeled suitcases, others are loaded down with shopping bags. Amanda can hear the tannoy announcing a platform change.

It's a busy lunchtime at the city's central train station. People heading to meetings, home or across the country to towns and cities she has never been to. She wonders what life could be like for her somewhere else, far away from Lexington and hairdressing, far away from everyone she knows.

She doesn't know how much more she can take of the salon and the mess left by that builder, of being a part-time mother to a child who clearly prefers to spend time with his dad, and being the wife of a man she can't trust.

The message came through on David's iPad when Amanda arrived home at teatime the day before. It was on charge by the kettle in the kitchen, propped up against the tiles and the alert sounded, a loud beeping, made her jump. She'd looked at the tablet for a long time, contemplating whether she should lift the protective cover and see what the alert was for; after all she had promised to never snoop through his stuff again. But what if it was important? And it wouldn't do any harm really. It could be a courier firm confirming the date and time of a delivery, confirmation of an appointment to the dentist or something. Her hands made the decision before her brain did. She pulled the cable out and lifted the cover and nearly died on the spot.

I want you inside me again, Davey.

She staggered to the kitchen table and sat, waves of nausea rumbling through her, reading the words over and over. She couldn't access the device because David had changed the password and that made her more suspicious. Whoever the sender was, they weren't in David's contact list because no name appeared, just a mobile number. One she didn't recognise.

When David arrived home, he never mentioned the message yet he must've seen it because it would have appeared on his phone at the same time. A short while later, the message had disappeared off the tablet screen when he presumably deleted it off his phone. Perhaps he had responded to the message with a jokey reply like, 'Are you sure you've got the right person?' But perhaps she, whoever she is, had got the right person and "Davey" was their affectionate term for him.

Amanda watched his every move that night and, though he did nothing else to arouse suspicion, she knew it was solely because he assumed she knew nothing about the sordid message. He was relaxed that he'd got away with his infidelity.

That night, a devastated Amanda lay awake, allowing the betrayal to grow to massive proportions, desperately trying to decide what to do. Should she wake him up from his gentle snoring and confront him? Should she leave a note for when he got home, demanding he collect his belongings and leave her house? Should she follow him?

When she awoke, David had gone to work and she had a train to catch. Upon her arrival in the city, she spent ages outside the exhibition centre debating whether to go in since the ticket was paid for or just turn around and go home. She couldn't be bothered with it. Pasting a smile on her face, being on guard for hours trying to keep it in place should it start to fall, making pleasantries with people she hadn't seen for a while, nodding and saying, 'Yes, business is good, Oliver's great, married life is heavenly.'

Now she sits in a cafe surrounded by lots of people and she has never felt more alone, and her mind releases the many questions she has for herself. What are her options? Not only for the now, but more importantly for the long-term. If she leaves Lexington for a short time, it will give her breathing space but all her issues will still be there when she returns. And it'll be worse because, in her absence, some decisions will need to be made and that will fall to David, Holly, her parents, Declan. They'll have a hand in her future. Does she want them to continue dictating to her?

David must have cheated on her. He came home early that night he spent in the pub with Jake, afraid she'd kick him out and that he'd lose his home, the potential for money, and he buttered her up with his apologies and pleas to try again. She fell for it, caved in against her better judgment and ordered him hundreds of pounds' worth of brewing equipment. And to repay her, he'd fucked some tart on the side.

Like he was always going to.

She should never have married him because, even if he hadn't done this, she would never have really trusted him. How can you trust a man like that when you're damaged yourself? The situation is hopeless.

How can you be happy when you can't trust someone?

She doesn't know what will make her happy.

Amanda gives in to her dark thoughts; they've taken her here before. What if she got on the next train out of here, anywhere, booked herself into a hotel, and climbed into the bath with a stack of paracetamol and a bottle of gin? Or bought a rope and climbed a hill to a tree standing atop?

No one would find her in time. No one might find her at all.

Chapter 17

Present Day

William

'No pressure, but it's imperative that you pass first time,' I tell Shaun. 'There isn't a Private Investigator in the whole of England who isn't mobile. And if they aren't, they've probably been done for drink driving.'

Across the round coffee table, my young assistant rolls his eyes.

'I got this, Will,' he reassures me, his tone slightly condescending. 'Trust me.'

I frown with annoyance. 'Look, Shaun. Until you've got a set of car keys in your hand, there are certain tasks I cannot let you undertake. I need to know that you can exit a sticky situation lightning quick. I mean, if you were caught photographing a honey-trap from a strategic position by *our* target, no amount of quick-thinking chat is going to prevent you from getting a black eye or pissing off our client when they discover we fucked up.'

'Will, quit worrying. My mum is taking me out every night this week for practice. I can't do any more. I am ready for this. Anyway, I've got my own added incentive to pass first time. My twin sister has her test two days later.'

'For God's sake, don't let a girl beat you.'

'She thinks, because she's three minutes older, she's got the right to beat me to my licence.'

Shaun has been my apprentice for twelve weeks and, when I discovered I'd be the one to ferry us around, I nearly told him to sod off. How can you get to twenty years old and be unable to drive? But as Shaun explained, it's a lot more common than I might think and my lack of awareness of this has made me feel older than my late thirties. At my insistence, Shaun started taking driving lessons. Turns out he's a natural. A bit too much of a natural. He's already developing habits. Occasionally he fails to indicate, exceeds the speed limit by a couple of mphs, and the one that *really* pisses me off: rests his hand on the gearstick. These are all offences that will prevent him from passing his test next week.

The reason why he's working with me and why I'm caretaker manager of Nisha's business is because she's on maternity leave, just a couple of weeks from giving birth to her second child.

One of the main reasons why I want Shaun mobile is so he can take over a chore that I'm fed up doing: being the bait in the honey traps. It's hard work pretending to be interested in people when you're just getting paid to. And although women aren't his preference, Shaun is a good-looking lad, the ideal choice for honey-traps. Five feet nine, slim with a budding muscular physique which is being honed at the gym several times a week. He has recently restyled his chestnut-coloured hair into a trendy short, back and sides with a razor-sharp side parting. With his big blue eyes, flawless skin and perfectly sculpted features, Shaun could easily pass as a male model. And he's got charm and a friendly disposition.

Shaun gets up from the comfy office chair to collect my lunch debris. I reach over to plump up the squashed cushion. We have a meeting at two o'clock. We've arranged the comfy chairs around the coffee table in front of the floor-to-ceiling windows. The April sunshine streams through the glass and I get up to open a window, to let out the stench of cheese and onion crisps and Shaun's horrible sweaty-smelling pasty.

Three months ago, Nisha and I were asked to defend Shaun's friend who'd been accused of murder. During my conversations with him, I saw a quick-thinking and loyal lad with promise. Initially, Nisha was very sceptical about taking him on in case the animosity between me and Shaun's dad Hock, a thug of a man I have bad history with, might get in the way of our work but she's given him a chance and, since she left, Shaun is intent on grabbing every opportunity with both hands.

The last time I met Hock senior, I punched his lights out so employing his son goes some way to making amends and prevents him from taking revenge. I actually quite like my face. Plus my hands have only just properly healed from a knife attack I suffered three months ago courtesy of a bloke who hired me to test the fidelity of his wife in a honey-trap. The same enraged husband later accused me of stealing her away. It's going to be the best decision I've ever made, letting Shaun do these honey-traps. I'm tired of kissing women I don't fancy.

'How's the arm?' Shaun asks, picking up the bin and leaving the room. His voice floats down the corridor. Seconds later I hear the sound of running water as he puts the kettle on.

'Sore, but once I get these antibiotics at least my arm won't drop off.'

The ache in my upper right arm is difficult to ignore; it nags something terrible. It's an infected insect bite and it's the last time I offer my gardening services to Mrs Penn, my landlady.

There's a knock on the outer office door and Shaun gets it. I hear him making pleasantries, offering to take the client's coat, make a drink, show her the way.

I stand in the doorway ready to receive Mrs Davies.

A short smartly-dressed woman in her mid-seventies enters the room. She has short grey hair and wears red horn-rimmed glasses, which match her red coat. She smiles nervously and there's a sadness in her blue eyes. I smile back, hoping it puts her at ease. I introduce myself and offer my hand.

I gesture towards the comfy chairs but she politely declines, explaining she has a sore hip, so I position a hard-backed chair near to the desk, pleased because I prefer a barrier between me and the client. Shaun hangs her coat up behind the door and offers her a drink, which she declines.

'Take a seat,' I say, sitting down behind the desk.

'Thank you,' she replies in a well-spoken voice. She places her bag on the floor before sitting down and smiling nervously again.

'You said on the phone that you desperately need my help,' I prompt.

'I do, yes, very much so,' she says nervously, clasping her hands together. I notice the large ruby ring on her finger.

I wait.

'I don't know where to start...it's my daughter. She went missing nearly seven years ago... and I...' Her voice starts to crumple and she takes a few moments to gather herself before breaking down again. 'I can't bear it. I must know what happened to her, Mr Bailey...'

'Okay,' I say patiently. 'Take your time. Let's start with your daughter's name.' I need to know the name of the person who's going to be the centre of my investigation. Should this require one.

Mrs Davies smiles with relief as if finally, after a long battle, someone is prepared to listen to her. Beside me, Shaun is holding his breath. The nib of his biro rests on the blank white paper. This could be the first investigation he's involved in.

She closes her eyes for a moment, takes a deep breath and tells me, 'Her name is Amanda.'

Chapter 18

Mrs Davies gives us a brief outline of who Amanda is. It helps me build up a picture of the person. And talking of pictures, Mrs Davies reaches into her handbag and hands me a photo. Shaun leans over to look at it.

In the photo, Amanda is an attractive woman in her mid-thirties with green eyes and long amber-coloured hair expertly styled into a chignon. She's wearing a long and floaty dress and stands on a well-cut lawn. In front of her is a little boy, primary school age, blond-haired, smiling shyly.

'Amanda and her son Oliver. He's fourteen now,' Mrs Davies explains. 'This was taken the year she went missing.'

Mrs Davies continues her background account on Amanda, whilst nibbling chocolate digestives and sipping the coffee Shaun insisted on making. Amanda was 37 when she went missing in October six and a half years ago. She was the owner of a hair salon called the Colour and Curl Hair Studio. She had been married for 8 months to David Bywater, twelve years her junior, and they lived in Amanda's four bedroom house on a nice development in Lexington. Amanda has one son who has lived with his dad, Declan, since he was small. I wonder why that is and jot it down. My list of questions starts to grow, mostly what happened to her assets after she disappeared and, of course, who benefits from her will. It makes me think of my personal experience with a missing person namely my best friend Claire who disappeared in the last four months of my prison sentence, another story. The mortgage on her flat was paid by her wealthy parents until I discovered Claire's body buried in a mechanic's pit in the garage belonging to her half-sister. It was soon put on the market. The flat that is.

I tune my ears back onto Mrs Davies.

'We haven't heard a word from Amanda since that day, Mr Bailey. There's been no activity on her mobile or her bank accounts. No one has seen her; there have never been any sightings of her. There's never been so much as a blank postcard. It's like she just stepped into a black hole.'

'What are the circumstances of Amanda's disappearance?' I ask. 'Where did she go missing from?'

'She drove to Lexington train station, caught the 0955 to Fradlington and made her way to the Exhibition Centre, to a trade fair. She went every year.'

I did my police training in Fradlington. Big sprawling city. Great for weekends away: designer shops, trendy bars, posh eateries. Lots of green spaces too: well-kept parks which house open-air concerts. It has a business district too, glass sky scrapers, the centre of money and law. The residential areas are a mixture of leafy suburbs and high-rise flats. On the outskirts is the exhibition centre, accessible via a tramline. Also, Fradlington has a huge train station which has several lines stretching in all directions and the airport is only a short train ride away. If she went missing from such a big city, she could have gone anywhere.

'The trade fair was a hairdressing one, I take it?' Mrs Davies nods. 'Did she arrive?'

'Yes. A couple of the exhibitors spoke to her, gave her some samples. The police obtained CCTV footage of her at Fradlington train station sitting at an indoor cafe alone. This was recorded around noon, a little while after she left the fair. There's no other footage.'

'Did the cafe staff remember her?' Mrs Davies shakes her head sadly. 'Did Amanda buy anything from anywhere?'

'A magazine from WH Smith in the train station before she went to the cafe.'

'What magazine?' Shaun asks. She blinks at him. 'I'm just thinking, if it might give us a clue…'

Good thinking, I say to myself. *Boating Holidays on the Norfolk Broads.*

'*Take a Break*,' Mrs Davies replies. 'Amanda bought it to read on long journeys.'

Shit, I think.

'Was there any other reason Amanda might go to the city? Does she have friends or family there?' I ask and Mrs Davies shakes her head. 'Did she take anything from home? Was there a missing suitcase, empty hangers in the wardrobe? Was she on medication?' I'm thinking about Claire's antidepressants. Her half-sisters didn't know Claire was on them so failed to take the pills when they were trying to suggest Claire had done a runner.

'Nothing was missing. Her passport was still there and she wasn't on any medication. It all suggested Amanda was coming back. She had plans with Oliver for the half-term week.'

Something suddenly occurs to me. 'You said Amanda drove to Lexy train station. Was her car still there?'

'David found her Range Rover in the car park.'

That rules out a sneaky return. 'Who raised the alarm that she hadn't come home?'

She explains that Amanda wasn't due to return to the salon, but when she hadn't arrived home by early evening, David starting phoning people: the salon, her son's father Declan, Mrs Davies, but no one had heard or seen Amanda. I ask if her own address is on the way from Fradlington, but it isn't. It's about twenty miles in the wrong direction. Finally when David had phoned everyone he could think of, he contacted the police and for that, I need to speak to them, which will be no easy task.

'Tell me about David, those closest to her.'

Mrs Davies gives us a quick rundown on Amanda and David. Basically one day, Amanda phoned her parents to say she was going to the Caribbean for a fortnight and returned with a husband. And, apparently, Amanda was nearly six months pregnant with Oliver before she told them that she was making them grandparents.

So Amanda had kept key things from her parents. Marriage and babies are major milestones in a person's life. What else could she have been keeping to herself? And not just from her parents. What about David? Her staff? Her friends?

Did these secrets get too big for her to cope with? If Amanda was struggling with anxiety in the weeks leading up to her disappearance, was this something else she decided to keep from her parents? Was David a cause? Was he trying to help? Did he even have any idea how bad things might have been for her? I wonder if marriage to an older woman was a shock to his system or if everything was heavenly? Did they row? Did Amanda treat him like a child? And as a result, was he petulant?

As if reading my mind, Mrs Davies reiterates how much she thinks of David, how hardworking he is and that he runs his own small brewing company and that he sells his wares to local pubs.

'He was a lovely husband to Amanda,' she adds with emphasis, almost as if she knows that by being her husband, David tops my suspect list.

I'll be the judge of that, I think.

I ask Mrs Davies who were the key people in Amanda's life. After a few minutes, I discover that there aren't many. No friends, no notable ex-boyfriends; she had no known contact with previous colleagues or managers; in fact Jean Davies can't give me the name of one single person Amanda might have visited that day. Amanda must have been more of a loner than me. She didn't do social media; the salon didn't even have a Facebook page.

I ask if Amanda had a favourite place from her childhood that gave her particularly happy memories. I'm thinking she might have started a new life somewhere she had fond memories of, but I know the police would have already considered that.

The question appears to have stumped Jean, perhaps they never went on holiday. Interestingly, Shaun gives one of his own examples.

'When we were little, my mum and dad took us to a place just outside Keswick, in the Lake District.' He smiles whimsically. 'It was a great campsite.'

And I laugh out loud. The vision of Hock heating a tin of sausages and baked beans over a tiny stove, or him traipsing across a muddy field, rolled-up newspaper under his arm as he makes his way to use the bog, unexpectedly amuses me. I haven't found anything this funny for ages. Shaun frowns at me but I ignore him.

'Mrs Davies, can you think of anybody at all who'd want to harm Amanda?' I ask. 'Had she had any recent arguments? Disgruntled customers, someone from her past maybe...'

But Jean doesn't give my question any thought before she emphatically shakes her head. 'No. Amanda got on with people. She could be a strict boss but she had a business to run. She was a lovely girl.'

Who had no friends and no enemies. No one goes through life without pissing someone off. I know I have. But if Jean really believes someone killed her daughter then somehow along the way, Amanda had done what we've all done.

'Mrs Davies, what is your theory about Amanda?'

She sighs with sadness. 'Amanda attempted suicide when Oliver was young. Before my husband passed away, he said she was dead. He—'

I interrupt. 'Mrs Davies, what's *your* theory?'

Her eyes fill with tears, again like it's the first time she's been asked for her thoughts. 'Before, when she tried to...she booked a room in a hotel, took an overdose. If she had been successful, she would have been found the next morning. If she's killed herself, then where is her body? Why hasn't it been found? In a hotel room, or at the foot of some cliffs? Amanda would hate to never be found. The idea of being lost somewhere, rotting out in the open. None of it make any sense.' She sniffs loudly, fishes in her handbag for a tissue; Shaun reaches for the box off the nearby table. She grabs two, wipes her nose and looks at me with a serious stare.

I wait.

'I think Amanda is dead and, though I have no idea who would want to…I think someone killed her.'

Chapter 19

I lock the Mazda and make my way across the car park to the supermarket, prescription and list in my pocket. I grab a basket from the stack by the front entrance and start my route at the fruit and veg. I consider buying my mum a bunch of flowers as a thank you for doing my ironing, but the flowers in the dry black buckets have all wilted. Perhaps a bar of dark chocolate would be better. I stroll on, past the meat and fish cabinets towards the pharmacy counter.

The store is fairly quiet mid-week just before 6pm. A staff member is placing cardboard trays of fancy yogurts which taste like desserts on the end of an aisle and I pause to grab an apple crumble and custard one.

Before I locked the office up, earlier than I normally would, I googled Amanda's disappearance to see what the local rag was reporting at the time. Not much by the looks of it. The police weren't publicly suspecting foul play. Certainly no persons of interest were interviewed. Like they did with Claire, did they just assume that Amanda, being a responsible adult, had left Lexington to make a new life somewhere else in the country? They would have looked into the circumstances of her disappearance and who might have been involved. I need to know what they found, but it's been a long time since I had anything to do with the police, not since I went to prison. Ideally, I need someone in the job who I know, not the officers who looked into the case at the time. They are under no obligation to tell me anything. Who though? Who will speak to a disgraced ex-police officer sentenced to two years for perverting the course of justice?

The short queue at the pharmacy counter moves forward another space and I think of Amanda. It is possible that she committed suicide. If she went to a remote location to do it, then it's unlikely her remains will ever be found. I'm certainly not going to find her. Maybe some poor sod out walking their hound will find her remains half buried in woodland.

It is also possible that Amanda's life wasn't fulfilling and she decided to make a new one. She could have spent months preparing for it: filtering money off into a new account under an assumed name, buying new clothes and other much needed items and sending them ahead to her new address. If someone wants to change their name and hide their original identity, it's a lot easier than people might think. I've got about as much chance of finding her now the trail

114

is stone-cold as I have of finding her remains. Which leaves one alternative, or two if you count abduction and imprisonment.

And to find her potential killer, I need to know who had it in for her, who gained from her death however insignificantly. I'm going to have to meticulously take alibis apart, ask awkward questions and massively piss people off. People who have relied on a statement six years old are bound to make mistakes when reinterviewed. The things that they've relied on back then will have been forgotten and so there's a tendency to make it up. What they won't know is that I'll have an upper hand if I can get my hands on the MISPER file.

I move to the front of the queue and, predictably, the Pharmacy Assistant asks me to return in ten minutes so I take my basket and start the shopping. I add a can of deodorant to my lonely yogurt, dodge around an old man with a trolley, cross the central aisle heading for the microwaveable pasta and rice dishes, still thinking about Mrs Davies. But just as I'm about to step into the aisle, my eye catches sight of a familiar female figure standing several metres away, trolley parked by her side as she studies two jars, one in each hand. My feet stop abruptly, the corner of the basket bangs into my leg, but I barely notice the pain.

It can't be.

I blink.

Bronwyn.

I haven't seen her in three months. Not since she walked out of the restaurant and left me with the bill to pay and a load of grief. My heart thumps madly, reverberating in my throat.

I hide behind the gondola end but glance down the aisle, tilting my head to the right to see around the other shoppers. She's still studying the cooking sauces.

'Don't tell me you eat curry now,' I mutter. The irony of it. She wouldn't even entertain the idea of going to an Indian restaurant with me so we could talk about taking our friendship further, but I bet *he's* got her into them, just like he coerced her into dropping me.

Bronwyn chooses a jar, and shoves the other back on the shelf, probably in the wrong place if I know her.

I study her. She looks good.

She wears a bottle-green office dress, the hem skimming her knees, a shiny black belt pulled around her slim waist. Green suits her blonde hair and green eyes. She always wore the colour a lot. Her black heels, as usual, are completely impractical for walking in. I don't know how she does it.

My eyes narrow...there is something...

It's her hair. It's longer. Her spiral curls nearly touch the top of her shoulders. It's testament to just how long it's been since I saw her.

'Excuse me, please,' says a voice, making my heart leap.

It's a customer trying to reach for the goods on the promotional end. I mutter an apology and step out of the way, hurrying across the mouth of the aisle in case Bronwyn should look up alerted by the voice.

This is silly, I tell myself. Get a grip. Why am I standing here, spying on her? We're grown-ups. I should either walk away, which means I won't learn anything new and I'll have to live with a missed opportunity, or I need to go over and say hello. If she tells me to sod off, and why would she? then at least I know there's no hope for a reconciliation. I can really move on then.

I glance again and Bronwyn is now looking at the boil-in-the-bag rice on the bottom shelf.

A strange spear of jealousy pierces my chest that she is gathering ingredients to cook a meal for two: her and *him*. With me out of the way, Michael has Bronwyn all to himself. It's no wonder I haven't heard a word from her. I'm out of sight and very much out of mind.

I could walk past her now, see if she notices me and then, judging by her initial expression, frosty or warm, I'd know whether she had missed me as much as I've been missing her.

'Fuck it,' I mutter loudly, stepping into the mouth of the aisle, my heart still thumping, making me feel as nervous as hell like I'm a teenager approaching a girl I have a crush on.

But her hand is digging around in her handbag; I detect the faint sound of a ringing mobile and I almost turn back defeated, and yet I smirk to myself because the last time we were together, she allowed a phone call to interrupt us.

I continue my journey, bracing myself for the sudden cry of, 'Will! Is that you? Oh my God. How are you?'

But it doesn't come. She allows it to interrupt us again.

'Hello, you! Are you back?' she says into the phone, excited.

The warmth in her voice instantly deflates the small balloon of hope I have in my chest. I glance at her shopping as I approach, desperate to see what sauces she's bought, but it's difficult to tell in a couple of seconds what items she has placed into her full trolley.

When I reach the other end of the aisle, all I have to show for my efforts are a nostril-full of her perfume and a deviation from my route around the supermarket. I glance back, for one final time, at my ex-friend but she's chatting into the phone.

I have my answer. It wasn't meant to be. We were not meant to be. And this fruitless freak meeting proves just that.

I return to the pharmacy counter for my antibiotics, pay for my goods at the self-service till and exit the supermarket. And now that I know, I can put all my effort and concentration into finding Amanda Davies. This investigation has come just at the right time.

Chapter 20

The next morning, I get up nice and early to go on my every-other-day run in an attempt to permanently drive out thoughts of Bronwyn by pounding the paths of my local park. It appears to work too and I arrive back at Mrs Penn's breathless and hot, my thoughts on the day ahead. I unlock the front door, deposit my trainers in the porch but leave the baseball cap on. No one is seeing my normally styled quiff soaked flat against my skull.

Mrs Penn is exiting the lounge as I shut the door behind me. She's a multi-divorced woman in her mid-fifties. Currently she is seeing two men. Both are aware of each other and neither seem to mind. She definitely doesn't let them stay overnight.

'I'm only after a bit of fun,' she regularly assures me. 'I'm not looking for husband number four, or is it five?'

Aside from me, Mrs Penn has one other tenant, but he only stays here in the week, driving the hundred or so miles back home every weekend to see his wife and family. Both of them have better social lives than me, which means I frequently have the house to myself in an evening. One of Mrs Penn's exes left part of his extensive Blu-Ray collection behind and so far, I have worked my way through the Westerns, which remind me of my dad who loved them.

'Morning Will,' she says, brightly. 'How was your run?'

Her lipstick is blood red, her dress leopard-skin, her heels as tall as skyscrapers. No wonder men admire her, no wonder her two adult daughters are worried about their good-time mother. I would if she was my mum too.

'It was good, thank you,' I reply, wiping a tear of sweat off my cheek.

'Good, good. The toaster is still out, but we've run out of strawberry jam. Have a lovely day,' and she grabs her handbag off the hallway table and rushes out of the house.

I lock the door behind her and make my way upstairs, peeling my sweat-soaked top off. After a quick and very hot shower, I stand in front of the bedroom mirror, my sore eyes adjusting to the new contact lenses, and style my dark hair, a task which can take several minutes, three different hair products and a hair dryer.

Afterwards, I make myself a travel mug of tea, wrap two slices of toast in a sheet of tinfoil and head for the motorway and the last place I ever expected to visit again.

*

I park in the street outside her smart three bedroom semi-detached house with its white painted gate. I notice that she's changed her sporty little hatchback for a more robust 4x4 lookalike, which shouts I-drive-my-grandchildren-around-a-lot. She's still got her personalised reg though. I walk the three minutes back to her place of work and wait outside the security gate. Overhead, a dark rain cloud moves into position and, typical for April, a shower starts, dotting the pavement. Only then do I remember the umbrella in my boot. I could walk back for it but, if she appears and I'm not here, I'll have missed valuable minutes. I snuggle into my coat, pulling up the collar, and hope that she's on her way down from the third floor.

I look at the gold plaque set into brick wall which announces the address: Fradlington Police HQ. The wall forms the beginning of its bricked perimeter and my eyes follow the meandering driveway up through well-kept grounds, up a slight hill to the building, which looks more like a stately home, with faded white columns outside its main doors and a grand entrance.

I check the time as the rain spots start to get heavier. One minute past twelve. She can't be much longer unless she's changed her lunch-hour, but she always used to leave at noon because it meant she'd be home before her husband started his afternoon shift. It's a habit she'd be unwilling to break.

A couple of cars, marked and unmarked, are driving slowly towards me, but they don't give me a second glance as I'm standing near to a bus-stop. Just when I'm beginning to have second thoughts that I should've stayed with the Mazda, I look back up the driveway and spot a promising figure: 5'5", slightly overweight, with short blonde hair, and carrying an umbrella with a rainbow on it.

This is her. I straighten up, step out from behind the lamppost so she'll have to walk into or around me, and smile with anticipation. She sees me and her pace slows; the umbrella tips backwards exposing her bright smile, which instantly helps to diminish my nervousness.

'Well, well, well. If it isn't DC William Bailey as was. How the hell are you?' Yvette Wallace moves the umbrella completely out of the way and stretches up to give me a hug.

'I'm good, thanks, Sarge,' I reply, hugging her back.

She laughs. 'Now, now, I'm no longer Sarge. I'm just plain Yvette.' She holds me at arm's length, studies me from toe to quiff. 'You've changed. Lost some of that awful bulky muscle

119

I always hated, but I suppose prison does that. You look slimmer, healthier. Are you coming for a quick butty? Here, have the brolly,' and she thrusts it at me. 'I've got a hood.' She yanks the hood of her blue waterproof over her hair.

I hold the brolly over my head and walk alongside her as she leads the way back to her house. 'I searched for you on social media. I know it wasn't your scene, which is why I never found you, but I wondered, you know, how you were doing. What *are* you doing these days?'

'Private Investigator in Lexington.'

'Good to hear you're putting those skills we taught you to good use. How was it inside? Bad?' She looks at me.

'I kept my head down, mouth shut, and eyes averted. It passed without incident.'

'I'm glad to hear it. How are your parents and Eddie?' she asks, referring to my younger brother, who's also my partner in crime. It was his car-related offence I was trying to help him evade when it all went tits up.

'Rebuilding his life, got himself the love of a good woman and is going back to uni. My dad died last year. Alzheimer's.'

'Very sorry to hear that, Will. Did you get to spend some quality time with him beforehand?' I nod. 'And your mum?'

'Rebuilding her life too.'

Yvette smiles. 'Here we are,' she announces, coming to a stop outside her house. 'Yours?' and she points her house key at the Mazda.

'My dad's.'

'Nice car. Come on then. I'll get the kettle on.' She unlocks the front door, disarms the house alarm and gets straight to work, filling the kettle, halving the sandwich her husband has left for her in the fridge and tipping a big bag of crisps into a bowl for us to share.

'Tuck in,' and she slides the plate across the counter to me.

I take a seat at the pine kitchen table and grab a handful of ready salted crisps. When Yvette was my Sarge back in the good old days, we used to regularly pop back to her house where her husband Alan would have lunch on, either a chip butty on white bread, tomato soup with croutons or a good old cheese and pickle sandwich. She was like an auntie to me. And I know it hurt her when I got sent down.

'How's the family?' I ask, crunching on the crisps.

'They're all good,' and she flicks the teaspoon at the windowsill where a row of framed photos stand. Yvette is a real family person with three kids. I spot a couple of graduation pictures, one daughter in a paramedic's green jumpsuit, several more of young grandkids, dressed in pink or blue, on swings, laughing in high chairs, chocolate smeared on their faces.

I take a bite of the sandwich. Smoked cheese and breaded ham with a smear of Branston's pickle. Alan still knows how to make a nice sarnie.

She places the tea and a box of chocolate marshmallows on the table and joins me. We eat in silence for several minutes. The food fills a gap and I sit back, stripping the foil from the chocolate domed marshmallow.

'You're here on business then?' she asks. 'Can I assume it is not just a coincidence that you are visiting your old teacher?'

'It's not, no. Hope you don't mind.' She shrugs. I know it bothers her that I've only shown my face because I need something, but I know Yvette understands how hard it is for a disgraced copper to make the first move.

'What do you need, Will? If I can help, I will.'

I leave the little ball of foil on my plate, sip my tea and begin. As an ex police tutor, in particular my old tutor, Yvette is now a civilian specialist in forensic data recovery and I know she can easily hide her trail as she locates the MISPER file on Amanda Davies.

*

When I get back to Lexington and fish my mobile out of the glovebox, I see that I have two missed calls from Nisha, and a voicemail message. I lock the car and make my way back to the office. Honestly, hasn't she got anything better to do than check up on me? I half expect to find her sat at my desk going through the paperwork when I unlock the office door.

I call out but there's no reply. Unless she's in the toilet, complaining that the baby is pressing on her bladder. I don't miss those quips. I flick the switch down on the kettle and make my way down the short hallway to the office, mobile clamped to my ear as I replay the voicemail.

'Oh,' I say with surprise. It isn't from Nisha, but her husband Matt.

Two weeks early and the baby is ready to make an appearance. Nisha has gone into labour.

Chapter 21

'Do you need to go shopping?' Shaun asks, bringing the Mazda to a standstill at the traffic lights and gently applying the handbrake.

I look across from the window. 'For what?'

'Baby clothes,' he tells me like I should know. 'You can't visit Nisha empty-handed. You need to get some flowers too. There's a new boutique opened just down from my dad's paper shop…'

'I can't afford boutique bloody prices,' I reply sharply. 'How much money do you think I make? Nor do I know what colour clothes I'm supposed to…'

He gasps. 'You don't have to buy pink just because it's a girl—'

'I don't know that it *is* a girl.'

'Or blue just because it's a—'

'Enough, Shaun!' I shout. 'Don't give me any of that gender rainbow crap. I will wait until I am told what sex the baby is before I make any such purchases and, if I do buy it anything, it'll be a neutral colour and cheap, accompanied by a one pound bunch of daffodils since they're in season. Would you like me to add your name to the post-it-note I stick on the outside of the carrier bag or are you going to spend a fortune on an item that won't fit the baby by the end of the week?'

Shaun stares at me, mouth open and eyes wide, and it's only when the driver behind beeps their horn that it startles him out of his trance and back into learner driver mode. He shakes his head as he turns left and casually rests his hand on the gearstick.

'Take your hand off the gearstick,' I snap. 'It's an automatic fail.'

He snatches it back and places it on the steering wheel, keeping his hands at ten to two like he's been taught. He remains silent for a few minutes before giving a little throat-clearing cough and asking, 'How was your jolly to Fradlington yesterday?'

It's one of the many things I like about Shaun that he can't tolerate heavy silences like I can, and he's always the first to break such awkward ones, unlike me.

'It was good and it should bear some fruit later.'

He doesn't follow up with a repeat comment of "What do you mean?". Shaun never pries or asks the same question twice, knowing that the second time round my answer will be unchanged. Once we arrive at our destination, Amanda's house on a leafy avenue in a nice area of Lexy, I instruct him to execute a parallel park and slip the Mazda in front of a skip parked outside a neighbours house.

'Nicely done,' I tell him and he beams. 'And we'll have a three-point turn on the way out.' I get out of the car and look at Amanda's house. It's a detached house with an integral garage. A white transit van is parked on the driveway. The front garden has been gravelled with purple stones. Several low maintenance evergreen shrubs, the kind you see in council car parks, add a green focal point. I wonder if David has made any changes to the house and garden to suit himself or maybe Amanda didn't care for gardening.

We approach the house. Shaun's eyes are everywhere, drinking it all in: the signage on the side of David's van, whether it's curtains or blinds in the windows, any clues anywhere. I see the vertical blinds swing in one of the downstairs windows and seconds later the front door opens, and a man in his early thirties with blond hair and wearing black cargo trousers, a navy t-shirt with a white stripe across the front and black work boots smiles apprehensively. Down one arm is a colourful tattooed sleeve.

'David?' I say. 'I'm William Bailey and this is my colleague, Shaun Hock. Thank you for sparing the time to talk to us.'

'It's alright,' he replies. 'To be honest, I don't know what I can tell you that I haven't already told the police.'

I'm getting tired of hearing that but I keep my irritation hidden from my face and voice. 'I'm afraid I won't get access to the MISPER file,' I lie. I had hoped it would have arrived by now. I would have preferred going into this meeting with a knowledge of his account.

'Come in.' We step inside. The hall is light and airy. The walls are a light blue, the hard floor is dark wood.

'Your handiwork?' I ask and David turns questioningly. 'The floor. Did you lay it?'

He smiles, visibly relaxes. 'Yeah. It's how we met. Me and Amanda, over the floor.'

Sounds rude, I think. Confessions of a floor installer. We follow him down the hall, looking around, but the place is tidy, no pictures on the walls, completely uncluttered and I wonder if he had to tidy up big style before our arrival. He shows us into the kitchen/diner, a room the entire width of the house. Beautiful white cabinets, spotlessly clear worktops, a shiny Belfast sink and a dark wood kitchen table with four chairs.

'Sit down,' he says, pulling out the nearest one to the window. He doesn't offer us a drink.

We settle ourselves down. Shaun gets out his notepad and pen.

'You were saying, you met over the floor,' I begin with a smile.

David nods, nervous again. 'Amanda bought a new floor. I laid it.'

The seduction chat must've been sparkling. What did she see in him? But then he is easy on the eye and maybe laying floors isn't all he's good at. Did she see him as a trophy husband?

'We got chatting. Which is not hard when you're the only two people in the house.' David chuckles. 'She was a really interesting person. You know, running her own salon. She asked me out,' he adds quickly. 'Good-looking woman like that. Amanda wanted to move us along quick. We'd only been seeing each other for a few weeks before she popped the question.'

'Very spontaneous. Why did you say yes?' I ask. He blinks. 'To the proposal?'

The question throws him, but surely he's had loads of people speculating why Amanda asked a handsome younger man to marry her and why he would say yes.

'I fell in love,' he eventually answers. I smile and wait for him to elaborate. 'A life with her was promising. She had her own things. Being her husband made me feel like I could have something too, I could have a chance to do better. Does that make sense?' He shakes his head. 'I bet you're gonna think I'm a right gold-digger.'

'No, David. I don't. People marry for lots of different reasons. So life with Amanda was good?'

He admits that mostly it was good, but it was an adjustment. They were getting to know each other whilst getting on with married life and allowing each other to do the same things as they did before.

'What sort of things did you want to continue doing?'

He hesitates. Perhaps he doesn't think I'd question him like this.

'I brew my own beer.' This time he smiles brightly. Beer is his passion. Interesting. He briefly tells me that he and his mate used to brew beer when they were teenagers, just as I predicted. Amanda allowed him to turn the garden shed into a place to brew and from there it grew and grew. Just before she went missing, a couple of the local pubs started to flog his IPA brand in their establishments. I ask him the name of the brand, wondering if I've seen it anywhere. He tells me it's called The Filthy Pig and the reason is a long story, unrelated to Amanda.

'What sort of things did Amanda want to continue doing?' He looks puzzled. I explain. 'Did she have a weekly night out with the girls? A male friend she liked to go out with?'

'Nothing like that. She went to work and came home. She did what she wanted.'

'She was the boss?' I joke. David smiles tightly. Of course she was. 'What did you two argue about?'

'We didn't have arguments.'

'All couples argue, David. I mean in general. Was she supportive of your brewing endeavours?' I ask and he nods. 'Did it ever cause rows?'

He bites his lip. 'Occasionally. It's time consuming. I don't know how much you know about brewing.'

I tell him that I only like to drink beer.

'We occasionally argued about the usual stuff. Whose turn it was to cook, put the bins out. That sort of thing. We were your typical newlywed couple.' He smiles suggestively, raising an eyebrow.

'Can you tell me your movements on the day Amanda went missing?'

David leans forward, rests his hands on the table. 'I got up before her. I had a few big jobs on that day and wanted to get a head-start. Amanda was going to this trade fair in the city. I never heard from her all day, which wasn't unusual. We were both always busy. I went home about six and my mate, Jake came round.'

'Can you give me the contact details of the customers you saw that day, please? I'll need Jake's too.'

He stares. 'You're joking? It was seven years ago. I've laid hundreds of floors since then. I don't remember their names.'

'I assumed their details would be ingrained in your memory as it was the day you lost your wife.'

'Well, they're not,' he snaps.

I smile patiently. The MISPER file will have them. 'You can give me Jake's details though, can't you?' His stare intensifies.

'Of course I can. Jake Bunby.' David reels off the number quickly in an attempt to outwit Shaun, but I've been giving Shaun lessons in how to absorb details like this. He scribbles the digits quickly. 'Jake stayed until 7 maybe. That's when I started to get concerned about Amanda.'

'Was it a common occurrence, Jake coming round?'

David nods

'Did Jake and Amanda get on?'

'Yeah. Okay...'

'Really? You don't sound so sure.'

David looks flustered. He shifts in the chair, sits back and folds his arms defensively. 'They were jealous of each other. Jake helped, *helps*,' he corrects, 'with the brewing. Amanda wanted me all to herself.'

'You were newlyweds,' I point out using his word. 'And you argued about Jake?' Reluctantly, he nods. 'Understandable she was jealous. What time did you expect her back?'

'About seven. When it got to quarter to eight, I rang her, but there was no answer. I tried the salon, Declan, everyone I could think of, but no one had heard from her. I headed to the train station, thinking that she might've had an issue with the car.'

'Wouldn't Amanda have phoned you?'

'Yeah,' he replies defensively, 'but where do you look when you've run out of places? Her car was there and no sign of her. The next train wasn't due for another hour. Once that came in and she didn't get off, I called the police.' He pulls a face as if to say "I know nothing more", and relaxes his folded arms.

'What do you think has happened to your wife, David?'

He huffs, shrugs, pulls a confused face. 'I've gone through every single scenario I can think of: suicide, kidnapping, accidental death, she's got a new identity with a new life doing something as far away from hairdressing as you can get like dairy farming.' He chuckles.

'Murder?' I suggest, noting its absence.

He looks at me. 'Yeah, that too.'

'What would you say if I told you that that's why Mrs Davies hired me? That she thinks someone murdered Amanda.'

'I'd say it's a possibility. It would explain why Amanda's never been seen again. How can you find a murderer when you don't know who you're looking for? The city is a big place.'

'Mrs Davies doesn't think a stranger murdered Amanda.'

David recoils, his head flings back as if he's been struck by a fist. His eyes widen and he shakes his head. 'You're joking? What? One of us? Someone who knew her? You mean me?'

He laughs without humour. 'That's why you've been interrogating me. I didn't kill my wife. I loved her!'

'David,' I begin patiently, 'I wouldn't be doing my job if I didn't question you…'

He shakes his head again. 'I didn't kill her,' he states forcefully. 'We had our issues. And it's breaking my heart to do it…it really is…but it's been nearly seven years. Amanda isn't coming back. I know that. I asked Jean if she wanted to do it, but I knew she'd find it difficult. I'm trying to save her the agony…'

I frown.

David's expression changes and he suddenly looks sad, guilty. 'It'll give us all closure we need so we can move on. *I* need to move on. I need to be independent, stop living off Amanda's earnings from the salon.' I nod encouragingly. It's just as I thought. 'Finally I can apply for a declaration of presumed death.'

*

'Which means what?' Shaun asks, resting his hand on the gearstick briefly before I throw him the filthiest stare I can muster. He removes his hand. 'Sorry, Will. What does it mean?'

'It means if he's in the will, he'll get his hands on a slice of Amanda's estate, which could be a sliver or a generous wedge. We need to know who benefits from Amanda's death.'

'He's been benefitting every night for the last six years. It's not exactly a borstal cell, is it? Not that I'd move out either. What's his alternative? Back to his mum's?'

'Jean did say that he had offered to move out but she insisted it was his home too. I don't necessarily mean who's in her will. Like you say, there are other ways to benefit from someone's death. I think it's odd that she never took his surname.'

'Maybe she didn't want to be called Amanda Bywater. But since she wasn't married to Declan, she wouldn't have the same surname as their son. Unless he has a trendy double-barrelled one. By keeping Davies, she retained part of his name.'

'I was actually thinking more along the lines that she didn't see David as a long-term partner. Almost like she knew it wouldn't last.'

'I tell you what is bullshit,' Shaun begins knowledgeably. 'That he's not had a girlfriend since his wife went missing. Either that or he's got to know his right hand intimately,' and he takes his hand off the wheel to make a wanking gesture.

'Another automatic fail,' I remark drily.

He laughs and sticks his middle finger up. 'And another.'

Chapter 22

'No, we haven't chosen a name yet,' Matt chuckles down the phone. 'We were going to call her Jasmin, but now that we've seen her, she doesn't look like one.'

His pride at being made a dad again positively oozes down the line and into my ear like warm oil. I resist the urge to ask what a Jasmin looks like and instead say, 'You've got a few days to find one...' I scroll through the MISPER file which arrived at 7.30 this morning. I couldn't wait to get to the office and get cracking with it. I was like a child with a new toy. I even texted Shaun at 7.33 and ordered him to get the coffees and breakfast muffins in.

'Do you know, it's actually…' Matt trundles on and I roll my eyes, wishing he'd get on with revealing why he's phoned so I can get on with my job. The file is a goldmine of information. Finally I can make some headway.

'Are you available then, Will?'

Shit. 'What was that, mate? I was distracted.'

'I asked if you're free this afternoon to pop over and see us all. I'm sure our beautiful daughter will love to meet her Uncle William.' I hear the amusement in his voice and, if Nisha is in earshot, she'll be laughing like a bloody drain.

'I'm sure she will,' I say, through gritted teeth. 'The thing is, I've got a couple of appointments on after lunch and I might not—'

'Before lunch then! We won't keep you long. Half an hour tops. Twelve thirty, okay?'

It's pointless arguing any more or trying to come up with another excuse. I might as well get it over and done with. I tell him yes.

'Great stuff…oh, and Will, there's no need to bother with gifts. Your presence is all that we require. Bye.'

Which will save me some hard-earned money. I chuck the mobile on the desk and lean back in the chair. Babies, I think. I'd much rather be chasing after ghosts all day than a screaming brat.

*

'He might not have remembered his customers details, but everything else David told us is exactly as stated in here,' and Shaun taps the back of his hand against the paperwork, a gesture I've seen Nisha do many times. 'He went to work, went home and his mate came round. It couldn't be verified by the neighbours because their lounge is on the back of the house and not the front like Amanda's.'

I flick through the pages until I find the important bit: the police's initial searches. No unknown females in the two district mortuaries or hospitals; no females matching Amanda's description had booked themselves into the surrounding hotels or hostels. A search of the house and grounds hadn't revealed anything of interest: no newly dug areas in the garden, no signs of a struggle in the house, no newly plastered walls or raised floorboards, no recently moved items of furniture like a wardrobe, no missing rugs. The only item of interest noted was in the loft. A box had been opened and some items removed and stacked on top of a black bin liner containing old clothes. The removed items were old exercise books and photo albums of Amanda's: trinkets like friendship bracelets and cheap jewellery, the stuff a teenage girl might keep for sentimental reasons. Had she been searching for something in the days before her disappearance or was it much longer ago? And were they significant items? When asked, David replied that he had no knowledge of Amanda entering the loft; in fact he'd only been up there once or twice himself. David didn't store any of his things up there. Whatever it was, Amanda had journeyed up into the loft herself.

I reach for my takeaway cup of coffee but of course it's still empty. I stretch my legs out and feel my knee click painfully. I get up and go to the kitchen. As I fill the kettle, my thoughts wander back to the MISPER file. There are very few witness enquires contained within the file. The police naturally spoke to her parents who were right where Jean said they were, staying at her sister's house a hundred miles away, confirmed by the sister and her friends who she had invited around to celebrate her birthday.

The police spoke to Amanda's staff. A dozen witnesses confirmed the stylists' presence in the shop from 8.30 until 6pm. Another colleague, Tamsin, had rung in sick that day. She was at home in bed all day. No one to confirm it, but no obvious motive to harm Amanda either.

All her employees claimed to have excellent relationships with their boss. Can anyone really say that? I love Nisha as a friend, but bugger me she can be infuriating. With her nitpicking, occasional bossiness, the constant talk of babies and all things maternity and her sarcastic jokes. Who's to say, one day, when I'm really pushed to the limit by something or someone else, that one wrong word from Nisha, might have me reaching for her neck to wring?

All-women environments are catty places. Claire used to tell me how bitchy her office was because four women spent eight hours a day with each other. Male habitats are the same, and it needs a member of the opposite sex to prevent these toxic situations happening. Why should a hairdressers be any different to an office? Was Amanda a tyrant boss and did the other women get together to bitch about her? Did Amanda deny one a pay rise? Did she even sack one of them and, as downtrodden "sisters", have they all played a part in covering up Amanda's death?

I carry the tea back through to the office and place Shaun's mug on the table by his side. He mutters his thanks but doesn't look up from the papers he's reading. I settle back in my chair and reach for a line of enquiry when suddenly Shaun announces, 'Everyone's alibi seems pretty watertight. Declan the ex worked until noon and had the afternoon off which he spent completing the long list of jobs his girlfriend left. He picked the kids up, went back home and started tea. There's no way he could've driven to Fradlington to abduct and kill Amanda.'

'Don't believe everything you—'

'And the same goes for Tamsin. She was at home sick in bed. No one can confirm it; her parents were away.'

'Shaun…'

'And that's it!' He throws his hands up in frustration. 'We have one, two, three,' he stabs his finger at the statements which dot the coffee table. 'Four…'

'Shaun,' I snap loudly. 'People lie. These are witness statements. In fact you can't even call them that. They're lines of enquiry, not to a murder, but to a disappearance. Don't forget, there will be people out there never interviewed by the police because their connection to Amanda has never come to light. You must understand, Shaun,' and I lean forward, elbows resting on my knees, 'that we may never find Amanda. She could be homeless, in which case we will never find her. If she's relocated and changed her name, then you can bet your life she is eagerly awaiting David's court application to declare her dead. Finally, she can raise her head a little.'

'This could all be pointless then?'

'No. Mrs Davies will know she did everything in her power to find her daughter. She either accepts Amanda's dead or continues to have a tiny bead of hope that one day, Amanda will get in touch. Sadly people who change their identity usually remain hidden for the rest of their life. This agency gets paid and you learn a valuable lesson in investigative work. That it is painstaking and laborious, but bloody interesting.'

It prises a smile out of him. 'Yeah, you're right. It'd be no fun if we found her quickly.'

'Rest assured, if I find something, you'll be on the front row to see it. Now, I must get going and see my delightful boss' new baby.'

'Is there anything you want me to do?'

'Yes. Start ringing David's customers up, verify his whereabouts for the entire day.' I grab my coat off the peg. 'At the moment, he's our number one suspect.'

*

On the windowsill of the lounge, through the open curtains, I see rows of congratulatory cards propped open. Shit. I forgot a card. Shows you how out of practice I am with other people's good news.

Matt opens the door and beams. 'Hi Will. Come in, but you'll have to whisper; I've just got her off to sleep.'

'Who? Nisha?' I quip, laughing at my own joke.

I step into the hall and spy the evidence of a new baby already. A pack of disposable nappies for newborns stands at the bottom of the stairs along with pink gift bags decorated with cartoon storks and babies with pink bows in their hair.

'Before you go into the lounge,' Matt tells me, 'there's something you should know.'

I feel a sudden dread in my chest. Is this why Matt was so insistent I come today? Is there something wrong with the baby?

He smiles awkwardly. 'Bronwyn is here.'

The dread in my chest quickly erupts like a firework sending a burning sensation up my throat. Bronwyn is here, just a few metres away. I wonder if they've told her I'm coming.

'I understand if you want to go,' Matt continues. 'She said she has meetings all week and didn't want to—'

I interrupt. 'It's alright, Matt. We're grown-ups. I'm sure we can be civil to each other in your house.' At least I'll know what her reaction would have been that day in the supermarket.

Matt opens the lounge door. Nisha is curled up on the brown leather settee, wearing leggings and a long jumper. She gets up, smiling brightly and gives me a hug.

'Congratulations,' I whisper.

'Thank you, Will. It's so good to see you. Everything alright at work?'

'Everything's fine. Was the birth very painful?' I ask.

She nods. 'Not as bad as the stitches.'

I grimace. 'Too much information.'

She laughs.

'You look good,' I tell her. 'Motherhood has cleared your spots up a treat. And saved you a fortune on expensive facials.'

'Piss off,' she laughs. A quiet complaining mewing from the cot at the end of the settee instantly shuts her up and we smile at each other. 'Want a peep?' Nisha peels back the corner of the soft white blanket and I look down at the baby. Her hair is wispy and dark. She has the tiniest fingernails. 'Will, meet whatever we decide to call her.'

'She's very pretty. Obviously takes after her dad.'

Nisha smiles. 'Bronwyn's putting the kettle on if you're staying for a brew.'

'I'd love one.'

'Go on then,' and she pushes me towards the other door in the room which leads into the kitchen.

It takes an eternity to cross the room. Just say hello, help make the tea, keep it short, smile politely. I open the door. Bronwyn is pouring hot water into a striped mug; steam curls upwards and in those brief moments I look her over. Being this close, closer than I have in a long time, makes my heart unexpectedly yearn. She's wearing another dress I've never seen before. Dark grey knee-length, with a trail of tiny dusky pink and silver flowers climbing from the hem over her hip and flank. Her blonde curls are up, secured by a sparkly pink clip, revealing her pale slim neck, the dainty white gold earrings. She looks so nice, so fanciable. No, I tell myself. She was only ever your friend; she'll never be anything else. She chose him over you.

'Hello Bronwyn,' I say formally.

She jumps, sloshing water onto the work surface and putting the kettle back onto its base with a thump. She turns and I expect an annoyed glare. I'm poised to give a sarcastic apology but her expression changes like a flower suddenly coming into bloom and she grins, making my heart feel like it's being tugged out of my chest.

'Will!' she says, with a gasp. 'Hello. How are you? It's really good to see you.'

133

I'm taken aback by her enthusiasm and wonder if it's nerves.

'Yeah, you too.' I close the door to stop Nisha from eavesdropping, and lean against the doorjamb.

Bronwyn mops the spilt water up and asks if I want a drink.

'Tea please, one sugar.'

'I remember.' She refills the kettle, fetches another mug out of the cupboard and, whilst she's waiting for the water to boil, she says, 'Beautiful baby, isn't she? I'll just take these drinks through before they get cold.'

I hold the door open. As she levels with me, she looks up, smiles shyly and mutters thank you. I get a whiff of her familiar perfume, the scent of which used to fill my Mazda every time I gave her a lift. It still lingers in the leather of the passenger seat.

Whilst she's gone, I make my tea and notice that she's left her own coffee behind. I pick the mug up and am about to take it into the lounge when she returns.

'Nisha's just feeding the baby. We could stay in here…have a catch-up,' she suggests hopefully, nodding at the wrought-iron table and two chairs against the wall.

'Yeah, okay.' I reply reluctantly, placing the drinks on the table mat. I pull the chair out and sit. My heart is pounding, my throat dry so I try the tea but it's scalding. She sips the coffee, keeps her hand through the mug handle, her thumbnail begins to scratch the striped ceramic the way it always does when she's deep in thought.

I remember so much about being with her: the lime and mandarin of her perfume, this telltale sign with the thumb, the colour of her eyes like springtime ferns; it comes flooding back and yet I've never felt further apart from her. What has she been doing during my absence? Has she missed me? Has she thought about me at all?

Suddenly, like she's collected her thoughts and knows what to say, she smiles at me, sending my heart rate up. 'How have you been, Will?'

'Yeah, okay. You?'

'Yes, fine. Work's a little bit, you know,' she frowns, searches for the right word. 'Hectic. It feels a bit naughty that I've sneaked out of the office to come here, left everyone to it, but I needed a break and seeing Nisha's baby is the perfect escape. How's your mum and Eddie?'

'They're fine.' I'm aware my answers are only two words long; I should try harder, but what can I say? 'My mum moved into her new house. She's settled in really well.'

'That's great. How have you settled in?'

'I don't live with her.'

'Oh. I thought that you'd…sorry. Where do you…sorry. I shouldn't pry.' She takes a deep breath and admits, 'This is really awkward, isn't it?'

'Yeah.'

For several moments, she says nothing. Finally she takes a long gulp of her coffee like it's alcohol offering Dutch courage and says, 'I am so sorry, Will, for my behaviour in January; it was appalling. We were meant to be friends. You were having a terrible time and I was crap. Will you forgive me?' Her eyes are regretful, her smiles wanes, and I see that making up means as much to her as it does to me. I have missed her so much.

'I was difficult. I *am* difficult,' I admit. 'I shouldn't have called you a poor substitute for Claire. It was unkind and untrue. We should forgive each other.'

Her smile broadens. 'That's a very good idea. I really miss you, Will. And I know what you're thinking, "Why didn't you get in contact before?" But the longer I didn't, the harder it was to. I took some bad advice.'

And I bet I know who that came from.

'I want to show you something,' and she reaches for her handbag off the back of the chair. She removes her mobile, flicks her fingertip across the screen and taps away before finally presenting the phone to me. 'Do you see all those unsent messages?'

I frown in puzzlement. 'They go back as far as the 18th January,' she explains. 'The day after our…when I walked out of the restaurant. Read one. Please.'

I scroll through them. She drafted three on the 18th, two on the 19th…the list whizzes past as I move nearer to today.

'Bron…' I begin uncomfortably. 'It wasn't—'

'Please. Pick a message, any message,' she jokes sadly.

I scroll back through them. Click on a date in February. Let's see how she was feeling a month later. It opens up. It's a long message.

I read it aloud. '"Hi Will. What are you up to? I'm here at home on my own on a Saturday night. It's horrible. You're not here to tease me about my lack of film knowledge, make me a hot chocolate the way I like it, or take my rubbish to the bin because I hate going out in the dark. I'm so lonely without you".'

135

I look at her, my heart tugs again, harder, painfully. 'I had no idea...'

'Read another.' I question her with a look. She looks so upset. Why is she punishing herself?

'Please.' She waves her fingers at the phone. 'One more if you want.'

I look back at the list and choose a more recent date. There's one from that day.

I read aloud. '"I saw you today".' I stop. She saw me? Where? '"In the supermarket. I was heading down the cereal aisle and there you were walking past the back of the tills. I couldn't believe it. I was so excited. I called your name but you were in a hurry and there was a screaming child making too much noise. I wished you'd seen me, Will. I'd have given anything to speak to you".'

I look up, stare at her speechless. She saw me. After all that about missed opportunities and fate and things that were not meant to be, she did see me. Fuck's sake. I could kick myself. I should have done another loop round the aisle, not given in and walked away at the first hurdle.

She drops the phone into her bag. 'Will, can we...would you like us to be friends again?'

Surely it can't be like it was before. We spent so much time together. From nights in, days out, me driving her to the supermarket. I'm sure her boyfriend will be thrilled when the three of us settle down on a Friday night to share a takeaway and watch a good film. But the occasional coffee would be nice. Even better if I don't have to extend my friendship to him. Isn't something with her better than nothing? That all depends on how the painful the something is. But, if I'm around, then every day will be a reminder of what our friendship meant to her. I know what will be satisfying. Wait until precious fucking Michael finds out about our reunion.

I smile at the thought.

'Yeah, why not?' I reply.

Happiness and relief radiates from her smile and she reaches across the table for my hand. I put the tea down and meet her halfway. I need to know what she still feels like, if her touch will have a repeat effect on me. Our fingers reach up like they're making a tent, they interlink and clamp together; her touch is warm, soft, and it sends an almighty bolt of electricity up my arm and into my chest. Yes, exactly the same. Just like I knew it would be. I still feel the same way about her. Slipping back into the role of being only a friend is going to be very bloody hard and will take a colossal amount of strength.

I look down at our entwined hands. Dare I? Should I? Why the hell not? I stroke my thumb along hers, over the bone, down and under to her palm, rubbing gently across the smooth skin. I watch as her smile grows like turning up a dimmer switch and seeing the light brighten. Could it be…that she feels…no….I doubt it…

I pull my hand away abruptly. 'Hadn't we better have another look at this baby?' I suggest, pushing my chair back.

She holds her hand to her chest like it's been wounded and nods. I notice that her smile has lost a handful of its sparkle. 'Yes, we should,' she sadly agrees.

Chapter 23

Being friends again, even if that means I won't actually see that much of her, doesn't mean that Bronwyn won't be in my head every minute of the day. This is going to feel more like a punishment. If I text or ring her, suggest a coffee, will she really come, or will she make an excuse? Or worse, will she bring Michael along so we can all be mates? Maybe she wants to be friends on paper only.

I push thoughts of Bronwyn away and concentrate on the task in hand. The Colour and Curl Hair Studio. Jean told me that in the ensuing years, Holly wanted to make changes to the salon, modernise and revamp the place with Jean's blessing. It looks like a private health clinic. Black wooden floor, white leather furniture, chrome-surround mirrors, LED spotlights. The staff are all good-looking young women with hairstyles straight out of a hair magazine. The noise is tremendous: hairdryers, loud chatter, music from hidden speakers, the metallic snip snip of scissors. The heat and smells are overpowering: hot hair and chemicals.

I approach the counter where a woman with ruler-straight black hair is on the phone. She mouths that she'll be just a minute. I wait and look at the selection of hair products for sale in a glass cabinet mounted on the wall. I'm running short of hairspray. I'm getting through nearly two cans a week, which is what happens when all you can afford is the cheap stuff. I either need to change my hairstyle or fork out for a better make. Perhaps, if I can sweet talk Holly, then she might give me a can to try…

The girl ends her call and smiles brightly at me. 'Thank you for waiting. How can I help you?'

I make the usual brief introduction: name, business and who I've come to see.

'How exciting. I've never met a PI before. Take a seat,' and she points to a row of fake white leather chairs, 'whilst I get Holly.'

I sit down in the nearest chair and reach for a can of hairspray, which promises an ultra tornado-proof hold. Sounds ideal. I turn the can around to read how it can come up with such claim when I clock the price tag. *How much?* That's nearly a tank of fuel. I shove it back on the shelf.

'Hello. I'm Holly,' says a voice.

A mixed race woman in her late thirties with short curly hair and friendly brown eyes smiles nervously at me. Her pregnant abdomen strains against her tunic.

I stand. 'Pleased to meet you.'

'Let's go in the back where it's quieter.' She leads me across the floor and through a door into a smaller room where three backwash basins are housed. One of the basins is occupied by a very chatty lady who is babbling away to the girl washing her hair about how extortionate it is these days to have her poodle clipped. Holly leads me further down the corridor until we come to a door with a frosted pane of glass in the middle. A little wooden sign hanging off the door handle says *Staff only*.

The staffroom is comprised of a small round table and four chairs. Worktops down one wall house a microwave and a toaster. There's a fridge and sink.

Holly flicks the switch down on the kettle and shakes an empty cup at me. I spy a box of powdered cappuccino on the side and say, 'Yes, please. One sugar.'

She makes the drinks and starts telling me that she worked for Amanda since the salon opened. That it was actually Amanda's influence that inspired Holly to take up the same career.

'I never wanted my own business,' Holly explains. 'I only inherited this as favour to Jean and David until they appointed someone else, six months or so, but they both said they wouldn't want to trust a stranger with something that Amanda had worked so hard to build.' Holly places the drinks on the table and eases herself into a chair, one hand on her back. 'Running a salon is hard work. It's a competitive industry. There's three salons in this high street alone. I think hairdressing is only one of a few careers where you can leave one job and walk straight into another. It is hard work but it's fun...'

'Was it easier for Amanda?'

'Yes, very. She was very business-minded and ambitious. An excellent teacher and a fair boss. I should've paid more attention years ago. I could've learnt a lot.'

'What about her suicide attempt?'

Holly's eyes flash with annoyance. 'It was more a cry for a help.'

'You don't think she intended to kill herself?'

'She had everything to live for. I would have loved even a quarter of what she had. Amanda had no reason to do what she did; she had loads of people to reach out to.'

I keep my expression blank. Obviously Holly understands very little about depression, that someone can be wealthy and popular, with a fantastic job and a loving family, and still feel lonely.

'Did you notice any changes in Amanda in the weeks before she disappeared? Was she quieter? Did she have any money worries? You must've seen the accounts. Were they healthy?' Holly tells me the business was and is solvent, and there were no obvious changes to Amanda's mood.

'Had she fired anyone recently? Were there any unhappy customers? Anyone she might have had a row with?'

Holly raises the cup to her mouth and shakes her head.

'What about her marriage?'

'Things were good as far as I could tell. But I really wouldn't know.'

'Do you know David well? What do you think of him?'

She shrugs. 'We've got to know each other pretty well over these years. He's a nice bloke. They were good together. He used to pop into the salon now and again and surprise her with a chocolate bar or a bunch of flowers. It was so romantic,' she says dreamily. 'I should be so lucky.'

'Did she like him doing that?' She frowns at me. 'You said he *used to*. That implies it stopped. Why's that?'

Her mouth opens but she gives it some thought. 'She said his presence distracted her. Good-looking younger husband like him, you know.'

'She confided in you?'

Holly nods, face hidden behind the mug again. 'She mentioned it once, you know.'

'Can I ask where you were the day she went missing?'

'Here. We had a full day. I hoped that Amanda would change her mind about going to the trade fair but she insisted. Tamsin had phoned in sick too…it was mayhem.'

'Tamsin? Is she here today? Can I—' but Holly is shaking her head.

'She left shortly after Amanda disappeared. She took it hard.'

'Was it usual for Amanda to go alone to trade fairs?'

'Yes. The only exception would be if we had a new starter, Amanda would always take them. It's a chance to see new products, network, get free samples,' she smiles. 'Jenny went the year after Amanda…you know…Tamsin the year before.'

'I'll need to talk to Tamsin at some point, if you can write down her full name and where she's working now.' I slide the pad and pen across the table.

'She's not hairdressing anymore. She's a stay-at-home mum.'

'Whatever you can remember. Where she might have gone after she left here. Has anyone else left the salon?'

Holly thinks, scribbles on the page. 'Jenny. She's at Masquerade now. The posh salon in Kelsall. She's done really well for herself.'

I say thank you to Holly. 'Just one more question. What do you think happened to your cousin?'

She ponders her answer, gets up and puts her empty mug in the sink, runs water into it. I struggle to hear her over the rushing water. 'I think she's dead,' she says sadly. 'I know Auntie Jean thinks someone murdered her, but I have no idea who would do that. Amanda didn't have enemies. People liked her.'

I get back into the Mazda and ring Shaun. 'Everyone liked Amanda,' I tell him, in a mocking tone. 'I didn't see the many Best Boss in the World trophies but I bet ten quid she won one every year.'

He laughs. 'Did Holly stick to her statement?'

'Like glue. We've got a list of customers she saw that day, but I see little point in contacting them. I doubt Holly managed to sneak out of the salon unnoticed for a couple of hours to abduct and murder Amanda.'

'If you're sure you want to leave that stone unturned. Could she be involved some other way?' Shaun asks.

'She did provide Jenny and the other employees with alibis, but I doubt any of them murdered Amanda. And talking of Jenny, her last known place of work is a salon called Masquerade in Kelsall. Get over there and interview her. Find out if she thought the sun shone out of Amanda's arse.'

Shaun gasps. 'Seriously, Will? You want me to go?

'Yes, tomorrow…'

'Why can't I go now? I can organise a taxi and be there in half an hour—'

I interrupt. 'Because you've got to be at the pub in an hour or have you forgotten you have another job?' I can almost hear his disappointment hit the floor and smash into tiny pieces.

'Oh, God,' he groans. 'I can't believe it. You know I'm not going to be able to concentrate on wiping tables and putting handfuls of salad leaves on plates after what you've just said.'

'Yes, you will. Use the time to think of what questions you're going to ask her. I'm hoping one of these other employees has a different tune to play because this one is already getting on my wick.'

Chapter 24

Tamsin Archer doesn't prove too hard to find. After giving Shaun his marching orders, I head back to the office and phone the salon Tamsin started working in after she left Amanda's.

'After the allegation of theft, Tamsin told our valued client to fuck off,' the manageress tells me, 'I had no choice but to fire her.' She goes on to explain that she saw Tamsin about eighteen months later with a pushchair. 'I think she lives in Meadow Road, at the back of Aldi. I have no idea what number.'

But Isla, my contact at Lexington General Hospital, confirms the number: 27C. She has access to the patient database. If she was ever caught, and she assures me that won't happen, she'd be sacked, but Isla knows the things I ask of her all go to ensure that justice is done.

There's limited parking at the flats so I park on Aldi's car park which allows me a max of two hours free. I follow the path away from the supermarket and in a couple of minutes' walk, the path empties into another car park overlooked by three blocks of flats. Twenty-seven C turns out to be a flat on the second floor of block 2. From the outside the blocks look nondescript, box-shaped with large windows set into brown-painted window frames. A couple of the downstairs flats have window boxes containing purple and yellow pansies which shiver in the breeze.

I head for the communal entrance and find the scratched metallic panel housing the doorbells, which someone has very kindly deposited their blob of chewing gum on. Nice. I press the button and wait. Silence. Don't tell me she's out. I press the button again, hold it for longer. A crackling emits from the speaker and a sharp voice asks, 'If you're after Brett, he doesn't live here anymore.'

'That's great because I'm not looking for him. Are you Tamsin Archer?'

'Who are you?'

'My name is Will Bailey. I'm a Private Investigator.'

'A what? Put that down, Ethan!' she shouts. 'I said no…' I hear indistinctive shouting and a child wailing.

'What are you investigating? I haven't done anything. As I said before, Brett doesn't live here.'

'Your old boss, Amanda Davies.'

'You're shitting me. That was fucking years ago. Why are you raking that up?'

143

'I can explain it all to you if we could talk face to face. Have you got a few minutes?'

'What? Now?'

'Please Miss Archer. Sorry, mate,' I say to the skinny man who suddenly appears wanting to get in. He wears a dirty baseball cap and carries a faded Waitrose bag. I hear the unmistakable sound of clinking glass. He gives me a filthy look and doesn't say "thank you" when I step out of his way.

'Oh, alright. Come in.'

I catch the door before it closes and step inside the lobby. I let the male resident get ahead of me. The lobby stinks of stale cigarettes and fried food. On the right-hand wall are the individual letterboxes, which are crammed full of paperwork, in particular those colourful adverts for cheap supermarkets and fast-food joints. Several dried leaves and empty food wrappers have blown against the skirting boards. I look for box number 27C but it's empty and the little door is hanging on by only one hinge. I head for the staircase, not trusting the lift.

I find number 27C. The front door is red and paint-chipped with a foot-shaped indentation in the middle of the wood. I rap the door with my knuckle and a petite woman opens it. She wears no make-up and her dirty blonde hair is tied back into an untidy ponytail. There are rips in the knees of her jeggings and her black vest top has a food smear down the front.

'William Bailey,' I tell her, holding out my ID card for her to scrutinise.

She ignores it. 'Come in,' and she pads back down the dark hall, leaving me to close the door. I follow her into an untidy living-room. The curtains are drawn and the standard lamp is switched on, casting a yellowness across the room from under its tilted tasselled shade. There are toys everywhere. A football on the armchair, plastic dinosaurs and other animal figures are on every hard and soft surface. I step over a half-built Lego building in the doorway. Tamsin drops onto a sagging sofa, picks up her mobile, but slaps it back down on the arm of the chair with a disappointed sigh. On the junk-filled coffee table is an ashtray containing half-finished cigarette butts and the remnants of a joint.

Kneeling on the floor, colouring in a picture of a steam train, is a little boy aged about four years old. He doesn't look up.

'Ask away, Mr Bailey,' Tamsin says, reaching for the pop bottle containing cheap cola. 'I'm all ears.'

I get a whiff of alcohol on her breath. Is she drunk? Down the side of the settee, standing atop a stack of magazines and kids' comics is a clear glass bottle with a red screw-cap. Vodka, I suspect. I keep it brief in case she's so bladdered, she nods off before I finish. I explain why I'm raking up Amanda's disappearance and that my investigation has taken me to the salon. 'I spoke to Holly.'

Tamsin laughs. 'That bitch. Lucky you.'

'Why do you say that?'

'She just is, alright?' Tamsin takes a slug out of the bottle.

'She told me that you left the salon shortly after Amanda disappeared.'

'I did indeed. Best thing I ever did.'

'Was your leaving anything to do with Amanda?'

The little boy gets to his feet, with a handful of felt-tip pens in his fist. He sits in front of the wall to the side of the television which shows a cartoon on silent.

'I had these bright ideas, you know. A friend of mine works on cruise ships. She goes all over the world. She spent New Year in the Caribbean. Another friend works in a salon in London. London! Can you imagine it? I've only been to London once on a school trip. All I wanted was to bag a nice man, I had one once, raise a family and cut hair. I didn't aim high.' She laughs again. 'This is my life now. It couldn't get any lower,' and she throws a dirty look at the boy.

I glance at him. He's scribbling on the wallpaper with a pen in each hand. His scribbles reach quite high. Has he been standing on something?

'Tamsin,' I warn,' should he be doing that?'

She turns her head and it sways. She blinks. 'Don't mind Ethan. He does exactly as he pleases, don't you, you little shit?' and she reaches over to tousle his brown hair. The boy flinches, opens his mouth and screams once. The sound pierces my ears painfully and I flinch, but a second later, he's resumed his drawing as if nothing happened.

'They told me that I'd get used to his ways, but I won't,' Tamsin tells me. 'I nearly had an abortion, you know. Wish I fucking had.'

'What was Amanda like?' I ask, steering the conversation back on track.

'She was nice.' Tamsin laughs. 'The bestest boss I ever had. We were very close. I miss her, you know. If something happened to you-know-who,' and she points at Ethan, 'I wouldn't give a flying fuck, but Amanda...I cried my heart out. I couldn't stay there after that, Mr Bailey.' She slurps from the bottle, spills it down her neck. She wipes it off with a finger and licks it. 'Too painful.'

'I see. Do you recall where you were the day she disappeared?'

'I do, yeah. The night before, I'd gone out on the lash with a friend; I was mega low, you know. I picked up this gorgeous-looking blond guy. I like blond men,' she whispers tipsily, 'but they don't like me. Strange that. Anyway, I had the most mind-blowing night of sex I've *ever* had. But the next morning. Wow! I had the worst hangover. I couldn't get out of bed all day. Sore head, sore everywhere if you get my drift.' She giggles.

Jesus, I think.

'Those wild days are over now. Sadly. Are you single?' she asks me.

I debate whether to lie that I'm taken but then she doesn't like dark-haired men so I should be safe. 'I am, yes.'

'Stay that way,' she tells me wisely. 'Women might break your heart, but men, believe me, men will fucking stamp it into the ground.'

*

I climb back into the Mazda, relax back into the seat, close my eyes and sigh deeply. I feel wrung out. Bloody hell. She's messed up. What a miserable fucking life she's got and what a shit prognosis. She's what? Late twenties? Poor girl. What the hell caused that? A man, the allegation of theft and the subsequent sacking, the child and his problems, what? It can't be Amanda. I don't buy that. Her sentiment sounded too forced. "The bestest boss? I cried my heart out". And like Holly, Tamsin has stuck to her original story. She knows of no one who would want to harm Amanda and things in the salon were fine. 'There were no dramas,' Tamsin had said. Funny way of putting it.

Tracking down her one-night stand is going to be impossible and what can he confirm? Unless he stayed with her all day and held her hair up whilst she threw up in the toilet? That's if she stayed home. That's if she went out the night before. She might have had the day off because she didn't fancy working a busy day but why go after Amanda? There's no evidence, as yet, of any animosity between them.

On the passenger seat, my phone beeps. My heart leaps when I see who the sender of the text is. Bronwyn. It's only been a few hours since I last saw her.

Hi Will. Are you busy mid-morning tomorrow? Fancy a coffee? I'm buying.

I read the text over and over, trying to work out if there's an unseen message in the words.

Oh, of course. It's an invitation to meet Michael. She wants us all to be pals. How nice. I start thinking up a plausible excuse or at least a way of finding out if he's coming too.

The phone beeps again. Bron again.

Stop trying to think of a way of getting out of it. It'll be just you and me x

I grin. My heart flips over and my fingers type a reply: I would love to.

I turn the key and the Mazda fires up. I glance at Tamsin's window. They do break your heart, I agree, but we all go back for more.

Chapter 25

Bronwyn tears the top off the little brown packet and tips the sugar into her large Americano. She stirs the coffee and tucks the paper under the spoon to stop it flying off in the breeze. She suggested we meet at a café a few minutes' walk from her building. When I got here, she'd bagged the table in the corner of the outdoor seating area. A clematis with white and purple flowers is climbing up a trellis attached to a brick wall. I stir the dusted chocolate powder into the cappuccino and lick the spoon clean.

'Everything alright?' I ask. She hasn't said much since I arrived, her expression unreadable behind her sunglasses.

It's a warm day for April but very breezy. The strong gusts are blowing her curls everywhere, making her hair look like Medusa's. She's wearing a black sleeveless dress with a thin black cardigan over the top.

She looks up at the cloudy blue sky. 'It might rain the rest of the week. Typical for April, I know, but I thought today was the best day to meet up.'

'Any day is great to meet up but I only saw you yesterday.'

'We've got three months to catch up on. How's your investigation going? Nisha told me… only the bare bones, that it was a missing person case.'

I keep it brief. I don't mind discussing things with Bronwyn. She's helped me many times with previous investigations but this time, because of the timeframe, there really isn't much to tell, and I get the feeling that this isn't the reason she's asked to meet up. Yesterday, in Nisha's living room after our reconciliation chat, no one mentioned Michael. It was obviously a deliberate avoidance for my benefit but it can't be ignored forever. Best to get these things out in the open from the start.

I broach the subject head on. We're friends again; I can ask what I like. I move the cappuccino aside and say, 'Take your sunglasses off. It's not that bright and I find them disconcerting. Can we talk about the elephant in the room?'

She lifts them onto her head and looks around the half-empty courtyard with amusement.

'Are we in a room?' she jokes. 'Is that better?'

'Yes, that's better. Can we talk about the elephant in the outdoor space then?' She nods. 'Are you still seeing Michael?'

She guides the heavy ceramic cup back down, but it clumsily knocks the teaspoon out of the saucer, allowing the breeze to catch the empty sugar sachet and lift it up into the air. She watches it flutter away before looking back at me. I cock an eyebrow.

'Yes.'

I knew she was. I made Nisha promise to tell me if Bronwyn and he ever split up. Not that I'd tear round to her flat to comfort her but I would want to know. I open my mouth to ask if he treats her well but she gets in first, asking, 'Are you seeing anyone?'

There's no point in lying. She may well have asked the same of Nisha, and she certainly knows I'd never use a dating site.

'No. How's it going with him?' I ask, trying not to let jealousy creep into my tone.

'Okay. Or it was at first. He's a nice man. Attentive, considerate.' I keep silent, wait for more because I'm sensing a but. 'He works in IT. His department sorts out all our IT issues so he's popping up to our office all the time. People like him. Some of the women say he's a real catch.' I nod, prompting her along with my attentive stare. 'But then,' she pauses. Here it comes, I think. All is not rosy.

'The company he works for are having a restructure so people are being made redundant and, though his job should be safe, he doesn't stop talking about the effect it's having on him. Not those facing job losses, but *him*. He can't sleep, eat, concentrate. You know, the other day, I told him what a bad day I was having. Everything that could go wrong, went wrong. And I assumed he'd do me the courtesy of listening but all he said was, "At least you've got a job, Bronwyn. Some of my colleagues haven't".'

I smirk at the ridiculously deep voice she puts on.

'Are you laughing at me?' she asks, affronted.

'Sorry,' I say, 'I've never heard you do a voice like that.'

She smiles but quickly her face falls again. 'I feel like I'm his emotional crutch all the time. I don't mind listening to a point, but he never stops going on. If it's not redundancies, it's his family. They all seem to be old and ill, or young and ill. I've tried to steer him onto other subjects, but he always brings it back around to him and his issues. I'm tired of it. A month ago, I decided I was going to end it. I mean really end it, not threaten to. It took me ages to get my nerve and do you know what he said?' she demands.

'I promise to change?' I suggest.

'Yes!' She slams a palm on the table. 'I promise to change. And he did. For one day. I shouldn't have given him that chance. I'm an idiot.'

'It's not easy to dump people.'

She looks at me like I've said the understatement of the year. 'It's a horrible thing to do. Worse when you're dumping someone because they're boring and needy.'

'Yeah, I suppose so.' Personally I'd take a lot of pleasure in dumping this melodramatic idiot but then Bronwyn has always been a soft touch, too nice for her own good.

She sips her coffee, takes a deep breath and launches into round two. 'He's invited himself around to my flat tonight. He made me feel like I'd asked him, but I haven't.' She throws her hands up.

'What's he coming round for?'

She huffs. 'To talk about his poor brother who has neurological symptoms. I don't know of what; Michael's very vague. And I know it must be an awful worry and I don't mean to sound heartless, but he'll sit there, snivelling and crying, using up my tissues. It's so irritating. All I want to do is watch the telly and paint my nails with a glass of wine. I don't mean paint my nails with wine. I mean—'

'I get it, Bron,' I say with a smile.

'And just when I'm about to call time and say it's late, he'll tell me how wonderful I am, that he can't live without me.'

'I managed it for three months,' I quip.

She pulls a face. 'And then he'll try and get me into bed.'

My eyes widen. She stops talking and looks at me before laughing. 'I'm not having sex with him.'

'It's none of my business if you are,' I say, holding up a hand. This I do not want to hear about.

'I'm not. I've been celibate for two years. I feel like a bloody virgin.'

'The next time's for love?' I joke. Celibate? Why? When was the last time I...I do a quick calculation on my fingers under the table. Shit. Ten months! Does that make me celibate too?

'Maybe. Hopefully. But it won't be with him. Sorry, Will. Honestly, I didn't invite you for coffee to listen to me go on and on. Are you okay listening to this?'

'That's what friends are for. If you can't tell your best friend, who can you tell? But maybe leave the sex stuff for Nisha.'

She leans back in her chair, smiles. 'I think I'm done.'

'With him too?'

She nods. But a few seconds later, she frowns thoughtfully and says, 'I should finish with him. It's not what I want from a relationship. He doesn't make me feel all giddy or give me butterflies in my tummy. Do you know what I mean?'

I nod. I know exactly how that feels.

'Finishing with him will make me feel like I'm stabbing a helpless puppy through the heart. I have to do it or I'll go mad.'

'I will too if I have to listen to this crap every time we meet. Just send him a text. "Michael, it's over because you're a pathetic needy cretin. Don't contact me again." Something along those lines.'

Bronwyn shakes her head. 'I see you haven't lost any of your warmth, Will.'

I shrug and smile. 'What do you expect me to say? He took my friend from me.'

'I came back, didn't I?'

'You took your time,' I joke and she smiles. Beside my cup, my phone starts to ring. I turn it over to see who's calling. Shaun. I answer it. 'Hello mate. I'm at the Cafe in the Square. Yeah, in the courtyard. What is it? Are you alright?' but he hangs up. He sounds breathless like he's been running with excitement. 'Shaun,' I explain to Bronwyn. 'My maternity-leave helper.'

'Nisha told me about him. Wise move employing your enemy's son. I see no old bruises or scars on your face so I'm guessing Shaun the Shield is working out.'

'He is. He's keen, a quick learner. Nothing like his dad. Well, you'll see in a minute when he rocks up with the fruits of his endeavour. I sent him to interview a witness.'

A few minutes later, Shaun stumbles into the courtyard, bag slung across his chest. He looks around, over our heads even though I've raised a hand. Finally he spots me, weaves a path over, clattering into chairs and customers, before dumping his bag on the table and falling into a chair. He sighs with exhaustion, plucks the EarPods from his ears and turns to me but his eye catches Bronwyn and he smiles brightly. He raises an eyebrow at me.

'Sorry. Am I interrupting? Are you guys on a date?'

'I'm Bronwyn, a friend of Will's. We haven't seen each other for a while. Would you like a drink, Shaun?'

'Yes, please, that'll be great. Can I have a large triple chocolate Frappuccino with cream?'

She pushes her chair back and heads inside the cafe.

Shaun sits up and leans across the table to me. 'Wow, Will. You said you didn't have any friends and now you pull her out of the hat. I love her hair. Naturally curly, is it?'

'How would I know?' I say.

'It obviously is. Is she more than a friend? You can tell me; we're mates. And if you want me to piss off and leave you alone, then I'll take my drink and—'

'Don't start, Shaun. She's a mate. End of. She has a boyfriend.'

'Oh,' he says and winks. 'I get it. You don't like him. Neither do I then. Can we talk in front of her? Boy, have I got some gossip for you!'

'Yeah. She's completely trustworthy.'

Bronwyn returns with Shaun's very chocolatey drink. She sits down and uncaps a bottle of water.

'So,' I say to Shaun after he's sucked up enough of his ice-cold drink to give himself brain freeze, 'what did Jenny tell you? I hope I haven't sent you all across town to come back with the same old shit.'

Shaun is shaking his head, his grin stretches from ear to ear. He looks at Bron, then me and, in a tone I've never heard before, he announces, 'They're fucking lying. All of them.'

Chapter 26

'They're Jenny's words, not mine,' Shaun clarifies. 'I'd only just started my spiel on why I'd contacted her and what I needed to know and she comes out with that. "They're fucking lying. All of them." And my first thought was, "Wow, she's bitter. What's happened to her?" I asked who she meant and...hang on, I've got it written here,' and Shaun unzips his bag and yanks out a hard-backed notebook with a picture of a llama wearing a party hat on the front. He catches me smirking at it. 'Kid sister bought it for me. She has a thing for llamas. She was hoping I'd let her have it.'

Bronwyn laughs. She's going to love Shaun.

Shaun flicks through the pages; many of them are marked with little coloured tabs. I'm impressed with the amount of notes he's taking. Lots of the sentences are highlighted in fluorescent colours.

'Here we go...oh, let me have another slurp,' he sucks hard on the straw, wincing with pain. '"Those devious bitches from the salon.".'

'As I recall, her statement was nearly word for word the same as theirs. Was she lying too?' I ask.

Shaun nods sadly. 'She admitted it, but the reason was because Holly took her aside to tell her what she and Tamsin were going to say and, if Jenny wanted to keep her job, then she needed to make sure she did the right thing. She was very regretful.'

'Did she cast any light on why they lied?'

'It was a combination of wanting to protect Amanda's name and themselves. If they admitted to the police they all despised her, like I think they did, how would it look? Like they're suspects. Jenny gave me some new information too. A brand new suspect,' he tells us dramatically.

'Who?' I ask, leaning forward with interest.

'First things first. Let me give you a bit of a background into Jenny. She's fun and no nonsense. Generous too. She gave me some samples to try,' and he fishes in the side pocket of the rucksack and comes out with more than a handful of black tubes and pots. Blimey. All I got was a powdered cappuccino that tasted like anything but coffee.

Shaun tells us that, after Amanda disappeared, Holly ramped up Jenny's training and she stayed 18 months before moving to Masquerade. She worked there for another year before it all became too much.

'She says working with women is torture.' Shaun refers to his notebook for her exact phrases. '"The backstabbing and bitching is horrendous. I blame these all-women salons". So she applied for a job at Men Only, which is a salon solely for men.'

'What's her true opinion of Amanda?' I ask. 'I seem to recall she admired her…'

'She said Amanda was "hard-faced and didn't take crap from anyone" and the worst person to give her crap was…' he pauses for dramatic effect.

'Tamsin?' I guess.

Shaun points his finger at me. 'Got it in one. They hadn't always not got on. At one point they were quite friendly, not outside of work, but pally enough. In the last eight months or so before, Tamsin changed. She was often late, hungover, sloppy, had a poor attitude. She had loads of run-ins with Amanda.'

'Was she sacked?'

Shaun shakes his head. 'No. Also, Jenny often witnessed Holly and Tamsin bitching about Amanda, usually in the staff room. They wouldn't involve Jenny which is why they often forgot she was in the vicinity.'

'What does she think of Holly?'

'She doesn't care for her much at all. She said Holly was worse. And being her cousin with perhaps more influence, she never spoke to Amanda and asked her to ease up on Tamsin, who was obviously having personal problems. Oh, and another person Amanda didn't take shit from was…David.'

Of course she didn't. Stands to reason that, if she's not going to take crap from silly misbehaving juniors, she's not going to take it from a husband twelve years younger. My, how she must have lorded it over him.

'When Amanda introduced David to everyone, Jenny said she was draped possessively over him like a cape. A fortnight later, after he'd visited the shop a couple of times to say hello because he was passing, Amanda did the worst thing. She deliberately humiliated him in front of everyone.'

'Unforgivable,' I say and Bronwyn looks sharply at me. 'A lesson for you to learn,' I tell her, mock-serious.

'Since when have I ever—' she protests.

'I can name at least three occasions...'

Shaun interrupts. 'You pair sound like my parents. Anyway, Amanda accuses him of "embarrassing me with your constant pestering". Ouch. Like you say, unforgivable. Maybe he didn't forgive her. Jenny felt terrible for him; Tamsin even went after him to make sure he was okay. He never dropped in again.'

'What does Jenny say about Tamsin?' Bronwyn asks, glancing at her watch but dismissing the time with a shake of her head.

'She feels sorry for her, that if Tamsin hadn't made some dodgy decisions a few years ago, things could be so different for her. Apparently, she got pregnant by "some low-life scum one-night stand" and that was her future set in stone.'

'What did she think of her when they were colleagues?'

Shaun smiles. 'She reckons some bloke had done a good job on Tamsin.' Bron and I look at each other, perplexed. 'Come on, you know what that means. No? Broke her heart. Jenny said Tamsin looked sad; she thinks that's why she had so many casual shags. She missed *him* so she filled the void with whoever would take her home.' Shaun picks up his drink which has liquefied. He slurps at it loudly.

'If Jenny is saying that Tamsin's behaviour only changed in the last 8 months pre-Amanda's disappearance, then she had her heart broken around that time. Is it relevant?'

'Depends who the bloke is,' Bronwyn says.

'Who's this new suspect?' I ask, reaching for Bronwyn's bottle of water. I take a big gulp and swat her hand away as she makes an attempt to grab it back.

'Ahh, well, when you visited the salon, Will, you must've noticed it looked very different to the photos Jean showed us.'

'I did,' I agree, 'Nothing gets past me.'

'It's bigger and there's an extra couple of workstations. A local builder was hired to do the work.'

'Okay…and your point is…'

'The builder is the same guy Amanda sacked not two months before.'

'Sacked?' Bronwyn repeats. 'Amanda hired and fired him? And then he was rehired?'

Shaun is grinning and nodding. 'You haven't heard the best bit…Amanda sacked him after just one hour and fifteen minutes of work.'

'What the hell... Why?'

Shaun shrugs. 'Jenny hasn't got the foggiest idea. All she knows is this guy turned up, a day late for some reason, to knock a wall through and refit some other stuff, and after an hour or so, Amanda gives him his marching orders! No one knows why. Well, the builder does if you can find him. Jenny doesn't know his name.'

'Would he have a motive to harm Amanda?' Bronwyn asks. 'Was his work inferior? And how would you know unless you were an expert in renovation, in which case you'd do the work yourself. Unless the surrounding walls fell down the next day. It can't be related to work surely.'

'Maybe this builder bloke took the sacking as a huge insult, bided his time, abducted Amanda and bricked her up inside a wall.' Shaun chuckles.

Bronwyn looks at me. 'He's been spending too much time with you. The obvious thing is if he touched her up or said something inappropriate. She might not tell her husband if she feared he'd go to this builder's house and punch him.'

I look at Shaun. 'Did Jenny mention if this builder made any farewell remarks? Something like,' and I put on a deep voice: "Your tits were shit anyway" or "You stuck-up ugly bitch".'

Bronwyn laughs, Shaun looks worried. 'I've never heard you put on a silly voice before, Will. I did ask that question and he didn't say a word. Whether he'd said all there was too say, I don't know, but Jenny didn't hear any shouting.'

'Strange,' I comment. 'He accepted the firing without a word, or at least a loud one. So, in conclusion, we have three women who've conspired to lie to the police about their relationship with Amanda and to conceal a possible suspect and his motive. Why?'

'Maybe they felt sorry for the builder, that he was badly treated by Amanda. They may not know why he was sacked, or they do and they don't care,' Bronwyn says.

'Sounds to me,' begins Shaun, 'they're all glad to see the back of Amanda. That she wasn't as nice as we were initially led to believe. She pissed people off. Four of them so far. But we can rule Holly and Jenny out as they were working all day. And Tamsin really. Why would she want to harm Amanda? She hadn't been sacked.'

156

'Why this one-night stand?' I ask. They frown at me. 'Tamsin made drunken flings part of her life. But absences from her job weren't on the list of offences: being late and hungover were. Tamsin usually dragged herself into work but, on an extremely busy day, she decided to stay in bed. At least she would have us believe.'

'Do you think she tracked Amanda down in Fradlington?'

'Why not? She knew where Amanda would be. She could narrow her search down to the fair...' my voice trails off as an idea comes to me. Should be easy enough to check out. 'Come on, young Hock, finish your slush, we've got work to do.' I push my chair back, hand Bronwyn the nearly empty bottle of water. 'Thanks for the coffee, Bron. It was lovely to see you.'

Beside me Shaun slings the rucksack onto his back and takes the car key from my outstretched hand. 'I'll fire up the Mazda,' he says. 'Nice to meet you, Bronwyn.'

'You too, Shaun. Will, have you got a quick second?' she asks nervously.

I watch Shaun leave and turn to her. 'Everything alright?'

'Yeah, great. I've really enjoyed this,' she replies with a smile. 'It's the first time I've felt happy in absolutely ages.' She fidgets with the bottle cap. 'It's Easter Sunday this weekend.'

'Is it?' I question. I hate long weekends. Four days off against my will. Four days I will go into the office anyway because what else is there to do? I haven't even noticed the Easter crap in the window and I must've missed the seasonal aisle in the supermarket the other day.

'Are you free on Sunday? Would you like to come for dinner? It'll just be me and you. Michael's asked me to go to his parents but I'm not going. It's unfair when I'm going to finish with him. I could help you with your investigation and there'll be roast beef,' she says temptingly.

'Beef at Easter?'

'I don't like lamb.'

Me and her in the flat, lazing around, maybe watching a film. It'll be like old times. And she's finishing with him. This could mean my number of friends rises to three. I can't think of anything else I'd rather be doing, but I hide my enthusiasm as I reply, 'Yeah, okay, sounds great. Text me what time.'

Bronwyn beams and steps around the table to hug me. Her touch sends a thrill through me but I keep it brief, reminding myself she's very tactile and we're only friends.

157

'See you Sunday,' I tell her. 'Looking forward to it.'

And now I'll have to buy her an Easter egg.

Chapter 27

'Lawrence Hayden,' Shaun tells me, turning the laptop round to show me the builder's Facebook page. But there isn't a picture of the man himself; it's strictly for business purposes only. Very disappointing. There are lots of photos of his handiwork though: freshly painted and wall-papered rooms, rows of fence panels, tiled walls, and so on. He assures all visitors that "no job is too small, give Lawrence Hayden a call". Very catchy.

I scroll through the posts which hide the identity of the customer but in stilted words, Lawrence's accompanying comment to one photo, boasts: "Mr F was pleased with his raised bed. Now he can plant lettuces in it.". Lawrence has some starred reviews too. Sammie awarded him five stars for this: "Laurence (careless misspelling of his name) dun a gr8 job re-plastering our front room wall'.

He has built up quite the reputation for small and big jobs. I wonder what he was bragging about six years ago, if the hair studio was one of his triumphs, but unfortunately, the profile is only four years old. Lawrence is starting to come over as a reluctant Facebooker. Maybe he's bit old school and had to be dragged onto social media by his wife if he's married, or his children if he's spawned any.

But where had Amanda found out about him? Holly couldn't answer that question. As Shaun drove us back to the office, I tried David's mobile first but he wasn't answering. Holly gave the name up in the end and denied trying to keep it from me or the police. Once again, she couldn't offer any explanation as to why Lawrence was sacked or why he was rehired, claiming the decision was David's.

'There's no personal profile for Lawrence Hayden,' Shaun says, after he's had another thorough search. 'Well, not one in this area. There's nothing for Larry, Loz or Lol Hayden either. What else can you shorten Lawrence to?'

'Forget it,' I tell him. 'There isn't one. This is a man who doesn't like his picture in the public domain. I feel the same. Chuck us my phone. Let's ring him and see what he has to say.'

I dial Lawrence's mobile as stated on his profile and, after six rings, a gruff voice answers, 'Hello, Lawrence Hayden.'

He has an accent I can't place but it isn't local.

'Hello Mr Hayden. My name is William Bailey and I'm a private investigator. Do you have a few minutes for a quick chat, please?'

'What about?' he asks suspiciously.

'Amanda Davies. She was the owner of a hair salon called The Colour and Curl Hair Studio. Six and a half years ago, Amanda disappeared and her family have hired me to investigate that.'

'I don't know what you're talking about. Look, I'm in the middle of a job. I've got—'

'My understanding is that Amanda hired you to refurbish her salon. Two months later, her husband rehired you. David Bywater? Do you remember him?'

'Name rings a small bell, but…it was…what…six years ago,' he snaps. 'I've been to bed since then and I've done hundreds of jobs. I can't remember—'

'This one should stick in your head because Amanda fired you after just an hour's work. Does that happen often?'

'What?'

'Are you often sacked after an hour's graft?' He doesn't answer. He remembers alright. 'Mr Hayden, I need to know why she sacked you. I believe it's relevant to my investigation.' I glance at Shaun who is grinning with amusement. Silence on the receiving end; time to prod him a bit. 'Did she make an accusation against you? Did you say something inappropriate? Did you touch her?'

'What? No, I fucking did not,' he shouts. 'What kind of pervert do you think I am?'

'A forgetful one?' I suggest.

'Listen, pal,' he hisses, 'I don't care what you're fucking investigating. Leave me the hell alone. I don't remember her.'

'I'm investigating a possible murder, Mr Hayden. Amanda's. And at the very least, you're a witness. I'll text our office number to your mobile. Please get in touch when you can spare the time. This is very important.'

'I never laid a hand on that bitch.'

'Bye, Mr Hayden,' I say cheerily. I end the call and look at Shaun. He raises his chin expectantly. 'Oh, yes, he remembers her, alright. He called her a bitch.'

Shaun grins. 'Knew her well, did he?'

*

'All I know, Mr Bailey,' David says with a tired sigh, 'is that Amanda sacked him. I don't know why; I asked several times, but as usual her business was none of mine. I know you probably think I'm grossly exaggerating this, but Amanda really didn't tell me. She might have said hiring him was a mistake. So I pointed out that sacking him was too, since she wasn't going to find a replacement quickly.'

I consider his words. Down the phone, he sounds genuine; face-to-face may be different. It's hard to tell. 'Why did you rehire him?'

David sighs again. 'The salon was in a mess. Piles of plasterboard and bags of crap everywhere. Two inches of dust on the surfaces. It was a wonder no one went down with respiratory failure. Me and Jake did our best to tidy it up but it was obvious we couldn't do much else. Made sense to rehire Mr Hayden.'

'Did he take much persuading?'

David hesitates. 'Yeah, well, naturally he wasn't going to do it for his original quote. I had to give him a bit extra.'

'And how was his work?'

'Top drawer. It looked good. Everyone was pleased.'

'So why wasn't Amanda?' I persist. 'What was it about Lawrence Hayden that she didn't like? Did any of the stylists tell you or Holly that they found him creepy? Did he say—'

'Nothing like that at all,' he replies firmly. 'He's a hardworking bloke who keeps himself to himself. There's nothing wrong with that.'

'Sounds like you know him well, David. Do you? Have you seen him since?'

'No. I might've spotted him in a supermarket and nodded in acknowledgement but that's it.'

'Wasn't it a bit risky rehiring Lawrence? What if Amanda had returned and found out what you'd done? How would she have reacted?'

David chuckles. 'She'd have torn a strip off me. But she'd have done the same if I'd left the salon in a mess too. I need to go. The oven's on and I don't want my lasagne for one cremated.'

Sounds a familiar meal. 'Thanks for ringing me back, David. Just one more thing…there isn't anything else you're keeping from me, is there?'

'What like?'

'Anything similar to this. Every event you deem insignificant, I need to know about. And don't forget to tell me the big stuff too. Enjoy your pasta.' I end the call and shake my head with frustration. How many more witnesses/potential suspects am I going to find? And I've still got to contact David's mate Jake and Declan. I opt for Declan. It's nearly teatime and he's a father. With any luck, he's at home, sitting down to eat with his family. I like nothing more than interrupting people at mealtimes. Put them on the back foot, and they tend to agree to anything.

I dial the landline and wait and wait and eventually, after nine rings, it's answered by a child. Hard to tell if it's a boy or a girl; they sound the same at that age.

'Hello,' I say in that voice that people who rarely have anything to do with kids use, 'is your daddy in, please?'

'No. Mummy is. Do you want her? MUMMY!' the voice shouts, piercing my ear with enough shrillness to dent my eardrum. I hold the phone away and mutter an expletive. Which is why I'm not good around kids; they're too noisy. My own mum can, at least, rely on my brother to provide her with grandkids. She's got no chance with me.

'Hello? Who is this?' a female voice unexpectedly demands of me. 'Go and finish your nuggets, Lucas. Now, please.'

I make the usual introduction and ask who I'm speaking to.

'I'm Kerry, Declan's fiancée,' she replies affronted. 'Declan's at work. His shift doesn't finish until 10 tonight. What do you want him for?'

'As I explained, I've been hired by Amanda's family to look into her—'

She cuts me off with the sharpness of a knife. 'Why bother? You're not going to find her after all these years. The woman's dead. Everyone knows it. Do you know how hard it's been for Oliver? Poor lad. And here you are, dragging up a shitty time again.'

'It hasn't been very nice for Mrs Davies either,' I remind her.

'Yeah, I know that, but he's only a child. What do you want with Declan? He doesn't know nothing. He had a good relationship with Amanda. Oliver has lived with us since he was a toddler. That was Amanda's decision and she didn't want to change that.'

'I'm sure she didn't.' Why mention it then, I think. 'I do need to speak to Declan. When's the —'

'What about? You tell me what you want to ask him and I'll—'

'I'm afraid, Kerry, it doesn't work that way. I can only discuss this with Declan, so please, when is the best time?'

She doesn't reply but I can hear her snorting with annoyance. I bet she's the mouthpiece of the act, telling Declan what to think, speak and do.

'Ring tomorrow after half six, but not before because I'll be putting the tea out. And don't keep him long either. There's four kids in this house and it's the Easter holidays. I need a break too,' and with that she hangs up.

'That told me,' I mutter, closing the case on my mobile, but I don't think I'll ring him. I'll take Shaun and we'll make a house call on Declan, see if we can't upset his mealtime.

Chapter 28

Jake Bunby lives in a two-bedroom bungalow on the Coleshill estate, a place known for its council houses and trouble in the form of drug pedlars, vandalism and neighbours from hell. His home is on the main drag through the estate, round the corner from the Premier shop, a chemist and a Chinese takeaway. From the outside, it looks well-kept with small patches of mown lawn. The inside is something different and, for a sole occupant, he really knows how to make a mess. The place is a tip. A row of trainers lines each side of the hallway, their toes pushed against the skirting boards. There are two dozen maybe, and all different colours and brands. Adidas, Nike, Converse. On the hall wall, in a dusty frame, is a large painting of four dogs sat round a table, but they're not playing cards. Large cone-shaped spliffs protrude from their snouts and, on the table, are lines of white coke, credit cards and a rolled-up old fifty pound note.

Jake sees me studying it. 'Love that picture,' he says and opens the door to the living room. Predictably, he has a massive television balanced on a black glass and chrome stand. All sorts of dusty black cables are bundled between the shelving and the floor leading to a Sky box, a Blu-Ray player and several games consoles. On one of the armchairs are half a dozen remote controls. On the coffee table under the window are several cigarette packets, plastic lighters, Rizla papers and a large overflowing ashtray in the shape of a cannabis leaf. The room stinks of old joints. It's the sort of stench that gets into everything: curtains, upholstery, the walls. Balanced on top of an already full bin is a tinfoil container and a cardboard lid stained yellow.

'Last night's tea,' Jake explains, hobbling ahead of me and Shaun. 'Chicken dopiaza. And this morning's brekkie. Take a pew, gents. Chuck those jazz mags on the floor, mate.'

Shaun lets out a small 'Ugh' which makes Jake laugh loudly. They aren't jazz mags but magazines on home-brewing and true crime. I give Shaun a withering look and he sits beside me on the sagging settee. Jake takes the other armchair, props his crutch against the windowsill and smiles at us.

He's a thin bloke with hardly any meat on his bones, dark receding hair he'd do better to shave off. It might take some years off him because, although he's the same age as David, he looks in his midforties. The crutch indicates either he's swindling the DWP or has genuine mobility issues.

164

I ask about the crutch and he's only too eager to explain.

'I used to work in the abattoir on the Collingwood Industrial estate. I got side-swiped by a bastard of a pig on a hook. It floored me, broke several vertebrae and some other bones and put me on an orthopaedic unit for months.' He shakes his head. 'Health and safety was non-existent, which meant I got a huge payout. Now *I'm* fucking paying for it. I had a scan last week. I've got the bone density of an eighty year old. I'm fucked. I'm in agony day and night.'

'Isn't there anything the doctors can do?' Shaun asks, politely.

'I need hip replacements but I'm too young. I could actually do with a new fucking skeleton, mate.' He laughs. 'You know, you look familiar. Are you any relation to Phil Hock?'

Oh, I think, Jake knows Hock senior. And I bet I know how.

'I'm his eldest son,' Shaun replies tightly.

Jake grins and clicks his fingers. 'Yeah. You look like him.'

I raise an eyebrow at Shaun and he looks back. I don't see a likeness myself. Hock is a beast of a man with all the charm of rabies. Shaun, by comparison, is as far away from his dad as you can get.

'Do you know my dad well?' Shaun asks, taking the opportunity to start the questioning like I've taught him, and what better target than Jake Bunby who has drug dealer practically tattooed onto his pale sloping forehead?

'Yeah, everyone knows Phil Hock. A great bloke. We've done a bit of business before. Oops,' he says, putting his hand over his O-shaped mouth. 'Should I be saying that in front of an ex-copper? You're not gonna tell your mates in the Drugs Squad, are you?' He stares wide-eyed at me.

'Who says I'm an ex-copper?' I say, with interest. It always intrigues me that you can remove that invisible police officer coat, but somehow it remains ingrained in you somehow. But *you* can't see it yourself, otherwise you'd be trying to scrub it off.

'You don't have to, mate. I've had a couple of dealings with them in the past. I can tell a pig, oops, sorry, a member of the police constabulary from a mile away. Don't forget I've had a close relationship with porcines since my slaughterhouse days,' he laughs.

'Anything you tell me today is strictly confidential,' I assure him.

'Fair enough. What do you wanna know?' and Jake leans over to the table for a packet of cigarettes. He taps one out and lights it. Great and now we're both going to stink of fags.

'Let's start with the relationship between you, David and Amanda.'

'Whoa, mate,' he says, putting his hands up in mock disgust, 'it weren't a love triangle! There's an image I don't need in me fucking head. Me and her hated each other. She was a stuck-up, selfish and possessive bitch, but David loved her to bits, made a lot of excuses for her. He called her "damaged" once.' Jake grins and taps his temple with a nicotine-stained fingertip. 'Damaged in the fucking head.'

'Stuck-up, selfish and possessive how?' I ask.

'She looked down her nose at *everyone*. Thought she was something special.' Jake pulls a face. 'I don't know why he married her. David had some lovely girlfriends in the past. I tried to set him back up with an ex after one fight he and Amanda had. He wasn't having any of it. Stupid sod.'

'What about the ex?' I ask. 'Was she keen on a reunion?'

Jake laughs. 'She didn't fancy taking Amanda on. Anyway, she was too immature. David likes old boilers, or should I say mature and wealthy women.'

'What was this fight they had?' I ask. 'When was it?'

Jake taps cigarette ash into the ashtray, which spills onto the table. 'A week before she pissed off. Turns out, for months Amanda had been secretly going through his stuff: rucksack, pockets, phone, his van and one day, *we* walked in on her trying to break into his iPad. It was one of the best days of my life, watching that bitch squirm. Fucking hell she was humiliated. I told her, because Dave the Gutless Wonder wouldn't, exactly what I thought of her.'

'What did David do? Was he angry? What did he say?'

'Nothing, because Oliver was there. Last thing he'd do would be to cause a shit storm in front of a kid. A couple of days later, in the pub, Dave tells me that he had it out with Amanda, told her he was gonna leave if she did it again. It was all bollocks. He had no bottle. Anyway, next thing I know, she's offering to buy David a load of home brewing gear to make up for it. Maybe he finally grew a pair and threatened to leave her.'

The cigarette smoke is tickling the back of my throat. I could do with a drink but I dread to see the state of the kitchen. Out of the side pocket of Shaun's bag, I see a metal water bottle. I reach for it and take a swig. It refreshes my throat but does nothing for my stinging eyes. I should have worn glasses instead of contact lenses.

'You told the police that, on the day Amanda went missing, you had a hospital appointment.'

'Yeah, in the morning at Lexy General. Then I came back here for some dinner, watched TV, dossed about and then went to David's house.' Jake grinds the butt into the ashtray, waves the smell away, dispersing it in our direction.

'It was usual for you to be at their house? You say that Amanda didn't like you, but she didn't mind you being in her house?'

'I wasn't in her house; I was in the shed,' he explains. 'That's where we run the brewing business. I'd have it in my garden but it's not big enough to put a shed in it. I rarely went in the house unless I needed a piss or a drink, and then never when she was home.'

'What time did you arrive and when did you leave?'

'I met David there about six, I think. Stayed until 7.15. He started getting his knickers in a twist about Amanda coming home and finding me there, the usual crap.'

'What were you doing in the shed?'

'Tasting his latest IPA. I'm chief taster,' he laughs. 'We were discussing our game plan. Back then we were trying to get our IPA into local pubs.'

'Have you tried The Smoking Gun?' Shaun asks Jake. 'On Shenfield Road? I work there part-time and my boss, Ben, is a connoisseur on IPAs. You should have a chat with him. I see you like pubs,' and he points to a picture frame on the wall. It's about the size of a noticeboard and contains lots of photos of David, Jake and other males holding beers up in a toast. The photos have been taken in gardens, underneath pubs signs and against bars.

Jake smiles fondly. 'Taken back in the day, you could go on a pub crawl without the need for a fucking taxi. Proper boozers, with proper alkies, old blokes in the corner nursing their pints of mild and bitching about the past. Nowadays it's all about two-for-one meals, annoying kids running about the place like it's a playground, and raspberry-flavoured gins. Who the fuck drinks gin? Benders and middle-aged women who think they're fucking twenty again.'

Shaun emits an almost silent huff. I smile politely. 'Pubs certainly have changed.'

'Which is why I miss these places. See that photo in the bottom left corner? David's in the green shirt, I'm wearing an England football shirt.'

167

I lean over the arm of the chair to focus on it. The lads look out of their trees, wearing drunken grins and, hanging above their heads, are blurry brass objects on dark wood.

'That was taken in the Jester,' he explains. 'Cracking pub. It's derelict now. The picture in the bottom right corner was taken in the Black Swan. His mum ran it. He comes from a family of publicans. It was inevitable that he'd go into brewing. Beer's in his blood and mine. There's a lot of it in mine,' he laughs before coughing. He has a smoker's cough, chesty and full of muck.

'I had this idea that me and David could break in and run our brewing business from one of those abandoned pubs. David wasn't keen. He likes to do things by the book. Which means it takes twice as fucking long.'

'Sorry,' Shaun says politely and flicks back through his llama notebook, 'but can we just go back a bit? Jake, you said that David called Amanda "damaged". Did he say why?'

Genius, I think. Get him on his favourite subject: hatred for Amanda.

Jake rubs a hand over his forehead. 'David never really talked about the finer details of his marriage. Most of my mates who are hitched talk about their other halves. They'll brag about how many times a week they're doing the dirty, what she likes between the sheets. You two know what I mean, right?'

Shaun and I nod in agreement, but I would never betray the confidence of a woman I was seeing by discussing it down the pub. I'd hate it if she did it to me.

'David wouldn't, but occasionally, usually after one too many of his own beers, he'd let something slip. He confessed that Amanda liked drinking red wine to rev herself up. She needed it to relax. David also thought for an older woman, she'd be more experienced in the sack, but turns out she wasn't; she didn't know what she liked. She was a frigid cow. If she hadn't had a child, I'd have said she was a virgin. I don't know what he saw in her. He was devastated when she went missing though.'

'What do you think happened to her?'

'I don't buy this bollocks that she committed suicide or someone did her in. I think she pissed off somewhere, got herself a fake passport. Easily done,' and he looks at Shaun. Again Hock Senior will know a man who can sort that, I shouldn't wonder. 'She's set up a salon in Spain on some estate colonised by Brits. And maybe in a few years, she'll turn up and say to David, "I've been waiting for you to come and find me. Didn't you think to look abroad?"'

'Let's just say, someone has harmed Amanda. Any ideas who?'

'I pity the person who decided to take Amanda on. She'd fight dirty. I don't know, mate. Declan maybe,' Jake laughs.

I frown. 'Why him?'

'He's got the kid all to himself and didn't have to go through a court to get him.'

'Were Amanda or Declan threatening to take the other to court over childcare issues?'

'My sister had issues with her ex over their kids. I know applications to the court cost a lot of dough. But it's amazing how quick someone can be made to get used to the sight of blood for a few quid,' he says cryptically, leaning back in the chair. A look crosses his face, a thoughtful frown. Suddenly he emits a sharp, 'Oh!' and his beady eyes widen. 'I'd forgot that.' His finger starts wagging and he tries to recall the memory. 'There is someone you should speak to. Fucking hell. Memory ain't what it…Martyn Hepworth.'

I raise an eyebrow.

'He's head of PE at Lexington Secondary,' Shaun explains. 'He taught me.'

'He's a fancy pants swimming coach an' all,' Jake adds. 'Claims to have won gold medals. He was me and David's teacher too.'

I make a mental note to ask Mrs Davies what school Amanda went to and if she was into swimming, but I see that Shaun is writing the note down.

'One night, I'm on my way to The Crown and who do I bump into, stepping straight out of the salon, after hours, but that dirty old bastard.' Jake laughs. 'I made some crack about him getting a trim of his bush or a late-night leg over with her, even though she likes them younger. I pissed myself at the haughty look on her face. It was almost as good as when we caught her going through David's iPad. Classic!'

'Did they know each other?' I ask.

'Fucked if I know. What else could he have been doing there? They weren't in mid-convo.'

But there are many reasons why a PE teacher could have been exiting the salon after hours. Perhaps he had gone for a trim or gone to make an appointment. If he's married, had he gone to pick up something his wife might have left in the salon during one of her appointments? No wonder Amanda glared at them both. Very humiliating, especially if what Jake has said about her is true, that she was shy about sex. Most women would be appalled. Others might have sworn at them both and slammed the door in their laughing faces.

'Speak to him. Right, gents, I'm gonna have to ask you politely to leave. I have a doctor's appointment and I need to pop to the paper shop, see your dad. Shall I say hello for you?'

Shaun smiles politely. We stand and Jake hobbles after us to the door, complaining that his back has seized up.

'If I think of anything else, I'll give you a call. Thanks for the card.' He waves my business card at me. Shaun and I walk back down the path to the Mazda. Shaun settles himself behind the steering wheel, checking his position even though he drove over here. His test is tomorrow and he's as nervous as hell.

'There was a perfect example of a bromance,' Shaun jokes.

'A what?'

'Bromance, you know? Close friendship between two members of the same sex. Haven't you ever had one, Will?' he teases.

'No, I have not,' I snap. 'Get me some intel on Martyn Hepworth.' I unscrew the water bottle and pour half of the water into my mouth. The smell of Jake's fags has burnt the lining of my throat.

'I'll get straight on it as soon as we get back.' Shaun pulls away from the kerb. At the junction, he asks, 'Why do you think Jake called Mr Hepworth a dirty old bastard? Because he assumed he was "getting his leg over"?'

'Either that or Hepworth likes young boys. Did he ever…you know… you.' I nod at him.

'What? Touch *me* up? The local villain's son? Not if he ever wanted to swim again.'

Good point, I think.

Chapter 29

I had asked Shaun to ring me as soon as his driving test was over, but it's been over two hours since it ended. He could have returned to the Smoking Gun, preferring to be kept busy and amongst people who will raise his confidence levels. That's if he's failed. And it'll be on something stupid. Resting his hand on the gearstick or driving one-handed around a roundabout. He knows I'll give him major grief if that's his offence. I pick my mobile up off the desk, but there's no message or missed call. I think about putting the kettle on but I've got to leave in fifteen minutes in order to interrupt Declan's mealtime just right and I've drunk too much tea already, convinced that someone always contacts you when the kettle's on. I turn back to Declan's statement and refresh myself with his claim. As confirmed by other people, namely Jean, Declan was entrusted with Oliver's care following Amanda's meltdown, which she agreed to when she was recovering. They agreed the contact arrangements without the court's intervention, which is testament to their amicable relationship. Oliver stayed at Amanda's house every other weekend and at least once a week when she would pick him up from school and take him back the next morning. They split other holidays like half-term and Easter. Declan claims that Amanda could have Oliver over any time she wanted and the boy did stay more often due to his blossoming relationship with his stepdad. However, Declan goes on to state that Amanda in no way wanted to alter the arrangements. But if she did, he would agree if it was in his son's best interests.

'Hmm,' I mutter, leaning back in the chair. Amanda's been accused of being a hard-faced boss with little respect from her staff and no friends; she was also a selfish possessive wife who may have had sexual inhibitions. And yet, the relationship she had with the father of her child, a child effectively taken from her, was amicable and on friendly terms. Is that likely?

Now she had support at home and was making changes at work to accommodate another stylist, might Amanda have wanted to change the contact arrangements for Oliver, especially since the boy was growing close to David, who let's face it, was probably more fun than his dad. If I ask Declan or that fiancée of his, and she sounds a right battle-axe, are they going to be tell me a pack of lies? Who else would know if there were issues? Oliver? Perhaps I can engineer a quick chat with the kid.

On the day of Amanda's disappearance, Declan was at work until 12pm at a distribution warehouse in Lexington, he went home, picked the children up after school and returned home. The neighbours report seeing his car leave home early afternoon. There is a three hour window of opportunity, mid-afternoon, in which Declan could conceivably have driven to the city, or lain in wait at Lexington train station for Amanda, but it's pushing it.

I glance at the time. I need to get going. I close the folder and pick up my stuff just as I hear movement at the office door. Footsteps and a door handle being turned. Shaun. I catch my hip on the desk corner as I race for the door.

I call his name and a despondent voice replies, 'Yeah.'

He closes the door, back to me and I see there's no passing certificate in his hand but do they give them out now? He turns to me and he looks devastated. Shaun normally holds himself upright. He never slouches or drags himself around, but he looks defeated,

Oh, shit. 'What was it? Hand on the gearstick? I told you, didn't I? It's an automatic—'

'Pass!' he shouts, jumping into the air, his face breaking into the biggest grin. 'I've bloody passed!'

'What?'

He laughs loudly, continues jumping up and down, his feet thudding on the floorboards. Our neighbour below is going to have a fit. 'I've passed! First time. Suck on that, twin sister.'

'Well done, mate,' I say, holding out my hand. He stops and pulls me to him, giving me an awkward hug.

'Thanks for everything, Will,' he says into my shoulder. 'I would never have passed if you hadn't made me drive everywhere.'

'My pleasure.'

He releases me and grins. 'Are we heading to Declan's? Do you want me to drive?'

I chuck him the car key.

*

Declan lives in a three bedroom semi. The front garden has been paved to make way for a ten-year old people carrier and a large saloon with an enormous boot, both parked at diagonals across the crumbling driveway. A child's drawing has been taped in the front window so it looks out across the trio of different coloured wheelie bins parked underneath the windowsill. It depicts "my family", two adult stick people, one wearing a triangular skirt; and four smaller ones, two boys and two girls each wearing similar-shaped skirts to the adult female. The house they stand beside is nothing like this one. It has a fence, a tree with a hollow, and acres of land around it.

We can all dream, I think, raising my fist to knock the red-painted door. I wait for a few moments, knock again, louder, and eventually a small figure appears at the frosted glass. It reaches up on tiptoes to open the door. A small blond boy with ketchup plastered over his hands and chin smiles warily at me.

'Do you want my mummy or daddy?' he asks and this is the kid who nearly pierced my eardrum the other day. I step back, brace myself and say, 'Your daddy, please.'

He takes a deep breath and at the top of his voice, bellows, 'DADDY!' And runs away, feet thudding on the floor. Down the dark hall, I hear a crash, a shrill yelp and a reprimand. 'Will you stop running about the place and screaming?' a voice ironically shouts.

Several moments later, a figure appears but it isn't Daddy. This must be Kerry. An overweight woman around forty years old, wearing a long grey t-shirt, the emblem on the front faded, over black leggings. The pointed end of her untidy ponytail lies curled on her shoulder like a lemur's tail.

'Yeah?' she says, defensively.

'Hello Kerry. I'm William Bailey. A private investigator. We spoke the other—'

'Yeah and I said *after* six,' she complains. 'We're having our tea.'

'I know and I do apologise for my timekeeping. Is Declan around?' and I look over her shoulder into the hall behind.

'Come in. Lucky for you we're on pudding,' she sighs, letting us into the hall. Children's shoes, in various sizes, are all over the laminate flooring; dozens of coats and schoolbags hang off the stair post and the rows of pegs on the wall. From a nearby room, I can hear muted chatting and that little boy shouting for raspberries.

'In there,' and she flings open another door, which opens into the lounge, a large room, nicely decorated in bold colours. A black fireplace with two large leather sofas face a wide-screen TV. A box of kids' toys, all tidied away, stand on the other side of the fireplace. Hanging on the wall over the fireplace is a washing-line. Little wooden pegs hold photos of the family like bunting. I study them. Oliver now in his early teens has gained some resemblance to his mother. His hair is amber-coloured, his eyes the same shape as Amanda's. He stands beside

173

his stepsisters, a similar height, both blonde, wearing experimental make-up; and the little boy who shouts, grinning a toothy grin.

I move along the pictures. Declan is slightly overweight, his paunch straining against his white and blue striped rugby top. His hair is shaven but it doesn't make him look hard like it does most men. He looks like a middle-aged, chubby dad.

He and Oliver playing swing-ball. Declan and Kerry kissing; Kerry chasing the children with a hose; Declan pushing the little boy down a chunky plastic slide. They look a happy family. Did Amanda threaten that?

'Hello,' says a croaky male voice.

I turn to Declan, smiling confidently. His nervousness is coming off him in sweaty waves. His hands are deep in the pockets of his faded jeans like a naughty kid going before the headteacher. He hasn't lost any weight but his hair needs a shave. He coughs, yanks his hands out and offers us both a seat.

'Thank you for agreeing to speak to us. I'm William Bailey and this is my colleague Shaun Hock.'

Declan reacts to the name. His brown eyes widen and stare. 'Hock?' he repeats, his hands clench tighter.

Oh-oh. We have another one.

'Phillip Hock is my dad,' Shaun confirms. 'Do you know him?'

'I've heard of him,' he says, stumbling over the words, shrugging casually but he can't hide the panic on his face. 'What I mean is that I know where his paper shop is,' comes the pathetic explanation. But who would know who owns a paper shop unless they visited it every day or they'd had dealings with the owner, which didn't involve the procurement of magazines and sweets. What sort of dealings does a person have with Hock? Drugs? Declan doesn't look your typical addict and neither does he look like a dealer. He could have done some casual work for Hock, but there's never anything casual about work done for that man. He could have been on the unfortunate receiving end of Hock's violence. Or he's crossed paths with Hock somehow, like me. The last option is how my friend Claire knew him. Her debt was sold to him because he's an occasional loan shark.

'You're not the first person we've interviewed who's had dealings with Mr Hock,' Shaun admits, remaining professional.

174

'I didn't say I'd had dealings with him,' Declan protests.

'Jake Bunby was the other one. Do you know him?'

Declan's eyes wide again. 'No. Well, I know he's a mate of David's. C-c-can we get on with it? It's teatime and Kerry will be...' I make a hand gesture for him to continue. 'I don't know what I can tell you, Mr Bailey. Erm, I went to work…'

'I'm aware of what you told the police, Declan. What can you tell me about your relationship with Amanda?'

'We didn't have one…we were a drunken one-night stand. A nice one though,' he adds, but I'm guessing that's only for my benefit so I don't suspect him of harming her.

'I meant more recently.'

'Things were good. Civil. We all got on okay.'

'Following Amanda's marriage, which gave her that all important support network that had been missing during her depressive episode, did she want more time with Oliver? Did she request a change to the contact arrangements?'

'Yeah, a bit...but it was because Kerry fell pregnant. We hadn't planned it, well, you know, how it is, you don't but it happens. Amanda knew the demands a new baby would have on us, and she offered to have Oliver more. I was okay with that.'

'Very kind of her,' I remark and very unlike her. 'Did either of you want to make the changes to the arrangements formal?' Declan stares, clenches his hands together. This is becoming his tell-tale sign. 'A court order?'

He shakes his head so hard, it looks like he's trying to detach it. 'There was no need. We were always able to sort stuff out between ourselves.'

'Costs a great deal of money to make applications to the court. If you didn't have that sort of money, and who does, you might need a loan.'

'From my dad?' Shaun suggests.

'Indeed,' I agree.

'No,' Declan states, shaking his head some more. 'I didn't get a loan from Hock. I didn't need one.'

A loud knock at the closed living room door makes Declan jump and he instantly shuts up. For fuck's sake, I think. That fucking Kerry and her protectiveness. She's like a lioness with a cub. The door opens but isn't Kerry. It's Oliver and I can see the ever-growing resemblance

175

to his mother. I don't remember seeing any photos of Amanda on the washing line. Are they not keeping her memory alive? Interesting.

Oliver smiles shyly at us but in a quiet voice says to Declan, 'Dad, sorry to interrupt but Charlie's going now. His mum's here.'

Behind Oliver, another teenage boy appears, his head above Oliver's shoulder. He has dark hair and wears black-rimmed glasses. He smiles apologetically at us.

Declan swivels on the settee to face Charlie. 'Tell your dad I'll give him a ring in the week about the patio.'

Charlie salutes. 'Will do. Thanks for tea again. It was great.'

'You're welcome,' Declan says and it's the first time he's sounded relaxed. The door closes and he faces us again. 'My son's friend, Charlie Hayden.'

Hayden? You've got to be kidding me? I stand quickly and walk to the window, pulling aside the vertical blinds. Parked up on the kerb, is a red 4X4 with a black roof. Kerry is talking animatedly to a slim woman leaning against the vehicle. She has shiny dyed red hair and wears a tight purple t-shirt. Is that Lawrence's wife? I can't hear their words but they're clearly pally, laughing and chatting with ease. Mrs Hayden could be a route to Lawrence.

'Does Charlie live nearby?' I ask casually, letting the slats fall back into place.

'Beckett Drive, by the petrol station.'

'Is Charlie's dad a builder?' I ask. 'You mentioned a patio.'

'Oh, he does odd jobs, you know.'

'Did Amanda know him?'

'No,' Declan lies. 'The boys became friends after she disappeared.'

Easy way to check that out.

I return to my seat. 'I'd like to turn to the day Amanda disappeared. I've read your statement, Declan, and I have only a handful of questions. Were you aware Amanda was going to a hairdressing exhibition at Fradlington that day?'

'No. Why would she tell me that? The salon was none of my business. It wasn't a day she was due to have Oliver. We only ever discussed Oliver. Schooling, holidays, maintenance—'

'Maintenance?' I pounce. 'Of course! The child lived here which meant she paid *you*. It always tends to be the other way round, doesn't it? How much money was Amanda giving you each month? Was it monthly or weekly?'

176

'It's none of your business,' Declan replies uncomfortably and folds his arms.

'Roughly. A hundred? One fifty? Two? Two,' I say triumphantly when Declan snorts. 'Generous amount. Obviously a boy who went for nothing.'

'Hang on. I wasn't taking what I wasn't owed. Oliver was a growing boy. Every penny went on him. I didn't spend it on me,' Declan argues.

'Did she accuse you of spending it on the other kids? Or maybe she accused you of neglecting Oliver.'

'No,' he argues, his voice rising. 'She did not.'

'If Amanda was paying you what the government recommended, that would be based on what?' I turn to Shaun who has the answer waiting.

'Will, it's based on earnings and how many nights the child stays with the parent,' he explains.

'Thank you, Shaun. Very helpful. If Amanda offered to have Oliver more, wouldn't that mean she'd slash the maintenance? After all, there's no point in paying for food for Oliver when he was getting fed at her house. That'd cost her double and she was paying for renovations to the salon. Or supposedly...if she hadn't sacked the builder.' I smile at Declan, pleased with myself. 'Did she?'

'Did she what?'

'Slash the maintenance?'

'No,' he snaps. 'Look, what are you getting at? My finances are none of your business…

'Declan,' I say patiently, 'I'm just trying to ascertain that *if* Amanda had Oliver more often, she'd slash the maintenance which might mean you went short every month. That might make you look at loan options,' and I gesture to Shaun.

'I did not get a loan from—' he bawls.

'And it might cause friction between you and Amanda, whereby your only option would be to get rid of—'

'I did not kill Amanda,' he shouts.

I smile. 'I'm glad we cleared that up.'

Declan snorts loudly, his nostrils flare so huge that I can see the tiny black hairs inside. 'Have you any idea what this investigation is doing to Oliver? He's come to terms with losing his mother and now he's got to go through it all again. This stupid idea of his Nan's that Amanda has been murdered is cruel. Who would want to do that?'

'That is what I'm trying to find out, Declan. Surely you want closure for Oliver. I cannot investigate Amanda's disappearance if I can't reopen the questioning. Let's turn back to the day she disappeared, please? I shan't keep you much longer.'

'Fine,' and he sinks back into the seat. 'My shift finished at 12pm. The shift leader confirmed that, I think?' He waits for me to give my acknowledgement. I nod. 'I went home, had my dinner. It was a ham sandwich and started the jobs Kerry had left for me. Mow the lawn, wash up the breakfast bowls, fix the curtain rail in the girls' bedroom because for a week we'd have to pin the curtain to the wall. I finished sorting the garage out and emptied Oliver's room of junk. Then I drove to the school, about ten past three, confirmed by my neighbour, who sadly died three years ago, picked the kids up and drove home for tea. Spag bol, I think. Kerry was already home. Her mate gave her a lift. That's it. Okay?'

'What about the evening?'

He sighs. 'Helped the kids with their homework, read them a story, watched the telly, went to bed and then the next morning went to work.'

'Oh. I see. Don't you remember David phoning to see if you'd seen or heard from Amanda?'

My question stops him dead and wipes the smug grin off his face. 'Shit. Yeah, of course I do. He was frantic. But I couldn't help him. I told him to ring the police.'

Sympathetic, I think.

'What do you think happened to Amanda?'

'I've spent nearly seven years watching what I say in case I upset Ollie. He has hope that one day she will come back, but,' Declan shakes his head, 'I don't know how but I think she's dead. This application that David is making will help Oliver. It'll be an end to it. He can end his grieving and move on.'

I watch Declan for a few moments. He stares back, begins to shift in his seat like there's a thorn in his arse. He looks away first. 'Is that it?'

I smile and stand. Declan visibly relaxes. Shaun finishes his scribing, clips his pen onto the front cover of his notebook. Declan gets his feet, shoves his hands in his back pockets. He looks victorious, confident that his weak alibi is enough to deflect the spotlight onto someone else. If he wasn't silencing Amanda, twenty quid says he was up to no good. And I know just the man who knows. Whether he'll tell me or not, is another matter.

Shaun leads the way out, but I pause on the threshold and turn to Declan. 'Are you still getting paid? Only fair if David's living in her house and Holly's running the business. After all Oliver is her son and heir. He takes precedence.'

'Yeah, I get money,' he replies defensively. 'But Amanda would have been worth more to Oliver alive than dead.'

'Yes, she would,' I agree, 'but not to you.'

We return to the Mazda and I settle in the passenger seat, reach for the bottle of water out of the door panel and take a swig. Shaun starts the car, looks back at the house.

'He's watching us,' he says.

'He's lying through his teeth,' I say, wiping my mouth on the back of my hand. 'Like the rest of them.'

'He knows my dad, alright.'

'We need to speak to Oliver's old primary school teacher.'

'The schools have broken up for Easter. It won't be an easy—'

'Shaun,' I say gently. 'A small obstacle.'

Chapter 30

Shaun has done an excellent job tracking down Oliver's primary school teacher. He went to the school, spoke to the nearest neighbour who told him where he could find the caretaker. Helpfully, he only lived two doors away. The caretaker explained that, if the teacher still worked at the school, he'd respect her identity and tell Shaun to bugger off, but it seems that five years ago, Lucy Benson jacked her job in and took up a managerial job in Waitrose. I was so impressed with the result, I sent Shaun on another mission: track down Oliver and interview him about his mum. And not to forget intel on Martyn Hepworth.

I find Lucy Benson assisting a colleague down the Wines and Spirits aisle and she agrees to a chat. We meet outside and she leads me around the corner from the entrance past the trolley park, her high heels tapping loudly on the path. We enter a delivery gate where we nestle against those huge lidded dumpsters, sheltered from the brisk wind.

Lucy's a good-looking, mid-thirty year old. Her dark hair is in a tidy bun at the back of her head and she's wearing a dark blue skirt and jacket over a white blouse.

She makes sure we're out of sight of the loading bay staff before lighting a cigarette.

'Busy morning,' she explains. 'But not stressful, unlike teaching. I used to like kids, thought of having a couple one day when I met Mr Right, but teaching puts you off. Kids never do as they're told and even 7 year olds are cheeky little sods. I blame the parents. They actually think it's the responsibility of the teachers to teach them even basic manners! Sod that for a game of soldiers. So I had a complete career change and this is where my heart is: retail. I'm much happier.' She laughs, before issuing a quick apology. 'I'm sure you don't want to hear all this. How can I help?' She flicks ash onto the ground.

I briefly explain why I'm currently confused about the investigation and that I need an independent witness to cast some clarity on the situation. Lucy listens, occasionally nodding.

'Charlie Hayden started at the school in September. His parents moved to the area, I don't know where from. He met Oliver in one of the after-school martial arts classes. They were inseparable, sat together in class, played together at playtime. It was a nice friendship. The sort you get in Hollywood films that stands the test of time. And yes, they were friends before Ms Davies disappeared. Absolutely,' she confirms.

'I've been told that Amanda didn't know Lawrence Hayden, but I know this was a lie. I get the impression that there was friction between them. Amanda hired him to refurbish the salon and fired him after just an hour. No one knows what the reason was and Mr Hayden is proving to be extremely hostile.'

'I bet he is.' Lucy smiles mysteriously. 'At Charlie's first parents' evening, Lawrence Hayden sat opposite me and hardly spoke, just glared at me and the other teachers. His wife is a mild version of him. Bit less unpleasant. And you're right, he and Amanda were definitely acquainted.' Lucy takes a long drag of her cigarette, blowing the smoke away from us before launching into her story. 'One day, it must've been a few days before Amanda went missing, I was standing in the classroom at home time, watching the kids filing out. Outside the school gates, I saw Lawrence Hayden confront Amanda. They were nose to nose.' Lucy pauses to take a long drag on her cigarette. 'They were shouting at each other and pointing fingers. It was quite a spectacle. Fair play to Amanda, she was giving as good as she got. A couple of the other parents tried to intervene but Mr Hayden told them to sod off, or words to that effect. I had no idea what it was about. But the next morning when Amanda bought Oliver to school, she asked for a quiet word and we went into the staffroom. She wanted Oliver moved to another class because she wasn't happy about him being friends with Charlie. I stuck up for Charlie; he was a polite lad, but she wasn't having any of it. I told her there were too many kids in the other class and the Head would never agree.'

'That's all she said? She didn't offer any further explanation?'

Lucy shakes her head. She grinds the cigarette out on the nearby brickwork and slides it under the bin lid. 'I thought she'd take her request to the Head anyway, but she said she was going to change Oliver's school instead. That that would be a better solution.'

'Why would it?'

'She'd been thinking about it for a couple of weeks and said it would make sense since Oliver was going to be living with her.'

'Living with her?' Very interesting.

Lucy nods. 'I remember thinking what a loss it'd be to my class and to Charlie. Oliver was a nice boy, and they were in short supply.'

'Did she say anything else?'

Lucy rubs her fingernail down her thumb as she thinks. 'Oh, yeah. I asked, "How does Oliver's dad feel about Oliver moving school?" and she replied, "He can like it or he can take it to court.".'

I find Shaun seated at his desk, earphones in and sipping tea as he writes his notes up. He jumps a mile when I touch him on the shoulder.

'Christ, Will,' he says, clamping a hand on his chest and breathing hard. 'I nearly had a heart attack. Do you want tea? Kettle's not long boiled.'

'I'll do it.' I cross the corridor to the small kitchen, flick the switch down and get the tea things ready. 'How did you get on?' I shout.

'Very interesting,' he replies from the doorway. 'You go first.'

I recite the conversation with Lucy Benson, concluding that whatever the issue was between Amanda and Lawrence, it probably wasn't anything to do with his workmanship.

'They hated each other and nearly came to blows. Lawrence was the instigator and thought nothing of publicly confronting her.'

'It was unlikely they were having an affair,' Shaun says. 'You wouldn't risk arguing with your lover in front of your kids' school. I found out something interesting…'

'I should hope so.' I pour the milk into the tea and carry the mug into my old office where Shaun has set himself up. I take a chair and wait for him to begin.

'Oliver misses his mum,' Shaun begins. 'He was tearful. Although he's come to terms with the fact that his mum isn't coming back, he desperately wants to know what happened to her. It was sad, Will. How can any of us understand what it must be like for a child to lose their mum like that? He gets on with Kerry, says she's great but, since his younger brother came along, he's been pushed to the background. Oliver doesn't see as much of David as he'd like. He sends birthday cards, even Father's Day cards; they text often but he hasn't seen David for a while.'

'What did he tell you about Charlie?'

'They're best mates. They often go to each other's house for tea. In fact, Oliver told me that Charlie's going to ask his parents if Oliver can go on holiday with them in the summer. They're going to Ibiza. He didn't think Declan would object.'

I smile. 'Amanda would have.'

'Yes. Oliver says that he vaguely remembered an incident outside the school between his mum and Mr Hayden. He has no idea what it was about, but it made him feel like he wouldn't be allowed to be friends with Charlie anymore.'

'Did he tell you anything specific about Lawrence Hayden?'

Shaun nods as he drinks his tea. 'Yeah. Charlie and he play darts. Declan put a dartboard up in the garage and they play for hours. Oliver says it's improved his maths.' Shaun smiles.

'That's great,' I say, my tone bordering on sarcastic. 'We all need to subtract correctly. And this helps me how?'

Shaun's smile broadens. 'Because Lawrence played darts. Apparently he was good. Really good but he's not a professional player because I've googled him. Oliver didn't know where the family moved from. Charlie told him that they weren't allowed to tell anyone ever because their "dad told them to keep it a secret". So they have. Rachel Hayden is a nurse on the geriatric ward at Lexington General. She works permanent nights. Oh, and I got their exact address too. Twenty five Beckett Drive.' He sits back and grins proudly. 'A house call maybe…'

'When do you get your car?'

Shaun pulls a face. 'Friday night. I'm not looking forward it. What if it's some old banger, banana yellow with a pair of furry dice in the window and regularly breaks down. How can I pretend to be over the moon with it? My mates will rip the piss out of me.'

'Surely your dad can nick something better than that?'

Shaun laughs. 'You would hope so.'

I check the time. Mid-afternoon. 'Finish your tea,' I tell him, lifting mine to my mouth. 'Let's go and see if Rachel Hayden is around.'

*

The red 4x4 I saw yesterday at Declan's is now on the drive at Lawrence's house. There's no sign of a van. The house is a very tidy detached property. The front garden has been ripped up and tarmacked. In the lounge window on the windowsill is a glass vase containing a bunch of white lilies. I glance through the window into a tidy, smart room. Large TV and comfy sofas. Wide mirror on the wall over the white mantelpiece.

I knock the door and wait. A dark figure approaches the frosted glass panel of the door and hesitates before opening the door. Rachel Hayden's face appears in the narrow gap. She raises her chin, her tired eyes narrow suspiciously. There's a small silver hoop in her left nostril.

'Can I help you?' she says coldly.

'Hi Mrs Hayden. I'm William Bailey, this is my colleague Shaun Hock. We're Private Investigators. My card,' and I hold up my ID card. Her dark eyes squint at the small writing.

'What do you want?' Intrigued, she opens the door a little more. She looks like she's come in from the garden. Dirt is under her fingernails and there's a streak of mud across the front of her white t-shirt which has faded writing on the front and an odd-shaped emblem on the top left corner of her top.

'I've been hired by the family of Amanda Davies to investigate her disappearance six and a half years ago and I understand that your husband was acquainted with her.'

She mashes her lips together and shakes her head. 'Don't think so.'

'Ms Davies hired Lawrence to refurbish her hair salon, The Colour and Curls Hair Studio in Lexington?'

She shrugs as if to say "Never heard of it."

'It was a fairly big job which would have taken up a considerable amount of Lawrence's time and, had he completed the job, would have paid a fair packet too. Unfortunately Lawrence was sacked just an hour into the job.'

She shrugs again. 'Are you sure you've got that right?'

'Yes, I'm quite sure my information is correct. This may jog your memory as the circumstances are unusual. A little after Amanda disappeared, her husband, David Bywater, rehired Lawrence to complete the job.'

'I really don't remember. When did you say this woman went missing?'

I tell her and she shrugs again. The little jerk upwards of her shoulders is starting to irritate me.

'I'm sorry I can't be of more help, gents. There's no point in asking Lawrence either. He has a shit memory,' and she gives a short snappy mocking laugh.

I smile patiently. 'But you do know Amanda in a non-professional capacity. Her son, Oliver Davies-Page, is Charlie's best mate.'

'Really? I thought Kerry was his mum. I wondered why he called her by her name. I thought it was a family joke. Kids, eh?'

'Their primary school teacher, Lucy Benson, has confirmed that the two boys were friends *before* Amanda disappeared. Perhaps that's how Lawrence got the job. I hadn't considered that.' I look at Shaun.

'Nor me,' he agrees, with a bright smile.

I turn back to Rachel and smile. 'Anyway, the reason for Lawrence's untimely dismissal is unfortunately only known by Amanda and your husband. But a couple of weeks later, they obviously decided to broach the subject again because they were witnessed arguing outside the school gate. In fact, at one point, it looked like they might come to blows. One of the other parents attempted to calm the situation...'

Rachel shakes her head. 'Lucy Benson is talking out of her arse. Lawrence never picks the kids up. He's always at work in the day. I pick them up because I work nights and I'm awake in the afternoon. Maybe it was another dad Amanda squared up to.'

'No, it was definitely Lawrence,' Shaun says, reaching in his bag for something. He pulls out a plastic document wallet. Inside is a sheet of paper. His eyes move quickly left to right across the lines of writing. After a few moments he looks up. 'This is an account given to me by Mrs Andrews. She's the mother of Dylan, who also attended karate club with Oliver and Charlie. She knows Mr Hayden because he re-roofed her garden shed the week before. She states, "At 3.15pm, I was standing with"...oh, let me skip this part...here we go..."when I saw Lawrence Hayden walk up to Amanda Davies who was standing with the two boys. He started shouting and pointing his finger in her face. Amanda repeatedly asked him to back off but he refused. He told her she wouldn't get away with firing him and he wasn't going to stand aside and let her ruin his career."' Shaun stops and looks up. 'Mrs Andrews went on to say that she approached Mr Hayden to ask him to calm down as a number of the children including his own son was visibly upset. Lawrence Hayden told her, excuse my French, to "fuck off".' Shaun smiles apologetically.

I look at Rachel. 'Does that sound like your husband?'

She stares at me. 'What do you want?'

'I want to talk to him about his acquaintance with Amanda Davies and what her problem with him was. I need to know where he was on the 15th October, six and a half years ago.'

'How the hell is he supposed to remember that? Do you want to know where we all were? I'll tell you where I was. You might want to write this down, kid, because I'm only going to say it once.'

Hurriedly, Shaun opens his notebook and takes the pen out from behind his ear.

'I had worked a twelve-hour shift chasing dementia patients around a ward, doing their obs, feeding them, listening to their constant cries of "Help me, please". I lost three patients that day. It was a horrible day. I went home to bed, got up in the afternoon and picked my daughters up from school. Charlie and Oliver had karate club until 4.30. I took the girls for a milkshake and then returned to collect the boys. Oliver came to our house for tea. I might have done fish fingers and curly fries. Lawrence was home at his usual time of six-ish. He ate with his family and looked after our kids whilst I took Ollie home about 7.45. Later than normal because the boys were playing darts in the garage. At Ollie's house, I remember Kerry was frantic because someone called David had phoned; his wife hadn't come home and he wanted to know if Declan had seen her. But Declan wasn't answering his phone. Perhaps they were together.'

'Declan wasn't there?' I ask.

'No,' Rachel replies slowly like I'm stupid, 'that's why Kerry was ringing his mobile but it kept going straight to answerphone. Kerry was stomping around the place and complaining. Her daughters looked scared. I put all the kids in the lounge, gave them biscuits and squash and stuck one of the *Shrek* films on. I stayed for twenty minutes and left her to it.'

'Where did she think Declan was?'

Rachel shrugs again as if it's not her problem. 'A mate, work, another woman. I don't know.'

'Did she ever tell you where he'd been?'

'No, she did not. Our kids are friends, we're not.'

'You have an incredible memory, Rachel,' I tell her in a tone that isn't meant to compliment her but to warn her that it sounds like she's prepared her answer for such a question.

'The day sticks out for me. If you want to speak to my husband, I suggest you call at a more convenient time. Now, if you'll excuse me, I'm going to carry on with my weeding.' She steps back from the door and closes it in our faces.

I look at Shaun. He's still scribbling. His knuckles have turned white from holding the edges of the notebook. He has a strange half-smile on his lips as if what's she told him is gold dust.

'Let's go, mate,' I say. 'I'll drive. You can carry on in the car.'

I start the engine and pull away from the kerb, picturing Rachel on the phone to her husband, telling him all about our visit. The account Shaun read out is pure fiction, designed to provoke Rachel, which it certainly did, but not the way I expected. Oliver was not picked up from school by his dad as claimed and nor did he eat his tea at home. Declan was not being the dutiful father. And if he didn't pick Oliver up, what's the betting he wasn't there to pick Kerry's kids up either? So, what was he doing?

He was somewhere he can't admit to and, by an unexpected fluke, someone else has blasted his alibi out of the water. It doesn't give me much of a clue but he'd clearly lied to Kerry, which is brave judging by the way she throws her weight around. Was he up to no good? Will it be somewhere juicy or will it just be a case of seeing another woman? I tap my fingertips on the steering wheel thoughtfully. Perhaps he isn't protecting himself, or someone else and could that person be—?

'Did you notice Rachel's t-shirt?' Shaun asks, looking up from his mobile. His notebook pokes out of the top of his rucksack.

He hasn't said a word for a couple of miles and his voice breaks the silence, making me jump.

'I could only make out its colour. It was covered in dirt, paint splatters…'

'I thought you said nothing gets past your eyes,' he teases.

'Perhaps you didn't notice but *I* was doing the questioning. You're the scribe.'

Shaun laughs. 'Well, whilst you were interrogating Mrs Hayden, I *did* notice her t-shirt and I've just discovered that she used to work at GRATH. Greater-Ridley and Trindle Hospital. About two hundred miles north-west of here. Did you see the emblem on her t-shirt?'

'No, Shaun, I just said…'

'Two birds in mid-flight, holding what looks like a scroll; that was the clue. Perhaps she did a charity run for a hospital fund and kept the t-shirt to do gardening work in. Like people do. Lucky for us we called round when we did or she might have been wearing a different outfit. I've googled what we know: Greater Ridley, Lawrence Hayden, her name, but the signal is crap. It keeps buffering.'

I brake hard, pissing off the white Transit van driver behind who was driving with his nose in the Mazda's boot anyway. He thumps the horn but I ignore him and turn the wheel hard right, just making the junction without kerbing the car. Ahead, just past a Tesco express store and small car park, is a red brick building. I spot a parking space and I stick the Mazda in it.

Shaun looks through the window and then turns to me horrified. 'Why have you bought me to work, Will? It's my day off,' he whines.

I unclick my seatbelt and open the door. 'Free Wi-fi,' I tell him. 'And I could murder a drink.'

Chapter 31

I shift the bunch of purple and white tulips into the crook of my elbow, the cellophane wrapping crackling noisily, and pick up Bronwyn's Easter egg. I close the boot and look around. The only other vehicle parked in the small private carpark is a white Mercedes S-Class cabriolet. It's suspiciously close to her front door and since Bron doesn't have a car, I wonder if Michael has called in to beg her to attend his parents' swanky lunch, but I'm sure she would have texted me if she'd changed her mind. I'm going to be very pissed off if I've driven over here to find him here. I could be stuck in my room now eating a microwaveable chicken dinner for one and working my way through a Western.

Bronwyn's ground floor flat is one of six in a large white Georgian-style house with black-painted window frames. I walk around to the left, feet crunching on the yellow gravel. The window box on her kitchen window sill contains dwarf daffodils. Very Easter-like. The vent high up on the wall is blowing kitchen smells at me: roasted beef and herbed potatoes. My hollow stomach grumbles. Suddenly her black front door flings opens with force and Bronwyn grins at me. I resist the urge to gasp. She looks beautiful. Her dress is bottle-green with a pattern of white and wine-coloured flowers. Her shoes are green and emerald earrings grace her ears.

I glance down at my own clothes and wish I'd taken my mum's advice. "For God's sake, make sure you look smart. You're having Sunday lunch, not fish and chips wrapped in newspaper." I knew I should have gone clothes shopping but as usual, money is tight this month.

'Hi Will,' she says, beaming at me.

'Bron. How are you?' I ask, suddenly feeling nervous.

'I'm great. I've been looking forward to this all week; it's like old times, isn't it? Come in. Hope you're hungry. I seem to have gone overboard with the food somewhat.'

My feet don't move. I need to know who else is here. 'Whose car is that? The Merc?'

Her grin widens and her green eyes glint with pride. 'It's mine.'

'Since when?'

'Since two months ago. Come in,' and she gestures at me, 'and I'll tell you *all* about it over a cheeky glass of pre-dinner wine.'

I step inside and look around, slyly because I don't want her to catch me, but I need to see how much Michael has infiltrated her flat. The hall has been repainted in pale grey and there's a mirror on the wall that wasn't there the last time I was here. It helps to reflect much-needed light into a dark area. A few metres outside her front door is an ivy-covered six foot brick wall belonging to the neighbouring property. Underneath the radiator are a selection of her shoes: pink sneakers, slippers, half-Wellies. On the coat pegs are two coats, both hers. All good so far. He hasn't been allowed to leave a pair of slippers here. Unless they're under the bed.

'Red or white? Strictly speaking it should be red since we're having beef.'

'Red's fine,' I tell her, following her into the kitchen. 'I'd better have a big glass of water too. I don't want it going to my head.'

'I don't know…that could be more fun…' She grins at me before turning her attention back to dinner. Three pans are on the stove, their lids rattling. The oven is lit up and is kicking out a furnace-type heat.

I open the cupboard and take out two large wine glasses. There are two bottles of red wine on the work surface but since I know nothing about wine, I choose one randomly and unscrew the cap, pouring more into one glass than the other. Then I get myself a large glass of water and deal with the tulips at the same time.

'Are they for me?' she asks, sticking a fork into whatever is boiling on the hob.

'Yeah, to say thanks for inviting me. They're not a thank you for dinner; I need to eat it first and if it's edible, you can have your Easter egg.'

'You're spoiling me. I like that. They're beautiful tulips, Will. Thank you,' and she whips around from the stove, fork held high in the air, away from my head, to kiss me on the cheek. Her soft touch sends a spark of longing into my chest and I can still feel the imprint of her lips seconds after she's turned back to the pans.

I lean against the fridge, sipping the wine and gulping the water. 'So this car then?'

'Oh, yes. Well, after we…you know…' she begins awkwardly. 'I realised how much I'd come to rely on others for a lift so I looked into getting my own wheels.' She takes a long drink of her wine and smiles appreciatively. 'Rather stupidly, I asked Michael and he advised me that all I needed was a city car, because I'd only be doing low mileage and it was pointless getting anything bigger than a one litre. Talk about condescending. A friend from work said that I should ignore him and get what I want since I'm the one who's going to be driving it. One lunchtime I went to the Mercedes dealer, spoke to a really helpful salesman and bought what I wanted. Do you like it?'

'It's very nice,' I tell her.

'It's a wonderful drive. My friend says it's sexy.' She grins at me. 'Perfect for making out in.'

'Yeah, I can see why it might be good in that department. Does the table need setting?' I ask, changing the subject. Fucking hell, it's hot in here or is it me? Is she flirting with me? How much wine has she drunk before I turned up?

'It's all done. I've been up since seven: cleaning, hoovering, chopping, cooking. I haven't been drinking. This is the first drop I've touched,' and she grabs the wine and takes another long swig. 'Take a seat in the lounge if you want, Will.'

'I'm alright here unless I'm in your way.'

'You're never in my way. How's the investigation going?'

'Oh, it's taken a very interesting turn.' And I explain about the interview with Mrs Hayden and what we discovered when we hijacked the free wi-fi at The Smoking Gun. We sipped our alcohol-free IPAs and bent our heads over Shaun's iPhone. 'Turns out Lawrence Hayden is his new identity. He was called Killingworth.'

Bronwyn turns from stirring the gravy, wooden spoon in one hand. She frowns. 'Why do I know that name?'

'Let me tell you how we did it first. I think you'll be impressed, Bron, with our powers of detection,' I tell her, mischievously. If she can flirt, why the heck shouldn't I?

'I'm sure I will be.' Her smile widens and with one eye on the bubbling gravy, she settles back.

'Eagle-eyed Shaun noticed that Rachel, Lawrence's wife, was wearing a top with the name of the hospital trust emblazoned on the front. We already knew she was a nurse. We put together what we knew about them. They either moved from Greater Ridley or Trindle, his name, and darts.'

Bronwyn raises an eyebrow. 'Darts?'

'Oliver said that he and Charlie, their son, play darts because apparently Lawrence was really good. Possibly BDO good. I'll explain that some other time. We googled various combinations and, on the fourth go, we struck lucky. We found an article from the Trindle

Chronicle with the headline: "Local builder scores double top". Lawrence Killingworth had the potential to become a professional darter until…' I pause dramatically. 'Nine years ago, Nathan Killingworth, Lawrence's older brother went on a killing spree, murdering four people and seriously maiming two others with a shotgun. He received six life sentences.'

Bron shudders. 'Bloody hell. Really? That's awful. But why has Lawrence changed his name?'

'His journey into the world of darts came to an abrupt halt at his brother's trial. In front of TV cameras, the press, he denounced Nathan's wife, firmly planting the victims' deaths at her door, saying that the way she treated Nathan after the death of their child was the cause and catalyst for the murders. He said she had blood on her hands. The backlash from the community was almighty. Patients refused to be treated by Rachel, their kids were subjected to bullying, Lawrence's customers cancelled him, his van was set on fire. He had no choice but to uproot his family and move. I can only guess that somehow Amanda discovered his secret and that is why she sacked him.'

'Is he a suspect?'

'Yes, he has to be. I believe the teacher's account that she saw the two of them arguing. Amanda mightn't have let it drop. I reckon Mr Hayden will be spending the bank holiday weekend with his family. You know how I like to make people's days. He's probably going to tell me to fuck off but, if I can goad him, I might get something.'

'Other than a black eye?'

I turn my palm over and touch the scar from the last time I goaded someone. Wounds heal. And you don't get anywhere if you don't provoke and poke.

'I can always duck.' I smile.

'Here's to goading murderous brothers,' and Bronwyn holds her wine glass out. Carefully I clink the fragile glass against hers and we sip the wine. Our eyes lock over the wide rims and, for several seconds, I lose myself in her green gaze. Alcohol-infused blood courses through my veins at an alarming rate making my head sway. All I want to do is push her against the work surface and kiss her hard. The need to touch her is almost too much to bear and I tear my gaze away, plonking the glass down hard, nearly snapping the stem.

I mutter something about the toilet and escape the heat of the kitchen, heading for the bathroom, the coolest room in the flat. The white tiled walls offer me a place to chill my warm forehead and hands. Get a grip, William. How can you eat a meal if you don't snap out of it? She's your friend. Not in love with her boyfriend but that doesn't make her yours.

I flush the toilet for effect and run my hands under the cold water for several minutes until my fingers go nearly numb. Keep the conversation on neutral topics: the investigation, Easter, Nisha and the baby, Michael even. My thoughts trail off. Who am I kidding? I'm lazy at keeping up pretences.

'Will?' A soft knocking on the closed door. 'Are you ok?'

'Yeah,' I call loudly. 'Just drying my hands.'

'Dinner's ready.'

I take one last look in the mirror, decide my game plan and open the door.

*

I fold the dirty napkin up and neatly place it on the table next to my empty plate. 'That was fantastic, Bron. Thank you. I won't need to eat for a week now.'

She smiles proudly. 'You're welcome, Will. It's so nice to cook for someone. I try not to rely on microwaveable meals for one. They might be convenient but they're full of crap. I find cooking quite relaxing, even when things get a bit hectic and pots start boiling and the oven timer is pinging.'

'Don't you cook for Michael?' I ask, reaching for the water and sitting back.

'Oh, God, no. I'd never get rid of him if I invited him round. The other night when he turned up was awful. I had to fake period pains to get rid of him. He came up to my office on Thursday. There's a rumour going around that there'll be more redundancies. He's worried about how he's going to pay for his new kitchen. He's just put a deposit down. And then he catastrophized it, saying he might lose his house; never find work again, have to move back in with his parents. After fifteen minutes of his self-pitiful cries, I had to make up a meeting to get rid of him. I've instructed our receptionist that on the next time he appears to tell him I'm in an all-day meeting. I can't take it anymore, Will.'

'No closer to ending it then?' I say.

'Yes. I'm going to see him tomorrow and finish it. I'm going to feel like a right bitch but it's not fair to go on like this.'

'No, you're right, it isn't.' I start to stack the crockery, noisily clattering the cutlery on top of the plates. Anything to escape the subject. It's my own fault mentioning the weirdo.

'Don't worry about the plates; I'll do them later,' she calls out.

'I don't mind,' I tell her, carrying them through to the kitchen where I fill the sink with hot water and apple-scented washing-up liquid. I look at the time. Four thirty. Her flat is too comfortable. The sort of place I wish I had. Mrs Penn has all her family over so Bronwyn's invitation has done me a favour. Otherwise I was going to have to spend most of it in the office or my room, like a naughty boy who's sent upstairs. I could be living in a place like that for the rest of my life. What a fucking depressing thought.

'You okay?' Bronwyn asks, appearing behind me.

I snap the tap off. 'Yeah,' I reply, pasting a smile on my face.

'Do you want some more wine? I can open another bottle,' and she waggles the bottle from side to side so its base see-saws on the work surface.

'I'd better not. I'll be over the limit if I have another drop. Shall I put the kettle on?'

'Good idea, Will. I bought some decaf coffee if you prefer. Let me know when you're ready for pudding. You're not going yet, are you?' she asks, sounding horrified that now I've eaten I'm going to leg it.

'Not if you don't want me to.'

'Course I don't want you to,' she tells me, putting a hand on my arm. Her fingernails are painted dark purple like ripe plums. 'You sit down and I'll make the coffee. Put the telly on if you want.'

In the lounge, I finish tidying up, bringing more crockery through to the kitchen and abandoning it on the work surfaces for later. I drop onto the settee, adjusting a cushion behind my back. She's placed the tulips pride of place on the low coffee table. I put her *Galaxy* egg beside it.

A few minutes later, she carries a tray through loaded with a cafetière, cups and saucers, jug and sugar bowl.

'My favourite! Thank you,' she cries when she sees the box.

'You're welcome. After such a great dinner, it's the least I can do.'

She smiles shyly and presses the plunger down on the coffee. I watch as she pours the hot liquid into the cups and adds sugar and milk. She kicks her shoes off and drops onto the settee beside me, curling her legs up so her knee brushes my leg. We sit in silence, sipping our coffee. Desperately, I try to think of something to say. It just goes to show that, these

194

days, I really do have limited conversation. How the hell would I fair on a blind date? There is literally nothing interesting going on in my life. I don't go to the cinema, or restaurants; a visit to a pub is a rare occurrence. I don't go on holiday, day trips, don't play sports. I have a fairly interesting job that I'm not allowed to discuss. Customer confidentiality silences me, but who wants to hear about adulterous couples and missing persons?

I glance at Bronwyn. She's watching me. Her expression is unreadable.

I squirm uncomfortably. Has she been watching me as my mind has been racing to find something to talk about? I smile awkwardly. We're not normally lost for words. Maybe the three month hiatus has dented our friendship. Perhaps permanently. We might never get back to the way we were. Maybe I haven't asked her enough about her life.

I open my mouth. 'How's work?'

I hear her take a sharp intake of air before she says, 'Will, do you remember in January when we went out for a drink with your friend Chris?'

Her question throws me. I've only seen him once since the work Nisha and I did for him was completed. We went back to the Oak and Cedar for a drink but it felt awkward listening to him go on about his wedding plans and how happy he and his girlfriend were. I ignored his follow-up text message and he never bothered again. But then I wasn't in the best place. Has Bronwyn seen him recently?

I nod and taste more coffee. It's nice. Strong. Glad it's decaf though or I'll be up all night.

'He thought we were a couple and you told him we were just good friends,' she continues.

I want to ask why she's bringing this up now. Does she still feel bad about walking out of the restaurant that day? Has the wine made her feel melancholy? I clearly remember Chris' assumption that there must have been more between me and her and, because she'd always been quick to correct people who assumed the same thing, I just told him what I knew she'd say. But something changed for me, like his words had broken a spell. Maybe it did for her too, but for me it was permanent. For the first time, I looked at her differently, wondering what it'd be like if we were more than friends. But then Michael came along and she allowed him to take her away. Not seeing her gave me a chance to put my feelings away, but her recent return has caused them to resurface. And now, along with this investigation, she is all that I think of.

'Will?' she asks, her voice urgent. She's not going to let this drop. Why is she raking this up?

'Yeah, I remember it vaguely,' I reply, playing it careful. 'Not his exact words, but something…you know. Why are you asking me about that evening, Bron? It was ages ago.'

She lifts her legs more onto the settee so she's turned her whole body towards me. Her chest heaves upwards as she takes a deep breath. 'The thing is, Will…how I feel about you changed months ago. I *liked* you. I still do.'

It feels like my heart has stopped for a split second, as if taken aback by her revelation. 'I don't understand…' I say, my words stuck in my suddenly dry throat. 'What are you—'

She hesitates, bites her lip. 'I should never have got involved with Michael when it wasn't him I wanted…I must know how you feel about me, Will, whether it's the same because I can't go on not knowing.'

She's clutching her hands together and she looks distressed, desperate for answers. She's saying what I've longed to hear for so very long but can this be true?

'Please,' she implores.

Her pleading causes my resolve to collapse and I give in; my words pour out like wine from a bottle, flowing and steady, without any thought.

'I think about you all the time. I can't bear the thought of never being in your life. The three months without you were nothing short of torture,' I tell her, my hand reaching for hers, unlocking her fingers. 'I ache for you.'

She smiles at my heartfelt words and I place our entwined hands to my racing heart. Her fingers grab the front of my shirt, bunching the material, and pulling me closer. I smile at her.

She leans towards me and I feel like I can't breathe, like she's sucking the oxygen out of my chest. Her eyes, the colour of fresh basil, bore into mine and I need to kiss her or I will explode.

'Kiss me, William,' she whispers and the sound of my name on her lips is all I ever want to hear.

I kiss her softly. She shudders, groaning low in her throat. She falls into me and I hold her close, wanting her so badly, my hand in her tangerine-scented curls, her bare leg resting over my knees, her skin hot against my arm. And then I'm kissing her hard and she responds, fierce and devouring, fingers fumbling with tiny buttons, touching my chest, setting me on fire, making me ache for more, much more.

Chapter 32

'Will, what time did you get here?' Shaun asks, dropping his heavy rucksack onto the nearest chair, the weight almost pulling him with it. 'Have you been here all weekend?'

'No. I got in about twenty minutes ago,' I reply. 'I've been reading up about our water baby, Martyn Hepworth, since the intel from you has been somewhat delayed.'

'I haven't forgotten, Will. I have everything you need to know in my notebook, plus I've interviewed witnesses.'

'He's had quite a career. I won't bore you with the sporting details, but he's had his face in the local papers a few times. Coaching swimming stars of the future who funnily enough have disappeared down the plughole. There's one, two, three...' and I count them off on my fingers.

'Was Amanda one of them?' Shaun asks, unzipping his bag to remove his llama notebook, which I notice has little bits of paper sticking out, paperclips hooked over pages and now a thick elastic band is wrapped around it holding it closed.

'Sadly not. Mrs Davies said Amanda didn't like swimming, didn't like getting her hair wet. Neither did she attend Lexington Secondary. However, she did play hockey for her school and obviously travelled for games so there's a chance she might have played Lexington.'

'How old would Hepworth have been then? It's so nice not having to refer to him as sir. He really was a bastard to those of us who hated PE.' Shaun removes a brown paper bag from his rucksack and tears into a blueberry muffin.

'I'll let you be bad cop when we interview him if you like,' I offer.

'I'd really like that, Will, thank you,' he says, spitting crumbs down his t-shirt.

'There's eight years between them so he'd have been 23 when she was 15. And you might find this interesting because I certainly did: the campus where he did his post-grad teaching degree is a mere ten miles from where Amanda spent her teenage years. Mrs Davies suspected Amanda of having a boyfriend when she was around 15, but she never brought him home to meet her folks. And guess what?'

Shaun shrugs.

'Amanda went to an all girls school. So where did she meet boys?'

'If she was involved with Horrible Hepworth, how did she meet him?' Shaun asks.

'I have no idea. That's the flaw in my theory. That's assuming Hepworth likes teenage girls, or that Amanda's boyfriend was him and not a teenage lad. But I went back through the MISPER file,' and I rummage around for the relevant page on my now untidy desk. 'Here it is.' I lift the empty cup up and read the items found discarded from the opened box in Amanda's loft. 'Friendship bracelets, photographs, cuddly toys, exercise books...' I look up. 'Where's the teenage diaries?'

'She didn't keep one?'

'I guarantee you, Shaun, if she ever had a teenage boyfriend then she kept a diary. Your first crush, kiss, petting session, sneaking out to meet an older boyfriend, you want all that documented for posterity. You want to remember it. Get off on it when you're on your own.'

Shaun raises an eyebrow. 'Okay. Where are the diaries then?'

'Missing. Like their author.'

'She took them with her that day? Or hid them? Why remove them from a loft and hide them somewhere else? Do you think David found them?'

I shrug. 'It's possible. A loft is an obvious place to store stuff like that. You'd remove them if you were concerned about their safety. And you'd be concerned about their safety if there was something contained within their pages that was detrimental to you, any persons mentioned or anyone who could come across them like David or Oliver.'

'She might have destroyed them,' Shaun suggests.

'Not a chance,' I reply. 'Unless under extreme duress. Why keep them secure in a loft for twenty odd years and then get rid of them? They're hardly taking up room. No. If she got rid of them, and I don't think she did because she was her own free person, then the only person who could have that level of persuasion is any person mentioned in her pubescent ramblings. And by persuasion, I mean a threat of violence or exposure…. Or they paid her. Amanda doesn't strike me as a pushover. She'd move the diaries first and goad them. "Come and find them if you want them", that sort of thing.'

'Lawrence?' Shaun suggests. 'He was witnessed threatening her.'

'According to the newspaper article on his darts career, he's Trindle bred and raised.'

'Oh, okay. What else did you find out about Hepworth?' Shaun asks, pulling the elastic band off his notebook and leaving it on his wrist like it's a bangle.

'Back in the day, when he first got his face published, you can see what a good-looking rugged bloke he was. Blond, broad and blokeish.' I hold the iPad up for Shaun to see. He pulls a disgusted face. 'A teenage girl's heartthrob.'

Shaun pulls a face. 'He wasn't a heartthrob at our school. I asked my evil twin sister…'

'Oh,' I say, suddenly reminded of something. 'Did you get your Easter car? Have you come in it?'

Shaun smiles smugly. 'It's outside. I'll take you for a spin later. My dad has excelled himself with these hot wheels, I'll tell you. My mates are dead jealous. Anyway, I spoke to my sister about Hepworth. Obviously he never took her for PE; it not being allowed in case male teachers are paedos.'

'Nicely put, Shaun.'

He grins. 'But I wanted her take on him. Now, she is much sportier; she played for her house and the school so it's a pretty safe bet that she knows what she's talking about.' Shaun glances down at his notebook and frowns. 'Hepworth's office overlooks the all-weather pitch and she swears that, several times, she and her mates would see the vertical blinds in his window swinging madly and his face disappearing quick smart.'

'Any formal accusations?'

Shaun shakes his head sadly. 'I know teenage girls are rowdy so, unless he has an issue with noise and disturbance and is peering out the window like a nosy neighbour, you could conclude that Hepworth got off on toned legs in short, pleated PE skirts.'

I nod in agreement. 'Bit of a conclusion. We can't steam in there and accuse him of being a predatory paedophile. But there's a couple of witnesses in these articles who may be able to assist. If we can track them down. Otherwise we're a bit stuck.'

Shaun drops into a seat, kicking his legs over the arm whilst skilfully throwing the screwed-up paper bag at the bin. He scores a hit.

'How was your Easter, Will? How many eggs did you get?'

'One,' I reply. What did I do with it? I don't remember putting it in the boot or taking it up to my room. I certainly didn't eat…oh, I know. I left it in Bron's flat. But then my mind wasn't on hollow chocolate shapes.

I sit back in the chair and think back to yesterday. A half-smile plays on my lips and, though I know Shaun is watching, waiting for a less vague answer, I ignore him and replay the events for the hundredth time that morning. This investigation helped to prevent Bronwyn from encroaching on my thoughts 24/7 but now…after last night and this morning, I never want to block thoughts of her out of my head. I will never tire of thinking about her and the way she makes me feel. I came so very close to telling her that I'm falling for her. Holding her in my arms, on crumpled bedsheets, sweat glistening on our skin, chests rising with exhilaration, my heart literally bursting at the seams, to turn to her and say those words felt like a cliché. I daren't say it until she's finished with Michael. That's why it doesn't feel right. At the moment it feels like unfaithfulness even though they're not sleeping with each other; they're perceived as being a couple, at least to him. He has to be told it's over and Bronwyn is doing it today. This is why I need to work today. I cannot spend the day doing nothing, waiting for an outcome I have no control over. His misery will be my happiness.

And then, when she tells me it's over between them, I'll be free to tell her.

'Will!' Shaun shouts, clicking his fingers loudly. I snap out of my thoughts. He grins at me.

'Good Easter, was it?'

'Yeah. Not bad, you know.'

'No, but I can see you do. Boyfriend been given the Spanish archer, has he?'

'What?'

'El-bow,' and he sticks his elbow out and erupts into silly laughter.

I push my chair back, close the cover on the tablet.

'You never want to talk about things, do you?' he complains, swinging his body out of the seat, face still creased with amusement. 'I'm here if you want to. We're friends.'

'That's very kind of you, mate, but there really isn't anything to say. Right, let's fire up this stolen car of yours and pay Mr Killingworth a visit, see if we can't rattle his cage.'

*

The black Corsa pulls up so sharply against the kerb that the pine tree-shaped air freshener hanging from the rear view mirror swings like a pendulum. I release the door handle and look at Shaun.

He grins. 'What do you think, Will? Pretty cool, isn't it?'

'What is it? 1.2, 1.4?'

'1.4 but it's got some poke, hasn't it? I love it,' and he smooths his hands over the steering wheel.

200

It's just like Hock to buy his son an unsuitable car as his very first vehicle. The man's probably trying to show off. At least it's not brand new. If Shaun does dent it or God forbid, total it, it won't hit Hock too hard in his pocket. That's if he paid for it. And thank fuck Shaun drove it here relatively safely.

'It's very nice, Shaun. Just take care driving it. You're quite important to the agency and to me. I like to think you're safe on the road.'

'Thanks, Will. That's really kind of you to say and you are to me too.'

'Right, now we've got the soppy shit out of the way, let's ruin Lawrence's Bank Holiday.'

We exit the car and I watch with amusement as Shaun locks it, walks around it, pulling on the door handles to make sure it's secure. Thankfully it's only two-door. I used to do the same thing with my first car.

Today Lawrence's van is parked on the drive, squeezed tightly against the 4x4. It's bigger than a transit with a higher roof. There are no ladders on the roof rack and the printed advertising down the sides and back doors are everything you need to know: his name, the business he's in and contact numbers. There's also a warning potential thieves there are no tools kept inside overnight.

I knock the front door and stand behind the faded welcome mat. A few moments later, Charlie opens the door and smiles at us. In his hand is gold foil paper, a splinter of Easter egg pokes of out the top.

'Hello. Oh, hi Shaun.' He raises a hand in a bit of a wave. 'How are you?'

'Fine, Charlie. How was your Easter?' Shaun asks.

'Yeah, good, thanks.' He brings the door closer to his shoulder in an effort to conceal our presence from whoever might be behind. He glances quickly over his shoulder. 'Have you got more questions for me?'

'I'd like to speak to your dad, please, Charlie,' I say.

Charlie looks puzzled. 'Dad? Why? What can he tell you?'

'Is he home?'

Charlie nods. 'He's fixing the back gate. What do you want him for? Is this about Ollie's mum?'

'Can you ask him to come to the front door?'

Charlie looks at Shaun for confirmation.

'Please, Charlie, mate,' Shaun persuades in a pally tone.

Charlie nods compliantly, but he looks crestfallen that it's not him we want. He leaves the door ajar and disappears back into the dark hall. When the taller, broader figure of Lawrence appears, Charlie is trailing after him until a deep manly voice orders him to stay away, but instead the nimble figure of his teenage son races upstairs.

Lawrence Hayden walks into the light and it's at times like this that I'm glad I'm fairly tall. He snatches the front door close to his shoulder even though there is absolutely no way I could physically barge my way past him. He's easily 6' 4" and as broad as a heavyweight boxer, slightly podgy around his middle. His dark beard contains threads of grey and is clipped short. His hair is neatly cut with a razor-sharp side parting. His dark blue eyes blaze angrily.

'Morning Mr Hayden. How are you?' I begin pleasantly.

But he's in no mood for pleasantries. 'I've got nothing to say to you or you,' and he jabs a finger aggressively at each of us in turn. Behind me, I hear Shaun shift backwards a couple of feet. 'I do not appreciate you hassling my family. For the very last fucking time, I did not know Amanda Davies.'

I interrupt. 'I don't expect you did. You were only in her salon for an hour and fifteen minutes, and on the other occasion, outside the school, you were probably in conversation with her for ten minutes maximum. I doubt anyone could claim to *really* know her in such a short time.'

'Listen, smart arse,' and he leans his upper body over the threshold, 'this is my Bank Holiday. I rarely get time off to spend with my family. I work hard six days a week. I do not intend to waste my precious time talking to you pair of jokers about something that's got fuck all to do with—'

'Why did Amanda sack you?' I ask. His jaw clenches tight. 'David Bywater told us that you did an excellent job refurbishing the salon the second time around, so I can't imagine it was anything to do with the quality or speed of your work. Were you Amanda's lover?'

'What the fuck?' he shouts, coming back alive. 'No. I wasn't shagging her. Jesus Christ…'

'The only other reason I can see is that she somehow found out who you used to be.'

His eyes widen with surprise before narrowing until they're just slits.

Momentarily, I think back to the conversation I had with Bronwyn, how if I goaded Lawrence that I might need to duck. A glance at his hands reveals he hasn't made them into fists but he might be quicker swinging them than I am on my feet. Oh, what the heck? Bruises heal. 'And that didn't sit well with her. Hiring the brother of a spree killer.'

'You fucking…leave my brother out of this,' he shouts, spittle flying towards me. I jerk my head back; I've already had one shower today. 'Nathan is none of your fucking business. Do you have any idea how hard it's been?'

'Mr Hayden,' Shaun begins, shuffling forward, 'we're not here to criticise Nathan or yourself. Your name came up during our investigation and we are obliged to ask you questions pertaining to that. If you could please just spare us a few minutes.'

His tone is staggeringly polite but his voice is unnecessarily loud considering he's just a few metres away.

'Where were you on the 15th October? Were you working? It was a Wednesday if that helps, the week before half-term.'

'I don't have to tell you nothing,' Lawrence retorts aggressively, glaring at Shaun like he wants to tear him limb from limb.

'I know you don't, which is why we appreciate your time. Do you keep records of your customers? Could they vouch for you?'

'What? You want me to trawl through my records, finding people and jobs I've long since forgotten to prove where I was on some random day in October six years ago.'

'It was the day Amanda Davies went missing,' I remind him, following Shaun's lead by speaking clearly and loudly as if Lawrence has a hearing impairment.

'Oliver is her son,' Shaun reminds him. 'I know he spends time with your family because he told me. He thinks of Charlie as a brother. Please Mr Hayden, take the time to remember where you were. If not for Amanda, for Oliver. He is desperate to know what happened to his mum.'

Lawrence snorts, but I can see he's considering Shaun's reasonable request. After a brief stalemate, Lawrence looks up, fixes his steely gaze on both of us and says, 'No. Now fuck off, both of you and don't bother me or my family again.' And with that, he slams the door in my face.

I turn slowly to Shaun and shrug. 'You almost had him then. I thought he was going to spill.'

'I can't understand why he won't help Ollie,' Shaun ponders. 'I know he thinks a lot of him. He's been teaching him how to play darts. It's so sad that he won't acknowledge a young boy's pain.'

I stroll around Shaun who appears to be rooted to the path. 'We could always try waterboarding or denailing him. He'd probably get a kick out of it. Some people don't have empathy,' I say. 'You'll realise that quickly in this job.'

'He's a family man,' Shaun says. 'He knows what it's like to lose someone he's close to.'

I stop at the car. Shaun has dawdled down the driveway and is fishing his key fob out of his pocket.

'I'm sure we'll find another way to the truth,' he tells me confidently, his voice still loud.

I shake my head at his strange behaviour. Perhaps listening to really loud music in his earphones every day is affecting his own hearing. He'll be deaf by the time he's forty if he doesn't turn it down.

Shaun unlocks the doors and we get in the car. As we click our seatbelts on, in his usual tone of voice, Shaun suggests a cheeky drink on the way back to the office.

'Yeah, why not?' I wonder what time Bronwyn is meeting Michael and when she'll tell me how it went. She might even ask me over later.

As Shaun pulls away, I look through the passenger window back at the house. In one of the upstairs windows, a figure has their back to us, an elbow stuck out, as if they're holding a mobile to their ear.

You little beauty, Shaun, I think.

Chapter 33

Normal service resumes on the Tuesday. The kids might still be off, which means the roads are quieter but most of society has gone back to work. Shops are open and I feel less of a freak now I'm allowed to be back in the office. Shaun is working until the early afternoon. I won't have him tagging along or pulling a face when I tell him he can't come with me. I head off on my own to see Bronwyn. I spent the rest of Bank Holiday Monday at my mum's house. Silently suffered her complaints that I only come round when I want something: food, the laundering of my clothes or to borrow money until pay day. It was her short loan, one I won't pay back, that paid for Bronwyn's flowers and Easter egg. I don't tell Mum that I spent the night with Bronwyn. She likes Bron and, until I know for sure we have a future, there really is no reason to raise Mum's hopes. There's nothing she'd like to see more than her eldest son hooked up, loved up and wed.

Bronwyn's place of work is on the eleventh floor of a 20 storey tower block on the outskirts of Lexington. The other floors house solicitors, private medical services like an osteopath and a psychiatrist, recruitment consultants and IT specialists. It's a stylish if minimalist building. Fake potted plants with a tropical feel, wide armless chairs surrounding low coffee tables, a black shiny floor and a receptionist behind a crescent-shaped desk. On the wall by the twin lifts is a noticeboard helpfully reminding people what's on which floor.

I press the call button and wait. I was really hoping to hear from her last night. Should I be worried? Maybe Michael was busy with yet another family drama or, if he knew what was coming, he might've made some flimsy excuse to avoid meeting up with her. Maybe she needs more time to finish with him. It's alright me saying dumping Michael is easy but I'm not the one who's got to do it. When was the last time I finished a relationship? Years ago, and I bet I could have done it more sensitively too.

But this situation and the suspense it's creating is killing me. A short text message from her would have sufficed. A "Yes, I've done it" or a "No, I've chickened out" is all I want. For now. I've found one of Hepworth's protégés, one who didn't make it big in the world of swimming. Heather Hughes was featured in a newspaper article when she came third in a competition for the 200m breast stroke and also because her mum was a name in the council. Now she runs her own gift shop just round the corner from Bronwyn's workplace. I'm going to call in and see Bron on my way to the gift shop.

The lift pings its arrival and the doors clunk and slide open with astonishing slowness. The lift is empty and I press the button for the 11th floor and wonder if I should have texted her that I was coming. She might be in a meeting. I suppose I can leave a message with the receptionist if she's busy.

'Floor seven,' an automated female voice announces and the doors slide open. I step back, allowing two more passengers to step inside. Two women wearing dark suits and carrying briefcases don't give me a glance as they resume their conversation about how much Prosecco they drank over the bank holiday.

'Enough to fill my bath,' the one woman says with a laugh. 'Twice over.'

'I can't even remember cooking the bloody dinner, I must've been out of my tree,' laughs the other.

'Wait for me,' a male voice calls and quickly I reach out to press the button to hold the doors. A man in his late thirties jumps into the lift and, in a slightly out of breath voice says "thanks".

'I need to get back in the gym,' he tells me with a laugh. He looks at the buttons, his finger reaching for 11th floor but he sees that the button has already been pushed and is illuminated so slides his hand into the trouser pocket of his dark blue suit and relaxes a shoulder against the side of the lift.

I'm presented with a side view of the man who is also wearing trendy brown shoes with pointed toes. I look down at my Adidas trainers and notice a black scuff mark on one of the toes. The movement of the man adjusting his position against the lift wall wafts the scent of his aftershave. It smells expensive. He looks expensive, like he has a good job, good prospects, his own home and is not driving around in his late dad's twelve year old MX5.

I feel a mess. I should've made more of an effort. This is where she works. It's not like her flat, a café or a bloody supermarket where it doesn't really matter what I wear, but here her colleagues will look at me and wonder what she sees in a man who dresses like this. Even my hair needs updating; I've had the Morrissey look for nearly twenty years. I glance at the man. His hair is dark blond and cut into a textured crop, tousled and styled. He's better looking than me with a chiselled jaw and dark blue eyes. Hopefully he's a twat, women despise him and children cry whenever he comes near.

206

The automated voice announces our arrival at floor 11 and the doors opens. The man exits first, knowing exactly where he's going. The women head left, leaving me to stare at the notice board opposite, checking the directions to Bronwyn's workplace. I turn right and walk the carpeted passageway towards a set of double doors. Ahead, the man has paused to speak to two people standing by a fire extinguisher but, as I'm about to overtake him, he says a quick goodbye and races ahead, pushing open one of the double doors, leaving it to swing back at me. I catch the handle before it slaps me on the forehead and yank it open. Inside on the right is a large reception desk manned by a pretty red-haired woman wearing a headset. A large vase of white lilies stands on the desk beside a register. Before I even get a chance to ask where Bronwyn McCartney's office is, I see her expression change. She rises out of her chair, lifting a hand and opening her mouth to speak to the blue-suited man, but he speeds past without a word or a glance in her direction. When she turns to me, her face alters again to one of horror and her gaze swings back to the man striding ahead.

'Hi,' I say to her, 'sorry to bother you but I was wondering if it's okay to have a quick word with Bronwyn if she's about. She's not expecting me; I'm a friend. Just wanted to say hello.'

'Yes, of course,' the receptionist replies with a big smile. 'I recognise you, Mr Bailey. Bronwyn showed me a photo of you last week. Her office is in the far corner.' And she points across the open plan office. 'Just follow that man.'

'The man who's just come in?' I search for him. He's striding purposefully across the floor, waving at people who turn to say "hello". He weaves a path around desks, printers, water coolers and more potted plants to the office in the far corner: Bronwyn's office. He's in some rush. Is he late for an appointment?

But suddenly, a woman rolls her chair away from the desk to look underneath it, causing an obstacle. He emits a sharp, 'Watch it' and swerves but has a nasty collision with a young lad carrying a stack of box files. They fly into the air as if he's stepped onto a mine, spilling their contents everywhere like confetti. Surrounding people react, stooping or dropping to their knees to gather the fallen items up.

I use the distraction to my advantage and speed up, determined to get there first; my stride is longer. The blue-suited man thrusts a couple of boxes into the office worker's arms, useless without the paper inside. Inside her glass office, Bronwyn suddenly stands like a meerkat on sentry duty, a mobile clamped to her ear, chatting away merrily. She looks for the cause of the commotion and I watch with increased interest as her expression exactly matches that of the receptionist: dread. She squeezes her eyes closed for a second, perhaps hoping he is a mirage. When she opens them again, he hurries across from my right and her head follows his movement and then she's looking straight at me, then back to him and then me like she's watching a tennis match. I know, judging by her expression, that her worse nightmare has come true. Her boyfriend and her lover are finally meeting. Not the way I would have liked it either but you can't interfere with the ways the Gods set you up.

My hand touches the handle first. His retracts quickly before it lands on mine and we look at each other.

I regard Michael. 'Still out of breath?' I quip.

He looks confused and I'm pleased to notice his chest is rising quickly. My running has paid dividends; I'm definitely the fitter. The door opens and Bronwyn looks at us, trying to hide the mixture of her feelings: horror and nervousness.

'Hello Bronwyn,' I say confidently.

'Hi,' she replies in a small voice. Her eyes dart to Michael who doesn't appear to know who the hell I am.

And that one word from her tells me everything I need to know. Disappointment shares a space in my chest. But I ignore it. I'm here now, time to stir things up.

'Do you know this guy?' Michael asks her, his tone suspicious.

'Where are my manners?' I say to him. 'Pleased to finally meet you, Michael. I'm William Bailey,' and I thrust a hand at him.

His hand awkwardly rises to mine and we shake. His eyes are as wide as saucers, his mouth opens like there's a dozen things he wants to say but his voice has abandoned him. I expect his handshake to be loose and weak, but it's firm. Maybe he does a lot of handshaking in his job. Or at home if his sex life is non-existent.

His recovery is impressively quick and I know he's measuring me up. Is he harder than me? Broader and taller? More intelligent? Does he have better luck with the women? I know where my advantage is. I might not earn anywhere near what he does, I don't have my own house or a girlfriend, I don't dress in fancy suits and shoes, but I have been preparing for this meeting since it was apparent he was a permanent fixture in Bronwyn's life. It doesn't look as if he ever thought he'd encounter me, assuming that his words and actions early on would be enough to keep me and her apart.

'Come in, please,' Bronwyn says, her tone formal and uneasy.

I gesture for him to go first. Bronwyn takes the opportunity whilst he can't see us, to widen her eyes and gently shake her head. My smile is non-committal.

But Michael can do something I can't. Once the door closes, he goes up to her and kisses her, forcing her to step backwards with the force.

I look away to the window and say, 'Nice view, Bron. I didn't realise you could see where I live from here.'

Michael lets her go, snorting with annoyance that I've missed him stamping his ownership on her like she's his property.

'I think it's fantastic that the two of you are back in contact after… how long has it been since you last saw each other?' Michael asks, shoving Bronwyn's mouse over so he can perch on the corner of her desk. His hand reaches for hers. I see her fingers flinch from his touch. 'Three months, wasn't it? I know she's missed you something terrible.' He squeezes her hand and she smiles tightly.

'Let me just,' she says vaguely. In her other hand is her mobile phone. She uses it as an excuse to pull out of Michael's grasp and goes to the cabinet against the wall where a charging cable rests on its top. She plugs the phone back in, glancing at me.

'Good to know,' I say. 'It was worth her seeking me out then.'

His eyes narrow slightly. 'Yes, it was. Bron is an amazing friend. I'm biased obviously.' He smiles lovingly at her. 'But I appreciate everything she does for me. I had some bad news at the weekend.'

Oh good, I think.

'My brother isn't well, having lots of hospital tests. It's a huge worry for me, my sister and our parents. They're in poor health too. And then I have the added worry that I might lose my job.'

Out of the corner of my eye, Bronwyn takes a position against the cabinet and folds her arms.

'The doctors want to do some tests on me too. To see if it's hereditary.'

'To see if what's hereditary?' I ask.

'Whatever is wrong with Jamie. Bronwyn has very kindly offered to take me to the hospital and accompany me to my appointment. I can't thank her enough. But I can start with this,' and from the inside pocket of his jacket, he removes a gift-wrapped box about the same size as a bottle of perfume, which is obviously what it contains. He presents it to her like he's opening the box of an engagement ring. 'Thank you for being there for me. You're the best girl a man could have.'

'You didn't have to,' she says in that irritating small voice. She takes the box with stiff hands, makes no move to open it.

'I wanted to,' and he leans over to kiss her again.

I stare at her, willing her to look at me now but she keeps her gaze averted. Why am I still standing here taking this crap? Disappointment shifts over to make room for anger. But I can't show him I'm bothered. If we're point-scoring, I'll be handing him a bonus ten points.

'I must go,' I announce. 'I'll leave you two alone. Give me a call in a couple of weeks, Bron. My investigation might be finished with then. Maybe the three of us could go out for a drink. Nice to meet you, Michael.'

Bron looks positively alarmed but hides it quickly and, maybe it's the thought that I'm leaving her alone with him, or that I mean what I say, but she comes to life, shoving the unopened box onto her desk and protesting, 'No, Will, we haven't discussed that private matter yet.'

'What private matter?' Michael enquires.

'It's *private*, Michael. Which means it's nothing to do with you. Hadn't you better get back to work? You've been away from your desk long enough. Your boss will be sending a search party out.' She strides confidently across the carpet in a way that makes her look as sexy as hell and throws open the door. My heart rate increases, my breathing becomes shallower. I fancy her madly when she's like this: in control and wearing those heels.

Michael mutters something about her being right, that he's sorry he won't see her for lunch. His attempt to say "goodbye" isn't as confident as his kissing and he skulks out of the door and down the open plan office.

Bronwyn firmly closes the door and goes around the office windows, turning the blinds away from prying eyes. I watch her, my pulse nearly through the roof. Finally, she chucks his gift into a desk drawer and slams it shut. She looks at me, her green eyes tear right through me and like before, my breath catches in my dry throat. I can't stand to have her this close and not kiss her. I pull her into my arms, pressing my mouth on hers, my hand on the small of her back. Her fingernails scratch my scalp as she plunges her hand into my hair and slides her knee between mine.

'Sorry, Will,' she whispers in my ear, 'that I didn't do…I tried…but he kept avoiding the issue…he only wants a lift…'

I tear my mouth away and look at her. 'What do you mean he only wants a lift?'

She blinks. 'The hospital. He hasn't asked me to go his appointment; he only wants a lift back. Says he won't be able to drive afterwards.' She shakes her head. 'I'm so sorry, Will. I wanted to ring you, but I'm ashamed. I'm weak…I'm—'

'Shut up, Bron. I don't want to talk about him,' and I kiss her again.

A couple of minutes later, we're torn apart by the sound of her desk phone ringing. 'It's Fay, our receptionist,' she tells me, reading the caller ID. 'It must be important. Hang on.' Bronwyn grabs the receiver, talks and listens, whilst smoothing her dress down. She put the phone back and smiles regretfully at me. 'I've got a meeting with the Finance Director. Will you be busy at 1pm?'

'What? Today?'

'Yes, today, obviously. Can you meet me at the flat? We still need to discuss that private matter. We made a start but I really feel there's more we need to go over.'

'Yeah, I suppose so.'

'Sorry. Am I putting you out?' she teases.

'No. See you then,' I say, reaching for the door handle, but I pause and turn back. 'I don't appreciate how hard this must be for you. Dumping that idiot. He is a drip, but he seems okay. Like you said, stabbing a puppy.' I open the door and walk back across the office, raising a hand to the receptionist who coos "bye bye".

*

The lift arrives at the ground floor and the doors take an age to clunk open. With a spring in my step and a promise in my heart, I skip across the shiny floor, calculating how many minutes I have until she's back in my arms. But leaning on the wall close to the revolving doors is Michael. He slides the mobile back in his pocket and pushes himself off the wall. He walks over and I can tell by the way he's holding himself that a confrontation of some sorts is on the cards.

'William,' he calls. 'Can I have a quick word?'

I stop and wait in the middle of the floor, making a small island people need to walk around.

'Why did you come back?'

'I never went away, Michael.'

He huffs. 'You know what I mean. Bronwyn is confused; she's moved on.' He steps closer. I stand my ground. Here it comes. I've never been one side of a love triangle before, never had another bloke threaten me over a woman. First time for everything, I suppose.

'I love that girl and your reappearance is jeopardising everything I'm planning. My future is with Bronwyn.'

'Mike, mate, we're just friends.' I hold my hands out.

'I'm not your mate. If you care anything for her happiness, you'll back off, make yourself busy next time she wants to meet up.'

'I will only do that if she asks me, and Bronwyn's happier with me in her life.' I tilt my head to his, lower my voice warningly. 'You're going to have to get used to that. See you around, Mike.'

Chapter 34

The Original Gift shop is inside a small indoor shopping mall between a florist and a lingerie shop. I look up at the trio of shops and smile. Do I need any more hints to buy Bronwyn a present? It won't compare to Michael's perfume, which no doubt costs more than I can afford.

The door to the gift shop is open and I stroll inside. On the left are two rotary stands. One contains fancy paper serviettes, the other greetings cards with pictures of cute animals, woodland scenes and flower arrangements on the front. The air smells of lavender and citrus fruit, and it feels warm and cosy in here. There are so many glass and chrome surfaces, reflecting the heat back. A woman in her early fifties is chatting to a customer as she slides a handful of cards into a smooth paper bag with the shop's motif on the front: a wrapped gift box, not unlike the one Michael had, with the bow being undone by invisible hands.

I head down the shop. On the right are well-polished glass cabinets containing little crystal animals and decorative plates; vases crammed with fake flowers of all kinds from anemones to tulips. On the right are yet more greeting cards for every conceivable event: Happy Teacher's Day to Happy Birthday to my mum's wife. At the back of the shop are shelves crammed with cuddly toys, those horrible ones with the really big glass eyes; scented candles; and the obligatory adult humour section, none of which make me laugh. I do a lap around the aisles and head back to the till but a mirrored door marked "Staff Only" opens. A woman in her early twenties exits carrying a plastic bag of cuddly toys, their faces squashed against the inside of the bag like fish caught in a net.

'Hello,' she says, with a pleasant smile. 'Is there anything you're particularly looking for?'

'Yes, Heather Hughes if she's around.'

'I'm Heather. How can I help you?' She has the physique of a swimmer: triangular upper body and strong shoulders. Her hair contains blonde highlights and is tied back into a neat ponytail with a fringe.

I show her my card and ask if there's anywhere quiet I can have a quick word.

She looks at the door she's just exited and hesitates. I tell her I don't mind talking in the shop but I'm sure, once I start the questions, she'll want to move the conversation somewhere quieter.

'Let me just give these to Bernie.' She holds up the bag of entangled toys. 'Now Easter's over, I need to clear all the rabbit and chick stuff out and fill the shelves with something else. Two secs,' she tells me, heading for the till.

When she returns, she punches the door code into the key pad, shielding the numbers from my eyes. The passageway is lovely and cool away from all those lights and she leads the way through two storerooms before entering a tiny staffroom containing two chairs, a sink unit and a small fridge.

She rearranges the chairs and offers me one. I sit and remove my notebook.

'I've never been interviewed by a private detective before,' she admits, smiling nervously. 'I can't think what I can possibly help you with, Mr Bailey. Fire away. Is it something to do with the shop or a customer?'

I shake my head. 'Nothing like that. Please call me Will. I appreciate you giving me a few minutes of your time. I'm hoping you can help me with a new line of enquiry I have regarding a missing person.' I briefly explain that I'm investigating the disappearance of Amanda Davies. As soon as I mention the name of the salon, Heather reacts.

'I know it. I had my hair done there before my prom. The hairdresser was really helpful, advising me what I could do to best protect my hair from chlorine.'

I take out my phone and show her a photo of Amanda. She grabs the phone, nodding enthusiastically. 'Yes, that's her. So sad. Her poor family.' She hands the phone back. 'I never knew her. My mother treated me to the haircut.'

'A witness states that Amanda may have known Martyn Hepworth.' I watch her closely for a reaction but there isn't an obvious one.

'The swimming coach? I wouldn't know that. Have you asked him? He's still working at Kelsall baths the last I heard, but that was a couple of years ago.'

'They were seen in her salon together talking, which is something not previously known. I'd prefer some background before I approach Mr Hepworth. How he might have met her, the nature of their relationship, that sort of thing.'

'Oh. I still don't know how I can help you, Will.'

'I understand Mr Hepworth was your swimming coach?' A nod. 'Do you still swim?'

She laughs. 'Only on holiday. And only for fun. Thank God those days are over. I do not miss getting up early to get into a cold pool, half-asleep.'

214

'What school did you go to, Heather?'

'St. Julia's.' Not Lexington then.

'How did you get into competitive swimming?' I ask, casually, crossing one knee over the other. She mirrors my actions, releases her knotted hands.

'It was my dad's idea. My parents were going through a nasty divorce and he thought, if he pushed his children into taking up a sport or a hobby, then we wouldn't notice the constant fighting. My mum knows Martyn's wife. They both work for the council. My mum said something to Mrs Hepworth, Martyn got in contact, offered to come and see me swim, see if I had potential. I never thought I was particularly good, certainly not good enough to compete but Martyn said, with proper tuition, I could be.'

'How old were you?'

'Sweet sixteen.' Another teenager.

'Was Martyn a good coach?'

'Oh, yes. Absolutely dedicated to his students. He told me I had the perfect swimmer physique,' she giggles childishly. 'He put so much energy into me. In every aspect: diet, technique, mental health, everything. And it did me some good. I won a medal. But I got a shoulder injury that I just couldn't shake. I lost my form, stopped going to training, got a boyfriend and knuckled down to my exams.'

'Martyn must have missed you?'

'Yes, he did. He kept on trying to persuade me to go back. It was very sweet of him,' she says, smiling fondly and here is my biggest warning yet to tread carefully. There's no way I can go straight in and ask if he abused her. She'll get defensive, especially if she doesn't think it was abuse, and she'll close this conversation down quicker than you can say "gift card". Thankfully there's more than one way to skin a cat.

'There's a suggestion,' I begin, choosing my words wisely, 'that Martyn and Amanda might have had a relationship several years before. At the time, Amanda would have been 15 and Martyn would have been a young newly qualified PE teacher. They obviously chose to keep the relationship quiet, which is understandable considering the age difference.'

Heather nods her understanding.

'This relationship ended at some point. Both Amanda and Martyn married other people, had a family, but it appears they kept in contact and some twenty years later were still close. Hence the reason he is a line of enquiry.'

'I see,' Heather replies. 'I last saw Martyn about three years ago. Bumped into him in The Grapes. It's a pub around the corner. He was with a swimming student then.'

'Good to know he's still coaching. He must have chlorine in his blood.' We both laugh. 'Was the student a lad?'

She shakes her head. 'A girl from St. Julia's too. I remember saying to her, "Watch him". Martyn's face was a picture. I don't think he knew what I was going to say. Cruel, I know. I told her that at times he's real drill sergeant. Like one of those you see in American war films, carrying a cane and shouting, "Sound off, one, two, three, four". Anyway, Martyn was so pleased to see me; it was like we'd never been apart. He asked how I'd been getting on. He even remembered that I liked ladybirds. I had a swimming costume covered in them. Wasn't allowed to compete in it sadly. Did Amanda swim? Is that how they met?'

'Her mother has told me that Amanda wasn't a swimmer, so I don't yet know how they met. I do know that Amanda didn't tell her husband about her friendship with Martyn. But sometimes people don't. You worry that your partner will disapprove of them, but sometimes it's nice to have a secret between friends.' And I think of me and Bronwyn. Are we having an affair? Is that what you'd call it? It sounds very clandestine, naughty and sexy. I'd much prefer to call it a relationship.

'That's true. I mean my mother would have gone up the wall if she knew Martyn took me for a drink after a session. Alcohol at 16! Or we'd just go for a drive, park up and talk. He was such a good listener.'

'You spoke about swimming, your parents?'

'Oh, everything. School, exams, boys..'

'You started to feel good about yourself?' She nods. 'All that swimming helped me lose a couple of stone, it toned my arms and legs. Suddenly, I was good-looking,' she announces.

'Boys at school told you that?'

She shakes her head. 'Martyn did,' she replies, lowering her voice conspiratorially.

Fucking hell, I think. I keep my face passive. I wait for her to continue, have a question ready in case she clams up. But she doesn't.

216

'He was always lovely to me.. Two days later he kissed me. Said he was falling for me. He was stuck in a miserable marriage with a cold-hearted wife. He told me they hadn't had sex in five years and that he needed to be loved. Five years! Can you believe it?'

I say nothing, tilt my head encouragingly.

'Martyn told me that I made him feel good about himself,' she confesses proudly. 'That made me feel powerful, like I could conquer anything: school, worries, swimming, love. Those feelings are amazing.'

'Yes, they are,' I agree, thinking of Bronwyn again.

'You don't think Martyn hurt Amanda, do you?' she asks, serious.

'Do you, Heather? Did he ever give you cause for concern?'

She shakes her head emphatically. 'Not at all. There's not a nasty bone in his body. He had so much patience and never shouted at me. I didn't even have to call him "sir". Unless he begged me to,' she laughs.

Oh God, I think. I've never been involved with investigations of sexual assault or rape, or even interviewed the victims when I was a copper. There are specialised units for that. But, if I've learned anything, it's surely that Martyn was grooming her so he could get his hands on her.

What a fucking piece of scum. Grooming young women, vulnerable in some cases, telling them they have potential, nurturing their skill, getting inside their heads, abusing them and then holding out a hand of eternal friendship, just in case one of them is tempted to make an allegation of sexual assault.

Is that what Amanda did? Made an allegation against him. Did she eventually work out what he'd done to her all those years ago, what he was still doing to her? Why he was still visiting her, being her friend? I wonder how she worked it out. Did she see something? Him talking to a teenage girl? This girl?

'Heather,' I begin, 'just one more thing. When Amanda did your hair that time, did you two talk? I know hairdressers like to chat.'

'Oh, yes, Amanda was really chatty. She was intrigued I was going to a prom. She said they didn't have them when she was at school. She asked if it would be like the American ones. You know, was a boy taking me? I said "no", that I did have a boyfriend, but he was older, and you could only go with boys from the school.'

'You didn't tell her it was Martyn?'

'God, no. Martyn told me to keep it a secret. I did tell her one thing though. I couldn't resist it. I mean, how would she ever find out it was him, right?'

'Right. What was it?'

'I told her he had a tattoo.' And she lays a hand on her upper chest, just under the clavicle. 'An eagle owl.'

There's a question for Shaun. As a male pupil, I wonder if Shaun has ever glimpsed his PE teacher take his top off. Bizarre maybe, but how else am I going to find out if it's true? I could ask Hepworth, I suppose. His reaction should answer it.

I thank Heather for her time and make my excuses. I exit the shopping mall and head back to the car. I may never know how Amanda met Martyn, unless I ever find her diary and what are the chances of that? Did he somehow find out Amanda documented their relationship? And where was he that day? Did he follow her to the city to demand the diary's destruction? Or instead, did he head to her empty house and begin his search?

I pay the extortionate car parking fee and jump into the Mazda. I want to head home first and freshen up. It's nearly noon and I don't want to lose a single second of being with Bronwyn.

Chapter 35

'Heather Hughes does not consider it abuse. She didn't come out and say they were having sex, but reading between the lines, it was certainly inappropriate behaviour. If we present that and Jake's account to Hepworth, he will tell us to fuck off. And I don't blame him. We need more. How we get it…I don't know,' I admit with frustration.

'I don't remember seeing Hepworth with a tattoo. He certainly wouldn't have taken his top off in front of us lads,' Shaun says.

'It doesn't prove that much really. He can easily explain a tattoo away; he's definitely not going to show it to us.'

'I don't want to see it,' Shaun replies, horrified.

I sit back in the chair exhausted. My mind tries once more to turn what we know over again but it feels like a wheel that's got something caught underneath it. It's no good. I look at the windows. Are they open? It's boiling in here. April is feeling like August on a Greek island. The long voiles Nisha hung in the windows to give the office some privacy from the building across the street, billow gently, moved by the cooling breeze. I could do with another shower, my third today, which teaches me the downside of having sex at lunchtime. As fantastic as it was, it doesn't half interrupt your day. Taking your mind off focus and putting it on something as far away from missing people as possible, and then you're thrust back into your day, hot and unable to concentrate.

Bronwyn had another meeting at 3pm. How can she sit in a room full of people talking about shoes? My mind keeps wandering back to our afternoon, hoping it'll happen again soon, hoping that she'll have some news later that Michael has been given the heave-ho. Somehow I don't think so.

'Why would Jake lie that he saw Hepworth leaving the salon?'

Shaun's question brings me back into the office.

'I suppose he might have been trying to deflect our attention off him,' I reply.

'He did admit he hated Amanda. And he has a bromance with David. I suppose he might have been assisting him. But why would David harm his wife?'

I throw my hands up. 'Shaun, he's living in her house. Mrs Davies hasn't asked him to leave. Plus once he's had Amanda presumed dead, he can get his hands on his share of the will. Even the small slice she bequeathed him. He's free to leave town with Jake and set up business and home together if they want. Maybe he didn't mean to kill her; or maybe they planned it from the start, the day he laid her floor. Now there's a thought.'

Shaun pulls a face. 'Sounds like something out of an Agatha Christie novel. I thought we were talking about Martyn Hepworth anyway.'

'Well, you brought Jake up. Not me. We need more dirt on Hepworth. Let's go back to David, have a look at those boxes in the loft. I'll text him, see when he's home.' I reach for my phone off the desk and type a quick message as Shaun collects the empty cups and heads off to put the kettle on.

I hear him banging the cupboard door as he takes out teabags, the sound of a teaspoon spooning sugar into the cups. As the kettle boils, he dawdles back down the corridor and leans against the doorjamb, frowning thoughtfully.

'If what Jake says *is* true, that Hepworth *was* coming out of the salon, what was he doing there? I don't mean talking to Amanda about whatever, but what was his "excuse"?'

'How do you mean?'

'Just say his wife is driving past at the exact moment he's leaving; when he gets home, she says, "Oh, honey, what were you doing coming out of a hairdressers?" A salon is a weird place for a forty-something male to be. And it's not exactly the sort of place where you can hide inside. It's got huge plate glass windows, brightly lit, pastel-coloured background. If he really didn't want to be seen there, he'd have snuck out the back way. He had to have had a reason for being there. A cover story. Oh, the kettle,' and he jogs down the corridor to deal with it.

I give it some thought. He could always say that he was enquiring about a haircut, or treating his wife to one. Hang on…what were Jake's exact words…I reach for the papers, sift through them. Shaun's notebook. He was making notes. He returns with the tea, a packet of custard creams tucked under his arm. I stand and take my tea off him, thrusting the llama notebook at him with the other hand. 'Find the notes from our chat with Jake.'

Shaun sits, balances the open book on his lap and flicks through the pages with a moistened fingertip. 'Here we are.'

'What time did Jake say he saw Hepworth?'

'Hmm…just said after hours. Why?'

'According to Holly, the salon only stayed open late on a Thursday, although Amanda often gave her clients later appointments on any day of the week. So was it a regular occurrence Hepworth popping in? And like you say, what was his reason?'

'What we know about Hepworth is that he remains friendly with his victims. It's his safety net. So we can assume he and Amanda were friends.'

'But if he was keeping this liaison from his wife, he'd need a reason. Neither the school or the pool are nearby; he doesn't live round the corner, so what else is close by?'

Shaun googles the street and reels off the amenities in the immediate area.

'Several pubs, couple of Indian restaurants, lots and lots of charity shops, a supermarket; they close at 9pm.'

'Bit late to go food shopping. Bit of a crap excuse too if there's a Spa or something round the corner when you urgently need a pint of milk.' I reach for my tea but a hard knock at the door makes me jump and hot liquid sloshes over the rim onto my hand.

'I'll get it,' Shaun says, passing me the box of tissues. I mop the mess up and throw the sodden tissues into the bin. What a time to interrupt a meeting. Afternoon cuppa. Some people have no respect.

'Er, Will,' Shaun says from the doorway, his voice hesitant.

'Er, Shaun,' I say, mimicking his unusual tone. 'What?'

'Charlie and Oliver are here to see us.'

I frown. What on earth for? What can they possibly want? 'Let me just….,' I say, gathering the MISPER file together and hiding it away. 'Show them in.'

'Take a seat, lads. Do you want a drink or anything?'

The two boys traipse nervously into the office, each looking at the other, each reluctant to go first. They're wearing shorts and t-shirts. Charlie has a rucksack over one shoulder, Oliver has a half-empty bottle of coke. They plonk down on the settee with a bounce and glance at each other. Shaun gives me a wide-eyed look over the tops of their heads and settles in a chair.

Shaun smiles at them, leans forward in his chair and says, 'It's a pleasant surprise seeing you both again. What can we do for you?'

Charlie coughs and, in a very nervous voice, says, 'When you came to my house to see my dad, I knew he wouldn't tell me what was going on. He and my mum have been talking a lot behind closed doors. When he told me to go away, I went upstairs to my room. It overlooks the front door. I heard what you said through the open window.'

Which is why Shaun was talking louder than normal; he knew Charlie was there.

'I don't think my dad hurt Ollie's mum and I don't know why he wouldn't help you. I rang Ollie and we both agreed that we should help you.'

'Do your parents know you're here?' I ask.

The boys shake their heads.

'They think we're down the park playing football,' Oliver explains. 'They wouldn't understand. Dad doesn't talk about Mum. It's like she doesn't exist. It's not fair. I want to know where she is.'

Charlie smiles sympathetically at his friend and turns to me. 'I had to do something. Ollie's my best friend.' He unzips his rucksack and removes several sheets of paper. 'I took it from Dad's filing cabinet, photocopied it on his printer.' He hands it to me. 'It's Dad's diary from the 14 to 16 October.'

I look at the paper. It's from an A4-sized diary, one of those hard-backed ones that are usually blue, where each day has its own page. Scribbled in large backwards slanting scrawl are the details of a job. Painting hall, landing and stairs, all woodwork, Mrs Valerie Tierney, 24 Grey Gate Close, Kelsall, and a mobile number. This is all Lawrence had to produce. So, why didn't he? Is he being deliberately awkward or is there a reason he doesn't want me to talk to his customer?

'The job was for three days,' Charlie points out. 'I haven't contacted the lady. Hope she still lives there.'

'The other sheet of paper,' Oliver says, 'is the receipt. She definitely paid Mr Hayden. And she'd have only done that if he completed the work.'

I sift through the paper. It is a receipt indeed. In the same scrawl are the words: Paid in full, dated 18th October, paid by bank transfer. I pass the sheets to Shaun who studies them with interest.

'Have you found any sign of my mum yet?' Oliver asks, nervously playing with the coke bottle.

'It's ongoing, Oliver. I'm only permitted to discuss my findings so far with your nan. Have you seen her lately?'

'No. Dad never has the time to take me.'

'She doesn't live far from you. He could see you safely on the train, get your nan to pick you up the other end. I know she still drives and I'm sure Charlie would make the trip with you. Right Charlie?'

Charlie grins. 'My mum could take us to the station, Ollie.'

'I appreciate your sleuthing efforts, boys,' I tell them sincerely. 'This is a massive help.'

'There is something else,' Charlie begins, adjusting his spectacles. 'I heard Mum mention it to Dad last night. They were sat in the garden; they didn't see me in the kitchen. But on the 19th October, that year, Uncle Nathan tried to kill himself.'

'Do you think that had something to do with my mum?' Oliver asks and I can see by the way he's gripping the bottle neck that this lad is so close to the edge. I feel sad for him. How can any of us know what he's going through?

'I don't know, Oliver. But if it has a bearing on it, then I will find out. I promise. You know, you two should be out in that sunshine, making the most of the Easter holidays.'

'It feels like we've been off school for ages,' Charlie complains. 'I can't wait to go back.'

'Kerry says when I turn 16, I've got to get a job. She says there's nothing wrong with pushing trolleys or stacking shelves,' Oliver tells us and I can picture that exact scene. 'That's how she started at Asda. Straight out of school, on the till, her dad picking her up from her shift.'

School leavers, sixteen, trolleys and supermarkets…suddenly I look at Shaun and, judging by the way he turns to me, we've both had the exact same thought.

'How old is his eldest child?' I demand, referring to Hepworth.

Shaun grabs the notebook, flicks frantically through the pages. 'Here it is. Sarah. She was seventeen at the time.'

'Ideal age to be working in a supermarket. Possibly hasn't passed her test yet which means she's reliant on her parents for a lift.'

'And it's over the road.'

I grin. 'That's it; that's what he'd say if he was ever questioned. I was picking my daughter up.'

Charlie and Oliver are frowning at each other in confusion. I stand, signalling it's time the boys headed home. I thank them again, encourage Oliver to contact his nan.

We need to get on. We need to find this daughter of Hepworth's and I need to get in that loft.

Isn't Hepworth in for a nasty surprise?

Chapter 36

Amanda's loft is tidy and organised. The heat of yet another warm day has risen and is now trapped under this ceiling. Sweat runs down my back, glueing my clothes to my skin.

The loft is only partially boarded so I tread carefully, moving the white light from the heavy-duty torch over the objects. A long box, sealed with brown tape; a product sticker on the side indicates this is the Christmas tree. Nearby boxes with "Xmas Decs" written on the lids are self-explanatory. I wonder if, each year, David hauls this box down and puts up the tree or whether he doesn't bother. Personally, I think sticking a tree up in your lounge for one day or twelve days, depending on your tradition, is a waste of time but I keep my opinion to myself or risk being called a misery guts.

Two plastic boxes with tightly sealed lids are empty.

'David!' I hear the sound of his boots on the metal rungs of the loft ladder as he climbs up and sticks his upper body through the hatch.

'Yeah? You found anything?'

'These plastic boxes. What was in them?'

'Oliver's baby clothes. I gave them to Kerry when she found out she was having a boy.'

'Very kind of you,' I say.

'I'd like to think it's what Amanda would've done.' He grins. 'But it probably wouldn't have been.'

I silently agree and wonder if Kerry dressed her noisy kid in them or whether she threw them away in disgust. I move onto two black bin liners, their tops in tight knots. I look at David who remains watching me.

'Brewing equipment I don't use anymore,' he explains. 'The other contains old bedroom curtains. Amanda changed the decor when I moved in. She asked me what colour I preferred.' He shrugs. 'Like I cared.'

'Have you got rid of any of her stuff?' I ask, lifting the flaps on an unsealed box. A dinner service decorated with fruit traditionally found in a bowl. Must be one of those things your gran passes down the generations, never seeing a scrap of food, just confined to a box in a female relative's loft.

'No. It's not my stuff to get rid of. I asked Jean if she wanted any of it, but she said she had enough junk in her own house.'

225

I move onto two boxes, stacked on top of each other. The flaps are unsealed, the tape torn off and curled over like an animal's tale. The first box is half empty and contains old exercise books and assorted papers. Must be the rifled through box mentioned in the MISPER file. I position the torch so its beam points down into the box and begin sifting through the books.

'If it's easier,' David offers, 'I can bring the box down.'

'Yeah, you know it might be. It's boiling up here.' I fold the flaps over and test the weight of it. Fairly light. Carefully, I manoeuvre it through the hatch where David grips it and steadily reverses down the ladder. I look inside the second box. It contains clothes. I lift an item out. A blue vest top with a row of little embroidered flowers around the neckline. I check the size. Aged 13. I rummage through the neatly folded clothes and find a teddy bear missing an eye, a hard-backed Beano annual, rolled-up posters, the sort a teenage girl might put on her bedroom walls. The elastic band securing them is brittle so I leave it alone, taking a chance she hasn't defaced a pop star's face with Hepworth's.

When my fingers hit the cardboard base, I hastily put the stuff back and descend the ladder. David has placed the box I gave him on the bed in the spare room, on top of a bath towel, and waits for me, chewing his fingernail.

I open the box flaps. 'Take an item,' I tell him. 'I'm looking for any reference to a friend, female or male Amanda had when she was between 15 and 17.'

'What, like a photo or something?'

'Anything,' I tell him, choosing an exercise book. It's from her maths class and helpfully has the year written in it. She was 15. I flick through the pages hoping to see a love heart with AD 4 MH 4eva scrawled in it, but no such luck. Slowly, we start to pile discarded items on the bed. Woven coloured friendship bracelets, more exercise books containing absolutely nothing revealing. My heart leaps with excitement when I spy a Valentine's Day card. It's very pink and soppy…and uselessly contains no sender's name, just a question mark. The handwriting looks too childish to be from an adult male. But she kept it. Unless it was her first ever Valentine's card.

I move on. Brittle plastic wallets containing letters from college, confirming her place on a hairdressing course; GCSE certificates; MOT certificates for a Mini, obviously her first car; a photo of a teenage Amanda with a mixed-race girl, no name or date on the back.

I pass it to David, who looks up from an exercise book. 'Could that be Holly?'

He studies it. 'Yeah…there's the earring in the top of her ear.' He taps the picture with a finger. 'I'll show her that.' He smiles, puts it on the windowsill behind him.

A little gold-coloured box reveals a dried flower inside, nestling in tissue. Nothing scrawled on the box sides. Was it from a bouquet? Underneath the tissue is a tiny red bow, exactly like the kind sewn onto women's lingerie. A present from a boyfriend?

The bigger box is emptying rapidly and only a few items remain. Foreign coins: franc and lire; a pencil, one end chewed, the name of a museum written in gold letters down its length; a pen with a wobbly kitten on its top; heart-shaped notebook, its pages containing an exam timetable.

I remove the last item and resist the urge to swear. David looks at me, puzzled.

'Find anything interesting?' he asks.

I shake my head. 'Not what I was hoping for.' Shit. Another fruitless search.

'Hang on,' he says. 'What's that?' He reaches into the box, lifts the bottom flap and removes a small white envelope, which can only be seen from his position. Amanda's name is written on the front, followed by a trio of hearts which rise to the far right corner like the tail of a kite. He hands it to me and I open it. It's a card like those you get with bouquets. On the front is a large pink and sparkly number 16. A sprinkling of glitter sticks to my fingers and I wipe them on the edge of the box. I open the card. Could the bow be from the present that came with this card?

I don't read aloud the words.

"To my sexy sweet sixteen Amanda. Wear this for me tonight. Now, we're legal! Yours forever, Marty. xx"

'What is it?' David asks.

Hepworth bought her lingerie and she kept the card and cut off the bow as a memento. Legal can only mean one thing. Consensual age of sex. He was having sex with her before she was 16. It's certainly enough to goad him with.

'Will?'

I have no choice but to show the card to David. Why shouldn't he know the kind of person his PE teacher was? What was done to his wife? I hand it over and he reads it aloud and, in his voice, Hepworth's words sound demanding and sinister.

'Who's Marty?'

227

'Martyn Hepworth.'

He laughs. 'What, the PE teacher?'

I nod. Let my confirmation hang in the air. David's expression changes and the reality of the card sinks in.

'They were seeing each other when she was only sixteen?'

I shake my head. 'When she was younger. I suspect she lied about her age; he took advantage of her.'

David shakes his head, his anger brewing. 'How did you know about this?'

'Jake told me. He saw Martyn leaving the salon late one night.'

'What the fuck? Really? He never told me that and he's meant to be my fucking mate. Fuck's sake…you think you know someone. Do you think Hepworth knows something about Amanda's disappearance?'

I shrug. 'I don't know, David, but I needed something to prod him with…'

'And this'll do nicely?' he says scornfully.

'It will indeed,' I say regretfully.

*

With no time like the present and armed with the information gleaned from our teatime searching and interviewing, Shaun and I pay Hepworth a visit. He lives in an affluent area of Lexington in a nice detached house with a large front garden containing mature trees and shrubs. The block-paved drive is big enough to house more than the three cars parked on it. There's a double garage, the door of which is open and a young man in his late teens is winding a long red cable around his bent elbow. Nearby is a lawn mower, a green wheelie bin stands with its lid open. I park up against the kerb, just past the house, facing the way out. I look back at the lad.

'Know him?'

'Hepworth's eldest son,' Shaun replies with disdain. 'He went to the grammar school. Up his own arse, according to Sarah.'

'She certainly has it in for the male members of her family.' I unclip my seatbelt, open the door. 'Let's go, Bad Cop.'

Shaun laughs and follows me down the path to Hepworth's house. The son is pulling the garage door down and locking it.

'Hello,' I call out, my tone friendly. 'Is Martyn Hepworth home?'

He turns, straightens up, already on the defensive. He's Shaun's height but well-built, with strong arms and legs. His chin flicks up. 'Who wants to know?'

I bet he's one of those lads who, in a pub, is all mouth, but when someone offers to take him outside, he cowers behind his mates. Unless I'm judging him wrong. I make the introductions and show him my ID card. He tries to study it but it's too far away for him to read the small writing, unless he's got exceptionally good eyesight.

'What's it about?'

'It's a matter I'm sure Mr Hepworth will rather discuss with us. Is he home?' I jerk my thumb at the house and set off down the drive. Hepworth Junior leaps into action like a steeplechaser, jumping over a white-flowered plant in a decorative half-barrel and hurrying towards the house, throwing open the front door and shouting, 'Dad!' at the top of his voice in a panicked tone.

I find great amusement in people's reaction to a Private Investigator calling by. It's much the same reaction as when the police come round. They're in a state of panicked fear, completely unaware that I have none of the powers the police have. Which is a crying shame at times; it'd make my job a lot easier if I could throw my hostile suspects into a windowless room for a few hours.

Hepworth comes to the door, quick-smart, laughing at his son's odd behaviour. 'It's alright, son, I'll deal with it. Go and give your brother a hand with dinner. Evening,' he says to us with a big smile. 'How can I help?'

He's aged. I've only ever seen newspaper photos of him, which nearly always make you look good unless you're a criminal under arrest. Hepworth reminds me of retired ex-footballers you often see doing punditry on Sky Sports: podgy and wrinkled, who still think they've got the fitness of a twenty year old. Those who think swapping pasta and salad for kebabs and beer still means they've got what it takes.

Hepworth's hair is grey like wolf's fur and he's unshaven. He has a paunch which pushes against his black t-shirt. There's an emblem in the top left corner. Two arms, bent at angles, sticking out of three wavy lines, presumably denoting swimming pool water. I wonder if he's been coaching today and who might be the pupil. I wonder if he's still grooming. But then why wouldn't he? He has no reason to fear being caught. Or so he thinks.

'I know you.' He gestures at Shaun.

If I had a quid every time someone has said that during this investigation.

'Shaun Hock,' he replies with a tight smile.

'Yeah. I seem to remember you didn't much like PE. Nearly every rugby game, you'd be sat on the sidelines with your excuse note.'

'Rugby isn't everybody's cup of tea,' I point out. 'Cricket was my game. Hated swimming. Sorry, I know it's your forte. Hated getting my hair wet.'

Hepworth's grin shrinks. 'So, what do you want?' he asks me, assuming I'm the lead investigator.

'We're investigating the disappearance of Amanda Davies,' Shaun tells him.

Hepworth swings his gaze to Shaun, gives a little shake of the head as if to say "never heard of her". But then, as a lifelong paedophile, he's learnt to hide his reactions. 'Don't know her. How am I supposed to know her? Are you sure you've got the right Martyn Hepworth?' he says arrogantly.

'I'm quite sure. Amanda was the owner of the Colour and Curl Hair Studio in Lexington. She was married to David Bywater, one of your past pupils. She went missing six and a half years ago.'

'Christ. You can't expect me to recall every single lad I've taught PE. There's thousands of kids,' he laughs. 'And I don't know this hair salon. Curly what? I wouldn't be seen dead in a hairdressers. I shave my own head.'

Could he be any more of a man's man?

'Perhaps you remember David's friend: Jake Bunby.'

'Who? The crippled lad? I read about his windfall in the paper. He was another one who'd do anything to get out of physical activity, the irony being that now he can hardly walk. I haven't seen him for years and I don't know Amanda Davidson. I'm sorry I can't help you. But it was nice meeting you.'

It's a tired old trick deliberately getting names and places wrong that you've only just heard. Makes you look guilty rather than having a poor memory.

'During the investigation Jake told us that he witnessed you exiting Amanda's salon, which has been confirmed by Sarah Hepworth, your daughter.'

Nice touch reminding him he has a daughter and one he's estranged from.

'I know who she is,' Hepworth sneers and obviously his daughter is a wound he doesn't want prodding. Best prod away then. 'I don't know why either of them would tell you that.'

'Why would either of them lie?' I ask. 'What have Sarah and Jake got to gain by telling us a complete fabrication?'

'He's a troublemaking little drug dealer, that's why. As for Sarah…well, she has her own axe to grind.'

Shaun used Facebook to stalk Sarah Hepworth, discovering that she moved to Liliton to run an animal sanctuary. He sent her a message and, within the hour, they were chatting on the phone. A few years ago, Sarah dropped out of university, abandoning her biology degree when she met someone who changed her life. She fell in love with a woman and, when she told her family, she quickly discovered that her father was homophobic. Lucky for us that she does have an axe to grind. She was quite prepared to answer all of Shaun's questions.

'When she worked part-time at Tesco, you would pick her up from work, but you wouldn't be waiting in the car park. Your car was in the nearby high street and many times she would find you in Amanda's salon. Obviously she asked how you knew Amanda, concerned that you were having an affair behind her mother's back, and your reply was, and I quote "We're old friends, we go way way back". Now, do you remember Amanda Davies? I have her picture here if you think it might jog your memory.'

Hepworth snorts, his eyes narrow menacingly.

Shaun continues. 'Jake Bunby witnessed you leaving Amanda's salon a couple of days before she went missing and that the atmosphere between you was not friendly. What did you argue about?'

'I don't recall,' he replies.

'Okay. What did the two of you talk about when you visited her?'

He shrugs. 'I don't recall.' Which is as annoying as "No comment".

'The past?' I suggest.

He looks at me, says nothing.

'What was the nature of your relationship with Amanda?' Shaun asks.

'I was not banging her,' Hepworth states forcibly.

'Not then, but in the past, you were,' Shaun tells him.

'What? What did you say, you little poof? I did—'

'Whoa,' I say, holding out hand. 'There's no need for offensive name calling.'

'What? He just accused me of screwing a woman I don't know…'

'He's not accusing you of screwing a "woman". He's accusing you of abusing her when she was fifteen. Big difference.'

'What?' Hepworth's eyes widen until they look like they could pop. 'What the fuck? How dare you come to my house and make this unfounded allegation—'

'It's not unfounded, Mr Hepworth,' Shaun says, calmly. 'We spoke to Heather Hughes.'

He freezes, doesn't blink.

'She's a right little chatterbox,' I tell him. 'She sat me down in the little office in her adorable gift shop and told me all about her ladybird swimming costume and how you liked her to call you "sir". She told me about your tattoo. Here,' and I lay a hand under my left clavicle, 'of an eagle owl. Sarah confirmed the tattoo. Heather told me how you plied her with alcohol, told her some pitiful story about your wife refusing to have sex with you and how the two of you would have sex in your car. I know your game plan is always to remain friendly with your victims. That way you're almost guaranteed their silence. You did it with Amanda. And it worked for several years. Until something changed.'

Hepworth stares in horror, shakes his head in denial. 'I don't know what you're talking about,' he replies weakly. 'No idea at all.'

I look at Shaun and nod. He reaches into his pocket for a small laminated piece of paper. It's not the original, but a photocopy of Martyn's card. Shaun hands it to Hepworth.

He studies it, his expression changes. Clearly he remembers it, can't understand why we have it. If he managed to get into Amanda's house and into the loft, which is easy enough, he's thinking "Why did I miss this?" If he hasn't got the diary, is he wondering if I have it?

'I found it in a box in her loft.'

He thrusts the card back, gives us the only explanation he can. 'That could be anyone called Marty.'

'We know it was you. We think you argued with Amanda about her teenage diary which documented your abuse in probably extensive detail. We think that, whilst she was at the trade fair in the city, you took the opportunity to search her house which was empty all day. And when you couldn't find the diary, you had no choice but to silence the author. What have you done with Amanda?'

232

'You've got to be fucking kidding me?' Hepworth explodes. 'Are you accusing me of murder now?'

'Where were you on the 15th October? The day she went missing,' I demand.

'How the fuck should I know?' he shouts.

'Dad,' a tentative voice says.

We all stop. Hepworth turns back into the hall, mutters a few sharp words to the child and steps outside, closing the door behind him.

'I don't know where I was. Do you know where you were? Eh? Do you?' he shouts, spittle flying out of his mouth.

'I was at school,' Shaun replies, his voice calm. 'And, as it was a Wednesday, I had geography and double maths. I hated Wednesdays. And the days I had PE.'

'Perhaps you could look at an old timetable,' I suggest. 'Or ask a colleague. I need to know what you were doing until the early evening.'

'And why the fuck should I help you?'

'Mr Hepworth, you're helping yourself. Have a think. Here's my card.' I hold it out to him. He doesn't take it so I let it fall to the ground. 'Let me know. It's better that you talk to me. If I don't hear from you, say by tomorrow night, I'll be giving this information to the police. As an ex-police officer, I know there's enough here to warrant a chat with you.'

'You fucking pair of bastards,' he swears.

I touch Shaun's arm, nod at the drive. We turn, stroll away.

'What?' Hepworth is shouting. 'Mind your own fucking business, you nosy bitch.'

I glance back. He's yelling at a neighbour, spoiling the quiet affluent residential area. What a bloody hooligan. I'd certainly say his high standing in the community has been reduced by several notches.

Chapter 37

'A friend recommended Lawrence Hayden. Angela Newman, lives on Drummond Avenue.' Mrs Tierney offers me a biscuit from the plate.

'Thanks,' I say, sliding a chocolate-covered digestive off. Hang on, I think, the biscuit poised between my teeth. Drummond Avenue? Where David lives? I ask her what number and she tells number 13. David's next-door neighbour.

'Had Mr Hayden done work for Mrs Newman?'

'From what I remember, she and Bob had asked him to quote for some work but for reasons unknown they didn't hire him. You'll have to ask Angela.' Mrs Tierney frowns and lifts the cup to her mouth but, like me, holds the cup mid-air as a thought strikes her. 'She said she felt sorry for him. Which made me feel obliged to hire him.'

Which is an interesting comment I must ask Mrs Newman about.

Valerie Tierney was Lawrence's customer the day Amanda went missing. When I called round to her house, she was on the doorstep of her neighbour's with an Amazon parcel under her arm. She called out to me across the laurel hedge and raced round when I said I was a Private Investigator with a couple of questions. She dumped the parcel on the bottom stair, sat me in the conservatory and made coffee.

Mrs Tierney is a tall woman, in her late sixties with dyed black hair and plenty of tastefully applied makeup. On the wicker shelving unit are dozens of framed photographs of her family: lots of children, twice as many grandchildren, ranging from babies to small kids and graduates.

The ceiling fan is gently rotating warm air over my head and the wicker chair with its floral cushion is so comfortable. I've never considered conservatories before but I reckon, if I could ever afford one, I'd get a lot of use out of it.

'Her recommendation made you phone Mr Hayden?' I ask, steering the conversation back on track.

'My usual decorator had hurt his back and I wanted the work done quickly. Lawrence's quote to wallpaper the hall, landing and stairs and gloss all the woodwork was very reasonable. He said it would take three days, longer if I wanted him to strip the old paper off. I got my sons to do that bit,' she grins.

I smile. 'That's what we're here for.'

'He worked all day on the Tuesday, made a good start too, and it looked promising that he'd be done in three days. But on the Wednesday morning, he explained that there'd been a family crisis and he needed to leave at lunchtime. He'd only be a couple of hours and would be back late afternoon to carry on with the work. I assumed it was one of his children. I've got four so I know full well how they can turn your day upside down, but it was his brother.' Mrs Tierney gasps. Evidently it still surprises her. 'I remember wondering what kind of a crisis an adult brother would cause. Unless he had special needs. He was very apologetic but the tone suggested he had little choice in it.'

'Did Lawrence come back?' I ask.

'He did not.' And that still annoys her. 'I was most vexed. I never heard a word from him until the next morning when he showed up about 11o'clock.' She reaches for the coffee pot, tops our cups up. 'If the house wasn't in such a mess, Mr Bailey, I'd have fired him. Rolls of wallpaper everywhere, dust sheets on the floor, half a bucket of that gloopy stuff they slap on the paper and that bloody table thing. I could have screamed.'

'Why was he so late? What was the excuse?'

'Apparently,' she begins in a tone that suggests she doesn't believe a word of it, 'he'd had a long drive and didn't get back until late and slept in. What could I do? I was beholden to him to finish the job. And in fairness, he worked hard all day without a break but it was obvious he wasn't going to finish it on time. Very annoying.'

I nod in agreement. 'The work spilled over into a fourth day?'

'Yes and that's why I remember it so well. I was going away on the Friday and didn't want to cancel my sister again. One of my sons stayed here to oversee the work. I couldn't leave Mr Hayden in my house alone.'

'Rightly so,' I agree. 'Did he give any other details of this crisis?'

'No. I asked if his brother was alright and he muttered something like, "He'll have to get on with it. Like the rest of us". Something like that. I wish I could remember, Mr Bailey,' she says, frustrated.

'You've done an excellent job so far, Mrs Tierney. This long drive he'd done, did he happen to say where it had been to?'

She smiles. 'Yes, because I asked. I suppose I didn't quite believe his tale. I expected him to fumble a made-up answer but he didn't, plus it's somewhere I know. My late husband and I stayed there on our way back from a holiday in Scotland. Trindle. Do you know it?'

Trindle. Lawrence's hometown. What's in Trindle, because Nathan isn't? He's serving life not that far from Lexington, which is why Lawrence moved here, to be closer to him. Probably the worst mistake he made. I wonder if he's still at Nathan's beck and call like he was back then. Why go back up north? According to previous newspaper reports on the trial, their dad died years before and their mother moved away to be closer to her sisters. Perhaps he has other family up there. People from his wife's side of the family, cousins, friends. But if the crisis involved Nathan, had he asked Lawrence to travel all those miles back home? Did Nathan have unfinished business? Who's up there that Nathan knows? The obvious choice is his ex-wife. She chose to stay in Trindle because, again according to reports, what little family she had left, were there.

Could Lawrence have driven to see her, on behalf of Nathan who was having a crisis? There's no way I can drive three hours up there to ask her that.

'Another biscuit?' Mrs Tierney asks, holding out the plate.

'Don't mind if I do. Your friend, Angela Newman, is she at home in the day?'

'I'll ring her if you want. It's no problem. And if you're going, you couldn't take the NEXT catalogue with you, could you?'

*

'It was very embarrassing,' Mrs Newman explains, wiping her nose on a tissue which she shoves back up her cardigan sleeve. 'Mr Hayden was a nice man, and it was a very reasonable quote. A lot cheaper than others we'd had. My husband wanted to wait until after dinner to phone Mr Hayden. But there was a knock at the door. It was Amanda.'

'Why didn't you tell Lawrence there and then you wanted him to do the work? '

'It's what men do, isn't it? They let workmen stew.'

Yeah, I silently agree. It's what my dad would have done. The complete opposite of what my mum does.

Mrs Newman is around the same age as Mrs Tierney but not as glamorous. Shorter, dumpier, wearing a flowery skirt and white lace top. Her short hair is steel-grey. We sit in her cosy living room with pastel-coloured country scenes on the walls and lemon-coloured cushions.

'Are you sure you don't want a drink, Mr Bailey?'

'I'm sure, thank you. Your lovely friend Valerie plied me with enough coffee to keep me awake for a week.'

Mrs Newman smiles fondly. 'We lost our husbands within twelve months of each other. I really must ask if she's free for lunch. So, yes, Amanda. She knocked the door asked to speak to both of us, which I thought was very ominous.'

'What was she like as a neighbour?'

Mrs Newman ponders her answer. 'Pleasant enough. Always said hello, how are you? Her little boy was sweet. Very polite.'

'What about David?'

Her smile broadens. 'He's a lovely man too. They made an unusual but nice-looking couple. He's been wonderful since I've been on my own, doing little jobs, bringing the bin round, keeping a general eye on things. I shall miss him when he goes.'

'He's going somewhere?' I ask.

'Well, I know he's applying for a presumption of death. I assume he'll be moving out and on.'

'Let's come back to David in a minute. What did Amanda say?'

'She asked if we'd hired Mr Hayden. When we said it was for a quote, she said, "Thank God" and explained that he was refurbishing the salon but she'd had to fire him after just an hour because of his dangerous and incompetent workmanship. She didn't go into huge detail but she'd caught him cutting a dangerous corner which could have resulted in a support wall coming down and causing thousands of pounds worth of damage. Bob wasn't convinced, but he mentioned it to our son and he said we shouldn't touch Mr Hayden with a bargepole. He offered to pay for new fencing but it meant we had to go with my son's choice of workman.'

'You've regretted it since?' I ask, gently.

She nods. 'Which is why I suggested Mr Hayden to Valerie to do her decorating.'

'Did you phone Lawrence to tell him you were going elsewhere? How did he take it?'

'Bob phoned him. Lawrence was very gracious about it.'

'Did Lawrence know Amanda was behind your decision?'

'How would he know she'd been around?'

'Lawrence confronted Amanda outside the school a couple of weeks later. There was a great deal of animosity between them. What do you remember about the day Amanda went missing?'

Angela sips her tea. 'Both her and David left early. Neither vehicle was on the drive, which was part of the plan. By plan, I mean, that was the first day of our fence work. Amanda said it was okay if the workmen wanted to park their van on her drive, as long as they promised to be gone by 6, when David returned from work. They weren't coming until eleven, you see. But there was a problem with a couple of the posts being the wrong size or something, so they stayed longer than 6. I was in a right tizz because David was due back and I didn't want him to be unable to park his van...'

I frown. 'What time did David get back?'

'I'm not sure, Mr Bailey. Not by the time the men went and that was 6.30 because it was dark out. I can't be sure. Our lounge is on the back of the house, you see. But David knocked our door about half 7, asking if Amanda had been home at all; she was late and he hadn't heard from her.'

Very interesting indeed. Seems David and his little friend, Jake, have been lying to the police and me. He wasn't at home until much later. So where were they both?

'Oh, there is one other thing,' Mrs Newman says.

I raise an eyebrow.

'One of the other reasons the workmen parked on her drive was to get access from her garden. But around one o'clock, one of the workmen said he'd seen David at the house, spoke to him as he left through the backdoor.'

'He came home?'

She shakes her head. 'He couldn't have. His van wasn't out front. I know because Bob and I were tidying the front garden ready for winter. The description the workmen gave in no way matched David.'

'Who did it match?'

'No one I recognise. The stranger was at least 15 years older than David and had grey hair and wore a tracksuit. The workman said the man looked like—'

'A PE teacher?' I suggest.

She smiles. 'A non-league football coach, he said.'

Close enough, I think.

Chapter 38

I lean on the work surface, chin resting in my palm as my mind plays over the phone call I received just as I was leaving the office. Bronwyn is at the stove, stirring something in a pan, keeping an eye on the oven, sipping wine and talking nonsense. Well, it could be interesting, but it's definitely not as interesting as what I've just been told.

Mr Beattie, purveyor of professional hairbrushes, was one of the traders who had a stall at the trade fair Amanda attended. His name was in the MISPER file as someone who had spoken to her that day. He was one of the first people I'd spoken to after receiving the file and he had nothing new to add. Amanda seemed happy enough, he didn't know her all that well, but they chatted about business, brushes, and family life. Oddly, though, she hadn't told him of her recent marriage and this surprised Mr Beattie.

Why? Did she not feel married that day? Didn't she want to talk about David? And was that because they'd had another row, which David is denying like he's denying his whereabouts the day his wife went missing? The plot is thickening. And doing my head in.

Today's chat is a lot more interesting than the first. Mr Beattie's colleague had just returned from a two week cruise to the Baltics, and after he told her about the reopening of Amanda's case, she reminded him of that other thing, which he promptly got onto the phone to me about. It appears that Amanda wasn't the only familiar face he saw that day.

He saw Tamsin.

'At the trade fair? Are you quite sure?'

'As sure as a brush is a brush.' He laughed. 'She was stood in the queue for a coffee. I'd recognise that pretty face anywhere.'

Not sure he'd recognise her now, but I'd kept quiet.

'I said "hello" and she said she was looking for Amanda but had lost her in the crowd.'

Which completely and utterly blows her "I was hungover and shagged out" alibi clean out of the water and means I'm going to have to pay Tamsin another visit. I could send Shaun. He's back in for a couple of hours in the morning before he returns to the pub for a long shift. Now he's mobile, the extra money is coming in handy for fuel as he tanks it around town in his boy racer.

I have so much I need to do. If I was at home, I'd have all our notes laid out on the bed and floor; I'd be making a plan on who I need to visit, what I need to ask, what I…

240

Bronwyn's voice snaps me out of my daydream. I blink at her.

'What?'

She smiles. 'I was going to ask if you want another drink, but you haven't touched that one,' and she indicates the beer glass close to my right elbow.

'Sorry, Bron. My mind was elsewhere.' I sip the beer, but the head has flattened.

'Do you want another? You are staying tonight, aren't you? I've made up the spare bed.'

But my mind has already wandered back to Tamsin and is asking if 8am is too early to knock her front door.

'Spare bed?' I repeat dumbly.

She laughs, opens a cupboard above her head and noisily pulls two dinner plates out from underneath a stack.

'What are you cooking?' I ask. 'You said it was a surprise.'

'Can't you smell what it is?'

I sniff the air. It smells spicy, of cardamom, coriander and garlic. Some Thai dish maybe. I step closer. The lid is on the pan, hiding the surprise. I move the tea towel across to peer through the glass door of the oven. A baking tray with two palm-sized circles on it. Are they —?

I look at her and she's grinning. 'Any idea?'

'A flat toad-in-the-hole?'

She lifts the pan lid, releasing an unmistakable fragrance. I breathe it in. It smells fantastic and it's making my empty stomach growl with hunger.

'I never thought in a million years, you'd be cooking a curry.'

'I never thought I would either. Nisha gave me the recipe. She promised it was really easy to make; she even gave me the spices.' And Bron picks up a little glass jar containing tiny black seeds. 'I decided it was high time I ate what all the fuss is about. I hope you realise this is all for you.'

I smile and step closer, pushing all thoughts of liars and deceivers out of my mind. 'One day, Bron, you'll make someone a lovely wife.'

She plays along. 'You think? I'm handy with an iron too.'

'All you need now is Mr Right.'

'I think I might have already found him.'

It's always the way she looks at me, her eyes shining with playfulness; her voice flirty yet half-serious, that makes me doubt. Her words mean so much to me, but her actions could mean everything.

This "affair" because that's what it is, doesn't feel permanent, ever-lasting. I swing from feeling so confident about her, that there's an "us" in the near future, to feeling that this is just something to be enjoyed in the short-term, a kind of make the most of it fling. Sex in the afternoon, a romantic curry, an overnight stay, hardly screams happy ever after. I know I can't keep this up forever. Not much longer if I'm honest. My heart yearns so much when I see her, touch her, but at the same time, it feels so fragile, like it could crumble in my chest. But then, if I'm falling in love with her, that would explain my emotions.

I give the only answer I feel like giving. 'Best let him know then. I'll set the table.' I yank the drawer open, grab the cutlery and march to the dining room table. She's already put the placemats out, folded two napkins, put a tulip from the ones I bought in a vase in the centre of the table. I feel like a thoroughly ungrateful bastard, wanting more, not getting it and sulking about it. Today was Michael's hospital visit. She hasn't said anything about it so I know she hasn't dumped him. Is the curry to make up for her cowardice? Why can't she do the deed? Is it really that hard to tell him it's over? Has he threatened to harm himself if she does it? Claire would've dumped him months and months ago, probably after their first date. I know I shouldn't compare Bron to her, but this is so frustrating.

I finish putting the cutlery out, return to the kitchen to find her chopping coriander on a board with a wickedly sharp butcher's knife. Let's see if this spurs some reaction from her.

'Michael confronted me.' She looks up, the knife mid-chop. 'When I called in to see you at work. He waited for me in the lobby.'

'What?' Her forehead creases with anger.

'He told me you're in love with each other and my presence was confusing you. He warned me to back off.'

She laughs. 'What a load of crap. What did you say?'

'That I would only leave you alone if you asked me to.'

'I won't be doing that, not when I've waited three months to be with you. Michael only loves himself. He's one of the most self-centred people I've ever met. And I certainly don't—'

I interrupt. 'How did his hospital visit go? Did they probe his brain with one of those metal sticks with a hook on the end?'

She laughs. 'You mean a leucotome?'

'If that's what it's called.'

'I looked lobotomies up on Wiki. He didn't say very much. Complained how claustrophobic the MRI scanner was, how they'd drained him of so much blood that there wasn't enough to go around his body which is why he felt tired and lightheaded. I tried to talk to him.'

'Oh, yeah?' I say, stepping closer.

'Yes. I said that I'd been thinking about our future and that I didn't think we were compatible in the long run.'

'Short and sweet. What did he say?'

She pulls a face. 'Unfortunately, just before I started my speech, the office phoned and I was on the hands-free for a good ten minutes. He must've fallen asleep.'

'Was he putting it on?'

She shrugs. 'His snoring sounded genuine to me. No sooner had I pulled up outside his house and elbowed him, sharply I might add, than he jumped out of the car, muttering something about having forty winks.'

'Fuck's sake,' I mutter. He had to have been pretending. I look at Bron as she sprinkles chopped coriander onto the curry. Why didn't she wake him up? Or make him stay in the car while she repeated her words? Why did she let him go? Why is she keeping me and him hanging on?

'Bron,' I begin, 'if Michael turned up here tonight, would you finish with him, in front of me?'

She thinks about it, presumably picturing his reaction, how he might sob, threaten to top himself, how he might promise to change, plead that he needs her.

She smiles confidently. 'Yes, I would.'

If only I had his mobile number.

*

Equally annoying, I have no idea what the passcode is to unlock Bronwyn's phone so I can't even use that to text and invite the needy bastard over. I should have paid more attention the last time I saw her using it. What a shit detective I am. To hide my frustration, I volunteer to

243

do all the washing and drying up. I leave her in the lounge with the rest of the wine and a TV programme about endangered shark species.

On the work surface behind me, my phone receives a text message. I slide the Marigolds off and reach for the phone. It's Shaun. He's excited about my news.

I can be in at 7.30 for a recap before we head off to see Tamsin.

I type a reply.

See you then!

I smile. This investigation really is picking up pace. What was Tamsin doing at the trade fair? What was so important that she couldn't wait until the next day to speak to Amanda? And why lie about…I lower the phone, tilt my head to the half-open door. Voices in the hall. She must have a friend on speakerphone. I step closer, listen. Unless it's a neighbour. I turn back to the washing-up and the dreaded pan.

I slip the gloves back on and reach for the dish brush when the door opens and Bronwyn hurries in, closing it noiselessly behind her.

I smile at her. 'Nearly done. Shall I put the kettle—?'

'Michael's here,' she whispers, angrily. 'I don't bloody believe it. He can't just turn up like this.'

Michael. My wish has come true and I didn't even have to do anything.

'What does he want?'

'I don't know. To tell me about yet another personal disaster he's having. I've told him you've come round for your tea. With any luck he won't stay long. Can you put the kettle on, Will?'

'Are you going to tell him?' I ask, sliding the gloves off again. She looks at me. 'That it's over. You said if he came round, then you would—'

'I know what I said, Will,' she snaps, throwing open the door and hurrying out.

I stare after her, my irritation starting to boil. Surely making him tea is encouraging him to stay; it's certainly inviting him to talk. There's nothing he has to say that I want to hear. And why am I the one who has to make his sodding drink, while he sits all cosy in the lounge with her, as she grants him an audience? I manage to successfully wind myself up further and chuck the gloves in the dirty water. I've no idea how he takes his tea so he'll have it how it comes. I don't bother getting a third cup out of the cupboard; I know exactly how this is going to play out. I take my time making the drinks too, allowing my anger to brew and stew like the teabag until it's dark and strong.

I step into the hall and listen, the hot handles from the cups burning my fingers. They're talking in low voices, but I can't make out any words. I take a deep breath before pushing open the door.

They're sat on the settee, not touching but close enough to ramp up my irritation, and they both look up at me, smiling their thanks.

Michael is pale, his hair is disheveled, his clothes crumpled and scruffy, like he's been sleeping in them. Hopefully he is ill.

'Hi Will. Nice to see you again,' he says, croakily. 'Thank you for the tea; just what I need. I'm sorry for interrupting your evening. I needed to see Bronwyn,' and he reaches for her hand, holds it on his knee.

I grit my teeth, force a smile, knowing it doesn't reach my eyes. 'It's alright. It's no bother.' I take the armchair. If I'm sat with them, it doesn't get her off the hook; she can't give me a flimsy excuse as to why she couldn't tell him.

'I had an awful nightmare,' he tells her, rubbing his thumb along the top of her hand. 'It really frightened me. I had to phone Jamie, check he was okay.'

'What was it about?' she asks.

Who gives a shit, I think. Why are you indulging this moron?

'I can't remember all the details now. You know what dreams are like. They disappear so fast. But he was really ill, we both were, our parents were devastated. Much like they are in real-life. I don't know what I'd do without you, Bron.' He raises their hands and kisses the top of hers. 'I can only get through this knowing I have you by my side. I'm so scared for Jamie, for what either of us might have. How it might ruin our future.' He kisses her hand again.

Bron makes no reply, just smiles tightly. I resist the overwhelming urge to roll my eyes and laugh.

'You know, Will,' he says to me. 'You were so lucky to have Bron as your best friend for all that time.'

I nod; the irony being that the reason we fell out was because she wasn't there for me three months ago. Like she isn't here for me now. And it's starting to feel like she never will be.

245

'I made a mistake recently,' he admits. 'I had this mate I play five-a-side football with. He was a really good bloke, or so I thought. We used to work with each other at Elite IT many moons ago. I told him about Jamie, his symptoms, the worry it was causing his family, our parents. I thought he'd understand. Yesterday I went for training; I walked into the changing room and one of the other guys says to me, "Didn't think we'd see you again. Danny says you've got motor neurone". Can you believe it? I didn't tell him so he could blab to the others. It was bloody confidential.'

'You don't need mates like that,' I reply. But then if you didn't tell him to keep it to himself, what do you expect? Men can be gossipmongers too.

'I'm gutted, Will. I mean, how would you feel if one of your close friends betrayed your confidence and told someone one of your secrets?'

Strange question to ask. Like he gives a shit what I think.

Bronwyn is looking at me, waiting for my answer.

I shrug. 'Angry, I suppose. Luckily I don't really have secrets. Or friends.' I try a laugh but Michael's face is stoney. This is getting too serious and has ruined what was meant to be a nice evening. I'd definitely rather be at home studying my lying suspects' phoney alibis.

'Would it be the end of your friendship?'

I try to imagine one of my friends doing the same to me. Shaun? He has only nice things to say about people so probably not. Ryan? Haven't heard from him in ages, but we were once close. Chris? He's a solicitor, used to keeping things confidential. Eddie? Yeah, he's fairly trustworthy. I certainly have enough dirt on him. Claire? Never, she'd rather die first. Bronwyn? No way.

'Depends what and who they told. But I probably wouldn't feel the same way about them again.'

'Would you still trust them?' he persists, leaning forward so his body is close to Bronwyn's, his mouth inches from her ear, almost as if his words are intended only for her. 'Trust is the foundation of love,' he says knowledgeably.

Sounds like something written on those stupid little wooden signs women have hanging off cupboard doors and above mirrors. My auntie Heidi has a few, finding the ones about gin amusing. And what's love got to do with friends?

Bronwyn is still staring but her eyes have a faraway look in them. Perhaps she's as bored as I am with this conversation, in which case there is a different topic we could be discussing.

'No, I wouldn't,' I reply and that seems to satisfy him because his smile is triumphant as if he's glad he's not the only one who'd kick a so-called friend into touch.

Michael sits back, releasing Bronwyn's hand so he can reach for his tea. Suddenly she stands, catching her knee on the edge of the coffee table. She winces, but ignores the pain, doesn't stop to rub it or even say, 'Ouch,' just scrambles out from the settee. I watch her leave the room, her fingers pulling the door behind her. I look at Michael to see if he's noticed but he's smiling into the tea and I wonder what just happened here.

'Biscuit, mate?' I say, getting to my feet.

'Yes, please. Ask Bron if she's got my favourites in.'

I find Bronwyn in the kitchen, fishing the gloves out of the dirty water and hanging them over the wooden dish rack to dry. I watch her for a few seconds. Is she taking a few moments to prepare herself, to find the words and tell him to go and never contact her again? Something tells me she isn't.

'Bronwyn,' I say and she jumps, but doesn't turn around, just pulls the plug out of the washing-up bowl and dries her hands on a tea towel. 'What's all that about?' I know she can see me reflected in the dark window. 'All that bollocks about trusting friends. Will you please answer me?'

She turns around and I'm taken aback by her cold expression.

'I don't know what he's talking about,' she snaps. 'He can be weird and cryptic at times.'

I step closer, confused by the change in her demeanour. 'Are you going to tell him it's over?'

'Now is not the time,' she replies, turning away and reaching for the biscuit barrel off the work surface.

'What? *Now* is the perfect time,' I argue. 'You told me you were done with him. How much longer are you going to put up with this bollocks? How much more do I have to put up with? Do you have any idea how frustrating this is—?'

'Stop pressuring me, William,' she shouts angrily. 'I've had enough of you going on and on at me. I will do it in my own time. Is that okay with you?' She raises a hand, pushes me out of the way and marches from the kitchen.

I stare after her, feeling defeated. Fucking hell. Tamsin was wrong. Women can stamp your heart into the ground too. I have only a couple of minutes to make my next move. On silent feet, I take my coat off the hook and my rucksack containing toothbrush and other essentials from the bedroom. I linger outside the lounge doorway. Should I say goodbye? Fuck it. Fuck them both. She's made her choice. Him again. Carefully, I open the front door and step into the cool night air. In the distance I hear a police siren and freeze, glancing back inside the flat. I close the door and hurry to the Mazda, my feet crunching and slipping on the loose stones. I chuck the rucksack onto the passenger seat and start the engine. Any second now she'll wonder what's keeping me and get up, call out my name, but there'll be no answer. Will she seek out the rucksack only to find it and me gone? And will she call my name louder and race through the flat to the front door? I pull up to the driveway entrance, wait for a break in the traffic. A quick glance in the rearview mirror and there's my answer. No. She will not. Maybe she's forgotten I was ever there.

Chapter 39

I rub my hands over my eyes and down my face, propping my chin up in both palms as I stare at the desk and the papers spread out over its top. I've been here since 7am and, though I've read Tamsin's account twice, I can barely remember it. I slide the paper away too hard and it flies off the edge of the desk like a paper plane taking flight. What difference does it make what she said? It's what she says now that counts. It's a good job Shaun is coming along to keep me in check or I may go in too heavy.

Predictably, I slept like crap. After leaving Bronwyn's flat, I toyed with the idea of calling in to see my mum but she'd have taken one look at my face and known there was a problem. I couldn't stand to hear her take on things so I went home and unpacked the rucksack, kicking the bag back under the bed; I won't be needing that again. I sulked for ages, thinking about it all, concluding nothing. It was an hour later that I received the first phone call. I stared at Bronwyn's name on the screen. Two choices: red or green, listen or ignore. I chose ignore. I knew exactly what she was going to say, the tone she'd use. It went to voicemail but she didn't leave a message; her form of retaliation. Half an hour later she tried again and got the same cold response. She didn't try again and didn't text. How many texts has she drafted and not sent though?

I pick my mobile up, the screen is still blank. Nothing received. She'll be up though, getting ready for work, feeling like shit, I hope. Will she try again today? Should I? You're pressuring her if you do, I warn myself. Yeah. I slap the mobile face down. Good point.

'Morning!' a voice calls from the office door, followed by a load of bustling and huffing, and a hissed swear word. Shaun bundles his way over to where I'm sitting, balancing a travel cardboard carrier of coffees in one hand. His rucksack has slipped off his shoulder and is hooked over his elbow weighing it down. I get up, relieve him of the drinks, which I place on top of the papers, something I hate anybody else doing. I loathe coffee-stained papers. A sign of a sloppy worker.

'You alright, Will?' he asks, dropping the rucksack on the floor and unzipping it.

'Yeah, fine,' I reply in a clipped tone. 'Which is mine?' My hand hovers over the two takeaway cups.

'The one with a C on the side,' he answers, giving me a funny look.

'Thanks for the coffee, Shaun,' I say, retrieving the paper off the floor. I retake my seat, sip the cappuccino and tidy the papers up on the desk, keeping Tamsin's to the side. 'It's good to have you back.'

'Thanks, Will,' he says, touched by my kind words. 'It's good to be back. I'm sick of the sight of burger buns and salad leaves; they all look the same. I need to stimulate my brain.' He bounces into one of the comfy chairs, keeping his cup held high to avoid slopping coffee out of the tiny hole in the lid. 'I can be here all day tomorrow if you need me. Day off. I'm working the weekend. Double-time. Do you want me to come in?'

I nod. 'We need to start ruling these suspects out or in. We need to pay your old man a visit. Appeal to his good nature and find out what Declan was doing, because he definitely wasn't home.'

'Hang on, let me make a list,' and he pulls his llama notebook out of his bag, finds a blank page and starts scribbling down bullet points.

'We need to chase up Martyn Hepworth, shove the witness statement from the fence guy in his face, see if he reacts.'

'Are we going to the police if he refuses to assist us?'

'I don't want them barging into our investigation, trashing it and then telling us we've got nothing on Hepworth. The man is a nasty little bastard. If he's got any sense, and he must have, then he'll come to us first with this bullshit alibi. If we don't hear anything by tomorrow morning, we'll go round.'

Shaun nods enthusiastically. 'Can I be Bad Cop again? That gave me such a kick.'

I wouldn't mind getting heavy with Hepworth myself, but it'll do Shaun more good than me so I say yes. We carry on discussing each suspect and the corresponding alibis and what we know so far. I finish the coffee and, on top of the mug I had when I first got here, I leave Shaun to refresh himself with Tamsin's account while I go to the bathroom. When I return to the office, Shaun has slung his legs over the arm of the chair and is chatting away all pally with someone on the phone.

'Hang on, he's here now. Yeah, you too,' he says with a grin and holds the phone out to me. It's only then that I see it's my phone in his hand. 'The lovely Bronwyn.'

I back off, wave my hand, mouth, 'No.' He frowns with confusion and thrusts it at me. I take it, look at the black screen lit with icons. The timer tells me they've been talking for a nearly a minute. I stab my finger on the big red circle to end the call and chuck the phone back on the desk.

'Don't answer my phone again, Shaun,' I tell him, annoyed.

His face falls. 'Sorry, Will. I didn't mean to piss you off. It's just that it rang twice and, when I saw it was your friend, I thought it might have been important. Sorry.' And he reaches for his notebook, buries his nose in it.

I sit opposite him. A horrible spear of guilt pierces my chest. Why am I taking it out on him? He's the only person who actually wants to be here with me.

'No, look, Shaun, I'm sorry. I shouldn't have snapped at you.' He looks up, doesn't tell me it's okay. He wants an explanation, deserves one. Wasn't I commending him yesterday for his trustworthiness? From the desk, my mobile rings again. I ignore it. He stares at it. But he's of a generation where ringing and pinging mobiles are more important than the person they're with.

'Will, you can talk to me; we're mates. I won't repeat anything, but I know there's something. Recently you have seemed happier, more relaxed - but now you seem really on edge and secretive too.' He waits and I try to find a place to begin. 'Do you want me to guess? You and Bronwyn are involved behind her boyfriend's back. Yeah?'

'Yes,' I admit, with relief, 'but only since Easter Sunday.'

He shrugs, not caring when it started. 'Has he found out, what's his name?' I tell him. 'Michael doesn't know, but you suspect he knows?' I shrug. 'And Bronwyn is delaying telling him? See? I know a lot. If it was all in the open, you and her would be public and I'm guessing you wouldn't stop telling me how fantastic she is and how much in love with her you are.' He smiles. 'You taught me well, mate. I'm getting the hang of this investigating. What happened last night? Why are you ignoring her?'

I give him a fairly detailed account, including Michael's strange monologue about untrustworthy friends and what a sulky bastard I can be, and that I walked out without so much as a goodbye. It feels good to be confessing my poor behaviour.

'You owe her an explanation,' Shaun points out. 'What if she dumped him after you left and she's trying to tell you?' I shake my head. 'Either way you haven't given her a chance to explain. It does sound like he suspects she's going to give him the elbow, you know all that crap about family illness and redundancy; it's a classic way of making her feel sorry for him.

She sounds an intelligent woman. Why isn't she seeing through all the bollocks? Unless...'

He leans forward. 'Will, do you think he's got something on her?'

'What do you mean, like dirt?'

'Yeah. What's she like as a person? You know her.'

I hesitate, think, how to describe her? What do I like about her? 'She's nice. That's not the word, goes nowhere explaining what she's like. She's a good person, gets on with people, fun to be with.' Shaun starts to smile. He's probably never heard me be this complimentary about someone before. 'You've met her, Shaun. I know only for twenty minutes but that's what she's like.'

'What about work? Is she well-liked?' I nod. As far as I'm aware. 'Is she the type to lie on a job application form, sleep with her boss for promotion, get someone sacked?' I shake my head emphatically.

'She's one of the most honest people I know,' I tell him. 'Too much sometimes, to the point of being tactless. I can give you countless examples of her opening her mouth when she should've kept it shut.'

Shaun's smile broadens and I realise I'm talking about her fondly. I feel an ache in my gut. I can't let her go. I did that before and I lost her.

'I can't see her doing anything that bad, Shaun; she'd be unable to live with herself. I'm different. I've done plenty. Ask your dad. On second thoughts, don't.'

'That story about the dishonest friend, do you think Michael might have been warning Bronwyn? "You dump me and I won't hesitate to tell William about that thing you did". So when you ask her if she's gonna dump Michael, she reacts like that. She's terrified it'll put you off. Whatever it is, you won't trust her again. Like he said, trust is the foundation of love. And it is.'

I stop, think. I could never hate her if she'd done something dishonest.

'Does Bronwyn know anything about you that she might have told Michael?'

'No,' I state, with a shake of the head. 'Absolutely not. She knows I've been inside and for what, but nothing else. And my criminal past is easy to google. It'll be in the local paper..'

Shaun scratches his chin thoughtfully. 'Can I make a suggestion?'

'Go ahead.'

'Let me put Michael under surveillance. Him and his brother, just for a bit. Let's see if all this crap about them being ill is true. I might even be able to get dirt on him,' and he winks. 'If I find anything, it's her excuse for dumping Michael. She can't not do it then.'

As his boss, I consider his suggestion. It's very tempting. Shaun's been on surveillance with me many times. He's mobile now, has a quick exit if he needs one. He's clever and street-smart, but he is my responsibility and I care what happens to him. If something happens to him, it won't just be Nisha who comes down heavy on me, but his dad too. And Shaun being my colleague will not stop Hock from pummelling seven shades out of me.

'Okay, but there are dos and don'ts.' Shaun grins with excitement. 'I mean it, Shaun. Keep your distance. It's watch and learn only. When you get enough, get out of there and, if necessary, take the long way home. Keep your phone on Bluetooth in the car at all times and phone if you need me.'

'You got it, Will. I'll start first thing tomorrow. But promise me, you'll stop ignoring her.'

I look at my mobile, just as our office phone rings. Shaun picks up it, putting on his posh voice as he says, 'Good morning, King Investigation Agency. How can I help?'

I pick up my mobile, text her.

Busy all morning. I'll ring you later. Will xx

Her reply is instant.

Can I see you? Let's go out somewhere, out of Lexington, away from everyone. xx

Shaun comes back into the room, the phone dangling from his fingers. I look up from my reply, my sentence cut in half. He has a stunned expression on his face.

'What is it? You alright?'

He smiles weakly. 'That was Hepworth. Smug bastard. He has an alibi for the fifteenth.'

'Well, of course he does. He's had hours and hours to think one up. What is it?'

'Says he was in A and E with a sprained ankle. He did it taking the year 9s for rugby and was off for the rest of the week. I kind of remember it as well. We all thought it was hilarious.' Shaun shakes his head. 'We can't disprove this, Will. Patient records are confidential.'

I smile, feeling better already. Shaun has a plan for bringing down Michael, I'm seeing Bronwyn later and I have a way of checking out Hepworth's alibi.

I put my arm around his shoulders. His visits to the gym are paying off; he's definitely getting bulkier. 'Shaun, there's no alibi in the world we can't check out. Even confidential ones. Not when I have a person on the inside at the hospital. It's time you met Isla.'

*

But a trip to the mortuary at Lexington General Hospital will have to wait until after our quick chat with Tamsin. The same scruffy ungrateful man I encountered when I first came here is exiting the building as we arrive and he's just as obnoxious, but Shaun grabs the communal door before it closes in our faces.

'Stinks in here,' he mutters snobbily, looking around in disgust at the shit state of the lobby. By the bottom of the stairwell is a plastic carrier bag, bulging with contents, its handles tied together. On the side is a clue to what's inside: a cartoon fish wearing a napkin around its neck and holding cutlery. Someone's takeaway packaging.

Shaun wrinkles his nose and gives it a wide berth as if it might jump out and grab his leg. I lead the way up the stairs to Tamsin's flat.

'Is that a boot print?' he mutters, nodding at the distinctive shape in the middle of the front door.

'Wait until you see inside,' I say, knocking the door hard. I expect to have to knock several times to get a response but, on the second rap, the door opens and Tamsin yawns, quickly apologising, and pulling her flimsy dressing gown back onto her bare shoulder.

'What? Oh, I remember you. You're that private detective man, aren't you?' She waves a finger at me.

I smile. 'Morning Tamsin. Yes, I am. This is my colleague, Shaun. I know it's early but—'

'I've been up since 7. Wide awake. Come in, join the party,' and she waltzes back down the dark corridor, sashaying her hips. Shaun raises an eyebrow at me.

'She's probably still pissed from yesterday.' I lead the way inside the dingy flat, noting all the doors are closed and there's debris everywhere: clothes and toys, more scribbling on the walls, empty vodka bottles, their little metal tops arranged into a face on the floor.

A man's voice floats from the open living room door. 'What you drawing, mate? Is that a monster? If not, it's a cracking likeness for your mum,' followed by an unmistakable laugh.

Jake Bunby is sat on Tamsin's sagging sofa wearing jogging bottoms, huge white trainers. His crutch is propped up against the wall. The little boy is sat on the floor, his tongue sticking out with concentration as he carefully draws something on a large white pad. On the table beside him is a bag of fun-sized chocolate bars and plenty of empty wrappers. Breakfast?

'Morning Jake,' I say and he looks up sharply, his thin features brightening into a wide grin.

'Morning gents. Alright young Hock? How's your dad?'

Tamsin eases past me to drop beside Jake on the sofa. I look from one to the other, wondering, but it's Jake who quashes my thinking.

'No fucking way. Don't go there. We are not...'

'Having sex with each other?' Shaun suggests, trying to hide his amusement

'Christ, no,' Jake replies, horrified. He looks at Tamsin, pulls a face as if she's the last woman on earth he'd go with.

But Tamsin is frowning mock-serious at him. 'What you lying for, Jake?' She elbows him in the side, looks at me and makes a poor attempt to lower her voice. 'But he was really crap. I think he'd have preferred me if I'd had a dick.'

Jake's beady eyes widen angrily and he turns to her. 'You fucking what?' He half-rises out of the seat, wincing as his back protests at the sudden movement.

'Oh, come on, Jake. I'm just saying...it's okay to be gay...'

'I'm not fucking bent,' he shouts, trying to get past her but there's hardly any room between Tamsin's legs and the coffee table.

'You must be; I've never seen you with a girl,' she says, calmly. She lifts her knee up, attempts to kick him but there's no power in her bare foot and she laughs mockingly as he stumbles across the carpet and grabs the crutch off the wall.

I watch with interest as his rat-like face changes colour. It's a lovely shade of crimson and there's a swollen vein in his temple. Has she hit a nerve? Why can't he just laugh it off?

Tamsin sloshes vodka into a tea-stained mug and looks up at him. 'You still here?'

He glares back, steps closer. I inch forward, concerned he might hit her with the crutch since he's holding it like a shepherd's crook.

'You know,' he begins nastily, 'I thought you were a bitch back then but you're even fucking worse now. I know I did the right thing ten years ago.'

She stares at him, confused, and then suddenly furious anger crosses her face and she shouts, 'What did you say?' She jumps up, spilling liquid onto her bare knees, accidentally catching the little boy in the back. He drops his crayon and clamps his hands over his ears and squeezes his eyes shut. Tamsin doesn't notice. She trips over the table leg as she goes for Jake, who, like the coward he is, limps off down the hallway. I trail after the ongoing row. This is gold dust.

'Come back here, you bastard,' she yells but Jake has reached the front door and yanks it open with such force that as it bangs against the wall behind, reverberating throughout the flat. 'Jake!'

He disappears through the door, leaving Tamsin standing on the threshold, swearing and yelling at him to come back. I watch her shoulders lift quickly as she breathes hard and uncontrollably. Then she turns and bulldozes her way through me and back to the lounge, where she drops onto the sofa and tops her cup up with a shaky hand. Ethan has retrieved his crayon and resumed his colouring-in.

'Tamsin,' I say, taking the armchair and keeping my voice low in an attempt to calm her ranting. 'What was Jake Bunby doing here? What happened ten years ago?'

She looks at me in disgust. 'What do you think he was doing here? He's a fucking drug dealer and ten years ago he introduced me to drugs. I needed something, I rang him and he came. What? Are you going to tell the police I occasionally have a joint or—'

'No. I'm not interested in what he sells or what you take. I need to ask you a couple more questions about the day Amanda went missing.'

'God! Are you still looking for her? Six years later and she's still getting all the fucking attention. She's dead, alright?'

My eyes narrow. 'What makes you say that?'

'It's obvious. Where is she then? Why has she walked out of her perfect life?' she demands in a raised sarcastic tone. 'Maybe she's living like me. Hooked on drink and booze, with some horrible bloke's brat to raise, living in fucking squalor...'

'Tamsin, yesterday I spoke to Mr Beattie; he's the proprietor of a hairbrush company who attended the trade fair. He saw you there and spoke to you. Why did you lie to me?'

Tamsin shakes her head weakly. 'I wasn't there; he's mistaken.'

'He isn't. He remembered you from the year before when you attended with Amanda. You told him that you were looking for Amanda. Why? Can you put the vodka down?' and I snatch the cup out of her hand and slam it down on the coffee table. Bang goes my calm manner.

'I need that,' she complains sulkily, making a grab for the cup, but I slide it out of reach. I look at Shaun. 'Take Ethan in the kitchen. Get him a drink or something.'

Having several younger siblings gives Shaun valuable experience with kids that I don't possess. He takes the little boy by the hand, speaking softly and leads him away. I look at Tamsin sternly. 'What was the issue between you and Amanda? The truth? I don't want to hear any of this crap about you and her being good friends, because I know Amanda didn't have any. Everyone I've spoken to had some beef with her; you aren't any different. Why did you go to the trade fair? What was so important that it couldn't wait until the next day? Did you go there to kill her?'

'No!' Tamsin shouts. 'I did not kill Amanda. I didn't see her there. My drink. Just one sip, please,' and she points at the cup. I slide it over.

She slurps at it greedily. 'I did go out the night before and I did have a hangover and I met some bloke whose name I can't remember. I can never remember their names. Only the ones who hurt me. I was bitching about her to him. She was a fucking nightmare to work for. Nitpicking all the time, going on and on at me. She was impossible to impress. And this bloke I'm with listens, but then he's had enough because he's too busy trying to get into my knickers and he tells me to have it out with her. So the next morning I rang in sick and took the train to the city. That's it.'

'That's it? Bollocks,' I tell her and her head jerks back like I've slapped her. 'Your boss finds fault with your work so you decide to skive the day and have it out with her in public. I don't think so. What's the real reason? Had she sacked you?' Tamsin shakes her head. 'According to Jenny,' and Tamsin interrupts with a snort. 'Yes, Jenny. You and Amanda were once close but eight months before it all changed. Why? What happened?'

Tamsin mashes her lips together, looks away as tears prick her eyes, she reaches for the cup, but I move it away and she gives me a dirty look.

'Was it work-related or was it personal? The sooner you answer, the sooner you can have your vodka back.'

'It was work-related. She was doing the salon up to go part-time and spend more days with her precious family. She needed someone to run the place in her absence and I told her that I'd like to do it. She said "yes". But Holly saw the advert for the new stylist. Amanda lied; she wanted someone with managerial experience. She was keeping me down and I had

257

enough so I went to the fair because she'd be alone. But I couldn't find her so I got the train back. And later Holly phoned to see if I'd heard from Amanda because she hadn't come home. I felt bad because I never saw her at the fair. It was a last minute decision to go. That's it. Can I have my drink now?'

I study her. 'Is this why you despise Holly? Because, after Amanda disappeared, she was running the salon.'

'Well, obviously. Her precious parents and him, David, overlooked me again. That's why I left. I'd had enough of being treated like shit. Fucking Jake's the same. Every fucking man I've ever had has treated me like shit and I am sick of it.'

She has a chip on her shoulder the size of the British Isles. Angry at her boss, her colleagues, men, her drug dealer, the world. It's hard to have any sympathy for her when she's orchestrated her own shit life. I still don't buy that she went into the city to have it out with Amanda, but right now I've got nothing else.

Shaun is leading the little boy back, talking softly to him. Ethan carries a glass of orange squash with both hands, an apple clenched between his teeth like a pig on a spit. He kneels down to resume his picture. Shaun gives me a pleading look.

'Tamsin,' I say.

'What now? Can't you leave me in fucking peace? I've answered your stupid—'

'Where's Ethan's father?'

She tops her cup up. 'Prison. Dead. I don't care.'

'What about your parents? Do you see them?'

'Yeah, they come round, sticking their oar in, bringing sweets for him,' and she sticks her bare toe in the child's back. Ethan grunts, moves away.

'Don't do that,' I tell her. 'If you don't want to look after him, let *them* or contact social services. Because if you don't,' and I lean menacingly close, 'I fucking will.'

*

'Poor kid,' Shaun says as we return to his car. 'You know he can talk. Only a few words but he's not as silent or…I don't know what the word is, special needs as you might think. He needs some love and attention. You should have seen his face when I offered him my apple. Unbelievable joy. Poor lad.'

'Yes, you're right. It's not a good situation for him. Hmm,' I say thoughtfully. My eyes move down the row of cars parked on the opposite side of the road. They stop and flick back one car. I slap Shaun's arm with my hand and slow my pace. 'White Golf at two o'clock.'

Shaun stares. 'That's Bunby's car. Why's he still here?'

'Why indeed,' I mutter, glancing back at the flats. Second floor, fourth window from the right, the drawn curtains have been pulled back. A figure is watching. Ten quid says it's Tamsin. But is Jake watching us or her? And is she watching him or us?

Chapter 40

Across the table, Bronwyn is still smiling as I prattle on about my day. When I agreed to a meal out, I made it clear that last night was not to be a topic of conversation. Shaun's surveillance is the ace up my sleeve and the last thing I want is to be drawn into a conversation where I end up confessing our plan of action. I just want to be able to enjoy an evening where we can pretend we're in a normal relationship, where there's no risk of being seen by anyone we know or by Michael magically turning up. If he does, I might punch him. Which will undoubtedly make me feel a million times better but almost certainly end in an assault charge. Would Bron appear for the defence or the prosecution? I push the thought away before it takes hold and ruins what is turning out to be a nice evening. The Kelsall Smokehouse, where the burgers are stacked as tall as skyscrapers and the brisket falls apart like it's melting, is a fantastic place. The music is loud but not deafening and only American anthems are allowed. The alcohol-free IPA is straight out of heaven's brewery and the company is okay too. The decor is simple and effective: lots of bare wood and scaffolding pipes.

Bronwyn booked the table on the recommendation of her receptionist.

'Are you any closer to finding Amanda?' she asks, putting down the dessert menu. 'Are we sharing a pudding?'

'You pick, but not banoffee pie.'

Bronwyn sits back, horrified. 'You don't like it. What's wrong with you?'

'It's sickly. I'm not struck on bananas...'

'Nor me but I make an exception for—'

I interrupt her. 'In answer to your question, no, I'm not any closer to finding Amanda. What I have discovered is that, contrary to the MISPER file, Amanda had enemies, and they have pretty strong motives for wanting rid of her. When I find the suspect with the ropiest alibi, then I might discover Amanda's whereabouts.'

'You don't think there's any chance she's still alive?'

I shake my head. 'I doubt it. To be honest, I've always worked on the assumption that she's dead. Her mother gave me lots of reasons why Amanda wouldn't have left town or committed suicide, so where is she, where are her remains? She must be dead, and if not an accident, then it must be murder.'

'Have you disproved any alibis yet? The chocolate brownie with custard, please, but can we have the custard separate,' Bronwyn tells the waitress as she appears at the table, notepad in hand. 'And two spoons.' She turns back to me and shrugs. 'I like to put my own on.'

Briefly, I run through our discoveries so far. 'Tamsin, the stylist, claimed she was hungover and shagged out, but I recently discovered that was bollocks. She took the train to the city to have it out with Amanda. She wanted to know why she was being passed over for promotion.'

Bronwyn frowns. 'What was the urgency that she had to travel into the city, which would have been costly, to ask her boss that? Doesn't make any sense. Is she capable of harming Amanda?'

'Violence is in all of us, even you,' I point out. 'When you've put up with crap for so long, it's inevitable that one day you might snap. This bloke she had a one-night stand with had wound her up and advised her to have it out with Amanda. I don't buy it altogether. But how can I prove otherwise? Her motive isn't much of one, not compared to other people's. Plus there's not much to Tamsin. She's quite slim but she *is* heavily into drugs. Perhaps a snort of cocaine gave her the strength of ten men. She'd still have to find Amanda in a huge crowd, abduct, murder and dispose of her in a busy city, without being seen by a single passerby. Not impossible, but hard work.'

'She had help?'

'The obvious choice is the one-night stand, but she can't remember his name. She can never recall their names...' my voice trails off thoughtfully.

'What?' Bronwyn asks, raising her large glass of wine.

'She can be quite cryptic...I need to look back through my notes for her exact words.' I scratch the bridge of my nose, thinking of the remaining suspects and their alibis. 'I need to see Hock too. Not looking forward to that.'

'What's he got to do with Amanda?'

'Declan, her son's father, was working for Hock the day she disappeared. I don't expect Hock to tell me what crime Declan was committing on his behalf, but he can exonerate him. Probably at a cost to me and Declan. But that's his problem.'

'How long has it been since you saw Hock?'

'The day I punched his lights out. So what? Three months ago. I wonder if he still remembers it.'

'I doubt it,' she jokes.

If only. I think of the less than friendly reaction I'll get when I pay him a visit, which is why Shaun is coming along for a lesson on how to interview a hostile witness. I don't even think Hock will want to make a bad impression in front of his eldest son.

'Just be careful he doesn't even up the score,' Bronwyn says. 'I prefer your nose in the middle of your face.'

Her words briefly transport me back to the day Hock lured me to a dodgy car park. Shaun was an elusive witness in a previous case and Hock had taken umbrage with my interview technique. During the course of the conversation, Hock brutally reminded me that, with a wrong word in the right ear hole, he could destroy all that I had achieved since leaving prison. I'd be disgraced again. He topped this threat off with a derogatory comment about my dad's death. It was a risk hitting him but, after quickly weighing up the consequences, I went through with it and lamped him. Bronwyn, who was a witness to the assault, was in a terrible state of shock; she nearly crashed the Mazda driving us out of the car park. Yes, of course, I think, she was there. Sat in the car with the doors shut, but she was soon alerted by our raised voices and got out to intervene. She couldn't have heard what Hock said. What I did for him before, keeping quiet about the drugs and, whilst in prison, the messages I passed, the contraband I smuggled, the other stuff. Should I tell her? Would she care? Would it bother her if I confessed that it earned me money that I can't yet spend? Money I need, but would seriously arouse suspicion if I suddenly put a deposit down on a house or changed the car. I don't want secrets between us but, Hock knows too much and, if he found out about her, nothing, not even Shaun, could stop him from telling her.

'The brownie,' the waitress announces appearing at the side of the table and sliding an over-sized dinner plate in front of us. Sitting in the middle of it, a generous-sized helping, is the chocolate brownie. She leaves a jug of steaming hot custard, enough to drown ourselves in never mind the pudding, and two long-handled spoons, presumably so we can romantically feed each other across the table.

Bronwyn dives straight in, grabbing the jug and pouring custard around her half of the pudding. She hacks a corner off the brownie and shoves it in her mouth. Very unladylike.

'What about the other suspects?' she asks.

'In the immortal words of Jenny, "They're fucking lying. All of them". So if they weren't murdering Amanda, they were up to something else, something they don't want to admit to me, but I am determined to uncover the truth.'

Bronwyn stops, resting her spoon on the serviette and pushing the plate towards me, gesturing for me to eat. 'Are you able to stay tonight? I'd really like it if you could.'

I nod, glad that I had dug the rucksack out from under the bed earlier on and repacked it on the off-chance she'd ask me. Although I wish I had my own place that we could go back to. Being in her flat means we run the risk that, like yesterday, Michael could put in a surprise visit. Now he's done it once, he could do it again. Especially if he suspects something and, although my walking out did him a favour, it made me look like I had something to hide.

'You're frowning,' Bronwyn says. 'What is it? Are you worried you-know-who will turn up?'

I want to tell her it's not a joking matter. Why does she think sneaking around and living on the edge is normal? I'm in my late thirties. I'm not a twenty-year-old lad getting a thrill out of having flings. I never had those days but, if I did, they'd be over by now. Her comments make me fear that, in six months, I could still be living like this. No. I won't. Once Shaun comes up with the goods, and I've no doubt he will, this will all be over one way or another. Either embarking on our happy ever after or I'll be on my own, rebuilding my life again. However, until then…

'Shall I get the bill?' I say, pushing away the empty plate and looking around for a member of the waitering staff.

*

The only other solution to spending time with Bronwyn without fear of you-know-who turning up is to go away for the weekend. I'm sure she can invent a few days at her parents or with a couple of friends on a boozy shopping trip. She can even lie to him about which direction she's heading, so there's no way he can track her down. We could leave on the Friday and return on the Sunday. Two nights away with her would be heaven. I glance across at her and, in the darkness of the car, her smile is bright.

'When this investigation is over, how do you fancy going away for the weekend?'

'I would love to, Will. Anywhere in mind?'

'How about the Lake District?' I suggest. It's at least three hours from Lexington. A big place. Often there's no signal. I can't see Michael tracking us up there.

'Sounds wonderful. Shall I start looking for somewhere? A nice B&B, lots of romantic walks in the countryside. Can't wait. What a lovely idea.' She pulls the seatbelt away from her chest and lifts herself over the handbrake to kiss my cheek and whisper naughtily in my ear.

'We can't,' I say. 'The Mazda's not big enough.'

'We should've come in my car. Is that your phone?' and she plucks it out of the compartment in front of the gearstick where I keep some USB cables and my little bottle of hand sanitiser. The volume is low but the device buzzes in her hand. 'It's David,' she tells me, reading the screen caller ID. 'Want me to answer it?'

'Yes.'

'Hello, William Bailey's phone. I'm afraid he's driving at present. Can I...whose house? Hang on, David. Let us find a safe place to park up. No, I won't hang up, I promise. Just a second.' She lies the phone flat on her thigh and turns to me. 'He's in a right state, Will. He wants to know what's going on with his wife.'

'Shit. Hang on. There's a bus-stop here.' I flick the indicator down and pull off the road into an empty lay-by. I kill the engine and reach for the phone. 'David. It's Will. Are you alright? Where are—?'

'He won't open the fucking door,' David shouts angrily. 'Fucking cunt.' He's outside, the wind distorts his words, blowing them away from the mouthpiece.

'Whoa, slow down. Where are you?'

'Hepworth's. I'm sick of being kept in the dark. I want to know what he's done to my wife... you,' he announces, enlightened. 'You know something, don't you? Get down here now or I will put a fucking brick through this bastard's door and beat it out of him.'

David hangs up. I look at Bronwyn. 'I'd best go to him. He's threatening violence.'

'I'd forgotten what a good time you can show a woman, Will.' Bronwyn smiles cheekily.

'You love it,' I tell her.

*

David's van is parked on the end of Hepworth's drive. I park up behind it and get out of the Mazda. Bronwyn insists on accompanying me and we find David sat in the driver's seat, gripping the steering wheel and staring at the house with a face like thunder. I try a smile and he responds, his expression softening a little. But then he's reminded that I'm a source of information and that I'm withholding it. He throws open the van door and jumps out. He's still wearing his work clothes. I can see he's been crying.

'David,' I begin, keeping my voice low, 'are you alright?'

'No, I'm not,' he shouts. 'I saw Amanda's belongings in the spare room. I should've put the box back in the loft after you went, but I searched it again. And all I could see was *him* abusing Amanda.'

Beside me, Bronwyn inhales sharply. David looks at her. 'Who are you?'

I open my mouth to give the standard reply, which now feels like a blatant lie, but Bronwyn answers.

'I'm Bronwyn, Will's girlfriend.'

Also a lie but it feels nice to hear her say it.

'I can't take it, Will,' he tells me tearfully. 'Did you speak to him?' and he flings his arm at the house. I look at the property. Only the porch light is on and all of the curtains are drawn. I can't see a figure, but I expect Hepworth is peering at us, hopefully shit scared. After all, David is a young man, driven by anger and frustration that his wife was murdered by her childhood abuser. I wonder if Mrs Hepworth or their kids are home. I look at the neighbours' houses. Some of their curtains are open and lights are on. Hepworth is certainly putting on a show.

'Yes, I did. I gave him twenty-four hours to tell me where he was the day Amanda went missing or I'd go to the police..'

'Whatever his alibi is, he's lying,' David spits. 'He has to be.'

I give him a pained look, take his elbow and walk him down the length of the van, away from the house, so Hepworth can't see us. I pause by a tall conifer, keep my voice low. 'I'm not supposed to be telling you this…' David opens his mouth to protest but I hurry on. '*Only* because it could get my source in trouble. He told Shaun that, in the morning whilst taking a class for rugby, he injured his ankle and had to go to A and E. Afterwards, he went home and had the rest of the week off. Shaun remembers the incident because all the kids thought it was funny But it is true, kind of. Hepworth did sustain an injury but not when he said it was. He attended the hospital at 2pm. Four hours later.'

David looks at me sharply, frowning. 'What was he doing?'

265

'He had to take an opportunity. He faked the injury, got a colleague to take him to the hospital so he had a witness. Instead he got a taxi to your house. Or maybe he left his car at the hospital…anyway, he entered your house through an open downstairs window and started his search in the loft, the last place Amanda told him the diary was.'

'He was in our house? Fuck's sake,' David shouts.

'Shh,' I say, 'please. But in an ironic twist of fate, as he descended the loft via the ladder, he slipped and landed awkwardly, straining his ankle for real.'

David stares at me. 'How do you know all this?'

'I'm coming to that. Now he's handicapped and in considerable pain. Because Amanda moved the diary after she revealed its location, Hepworth had no choice but to search the rest of your house. He hobbled around the rooms, looked through cupboards and drawers, trying not to make a mess. He still couldn't find the diary. Time is against him and now there was another problem.'

Enthralled, David shakes his head.

'Your neighbours, the Newmans, were having a new fence.'

His face lights up. 'I remember.'

'Amanda granted the workmen access to your garden, effectively trapping Hepworth in the house. He continued to search the downstairs. Wouldn't you?'

David nods. 'He wouldn't get another chance.'

'Eventually he had to leave and, brazenly, because we know he's that kind of bloke, he unlocked the back door and walked right past the workmen, fronting it out. Both parties spoke; the workmen assumed Hepworth was the man of the house.'

'Wow,' Bronwyn mutters.

'There's more,' I say. 'With this injury, Hepworth was forced to go to A and E for real, but he didn't tell the attending nurse it was a rugby injury. He told her he landed awkwardly—'

'Coming down a loft ladder?' David suggests and I nod.

'The official documentation states he was in the hospital for three hours. His wife collected him because he couldn't drive. He couldn't have abducted Amanda. I'm so sorry, David.'

David's face crumples and he screws his hands into fists. Sensing he needs comfort, Bronwyn touches his arm and strokes it soothingly.

'But he abused her,' David complains.

'Without the diary, I can't prove anything.'

'I can,' and he shrugs Bron's hand off and marches straight for Hepworth's front door. He bangs the side of his fist on the door, demanding Hepworth open up.

I grab David's arm and he shrugs me off, kicking the bottom of the door with his boot. 'Open this fucking door, you bastard.'

'Get off my property,' a voice inside threatens. 'You've got ten seconds or I'm calling the police.'

'Good!' David shouts. 'Get 'em down here so I can tell them what a disgusting paedo you are.'

I look at Bronwyn. She's standing in the middle of the drive, looking at the neighbours who are gathering on the ends of the driveways and on grass verges. Lots of windows are lit up as some prefer to watch the scene unfold from the safety of their houses. I can only imagine the gossip that will be travelling around the school when the kids go back.

If I don't get through to David with this one remaining chance, someone will call the police and cart him off for disturbing the peace.

I touch his shoulder, lean close. 'Walk away, please, David. At the moment I have absolutely no evidence of his abuse, but I know he's guilty. Once I find Amanda, I'm certain I'll find the diary. Then, we'll take it to the police. Just give me time.'

His raised fist stops mid-air and he turns to me, tears of anger running down his face. I take his arm, coax it back down to his side. He sighs.

'Go home. Is there anyone who can be with you? Jake, your mum…' I lead him back down the driveway, throw Bron a knowing look and she hurries ahead to open the van door ready to receive him.

'Jake,' he laughs without humour. 'That lying little fucker. He never said a word to me. All these years he knew about Hepworth being at the salon and he never said.'

'I'll come and see you soon,' I say, ushering him into the driver's seat. 'I need to ask you a couple of questions about something else.' I pull the seatbelt out, hand it to him and he clicks it in place. I slam the door and he starts the engine. Neighbours start drifting away now that the show is coming to a close. Curtains are being drawn, shutting out the light, darkening the windows.

We watch the van speed down the road. I take Bronwyn's hand. It's cold. I lead her back to the Mazda, turn the heating on.

'What do you need to ask David?' she asks.

'His whereabouts the day Amanda disappeared. He and Jake weren't where they claimed to be.' I head to her place, eager to get home and take her to bed.

'You don't think he...' She frowns at the thought.

'Why not?' I shrug. 'Tonight might have been for my benefit, all for show.'

Chapter 41

Nisha adjusts the baby's position in her arms and uses the corner of a towel to mop milk from her daughter's mouth. She smiles lovingly, sliding her finger into the tiny hand where it's immediately grasped tightly. Nisha looks at me from where I'm sat behind the desk. I admire her skill at handling something so fragile so masterfully.

'Are you sure you don't want a hold?' she jokingly offers.

'I'm sure. Missing work much?'

'I haven't had time. It's been the busiest last couple of weeks. Matt's just gone back to work; Kiran's off school, Easter hols, so I've had just about everyone popping in to see us with arms full of chocolate eggs, presents galore for this little one, dozens of bottles of Prosecco, enough to drown ourselves in. It's been lovely, don't get me wrong, but now I need a rest. And a rest will be an endless loop of childcare and housework. Not that I'm complaining. I missed out on this with Kiran. But I do miss grown-up conversation…well,' she frowns at me and I know a dig is coming. 'As near as I could get to it with you.' She grins wickedly. 'How is Shaun working out? Is he in today?'

'He has an appointment first thing. I'm not expecting him until ten-ish. He's doing exceptionally well. Biscuit?' and I hold the plate out to her.

'Are we keeping him on?' she asks, biting into the chocolate digestive and scattering crumbs onto the soft blanket.

'That kind of depends on you, but I'd like to. He's a good lad, has a sharp mind and is resourceful and calm.'

She nods, dunks the biscuit into the mug of tea at her side. 'I'll be honest with you, Will, there's two reasons I called in today. Three, if you include to see how you are. The first concerns little Anya here.' She places the lightest of kisses on the baby's head before looking at me, her face serious. 'Matt and I would love you to be her Godfather.'

'What? Really?'

'I know there aren't children in your life yet. Not until Eddie becomes a father. Or maybe you'll beat him to it, but I think you'll be an excellent role model. There's loads you can teach her. Lock picking, how to land a punch, the art of disguise and, of course, your legendary sarcastic humour. Jokes aside, Will, we'd really like it if you said yes, but if you want to think about—'

'I don't need to,' I reply, 'I would love to do it.'

She smiles. 'Thank you. I've asked Matt's sister to be Godmother number one. Miserable woman has been complaining we overlooked her for Kiran's christening. I'll never hear the end of it if I don't ask her now, but to counterbalance her, for Godmother number two, I've asked my lovely friend Bronwyn.'

'Good idea,' I remark, keeping my face impassive.

'Makes perfect sense since the two of you come hand in hand.'

'I don't know what you're talking about,' I deny.

'Bronwyn tells a different story. You forget, William, that she and I have been friends for donkey's years. And we both know she can't keep her mouth shut when she's excited or upset.'

True, I admit silently.

'Seems that, apart from the rest of the world, the only person she's not telling is Michael. What do you think of him? Do you reckon he punches hard?' She tries not to smile.

'Not as hard as me,' I reply confidently. 'Ask Hock.'

Nisha laughs, plucks the bottle from the baby's mouth, sees that it's empty and drops it into the open bag at her feet. In one fluid move, she alters Anya's position so she faces downwards over Nisha's arm and rubs her back in little circles.

'What's the other thing on your list that you want to discuss with me?' I ask, draining my mug.

She looks at me, her expression becoming serious again.

'I'm not going to like this, am I?' I guess. 'You might as well come right out and say it.'

Perhaps she's thinking of extending her maternity leave beyond six months. Matt's family aren't local, which surely means requiring a childminder or a crèche. Unless...she's thinking of jacking it in. Shit, I hope not. I can't afford to buy the business; I'll be out of a job. Just when I thought things were on the up. This is gonna affect all other walks of my life: where I live, career prospects. What else am I supposed to do? Private investigating is about the only thing I can do.

Nisha shuffles to the edge of her seat and places Anya securely into her car seat, tucking the soft toy rabbit into her arm. She sits back, smiles. I brace myself. 'I have a business proposition for you.'

270

Shaun parallel parks the Corsa a few doors down from Hock's shop. I haven't been here for months. The high street has always reminded me of the repetitious background of a cartoon: pub, charity shop, takeaway, hairdresser, pub and so on. Hock's newsagents looms ahead. The door opens and a man with an amputated leg eases his wheelchair out of the shop. Tied to a handle of the wheelchair is a dog leash tethering a Yorkshire Terrier. The scruffy dog trails after its owner, narrowly avoiding having its paws run over.

I get my first glimpse of Hock in months as he holds the door open for his customer and receives a hearty thank you for his effort. Outside the shop, the man in the wheelchair whistles and, immediately, the dog leaps up and settles itself on his lap.

The shop front hasn't changed. In each of the large windows are two screens like you might use to partition two rooms, but half the size. Their aim is to hide the dodgy dealings which take place over and under the counter from prying eyes outside. Shaun pushes open the door and it chimes at the rear of the shop, heralding the arrival of another customer, or threat.

Shelving, reaching from ankle height to above head height, stretches from both windows to the back of the shop. Magazines ranging from angling to yachting, newspapers from red tops to broadsheets to local rags.

A central length of shelving splices the shop floor in two. Shaun leads the way down the left-hand aisle. I follow, glancing at the products on display: stationery including padded envelopes, Sellotape, gaffer tape, a basic assortment of greetings cards for those emergency moments when you forgot so-and-so's birthday or someone dies unexpectedly.

At the end of the aisle is a long counter. A till in the middle. On the right is a chilled cabinet containing soft drinks and juice cartons, and a chest freezer for ice-creams and lollies. I notice something new. An electronic set of scales and a notice displaying postage tariffs. Just like Hock to see the benefit in offering a Post Office service.

"One First Class stamp, please. Oh and an untraceable sawn-off shotgun too."

Or how about: "How much to have a broken kneecap sent to this address?"

I'm thrust out of my daydream by the man himself. From the brightly-lit doorway leading to the private area of the shop, Hock appears slurping from a bottle of diet coke. He looks less bulky, thinner around the neck. Maybe his beloved wife has put him on a strict diet. She is someone who I always envisaged to be the clichéd gangster's moll, protecting and defending her man until only death or prison can separate them. I always knew Hock's blood pressure must be dangerously high. That he'd be dead before 55 of a stroke. Well, we can all dream.

Upon seeing Shaun, his enormous face bursts into a wide grin and his pale eyes illuminate with joy.

'Alright, son? What brings you to this neck of the woods?' Then his cold eyes flick right and, upon seeing me, his face crumples and his huge shoulders slump. 'Oh, fuck, it's you an' all.' He slams the bottle on the counter, causing coke to erupt from the neck. 'Brought your protector, have you, Bailey?' Hock nods towards Shaun.

'Not at all,' I reply, my tone light. 'I thought this would be an ideal place to teach my colleague a valuable lesson on how to interview a hostile witness.'

'What?' he shouts, angrily. 'Are you calling me a hostile witness? You've got some fucking balls, Bailey, showing your face again.' Little droplets of spit land on the counter. Hock uses a huge paw to wipe them away, takes a deep breath to launch into another tirade. Then Shaun steps forward, holding out his hand as if to slow his father down.

'Dad,' Shaun says in a firm calm voice, 'I'm working. Will is my boss. Can you just remember how much I like my job? Don't ruin it for me.'

Hock snorts like a bull. He swipes the coke bottle up and glugs from it, delaying his answer which he's no doubt considering. He must save face in front of his son, set an example on how to deal with people like me without looking like a thug or a coward. In the end, though, Hock has no self-control, and his true nature will out.

'I know he,' and he jabs a finger a finger in my direction, 'only took you on so I wouldn't go round his house and knock his teeth out.'

'Dad,' Shaun complains, frustrated.

'Phil,' I begin, keeping my tone flat, 'that's really unfair. I took Shaun on because of his own merit. You should be very proud of your son. I am. He's an asset to our detective agency. It had nothing to do with saving myself from a beating.'

'Does this mean I can knock your teeth out after all?' Hock asks, with a grin. 'Because I have waited a long—'

'No, Dad, it does not,' Shaun interjects. 'Please, I'm working. This is important. I'm working a MISPER case.'

'Well, they're not here,' he laughs loudly, 'but you're welcome to search the place.' His hand sweeps around the shop to the private entrance. 'There's some stock back there that needs sorting too.'

Shaun looks at me. 'Ignore him. He's being facetious. Dad, can I have a—'

'Yeah, yeah, help yourself,' Hock's voice floats out from behind the counter. 'But not him. He has to pay.'

Shaun shakes his head, opens the door to the chilled cabinet and removes a bottle of Ribena. I take a bottle of water, leave a quid on the counter.

'Right, Shaun,' I begin after a cool swig of water refreshes my mouth. 'The police and courts have lots of different ways to deal with a difficult witness. Unfortunately, as a Private Investigator you have a lot less. But one thing you can do is promise that whatever they tell you is in the strictest confidence; that if it's pertinent to your investigation, you won't be giving their statement to the police. That helps to open up the lines of communication.'

Shaun nods with understanding. 'Do we keep our promises?'

'Absolutely. We're not getting paid to investigate a second crime. Our main concern, particularly in this case, is to learn what Declan, our suspect, was doing on the day Amanda went missing. We know he's lied because a witness has inadvertently revealed he was not where he claimed to be.' I step nearer, bringing the conversation closer to Hock who is all-ears, although he's pretending to be interested in a folder of paperwork. 'Declan won't tell us where he was, which automatically makes us suspicious because, although he was up to no good, he might or might not have been murdering Amanda.'

'But you think he was moonlighting? Not working for his main employer?'

'That's right. We know he had, or still has, money worries. We know he's worked for this second employer before and we have yet another witness account that lends weight to our theory. The problem we have is that this employer, this criminal kingpin, if you like, by the very definition of his line of business, is a hostile witness. He will not exonerate Declan easily.'

Shaun scratches his head with a pen, the notebook in his hand, open to a blank page. 'If the kingpin refuses to help, what can we do?'

'Lots of things. What do we know that might benefit the kingpin? Think. Have we come across anything useful in our investigation that we can use to barter with?'

Shaun stares thoughtfully at the floor, a deep frown etches his forehead. 'Oh!' he suddenly cries. 'Yesterday, we went to see…best not mention real names. Witness X, but witness Y was there, dealing…what was it? Cocaine, cannabis, Es?'

'We don't know what he was selling; he was very cagey, on account of him realising we had caught him in a very precarious situation. He certainly left in a hurry.' I glance at Hock who is standing rigid at the counter, his mouth open and his eyes wide. Talk about a sponge soaking up water, the man looks burst fit to burst. What a fruitful lesson this will prove to be.

'At what point should we use this information? Where all else fails?' Shaun asks, jotting notes down.

'Ask yourself: how soon do we need the information?'

He nods enthusiastically. 'I think I'll plough right in. After all, I think our kingpin has the gist of what I'm going to ask.' And together we turn to Hock, who quickly looks away, busying himself with the folder.

'Mr Hock,' Shaun begins formally, stepping up to the counter, placing his notebook on top, 'what can you tell me about the whereabouts of Declan Page on this date?' and he taps his finger on the open page. 'Right here, the fifteenth of October.'

Hock looks down and then back up into the good-looking but serious face of his son. 'Never heard of him.' There's a distinctive warm twinkle in his eyes that tells me two things: he loves his son and wants him to succeed, but more than that, he wants to know the name of this dealer.

'In the course of my investigation, I have evidence that Mr Page was working for you. I can assure you that anything you tell me will be treated with the strictest of confidence. I am searching for a missing wife and mother. I'm willing to do a deal. Tell me what I want to know and I'll reveal who I saw yesterday dealing God knows what drugs on your patch without your knowledge.'

'You drive a hard bargain, young man,' Hock tells him, tapping a pen on the counter.

Shaun looks at me and smiles. 'I had an excellent teacher.'

Hock snorts with jealousy that Shaun isn't referring to him. 'Give me a minute,' and he disappears out the back. Shaun grins at me.

A few minutes later, Hock returns with a ledger. 'I can't give you any specifics. No names and such like, but I can confirm that on the afternoon of the fifteenth of October, Declan was engaged in private work at my behest.'

'Until what time?' I ask.

'He left between half eight and nine o'clock. Said he was going home to put the kids to bed.'

'Are you certain of these times?' Shaun asks him and Hock nods.

'It was a lengthy job, involving physical exertion and concentration. Got me a good result too. I paid him that evening and he thanked me before going on his way.'

'Thank you for your time, Mr Hock. I appreciate your co-operation.'

Hock smiles with amusement. 'You're welcome. Now,' and he leans forward over the counter. 'I've scratched your back. The itch on mine is beginning to drive me up the wall, so what you got? Who did you see?'

Even with his son, Hock can deliver a menacingly glare but I suppose Shaun is used to it and rarely feels intimidated by it.

'Jake Bunby,' he replies.

Hock's eyes narrow. 'Little shit,' he mutters.

Yes, he is, I silently agree.

Chapter 42

It's a certainty that once we leave Hock's newsagents, information secure in our pocket, Hock will snatch up his mobile phone and make that call to Declan quicker than you can say, "You owe me". After all, Hock has just provided what most would deem to be the "biggest favour" one person can do for another: provide an alibi.

I don't know what the going rate is for alibis these days but I'm guessing they don't come cheap. Certainly Hock's special alibis are costly as they need no corroboration from another party. You can put his word in the bank, or he will put you through the wall.

Declan will owe Hock for quite possibly the rest of his pathetic life, a debt he will never be able to make the repayments on. And it truly is a fate he deserves for many reasons: failing to keep the memory of his son's missing mother alive, for lying about his whereabouts on the day she went missing, for not encouraging the relationship between grandson and nan and, mostly for being a snivelling coward under his domineering fiancée's thumb.

And let's not forget Hock's conversation with Jake Bunby.

I sit at the office desk, freshly-made brew in hand, feeling like I've already done a hard day's work. With any luck, Declan will get in contact with me and, once he's finished balling me out for going to Hock, explain what went on between him and Amanda. I want to be able to tie up that loose end. My mind drifts back to my earlier meeting with Nisha and her proposition.

She wants to spend more time at home with the kids. Understandable after she admitted that she missed so much of her son's early years. She wasn't there when he uttered his first word, took his first step, kicked his first football. The childminders experienced all that on her behalf and, of course, it's not the same thing at all. Nisha's mum isn't due to retire for another year and her dad still works part-time, spending his days off golfing or tending his raised beds. Nisha is sure when her mother does retire, she will have her own plans on how to spend her time.

'They've offered to help where they can,' Nisha told me, 'but they won't take Anya full-time. I can, of course, put her in a crèche; Matt's had a promotion. It's more responsibility and money for him, so we can afford the fees. But it means he's away more in the week and I'll still be running all over town: school, childminders, the office, the shops. And for what? To see my children for a couple of hours in an evening before bed.'

'It's a problem, I can see that,' I said. 'What are your options?'

Nisha smiled. 'There's only a couple. Sell the business. But I poured my heart and soul, not to mention wads of money, into it. Who would buy it? I know you can't afford all of it… which leads me to my second option. It makes perfect sense. If you're agreeable, Will.'

Nisha offered me something I've wanted for a while, something we've joked out. Me seriously, her jokingly. But she wasn't joking when she asked, 'Would you like to be my business partner?'

My reaction was to swear. 'Shit. Really?'

She nodded. 'Shit, yeah, really. You already *are* really. I know not on paper but that can change. I want to come back part time. I don't mind doing the boring mundane office stuff, which I know you hate. In fact, that'd suit me because I can bring Anya in to work. But the investigating and surveillance would be your responsibility. You take the lead on it. We keep Shaun, if he wants to carry on working here. Can't guarantee him full time but there's certainly a good chance of more hours.'

'I didn't expect this, Nisha. I really didn't,' I admitted.

And as an added incentive, she was proposing to grant me my one wish.

'I'll even change the name of the business to Bailey & King.'

I tap the end of the pen on the desk. It's very tempting. Nisha firmly told me that she didn't want an answer now, that I must think about it for however long I wanted, to get legal advice.

'Bailey and King,' I repeat aloud. I don't even bother saying the names the other way round; they don't sound half as good.

To be one half of a private investigation agency, to be an actual partner where my opinion will matter and I can make decisions, help manage the place, all with one of my very good friends, and Nisha is that. She was Claire's best female friend, and after Claire's death, Nisha has always been there for me. What's there to think about? It's an achievement. It's what I've been working for since leaving prison. To get back some credibility.

But Nisha isn't going to hand me a partnership for free. I need to pay. And that will take all of my paltry savings and the money I earned from Hock from doing his dodgy dealings. Crime really will pay for me.

What else am I going to spend the money on? I'd always put it aside for a rainy day: repairing the car or changing it since it's getting on in years; a deposit on a house, even though I'll never be able to make the mortgage payments on my own. But if I do have a problem with the car, I can maybe get a loan or my mum might help me out. As for housing, I can't see me moving out of Mrs Penn's. It's comfortable and clean.

Bronwyn, I suddenly think. Shit. How will I explain the partnership to her? Do I need to? Doesn't that kind of depend on what happens with us? If we part company, what business is it of hers? If we become a proper couple, I'll have to be honest with her. I don't want secrets between us. And if she decides someone as corrupt as me isn't for her, then so be it.

I glance at my watch. Nearly time to prepare for my FaceTime call to Julie Spinner, Lawrence's sister-in-law. She was superbly found on Facebook by Shaun. After Nathan was charged, Julie divorced Nathan and reverted back to her maiden name. As new information regarding the shootings came to light and the nearer the case got to trial, Julie was often interviewed by reporters and the first few words out of her mouth, reminded them she was no longer a Killingworth.

Which is why she was so easy to find on Facebook. Shaun sent her a message, explaining why I needed to talk to her. I remind myself of the messages as I finish my nearly cold tea. Her Facebook profile picture was of a black and white cat. Her friends list was hidden and other profile pictures were yet more of the cat. The only visible post was from a year ago and it was a photo of a smiling little girl with dark curly hair, a tiny tube inserted into her right nostril and running down her cheek. The accompanying words were: Mummy's little angel.

She was surprised to hear from a private investigator and was naturally interested in why one from so far away would want to talk to her. Shaun was as honest as he could be without saying that ultimately the reason for the call would be to exonerate her worst enemy in a possible murder enquiry.

I fetch a glass of water and arrange the sheet of paper with my questions on just in case I need prompting. I prop open the tablet and position it so it doesn't cut off one half of my face. I type her number and wait for the call to connect. On the second attempt, a woman's face briefly appears on the screen before the camera tilts upwards to point at spotlights set deep into a ceiling. A voice says, 'Hang on. Let me just…shift Polly…'

The woman reappears, apologising, blaming the cat for getting in the way. She's mid-forties, with long blonde hair, parted in the middle. She has a tiredness to her eyes and her skin is lined. She smiles nervously. My own face appears in a small square in the top left-hand corner of the screen.

I study her for a few moments. Her bright blue eyes are intrigued and friendly, yet they look nervous. To overcome such huge losses in her life and still be here surely denotes someone who possesses real inner strength.

'Hi Julie,' I begin. 'I'm William Bailey. Thank you for agreeing to speak to me.'

'Well, I couldn't really say no,' she laughs. 'I could've but eventually my curiosity would have got the better of me. How can I help? What are you investigating?'

I had toyed with the option of being upfront straight away, that honesty was the best policy but I don't think it's the best way to go here. This woman has every reason in the world to refuse to help. After all, providing an alibi is the biggest favour one person can do for another. But I doubt that favour would stretch to a worst enemy. If I can't find out what Lawrence was doing the day Amanda went missing, he may never be exonerated.

'First of all, I am not at liberty to discuss the case. Client confidentiality.' Julie pulls a face. 'And secondly, you need to know that this matter concerns your ex brother-in-law, Lawrence Killingworth.'

Her eyes roll upwards and she mutters, 'Oh, God.' She puts a hand to her forehead and closes her eyes. I give her time to think about what I've just chucked at her front door.

'I didn't expect you to say *his* name.'

'I know it's a shock, Julie. I would like to stress that I am not working for him. The case may or may not involve him. He has a connection, I don't know how strong, to the person at the centre of my case. I need to know his whereabouts on a certain day. It was six and a half years ago so you may not recall. I appreciate it was a long time ago.'

'Shock is an understatement, Mr Bailey. I've put him and his damn family behind me. That's the reason I changed my surname after I divorced his monstrous brother, why I removed his surname from my daughter's headstone.'

I nod my understanding and wait.

'This person at the centre of your case…Is it a man…?'

'A woman.'

'What do you suspect Lawrence of doing? Having an affair with her? Stalking her?'

'I can't say, Julie.' I tell her the date, hoping it pushes her along.

She shakes her head. 'I haven't seen or heard from Lawrence since he turned up at my house, the day after his hideous brother got six life sentences. I had to call the police after he stood in the middle of my front garden and publicly held me responsible for their murders.' Her voice starts to rise with anger. 'I wasn't the one with the gun. Do you know who Nathan killed and maimed that day, Mr Bailey?'

'Yes,' I say patiently.

'Let me tell you the order they died. Nathan drove to my mum's house, rang the doorbell and, when she answered in her dressing gown, he shot her twice in the chest. The postman found her. Then he drove to my sister's pub, banged on the door repeatedly until her husband answered and then shot him. He survived. But my sister, well, he gunned her down. She died later that night. They had three kids. My brother-in-law will never walk again.'

'I'm sorry,' I say.

'Then he drove around Trindle looking for Rob, my boyfriend. He was a binman. Nathan found the bin lorry on a round by the school Millie used to attend. He shot Rob three times, his colleague twice; they both died instantly. Then to top it off, he shot and injured an old guy who was wheeling his bin out to be collected. Then he drove to the cemetery and sat by my daughter's grave until the police came. Lawrence blamed all that on me.' Julie wipes a tear off her cheek and produces a tissue. 'I'm sorry,' she says eventually. 'I shouldn't have poured it all out like that. I've had a lifetime of counselling. Just hearing that bastard's name...' She stops and composes herself. 'I have an injunction on Lawrence; he isn't allowed within 50 metres of me.'

Doesn't mean he didn't come to see her on that day though.

'Why should I help him?'

'You won't be. You'll be helping the family of the woman at the centre of my case.'

'Tell me what it's about then. Tell me exactly who I'll be helping.'

I ignore her request. 'Lawrence was working this day in October, but had to leave work at 11am due to a crisis involving his brother.'

Julie smirks. 'Nathan was one big crisis.'

'Lawrence visited Nathan. But he didn't return to work like he was expected to. The following day Lawrence explained his absence by saying that he unexpectedly had to drive to Trindle. I'm aware that he moved away from the town following a community backlash. I think he came to see you at Nathan's request. There is no one else he'd travel all that distance to see. Nathan must have begged…'

'Nathan is highly manipulative,' Julie tells me. 'He wouldn't have had to beg much. He has Lawrence wrapped around his little finger.'

'Did you see or speak to Lawrence on this date?'

'I can't remember,' she says, nonchalantly.

I reach for my water, keep my eyes fixed on her face. She looks away to call Polly to her and the black and white cat from the Facebook photos appears at the bottom of the screen.

Stalemate. I'm reminded of Hock, what I said to Shaun. Barter with them. What do you have that they want? But it's easier with Hock. He likes information because he's always looking for an angle, a way to get the upper hand. Oh…upper hand. Perhaps it could work here too.

'Her name is Amanda,' I tell Julie and she narrows her eyes with interest. 'Thirty-seven years old, married only a few months before she went missing nearly seven years ago. She's who I'm looking for.'

'Does she have children?'

'One. A 14 year old son. Her mother, my client, wants one final investigation into her daughter's disappearance before Amanda is legally declared dead.'

Julie's hand moves across the screen as she strokes the cat. She mashes her lips together and looks down, muttering something to the pet.

'How does Lawrence know her?' she asks softly. Her eyes look tearful.

'He did some work for her.'

She nods, says nothing.

I wait. Sip more water. Think about my offer, how to word it.

'Julie, if you admit what you know, I will tell you the name he's now living under and his address. You can ruin his life like Amanda tried to.'

She looks up, her eyes bright with interest once again. 'She tried to ruin him? How?'

'As soon as she discovered his real identity, she fired him. And then told potential customers not to hire him. You can ruin Rachel's life too and his kids' future. Get your own back.'

Julie seems to sink into the settee. She stops stroking the cat and the purring subsequently ceases. Suddenly she can't hold my gaze. I wait.

281

Eventually, she looks up, her face softer, and in a calm rational voice, says, 'Yes, he did turn up here. About 5pm. He sat outside in the street until I came home just after half six. My neighbour clocked him. I told him to fuck off but he wouldn't, not even when I got out my mobile and threatened to call the police. I didn't want a scene; I've had enough over the years so we stood in the back garden.'

'What did he want? It must've been important to drive all that way.'

'Nathan sent him. The prison chaplain told Nathan that he needed my forgiveness to find peace, so he started sending me these pathetic letters.' She laughs. 'How am I supposed to forgive him for murdering the three people most dear to me after my daughter? I've heard all that crap about forgiving someone and setting yourself free, but I can't do it. To forgive Nathan is like saying it's okay.

'I told Lawrence no, not a cat's chance in hell would I ever forgive that monster. He said Nathan was threatening suicide. I said, "Good. We'll all get peace then". He got in his car and left. That was about quarter to seven.'

'Did he say he was coming straight home?'

She nods. 'He asked to use my toilet before he left. I told him he couldn't, but there was a service station three miles down the motorway.'

'Thank you,' I say sincerely. 'Have you got a pen and some paper? I'll give you the info on Lawrence…'

'No, Mr Bailey.' She holds a hand up. 'There's no need. Lawrence was a wreck when I saw him, running around the country after his brother. That's his punishment. He'll never be able to cut those brotherly ties.' She smiles, drawing the conversation to a close. 'Good luck in your investigation. I hope you find Amanda.'

I say goodbye, end the call and close the cover on the tablet. Of course I wasn't really going to give her the gen on Lawrence. How was she to know what I gave her would be true anyway?

If Lawrence followed Julie's advice and visited the service station, that would mean he wouldn't be back on his way to Lexington until 7.30pm, arriving ten thirty, maybe eleven. Later if there were traffic holdups. The drive back from Trindle wouldn't take him through Fradlington. To divert there, would add another forty miles to his journey. The trade fair was long over, Amanda wouldn't be there. Would Lawrence have been that bothered about tackling her after such a tiring day dealing with his brother, sister-in-law and a long drive? He had to find her first.

I shake my head. If I had a handwritten list of suspects, I'd draw a line through Lawrence's name. This leaves me with who? David who was not with Jake, so where was he and why has he lied? And where was Jake and why has he lied? And then there's Tamsin and her weak explanation for being at the trade fair. And how does she know Jake? Is he just her dealer?

I sit back in the chair, glance at the time. It's near enough lunchtime. I grab my mobile, check the screen for messages. Nothing from anyone. I lock up and head down the street to join the queue outside The Pickle and Cob sandwich shop.

'Hi,' I say to the young woman behind the counter, 'can I have the—' A vibration from my back pocket stops me. It's Shaun. 'Hang on, mate. Just ordering a sandwich,' and I lower the phone, but I can hear his excited voice drifting upwards. 'Roast chicken on brown, please. No tomato. Thanks.' I hold the phone to my ear and dig out my money. 'You alright, Shaun?'

'Will!' he shouts. 'Where are you? I tried the office. I—'

'I'm getting a sandwich; I've just said.'

'Mayonnaise?' the woman asks me.

'Yes, please, but can I have the chipotle-flavoured one instead?' I ask her.

'Never mind bloody chipotle,' he shouts in my ear. 'I've been following Jamie Nicholls for the last hour. Will, I think he's right.'

'What? Who?' I hand over the payment.

'Michael,' he shouts like I should know. 'I think it's true. I'm sending you a video via WhatsApp. Have a look, unless he's putting it on, this guy has got serious mobility issues.'

Chapter 43

I unfold the brown paper and smooth it out, revealing the sandwich. I immediately lost my appetite as Shaun's revelation hit home. I nearly cancelled the order, which would have been a waste of money. A headache begins to take hold at the back of my head so I fetch myself a drink, two paracetamol and settle down to watch the video back in the comfort of the office. I pick the decorative gherkin off the top of the sandwich lid and eat it, feeling my appetite return as the sweet tangy vinegar floods my mouth. Just because the bloke *might* have mobility issues doesn't mean everything is as Michael says it is. Or what if Shaun's got the wrong person? There might be two people called Jamie Nicholls living in close proximity to each other. Perhaps Jamie is exaggerating or lying about his problems so he can claim money he's not entitled to. You read about it all the time. People claiming chronic back ache following a fall from a ladder and, when they think they're in the clear, they're caught dancing on a table at someone's 60th birthday party.

Isn't it important to remain objective? Isn't this what I'm always telling Shaun? Don't believe everything you're told. People lie all the time. And I have Michael down as a pathological liar, highly manipulative, and a needy bastard.

And so what if the real Jamie has neurological issues. Is that any reason for Michael to wield personal information like that? Use it to manipulative Bronwyn into staying with him because he's terrified he might get dumped. Because someone might see that he's not that interesting after all.

I take a bite of the sandwich, wash the tablets down with water and press play. The video starts. It's a sunny morning and Shaun has clearly taken the video from the safety of his car, through the open driver's window. A dark-haired man is locking the front door of a house. The hedge is knee high so it hasn't obscured Shaun's view. The man turns with difficulty. There's a stiffness to his movements as if he's pivoted to the spot somehow. He moves down the path. I peer closer, awaiting his arrival onto the public path. A blob of reddish-pink chipotle falls from the sandwich, splattering across the paper.

The man appears. He has two crutches. Two grey plastic cuffs grip his upper arms and he swings his body towards a red hatchback parked against the kerb. His left leg is bent slightly at the knee, his foot off the ground. He wears dark blue jogging bottoms but it's clear to see his leg isn't in plaster. He pulls a pained expression as he manoeuvres his way into the car,

284

chucking the crutches across the rear seats and using the car roof for support as he sits in the driver's seat and swivels his legs into the footwell.

Shaun zooms in on the shot. He's spotted something in the back window but it's too blurry for me to see what it is.

'I'm going to follow him. See where he goes,' Shaun says quietly.

Suddenly, the phone emits a high shrilling, giving me a fright. The screen changes to Bronwyn's name and two circles, red or green.

Shit. I press green and swipe up the phone. 'Hello?'

'Hi Will,' she says hesitantly. 'Are you okay?'

'Yeah, fine. Sorry, the phone made me jump. I had the volume up too high. How are you? What you up to?'

'Nothing very interesting. Just doing some paperwork; very boring so I've been looking at B&Bs in the Lake District. I found some really lovely places. It just depends where you want to…'

'I don't mind where we go as long as we're there together.'

She laughs. 'You smooth talker, William. I tell you what, pop round tonight and we can have a look through them. And tomorrow I can book—'

'Er, why don't we go out again? I really enjoyed the other night. I could take you for your first authentic Indian meal. We can have a look at them over a poppadom.' This dating lark is going to cost me money I don't have.

'Will, you don't always have to come to my flat under the cover of darkness. It's perfectly safe.'

But the other night was one of the worst night's sleep I've ever had. Every noise outside: car brakes squealing or engines revving, every voice passing by the gated entrance, each gust of the wind, or even the pipes creaking, made me think Michael was outside and he was going to pound the door, demanding entry and challenge me to a duel. Or bore me with yet another story involving untrustworthy friends and sickly brothers. It's not that I'm scared of him, far from it. But if I do encounter him in such circumstances, I'm liable to punch him.

I can't rest at her place; I'm starting to detest being there. Maybe this is why affairs are typically conducted in hotel rooms and the backseats of cars. Why can't she just finish with him?

'Bron, have you ever met Michael's brother?' The question is out before I can think.

'No. I was supposed to meet him Easter Sunday but, as you know, I chose to spend it with you. Why do you ask?'

'No reason. I was, er…just thinking about this condition he's supposed to have and wondered how it's affecting him. Has Michael said anything more? I mean neurological is a bit vague. Could be memory, mobility, speech…'

'It could be, yes. All I know is that his brother lives alone because Michael was organising carers to possibly come in and help him with housework and personal care. He split from his wife recently. He has children. Why do you ask?'

'No reason. I'm being nosy,' and before she can question me further, I suggest we meet for a drink after work.

'Ah, I can't. I've arranged to meet Michael. I shouldn't be long though. We can get together —'

'Are you going to finally talk to him?' I demand. 'End it with him?'

'Well, I hope to. It was actually his idea to meet up. His GP has signed him off sick for a fortnight.'

Good. Hope it's serious.

'But you can still talk to him, Bron,' I insist. 'A conversation is a two-way street. You can't spend the entire time just listening to the prat go on and on.'

'That's a bit harsh, Will. I said *I'll* try, but it isn't easy to find the right words. I don't want to hurt his feelings.'

She prattles on in the same vein - that it's easy for me as I don't have a girlfriend I need to finish with. How would I like to be treated insensitively if I was in the same position? I want to remind her that she actually treated me quite badly three months ago but what's the point? The bloody cheek of her. I say no more on the subject.

'Anyway, I should be home before seven, or I can meet you somewhere after if you want to go for this curry.'

But now the idea doesn't appeal. She doesn't sound very enthusiastic about a curry. And I can't get it out of my head that she will have been with him, and though they're not having sex, his hands will have been on her, his mouth on hers, his hand in hers, his clothing fibres on her dress. Jealousy truly does eat you up. From the inside out. I push the half-finished sandwich away, my appetite has abandoned me. She says my name, prompting me for a response.

'I'll give you a ring later, Bron. Shaun's here,' I lie. 'Looks like he has some interesting news.'

'Okay. See you later.'

I end the call, swearing loudly. I stare at the black screen. Signed off sick. Why am I not surprised? Whilst everyone battles on in the face of redundancy, this coward gets time off. Yet another reason to despise him. And another reason for her to feel sorry for him. I'm not sure which of them is getting on my nerves the most.

I return to the video but the ending is simply Shaun promising to update me later. I type him a short message. *Remain objective. There could be any explanation.*

But I realise the words apply just as much to me.

*

'He has a Blue Badge, Will,' Shaun tells me in an annoyingly whiney voice that I didn't know he was capable of. 'I googled the criteria. They don't just give them out for a broken leg or really bad cold. You have to been diagnosed by a proper doctor…'

I resist the urge to joke that a fake doctor would be qualified enough, but I realise Shaun is as disheartened as me. I admire him for feeling bad on my behalf. The sign of a good friend.

'The bloke can hardly walk. He relies totally on his crutches; he frequently stops for a breather. Every time I saw his face, he was wincing in pain.'

'Where was he going?' I ask. 'When you followed him.'

'GP surgery. It took him several minutes to get out of the car and walk the few metres to their door. One of the staff came out with him, carrying a huge white paper bag of medications. She helped him into the car and he came home. I stayed for another half an hour and then went to work.'

'Is he definitely Jamie Nicholls?' I ask, moving the phone to my other ear.

'Believe me, I'd have asked a neighbour if one of them had been in the front garden. If I could have engaged him in conversation, I'd have asked the man himself.' Shaun sniggers. 'That's an option.'

287

'Don't,' I warn. 'Seriously, Shaun. You don't know this man. This is supposed to be stealthy surveillance. We have no idea how he will react if you admit you're watching him because his brother, who he might be devoted to, is a lying manipulative bastard.'

'Point taken. Look, I've got to go. Apparently, there are people in the pub who want feeding. I'll ring you later. Bye.'

I open the tablet, google Blue Badges and read all about how a person qualifies for one. On the face of it, Jamie Nicholls may be eligible. Shaun says the man can't walk far, relies on walking aids and is clearly in a lot of pain. It may be neurological like Michael suggests. But Michael would have us believe that his brother's symptoms, whatever they are, have only come on in the last few weeks. Jamie's already receiving huge quantities of medication. How, if he's not been diagnosed? How quickly do you get a Blue Badge once you've submitted your application? If you need to be assessed by a doctor, I bet that doesn't happen overnight. If Jamie has been like this for a while, why is Michael only mentioning it now? Because he can sense Bronwyn is close to finishing with him?

I scratch my head thoughtfully but my brain feels muddled, and tiredness feels like a heavy cloak around my shoulders. I should call it a day. Start again tomorrow with what I'm getting paid for. I need to speak to David and Jake.

I type a quick text to David, asking if he's around tomorrow and what time we can meet. I close up the office, see the name of the business stencilled in gold letters on the frosted glass door. I need to do something about Nisha's proposal. As I return to the car, I call my mum. See if she knows a solicitor who can offer me some advice. Even better if they'll do it for free.

Chapter 44

I wake the next morning and discover, much to my delight, that I have the beginnings of a cold. My head pounds and my throat feels like it's been slashed with a rusty razor blade. I drink the water from the night before. It tastes disgusting but down it goes. I pull the squashed pillow into a more comfortable position and lie back, thinking about yesterday. The only solicitor Mum knew was the one who dealt with the sale of her house and, although they work for a large firm who deal with all your legal needs including business advice, they won't do it for free or a reduced rate. It could cost me fifty quid just to take a seat in their plush office. Mum could hear my disappointment down the phone and, knowing I would only need a solicitor for an urgent matter, offered to ring my auntie Heidi later. Auntie Heidi, eleven years Mum's junior, has lots of friends. One of those people who receives lots of Christmas dinner and New Year's Eve party invitations from a multitude of people, including ex-boyfriends she now has platonic relationships with and friends of friends. Eddie and I used to call her "Little Miss Sociable" behind her back, then she heard us and loved it.

If there is such a solicitor out there who will work for free or nearly free, Heidi will know them. My yawn is wide, and I feel my jaw click. I grab my glasses and mobile off the bedside cabinet and blink with blurry eyes at the two texts from Bronwyn.

Will, what was that all about?

Will. I'm going home. Give me a call if you can be bothered. Definite terse tone of voice. If you don't know what it was all about, I think, then we are in serious trouble.

And a surprise text from Declan.

I want to speak to you. Who the fuck do you think you are?

This one makes me smile. Three guesses what that's about. I'm in no mood for anyone's grief. Not with this headache. Of course! The phone call. The one I made at precisely quarter to six last night. Whilst my tea of a cottage pie and accompanying side order of vegetables was going round and round inside the microwave, I decided that it was my turn to interrupt Michael. I phoned Bronwyn's mobile, a wicked glint in my eye and a ready-to-go sarcasm. It rang several times before it was answered.

'Hello?' she said, like she was expecting someone else.

'Hi,' I said confidently, 'you alright? What you up to?'

'Can I ring you back later? I'm just in the middle of something.' Oh yes, I was spot on with the timing. In the background I could hear the excited chatter and the tinkling of glass, synonymous with the sounds of a busy bar. I hope I've interrupted his flow and he's sat there, brooding into whatever pathetic drink he liked, cursing me. Served him right to have a taste of his own medicine. I smiled at my victory.

Then I heard his voice. Close by. Needy and irritated.

'...picks his moments, doesn't he?'

I wanted to laugh.

Bronwyn made an odd little noise. Perhaps she was warning him to keep quiet.

'What are you in the middle of?' I asked innocently. 'Are you out? You sound like you're in a bar.'

'Can we speak at a more convenient time, please?' she asked formally. She might as well have been speaking to a senior manager rather than someone she'd taken to bed.

'Which will be when? I'm only asking because I thought you wanted to meet after your... what was it? Social drink with Michael? Oh, shit,' I exclaimed, in pretence. 'Is that where you are? Hope I'm not interrupting.'

'It's fine,' she replied tersely.

'Is Michael really pissed off? Is he glaring into his Taboo and lemonade? Bet he's just as annoyed with you for answering my call. Tell you what: now he knows how I feel. Anyway, if you do finish with him before seven, and by finish I mean the drink or the relationship, let me know. If not, I'll catch you some other time. Apologies to Mike. Bye.' But I knew she wouldn't talk to him and I knew we wouldn't be meeting up. I hadn't got the energy for further pointless conversations so I turned my phone off.

It still feels good to be awkward and sarcastic. It gives me a tingling from head to toe. Maybe she'll realise how unfair she's being with me. I yank open the drawer and fish around amongst the keys, pens, notes, and other assorted junk for the packet of Strepsils and the paracetamol. I dose myself up, heave myself out of bed and into the shower.

*

'Honey and lemon, that's what you need,' Mrs Penn tells me sympathetically. 'I think there's some honey in here,' and she starts rooting through the cupboard by the oven. 'I can always pick you up a lemon on my way home.'

'I can get the fruit,' I tell her. 'Don't bother yourself about the honey. I'll look when I've had my toast.'

'Okay.' She closes the cupboard door, regards me for a few moments. 'You are looking after yourself, aren't you, Will?'

'You sound like my mum,' I tell her with a heartfelt smile. 'I've had a lot on lately with this investigation, my boss' job offer…'

'This new woman of yours?' She winks.

'It's not serious.'

'Are you sure?' she teases, tilting her head. 'I've been around enough lovesick men to still be able to recognise one. And you haven't been sleeping here a couple of nights. Look, I know I have this household rule about girlfriends not stopping over and—'

'Mrs Penn,' I begin, brushing toast crumbs off my fingers, 'your rule does not cause me any bother. Honest.'

'If you say this lass of yours is trustworthy, then that's good enough for me. If she wants to stay over, then all I ask is you let me know when. And I'd like to meet her.' She claps me on the back and waves her fingers in a goodbye. 'See you later, love. Don't forget the honey.'

I contemplate her offer. It's an option. There'd be no chance at all of Michael turning up out of the blue. Which is good because he'll be on a mission to get his own back now. What can he do? Hunt me down and hit me? Damage the car? Slash the soft-top roof like someone did three months ago? Take Bronwyn away for a romantic weekend and propose? What a quandary that'll put her in. What would *she* do? It actually doesn't bear thinking about. I may not like her response and I can't counterattack until Shaun concludes his surveillance. So far that's thrown up more questions than answers.

In actual fact, what if he followed me here? Shit. Best not bring Bronwyn home. I do not want to bring trouble to Mrs Penn's doorstep. I still need somewhere to live. Now more than ever.

*

I arrive at the office and put the kettle on to start making Mrs Penn's throat remedy. I slice the Tesco-bought lemon and drop two slices into a mug with a generous teaspoon of honey. I check my phone. Still no reply from David. I send him a follow-up text, and I'll give him until this afternoon to reply to before heading to his house tonight. I still need to know his real whereabouts the evening of Amanda's disappearance. And then there's his slimy mate, Jake.

I pour boiling water onto the ingredients and gently stir the concoction, melting the honey. Jake could have been with David, but definitely not at David's house, given what Mrs Newman said about the workmen parked on Amanda's drive.

If they were together somewhere, why have they lied? Could they have been having an affair behind Amanda's back? Shaun called their friendship a bromance, which is the oddest thing I've ever heard. What's to say that, like me and Bronwyn, they didn't take their relationship to a different level? Personally I can't see what anyone, man or woman, would see in Jake. He's not easy on the eye. In fact, he is quite ugly and a creepy fucker to boot. I would credit David with more taste.

They don't appear to be a couple now though. Although David's house was spick and span the first time Shaun and I interviewed hm. Jake might have helped David clean up, despite the shit state his own house is in. Or maybe they're keeping their relationship a secret until after Amanda is presumed dead, which would be kinder to Oliver and Mrs Davies.

Tamsin did make that crack about Jake preferring sex with someone with a dick. Rude, admittedly, and maybe only said in response because he threw her a dirty look as if to say she'd be the last woman on earth he'd go with. But what if there is truth behind her comment? Perhaps it's unrequited love. Perhaps David has taken advantage of Jake's feelings and persuaded him to be his alibi.

They've both colluded to mislead me and the police. So where were they and why have they lied? Was one of them murdering Amanda? Or were they both doing something completely illegal or illicit? Jake dealing, and David in bed with another woman. Certainly if David was with another woman, it would raise the police's suspicion level, like it would mine.

I sip the mixture, feeling the sweet and tangy liquid soothe my sore throat. At my desk, I rifle through my papers for notes on Tamsin. She knows Jake better than I initially thought. They have a rapport rarely seen between dealer and addict. Almost pally. Tamsin said he'd been her dealer for ten years but was she on drugs whilst working at the salon? Surely, if Amanda had suspicions, she'd have fired Tamsin. No way would she want drugs on the premises.

Hang on...Tamsin didn't say how long she'd been taking drugs. It was Jake who said something about having no regrets ten years ago, but she explained that he'd got her into drugs. That might not necessarily have been ten years ago. Other witnesses have said that, eight months before Amanda went missing, her relationship with Tamsin changed. Tamsin became difficult, slovenly with a bad attitude. Was that drug-related? Were drugs her way of coping with work issues, or even an unknown issue which was affecting her work? I can see me having to make a return trip to Tamsin's flat. Or worse, Jake's house. Not that I'll get the truth from either of them.

The sound of a fist banging on the glass of the outer office door makes me jump and does nothing to help the stuffiness in my head. Ten quid says it's Declan.

I open the door to a raging Declan.

'You're here, are you?' he demands.

'Well, yes. I work here. Everything alright, Declan?' I take a few moments to admire how unkempt he is at 9am. Has he been to bed? When was the last time he showered? I sniff the air. Stale sweat. There are small piles of dandruff on the shoulders of his black polo shirt, a colour that does not suit him. He's unshaven with dark circles under his eyes, and a semi-permanent flinching expression on his pasty face as if he's had hours of being shouted at. Probably courtesy of Hock and Kerry. And I can guess why. Hock for bringing his name into disrepute and her because, from now on, Declan will be working for Hock for free. There will be no more nice things for her.

'I texted you last night and you haven't fucking replied,' he shouts.

'Turned my phone off,' I explain. 'Got a cold so I went to bed early. What's up? Come in before the neighbours start complaining. What's on your mind? Down the corridor, office at the end. Want a drink?'

'No, I fucking do not.' Halfway down the carpet, he stops and sniffs. 'What's that smell?'

Oh, the irony of it. 'Throat remedy,' I say. 'It's working. I'll be back to singing baritone by lunchtime.'

He gives me a funny look and enters my office, looking around at the light airy room. I hold out a hand to the various chair choices but he opts to remain standing so I sit and daintily sip my remedy, forcing him to look down at me.

'What is it, Declan?'

He snorts. 'You know full well what it is. Phillip Hock. You've dropped me right in it with him. I am never gonna get out of his clutches now. It's like being caught between—'

'A harpy eagle's claws?'

He frowns at me, puzzled.

'They have the strongest claws of any bird.'

'I don't give a shit about a stupid bird! Jesus. Why did you have to go and see him? Do you have any idea what you've done? I'm in his debt for forever...I am—'

'All you had to do was admit the truth about your whereabouts the day Amanda went missing, but you thought you could outsmart me.'

He shakes his head, pulls out the chair opposite and plonks himself down with a thud, catching his elbow on the arm. He screws his face up. I wonder if he's going to suddenly release his frustration and despair and bawl his eyes out.

'What did Hock say to you?' I ask, my tone sympathetic, but really I just want to know.

Declan shakes his head as he relives the conversation which was probably long, tiring and absolutely to the point. He looks up, his eyes narrowing.

'He called you a sarcastic wanker and bollocked me for bringing you into his shop.' I smile, pleased I got under Hock's skin. 'He seemed to actually get off on the fact that he was my alibi. I'm sure he must have been stroking his hard-on when he phoned me.'

I shudder. There's an image I do not want. I can't resist a smile though. Declan's face cracks and he relaxes into the chair.

'He assured me that he hadn't revealed what I'd been doing, like that fucking mattered. So not only do I owe the bastard for the remainder of my miserable life, I have to drop everything when he clicks his fat fingers, and I have to sell him my children. If that wasn't bad enough, I got it in the neck from Kerry. She's addicted to the extra money. Spends it like it's going out of fashion, mostly on tat for the house.' He stops. His face creases thoughtfully. 'There is a bit of a silver lining under the dark thundercloud hanging over my life.' I raise an eyebrow expectantly. 'I probably won't be able to afford to get married now.'

'Disappointed?'

He huffs. 'Do I look it?'

I smile, shake my head.

'Do you usually leave piles of wrecked lives in the wake of your investigation?'

'Sometimes. The liars come off worse.' He opens his mouth to protest but I hold up a hand to silence him. 'Declan, Phillip Hock was never going to let you go. You must have realised that. Your only exit is to get dirt on him.'

'Dirt on Hock? I'm up to my fucking thighs in his shit. I can't use any of it. Not without dragging myself down.'

I finish the drink. 'Take some consolation from the fact that you're a lot better off than some people I could mention.'

He raises his chin with interest. 'Oh. Anyone I—?'

'Jake Bunby.'

He snorts with amusement and starts laughing. 'Hope you've dropped him in with Hock right up to his balding head. He deserves it. Vile little bastard. Another one who takes pleasure from other people's misery. I could tell you something interesting about him, something I guarantee you don't know.' He wags a finger.

'Oh. You know, Declan, I'm really glad you called round this morning. Brew?'

'Why not?'

Hurriedly I make the tea in case he goes off the boil. I carry the cups back in to the office, sloshing hot tea on my hand. I plonk them and myself down and prepare to be enlightened.

'For Oliver's 7th birthday, Amanda threw a party, invited a load of people. She'd only been married to David for a couple of months, so she let him ask a couple of friends along. In case he felt left out. Jake was the only one who turned up. Them pair are glued at the fucking hip. But not always.' He pauses dramatically to drink his tea. 'For part of the afternoon, Jake was sat talking to Kerry. They were having a right chinwag. On the way home, she told me this interesting snippet. Kerry used to work with Jake's older sister at Asda. I forget her name. Anyway, a few years before, big sis tells Kerry, as they're stacking shelves or filing their nails at their empty checkouts, that Jake and David fell out big time.'

I raise an eyebrow. Most friends have fallen out at some point. Me and Bronwyn certainly have.

'They must've been about nineteen, twenty. Kerry couldn't remember all the details, but she knew it was over a girlfriend, David's at the time. I've only ever known David to be a calm, easy-going bloke, but on this occasion, friendship was tossed out of the window. He storms round to Jake's mum's house, bangs on the door and, as soon Jake opens up, David lamps

295

him and then goes in with the boot. Kicks him all the way down the hall, shouting and punching. Wish I could have seen it.'

'Please tell me David put him in hospital.'

Declan nods. 'You haven't heard the best of it. Jake is pretty badly beaten up. Big sis and the mother have to drag David off. He fucks off, calling Jake fucking this, bastard that. They call the police, ambulance carts Jake off to A and E, but when the cops question him, he refuses to press charges.'

'He told them he fell down the stairs?' I suggest sarcastically.

'Something like that. Big sis goes up the fucking wall, threatens to go round David's house give him what for. And there's Jake telling her, if she does, he'll disown her.'

'David and Jake obviously forgave each other,' I say. 'Fast forward a few years and they're in the brewing game together, and Jake is a spare part in David's marriage.' Plus, they're each other's alibi.

'According to what big sis told Kerry, within a week of the beating, David and Jake were back to being best buddies like nothing had happened. I can't tell you any more than that. No idea what it was about.'

'Is it worth me speaking to Kerry?'

'Kerry doesn't like you. You won't get anything from her. Plus she'll be straight on the blower to warn big sis you're coming to see her. I know. I've been on the receiving end of her tactics. Try Jake's sister. But I don't know her name.'

I'll get Shaun to Facebook stalk Bunby. See if he likes tagging his big sister in his posts. Or there's always David. He can tell me her name later when I call round his house to see what he's playing at.

Declan finishes his tea, plonks the mug back down, wipes his mouth on the back of his hand. 'I'd best go. Shift starts at 11.'

'Tell me something before you go. Why did you start working for Hock? Was it for the money?'

He nods. 'Amanda threatened to take Ollie back full time and send him to some posh fee paying school. She told me, if I didn't like it, I'd have to take her to court. He's lived with me since he was two years old. I wasn't going to give him up easily. But neither could I afford court fees. I'm sorry she's not here to see her son grow up. But at the same time, I'm glad she's not here to ruin our lives. She was good at that.'

Chapter 45

I balance the bottle of Lucozade on the arm of the bench and unscrew the cap, my shoulder clamping my mobile against my ear as David explains the delay in replying to my messages.

'I'm working away...well, not *away* away, but not down the road,' he tells me. 'There's a group of us laying a floor in an office block. It's a big job, full on, going to make me a pretty packet. I'm back tomorrow afternoon if that helps, Will.'

I sip the drink, feel the fizziness ease the pain in my throat. 'It'll have to be,' I reply, my tone shirty. He sounds a different person to the angry one from the other night, threatening to kick down doors and punch faces. Has he dished out any threats to Jake? After the last kicking he received from his bestie, albeit several years ago, Jake must be terrified that this is the end of their bromance.

'Ring when you're back and I'll pop over,' I tell David.

'Can you give me any idea what it's about? Is it about Hepworth?'

'Enjoy your floor laying. Cheerio.' I hang up, rest my back onto the bench and feel the April sun warm my skin. It's nearly noon and the North Street park is getting busy. There's the usual runners, wearing all the fancy gear: wireless headphones, lots of Lycra vests and coloured trainers; dog walkers swinging those little poo bags by their side. Women with those enormous push chairs and lots of screaming pre-school kids in tow; office workers balancing early lunches on knees as they take time out for some fresh air.

This is my favourite bench. It overlooks the entire park all the way down the hill towards the expensive townhouses I'll never be able to afford unless I win the lottery. On the left is the fountain, devoid of water whilst the park keepers clean the hexagonal pond and repair the huge stone fish which spurts out the water. It makes a lovely relaxing noise when it is in use though. On the right is the start of the rhododendron walk. When the shrubs are in flower, which should be soon judging by this warm spell we're experiencing, the colours of the petals are spectacular.

In front of me, a groundsman wearing brown and green clothing is preparing the oval-shaped flower bed for planting. The wheelbarrow is filling up with weeds and litter, a hoe is propped up against its side. A robin is perched on a nearby railing, watching for any worms that may be unearthed. The man has EarPods in and occasionally I see his mouth move as he sings along to the unheard music.

298

Must be nice to work outdoors, I think, watching as he turns the dark brown soil over with a garden fork. Especially something as rewarding as gardening, where you can stand back and look at your creation. But then it's probably shit in the cold months. Freezing hands, numb feet, only leaves to rake up and litter to collect.

I considered getting a second job after my falling out with Bronwyn, not just for the money but for something to do at the weekends and evenings. I should think about it again, actually look into it this time, visit some job pages and sites, join a recruitment agency. I'm going to need more money if I agree to a partnership with Nisha. My nest egg will be gone, all used up, and should I need some for a rainy day, I'm going to be lacking. I can't go to my mum every time a loan is needed. It's embarrassing enough that she still does my laundry. I need to take up her offer of a crash course in ironing.

'Hello,' says a voice, but the sun is blinding and I shade my eyes with a hand. 'Can I sit down?'

'Yeah, sure.' I grab my drink and scoot along the bench, avoiding the blob of bird shit, leaving a significant gap between me and Bronwyn. She sits, sanitises her hands with a bottle of hand gel. The smell of alcohol fills my nostrils, which is good because it means that the cold isn't yet affecting my sense of smell. On her lap, she unfolds a small paper parcel to reveal a slice of Rocky Road cake. Just the one, I note. None for me then. That'll be because of yesterday. I don't even want cake but the slight stings a bit.

After Declan left, she phoned and this time I answered. Thought it best not to make the situation worse by ignoring her again. Her tone wasn't terse but it wasn't gushing either. She started with the usual "how are you, how's work". I kept my answers brief, didn't ask the same. I agreed to meet her but not at the suggested time of 1pm. If she's going to chide me, I'd rather get it over and done with.

I take a long gulp of my drink, watch her break the end off the cake. Why can't she just bite it like a normal person? I turn my attention back to the groundsman, who's now talking to a woman with two white dogs who sniff around the wheelbarrow wheels with interest. The people are chatting. The gardener points at the raked ground. Perhaps he's explaining his planting regime.

'Just gonna plant them in a row' or 'A staggered row' or 'white ones here, red there'. She seems impressed anyway. Perhaps that's the way to a woman's heart. Not chocolate or humour, or even sex, but the ability to really wow them with knowledge about your job. In his case, planting begonias or geraniums, or whatever else choice he has.

I look over. Bronwyn's halfway through the cake and is daintily dabbing her mouth with the tiniest serviette. I don't wait for her to start the conversation; it'll annoy her if I do it whilst she's eating.

'Cake's not a very healthy lunch, is it?' I quip.

She looks up, shrugging as if to say she doesn't care.

'Sorry I couldn't meet you at one. I can't spare the time to drive over to your flat today. I have a meeting at half past.' This is with the solicitor Heidi found me. I find out today if the business venture is worth me investing in. It's quite exciting but I say nothing to Bronwyn. She's frowning with annoyance. Oh shit. What now? Can I do anything right?

'I wasn't inviting you for sex, William,' she tells me, coldly. 'I didn't even mention the flat, did I?'

'No...I just assumed. Sorry.' Her expression remains unimpressed. 'I'm sorry,' I repeat firmly. 'Obviously wasn't thinking with my brain.'

'No. You're not doing much thinking with that particular organ these days, are you?'

'I disagree,' I say, my tone light. 'I've put my white and grey matter to considerable use these last few days with my investigation. I've narrowed my suspects down; that's assuming Amanda has been murdered and hasn't started a new life in the south of France under a different name. I just know that, around the corner, something unexpected is lurking that's going to throw everything into chaos. But that's private detective work for you.' I offer her a big smile but she looks away in disgust, screwing the cake wrapper up and uncapping a bottle of raspberry and mango juice.

'Now that you've demolished your emergency cake fix, are we going to discuss my little antic yesterday? That's presumably why you called this meeting.'

'It is. You catch on quick.'

'I am known for my sharp intelligence, Bronwyn. May I start? Thanks,' I say when she raises a hand to indicate "Go ahead".

'In my defence, I couldn't help it. I despise Michael. What irks me is that he's interrupted me twice, and it's gone unpunished. I know two wrongs don't make a right but, for a while, no, actually even now, I'm still getting a buzz from fucking up his night out with you. Was I successful?'

She nods and I smile.

'He's getting a lot more than I am. I get a bollocking in a park, with no cake, no smile, no kind word. And he gets your undivided attention with a glass of wine in a swanky bar. I refuse to apologise for my sarcastic and sulky behaviour.' I try a smile again. No response. 'Your turn.'

'You are getting more than him, actually, Will. A white wine spritzer in a dank run-of-the-mill pub, surrounded by screaming kids and their disinterested parents, listening to a pathetic man moan about his miserable life in no way compares to the many exciting evenings you spend in *my* flat in *my* glorious company.' I concede with a nod. 'Also, I grant you the privilege of making love to me. Don't I?'

I blush. 'You do. And it is out of this world so yes, you're right, I am in a better position.' I lean closer, mindful of the mess on the bench. 'You're so sexy when you scold me. I'm having heart palpitations,' and I clap a hand to the middle of my chest. It still doesn't make her smile.

She frowns. 'I'm being serious, Will. And just so you're aware, I got it in the neck too, so I'm sharing the telling-off. Michael knows you interrupted us on purpose, accused me of playing a part in it by not taking you to task about it on the phone.'

'What a twat,' I say, my annoyance level rising.

'Indeed. And for your information, I have reprimanded Michael too. Told him that he can't just turn up at my flat unannounced, that I have a life of my own, and also to try and get along with you. I told him that you are here to stay.'

I'd have done more than reprimand him. Thrown my drink in his face and told him to piss off for good.

'I know I'm asking a lot of you, Will, to put up with this, but it'll be just for a little while longer. I'm not good with situations like this; it's been years since I've had to finish a relationship. When Michael and I are over, I will still have to see him; it's unavoidable. His company deals with our IT issues. I can't jeopardise that working relationship. Do you understand?'

I consider what she's asking. How long is "a little while"? A fortnight, a month, until Christmas? But once Shaun finishes his investigation into Michael's tall tales, and I present my findings to Bronwyn, "a little while" will only be a matter of hours. How can she carry on once she knows the lies he's told? That's if there are lies. There better had be.

'What happened yesterday?' I ask. 'Why's he been signed off sick?'

She sighs, sits back onto the bench. 'He went to the doctor because of a really bad headache. All this with his brother has worked him up. His blood pressure was high so he was signed off for a fortnight with anxiety but, if it doesn't go back to normal, he may have to go on medication.'

I resist the urge to remark that I hope the figures were dangerously high. I should stop being childish.

'I only agreed to a drink in the hope that I could finish the relationship but, as usual, Michael bombarded me. He went on and on about it all. He's convinced Jamie is going to die. I went home feeling like I'd been through a mangle. I texted you twice and went to bed with my own headache. Woke up with it too.'

'You might have my germs,' I suggest. 'I'm getting a cold. Or tonsillitis. My throat is murder.'

Bron smiles sympathetically. 'You want to try some honey and—'

'Already taking it, my sweet.' I reach for her hand. She slots her fingers into mine. 'Bron, have you considered that he might be lying to you?'

She frowns. 'How do you mean? About what? His headache?'

'Everything. His brother's illness, the high blood pressure, his job. I'm just saying. It's a lot to happen to one person in one go. He's either very unlucky or...' I trail off.

'What, Will?' And she shakes our clasped hands to prompt a further response.

'He's a manipulative lying bastard.'

'Michael?' she laughs. 'I doubt it. He's never struck me as...do you know something?'

'I'm just asking you to take what he tells you with a pinch of salt. In my line of work, with the exception of a few people, most of those I talk to are liars. I've learnt to never believe anything unless I can verify it.'

'Does that go for your personal life too?'

'Especially there. Saves on a lot of unnecessary hurt. Come on,' I say, standing and pulling her to her feet. 'Let's take a turn around the garden.' As we stroll past the groundsman, I give him a thumbs-up and he nods back in acknowledgment.

'You know what?' I say, as we pass the empty fountain. There's a load of tarnished coins in the bottom. It's a wonder someone hasn't collected them up. 'Ignore the predicament we find ourselves in. I can honestly say I'm never happier than when I'm with you, Bron.'

She tugs my hand, putting the brakes on our feet. We face each other. Her smile is big, her eyes tinged with a different emotion.

'Remember you told me this, Will,' she urges, her voice gently pleading, 'because I feel exactly the same.' And without another word, she wraps our joined hands around her back, pressing herself against me, and kisses me with a passion I've never felt from her before.

Chapter 46

Jake's kitchen, the one place I didn't want to be invited into, is in a worse state than his living room. I knew it would be. The large kitchen window overlooks a tiny square of garden; the grass I'm guessing rarely encounters a lawn mower. There is a rotary washing line though and, pegged out like bunting, are several pairs of men's underpants, socks and two pairs of jeans. The point of such a washing line is surely that it rotates, propelled by the wind. However, not in this case. Jake has failed to notice that a metre-high sapling, has been allowed to flourish within the grass and is acting as a stop, preventing such movement. I hope he isn't relying on those jeans to wear. They may never dry.

A few minutes spent in his kitchen and I can see that it resembles one of those cartoons where you have to spot the health and safety risks. The man high up on a ladder precariously over-reaching for a box, or the puddle of oil on the floor right in the path of a man carrying a large box he can't see over.

The bin is overflowing with glass bottles, takeaway cartons, food remains. Recycling is not on his list of priorities. On the peeling lino is a pool of yellow-coloured liquid. Beer, cooking oil, piss? The double socket is overloaded with adaptors and plugs for the kettle, radio and two phone chargers.

He flips the frying bacon over with a fork and rests the utensil back onto the bare work surface, which he will no doubt forget to wipe. I wonder how many times a month, Jake suffers from vomiting and diarrhoea.

'Are you sure you don't want a cup of tea?' he asks, turning to me. But I've seen the inside of the fridge. The bacon was on the shelf above an opened punnet of grapes. And I bet Jake isn't one to wash fruit before eating it.

'I'm alright, thanks,' I say.

Using a dirty tea towel, he pulls the grill pan out of the oven and hurriedly turns the slices of white bread over. 'I don't know about you, but a hangover gives me a raging hunger.' He grins, knocks the switch down on the kettle and reboils the water for the third time. He spoons two heaped teaspoons of coffee into a mug and splashes water into it, stirring it vigorously. 'What did you want to talk about?' He blows on the scalding liquid, eyes me over the rim of the mug.

'Your whereabouts the day Amanda went missing.'

He rolls his eyes. 'What again? It's in my statement. Take some pity on me; I've got a horrible headache.'

'New evidence has come to light, Jake, which casts doubt on your alibi.'

He looks horrified, slams the coffee down, sloshing brown liquid which dribbles down the lower cupboard door. He makes no move to mop it up. 'You're fucking kidding? Now? From where? Whatever it is, it's bollocks. Me and Dave were at his house, in the shed, tasting beer and chatting. I'm not lying. Ask David. He'll tell you.'

'I've no doubt he'll tell me exactly the same. The problem is, Jake, you really need a third-party to verify it.' Suddenly, I get a whiff of burning. I move my head to the side and see smoke coming from the oven. The corner of the tea towel is on fire having got caught in the bars of the grill.

'Shit!' he says, whipping it out, nearly pulling the heavy grill pan clean onto the floor. He flings the cloth into the sink which is piled high with dirty crockery, and yanks on the tap. Water sprays everywhere, hitting the flat surfaces with immense force. The work surfaces and the front of his red t-shirt are absolutely soaked. And now the bacon is burning. I step forward, grabbing the handle of the frying pan and moving it off the heat. I switch the hob off and look at the crispy black strips welded to the bottom of the pan.

Jake is muttering to himself, flinching with pain at the cost of such sudden movement to his back. 'Fuck's sake. Ow, my fucking spine. Ah, Jesus.' He clasps his lower back with a hand and reaches for his crutch propped up against the back door. But his fumbling fingers knock it sideways and it crashes into the small kitchen table, threatening to topple all the crap piled high on top. He looks like he wants to cry. I retrieve the crutch and tell him to take it easy.

He looks at me, tears of pain in his eyes. 'I don't know how much more I can take of this pain. It wasn't meant to be like this. A couple of twinges I reckoned on, bit of hip pain. I'm in absolute agony.'

'Can I get you anything? Have you got any painkillers among this crap?' I flick my eyes over the surfaces.

'Cut it out, mate,' he pleads. 'You're beginning to sound like our Kat.'

'Cat?' I ask.

'Big sister. Kat, short for Kathleen. Never stops mothering me.' He smiles fondly. 'Pass me that tin. There. By the bread bag.'

I pluck out a battered old tobacco tin and watch as he removes a slightly bent spliff and lights it, drawing the smoke deep into his lungs. Great, I think, backing away. Now I'm going to smell like a pothead with the munchies.

'The only thing that touches the pain,' he explains. 'Open the door, mate. Let some of this bacon smell out.'

I unlock the back door and stand on the threshold, breathing the fresh air in deeply. I watch him puff away and the pain etched deep in his face eases off, his joints relax. I wonder if Jamie Nicholls suffers this much pain and whether he might have turned to a cannabis dealer. Perhaps Jake knows the dealer in that area. He might be his dealer. I ask him.

'I don't cover that area. I'm not allowed to stray off my patch,' he tells me with a quick grin, and I wonder if Hock has spoken to him yet. But knowing Hock, he'll want evidence he can beat Jake with. And then even cannabis won't be able to touch his pain. He'll need morphine. Or an induced coma.

'What's this evidence then?' he asks, stabbing the end of the joint onto a plate to put it out before returning it to the tin. 'Who says I'm lying?'

'How did you get to David's house? Did he pick you up? Did you go by taxi, bus...'

'I drove there. Hate public transport. It's not user friendly. You know with crutches—'

'Where did you park? Up on the kerb, outside a neighbour's...'

Jake smirks with amusement. 'On the drive like always. Behind Dave's van. Never alongside in case *she* came home before I left.'

'Did you know Amanda was at a trade fair?'

He shakes his head and starts dealing with the mess, using the fork to scrape the burnt offerings into the bin.

'Jake, can you stop that for a second and look at me, please?'

With a huff, he slams the frying pan down and leans against the work surface, arms folded.

'When you arrived at David's house, did you notice anything unusual going in the street? Or at any of the nearby houses?'

'Like what?'

'Like a party, or a water company dealing with a blocked drain in the road...'

Jake pulls a thoughtful face. 'I don't think so. Look, mate, it was nearly seven years ago. Can you remember tiny details like that?'

'But you remember driving to his house and parking on his drive alongside his van?'

'Yeah because that's what I always did.'

'It's always easier and safer to say what your normal routine is when you're lying.' He opens his mouth to protest but I talk over him. 'When in actual fact, on the day your best friend's wife goes missing, you should be able to remember the things that are not normal. Like the fact that you couldn't have parked on David's drive that day.' Jake frowns. 'Amanda's neighbours had workmen round to erect a fence and they parked their vehicle on her drive. They were supposed to have finished the job before either David or Amanda got home but they were delayed. They didn't leave until much later. Well after you claimed you were there.'

'And?'

'The neighbours don't recall David coming home until much later when he knocked their door because Amanda hadn't come back. Were you together? Where were you really?'

'You're having a laugh, aren't you? We were at his house, both of us. The neighbour's lying. Can they prove they had workmen at their gaff? Can the workmen say for definite they parked on the drive?' Jake shakes his head, laughs, and resumes his food scraping.

'They can, yes.'

'Good for them. Now if that's you done, can you fuck off now? I've got lunch to redo.'

'I understand that you might feel obliged to give your best mate an alibi. I would,' I admit, thinking of the crap one I gave my brother. 'Particularly if I had strong feelings for my friend.' Jake turns from the bin, his beady dark eyes narrowing, 'Feelings that went beyond friendship.'

He straightens up, dark flakes of bacon matter fall to the floor, missing the open bin.

'Anything you tell me is in the strictest confidence, Jake. I don't care what your sexual preference is. Are you in love with David? Did he ask you to give him an alibi?'

'What the fuck? Not you an' all. I am not a bender! He's my mate, that's all. Can't two blokes just be mates? You've been spending too much time around Hock's queer son.'

'You weren't always best mates though, were you?' I ask, bombarding him with my next point. 'A few years ago, David seriously assaulted you. Put you in hospital. Why did you forgive him? Was it because you loved him?'

But rather than ask me to leave, Jake slams the pan down causing the fork to spring out and onto the floor, scattering more mess everywhere. 'Who told you about this? Was it Dave?' I don't reply. 'It was a misunderstanding. And it wasn't assault. It was one punch. Just a well landed one. My sister took me to A/E as a precaution. Haven't you ever argued with a mate?'

'I have,' I admit, 'but it's never descended into violence. What was the fight about? What had you done?'

Jake laughs. 'None of your fucking business.'

'That's fine,' I say with a smile. 'I'll ask David. See if he can elaborate.' Jake huffs. 'It was admirable that you forgave him. Even more impressive that he reciprocated. Was it over a woman? You've admitted that you didn't like Amanda. Have you liked any of his girlfriends? Have you interfered in all of his relationships? Imagine what David will do when he finds out you've had a hand in his wife's disappearance.'

'What the fuck?' Jake shouts. 'I've got nothing to do with that. Just because I didn't like her doesn't mean I harmed her. You're barking up the wrong tree here.'

'Where were you then, Jake? Why can't you answer me honestly?' I'm loath to suggest he was doing Hock's bidding. He'll pounce on the idea like a farmyard cat on a mouse.

'I was at Dave's house with him, just like it says in my statement. So for the last fucking time, will you please get out of my house?'

'No. How do you know Tamsin Archer?'

'What?' Jake's eyes dart everywhere, flummoxed by the change in questions. 'I'm her dealer, aren't I? She came up to me in a club looking to score.'

'Score what?' He gives me a funny look. 'What do you sell her? Jake, you must know what she likes. Does she want to go up or down? Relax, lose her sexual inhibitions? Come on. When she phones you, what is she after?'

'Anything! She'll have whatever I've got: cannabis, cocaine, Es, fucking paracetamol if it knocks her off her tits. The woman's screwed in the head. She's got a miserable fucking life and she just wants out. One of these days, I'm gonna go round her flat and find she's overdosed in a pool of her own vomit, and you know what? I don't care. I'll sell her anything as long as she pays.'

'Your concern is touching. You're what...three school years above her?' He nods, confused. 'You must remember her from school?' He shrugs. 'What was she like?' He shrugs again.

'Was she shy?' He huffs. 'Ahh, she was confident. Pretty too. I can still see under that haggard face, she once had a beauty, which must mean lads liked her. Did you like her? Did she knock you back?'

'I wasn't fucking interested in her,' he shouts. 'She was a slag. She lost her virginity at fucking twelve,' he says appalled, but somehow I don't believe him. He sounds too bitter, untruthful. If it was a rumour at the time, I bet he helped spread it. 'By the time she was fourteen, she was shagging and sucking off anyone who'd let her. Older boys, younger boys, teachers probably. She was the same slut as an adult. I saw her all the time in nightclubs, copping off in the gents, down side alleys, up against cars.'

'What was the first drug she scored from you?'

He frowns in puzzlement. I repeat the question.

'Where were you both?'

'A bar, I think. No, a club. She was after coke.'

'Coke gets you high,' I tell him. 'It's a good time drug, one where you want to go higher, dance for longer, enjoy sex more. Why did she want it?'

He shrugs. 'What difference does it make why she wanted it?'

'Answer the question and I'll go, leave you in peace.'

'Someone told her it enhanced orgasms. I gave her a small wrap and watched her drag her boyfriend into the toilets. She hasn't been able to get off the white powder since.'

'In her flat the other day, you indicated that you've known Tamsin for ten years. You said, "I thought you were a bitch back then but you're even fucking worse now. I know I did the right thing ten years ago". What did you mean by that statement?'

'I don't remember saying that.' Awkwardly, he bends over to retrieve the fork, wincing with pain.

'Why was she a bitch? Bit of a harsh name to call a client. A long-standing one too. Had she been a bitch to you? Did she knock you back? Humiliate you?' Jake shakes his head but I sense I'm getting closer. 'Had she been a bitch to someone you knew? A mate?' He shakes his head again; his lips are mashed together as if scared the truth will fly out. 'David? Was it him? Is that why he hit you? Because you'd interfered in their relationship?'

'No!' he suddenly shouts, 'It was not David. But it was a mate. He's not around anymore. Joined the army. He's in Afghanistan or one of them other poxy countries. She was a tart, getting pissed, eyeing up other blokes. I told him the truth about her, that her drug taking was going to get him into trouble, and he dumped her. She never knew it was me that told him. That's all I meant, that I didn't have any regrets about splitting them up. And I don't. But I'm happy to sell her drugs.'

'I think she may be looking for another dealer after your remark the other day,' I say.

He grins as a pop song suddenly starts playing from Jake's person.

'You reckon?' and from the back pocket of his jeans, he pulls out a battered mobile and holds the screen up for me to see the caller. I squint at the name: Tamsin A.

'Alright Tam,' he says loudly. 'I'm at home with that private dick. Yeah, dick is the right word.' He grins at me. 'Yeah, still asking questions about your boss. I'm bored with it an' all. What do you need? Uh-uh. Yeah, I can get that...' Jake wanders out of the kitchen, closing the door behind him so I can't hear.

I take the opportunity to have a quick nose around his kitchen. On the table amongst this morning's post is the latest iPhone. One for business, one for leisure. Like a typical dealer.

I wake his iPhone up, but there are no unanswered messages showing. The kitchen drawers yield nothing interesting nor is there anything on the small kitchen table. On the wall is a cork noticeboard and there are dozens and dozens of photos pinned to it. I peer closer. Grinning, drunk faces of men and women. Some are toasting the camera, others each other, cracking half-empty pint glasses against stemmed glasses or beer bottles. In the background are wooden roof beams with brass gubbins hanging off them, a fruit machine with yellow and red flashing lights preserved blearily in time, beer pumps being pulled by out of focus bar staff. These pubs are all different. I study the faces. Some appear many times, others occasionally. I spot David in one, his tattooed arm slung around the shoulders of a blonde woman, whose back is to the camera. He's much younger, pre-Amanda. Jake and David, arms around each other, clinking glasses, their faces red with drunkenness.

I remove my own mobile, line the camera up with the top left hand photo and take pictures of the entire board. I don't know how it might help but I know I won't get a second chance. I'm just sliding the phone back in my pocket when the kitchen door opens and Jake comes back, pulling a face when he sees I'm still here.

'I'm going,' I say before he can speak and I make my way down the hall, the smell of charred bacon and cannabis lingering thick in the air. He shepherds me to the front door, telling me

310

that the next time I have questions for him I should keep them to myself. Outside the sun is heating the early afternoon up nicely. The neighbours' lawns are emerald green, sunlight bounces sharply off car roofs blinding me. I just need to be by a pool, glass of something cold in my hand, and peace and quiet.

I turn to say "goodbye" but Jake shuts the door with a slam that says "don't come back". And it's only when I slot the key into the ignition, I wonder why, if Jake indeed has any, his smoke alarms didn't go off.

Chapter 47

I study Jake's photos on my tablet where I can enlarge the faces and zoom in on the backgrounds. I have no idea what or who I'm looking for, or even if there is anything to see. I can't identify the many drinking establishments. Unhelpfully there are no signs stating *Welcome to the Red Lion* or *Monday night quiz at the Falcon*. And even if I could name them, are the pubs still open? Would the bar staff still remember the nights these pictures were taken? They could have been taken over ten years ago.

Jake certainly likes to remember the good old days. Taking photos is one thing, exhibiting them on a noticeboard is another. Putting that board up where he can reminisce every day he tries to set fire to his kitchen reminds him of a time when he was able-bodied and pain free. When he could run and jump and play footy with the lads, drink his mates under the table. The daily pondering of what was must be torturous and won't help his mental health. Like when I was in prison, the very last thing I wanted was letters from home telling me how beautifully sunny it was when I was only allowed to spend an hour outside. Nor did I want to read about new restaurants opening or day trips, when all I had was prison slop and an occasional game of pool with the constant threat of violence in the air. I consider Jake's mental health. Outwardly happier than Tamsin's. He lives in squalor but doesn't seem to mind mess and uncleanliness. He has friends...but does he? I've never seen him and David together. And if David has had words with him about his failure to disclose Hepworth being in the salon with Amanda, then maybe their friendship has hit the rocks. Who can Jake turn to then? There doesn't appear to be a girlfriend. Amongst these photos, I've seen no evidence of Jake with his arm around a woman. The only picture of him in close proximity to one is of him standing next to David, who has a girl on his other side. A girl who is kissing his mouth, a curtain of blonde hair falling over her cheek, obscuring her face. Tamsin said she'd never seen Jake with a girlfriend and she's known him for a decade. Her comment backs up Jake's eventual admission that they are more than dealer and addict; they knew each other socially from back then, whenever "then" is. Is he jealous of his friends' blossoming love lives and rather than find one of his own, he sets out to ruin others? He meddled in David's and got a kicking as a thank you. And what of this army friend? Did he enlist to get away from future interference? David seems to be the one he'd die for, but if Jake was convinced he was losing David to Amanda, did he decide to take action? How though? He doesn't look physically capable of abducting an adult female and he would need to be if his target was Amanda. She would not go willingly. I've no doubt any woman, when faced with her arch rival, would fight tooth and nail, this one in particular.

Maybe he got help? Who from? David? Another mate? But what would be in it for them? Money? Does Jake have that kind of money? Or did he persuade David that his wife could never make him happy, that she would only hold him and his brewing business back? If David forgave Jake all those years ago for interfering in a relationship, and I only have Declan's word that it was about a woman, how did Jake sell his idea to David? David seems to have been in love with Amanda. Certainly his show at Martyn Hepworth's house, threatening to beat him up for abuse, was convincing. Perhaps a little bit too much for show. I should have asked Jake if David had spoken to him about Hepworth, but why ruin the surprise? David is away; it might be a nice treat for Jake to get a punch in the face.

I reach for my mug, drain the last dregs of tea into my mouth and push my chair back, ready to wash up and go home for the day. The office phones rings and I snatch it up.

'King Investigation—'

'It's me.'

'Hello me,' I say to Shaun. 'How are things in the pub restaurant business?'

'It's drudgery. I'm so looking forward to being back with you tomorrow. I feel like I've been out of the loop too long. Have I missed loads?'

I laugh. 'Yes, you have. The investigation is really picking up pace. I suggest a nice breakfast meeting, like one of those they have in the city. You know, with freshly-brewed coffee and warm croissants, bit of fruit salad.'

Shaun laughs. 'I'll see what I can do. How's the love triangle going?'

'Whose?' I ask, leaving the mug upside down on the draining board to dry.

'Yours, of course. Has she dumped him yet?'

'What do you think, Shaun?' I dry my hands on the towel and turn the light off. 'I got reprimanded earlier for interfering. I'm beginning to wish I'd never got involved.'

'Well, it's your lucky day, Will. I have just received an extremely useful nugget of information from my source. My source, I might add, I had to woo by taking her for a drink.'

I smile. 'I did tell you that charm opens many doors, didn't I?'

'You did. Anyway, listen to this, Will, because this is gold dust.'

I sit in the nearest chair and listen to what he says. And he's right; it is useful, but it's more than gold dust. It's a big fuck off gem of information. A perfect diamond.

*

I step outside onto the bustling high street and flick the sunglasses down over my eyes. The sun is bright, dancing off passing car windscreens and off neighbouring windows. I take a moment to watch the people going by: school kids laden down with rucksacks and sports bags, mucking about on the pavement, getting under pedestrians' feet; parents with pushchairs; shoppers; a man over the road is cleaning the upstairs windows of the wedding dress shop; two dogs are sniffing each other as their owners chat and laugh. I savour the news I've just been told, replaying Shaun's words over again, his controlled yet excited tone, the dramatically hesitant way he delivered it. He toyed with me because both his hopes and mine were pinned on it. It was just like the moment I received the letter from the police saying I was successful in my application, like the time my fiancée accepted my proposal of marriage. A moment of pure elation. Because this nugget was solid granite evidence of Michael's lie. He had not been signed off by his GP. It's a reflection of his true nature, one he keeps hidden from Bronwyn because it would appall her. Once she hears of this, Bronwyn will have to finish with him. How can she justify continuing to see him, support him, let him touch her?

But I can't disclose it yet, not until I have the rest of Shaun's report which he assures me will be the icing on the cake. This nugget is the cherry. My smile widens. I have him. Michael cannot talk himself out of this; there were a dozen witnesses who can all verify what he said and the venomous way he said it.

With a jaunty spring in my step, I turn and head down the street feeling almost like Gene Kelly in Singin' in the Rain. My rucksack bounces on my shoulder and I twirl the car key around my finger. I must be careful later. Bronwyn has invited me to her flat for dinner. She assured me Michael wouldn't put in an appearance but, for the sake of what I know, I will decline the offer of staying over. I can't risk it accidentally slipping out. Being with her and wanting more is too much of a temptation.

I turn right off the bright path and into the shade of the passageway that cuts between the two buildings and is a short-cut to the car park at the back of our office. It's much cooler and damper here and is a short welcome relief. Behind the sunglasses, it is suddenly nighttime and when I emerge several seconds later, things are bright again. There are only a few cars

314

parked in the bays. A figure is walking towards me, away from a sporty hatchback, a white BMW, parked in the last space on the right, several away from the Mazda. They're drinking from a takeaway vessel through a straw, slurping noisily.

It's a man, wearing stylish sunglasses too, and I move aside to let him pass. He stops and says my name sharply as if he's an old friend and it's a surprise bumping into me. I stop too, lifting my sunglasses up.

'How you doing?' Michael says. He's wearing smart jeans and a pale blue polo shirt. He looks like he should be hanging around yachts or sipping G&Ts in some fancy seaside bar.

'Alright,' I reply, guardedly. I should've realised he'd seek me out, have another word, a stronger one.

He sucks the final few drops of the milky liquid through the straw and looks around. Failing to find a bin, he spies a dark corner where dead leaves and other litter has accumulated and he lobs the plastic container into it. It clatters noisily and the domed lid flies off, splattering milk up the brickwork.

Nice, I think, but say nothing.

'I'm glad you're okay, because that makes one of us. I'm having a really shit time at the moment,   in every aspect of my life: work, family and now I have this worry regarding a relationship. A relationship with a girl I'm in love with. Do you remember me asking you to back off from Bronwyn?'

Oh, it *is* another confrontation. Well, he's hardly here to ask after my head cold.

'Vaguely.'

'You're always there, aren't you? In the background. Her office, her flat with your feet under the table, on the phone. You're like an annoying fly that lands on the table when you're putting the dinner out.'

'Mike, she and I are friends. We go way back.'

'But you don't, not really. How long have you known her? I'll tell you. Not even a year. Ten months.'

Ten months. Is that all? I work it out. We met in June last year when Nisha coerced me into helping Bronwyn whose neighbour's death was entwined with a case I working on. Michael's right. It hasn't been a year yet.

315

'You've only known her three months,' I retort. But he's shaking his head, a grin stretches across his slightly tanned face.

'A year actually. Granted we've only been seeing each other for three months but we know each other well, which is why I know she's the girl for me. I love her,' he repeats, touching the centre of his chest. 'I want to spend the rest of my life with her. We've discussed marriage, the wedding we would both like. Do you see how serious we are about each other?' Marriage. I've never even heard Bron say that word, let alone know anything about the kind of wedding she would want. Maybe she never struck me as the type to want to get married.

'Let me show you something,' and he pulls out his mobile, presses a couple of buttons and holds the screen out for me to see. I read the small text. It's a booking invoice for a three-night stay at Hotel Ravenscliff in May.

'It's Bronwyn's birthday that week. I intend to propose and I have every reason to believe she will accept.'

'Good for you,' I say coldly. 'What's that got to do with me? Are you asking for my permission?'

He smiles, unfriendly-like. 'I'm warning you again to back the hell off. Your presence annoys me and I can live with that to a point. But I can't ignore the fact that you make childish phone calls to interrupt our dates.'

'Date?' I query. 'It was a drink.'

His smile widens. 'It was still a date. Bronwyn was so irritated by your call that she insisted we go out for a romantic dinner. As usual she stayed at my house.' He pauses, stares dreamily at the ground, remembering their fictitious night together. No way did any of this happen. 'Sex with her is always amazing,' he tells me, 'but that night was extra special. I knew I didn't want to ever let her go and I decided to propose.'

Yeah, right, I think, keeping my face blank. Deluded moron. I want to laugh. Tell him none of that is the Bronwyn I know. She doesn't do hand-holding over candlelit tables, flowers and champagne, white lacy underwear and declarations of love…but she does. She loves receiving flowers. She loved the tulips I gave her at Easter and she does own dainty and pretty underwear; I've seen it drying on an airer in the bathroom. I've seen the many perfumes on top of her dressing table where she stores all that other scented stuff: moisturisers, body sprays, make-up. I can identify her from the perfume she wears; it's

316

ingrained in the passenger seat of the Mazda. Bronwyn is like Claire. A girly girl. Stands to reason she enjoys romance. I'm not romantic. Sounds like Michael is though. Is that what she gets from him? Why she won't finish with him?

They can't be having sex though. Bronwyn admitted that she was celibate. But is that really true? She must've been with Michael…she can't have been waiting for me to come along. We'd fallen out, we might never have been reconciled. None of this makes sense.

'What I can't ignore is the way you intrude on her life,' he continues, snapping me out of my thoughts. 'The way she has to make time in her busy day for you. All I get is, "I must ring Will", "I must invite Will round for tea", "He's on his own. I'm his only friend". She uses up her valuable time to make sure you're okay, when you can't seem to do anything for yourself. You're clingy and needy. It's pathetic.'

I want to laugh. Needy? Me? I did perfectly well without her for three fucking months. I didn't seek her out. I didn't draft messages to sit unsent for weeks and weeks. I had my life planned out, Bronwyn-free. She was the one who intruded in my life. Is this what she tells him about me? That I need her company.

'And I thought you of all people, Bailey, would understand the importance of a proposal.'

My eyes narrow. What's that supposed to mean?

'You were nearly married yourself, weren't you?'

What the fuck? Who told him about Justine?

'It must've been very upsetting when it ended. I can't imagine how you felt. And then last summer, you had a glimmer of happiness again. But she left too, didn't she?'

He's talking about Gretchen. How does he know this?

'Tragic that something so intense ended so abruptly. You will never know what could've been. And I don't know how I'd feel if the woman I cared about for nearly twenty years, was cruelly taken from me. How did you come to terms with that?'

I stare. He knows about Claire, my best friend.

'Have you come to terms with the loss of these three important relationships?' He pauses for my reply but it isn't forthcoming and he ploughs on. 'It's completely understandable that you might believe you will never be happy again. And then Bronwyn, because she's a good person, gets in touch and everything changes. Suddenly you think, "My friend is back. I need

317

never be alone again". But she's in an important relationship with a future. You do the only thing you can: interfere and intrude. Because you're jealous.'

I shake my head weakly. I want to tell him that it was all her doing. I buried my feelings, I had moved on, but *she* engineered a reconciliation at Nisha's, *she* invited me to her flat on Easter Sunday, *she* insisted on talking about us, about what could've been, she wanted me to kiss her, take her to bed. All because she wanted me. Didn't she? Doesn't she?

But I say nothing. I am speechless. I feel sideswiped by something I never anticipated, something that has come from nowhere. Bronwyn has talked about me to him. She's told him about my previous relationships, that I am responsible for their breakups because I am some kind of fuck-up. I can't believe it. Why would she tell him all this? Has she been mocking me? My heart is thumping madly and my headache returns with a vengeance; it feels like a pair of hands are pressing down on top of my skull.

'Are you going to leave her alone, Bailey? Desist with this pathetic behaviour?' he asks, with contempt.

I raise my eyes from the ground, meet his hard stare. What can I say?

'She'll find out one day what a lying manipulative bastard you are,' I say in reply. I should keep what I know to myself, use it wisely to inflict its maximum impact, but why is he allowed to say all that and leave unscathed?

He raises an eyebrow.

'I know your GP hasn't signed you off sick.' I manage a small smile. His chin lifts. 'I know you're suspended for making an inappropriate comment in the workplace.' I frown. 'What will Bronwyn say?'

He regards me carefully.

'You can say it's a lie, but gossip like that spreads like wildfire around an office.' I take a deep breath, drawing the chat to an end. 'I must go. Thanks for the chat, Mike. Oh, and in answer to your question, if you want me to back off, best ask your girlfriend to leave me alone. Then I gladly will.' I force myself to smile broadly and walk away, chin held confidently up, leaving him with no reply to make. I walk down the car park, ignoring the Mazda; he doesn't need to know what car I drive.

I turn the corner, head back towards the high street to the front of my building. I pause in the doorway, lean my shoulder against the brickwork, try to calm my breathing and my erratic heart rate.

I contemplate returning to the office but he may follow me; it was clearly where he was heading before he met me outside.

Why would she tell him about my relationships? What else does he know? I feel betrayed, humiliated. How could she do this? It can only be from Bronwyn. You think you know someone. You think, "Here's a friend I can trust" and then you find out you've never had it so wrong about them. What about earlier, what she said in the park? The way she kissed me. Is it all bullshit? Do I annoy her? Is she playing me? Maybe she only lassoed me in on Easter Sunday to make Michael jealous and improve his behaviour, make him more attentive. Make him propose. Surely not. Surely she hasn't been using me these past few weeks...but then why not? Like he said, we've only known each other ten months. How well can you really know someone in such a short time? And every time, she thinks I'm pulling away, she yanks that rope tighter and brings me in. I'm such a mug.

'I can't do this,' I mutter, pulling my mobile from my pocket.

I can only postpone matters. There's still too much to be learned before it can be finalised, but right now, I want to be on my own. I type her a text.

Hi. Sorry but can't do tonight. Feel really unwell. Will.

Chapter 48

My nose tingles with a sneeze and I quickly grab two tissues from the box. I have a brief moment of having two totally clear nostrils before once again they're blocked and I have to resort to breathing through my mouth. I feel bloody awful. My head has a brass band playing in it, my nose is sore and I'm shivery.

From across the room, Shaun regards me with disgust. If he had a crucifix, he'd be holding it up protectively like a virgin being advanced on by a vampire.

'I've never heard anything like it,' he complains. 'You're almost as loud as my dad.'

Which is no surprise. A man like Hock must be able to move furniture and scare the birds from trees when he sneezes or blows his nose.

'I can't help it, Shaun,' I reply sharply, dropping the sodden tissues into the bin on top of the growing pile. 'It's not much fun for me either.'

'Hand gel,' Shaun says, without looking up from his mobile, which he's been glued to since he arrived thirty minutes ago. 'I do not want your germs. I can't afford to be off work.'

I squeeze a dollop onto my palm and rub my hands together. I popped to the chemist's on the way in and bought enough drugs to give Jake Bunby a run for his money.

'I can't remember what time exactly I'm meeting David Bywater,' I tell Shaun, flicking through the papers on the desk. I must have written it down somewhere. On a post-it-note perhaps? Or was it on the notepad? Didn't David text me? Where's my phone? No, hang on. I spoke to him because I was at the park waiting for…her. Don't go there, I tell myself. Not again.

'David's going to ring me when he's back home. Unless he forgets, in which case I'll phone him.' But I can't face driving all the way across Lexington to listen to yet another liar. I really don't have the energy. I can hardly think, let alone pose probing questions to a suspect. And where are those questions? I wrote some last night. I pull my rucksack onto the desk, scattering papers onto the floor. I glare at them with contempt. I don't actually think I should be here.

I pull my A4 pad out and then remember that the sheet of paper containing the questions is still at home, on the bedside table under the glass of water. Shit!

'Hmm,' Shaun is saying thoughtfully but he's not listening and hasn't noticed the mess I'm making. People mock the debilitating effects of man-flu, that us men greatly exaggerate our symptoms to the point we're knocking on heaven's door, but as someone who rarely suffers from a cold, certainly no more than the average two a year, I have never felt so ill. And it doesn't look as if my esteemed colleague and friend is going to offer me the tiniest jot of sympathy. I watch Shaun for a few moments.

As usual, his legs are slung over the arm of the chair, his feet occasionally kicking upwards as if to keep the blood flowing. There's a crease of concentration between his eyebrows. Whatever he's looking at is obviously more riveting than listening to me. Resting precariously against his thigh is his empty mug.

I open my mouth to say something before he knocks it flying.

'Will…there's a fire.'

'I can't smell anything. Is it outside?' I say, looking at the windows, but we're too high up to see down into the street below. As long as it's not this building, I don't think I care. There aren't any sirens.

'I'm on Twitter, Will,' he tells me like I should know. 'Lexington Live. Have you heard of it?' I shake my head. 'It's a Twitter handle. Tells you all the latest news in the area. Road closures, accidents, weather reports.'

I make a suitable face in response. Fascinating. If you care about local fires.

'They're talking about a fire in Gardenia Close. Isn't that where Jake Bunby lives?'

'It is, yes.'

'It says here,' and he pauses whilst skimming a finger over his phone screen, 'that it is a house. You know, not a bin or a bus shelter. Hang on, I'll ask if anyone can be more specific.'

'If it's his bungalow,' I joke, 'I'm not surprised the place is on fire. The bloke can't even toast bread without creating a near-999 emergency.'

Shaun doesn't laugh and I get up to put the kettle on. I think another Lemsip might be due. I grab his empty mug as I exit the office. He doesn't look up, but mutters, 'Thank you.'

I scroll through my mobile whilst I wait for the kettle to boil. No more messages from Bronwyn. The first arrived at 8.10am, asking if I was feeling better. I wasn't lying when I replied that I felt like death warmed up. She sent another an hour later, offering her nursing services, something ordinarily I'd have laughed at and taken her up on, but her words fell well short of their mark.

She's pitying me because I have no other friends. She feels obliged to make contact out of some sense of duty to a ten-month friendship. Ten months! I knew people longer in prison. You can't be best friends with someone after forty weeks. That's the length of a human pregnancy near enough. I ignored the second text so she sent a third asking if I wanted anything, that she hoped I'd be feeling better soon. I wasn't going to reply but I remembered what Michael said about them going away for her birthday. It's weeks away yet but I mentioned it, hoping she might suggest that we go away together.

I still await a response. Maybe she'll swerve the question and, if I want to know, I'll have to ask again. The kettle flicks off and I pour water into the powder, stirring vigorously. I won't ask again, but I'll find out if she goes away with him.

I find Shaun in a much different position when I return to the office. He's sat properly in the chair, leaning over his phone which he holds over his knees. He looks up, a weird expression on his face. What was he on about? A fire somewhere?

'Bloke here, one of the neighbours, says this. Are you ready?' he asks me.

'Is that what he said? "Are you ready?"' I joke, returning to my seat, sipping the scalding liquid.

He gives me a withering look. 'I asked what number house. LexyDave, that's the bloke, says, "Don't know the number. But it's a bungalow".'

'Shit. Really?'

'I asked who lived there and he says, "Don't know his name. He's that drug dealer scum". So, unless there's more than one dealer in Gardenia Close, there's a good chance this is Jake's place. Wonder if he was home. I'll tweet LexyDave; he seems to have his ear to the ground.'

'Nosy neighbour by the sound of it. What time did the fire start?' I ask, but Shaun shrugs as his fingers frantically type. If it started early, there's a chance Jake was home, unless he was down the pub. He'll be devastated if he's lost his precious noticeboards, all those photos curled up and burnt. Let's hope he has a good memory.

'It's been going hours apparently. Started around 3am. Shit,' Shaun says, dramatically. 'He must have been in bed. There's a photo here. Place is smouldering.'

'In bed?' I laugh. 'He was probably making himself a bacon butty.'

Shaun holds the mobile out for me to see. I peer at it but all there is to see is a thick plume of smoke against a grey overcast sky. Bet Jake's lost all his drugs too. That won't go down well with Hock. Losing the entire supply of coke and the rest. It'll be coming out of Jake's pocket. The ingredients of the Lemsip start to take effect. I feel warmer and the pressure in my head is easing like a valve has been released. Suddenly, Shaun emits a sharp expletive and looks at me, his eyes wide, a look of horror on his face. I jump and the band in my head starts up again.

'For God's sake, Shaun,' I complain, laying a hand on my temple.

'Will,' he says, his voice sounding hollow, 'they're talking about there being a fatality. What if it's him? What if it's Jake?'

'It won't be,' I reply confidently. 'Don't believe everything LexyDave tells you. He's probably loving being on the front row, tweeting a running commentary.'

'We should get down there,' Shaun says, jumping to his feet, grabbing his hoodie off the chair opposite. I give him a blank stare. 'Gardenia Close! It's the only way we'll know. Come on, I'll drive; you're drugged up to your eyeballs. You're more likely to get pulled over for driving under the influence.'

'It's a Lemsip!' I tell him, finishing my drink. 'It's not a line of fucking coke.'

*

There is definitely a major incident in Gardenia Close. A parked police car has formed a barrier across the road by the bus stop, so Shaun parks up on the kerbside away from the suspicious eye of the copper and we walk the rest of the way. I zip my coat right up and bury my hands in my pockets. Despite the spring sunshine, it isn't all that warm out.

Further along are more police cars, two fire engines, and an ambulance. The thick air stinks of burnt material. It must be strong if it can penetrate my blocked nose. A tickle forms at the back of my throat and I reach for the ever-handy bottle of water before I break into a coughing fit. Neighbours stand at a safe distance on the very edges of driveways, behind hedges or cars, watching, glued to the unfolding scene, listening for any snippets of information from the crackle of radios or the voices of those dealing with the incident. Some neighbours are in full flow, voicing their own speculation. I gaze across the road, past the fire engine and the huddle of firefighters who look to be wrapping things up.

Jake's bungalow has been reduced to a charred box. A flimsy one too. The outside walls look to be made of soggy cardboard and one strong gust of wind will blow it down. The panes of glass are gone, leaving two blackened holes either side of the front door, which has been broken down and lies on the lawn. The brickwork is black and the roof is open, exposing the wooden beams, some of which are fractured and have split in half.

The place is still smouldering, smoking and dripping at the same time. The lawn is ruined, trampled by booted feet and hose pipes, and scattered with unrecognisable debris. I look around for Jake. Surely he got out. A fatality must be a nasty rumour started by any of the spectators here. And then I remember yesterday as I walked out of his bungalow. The mini fire had failed to set off a smoke alarm. Maybe he realised from its silence that he needed to change the batteries and did so immediately. Even if he didn't and he lazily made himself another bacon butty, surely a fire would have woken him up. He'd have smelled the burning and hobbled straight out of one of the exits. He can't have been inside when it went up. Unless number 1, he was pissed. He'd have to be pretty drunk to sleep through intense heat, thick smoke and falling debris. Unless number 2, he had a head injury or a knife wound, or he was already dead. I stop my thoughts before they run away from me. There is nothing here to suggest he's dead.

The doors to the ambulance are firmly closed. He could be inside receiving treatment; a mask on his face, a paramedic making sure all his observations are normal before they take him to A and E, Jake joking about his near-death experience, crying over his lost drugs and photos. Or he's already gone to hospital, and this ambulance is surplus. Don't they often send two ambulances to serious scenes?

I glance around for anything to contradict my thoughts. A member of his family screaming about the loss of someone so young, who loved life, or a desperate addict lamenting the demise of a beloved dealer. Unless number 3, there isn't anyone to miss Jake.

A uniformed police sergeant is talking to two people dressed in normal clothes but I can spot a detective when I see one. Do they suspect arson? Now that is interesting.

'Oh,' Shaun says and I look at him. He nods to the left and from around the fire engine two paramedics wearing dark green jumpsuits appear, chatting to each other. They briefly speak to the uniformed sergeant and climb into the ambulance. They weren't treating Jake...unless he went in another ambulance.

'It's not looking good,' Shaun mutters and wanders off towards two neighbours. Two ladies well into retirement, leaning on a shared wall, heads together. Gone to use his newly acquired charm I shouldn't wonder. The ease at which he starts chatting them up is to be admired and, within a couple of minutes, they are telling this handsome young man everything that they know and everything they suspect.

I sip more water, step nearer. If necessary, I'll walk as close as I can, just skimming the emergency vehicle. Someone is bound to say something louder than they should. Or I'll just ask.

Shaun sidles back, a smile on his face to suggest he's picked up something juicy.

'Last night, Jake had some friends over. There was a couple of cars parked up the kerb and it caused an obstruction for other residents. The next-door neighbour went round to tell them to quieten things down and Jake promised him that his friends would be going soon. Apparently, Jake was well oiled. Swaying in the doorway, slurring his words, glazed eyes.'

'Doesn't surprise me. It's not a party unless you lose consciousness.'

Shaun shrugs. 'No one has seen Jake. But they admit they couldn't see much despite the huge orange flames. So it might be that Jake was whisked off to hospital hours ago or he stayed the night at one of his mate's houses. They don't know.'

'Have you identified LexyDave yet?' I ask. 'Which one do you think he is?'

'LexyDave has gone suddenly quiet,' Shaun admits sheepishly. 'He was probably never here.'

The ambulance starts its engine and we watch as it drives away, revealing a white transit van. Down its side and on its back doors, in police colours, are the words "Forensic Science Services". They are always going to make an appearance, even in a non-fatal fire, looking for signs of arson.

I keep my watchful gaze on the police sergeant. He looks to be in command. A tall well-built bloke with a shaved head and muscular arms. He looks in the direction we came from and I follow his gaze. Something has caught his eye. Could it be Jake? Maybe someone has located him to break the bad news and he's on his way to salvage what he can.

But it isn't a car.

It's a black transit-type van and, as it passes, I read the gold lettering down the side. "Private Ambulance". And that can mean only one thing.

There is a body in the house.

But is it Jake? It must be. I feel an unpleasant heaviness in my chest. I didn't like him. What was there to like? But he was young and there were others who did. Family, David, his clients. What a way to go. Killed in a house fire.

Shaun and I remain glued to the spot where we can see everything. Two middle aged men dressed in black suits, climb out of the vehicle, closing the doors without slamming them. They open the back doors and remove a large flat square item in a black carry case. With distinctive sombre movements, they talk to the Police Sergeant. They look to the charred entrance of the house, nodding again and finally walk up the path, avoiding the debris.

It seems a lifetime before they emerge. I drink most of the water and have to prop myself up against a lamppost, my head pounding and my weak body complaining with the effort. Shaun returns to his mobile and nearly drops it when I nudge him. The funeral directors are coming and they're not alone.

'Jesus,' I whisper in horror when I see the shape of the body on the stretcher. Normally a dead body is flat on its back, its human curves undulating like hills on a horizon: the head, chest, knees, feet. But this one is not like that. As the men follow the line of the path, one at each end of the stretcher, I get a brief sideways view of the body hidden underneath the black canvas cover. It's round, but not perfectly, a bit like a boulder. The body might be strapped onto the stretcher but it's unstable. It wobbles from side to side, threatening to topple over.

He might have died from smoke inhalation, but this shape suggests he was on fire. I've seen it before in the only other fire-related death I have attended. As a young police officer, I visited a local mortuary to watch a post-mortem. A man had been burnt in a factory fire. The smell of charred flesh was horrendous, but what was worse was the state of the body. The soft tissues and muscles burnt, splitting the blackened skin exactly like a sausage frying in a pan. The body's joints were flexed, pulling his hands up to his chest in a strange pugilistic pose.

When the mortuary technician started the evisceration, they complained his tough skin blunted their knife. Underneath the skin, his flesh was pink, slightly cooked.

It was fascinating to see, but impossible to forget. And for a while, it put me off barbecued food.

The Funeral Directors slide the stretcher into the van and close the doors.

Jake will be unrecognisable. It'll be too distressing for his family to see him. It'll be a job for a dentist to confirm his identity,.

'Poor bastard,' I mutter and Shaun looks over, nodding sombrely.

And suddenly I wonder, where was Hock last night? Could this be his doing? Did he set Jake's house on fire as a warning and Jake was collateral? Or was his death intentional? Fire isn't really Hock's style. Issuing a beating is. Now isn't the time to ask Shaun if he saw his dad in the early hours but it's worth bearing in mind. It could be a horrible accident, of course. But Jake is a drug dealer and you don't go through a career like that without pissing off a few people. Whether it's rising prices, lack of gear, treading on toes or angering drug barons, the road is not smooth.

Isla, my mortuary contact, will have more information but she won't know anything for a couple of days, other than what she might pick up from the funeral directors and the police when they book his body into the mortuary.

I dig my mobile out and type her a heads-up text. And then it occurs to me: should I tell the Police Sergeant I saw Jake the day before and he nearly set fire to the kitchen? It's a difficult one. It'll open up a right can of worms. The police will want to interview me and, when they find out who I used to be and what I do now, the questions will be unrelenting: What was my business with Jake? What did I ask him? What did I suspect him of? Do I know of anyone who'd want to harm him or send him a warning?

I put a hand to my throbbing forehead. I can't face hours in a police interview room on the wrong end of a grilling, not with this illness. I am not telling the police I was here. Jake can't and no one else knows.

I tap Shaun's arm, nod that we should go. He leads the way, walking in silence.

'When we get back to the office,' I tell him, 'I'm going home. I feel like crap.'

'Am I in charge then?' he asks brightly.

'You certainly are. You can boss yourself around to your heart's content.'

Chapter 49

With a hand clamped over his mouth and chin to contain his grief, David shakes his head again. He's cried several times in front of me, going through as many tissues as I did at the height of my cold. But it also means I'm making excruciatingly slow progress as I patiently wait for him to compose himself.

In front of him, the cup of tea he made himself when I arrived is cold, a film forming on top of the liquid. I empty his tea in the sink and put both cups in the dishwasher, ask him if he wants another.

'I don't want any more tea,' he complains, but I put the kettle on anyway. I could do with another. He hasn't answered my question on what time he got back the day before. He was due home in the afternoon but, after I left Shaun in charge of the office and went to bed, I forgot all about David. It seems he never rang my mobile or the office. And I want to know why.

I slept all afternoon, woke up for my tea, which I couldn't taste and returned to bed. I woke at 7am, feeling nearly as fresh as the proverbial daisy. Certainly my nasal passages are clear and the brass band in my head has left the stage. Time to get on with my investigation.

'I can't believe Jake's gone,' David says for the hundredth time, his voice wavering on his dead friend's name. 'In a fire as well. I could understand it if he died from a drugs overdose. He was taking all sorts to combat his pain. Or even on an operating table having one of the many ops he was due to have. But not in a fire. How do you die in a fire nowadays?'

I keep quiet. I'm guessing he doesn't really want me to explain smoke inhalation or how the body burns. Nor does he want to hear that Jake could have been incapacitated by drugs or booze or a head injury, that his smoke alarm was faulty. I'm never going to get answers to my questions if I add to his grief.

'Thanks,' he says when I put the tea down in front of him. 'I went to the bungalow this morning because I couldn't believe the news. I expected to find him watching the telly or playing a video game. I thought I was in the wrong street. I didn't recognise the place. I never expected it to look like that…that burnt.' David bites his bottom lip, his eyes well up. He reaches for the scrunched-up tissue.

Oh, Jesus, I think. Not again. I sit opposite. 'Try not to think about it.'

'I can't *stop* thinking about it,' he tells me, his voice rising. 'If I close my eyes, all I can see is Jake clawing at the door unable to open it, screaming and panicking. The fire engulfing him. He was burnt to a crisp, did you know that?'

'Who told you that?'

'One of his neighbours. They watched the undertakers carry him out the house. Jake's arm slipped out of the body bag. It was black, like charcoal.' David shudders.

'David,' I say gently, 'that didn't happen. Funeral Directors are professionals. They're not like a couple of clowns blundering around the place on crystal meth. You couldn't see what Jake looked like. I was there too. I know it's hard; believe me I do. I lost my best friend in tragic circumstances too, but you must try to put it from your mind or you'll drive yourself mad.' I push the cup towards him and he picks it up. I watch him. He looks tired. There's a dark lilac-coloured circle under his right eye and his face is unshaven. He's aged a decade.

'I don't know what to do with myself. I suppose I should have gone to work but the thought of going into people's houses, putting carpet down, making pointless chitchat made me feel like throwing up. I tried doing some brewing stuff, but what's the point without Jake? They're doing his post-mortem this morning.'

I nod. I already know this. Isla texted me yesterday. The coroner's paperwork came through quickly on account of Jake's family demanding the matter was expedited. Helps me out immensely. Isla has promised to ring me as soon as "he's back in the fridge and the door is closed". Such is mortuary humour. I'm expecting a lot of bad taste jokes later too. Isla does love to tease me. And I bet, for a fire death, she has a repertoire of them.

'How did you hear about Jake's death?' I ask. Strictly speaking the body hasn't been formally identified as being that of Jake but, since it is his bungalow and he hasn't been seen since, it's safe to assume it's him. I'm sure the dentist's examination will just be a formality.

'His sister phoned me. Do you know what my first thought was when I heard the phone ring?'

'It was Amanda,' I guess.

He smiles with sadness. 'Yes. I thought it was her ringing to say she's come back and she loves me, begging for another chance. You should have heard Kat's voice.' He bites his bottom lip, composes himself. 'She was wailing. "Jake's dead. My brother's dead. My baby brother". Fucking hell. It was horrible. His mum isn't well. Bad heart. This will finish her off.

Kat's having to deal with the police and that. I don't know how they're going to pay for a funeral. Funerals cost a fucking fortune. Thousands, you know. Thousands to cremate someone who's already been cremated!' David stops, rubs a hand vigorously over his face. He breathes deeply, tries to stop his grief consuming him. With a shaking hand, he lifts the tea, sips it.

I wait patiently. After a couple of minutes, I ask, 'What time did you get back yesterday afternoon?'

He blinks at me, the question momentarily confusing him. 'What, from the job? I got back late the night before. Around half eleven.'

So he was in town on the night Jake died.

'Why did you come back early?'

'The job finished and a few of the lads wanted to go out on the lash but I couldn't see the point of pissing all that hard earned money up the wall and I had a long drive home. I went to McDonalds drive-thru for a burger and went straight to bed.'

'You didn't call in on Jake?'

'No. I didn't even tell him I'd be home earlier because I knew he'd try and get me to come by for a drink. Jake's very persuasive. *Was* very persuasive. Shit. Wish I'd gone now. It might not have happened. I certainly would have made sure the house was safe before I left. You know, turned the appliances off. Made sure he wasn't frying some chips.'

I don't recall seeing a deep fat fryer in his kitchen, but then you couldn't see much for all the junk. And who needs a dangerous deep fat fryer when you can set fire to a kitchen with a grill and a tea towel?

'Wouldn't any of Jake's friends have made sure the place was safe?'

'Doubt it,' David mutters.

'How do you know who was there if you weren't?'

'Kat told me who else was at Jake's place. They're his mates, not mine, but I know what they're like. They were only there to see what they could get from him. A bit of dope, some booze, a few games on his many consoles. They aren't his friends. Not like I was. Fucking hell. He spent his last night with a bunch of freeloaders.'

'What did Jake get out of inviting them round?' I ask.

David snorts. 'Company, that's all. He got lonely. Everybody works. He spent a lot of time in the day on his own, so he'd want company in the evening. His back was getting worse and he found it difficult to get down the pub. The neighbours said Jake was absolutely out of his tree but his mates told Kat he wasn't.'

I interrupt. 'How does Kat know all this? Have the police spoken to her?'

David smiles. 'It's Kat Bunby. She phones you, you answer. She wants answers, you tell her. She's a fierce woman.'

'Where can I find her?' I ask, opening the notebook to a clean page. That's if she'll talk to me.

'She's got a couple of part-time jobs. Erm, Asda and a care home, but I can't remember the name. Well, I'm sure she's not at work anyway. She lives in Hopwood Close. Number 25. Are you going to see her?'

I nod. 'Sounds like she's in the know.'

'She won't rest until she finds out what happened to Jake.'

'How do you get on with her?' I ask casually.

David smiles. 'Fine.'

But a few years ago, Kat was dragging David off her baby brother, saving him from further injuries. And now, she's personally phoning David to break the bad news about Jake, rather than let him hear about it from someone else or via the local grapevine. Has she forgiven him for what he did? If I can find her, she may tell me the truth about the cause of their fight.

'David,' I begin, 'I saw Jake the day before he died. I had some questions for him regarding the day Amanda went missing. His answers were unsatisfactory. I know it's hard to remember stuff that happened all those years ago, but you might recall them more clearly.'

'Really? Ask if you want and I'll try to help, but I don't know what use I'll be. My head feels all over the place. None of this with Amanda seems important at the moment.' His expression changes. 'That's a horrible thing to say. I didn't mean it like that.'

I begin by asking him to recall what happened the day Amanda disappeared and he gives me exactly the same answer as before. Everything is spot on, including the timings.

'How did Jake get to your house? Did you pick him—'

'He drove. We were coming from opposite directions. I got there first, parked in the road and —'

331

I interrupt. 'Parked in the road you say?' He nods. 'You never mentioned this before.'

'Haven't I? I'm sure I have. Maybe you've forgotten what I said or you didn't write it down, but I definitely parked in the road and not the drive. Jake parked behind me. The Newmans, my neighbours,' and he waves his right hand at the wall to indicate which side they live on, 'were having some work done in their house or garden, I forget which, and Amanda had given them permission to park the workmen's truck on our drive. I remember being pissed off because, once they'd gone, I'd have to go out back out and move my van. It was an inconvenience.' David laughs. 'You didn't say no to Amanda either.'

'You definitely haven't told me this before,' I say suspiciously. But then I remember. *I* told him. The evening I stopped him from kicking down Hepworth's door, I explained how Hepworth had accessed his house and searched it for Amanda's diary, that he had walked right past the workmen erecting a new fence in the Newmans' garden. Did it remind him that he was supposed to mention their van being on his drive both to the police and me? And did Jake remind him a second time?

'I have,' he insists. 'Check your notebook,' and he waves the same hand at the paper in front of me, but I didn't bring that notebook because there's no room left in it, and I had left it in the office. 'You haven't got it with you. Well, check when you find it.'

'It's not in your original statement either,' I tell him.

'Show me,' he says. But I didn't bring that either. David shrugs. 'You can blame the police for that. It's not my fault they incorrectly recorded my statement. I told them. What did Jake tell you?'

I narrow my eyes. 'Exactly what you said, almost word for word.'

'There you go then. Do you want me to tell you what we did until Jake left? We went into the garden...'

'No, it's fine,' I reply tightly. 'That was the discrepancy. The witness...'

'Mrs Newman, you mean? Oh. Sorry. You don't need to tell me who it was. Breach of confidentiality and all that.'

'When was the last time you heard from Jake?'

'Let me see,' and he picks his mobile up and flicks a finger across the screen. 'The day I came home. Here.' I take his mobile and read the text from Jake. It's a photo of a pint of beer.

I look at David. 'Taken in a pub during one of his lunchtime drinks. It's one of my beers. I haven't actually spoken to Jake since last weekend. Check my call history.'

But they could've communicated via email or FaceTime or perhaps Jake rang David on his burner phone. Sly pair of bastards. Jake's final act was to protect his beloved best friend. I should have fucking known he'd be straight on the phone to David.

I hand the phone back. 'There is one other thing I want to discuss with you, David. A witness has told me that a few years ago you and Jake had a big falling-out, and that you assaulted your friend, putting him in hospital.'

David snorts, but my statement doesn't surprise him. Again I bet he's been warned this would be coming his way. 'I didn't put him in hospital,' he argues. 'Jake went to casualty as a precaution. And the falling-out is none of your witness's business, or yours for that matter. It has nothing to do with Amanda's disappearance or Jake's death.'

'What was it about? What made you turn on your friend? Very soon afterwards, you reconciled with him which suggests you both forgave each other.'

He glares at me, his face suddenly coming alive, and it's odd seeing the transformation from grief-stricken friend to fierce defender. Could he turn like this with Amanda? Perhaps he wasn't the downtrodden husband he pretends to be. Maybe, that day, he shrugged off his subservience and showed her exactly the man she married.

'You know what, Mr Bailey?' David demands, pushing his chair back from the table, 'I'm not having this conversation. My friend is dead. My *best* friend. I thought you'd understand since you lost yours too. I am not discussing a misunderstanding a day after my friend burns to death in a fire. You have all the fucking tact and sensitivity of a sledgehammer.'

'I need to know—'

But he cuts me off. 'No, you don't.' He pushes his chair all the way back and stands, knocking the table with force. 'It's in the past. Buried and forgotten about. Can you leave me alone? I've had enough.' He leaves the kitchen and walks down the hall to the front door.

My cue. I must've hit a nerve and, like Jake, David does not want to give me any kind of an explanation. Very suggestive that, whatever the reason for the assault, it has everything to do with Amanda and Jake.

David waits at the front door, his hand on the latch, his expression stern, unforgiving. That's alright. I'm not looking for forgiveness. But behind him, through the frosted glass pane, is a shadow. Someone is there. My heart leaps.

The soft knock at the door makes him jump and his eyes widen with fear. I couldn't have timed my pissing him off any better.

He opens the door cautiously. I move my head to the right to see beyond him.

'Oh, Dave, babe, I'm so sorry,' gushes a female voice and two arms slide around his waist. A head of curly brown hair appears on his shoulder, the woman's face buried in his upper arm. Who is that? The hair is familiar.

His hands grasp her upper arms and he eases her off him to a respectful distance.

'Thank you, Holly,' he tells her formally, his chin held high, and now I see it's Amanda's cousin and how interesting is her greeting? Very friendly and sympathetic; use of the affectionate term "babe" is telling. One woman calling another babe is usual, but a woman to a man is only indicative of one thing.

She looks confused and hurt by his cold shoulder and opens her mouth to speak, but something in his expression must have stopped her because her gaze swings to me standing in the semi-darkness and then she understands his tone. Not in front of the private investigator who will no doubt jump to all manner of conclusions. One of which will be correct.

She recovers quickly, smiles pleasantly at me. 'Oh, hello again. How are you?'

'Nice to see you again, Holly,' I say, stepping forwards. 'How thoughtful of you to call round and offer your condolences to your employer.'

'Well,' she hesitates, looks up at David who is as motionless as a statue. 'I wondered if there was anything you needed. Bit of shopping, a chat, you know.'

A sympathetic shag, I want to suggest.

'Don't let me disturb you; I was just going. Thanks for the chat, David. I'll be in touch.'

David huffs and steps aside, against the hall radiator. Then I see Holly's swollen abdomen and I'm reminded that she's pregnant. A mother-to-be visiting the father of her unborn child. How cute.

On the doormat, outside the front door, is the biggest clue this isn't a social call to offer her condolences. This is a woman calling on her secret lover to comfort him. There's no sympathy card in her hand, but on the worn welcome mat is a rucksack and a clear plastic carrier bag containing a toiletry bag. She obviously doesn't leave her belongings here, or are these items to replenish used ones?

Like Shaun remarked a couple of weeks ago, David either made friends with his palm or he found the love of another woman. I'd definitely say the latter.

But perhaps a more pressing question is, why are they keeping their relationship a secret? Is it so as not to hurt Jean? Was Holly a temptation for David during his short marriage to Amanda? Did he see more of a future with Holly, who is closer to his age? Was Holly the reason Amanda disappeared? Did she find out David was having an affair with her hair stylist and try to kick him out? Did David turn on his wife? Or did David want to remove Amanda from the equation, keep the house for seven years and carry on with Holly until the time was right, and did Jake help by providing an alibi? And now that the alibi goes with Jake to the grave, it's effectively set in stone forever.

I walk down the drive back to the Mazda, hear the front door close behind me. Another love triangle. Amanda, David and Holly. I feel surrounded by love triangles. But I'm not going to disprove David's alibi unless I can get harder evidence. I need a hammer to crack that open and, right now, I just don't see where that's going to come from.

Chapter 50

The sweat on my chest has cooled and I shiver. I retrieve my t-shirt off the nearby chair and slip it back on, settling back against the propped up pillow, pulling the warm winter duvet higher. Automatically I run a hand through my tousled hair to tidy it. Next week, I have an appointment at the barbers to change my look. I've had enough of time-consuming hairdryers and expensive products. I look to the half-closed bedroom door, which Bronwyn walked through ten minutes ago, and wonder what she'll think of the new William.

Then I remember Shaun and that he was going to text with any news. I reach over to the bedside table for my mobile, when something occurs to me. I glance at the door again, tilt my head and listen. Running water from the bathroom. Bronwyn's in the shower. Now's my chance. Like every suspecting partner, the temptation to sift through their belongings is too much. If Michael's sat in this place in this bed, he may well have left something behind. Something that will prove she's lying to me.

My fingertips grasp the little brass handle of the drawer and I slide it out, turning to see what's inside. Emery boards worn smooth, a packet of scented tissues, a cork bookmark in the shape of a fish, a birthday card with "To a Dearest Daughter" emblazoned across the top, a couple of pens, a tiny notepad, nothing interesting written on its pages, a tube of lavender-scented foot cream. My fingers touch cold metal and I fish something out from underneath paperwork. A weighty gold watch. Its dial is black with slim gold hands. The time is stuck on a quarter past six. I examine it. The glass is scratched suggesting it's well-worn. It's not my sort of watch, but it could be Michael's; it's showy enough to be. It needs a damn good clean; an unrecognisable crud is caught between the links.

It might have belonged to a favourite uncle, but wouldn't Bronwyn have taken better care of it? Put it in a box or at least wrapped it in a protective cloth? No, it must be his and, like I did with my own timepiece, he removed it before climbing into bed with her.

Annoyed, I throw the watch back in the drawer and slam it shut. I wouldn't put it past Michael to have left the watch there on purpose. I can't even ask her about it since I'm not supposed to be rifling through her bedroom. What's the point? In a matter of days, this will be concluded.

I reach for my phone, which out of courtesy I had put on silent. No messages.

'Shit,' I mutter. I don't know what's pissed me off more: the lack of messages or the watch.
I feel my bad mood start to return.

Earlier in the day when she asked me over for a meal, I had hoped to have learned the full extent of Michael's lies so I could make my grand reveal, but Shaun had received a message from his source at Michael's office that she had remembered something, something juicy regarding a female colleague. Shaun reckoned it was worth waiting for. He's taking his source for another drink later on tonight.

I'd been patiently waiting a week already, so what would another day matter?

I arrived at Bronwyn's flat late. I forgot that she'd asked me to pick up a bottle of wine. She didn't query my lateness so I didn't apologise. She was cooking pasta, not my favourite, but I didn't complain and politely ate it, choosing water over beer. After the washing-up was dried and put away, we sat in the lounge, watching an inane programme on the telly, our conversation nonexistent. It was only a matter of time before one of us made the first move. After all, isn't that what I went for? Isn't that why she asked me over?

The shower has gone quiet and the door opens. Bronwyn comes in, a fluffy white bath towel pulled tight around her, a sprinkling of water droplets on her bare shoulders. She smiles shyly at me and drops onto the corner of the bed with a bounce, dries her curls with another towel. I watch, breathing in the grapefruit scent of her shower gel.

She taps my foot where it's tented the duvet up. 'I've put a towel on the radiator for you. Should be nice and warm.'

Her thoughtfulness makes me feel like a bastard.

'Don't work it out,' I say, 'but have a guess how long we've known each other.'

She smiles with amusement, looks to the ceiling. 'I don't know…eighteen months maybe.'

'Ten,' I tell her. 'It'll be a year in June.'

'Really? Are you sure? Feels longer.' She frowns as she calculates it. 'Yes, you're right. Wow.'

'I've never written you a birthday card. I hadn't met you in May.'

'Then we'll have to make my birthday something to remember. Anyway, it's not how long we've known each other, it's how *well* we know each other. And I think I know you pretty well, Will.'

How wrong you are, I think.

She drops the towel and takes one of the many tubes of scented body moisturisers off the top of the dressing table. I watch her meticulously moisturise every inch of her skin, from face to feet. She blushes under my watchful gaze; she turns her back but coyly looks over her shoulder at me.

I wait until she's rummaging through the chest of drawers on her side of the bed before asking my next question. 'What did you say you were doing Saturday?'

Her eyes lift upwards. 'Visiting my parents. I haven't seen them since Mother's Day and they've been pestering me to drive down. I'm going early Saturday morning but should be back Sunday teatime. Why? Did you want to do something?'

I shake my head. Bronwyn hardly ever mentions her parents; I know they're a little older than my mum.

'What are they like?' I ask. She pulls a pair of pyjamas, pale blue and white stripes, out of the fourth drawer down and tells me that they both love retirement. Her dad and his golf, her mum and her gardening clubs. Plus cruises and lots of socialising with their retired friends.

'They tried for years to conceive,' she explains, 'with no success. Dad always wanted a big family. They'd given up hope. My father was dedicated to his career but my mum wasn't accepting it and tried everything to boost their fertility.' Bronwyn laughs. 'Herbal remedies; crystals; different sexual positions, complicated enough that it made contortionists out of them; drugs; all sorts. Finally, they achieved success with a long weekend in New York. The irony being that's where my dad was born.'

'He's American?'

'No. My grandmother went into early labour on a holiday out there. Mum says New York is a lucky place for us.'

'Never been,' I say.

'It's where I'd have my honeymoon…'

'I didn't realise you had any thoughts of marriage.'

She pulls the top on over her head, her voice slightly muffled. 'I think about it sometimes, what it'd be like to be married, have that stability. I think that's normal for an unmarried person.' Her head pops out of the neck of the top. She runs a hand through her hair. 'A lot of my female colleagues are married. Our receptionist gave me her bridal magazines to look at. I think she's been speaking to my mum. She's always nagging me that I'm getting on, my

338

biological clock is ticking, she wants to buy a new hat.' Bronwyn laughs. 'Don't you do that, Will? Think about marriage.'

I shake my head. 'I had the big wedding planned, remember? Threw it all away for a stint in prison. Claire reckoned I wasn't ready to settle down. And with three failed relationships behind me, I might not be cut out for wedded bliss.'

She doesn't react to my relationship comment. 'I think you'd make a great husband. Mine obviously.'

I laugh without humour. 'Very nice of you to say so, but there's no way I can afford to get married. Planning the last one nearly bankrupted me. Now I'd have to rob a bank to pay for it. Have you told your parents you're seeing Michael?'

The change of subject surprises her and her eyes snap upwards to my face but I keep my expression blank.

'It's fine if you have,' I tell her reassuringly. 'It is the truth. Have they met him? Bet they liked him.'

'They haven't met him and they won't either.' She frowns. 'Will, why have you mentioned Michael?'

'He usually gets a mention at some point in the evening. He is one side of this triangle,' and I draw one in the air. 'How's he enjoying his sick leave? Is he getting out much, seeing friends, you? He needs to be careful milking it. I know you can't technically fire someone who's off sick but a boss would find a way to.'

Bronwyn's frown deepens. 'What's going on, Will? You've been in an odd mood since you got here.' I shrug as if to say I don't know what she's talking about. 'Oh, come on, you have. You picked at the dinner, you barely said two words in the lounge. You could hardly look at me in bed, you're clearly not staying tonight but you're too cowardly to say so, then you ask me all these questions with the sole purpose of bringing up Michael. Why?'

'I'm only not staying because I've got to get up early tomorrow...'

'It's fine really. I'm starting to get used to it. I don't know when he's going back to work. I don't care either.'

'Just wondered,' I mutter.

'You know, Will, I've had a crap day today. But you don't ask after me, do you?' she demands, glaring at me, her arms folded. 'All the printers went down, I had phone calls and emails coming out of my ears, and then out of the blue, a troop of senior managers turned up and took my manager into the meeting room where he spent hours. Meanwhile, most of the office are speculating about the reason for their visit and they asked me what was going on, but I knew nothing. Still don't know anything. They could be making us all redundant for all I know.'

'I'm sorry,' I say guiltily.

She huffs, shakes her head. 'All that's got me through the day is the thought of coming home, locking the door, having a glass of wine and seeing you. Instead I get the full force of your bad mood, topped with the third degree on bloody Michael!'

I reach out a hand but she shrugs me off so I scoot down the bed to get closer, take her wrist and prise it away from her chest. I smile at her. 'Come here, please. I'm sorry.'

'Please don't tell me that I look sexy when I'm scowling,' she warns.

'But you do. You're beautiful.' She blushes. One final tug has her dropping onto the bed. 'Bron, everything will be alright because you have me. I will never let you down.' My own resolve to go home to an empty single bed crumbles. I'm so petty. I could be here all night with her.

I grasp her gently along her jaw and, unlike before, I kiss her ever so tenderly, tasting mint toothpaste on her warm mouth. She pushes me back up the bed until we're lying on our sides, face to face. In between kisses, I ask if she's forgiven me.

'Not quite,' she teases, sliding her cool hands inside my t-shirt and onto my chest. I jump from her touch, pull her closer, trapping her hands between us. She squeals, hooks her leg over my hip, pinning me to her.

I gaze into her eyes. 'I might have to up my game in which case, this leg,' and I pat her thigh, 'will have to come off.'

She forces herself to smile but her mind is far away. 'I'm sorry, Will. It's just that…I have a horrible feeling there will be redundancies. I heard a rumour a couple of weeks ago that the company needs to make cuts…slashing the workforce is one area they can save money.'

'Would they make you redundant?'

She shrugs. 'Why not? If they don't, they could relocate my job, forcing me to leave or move…'

I interrupt, panic rising in my chest. 'Move where?'

'London probably. And they'd expect me to go. Remember I have been on many secondments. Don't worry,' she says, squeezing my hip, 'I'm not planning on moving. I'll get another job. I could retrain. Become a nurse or a barista…quite fancy working in a coffee shop. All those fancy drinks and cakes. Hey, I've got an idea,' and her eyes widen with excitement. 'I saw Nisha yesterday. She told me she's going part-time. I don't blame her, but does this mean you need some help in the office?'

Nisha obviously hasn't told her about our partnership, which is good. 'Do you think I'm that run off my feet? And how much work would we actually get done if we spent hours together? Not much, I can tell you.'

'I suppose Shaun will be given more hours.'

Her tone is unusual and it makes me pull back and regard her. 'He's a hard worker,' I reply. 'He's very keen, with an inquisitive mind. Under my tutoring, he's becoming a very good investigator. I thought you liked Shaun, Bron.'

'I've only met him once. He seemed alright…but his dad is Phil Hock. Is it wise having his son work so closely with you? What if he reports back to his dad?'

'On what? An adulterous husband or a flirty wife? I doubt Hock gives a toss who is fucking who behind whoever's back. Besides, Shaun is one of the most trustworthy people I know.'

'Not all that long ago, he was lying to the police *and* you. Encouraged by his father. And you've had numerous run-ins with Hock. Look what he did to Claire, Eddie…he's a violent bully. He could be looking to get even; use something against you. How could you stop him?'

'Why would he want to get even? Everything is cool between me and him. I appreciate your misgivings but I think you're being over-cautious. Shaun's worked with me for a couple of months and not once as he pried into something that's not his business.'

But she stares quietly as if there's more she wants to say. She thinks the better of it and instead says, 'You're right, Will, Shaun *is* a nice lad, and you know him better than I do. Forget I said anything. Now, where were we? Oh, yes, you said something about upping your game,' and she unhooks her leg from my hip and pulls me to her, with a wicked grin.

I try to concentrate on Bronwyn but can't shake off her unusual criticism of Shaun or the strange concern that somehow I will be powerless to prevent Hock from muscling in on the agency. I can't fathom where she's got such an idea from.

Chapter 51

I have misgivings about parking in the staff car park of Lexington General Hospital. I spotted the strict warning signs about the prohibiting of visitor and patient parking here. A fifty quid fine I can do without, but Isla assures me she can put the Mazda on the orange list. She describes it as a magical list for visitors to the mortuary who are exempt from paying, such as undertakers and grieving families who wish to visit their loved ones. I suppose compared to what she's about to tell me about Jake's post-mortem, strictly forbidden for every reason under the sun: I'm not a relative, a doctor or a copper, her putting my registration number on this list, is a minor misdemeanour. And all this information will cost me is a sticky bun and a large bar of milk chocolate, preferably Cadbury's, but Galaxy will do.

I stroll through the rows and rows of vehicles to the grass verge which runs alongside the access road and path, past the bike shed, and the three wooden bench/tables. The first two are taken. Three nurses in pale blue tunics are eating out of Tupperware boxes and laughing loudly. On the second table, a young bloke wearing a smart shirt and headphones is digging crisps out of a family-sized bag and watching a video on his phone.

I toss the paper bag containing Isla's payment on top of the third table and sit on the seat opposite the entrance to the mortuary car park where I await her arrival. It's another sunny April day. Blue sky, wispy clouds and a cool breeze. Next week they've forecasted showers synonymous with this month. Mrs Penn was complaining over breakfast that the garden needed a drink. A big ball of dread started to grow in my chest, because rain on grass inevitably means it'll grow as fast as the fairytale beanstalk. By the weekend, it'll need mowing and, for that job, she looks to me. I did suggest she replace the lawn with aggregate or even Astro Turf, but she was horrified. Her friends, she explained, would not appreciate summery G&Ts and nibbles on the equivalent on a pebble beach or an indoor football pitch.

But at least the mower is a good one, so it should make easy work of the job. I hear voices on the breeze and see two figures walking away from the mortuary. Isla and a colleague, a woman wearing office clothes. Isla is dressed in navy blue scrubs and a red hoodie. Her long dark plaited hair appears to be wound around the top of her head like the soft ice-cream in a cone you get from Mr Whippy. I suppose you want to avoid your long tendrils trailing in the open cavities of a dead body.

342

Isla looks over, spots me and slyly raises a hand to waist-height in acknowledgement. At the door to the nearby building, Isla and her colleague part ways. Isla jogs across the road, her long scrub trousers tucked under her feet which are clad in white mortuary slippers.

'Hiya Will,' she calls, waving madly, like someone in a period drama frantically waving goodbye as the steam train departs the station.

'Hello Isla,' I say. Isla is genuinely lovely, and she never refuses to help, but after each meeting, I am shattered. She drains my energy. She's far too energetic but then she's only in her mid-twenties. She chats loudly and enthusiastically to me like we're old friends. She worked with Claire and, when I was investigating her disappearance, Isla was a huge source of information, providing me with much info on Claire's colleagues.

'It's brilliant to see you! I couldn't wait to wrap PMs up and get out here and give you a hug. Come here,' and she throws her slim arms around my chest and squeezes hard. I feel my ribs bend inwards and I pull my upper body upright to give my lungs room to expand. The top of her cone-shaped hair nearly pokes my eye out and I tilt my head to the side, replying it's good to see her too.

'Ohh, is that mine?' She grabs the paper bag off the table and rips it open, shoving the chocolate bar in the pocket of her hoodie and ripping off a corner of the Belgian bun. 'I'm starving.'

I've heard her say before how hungry post-mortems make her. The smell of decomposing bodies makes her ravenous, she claims. I'm never sure if it's mortuary humour said to gross me out or it really does affect her.

'We should walk,' she tells me, her mouth full, crumbs falling down her front. I nod in agreement. Too many ears nearby. We head up the access road towards many one-storey buildings, loading bays and past lots of blue and white signs pointing the way to pharmacy, pathology and estates.

'Oh!' she exclaims. 'I got that address you wanted,' and from her pocket she juggles the removal of a folded yellow post-it-note.

'Thanks,' I say, pocketing it without reading it. I'll look at it in the car. 'How's work?'

'Oh, you know, enough to keep me out of trouble. Easter wasn't too bad considering the Bank Holiday. It should ease up now anyway as we head into summer. Fewer folks dying. How's work with you? I was going to ask if you're inundated with cheating couples and missing persons, but I guess not if you're asking me about Mr Crispy. Unless he's the victim of a scorned wife?'

I smile. 'No. He was a witness in a MISPER case. I find his death wholly inconvenient. And I'm sorry to say, he died knowing a lot more than he was prepared to tell me.'

'What a bloody nuisance,' Isla agrees, pulling a face. 'Someone shut him up, do you think?'

I raise an eyebrow. 'I was rather hoping you could tell me that.'

'Well,' she says mysteriously and pops another piece of pastry into her mouth, 'he was a very interesting case because, as I told you on the phone, he wasn't treated to the bog standard post-mortem. He had a gold standard one, or a forensic PM.' At the top of the road, Isla turns left and we head down a road past a sign which says "Boiler house".

Isla continues. 'According to the police doctor who went to the scene, Jake had an obvious fractured skull. Apparently skulls can fracture due to intense heat, but usually along suture lines. You know, those wiggly black lines you might see in photos of skulls.' I nod my understanding. 'But not in his case. The bones of his head felt wobbly like a...' she pauses whilst she tries to find something to compare it to. 'Like a foil-wrapped Easter egg after you've whacked it on the edge of a table to break it.' She looks at me. 'Ever done that?'

But I have yet to bring home the egg Bronwyn bought me.

'Well, like that. But a round indentation. This size,' and she makes a circle with her thumb and first finger, roughly the diameter of an inch. 'When I removed the calavaria, there—'

I interrupt. 'The what?'

She smiles. 'Alright, for you: the skullcap. There was a significant amount of blood on the surface of the brain. Enough to strongly point to a traumatic injury.'

'By traumatic, you mean......?'

She slows her pace, looks at me. 'Not natural. The indentations suggest a hammer.'

My jaw drops. This is unexpected. After she told me Jake's death was being treated as suspicious due to the fracture, I was expecting to hear that Jake had tripped and cracked his head on a sharp corner of a unit due to too much booze, and that the fire started because the idiot was grilling toast. But a hammer attack. Fucking hell.

A hammer...it's so Yorkshire Ripper. Violent, brutal and angry. Why not a knife? But to stab and render a young man unconscious, suggests multiple wounds and there's a chance he could have fought off his attacker and turned the tables. I wonder what kind of a hammer was used. I ask Isla and she replies, 'Ball peen.'

I shake my head at the horror of whacking someone over the head with such a weapon. How much force would you need to knock them out or kill them? Horrible.

'Which room was the body in?'

'The lounge. The deceased was sat on the settee. Police reckon whoever did it whacked him over the bonce, took the hammer with them before starting the fire, which I'll come to in a minute, and left.'

I hold up a hand. 'Hang on, rewind. He was hit whilst he was sat in the chair. Not standing up?'

Isla shakes her head. 'Definitely sat down.'

I picture Jake's untidy living room. The mess, the position of the armchair with its back to the window, the settee opposite. He was sat, watching the telly, playing on one of his many games consoles, and someone…what…crept up behind him and smashed his head in? How is that possible? Did he not realise there was someone there? Or did he forget he'd let someone in?

'Which part of the skull?'

Isla touches the top of her head. 'The parietal. You see, Will, if you slip on ice, you go tits up, and you're more likely to bash in your occiput. Or if you hit your head on the corner of a unit, you get a fracture here,' and she touches her temple. 'But the parietal…you just don't hit it when you fall; it's a classic weapon over the head job and it's a thick bone so it takes significant amount of force to break it. The pathologist reckoned the blow was enough to render our victim unconscious. Unless our perp thought they'd hit him hard enough to kill him.'

I smile at the Americanism. 'How many blows did he receive?'

'One. When the fire started, he was out cold, slumped in the chair and unable to help himself. There were soot deposits in his upper airways too, which suggests that he was breathing. That's what did him in. 1a Smoke inhalation, 1b skull fracture and 1c hammer-wielding arsonist.' Isla laughs. 'Shouldn't laugh. It's not nice. He's not viewable. Black and crispy, hair and skin burnt off and his arms, up like this,' and she flexes her elbows to adopt a boxer's stance with her dukes up. 'Stinks too. Chargrilled.'

'Did he smell of alcohol?'

Isla tilts a hand from side to side. 'A bit. We took blood to see what the levels of carbon monoxide and booze were, but as you know, we won't get the results quickly. The report said he'd been drinking with mates at home and they consumed several bottles of beer. The history said Jake was alcohol and painkiller dependent.'

'Any illegal drugs?'

'History of cannabis use. Family said he was a habitual user on account of his past medical history. He had a nasty accident twelve, thirteen years ago. In an abattoir. Weird place to have an accident. Anyway, he broke his back and various other bones. It left him in considerable pain and with mobility issues. The lab will analyse his blood for toxicology too so, if he was on any class A drugs, we'll know. Not that it'll change his cause of death.'

'Any suspects?'

Isla shakes her head. 'I heard one of the police officers say that all his friends had alibis. The less pissed of the group drove the others home. Someone must've called round later and you know…' Isla raises a hand and brings it down sharply. 'But they have no idea who. Or they're not saying.'

I shudder. Yes, but why hit him whilst he was sat in the chair? Why not at the front door? Or whilst he was walking away down the hall? Was it a friend, a customer, a boss? My mind wanders back to Hock. I must speak to Shaun, have this difficult conversation with him. With any luck, he's had this thought and done some careful digging into his father's whereabouts.

'Anything on the fire?' I say to Isla.

Her dark eyes widen. 'Oh yes! Well, they didn't find any evidence of accelerant. It was a good old fashioned chip pan. Have you ever seen one go up? I watched a YouTube video. Whoosh! Literally in less than a minute the entire room is consumed. The deceased had no smoke alarms either. Not that he'd have heard them. I think the point was to make it look like he fancied some chips.'

'Had he peeled some potatoes?' I ask.

Isla laughs. 'You can do frozen chips in the fryer, Will. My mum still does it. They're nicer too, but not good for the old heart.'

I suppose Jake had enough problems going on without worrying what damage a few chips could do. Perhaps he was hoping a blocked artery might put him out of his misery. At the end of the road we do a u-turn and head back.

'Anything else of interest to note?'

'Not really. Dentist is coming over to ID him this afternoon so, if you know, it turns out to be someone else, I'll let you know,' she laughs.

'Yes, please do.'

'He'll be with us for a bit yet,' she explains. 'Poor family; they're desperate to have him back. The sister in particular is giving the coroner's office a hard time, which is why they're trying to organise a second PM quickly. There's no forensic evidence on him. The fire would have burnt it away.'

'Is there a hammer missing from his house?'

'I think the police are still making enquiries into that. Who has a hammer lying around in their kitchen?'

'Lots of people do if you've just put up a shelf or hung a picture on the wall.'

Did the murderer bring the hammer? It's certainly an easy weapon to conceal. A long sleeved top is all you need. Did they know Jake had one in his kitchen, or did they just think they'd hit him with whatever was to hand? Or did they not go there with the intention of killing him, but their chat got out of hand?

'Did the police mention who Jake might have had contact with in the last few hours of his life?' I ask. I'm thinking more of David than my calling around.

'Not that I heard. They did the usual house-to-house but, as usual at that time of the morning, no one saw anything. I heard he was a bit of a part-time dealer, so maybe he trod on someone's toes or sold some poor quality gear. I'm sorry I can't be of more help, Will, but you know what the police are like. Once the pathologist has finished, they all leave the PM room and chat in the office whilst I spend the next few hours sewing up and mopping up on my own. It's not easy to sew a burnt body back together either. You see, the skin is—'

I hold a hand up. 'Spare me the gory details, please, Isla. I haven't had my lunch yet.'

She grins. 'Sorry, Will.' We stop opposite the bench where we met up. 'I'd better get back. I've got your reg stored in my phone. You haven't changed your car, have you?' I shake my head. 'Thanks for the bun and the chocolate, Will.'

'You're very welcome and thank you for the information. You've been extremely helpful.'

'If I hear anything else I'll let you know. See you later, Will.'

She heads back to the mortuary, the top of her hair bobbing from side-to-side. I walk back to the car, my mind whirring with the information I've just been told. Did Jake let his attacker in? Or did they break in and find him intoxicated in the chair? And the hammer was to ensure he wouldn't wake up and save himself. In which case, why not just hit him a few more times? Why set fire to the place? Was it someone full of rage who wanted to destroy Jake or was it someone who wanted to eradicate any forensic evidence?

I reach the car and, when I'm safely in the driver's seat, my hand digs out the note from my pocket. I unpeel it and read the address:

131 Marlowe Road, Kelsall.

'You absolute lying bastard Bywater,' I mutter angrily.

I suspected David would give a false address for Jake's sister to send me in completely the wrong direction. So I got Isla to check it out. Seems David doesn't want me talking to Kat Bunby. After all, she's the only one left who knows the truth about the fight between Jake and David. Did the two friends have a rematch and, this time, did David finish the job? It doesn't seem that David got the chance to tackle Jake about his knowledge of Martyn Hepworth leaving Amanda's salon either. Did he save it until the night he returned from the big job he had on?

I'm not going to waste my time with David yet. He'll only tell me to piss off again. Let's see if Kat Bunby can shed some much-needed illumination on the matter.

Chapter 52

Marlowe Road is a mixture of bought and council-rented semi-detached houses. Most are very tidily kept. Trimmed privet and laurel hedges, daffodils and primroses in pots and neat borders. Some owners have even splashed out on block-paved drives. Parking is limited though. Driveways are only one car in length, making on street parking inevitable considering most families have two cars. I spot a suitable gap several doors away and build up a sweat squeezing the Mazda between an old Porsche, still in good nick, and a white transit van with a broken wing mirror. I look up and down the street. It's fairly quiet. I can hear a dog barking further down the street and the nearby sound of a vacuum cleaner. Across the road, a man has climbed to the top rung of a ladder and is leaning precariously across to clean the gutters out. Clumps of debris fall to the ground where his wife collects them up with a dustpan and brush.

I set off down the pavement towards Kat Bunby's house and pause outside the gate to number 131, halted by a warning sign on the gate: "Beware the Rottweiler". And to emphasis the point, the sign bears a cartoon picture of a dog's head, with evil red eyes and slathering jaw. Hopefully it's only a deterrent. I'm not a fan of big dogs. I look at Kat's house before pushing open the red-painted gate. The small lawn is neatly mown and there's a basket of orange and purple pansies hanging on a hook by the porch. Parked on the little slabbed area under the front window is a huge three-wheeled pushchair. A pink unicorn soft toy with big blue eyes hangs off the frame.

I move forward warily, should a rabid dog suddenly appear, and lift the ladybird-shaped door knocker. I step back, a foot's length the other side of the welcome mat. Kat Bunby must have a thing for ladybirds. The welcome mat is decorated in them. Through the vertical frosted pane of glass, a figure appears. I get ready to sprint to the slightly ajar gate, should they open the door, while holding the collar of said Rottweiler.

A young woman, around twenty years old, answers the door. She has a long dark ponytail and her foundation is bronzed. She wears tight black jeans, heeled boots and a very hairy ice-white jumper. On her hip, she carries a chubby baby, dressed all in pink, a teething ring stuck in her toothless mouth.

I glance quickly downwards. No growling dog at her side.

'Yeah?' she says, guardedly, her dark eyes regard me with suspicion. Her mouth is set in a tight line.

I smile. 'Hello. My name is William Bailey. I'm a Private Investigator.' I hold my ID card out for her to see. 'I was wondering if it's possible to have a quick word with Kat Bunby, please?'

'Is this about Uncle Jake? You know he died?' she points out aggressively.

'I do, yes. I am sorry for your loss. I met Jake a couple of times during the course of my investigation—'

'Are you investigating his murder?'

'No. I'm looking into a different matter but it does concern Jake. If it's not convenient, I understand. I'll come back another time,' and I take another step away.

'No, wait. My mum's very upset but if you're here about Uncle Jake, she'll want to speak to you.' She opens the door and moves aside. She shifts the baby to her other hip but the child promptly screws its face up and begins to cry. Evidently, she preferred the other side.

'Shush, Bethany. Mummy will get you a drink.'

I could do with one too. I follow her down the long narrow hall, gazing around. The wallpaper is patterned with red and white flowers. There is only one door open off the hall. I glance to my right and see into the living room. On the windowsill are dozens of propped open sympathy cards, vases of flowers and, in the centre like you get in a shrine, is a framed photo of Jake himself. Looking happier and healthier. He doesn't look that good now, I tell myself. Much more sunburnt.

I continue following the daughter. The air smells of vanilla, not Rottweiler, and on the shelf above the radiator is a dark bottle with thin wooden sticks protruding from it. Bronwyn and Mrs Penn are fans of these. They collect dust like nobody's business.

She pushes open the door at the end of the hall and we enter a very red and white kitchen/ diner. Red floor, white cabinet doors, black worktops and lots of red appliances including fridge door, kettle and a tree mug. She shows me into a pentagonal-shaped conservatory. Through the glass I see a tidy garden. Large lawn, patio, a brick fountain in the corner. A child's yellow and blue slide on the grass. On the edge of the patio, a woman with dark hair scraped back into an untidy knot is pegging baby clothes onto a rotary washing line.

'Mum's just putting the washing out,' the daughter explains unnecessarily. 'She won't be long. Sit down if you want,' and she waves a hand at the furniture. She steps outside and trots across the grass to explain my presence to her mum. Kat glances at the conservatory.

I raise a hand in acknowledgement. She looks a little like Jake. Same dark hair, but her features are fuller, healthier.

I look around the conservatory. The furniture is pale wood and the cushions are red and white striped. Against the wall is a one of those trendy NEXT shelving units. Essentially a propped open ladder, each "rung" is a shelf housing framed family photos. I peer at one in particular. Inside a red frame, is a picture of a young Kat and Jake, and a second lad, junior school age. I didn't know they had another brother.

'Having a good look round?' the daughter says, suddenly appearing in the doorway, her tone accusatory, her dark eyes annoyed.

I smile. 'Just acquainting myself with Jake's family. You look very close. Nice to see that these days.'

She huffs, says "Excuse me" even though I'm not in her way.

I watch Kat. She's still busy with the washing so I turn my attention back to the photos. Kat and Jake as kids with their parents, the mum holding a baby on her lap. David said Jake's mum was ill. Wonder where the dad is. Next picture shows Kat gazing lovingly into the eyes of man with a shaven head and a biker's beard. Her hair is up and decorated with pearls and diamonds. Her wedding day? Wonder where hubby is…

A sound at the open door startles me. Kat Bunby has dropped the empty washing basket on the hard floor and stares warily at me.

I smile. 'Hello Kat. May I call you Kat?'

'That or Mrs Williams. Keeley!' Kat shouts and the daughter suddenly appears. The baby now has a bottle shoved in its mouth and suckles hungrily.

'Get me a coffee, will you, love? Stick an extra spoonful in.' She doesn't ask me if I want one. I really must remember to bring more fluids with me. That settled, she turns to me, smiles in an unfriendly way and says, 'Sit down and tell me how a Private Detective knows my brother? Are you investigating his death?'

'Not at all. That's entirely in the police's hands.'

351

She scoffs. 'I don't hold out much hope for a conviction. Seems to me they haven't got a fucking clue who caved Jake's head in and set his gaff on fire. I'm sick of answering their questions. It's the same ones over and over. It's emotional enough as it is without them pestering the hell out of me and my family with the same shit.'

'As an ex-police officer, I know that the police will have many lines of enquiry. Sadly they're unable to share these with the family. Have you got any idea who would want to harm your brother?'

Or do you know he was a dealer and he worked for Lexington's finest criminal kingpin? I wonder if Hock has sent flowers or there's a sympathy card on her windowsill from him. Best not mention him. Although I wonder if he'll make an appearance at some point, casually enquiring after her health, offering his services, seeing if there's any member of her clan who might want to take over Jake's patch.

'Thought you said you weren't investigating his death. How do you know our Jake? Cheers, love.' She smiles brightly at Keeley who appears in the doorway and expertly performs a sort of curtesy and places the mug down on a cork coaster without dropping the baby. The coffee smells hot and welcoming.

Kat sips the black liquid, relaxes back in the chair and waits for me to begin.

'I'm investigating the disappearance of David Bywater's wife before she is legally presumed dead. Naturally, this requires me to look at the people closest to Amanda. Try to discover if anyone had a reason to harm her. David made a statement to the police regarding his whereabouts on the day she disappeared.'

'What's that got to do with Jake?'

'David and Jake both claim to have been together at David's house—'

Kat shrugs. 'That's where they were then. End of.' She smiles triumphantly.

I smile patiently. 'Evidence has come to light which proves they couldn't have been at David's house, although they might have been together.' And that's what I need to know. Where and what were they doing.

'I can't help you then. Jake moved into his own house years ago. How would I know what he was doing on whatever day it was? He doesn't check in with me! Reckon your witness is lying. How many years ago did Amanda go missing?'

I give her the date.

'I've got to say it, who cares? I mean, sorry for the family; must be shit not knowing, but surely they need to move on. Did David hire you?'

'Amanda's mother did. She wants one last investigation into her disappearance.'

'What can you find out that the police couldn't? You won't have their clout, will you?'

'Well, I discovered that David and Jake's alibi was a complete fabrication.' Kat pulls a confused face. 'Besides which, the police treated Amanda as a MISPER; I'm treating her as a murder victim.'

Kat gawps over the coffee mug. 'You're kidding? And you what? Think my brother done her in? No way. Jake was not violent. He wouldn't hurt a fly.'

'What was going on in Jake's life around this date?' She frowns at me. 'Could he have been on holiday? Was he working anywhere? Moving house?' I wonder if she remembers that he claims to have had a hospital appointment on the day in question.

Kat thinks. 'Not that I can remember. Jake's being living on his own since he was 22. He came away with me and the kids occasionally but obviously preferred holidays with his mates. Who wouldn't? As for work, he's been unfit for that since he was 21. Did you know he had an accident at work?'

I nod. 'He did tell me a little about it.'

'Then you know there's no way Jake could work; he was in agony just doing the housework. He should have had carers but he was too proud. Stupid sod. I did what I could. Bit of tidying up, changing the bed, washing his clothes. My husband mowed his lawn, did some DIY jobs for him. But of course, what young man would want his older sister going through his stuff.' She laughs and I'm guessing by "stuff" she's referring to his porn stash rather than his drugs stash. And if she was his housekeeper, she certainly didn't "clean" his place to the same standard applied here. From what I've seen Kat Bunby keeps a very tight ship.

'Yeah, Jake's been on benefits ever since his accident. Fucking paltry amount too. I can't add anything else, Mr Bailey. If Jake said he was with David at his house, that's where he was.'

'How long have he and David been friends?'

Kat thinks. 'Since junior school. My aunt used to clean David's mum's pub back in the day. The two boys used to go to after school clubs together: football, scouts. Jake was rubbish at sports but he liked to tag along. They were always out playing together. Down the park, in the beer garden. When David passed his driving test, he'd pick our Jake up and off they'd go, pubbing and clubbing round Lexy.' Kat smiles at the memory but quickly her eyes mist over and she gets tearful. She grabs two tissues from a box on the table and blows her nose. 'Sorry,' she says. 'Doctor says I'm in shock.'

I smile sympathetically. 'Completely understandable. So, they were very close? Best friends?'

'Yeah, defo. David's taken Jake's death very hard.'

I nod. 'I know. I visited him yesterday.'

'I'm worried about him. I've asked him over here loads of times to spend some time with us, but he says he wants to be on his own. Losing his wife *and* his best mate in tragic circumstances...how do you cope with something like that?'

'I have no idea.' Get yourself another girlfriend. A secret one, one that your missing wife's family or your best mate don't know about. Get her pregnant and plan the rest of your lives together...oh...once you've declared your wife dead that is. That's enough to take your mind off grief.

'Kat,' I say, changing the subject, 'do you remember Kerry Haynes? She worked with you at As—'

She interrupts boisterously. 'Kez! Course I do. She sent me a sympathy card.' She looks around for it before explaining they're all in the living room. 'Lovely girl. Getting wed in August. To Declan. Amanda's ex of all people. Small world, isn't it?'

'It is,' I agree. 'I heard, via Declan...' No point in protecting my source and why should I care if Kat has a go at Kerry or Declan for opening their mouths? 'That several years ago, David violently assaulted Jake.'

I pause, watch her reaction, but she hides it behind the coffee mug. Must've been why she demanded a drink. She anticipated direct questions, but was too nosy to tell me to bugger off. She says nothing and I continue.

'When this came to light, I asked Jake about it and he was reluctant to discuss it. It obviously still caused him pain and, of course, he was loyal to David. Possibly right up until the day he died. They were best friends, after all. What can you remember about the incident?'

Kat stares. She really does have her brother's eyes. Her jaw is tight. Perhaps she didn't realise I was so fully informed and by a good friend too. They'll be having a conversation later, I bet. I continue. 'I was told that David came to your mum's house. When Jake answered the door, David went for him, landing a superb right hook and then proceeded to kick your brother. If it

354

wasn't for your quick-thinking, Jake might have ended up in a more serious state. What did David say to Jake? What reasons did he give for the attack?'

'He didn't.'

'He said nothing? Most attackers say something, give a brief outline at least for the assault, even if it's something along the lines of, "You've spilled my pint. Are you eyeing my bird up? How dare you interfere in my relationship." Were any of those the reasons David gave?'

Kat says nothing, just runs a finger around the inside rim of her empty mug. I lean forward. 'Kat, you're not betraying Jake by talking to me. I don't care if Jake has interfered in David's relationships or his marriage, but I need to know what the issue was. I know Jake didn't like Amanda. He admitted that to me quite freely. Please. Why did David attack your brother? You should know that, when I asked David for your contact details, he deliberately gave a false address. That's raised my level of suspicion considerably. He must be worried that you can fill in the gaps. If he's lying to me, who else is David lying to? You, the police, himself?'

'I really don't remember.'

'He could have killed your brother,' I remind her. 'What do you owe him?'

She frowns as she debates if it's a betrayal or not. Moments later, she decides.

'It was teatime,' Kat begins, with a defeated sigh. 'Mum and me were in the kitchen. I heard a scream and a thud. We raced into the hall and found Jake on the floor, David stood over him. Jake was crying, saying sorry over and over. David punched Jake again really hard; it was sickening. I thought he'd kill him. David was shouting something about Jake's big mouth and his filthy fucking lies, and that Jake had never had a girlfriend so what would he know.' Kat shakes her head, her eyes fill with tears. 'And then he kicked Jake in the kidneys. He put a hand on the wall for support and kept on kicking so I grabbed my phone and called the police.'

'Sounds an extremely violent attack. Terrifying for Jake.' And a side to David I now know exists.

She blinks at me. 'It was. I remember telling the call handler our address and there was David, his finger jabbed in Jake's face, telling him next time Jake stepped out of line, he'd kill him.' Kat stops, heaves a deep breath and looks at me with tearful eyes. Her hand is shaking as she wipes her nose.

'I'm sorry. I really am,' I tell her sincerely. 'The last thing I wanted was to upset you.'

355

She waves my platitude away. 'It's okay. I'd just put it to the back of my mind, that's all.' She looks at the entrance to the dining room, calls for her daughter who appears quickly and asks for another coffee.

'What were the finer details? What did David accuse Jake of doing or saying?'

'Jake refused to tell me until I threatened to banish David from Mum's house forever. Eventually, Jake admitted it was about David's then girlfriend. He'd seen her getting off with other lads in nightclubs behind David's back. David didn't believe Jake; he was furious, accused him of interfering, trying to split him and his girlfriend up. But it wasn't like that. Jake was *only* looking out for David. He split up from her shortly after.'

'What was her name?'

Kat shrugs. 'He's had loads of girlfriends over the years. I can't remember their names. I could give you a name now, but it mightn't be the right one. What does it matter? She shagged around behind his back. Even the good-looking lads get treated like shit occasionally. Mates, you see,' she smiles, 'worth more than any girl.'

Her comment reminds me of Bronwyn and what recently-found information Shaun has on Michael. I push the thought away and dig out my mobile. I click on the photo file and hold the mobile out for Kat to see. It's the picture of David with his arm around a blonde woman, her face turned away. 'Could that be her?'

Kat studies it briefly before grinning. 'No. Defo not. That's my aunt. The one who cleaned David's mum's pub. Did you get these from Jake?'

'Yes. I took them on my phone when he was out of the room. What about this one?' I choose another. Jake and David together, a redheaded teenage girl with her face pressed between their shoulders. 'No. That was Lee's girlfriend. Younger brother,' she explains.

'I didn't know you had a younger brother,' I say, glancing at the photos of him on the shelving unit. 'Jake never said. How has he taken Jake's death?'

She stares. 'Well, he's gutted. Obviously. They were very close. We're a very close family. Aren't most people's? He's on his way home.'

On his way home? Where is he? 'Has he far to come?'

'Germany. He's in the army.'

Oh. Interesting. And I'm reminded of something Jake said. I turn my attention back to the photos and choose another. I hold it out for her to see.

'Hang on, let me see,' and she takes the phone, brings it close to her eye and squints. 'There. In the background. Girl with the dark hair and the silver top. That might be her.' She thrusts the phone back and I study the photo. The girl stands side on; her face is obscured by a raised stemmed glass. There is nothing distinctive about her. Kat could even be fobbing me off to get rid of me.

Keeley appears with another coffee. She gives me a sideways glare and once again, doesn't ask if I want one. I slide the phone back into my pocket.

'David and Jake made up, didn't they?'

Kat nods, tentatively sips the coffee.

'How soon after the assault?'

'About a week. Jake had his accident at the abattoir and David came straight to A and E. Visited Jake on the ward, took him to countless doctor and therapy appointments. Everything was all rosy again and Jake was over the moon.'

Over the moon? A fractured back and other assorted breakages, inability to work and loss of income that no amount of money was ever going to compensate for, a lifetime of pain and worsening mobility issues and he was thrilled to bits. And I start to wonder again if the accident couldn't have come at a more convenient time...

'Kat, is it possible that Jake exploited a situation at the abattoir? An accident waiting to happen scenario. Could he have somehow engineered his accident? And that it didn't go to plan, injuring him far worse than it was meant to?'

'What the fuck would he do that for? The money?'

'No,' I say, 'to get David back.'

I leave the notion in the air, give it breathing room, but surely Kat must've considered this. It's too much of a coincidence that the two friends fell out big style and days later, one has a serious accident, bringing the other back into his arms. So to speak. It stood out a mile for me when Jake uttered the words, "It wasn't meant to be like this. A couple of twinges I reckoned on, bit of hip pain."

Had Jake seriously underestimated how badly injured he'd be? Did he think he'd be out of action for six weeks? That eventually the bone would heal and with a bit of physio, he'd be back on his feet, fighting fit and living another day with his best mate?

Lucky for Jake that his plan worked so far as to bring David back. But as time has gone on, has the situation changed? Had Jake become a pain in David's neck? Needy and pathetic, complaining that he's alone all day because David is at work. He has no girlfriend, just porn; David's married, he has a wife to put first. Or maybe David paid Jake a late-night visit because he wanted to discuss the revelation about Amanda and Hepworth. David must have expected better from a best mate.

Or did something else happen? Did David tire of Jake and Amanda's demands? Did he coerce Jake into helping him rid himself of his selfish wife? And now he has someone else and, knowing Jake would have something to say about another side to the triangle, did David decide it was time to silence Jake forever?

If Jake found out about Holly and David's baby, he must have realised that he could never compete for David's affections against a baby. Did he remind David of the lies he told for him? The alibi for the night he murdered and disposed of his wife's body. It wouldn't take much for David to come to the conclusion that he's better off without Jake.

I raise an eyebrow at Kat. 'Well? Could Jake have engineered the accident to bring back David?'

'It's possible,' she mutters. I notice that her hand is shaking.

'In that case, it's not such a leap to consider the strong possibility that Jake agreed to give David an alibi? Is it?'

Kat stares for several moments. I hold her gaze. I half expect her to demand that I leave her house but she doesn't. Eventually she blinks, looks away, raises the coffee mug to her mouth.

'I still don't know where they were the day she went missing.'

But if she knows, she's definitely not going to tell me now. My punishment for pointing out the obvious.

'It's fine. I have other lines of enquiry. Has David offered to pay for Jake's funeral?' It's a good cover for anyone who doesn't suspect he might be behind his friend's death.

Her eyes widen. 'Yeah…how did you know…?'

'Just a thought.' Because he feels guilty. Because he has something he needs to make up for.

'David wouldn't harm Jake,' she defends, but her argument is rubbish when David attacked her brother. If you can do it once, you can easily do it a second time and, without someone to stop him, did he go too far this time?

358

I don't reply. Kat puts the mug down and continues, 'Mum never forgave David for hurting Jake. I thought I might ask if he wants to contribute towards the funeral after-party.' She forces a smile. 'Jake always called it that. He wanted to be cremated. Do you think the undertaker might give us a discount because he's partially done?' She laughs but tears well up in her eyes. 'Hospital humour.'

'Yes. I have a friend with one. What will you do with his ashes?' I ask.

'Jake wanted them split into different urns and placed on the bar in each of his favourite pubs. He should have gone into the pub game. He spent enough time in them over the years drinking and pissing away his payout.'

'Any particular favourite haunts?' I ask, thinking of the many photos hanging up in his house. 'Too many to mention. There's The Jester, Seven Stars, Red Lion. All nice pubs back in the day. Proper boozers. I don't mean spit and sawdust dives. I mean friendly places, where the other drinkers know your name and the bar staff know what you drink. Jake had this bright idea of breaking into one of them and setting the brewing company up inside. Some of them had great kitchens. Perfect for them, Jake said, but he couldn't persuade David. If he hadn't got wed, he might have been up for it. I heard his wife kept him on a tight leash.' Kat pulls a face and I pity her husband if he even so much as frowns at one of her ideas. But considering who David's bestie was, I don't blame Amanda for keeping him on a tight rein.

'He's got a lock-up now. Runs his business from there...oh,' she slowly smiles, her red rimmed eyes widen brightly. 'You didn't know about it? Well, you won't know where it is neither.' And her look says it all. What kind of a shit Private Investigator are you? A very shit one it seems.

'Where is it?' I ask, but what does it matter? If David rented it after Amanda's disappearance, what bearing could it have on the case? But still, it's a line of enquiry. One that I'll have to tie up or it'll irritate me. He could have hidden evidence there, I suppose. Moved it from elsewhere.

'Can't remember,' she answers, smugly.

'Not to worry,' I say. 'I must really get on. I've taken up enough of your time.' I slide my notebook away and stand.

'Can I just ask you something before you go, Mr Bailey?' I raise my chin. 'I really want to see Jake but the coroner's officer has told us we shouldn't. I need to know it's him.'

359

I open my mouth to explain about the Dentist but she holds up a hand, silencing me. 'They've explained about dental records.' She shudders, composes herself. 'The thing is Jake hadn't been to one for years. He had a tattoo. Here,' and she touches the top of her left shoulder. 'Would that still be there?'

According to Isla, there's not a bit of Jake that isn't charred. 'I'm afraid not. Kat, no one can stop you from seeing Jake but, should you decide to view him, you have to be prepared.'

She nods. Despite her hostility, I sympathise. I wanted to see Claire but people talked me out of it. I regret that now. I didn't want the last person she saw to be her murderer. It should have been me. Someone who cared about her.

'I'm gonna ring the Coroner's office,' she decides. 'I must see him.'

I smile. 'Good luck and once again I'm sorry.'

She stands. Her hard expression relaxes and her smile is genuine. 'Tanner Road. Number twelve. Dave's lock-up.'

Chapter 53

I fold over the pages until the front cover is on top and smooth down the diagonal crease in the left-hand corner of the stapled document. Shaun has excelled himself with his dossier on Michael. It was well worth the wait. Well worth it indeed. It's frankly eye-opening.

He has set out his findings under dated headings, describing in detail the scenes he's witnessed, the conversations with whom and where; he's included timings and weather conditions, should the evidence be criticised.

The document ends with a succinct bullet-point conclusion stating Michael's three main offences, each of them on their own a reason to finish the relationship. In fact, if you were only mates with him, it should make you reconsider your friendship.

I drum my fingertips on the desk top and shake my head a little. I can't believe that it's come to this. That I've been forced to intervene in something that should've been over ages ago. The evidence is overwhelmingly indisputable and will slap Bronwyn hard across the face. It will hold a mirror up to her behaviour and rightly have her questioning her own judgment.

This is what's been going on under your nose for too long. *This* is what you have refused to see and believe. *This* is how Michael has manipulated you. *This* is how stupid and naive you've been for the last four months. *This* is what I had to do to make you see sense.

Seeing what Michael is guilty of, the lies and the manipulation is shocking, and I can't help feel absolutely staggered that someone like Bronwyn, an intelligent woman with professional qualifications and a good job, can have the wool pulled so far down over her eyes all her senses are rendered useless. What is it about Michael that makes her such a soft touch? Why does she buy into his emotional tales of woe? I may never know. It's a question that perhaps only she can answer. This document and its stark revelations will fix all that and propel her into action. There is no way she can explain away the colossal amount of lies he has told. And if she attempts to, then she's not the person I thought she was.

I allow myself a smug smile that I am the one who bought this stupid situation to a close. God only knows how long I'd be waiting for her to do it. But I know my patience is nearly at breaking point.   Snatching a couple of evenings of sex, flirty text messages and many empty promises is wearing me down and, so many times, I have been on the verge of finishing it with her. Whatever *it* is.

I glance at the clock. Just after 3pm. Bronwyn is due here at five, but I know she'll be early. The slightly formal invite has amused her and her first question when I texted to invite her over was a naughty, 'Will we be alone?' Shaun will be on his way home then and, though he'll be keen to know the outcome, it's only fair I break the news alone.

And how to break the news. I see no point in sugarcoating the findings. When I hand over photos of spouses and partners committing adultery, I don't offer such pointless platitudes as, 'I'm sure it's an innocent kiss' or 'I bet her hand just accidentally fell down his trousers'.

I've never had to break bad news to someone I cared about before and the thought has me thinking about how Claire would do it. Which is easy because, if she was here, I'd be thrusting this dossier at her and telling her to get on with it. She was always more sympathetic towards matters of the heart. I know her advice would be to ask myself how I'd like to be told something similar. Easy answer. Straight to the point.

And once I've done the deed and Bronwyn leaves to ring Michael, around 6, once she's calmed down, I reckon I'll be sitting pretty by 7 tonight. Michael will be a very distant memory. Finally, we can move forward and I might actually have a name for what's going on between me and her.

And won't that be nice? Another piece of my life will slot into place. Soon I'll have a complete picture. And if not, I can move forward very much Bronwyn-free.

Shaun pushes the door open further with the toe of his red trainer, carrying a cup of tea in each hand, his llama notebook tucked under his arm.

I slide the dossier back into the drawer and close it. I reach for the packet of chocolate digestives poking out from the top of my rucksack, unpick the little red tab and unwind it, exposing the top three biscuits. Shaun accepts two, parking them on the corner of the desk, whilst he removes the two elastic bands from the book, securing them over his wrist where they join two plaited material friendship bracelets, which his sister made. He looks up, finally ready to start our meeting.

I smile. 'As predicted, Kat Bunby didn't know where Jake was the day Amanda went missing. Isla confirmed his attendance at an orthopaedic appointment in the morning, which is of little use since our last sighting of Amanda is at Fradlington train station at noon. There is a tiny window of opportunity for Jake to have driven to the city to abduct Amanda, but this is highly unlikely since no-one has reported an abduction taking place in a busy place. There would have been plenty of train staff milling about, along with plain clothes cops so I think it's safe to rule it out.'

'He's much more likely to have taken her from Lexington train station when she arrived back. But then he wouldn't need to abduct her if he and David were in it together. She'd have willingly got in his van…' Shaun says.

'Ahh,' I say, raising a finger. 'Would she? Think about it…her car's parked there. An expensive top of the range 4X4. She's hardly likely to get into David's van, and for what reason? What would make you get into your sister's car, rather than your own?'

'Lucky for me, she doesn't have a car on account of failing her test.' He tries to hide his smile but it's literally bursting out on his face.

'You look thrilled. Why did she fail?'

Shaun grins smugly. 'I'm positively over the moon, yeah. The examiner asked her to turn right at the next turning and silly cow was all flustered and couldn't see it. He had to take control of the car before she ran into the back of a parked vehicle. Automatic fail. Brilliant!'

He clamps a hand over his mouth and laughs. His shoulders jump and down, his eyes dance with mirth.

'Turns out Dad didn't have faith she'd pass because he hadn't organised a car for her.' Shaun pulls himself together and wiping tears from his eyes answers, 'A family emergency.'

'What?'

'A family emergency would make me get in my sister's car. If she had one. And one involving a close relative. Like if she told me Dad had had a heart attack and I was so upset that I was unsafe to drive.'

I picture Hock alone in his shop, when suddenly excruciating pain strikes his chest and left arm, his breathing becomes ragged and he collapses in a heap on top of a stack of newspapers, his heart coming to a standstill. Not sure I'd be so upset that I was unable to drive. My first reactions would be to crack open the bubbly and keep my fingers crossed that the next customer through the door didn't know CPR.

'Oliver is the only reason Amanda would get into David's van,' I tell Shaun. 'She'd be so panicked that she wouldn't even think twice about it. Particularly if he told her that the boy was in pain and crying for his mum. And I bet you know what wailing kids are like. When they want their mum, only their mum will do. My brother was like that,' I say. 'A real crybaby.'

Shaun nods knowingly. 'My younger brothers and sisters know they'll get more sympathy from my dad. He's a softie,' he explains. The revelation makes me raise a surprised eyebrow. 'My mum's quite hard-faced.'

Having never met her, I'll take his word for it.

'What we're saying is that David spun Amanda a yarn when he caught up with her at the train station. Oliver's had an accident; he's fallen off a climbing frame, broken his ankle and he's screaming A and E down for his mum. Amanda jumps into Dave's van, failing to spot Jake lurking behind the seats. David drives her to an unknown location where together, they murder and dispose of her body. We have no idea where that place is, how they murdered her or why.'

'No evidence either,' Shaun points out, using the blade of his hand to sweep crumbs into the bin.

'The lack of motive bothers me,' I admit, with frustration. 'Jake has one. He hated her, was jealous that she elbowed her way to number one in David's affections.'

'I can't believe he admitted how much he despised her though. Pretty stupid.'

I shake my head. 'No, it's clever. Admit something someone will point out. He thought we'd exonerate him because of his disability and weakness. There's no way Amanda would get into a vehicle with him if he was alone at the train station. She'd never buy the lie that something had happened to Oliver from him.'

'What if he'd told her David had had an accident?'

I shake my head, reach for another biscuit. 'No. She absolutely loathed Jake. Being in a confined space with him, would have repelled her. Which means Jake couldn't have done this on his own. He needed David.'

'He needed *someone*.'

I frown and wait for him to elaborate.

'Who's to say David was his accomplice? How the heck did he get David on board? We've got no evidence he and Amanda had an unhappy marriage. Alright, they had issues. Amanda was selfish with money, she was possessive and jealous. David was torn between his wife and bestie, she had very little experience with sex whereas David was a Lothario. All those issues can be ironed out with time and counselling. They'd only been married a few months. It was too soon to throw in the towel.'

I give it some thought. Jake and who? Who hated Amanda as much as him? Or who loved Jake enough to assist him in murder? Kat? I smile. She might have loved her brother with every bone in her body, but help him in his murderous endeavours? I don't see it. She wouldn't risk her freedom and family for him.

I chuckle with the irony of it. I didn't need much persuading to put my life on the line for my own brother.

Perhaps Jake had another friend who felt the same way. We haven't unearthed anyone else who fits this criteria. In fact Jake's only friend appears to be David.

'Hepworth?' I suggest, blurting out the name.

Shaun looks up from his notebook, considers it for a few moments but shrugs. 'Teacher and pupil joining forces against a common enemy. Hepworth certainly has the motive, but he had only contempt for Jake—'

'Or he was pretending to,' I suggest.

Shaun concedes with a shrug. 'Hepworth has an alibi.'

'Only on the day Amanda disappeared. What if Jake murdered her but Hepworth helped him dispose of her at a later…' my voice trails off as I realise the stupidity of what I'm saying. 'Forget it.' I rub my chin on the palm of my hand. 'Jake still had to store her somewhere and get her into his vehicle. Hepworth would still have been incapacitated, and there's no way in the world, Amanda would've got in a car with Hepworth. All he wanted was the diary.'

'Lawrence Hayden then?'

'No evidence Jake and he knew each other. And again, how did the two join forces?'

'A woman then.' Shaun rubs two fingers across his forehead. 'Tamsin! Jake knew her from school and was her dealer.'

'Maybe. She certainly hated Amanda enough. But did he know that? From my experience, most dealers spend just enough time with their addicts to make a transaction. They don't really do chitchat. Not the murderous kind anyway. Getting rid of Amanda was going to do exactly what for Tamsin? I got the impression that Amanda had little faith in the abilities of any of her staff. And we know that Holly was the one who grabbed the crown in the end. Tamsin left soon after Amanda's disappearance.'

'Guilt,' Shaun points out. 'Perhaps she thought if she hung around, people would see it written all over her face. There's a lot of animosity between Tamsin and Jake, which is typical for a dealer/addict relationship. I'm not sure, if I was either of them, I'd trust the other to keep their mouth shut.'

'I wouldn't have trusted Jake as far as I could throw him. He lied about his alibi. Holly's got more of a motive,' I say. 'She's done extremely well out of her cousin's disappearance. She's got her man, her business, a baby on the way, her feet firmly in Amanda's bed.'

'Has she got any other kids? Any around six years old?'

I laugh. 'Isla says not. This is her first pregnancy.'

Shaun screws his face up. 'Still...Holly and Jake...do you see it?' I shake my head. 'David and Holly maybe...unless the three of them were in on it...'

'Holly had an alibi for that day, unless she assisted them in disposing of the body. It's not inconceivable that Amanda discovered David had feelings for her employee. That's if he did 7 years ago. I can't imagine it would go down very well at all. Very humiliating. Amanda wouldn't hesitate in firing Holly and kicking David out, and there goes his home and his budding business.'

'What about Jake? Where does he fit into all this? He's not going to help David and his lover get rid of a wife. It puts him in exactly the same position: out in the cold. Even if David promised Jake things would be different, he's not that stupid. And wouldn't they then try to blame Jake for Amanda's murder? You know, plant evidence of Jake on her body? I would. But she hasn't even been found. She *could* be alive.'

I shake my head. 'She's dead. And one of this lot,' and I slap a hand on my notes, 'is responsible. We have to consider the strong possibility that the person who murdered Amanda, killed Jake too. Other than trying to hide his caved-in head and destroy evidence, I don't know why they burnt the house down. Like you said, if Jake is your accomplice, frame him, *then* kill him. But don't destroy the house and any planted evidence.'

'Maybe they didn't mean to kill him,' Shaun says, reaching for another biscuit. 'Perhaps they went for a chat but it got out of hand. They saw the hammer, gave him a forty whacks—'

I interrupt. 'It was just one.'

'One whack then. Of course you'd panic. Do you think it was someone who couldn't dominate Jake with words? Someone too emotional.'

366

I nod in agreement. 'David is emotional. They could have been tears of remorse the other day over Jake. He regrets it but knew it had to be done to shut him up. Perhaps Jake was threatening to blow the whistle on their phoney alibi. Because he found out about Holly and, with Jake gone, David's alibi is virtually sealed in concrete forever. There's no one to give him up. Holly might not even be aware of what he's done, or if she is, she's doesn't care. Sensibly she's better off keeping her gob shut unless she wants to be victim number three. David had to have had a motive.' I clench a fist. '*Something* must have happened between him and Amanda. He might not have meant to do it. People can flip just like that,' and with the same hand, I click my fingers. 'I bet she pushed him to his absolute limit. Don't forget we know she was rooting through his stuff. Who's to say she didn't "say sorry" and the next day, there she is going through his bag again. But this time he isn't so forgiving. He's had enough. He can't put up with this for the next forty years. They have a huge row. She gives him one day to get his meagre belongings together and get the hell out. There goes the nice house, his precious brewing company; it'll never reach its potential now and it's back to his mum's. His investment in marriage and Amanda has been cut short. He talks to his best friend. And Jake we know has every reason under the sun to want the bitch gone. This is the news he's been hoping to hear. He makes a tentative suggestion. Tests the water. Picture Jake, sidling up to David, arm slung around his mate's shoulder, whispering, "Don't fret, Dave, mate."'

Shaun starts giggling. Tears of amusement spring into his eyes. 'Jesus, Will. You sound exactly like him. Have you been practising? It's like you've bought him back to life. God, I miss his little rodenty face. He was like your favourite bubonic plague carrier.'

'You crazy sod. Anyway as I was saying, he's all over David, probably getting turned on too and he says—'

'Do the voice,' Shaun demands, with excitement.

'This is very unprofessional, you know. The man *is* dead. Okay. He says, "Don't fret, Dave, mate. I've got an idea. Let's get shot of the bitch and be quids in!"' I clap my hands and rub them together.

'Would you really kill your wife for going through your stuff?'

'Depends what she found. Evidence of another woman, or a man, drugs, something that appalled her. Maybe he stole from Amanda. I can picture him doing that. Remember Jake was encouraging David to break into one of those empty pubs to run their brewing business from it. Maybe nicking from his wife was more preferable. None of this helps if we can't prove it. Shaun, we may never know the catalyst, but he's involved.'

Shaun nods, finishes his tea. 'I don't even want to consider the possibility that the culprit is someone we haven't found yet.'

'We can't absolutely rule out a stranger killing but, if she died at the hands of one, they went to a lot of trouble to hide her body.'

A shrill beeping from my mobile cuts across the end of my sentence. I snatch the phone up, expecting it to be Bronwyn cancelling our meeting.

It's a message from Nisha.

"Hi Will. Hope you're okay. I'll give you a ring later but I wanted you to know that I'm thinking about Claire. Much love, Nisha xx"

'Shit,' I mutter. My mood does a u-turn. Claire. I remembered this morning, of course I did. The date will forever be etched into my memory, but since I arrived at work, the dossier and the case have pushed away the significance of today. Three years ago, I discovered who was responsible for Claire's disappearance and more importantly, I found her.

I remember the evidence which took me to the front door of Sally, Claire's youngest half-sister. I suggested that we talk in her garage because she wouldn't let me in her home. I recall Olivia, Claire's other half-sister, turning up supposedly to save both their skins, and Nisha's all-important phone call which couldn't have come at a better time, when I was floundering. Both Claire's half-sisters in it together. All I wanted to know: where was Claire? What had they done to her?

'Will? You alright?' Shaun touches my am.

'Yeah, mate.' I explain the significance of today. 'Time flies. Even when you're not having fun.'

'I googled it,' Shaun says. 'The trial. I always wanted to ask you about it, but didn't want to upset you. Besides, it's personal, you know. I read about them changing their plea…'

'They had no choice. How the fuck can you explain away a body buried on your property?'

I fall silent thinking about how long it took the workmen and Forensic Science Service to break through the concrete and release Claire from her tomb. The wait was agonising. The physical investigation was over, Claire had been found, the murderers were arrested and giving the standard advised responses of "No comment". Mentally the investigation felt far from over. Closure was months and months away and I knew the trial and the verdict wouldn't give me an absolute end to it all.

'Will,' Shaun says, breaking into my thoughts with a gentle voice.

I turn to him. 'Yeah?'

'There is something I'd like to know. Did Claire's half-sisters ever explain why they buried her where they did?'

'Once they changed their plea to guilty, they didn't have to take the stand, so no, they didn't. There was a mechanic's pit in the floor of Sally's garage,' I explain. 'It was the perfect grave, right size, right depth, no one would ever know—'

'I know, I read about it, but why bury Claire on their property? Why didn't they leave her where she was killed? Cover her with leaves and stuff, and leave her to be found by a dog walker.'

'There are lots of reasons why people hide and attempt to dispose of bodies. Firstly, it buys you time to formulate a plan. I defy anyone who murders for the first time not to go into immediate panic. Kicking leaves and twigs over a body is an attempt to hide what you've done, albeit a crap one. Hiding a body means you're hiding forensic evidence. If you manage to destroy the body, not an easy feat, and/or the scene, like Jake's house fire, you're destroying evidence permanently. That's what they were doing. The pit and the subsequent filling in of it meant they hid Claire and any evidence tying them to the crime. They could get on with staging the scene for Claire's supposed disappearance. And, with the pit being on Sally's property, it's effectively hidden. They'd thrown an old rug or something over it. Who looks twice at a garage floor?'

'You did,' Shaun points out proudly.

'The concrete was two different colours, but it was only when Sally glanced down at it that she gave the game away. You could argue that her actions tied her to the house forever but, even if they could afford to move, the next owner would be unlikely to open up a professionally filled-in pit. At least Sally and Olivia would always know where Claire was; there was never any danger of someone suddenly stumbling over her body like if they'd left her in the woods. I suppose it gave the sisters peace of mind too. They did get on with their lives reasonably well. Until I showed up that is.'

Shaun stares at the desk. I watch with interest, toy with the idea of making another drink, but I don't want to ruin his train of thought.

Then he looks up, a tiny crease between his eyebrows, his eyes bright with an idea. 'Do you think this is what was done to Amanda? Jake and David, or whoever, they hid her in a similar location. Somewhere secure. A place no one is going to stumble upon, or nose about in.'

I look for the MISPER file underneath the other papers. 'The police searched the grounds of Amanda's house; they found nothing. No disturbed soil, no newly erected walls…'

'No,' Shaun says emphatically. 'Not the house. David wouldn't be that stupid. She isn't at his house; one day he'll have to leave. He knows that. If she's at Jake's, the fire service will find her when they investigate the cause of the fire. But I don't think she's there. And no way could anyone dig a hole in the bungalow's garden and pop her into it without being seen by the neighbours. Did you see that Jake's garden is overlooked on all sides?'

'Yes,' I lie. Blimey, Shaun was eagle-eyed that day. Why wasn't I? Oh, yeah, I had that stinking cold and I wasn't even functioning at 5%. 'A grave in a garden is not as fool-proof as one in concrete. It could smell. A very tell-tale stench too.'

'I don't think even Jake would be stupid enough to agree to housing his best mate's dead wife on his property. We can rule out David's lock-up. The entire site is surrounded by CCTV, it's overlooked by houses and he only started renting it five years ago.'

'Why move the body from a perfectly good grave, which has been secure for a number of years, to a place that's in your name? It doesn't make sense.'

'Yeah,' Shaun agrees, flinging himself back into the seat with exasperation. 'I agree.'

'I certainly believe Amanda was hidden to give the illusion that she left to either commit suicide or start a new life.'

'Well, if they have hidden her, rather than attempted to destroy her remains, where could she be?' Shaun ponders. 'It would need to be local. Lexington or the outskirts of Kelsall. David's customers told the police the times he finished work that day and both he and Jake were seen at David's house later. They can't have gone far. A short van drive away.'

My mind races. Where did they have access to? What was going on in their lives at the time? Very little in Jake's…brewing, dossing about at home, drinking, watching porn, playing video games, pissing his payout up the wall. And David. Trying to make his marriage work, playing tug-of-war with his wife and best mate, drinking, pubs…brewing again…they were pretty obsessed with it...they always had been, spending their youth in pubs. Jake's photo collection is testament to that. I've never seen so many photos of public houses...they're like second homes, retreats. No wonder Jake wanted to break into one...

'Somewhere secure, remote…' Shaun is saying. 'A place that's—'

'Vacant,' I say, suddenly enlightened.

He turns to me, his eyebrows raised with interest.

'And there are plenty of places right here,' and my hands move the papers aside. Pages fly off the desk and zig-zag to the floor. Shaun attempts to catch them. I pat the desk for my iPad. I know it's here somewhere. Why am I so untidy…my hand lands on a hard flat object and I pluck it out, sending more paper into flight.

I unlock the screen, click on the photos icon. Lots of squares appear and I quickly scroll through them. They whizz past and I choose one at random. I hold the screen out for Shaun to see. Jake and David, their faces red with drunkenness, their grins lopsided. Behind David's left ear is a large bell on a thick rope.

'A pub,' I explain. 'A closed down one.'

His eyes dance with excitement and his fingers enlarge the picture until the bell fills the screen. 'But how can we identify what pub this is? It could be one of many—of course!' He grabs my arm, squeezing it. 'Ben. I should've realised. Why didn't I think of him?'

'Ben? As in The Smoking Gun Ben? Your boss?'

He nods vigorously, a smile spreading across his face. 'Ben is an aficionado of local pubs. Particularly ones from the past. Their history, the beers they sold. If anyone can identify these boozers, he can.'

'Get him on the phone,' I order bossily. 'Get his email address. I'll send them straight over.'

'On it,' Shaun announces with excitement, grabbing his phone off the desk.

A noise in the corridor alerts me and I tilt my head to the slightly ajar door. Footsteps, the outer door closing and a female voice calling out: 'Hi! Is anyone home?'

Bronwyn. I glance at the clock. An hour early.

Shaun looks at me, lowers the phone.

'In here,' I call out.

The door gingerly opens and Bronwyn smiles at us. Her attire surprises me. I thought she'd come straight from work…unless they've had a dress-down day. She's wearing dark maroon leggings, black ankle boots and a pale grey woollen top. Her hair is down, the spiral curls framing her pretty face.

'Hello. How are you both?' She takes in the scene. The paper-strewn desk, the empty cups, the biscuits and she knows what this means. We're having a case catchup, a where-do-we-go-from-here? session. Perhaps she can feel the sizzle of excitement in the air when she asks, 'Have you had a breakthrough in the case?'

'We hope so,' I reply. 'We've definitely discovered another line of enquiry.'

'I recognise that look on your face, William. I've seen it many times before. Am I interrupting? I can come back if you're busy.'

'Not at all.' I shove the iPad at Shaun, the screen still open. He drops the notebook and it falls open face down on the floor. 'Email Ben. Ask him to identify what he can. We'll get together in the morning. We need to know how far away these locations are from our three points of interest.'

He retrieves his book, secures it under his arm and nods repeatedly. 'I'm on it, Will. Nice to meet you again, Bronwyn. Can I get either of you a drink?'

'I'm fine, thank you,' she replies, moving aside to let him past.

'Me too. Cheers Shaun.'

At the door, just before he shuts it, Shaun turns to me, mouths, 'Good luck.'

I smile thanks. The door closes and I watch as she walks further into the room, her heeled boots noisy on the hard floor. She places her bag on the coffee table.

'You been to work today?' I ask.

'No. I've had the day off to indulge in some retail therapy. I had an utterly crap day yesterday. The atmosphere in the office was horrendous and I couldn't face more of the Senior Managers' bullshit. I got some new jeans and a lovely dress, really cheap and sparkly for my next night out. I've spent a ridiculous amount in *Paperchase* on stationery I might not ever use for a job I might not have by the end of the month. But what the heck? You can't take it with you, can you?'

'You can't indeed,' I agree.

'Oh. I got you something too,' and from behind the oversized handbag, she produces a paper bag with strong rope handles. She smiles at me. 'Hope you like it, Will.'

I stand and accept the bag. 'Thank you. You didn't have to buy me a present.' I remove a tall thin box. The picture on the side is of a black stainless steel water bottle. I clock the make. An expensive present indeed.

'Thanks, Bron. It's great. Much better than what I was using.'

'I've noticed how much water you're drinking. First thing you do at my flat is go to the tap.' She smiles. 'There's a carabiner too, if you want to attach it your rucksack.'

I slide the box back inside the bag and come around the desk to say "thank you" properly. She slides her arms around my waist and buries her face in my neck. We stand like this for several moments, her body warming mine.

'I could stay like this forever,' she whispers. 'I really needed this hug.'

Me too, I think. I need them from her every day. Michael's words from our last encounter come back to haunt me. I've known Bronwyn for ten months and I hardly know her at all. Yesterday she had a crap day at work and I wasn't the one she contacted to moan to. I wasn't doing anything special and if I had have been, I'd have shifted it aside for her. She could have ranted at me down the phone or face-to-face. Did she turn to him instead? Or was it a friend she rang? Either way it was not me. I want to be the first person she turns to when she's sad, angry, excited. I want to be the one to hear her sad or good news. I want to be her shoulder to cry on, her ear to bend when she's ranting. I want to be the one to accompany her on retail therapy shopping sprees, the one stood outside the clothes shops, hands sore from carrying the many shopping bags like other men.

If I was her boyfriend, I'd spend forever getting to know her properly.

Today, now, is as good a time as any to tell her what I know.

I pull gently away and she looks at me questioningly. I remove the dossier from the drawer, keep the front cover hidden and say, 'Do you want to sit down?'

Surprised at my sudden seriousness, she looks behind her and chooses a chair. She tenses up. After all she has no idea why I asked her here. She sits right back into the chair, lays her hands on its arms, almost braced for impact, a sudden vicious jolt that will throw her forward and turn her day into a horrendous one.

I take a seat opposite, try a smile, but it falls from my face too easily. My happiness and hers depend too much on this to treat it any other way than serious.

'Bronwyn,' I begin, 'there's something I need to tell you.'

Chapter 54

'What's that?' She nods, an intrigued smile on her lips. 'Is it your last will and testament?'

'No. It's some—'

'Phew. For a minute there, I thought you were going to ask me to be a witness. Which means I'm not a beneficiary…'

'I have very few worldly goods to bequeath. I doubt you want my aged Mazda.'

She smiles again. 'Is it a CV then? You're not applying for another job?'

I'm making her nervous. It's her way of easing the tension by making quips.

'With Nisha going part-time, it'd be silly to leave. You'll make an excellent—'

I interrupt. 'Bronwyn, have you spoken to Michael yet?'

The question erases her smile and she shakes her head regretfully, opens her mouth to deliver yet another reason as to why she couldn't find the words. I plough on. 'You know I've never believed the claims about his brother's illness and his work situation to be true. I've long since held the opinion that he's consistently lying to you and manipulating your feelings.'

Her shoulders tense, a little frown appears on her forehead and I know she's about to tell me the same old crap. That I'm being unfair, pressuring her, it's alright for me and so on. The idea of listening to that nonsense again makes me feel tired.

'This,' and I hold up the document. Her eyes flick to it. 'Proves I'm right.'

'What is it?'

I take a deep breath. Here goes. There's no going back. 'I've investigated his claims. They're bullshit. All of them.'

She stares at me, tilts her head slightly. 'When you say investigate, what do—'

'I put Michael and his brother under surveillance. Witnesses were inter—'

'Witnesses?' she queries. 'Who?'

'Colleagues, his brother, neighbours. An ex-girlfriend. People,' I patiently explain, 'who have refuted Michael's claims.'

She shifts uncomfortably in the chair, takes hold of the arms. She looks shocked. Her eyes are staring, her jaw clenched.

'Do you want to read it yourself?' I offer.

'No.'

I turn the front page over, crease it across the staple again. My heart thumps in my chest, reverberating against my ribs like a mallet on a xylophone. Straight to the point, I tell myself. 'Michael,' I begin but stop to cough. My throat feels dry. I need a drink. I could do with that swanky new bottle to be brimming with cool water. I swallow hard, cough again and try once more. 'Michael told you his brother, Jamie, recently began to suffer neurological symptoms of an unknown disorder and was undergoing tests at the hospital.' I wait for her to acknowledge with a nod or a noise but she doesn't. I continue. 'The truth is that Jamie has been ill for four years. He had a motorbike accident on the A5689 and sustained, along with rib fractures and concussion, a very nasty break of his left femur. He's had numerous operations to fix the break. Lots of plates and screws, but it's never healed very well. As a result, Jamie has been unable to continue in his work as a tree surgeon. He lost his business and has been receiving benefits ever since. Jamie sunk into depression and turned to alcohol.' I pause, examine her reaction.

'Four years?' she queries. 'Are you sure?'

'Five in September.'

She looks away down at the edge of the threadbare rug and frowns.

'A few months ago Jamie's wife left him, taking the children. This has only increased his drinking. Jamie suffers from alcoholic neuropathy, which is essentially damage to the nerve endings caused by alcohol. A condition which won't help his mobility and balance. He's made the decision to have his leg amputated and is on a waiting list for surgery. In the meantime, he is on a variety of medications and has carers to help with his daily living and pain management.'

'How did you find out about this?' she asks.

'He was observed,' and I flick the page over and hold the document for her to see the photos Shaun took of Jamie struggling to walk down the street with his crutches, the pain deeply entrenched on his face.

Her eyes widen and her hand moves to her mouth. I ask if she recognises him. She shakes her head, tells me she has never met him.

'Where did you get all the medical stuff from? That girl who works in the mortuary? Did she access the patient data—'

'No. Jamie was engaged in conversation in the Golden Swan public house. He volunteered the information.'

Bronwyn stares at me thoughtfully without saying a word. Several moments later, with a funny little chuckle, she says, 'You mean, you or Shaun bought an alcoholic a pint in exchange for his life story? And for a whisky chaser, what did he do? Show you his scars? How do you even know he's the right Jamie Nicholls?'

'It's the right one. This is my job, Bronwyn,' I tell her firmly. 'I have verified his identity. Plus, I have this photographic evidence.' I flick to the next photo. Michael walking up the same garden path to the front door Jamie was photographed leaving. And look: Jamie answering the door to Michael. Next picture: Michael embracing Jamie. 'Irrefutable, I'd say. Wouldn't you?'

Her eyes meet mine. 'Yes,' she replies quietly.

'When asked about the recent hospital tests he and his brother have undergone, Jamie has denied all knowledge. In fact, the only appointment he's waiting for is his pre-op assessment. But to back up these findings, we spoke to a neighbour who's been friends with the family for nine years. She confirmed Jamie's injuries. There is absolutely no evidence to back up Michael's claims that his brother has been struck down by an unknown disorder.'

I study her. She looks shell-shocked, like this is the very last thing she expects to be told. Her fingers entwine, her thumbnail scratches the dark purple varnish off the other thumbnail.

After several seconds of silence, she looks up and blinks.

'Carry on,' she says, her tone flat.

I remind her of Michael's claims that he's been signed off sick. Then I tell her the truth.

'He's been suspended pending an allegation of making an inappropriate comment in the workplace.'

'What?'

'There was a meeting regarding the recent redundancies. Several people, including Michael and his counterpart from another branch, were informed that they would need to reapply for their jobs. This effectively pits colleagues against colleagues. It was alleged that Michael said to his counterpart that she would be successful over him because, and I quote, "management would need a fat dyke in the office to fulfil their quota of employing people like you". Three of his colleagues complained and he was immediately suspended.'

376

'I…' she begins before trailing off and sitting very still, speechless. After a few moments, she shakes her head. 'I've never heard Michael make a homophobic remark. It doesn't sound like him.'

'How well do you really know him, Bron? When he's with you, he's on his best behaviour. If you've ever said anything positive about gay rights or mentioned a gay colleague, he's going to watch what he says around you.'

'How do you know it's true though, Will? What if they're making it up? His suspension gives his colleague her best chance of landing the job.'

'But he told you his GP signed him off with high blood pressure caused by stress over his brother's illness. An illness which doesn't exist. Have you seen his sick note?'

'No, but he would have sent that to his employer.'

'The receptionist at Michael's workplace hasn't seen his sick note and she opens the post. However, she told us that under no circumstances is she to let Michael into the office unless he has a meeting with HR. If he does turn up, she is to call security. Rather strict instructions for someone supposedly signed off sick. Jamie was also asked about Michael's blood pressure. He's not aware Michael has been signed off sick.'

'I can't believe you got so much information from Jamie. It's very odd that he was willing to talk about his brother to a complete stranger.'

'But he did,' I insist. I take a deep breath, try and calm down, ignore her arguing. It's a reaction, that's all. Not wholly unexpected. No one likes to think they've been taken for a ride. Of course, she's going to be angry with me since I'm the telling her this. But once she confronts Michael, the anger will be directed at the right person.

'There's one other thing you must know,' I say.

With a tired nod, she indicates I should go on.

This final piece is the most damning yet. The most serious too because it could have a direct effect on her once she finishes with him. She needs to know how he might react.

I begin by telling her the same receptionist contacted us with the name of someone we should speak to: Michael's ex. I explain that last autumn, Jane, an alias, began work as an admin temp to cover another colleague's long-term sick leave. After a couple of weeks of flirting, Michael and Jane started seeing each other. It all seemed to be going well, until one day Jane didn't turn up for work and the temp agency rang to say she wouldn't be coming back. Jane and the receptionist had also made friends and eventually Jane confided the real reason she left.

'Jane agreed to meet Shaun and told him that after a week of seeing Michael, he became controlling, insisting they always had lunch together, demanding to know what she was doing on nights he didn't see her. Several times, if he couldn't get hold of her, he would turn up at her home unannounced. She put it down to the age difference; she's 8 years younger. After speaking to her friends, she decided to finish with him. The following day, Michael posted photos on her Facebook profile of the two of them having sex. Revenge porn. She didn't even know he had set up a camera in his lounge and bedroom. She quit the job and...'

'Did she go to the police?'

'Yes, but the pictures had been taken down by then so no further action was taken.'

Bronwyn slumps back in the chair, hands over her face. She stays like this for several moments. I desperately want to reach out and touch her but I keep my hands on my lap.

'Michael isn't like that with me,' she tells me. 'I know he turned up at my flat when you were there, but he hasn't done it since. He doesn't control me.'

'You're a different person to her. You're older, more independent, and you're not having sex with him.' I pause. 'Are you?'

'What?'

'You told me that you were not having—'

'I'm not fucking him, William,' she snaps, her voice loud, argumentative. 'How many more times?'

I take a deep breath, don't respond. I keep the subject on track. 'He's obviously changed his tack. Now he prefers to spin bullshit sob stories designed to play on your emotions. Bron, these findings disprove Michael's claims. Surely now you cannot fail to see through his lies.' I hold my hands out to her. No reaction. 'Bronwyn...I did this for you.'

Suddenly she looks at me and it's such a cold angry glare that I'm taken aback.

'You did it for *you*. Because you only do things for yourself, William. I had this under control. I told you that I needed to finish it in my own time—'

'Own time?' I argue. 'I've given you all the time in the world. You've had countless opportunities to talk to him. I *have* been patient. I have waited for you...'

'It's alright for you,' she states, her voice raising. 'You don't—'

My shoulders sink with despair. 'Don't give me that crap about maintaining good working relationships because he deals with your office's IT issues. He's been suspended. In a short while, he might not even have a job. You're making excuses again. There is *no* right time to finish with him. It needed to be done. How are we supposed to move us along if he's still—'

'So you took control of the situation and undertook your little investigation into my private life? Am I supposed to be grateful, William? "Aren't I a clever dick, Bronwyn?"' she mocks in a voice that sounds nothing like me, but rather like an evil puppet from a horror film. '"Here's the evidence that you've been an idiot and your boyfriend is a lying, manipulative sexual predator!"'

'Boyfriend?' I repeat. 'You've never referred to him as that before.'

'Oh, you know what I mean,' she replies unpleasantly. 'It's just a word.'

But she defends him and criticises me. He does all these cruel, unjustifiable things, manipulates people, and I'm the one that gets it in the neck for revealing his appalling behaviour. I don't think I can win here. It's not going the way I planned, the way I hoped. I don't expect her to be grateful, thankful maybe. I don't expect hugs and declarations of love, but I do expect her to treat what I've said seriously and act on it.

She crosses one knee over the other, folds her arms tightly and turns away a few degrees. That's the cold shoulder, right there. For fuck's sake.

I take a deep breath, try another approach, keep my tone calm, even. 'I never set out to humiliate you or make you feel stupid, Bron.'

She huffs. Yeah, right.

'I am sorry if I have,' I say in a sincere and soft voice, sitting forward, resting my forearms on my knees, closing the gap between us. 'But you must understand how I feel…I care about you.' She glances at me. Not strong enough. I sound like a friend. Her gaze is icy. I try again.

'At Easter when you confessed how you felt about me…it was one of the most wonderful days of my life. I never thought we'd get another chance. Do you remember our recent walk in the park?'

She looks across, shrugs nonchalantly.

'You asked me to remind you of something I said. Do you know what it was?' She shakes her head a little. 'I do. I said, "I can honestly say I'm never happier than when I'm with you, Bron". And I'm not.'

Her demeanour softens. Her arms relax, her legs uncross and the beginning of a smile plays on her lips. She shifts in the chair so that she's facing me again. We look at each other for what seems like several minutes.

A little frown appears between her eyebrows and I hold my breath, waiting for her response. It's okay, I tell myself. She's over the anger. She'll do the right thing, the only thing. She'll dump him.

'I...' she begins, '…I'll speak to Michael, ask him—'

'*Ask him*?' I echo. 'What's there to ask? He's lying to you and this,' and I snap the dossier through the air, 'is proof of it. Bronwyn, how much more evidence do you need? What are you going to do if he says it's not true? It'll be his word against this dossier and which will you believe?' I stand, chuck the dossier on the desk. I pace the room, stop in front of her and stare down. She looks up, her eyes hard, unimpressed.

'Tell me,' I demand, 'which one of us is telling the fucking truth?'

'There's no need to swear,' she says, huffily.

I laugh. 'No need to swear? Are you kidding me? Do you have any idea at all how frustrating this is? I am sick of being second best to a snivelling wanker like him. You promised me we'd be together, that you'd finish with him and all I've had is excuses and grief.'

'It's complicated, Will,' she says weakly.

Something deep inside me, right in the core of my chest, snaps. It might be my temper breaking, or the last ounce of patience I have left exploding into smithereens, but on that break, my decision is made.

'Well then, let me uncomplicate it for you.' I stomp over to the door and fling it open. 'I want you to leave my office.'

She looks up, her eyes panicked. Her voice is hollow, frightened. 'What do you mean leave? We're talking…'

'We're done talking and I'm done with *this*, with you.' My heart is thundering like a wild animal flinging itself against the side of a metal cage in a desperate attempt to break free.

She gets unsteadily to her feet, like her legs possess no strength. She implores me with a look. 'Please, Will. You don't mean—'

'And that.' I gesture at the gift bag. 'I want nothing more from you.'

With trembling hands, she takes her handbag and the bag containing the water bottle and steps towards the doorway, looking at me the entire time. Now her eyes look sad, tearful and sorry, but it's too late. She's chosen her side. A side she was always on.

She staggers down the corridor, almost drunkenly, to the outer office door. On the left-hand side, Shaun appears in the kitchen doorway, tea towel buried inside a mug as he dries it. He looks at me, concern on his young face, then at Bronwyn.

Once she's through that door, I can never contact her again. Should I stop her from disappearing from my life, taking away my chance of happiness?

But there is no happiness. Just more of this.

She fumbles with the door handle and Shaun helpfully steps forward to assist. She pauses on the threshold, as if waiting for me to speak, stop her, tell her, yes, let's talk some more.

But I say nothing. I let her go. It's over.

She steps onto the landing. Shaun reaches out, maybe to see if she's ok, but she disappears out of view down the wooden staircase, her footsteps receding. He closes the door, looks at me. His concern is touching but I can't bear it at the moment. My heart feels like it's splitting wide open.

'Will,' he says softly. 'What—'

I cut him off. 'Go home, Shaun.' And I close the door, collapse into the nearest chair and give in to my distress.

Chapter 55

I toss the magazine back onto the low coffee table and sit back in the worn leather settee. I've been googling men's hairstyles for the past week since I made my hair appointment. The last thing I wanted was to turn up here, have Al ask, 'What are we're doing today?' and me meekly reply, 'The usual' because I hadn't given any thought to my new look. I've given lots of thought to it. I want something quick, slick and definitely something that doesn't require hairdryers and more than one hair product to style it. I want to look different. Not like me anymore. A new me.

I always remember Claire seeing this older lad when we were at sixth form. She thought it was great that he had a car, could get served in a pub, had more experience. She was besotted until he ended it. The first thing she did was hit the shops, the second thing was change her hairstyle. Her hair then was long. She had it cut to half its length, had a fringe installed and changed its colour.

She told me that it wasn't to entice him back, nor change her appearance because it wasn't working for her, but because it made her feel better about herself. Like putting a bandage on a wound. Change the way you look, become someone else and erase the hurt that went with the old you.

If it worked for her, it might work for me. I need to pick myself up, in more ways than one. But I can start here with the easy, if costly, task of changing my appearance. For too long, I've felt and looked scruffy. I'm a professional Private Investigator for God's sake; I should look like one. I'm not trying to compete with Michael but I do appreciate he looks good. I'm not doing it for Bronwyn either, because I doubt I'll see her again.

I intend to ditch the jeans and trainers, the rugby tops and the Morrissey look.

I look around the barbers. The red leather chairs, the bare brick walls and the industrial-style light fittings. I can just hear swing music playing under the snip-snip of scissors and the buzzing shavers.

Al finishes dealing with his client, bids him farewell and comes out from behind the reception desk, beaming at me. He has great style and today is no exception. His crisp shirt is brilliant white and his pale blue jeans have been turned up exposing the black 8- eye Doc Marten boots.

He takes the studded green leather chair opposite me and says, 'You're two weeks early, William. I have you booked in for May.' He spies the untidy magazine and raises an eyebrow. 'You don't normally peruse new styles.' He moves to see the back of my head, checks the length of my locks, whether my hair is creeping over the top of my ears, if the weight of it is too heavy to hold the style.

He turns in the chair, extends a tattooed arm across its back.

'You're after a new look?' he correctly guesses. 'What d'ya fancy?'

'A serious change.' I hold my phone out for him to see the photo. He nods appraisingly.

'I can do that. I can do one better too. Let's get you prepped.' He winks and jerks his head over his shoulder.

I put myself in his skilful hands and follow him across the salon, towards the backwash stations.

*

At noon, I stroll into the office looking considerably different than how I looked last night. I close the door, hear Shaun on the phone in the nearest office.

'What *time* did you stay up to? There was hundreds of photos…well, it seemed like there were. Yeah. Yeah. That's a good idea. One o'clock should be fine. I'll ask Will when he comes in…hang on. This might be him now.'

I hear the wheels of the desk chair roll across the wooden floor and Shaun's head appears at chest-height in the doorway.

I smile, raise a hand. 'You alright?'

'Yeah…are you?' he asks with concern. He clocks the different hairstyle, and grins. 'Can I ring you back in a sec, mate?' he says to the person on the end of the phone.

I put the kettle on, get the things ready for tea. Shaun appears in the doorway, rests his left shoulder on the doorjamb. From the corner of my eye, I see him looking my hair over.

'Like the hair, Will. It really suits you. Crew cut, is it?'

'Yeah, with a quiff. My barber suggested it. He reckoned I'd miss my quiff if he cut it out.' I chuckle. 'I think it's one of his favourite things to create for his clients. He assures me that it'll take only a quarter of the time the old style took. I'm sick of being a slave to my hair.'

'I've often thought about having a crew cut.' He reaches a hand unto his own head, touches the side-parting. 'Maybe next time I will, since this looks good on you.' He opens the fridge door, hands me the milk.

'I thought since I'm going to be your boss, well, one of them, the one you'll see the most of, I should look the part.'

'Well, you definitely do. Nothing like a bit of retail therapy from time to time.' He uses the exact same phrase that *she* used yesterday. I feel a little jolt in my chest but push it away. Don't dwell on it, I tell myself. You spent too many hours going over and over it. Time to move on.

I slide his tea over and tell him we'll talk in the other office. I pick the rucksack up from the floor where I rested it against the wall and lead the way into the office. Shaun has kindly tidied the papers away and removed the dossier.

He takes his usual chair, watches me again and asks in a gentle concerned voice, 'Are you alright?'

I delay my answer. I put the tea down, hang my jacket on the hook behind the door and sit down.

'It's okay if you don't want to talk about it; I understand. I just want to know that you're okay.'

I look at him and he really is concerned. 'I'm not brilliant,' I admit with a steady voice, 'but I will be in time. I went to bed without any tea and slept utterly crap. At half three this morning, I was watching stupid videos on my iPad. At half six, I headed out for a run, but with no rest and no fuel, I only managed half a mile before I had to turn back.' I smile.

He nods, but I can see there's another question on his mind.

'Just ask it,' I tell him, 'it's fine.'

'What happened yesterday?'

I sigh, rest my back in the chair and shrug. I give him the condensed version, omitting the really personal parts about how it made me feel.

'It was when she said she'd ask, it was that word: ask, Michael about it. Suddenly I realised there was a chance he'd be able to talk her around. I wasn't going to waste any more of my time and energy and I told her to leave.'

'Shit, Will. I don't get it. I was so fucking sure she'd dump Michael...'

384

'She may well have done but it's none of my business.'

'Has she contacted you?'

I shake my head. 'I'm half-expecting a text at some point, asking if we can talk, but unless she's going to tell me what I want to hear, then I'd prefer her not to bother. I need to move on, Shaun. Draw a line under this sorry fucking mess and start again. I might even try online dating.'

Shaun shrugs as if to say why not?

I laugh. 'Maybe not for a bit, but it's an option. Right,' I clap my hands, 'onto the important stuff. Have you heard from Ben? Was that who you were on the phone to when I arrived?'

'Yeah.' Shaun grins. 'He is one happy dude. Old pubs and a private investigation and he's in heaven. He was bursting on the phone when I explained that we needed his help. Which is weird for him. Ben rarely gets excited. He sat up until after midnight studying the photos.'

'He is taking this seriously.'

'He's invited us over to go through his progress so far. I said yes. Hope you don't mind. I thought a trip out would be just what you needed.'

I smile. 'Excellent initiative, Shaun.'

*

Ben and his wife Betsy have worked hard on creating their brand and making The Smoking Gun what they want it to be: strictly adult only, which is why there are no child-friendly food items on the menu. You won't find chicken nuggets and baked beans here. The pub has the ability to appeal to a mixed group of patrons, including those calling in for a drink on the way home, young adults taking their visiting parents somewhere nice for lunch. Lone drinkers can bag themselves a table in the corner, get out their laptop or iPad and sit for a while with a trendy IPA and remain unbothered. Thankfully, the pub also manages to exclude those who might ruin a nice pub. Cackles of fun-loving girls won't find fruity gins here, men looking to get tanked up before a football match will have a hard job finding piss-poor lager on draft. And there's definitely no football allowed on the TV screens. It's rugby, MotoGP, news or the TV goes off. Ben's rules and he enforces them strictly.

I discovered this place in January during the investigation into Shaun's friend's murder charge and was impressed as soon as I walked through the door.

It's a wedge-shaped bar area, about the size of the ground floor of a standard-sized detached house. Intimate yet spacious. The tables are set far apart for privacy purposes. The walls have been wallpapered in mock crumbling brickwork paper. It makes you want to reach out and run your hands over the pretend rough surface. The bar itself is tiled in multi-coloured square tiles featuring cartoon pictures of unknown characters, flags, emblems, words. Something to look at whilst you're waiting for your IPA. The selection of beers is out of this world: from European and American IPAs, to a small selection of real ales, fruity beers and those from local breweries.

Shaun leads the way inside, his domain, and goes up to the bar. He greets the barman, a young bloke with blond hair, and orders himself an alcohol-free IPA. He's the designated driver. I grab a beer menu and scan it for something that sounds interesting, and right there, under the underlined heading of local breweries, I spot one. 'Many a Hog' created by The Filthy Pig Brewery, Lexington. David and Jake's brewery. Or is it just David's now? I ask for a half, considering its alcohol content is over 6%.

Across the room Betsy, Ben's wife, is talking to a middle-aged couple. Under the table lies a Jack Russell chewing on a doggy treat. Betsy has one knee resting on a nearby chair. I can see the bottom of her yellow sandal. She wears some quirky clothes, which on anyone else would look ridiculous but somehow on her, they don't. Today she's wearing a yellow dress with blue flowers on, a thin crocheted green cardigan, and in her pale red hair is a lilac hairband.

Our drinks arrive and Shaun asks his colleague to tell Ben we're here. Moments later, Ben arrives, through the door marked Staff only, carrying a laptop and a tablet under his arm.

He thrusts his hand out to me. 'Hello Will. How you doing? Alright Shaun?'

'Good, mate, thanks.' Christ, his grip is strong. Must be all the heavy lifting he does. He's much shorter than me, but broader. His head is shaved, which only makes his black beard look longer. He nods at a table in the window. Shaun and I take the cushioned window seat. Ben gets to work, opening the laptop and tablet, arranging his findings on the screens.

'Right then...oh, hang on. Let me get a drink too.' He leans back on the stool, calls to the barman who is loading the tabletop-sized dishwasher. 'Leo! Can you bring me a diet coke? No ice.' His eyes flick upwards to my hair. 'New Barnet, Will? Looks good. Right, on with the show. Here are your photos,' and he turns the propped-up tablet around. The screen shows

386

row upon row of photos. 'I've annotated the photos with the initial letters of the pubs I've successfully managed to identify.' He points at an example. Written in the top left-hand corner are the initials TJ.

'The Jester,' he explains. 'Some photos are of the same pub, but different parts. You know, the lounge, public bar, smoke rooms, when they had them. Even the bloody toilets. They certainly liked their boozers, these blokes. There's a small number of pubs I can't identify. There's either not enough in the frame to say for sure which pub it is, or they could be pubs out of the area. Which, Shaun,' and he flicks a hand at Shaun who has leant his elbow on the table in order to see the screens, 'said you wouldn't be interested in.'

'I wouldn't, no,' I confirm. There's no way that David and Jake could have driven miles and miles out of Lexington into the surrounding towns to hide Amanda and make it back in time for David to to be seen by the Newmans.

'From there, I googled each pub to see if it's open, i.e. still trading as a pub or if it's something else like a cafe or flats. If they're closed, I tried to find out what they are now. And *if* they are still closed, why they did and how long they've been closed for. Shaun gave me a parameter of between eleven and seven years.'

I look at Shaun and nod my praise.

'Cheers, Leo.' Ben swipes up the coke and takes a long gulp. He starts tapping away at the laptop keyboard and brings up a document. I peer closely at it. It's a spread sheet. The columns are labelled: name of pub; location either Lexington, Kelsall, Lilliton; year opened; year closed; reason for closure; current state; distance from David's customer; distance from Jake; distance from David's house. There's over twenty names. He's not kidding. Beers and pubs were their life.

Ben looks up. 'I'll print it out before you go. Let me give you a quick example. Here.' He chooses one halfway down the screen and tells us about The Red Dagger, which opened over thirty years ago in Kelsall and closed down for two years before reinventing itself as The Tandoori Grill. It's close to Jake's house, but eight miles from David's last customer of the day.

'You can easily exclude pubs that have become something else, but I've left them in case there's any buildings on the land that haven't been renovated. I know the Lexington Hive has several outbuildings. It's a micropub now, but once was quite a place. You might find who you're looking for tucked away under a trapdoor.'

God I hope they haven't stuffed Amanda's body somewhere like that. How on earth am I going to locate her without drawing attention to myself? I'm hoping for somewhere remote, with no other buildings around, but I know that's unlikely. Most pubs that go out of business are high-street ones where the competition is high. I did some research of my own last night and found that the smoking ban and changes to licensing laws have put a lot of pubs out of business. And unless they can evolve into food places, swap beer for wine and fancy gins, stick some climbing frames and swings in the grounds, then they've got little chance of surviving.

'Once you disregard the still open pubs and those that evolved into something else,' Ben explains, 'it gives you a list of four possible locations for a disposal site: Lexington Exchange, The Perching Buzzard, The Jester and The Black Swan. The Jester is a listed building. The Black Swan featured heavily in the photos. It did nice food back in its day. They've also all been closed down between 8 and eleven years. It's a shame they haven't become something else; they have potential but I suppose no one wants to see places which had a lot of character become something so featureless as a Tesco Express or yet another Indian restaurant. Although rather that than see them standing derelict. Nothing sadder than a neglected pub. Betsy and I saved this place from that,' and he looks around at his castle, holds his gaze for several moments on his wife who is wiping down tables and clearing away dirty glasses. She looks up as if feeling his eyes on her and smiles lovingly back.

'This is great, Ben,' I say gratefully. 'It would have taken me God knows how long to identify these places.'

He smiles. 'You're welcome, Will. The thing is, we looked into taking over a couple of these places, before we got lucky here. In my youth, I spent a lot of time in pubs. Not drinking so much. I love the history and culture. Some of the places I know so well. It's been a nice trip down memory lane. Oh, Shaun,' Ben exclaims, swivelling in his seat to face him, 'before you go, can you work this afternoon? I know it's short notice but bloody Lara's rang in sick again. And she'll be off the weekend too.'

'What again? How many episodes is that this month?' Shaun asks. 'And yeah, I'll come in. I could do with the extra money.'

'Too many to keep track of. Completely unacceptable.' Ben looks at me, shrugs. 'Decent staff are hard to find. Present company excluded,' he says, nodding at Shaun.

'What you looking for? Bar staff?' I ask.

'Yeah. Someone to do a couple of evening shifts, the occasional impromptu one. No one wants to work; they want to socialise instead. What I need is someone who doesn't have friends,' he ticks them off on his fingers, 'no social life, no partner…'

'What about me?' I say, ticking two more points off on my hand. 'I'm also hardly ever ill and I could do with the extra cash too.'

'Seriously?' Ben glances at Shaun to see if he's in on the joke. Shaun shrugs. 'You worked in a bar before?'

'No, but I'm a quick learner and I'm reliable.'

'Good. I've just got the one worry: if I pair you two on the same shift, am I gonna get any work out of you?'

I laugh. 'Ben, mate, I'm his other boss. I'll work him like a dog.'

'Great, just great,' Shaun mutters and puts a hand to his forehead, shaking his head gently.

Ben laughs. 'Call in around four this afternoon and I'll show you the ropes, see how you are at pulling pints.'

I smile. New hair, second job, and a new line of enquiry. Things are beginning to look up.

Chapter 56

Shaun follows the road as it winds upwards like a helter skelter all the way to the top where The Black Swan sits like some kind of castle up a mountain. I stare out of the window at the grass verge which disappears into thick hedging and beyond that, into an unseen drop. Are there are any breaches in the shrubs? A way through? It's possible, but it won't be easy to navigate in the dark. We could be seen now. A dog walker or kids using this long winding drive as somewhere to skateboard or cycle down at speed.

Shaun reaches the top but is prevented from going any further by a huge row of fencing, the sort used on construction sites to keep trespassers out. The fencing is made of mesh panels, criss-crossed lengths slotted into a tubular steel frame, but there's no frame across the top of the panels. By leaving these parts exposed, they effectively form a very sharp, almost razor-edge, which will cut the hands of anyone attempting to scale them. The legs of these frames are embedded inside heavy unmovable stone plinths, which cannot be knocked over or lifted out.

Serious stuff.

I peer closer. Someone's breached the perimeter. On the flaking white painted outside wall is unreadable graffiti. Interesting.

Shaun turns hard right and brakes, parking us parallel to the fencing. He leaves the engine idling, rests his hand on the gearstick and we stare out of the window at what was once one of the greatest pubs in Lexington. It's a ten minute walk from where my parents lived and I remember on Christmas days, how my dad would leave my mum to the cooking, Eddie to his toys and together he and I would escape to the pub for a couple of swift pints.

It was nice inside. A mixture of hard wood flooring and soft carpets with a swirly pattern on them. Brass bars running along the length of the bar at ankle height; somewhere to rest your foot when you were waiting to get served. Lighting, above tilted mirrors, cast soft yellow light on the highly polished bar top. I remember the bucket of ice, the bowl containing half-moon lemon slices glinting under the bright lights.

Dad would always head for the same table. The one close to the fruit machine, with good views, of the door and the rest of the pub, so he could watch the comings and goings of fellow drinkers and diners. The pub did nice food. Often when it was a family birthday, Mum would book a table and we'd come here to celebrate. Their steak was good. It came with fried tomato, onion rings, mushrooms. My mum never did all those trimmings if she did steak at home, so it was a luxury.

The landlord threw a decent New Year's Eve shindig. It was ticket only and you had to book early. It was popular with young people so that's perhaps why David liked coming here - a better class of young women to pull. Jake tagged along to see how it was done, probably left empty-armed though.

I think back to what I remember about our visits here. At the foot of the drive is a larger car park, used by both patrons of the pub and patients of the doctor's surgery and the dentist's, housed in two cottages which stand opposite the entrance to the car park.

I frown. The Black Swan is the local pub serving the surrounding housing estate. Many people would walk here, but they wouldn't walk up that drive. There was another route up. A path for pedestrians, cut into the hill and constructed of wooden slats covered in a non-slip surface. It must be on the other side of the hill, accessed from a nearby street. Is that how the graffiti artist accessed the area? If so, how would David and Jake get Amanda's body through this fencing? Surely they didn't cart her up that path? Unless the fencing wasn't here back then. It could be a recent installation, done to stop people from parking their caravans up.

'Go back down,' I say to Shaun. 'Park in the bottom car park.'

Minutes later, we exit the car and find the pedestrian path and start climbing the crumbling steps. Some of the wooden slats are collapsing, the non-slip surface is peeling back like a badly laid carpet. Unsurprising really since the pub closed ten years ago. Who comes up here now? It goes nowhere.

Shaun pauses to unzip his hoodie. His face is getting red and I'm guessing, since he hated PE, that this is the most exercise he's done in years. He might do weights at the gym, but it's time he jumped on that treadmill.

The end looks to be in sight. The trees are thinning out and the path is widening until it ends in a gate, sturdily padlocked, although it is of a height that's easy to climb over.

Shaun grabs hold of the nearest wooden post but it suddenly gives way like a wobbly tooth and plunges him forward. I reach out and grab his hood and pull him back before he lands in a nasty thorny bush.

We look at each other and smile.

'Our way in.'

We squeeze through the gap between the post and the gate, arranging it back in place behind us, and follow the path round. The beer garden was always lovely in the summer. A brick-surrounded pond, lots of wooden tables and chairs, landscaped garden, well cut grass, all overlooking the surrounding area. A nice view in the summer with a cold beer.

Now, it's sad, abandoned and overgrown. The grass is full of moss and weeds. The pond is murky and full of leaves and rubbish. A soft drinks can bobs up and down in the water. The pub isn't fairing any better. Many of the windows are boarded up. There's a huge sheet of metal screwed into the brickwork over the patio doors. There's been an attempt to crowbar the sheet back, but it's held its position well. Shaun follows me around to the front entrance. The double doors are locked, the glass panels covered with wood, graffitied also. I tap Shaun's arm and point at a wooden structure attached to the side of the pub. It looks like a kind of shed and covers the service entrance to the kitchen where deliveries were once made. I remember once when we arrived for a birthday meal, that the gate was wide open and I looked inside to see a man dressed in chef's whites having a crafty fag. He saw me looking and abruptly kicked the gate shut.

Could that be an easier way in?

'Go and see if that's a way in,' I tell Shaun quietly. He walks over, his feet light as if heavy footsteps would give the game away. I leave him to it and look up at the front of the pub for any cameras or signs the place is rigged up to an alarm system. Nothing obvious and, to be fair maintaining cameras is going to be costly for the owner, especially since the place has been closed down for over a decade.

'Will,' Shaun whispers urgently, appearing at my side and giving me a fright. Christ. I hope I'm not going to be this jumpy when we do enter these properties. I'll be having a bloody heart attack.

'What, Shaun?'

'The gate's open. The padlock came away in my hand,' and he holds out his palm. I take the very rusty padlock and examine it. The shackle, the thick u-shaped metal part which slides into the body of the lock, is loose and, when I peer closer, I can see something inside the hole which is preventing the shackle locking into position.

'Helpful,' I reply. 'Let's have a closer look.' Together we go to the service entrance: double doors made of solid wood, no glass panels. A sign screwed into the brickwork says: "ring for attention". Underneath is a little white button. I try the door handles. Locked. And the doors are firm in the frames. I won't be kicking these doors through. But interestingly, there's just one keyhole. Could it be that easy…

I slide my mobile out, switch to camera mode and take some photos of the doors and the lock. If we're going in, we need to be prepared.

'Let's go,' I say to Shaun. I close the gate behind us, refit the padlock so it looks secure. We walk back round to the beer garden and start our descent.

'Will?' he whispers. 'Are we going in?'

'Yes. But we need to check the other places out. We won't be able to do them all in one evening, but I reckon we can spread them out over a couple of nights. You're not busy tonight, are you?'

'I finish my shift at eleven…'

'Perfect.'

'Will!' he hisses urgently.

'Shaun, not in the open. Wait until we're in the car.' But once in his car and the doors are closed, Shaun turns to me, his arm resting across the steering wheel.

'Are you serious about breaking in and entering into these places?' he asks.

'How else are we going to find Amanda if we don't look for her? What's the matter?…Oh, I see. This is your first crime. Don't worry, Shaun. We won't get caught…'

'How can you be so sure? We only need someone to spot us and—'

'We won't be seen. Shaun, the key is preparation. I can't afford to go back to prison. I suppose it's different for you, isn't it? If you're arrested, does this mean you've passed some kind of initiation test and now you can join the family business?'

Shaun stares at me.

'I'm joking, Shaun,' I say, with a chuckle. 'Relax…'

'Well, yes. That is how Dad might see it.'

'Shaun, strictly speaking, we're not breaking and entering…alright, we are entering. But we won't be breaking our way in. Trust me,' I say, tapping the side of my nose. 'I have just the tool for the job.'

His frown deepens and he sighs noisily. He doesn't look reassured.

'Mate, I'm not about to deliver you into the hands of your father or his business. No way. Come on,' and I click the seatbelt into place. 'Next on the list: The Perching Buzzard. Take a right at the end of the road.'

*

At The Perching Buzzard, we get an unexpected surprise. The builders are there. The place is a construction site: scaffolding; lots of hi-vis wearing builders traipsing across a muddy debris-strewn car park; skips crammed full of interior doors, long lengths of wood; identical unmovable fencing but these ones have signs cable-tied to them warning potential trespassers that this is now a building site and of the various dangers.

A builder wearing a yellow hardhat and a hi-vis coat informs me that, in a few months, I can book a table and dine in a swanky new fish restaurant.

'Some local celebrity chef has bought it,' the foreman told me, jerking his head back at the building in case I thought it was the place next door.

'How far has the refurbishment got?' I asked.

'Place is gutted. There's nothing left.'

'Have you gutted everywhere?'

'Yeah, from the attic down to the cellar. Place is an empty shell.'

'Find anything interesting inside?' I asked.

'What like? A dead body stuffed into a wall?' he chuckled.

'Yes. Exactly like that.'

His expression changes to one of horror. 'Shit, no, man. What? You think…' He jerks a thumb over his shoulder.

'Thanks for the info, mate.'

The look on his face makes me laugh all afternoon, despite Shaun not finding it in the slightest bit amusing. He's worried to death that the workman might contact the police. Or worse give them Shaun's vehicle reg. What would Hock say if the police turned up at his home? What if we were questioned and they got wind of our late night intentions?

In the end I tell Shaun to shut up, which he takes badly, and for the first time ever, sulks. Which makes me feel bad considering the shit day I had yesterday.

A drive-thru McDonald's cheers him up. He drops me off at the office and heads off to do his afternoon shift at the pub.

With no messages to deal with, either personal or work-related, I go home. I have a few things to sort out.

I open the wardrobe and the chest of drawers and hunt for any dark clothing. I search through everything, which takes all of five minutes, and come up empty-handed. Defeated, I plonk myself down on the corner of the bed and look at the mess I've created on the floor. Why do I never have what I need? But when was the last time I needed black clothes? Black does not suit me. I spy my darkest pair of jeans, chucked over the back of the chair. On the back of the door hangs my dark grey waterproof and I'm sure I've got a dark enough hat or cap somewhere. They'll have to do. I can't spend money on black clothes I'll only use for a couple of late night activities.

Hastily, I shove the clothes untidily back on hangers and back into drawers and then kneel on the floor, flicking the lopsided duvet back over the bed.

I stare at the flattened black rucksack in which I used to take my overnight gear to Bronwyn's flat. I won't be needing that again. I unzip it and look inside. My spare toothbrush and well-squeezed tube of toothpaste, wrapped in a dry flannel. A balled up pair of socks and a spare T-shirt. I empty the bag, chucking the items on the bed to sort out later.

One last thing to find. I tug out the clear plastic storage boxes which contain those items I thought I might need more often, but it turns out I haven't needed. Books I haven't and probably won't read; the box for my tablet; a pair of walking boots, far too clumping for my purpose and caked in dried mud; a small photo album containing pictures of my childhood; a couple of Blu-rays; and here: a smaller cardboard box. I lift it out, shove the plastic storage box out of the way. I lean back against the bed, my legs across the carpet and remove the cardboard lid. More boxes are inside, made of plastic. Each contains metal padlocks and barrels. I stack them to the side. I need to give myself a lesson before I go out later, remind myself of a skill I got quite good at. I need to flex my fingers, retrain my ability to focus my attention and precision on very small and fine workings.

I remove a leather case, unzip it and take out Bronwyn's Christmas present. It was something I asked for, not expensive, but something that was targeted advertising as if the company knew one day I would need it.

It's probably the best present she could have ever bought me.

I slide a pick out of its elastic binding, press a fingertip to its rounded end.

If stopped by the police, with this case in my possession, I could get done for going equipped.

But without it, how else can I enter these closed-down pubs?

Chapter 57

Beside me, Shaun shivers. I can feel his upper arm trembling against mine. The circle of bright white light starts to jiggle and the rustling of two different fabrics touching distracts me. My attention starts to wander and as a result my fingers release their grip ever so slightly. The tension wrench and pick loosen their hold and, inside the barrel, the pins drop back into position.

'Fuck's sake, Shaun,' I hiss. 'Keep still.'

He moves the torch away, dropping the light onto an area of the door several inches away from the lock. 'Sorry,' he mutters, bringing his aim too sharply upwards and temporarily dazzling me with the light. 'Sorry, Will.'

'Just hold it there.' I stretch my fingers out and once Shaun shines the light on the lock, I insert the tension wrench into the keyhole and, with one finger, turn it slightly to the right. Then I slide the pick into the keyhole, feeling the outline of the hidden pins. I was nearly there before Shaun lost his nerve for the hundredth time. The first pin springs upwards almost immediately and I quickly move onto the next.

It's not that the lock to the kitchen entrance is tricky. It's no harder than the practice padlocks and barrels which came with the set. I spent two hours sat at the kitchen table practicing my skill, until my arse got sore from the hard seat and my eyes started to blur with the effort. I knocked it on the head for a while, watched the remainder of a Western on the telly, and got back to it. This time on the bedroom floor. I couldn't risk Mrs Penn or the other lodger coming home and finding me picking locks in the kitchen.

'Better,' I mutter encouragingly to Shaun. 'Just a little…bit…longer…' Suddenly I hear a soft click and the last pin springs up; the tools clenched between my aching fingers jump as if receiving a spark of electricity and I pull them out. 'We're in,' I whisper excitedly. 'Great stuff.' I stand up, feeling the ache in my ankles from being held in such a position.

Shaun holds out the leather-bound case and I drop the tools inside, quickly zipping it back up. He looks both terrified and relieved. He doesn't move until I spin him around by his shoulders and drop the case back into the rucksack on his back.

'Shaun, get with it,' I whisper harshly. 'You know the drill. Quick, thorough and silent. We're out in ten minutes max.'

He removes another torch from his pocket, switches it on and hands it to me. I ask if he's ok and he nods, forces a smile on his face.

It'll have to do. We don't have the time to discuss matters.

I turn back to the closed but unlocked door, take a deep breath, grasp the door handle and brace myself. Christ, I hope there's not an alarm system installed. It didn't look like it from the outside…I open the door…silence. A good start. Normally an opening door would break the contact between the two points and trigger the alarm.

I shine the light inside. A dark dank passageway stretches away, ending in another closed door. I step forwards onto a tiled floor and shiver. Fucking hell, it's freezing in here. I lift my hand to my mouth and breathe hard on it to warm my frigid fingers up. I wish I'd opted for insulating gloves rather than flimsy Nitrile gloves. Who the hell is going to be looking for fibres or fingerprints if they don't know anyone was in here?

I get on with it. The ceiling is low, the walls are painted white; flakes of peeling paint are scattered on the floor near to the skirting boards. The place is oozing dampness like an underground cave. Behind me, Shaun follows me, keeping close. The spot of white light from his torch moves quickly across the surfaces like a prison searchlight. On the wall ahead is a noticeboard, devoid of notices but several drawing pins are still stuck in the cork. At the end of the passageway is another door, a wide one and it's unlocked too. I push it open and shine the torch around.

The kitchen. Steel-topped units pushed back against the walls, industrial-sized ovens, steel sinks. A pale tiled floor. No pots, pans or crockery though. The windows are grimy. Cobwebs hang in the corner of the frames and there's a collection of crusty dead insects on the windowsills. I look at Shaun. He nods nervously and we separate, moving around the sides of the area and meeting at the back. I find a white door with a lever as a handle. I pull on it and slide the heavy door to the right. I look inside. A freezer? Completely empty. Behind me, Shaun is sliding open the doors underneath the units, moving swiftly onto the next. Within a minute, we meet at the back of the kitchen and move through the double doors. One marked "exit", the other "entrance". Another passageway. The floor is wood, the walls papered, a dado rail runs along the walls at waist-height. On the right is a door marked "private". The living quarters. I continue, leading the way deeper inside, through more double doors.

I pause on the threshold, move aside to let Shaun stand beside me. Together we shine our lights around the interior of the Black Swan. Memories come flooding back. Family meals out, drinks out with girlfriends, picking my parents up after one New Year's Eve. Dad drunk in the back of my car, Mum laughing tipsily in the front. I was terrified they were going to throw up on the seats.

The pub is split into two levels. Two or three steps, with smooth wooden handrails, lead up to the next level which opens onto the beer garden through French doors.

We direct our light over the papered walls, unhindered by a lack of surfaces because the entire pub is empty. There are no fixtures and fittings. No tables or chairs, no light fittings, no mirrors behind the bar, no glasses, pumps or bottles. I nudge Shaun's arm and he looks at me, his face pale and worried.

'Toilets,' I say, nodding at more double doors to my left. 'Be quick.'

He nods, hurries off, his tread soft on the carpet.

I walk around the pub, on both levels, looking for a sign that anyone's been in here. Something that looks out of place. Signs of squatters, break-ins. I don't expect to find Amanda's remains propped up against a wall or sat behind the bar, but I must look. I sniff the air. It smells stale, dusty and cold. No hint of rotting flesh, but I'm sure, if she had have been dumped here, the smell would have almost certainly attracted vermin and rats have been known to gnaw through wood and concrete to get to food. I shiver inside my waterproof, but I can feel sweat on my skin, dampening my clothes. A sliver of moonlight has managed to breach the wooden sheets nailed over the window frames. It crosses the carpet and shines against the brass rail running along the bar.

This is so fucking sad, I think, continuing my route back round to the bar. This was such a great place in its day.

Shaun appears and shakes his head. Only one place left to look. The living quarters upstairs. We head back to the passageway, through the door marked *private* and up the carpeted staircase. Yet another door opens into a small hallway where a dusty mirror hangs in a small alcove. On the floor, embedded in the carpet, are four round indentations signalling a table once stood here. We investigate each room together. A large sitting room overlooks the front of the pub. It's bitterly cold. Cobwebs hang in the windows and yet more desiccated insects lie on the windowsills. It's empty of furniture and fittings. The next two rooms are bedrooms. Both empty but the carpets bear the indentations of heavy furniture.

The bathroom has a green suite in it. It is disgustingly dirty. The shower curtain is mouldy. The plastic looks brittle. The mirror of the cabinet is dusty and the doors squeak when I prise them open, not that I expect to find part of Amanda bundled inside. I leave it open in case closing it makes it crash to the floor.

'Only the apartment's kitchen left,' I say to Shaun and he nods quickly and steps aside to let me go first again.

The kitchen overlooks the beer garden. The cupboard doors are that farmhouse wood that was the rage all those years ago. This time the cupboards do yield a couple of items: a spray bottle of kitchen cleaner, a tea-stained mug, a couple of screwed-up rags.

I push past Shaun who appears frozen to the spot. There is one other place. I stand in the bedroom and shine the light upwards. The loft hatch.

I look at Shaun. His eyes widen and he shakes his head. Who would go to the trouble of stuffing Amanda's body in the loft? How on earth would they get it up there? It's unlikely David or Jake brought along a pair of step ladders.

That's assuming I can even open the hatch without one of those special poles with a hook on the end and if there's a fold-down ladder inside.

'Balls to that,' I mutter. 'Let's go,' and I tap Shaun with the back of my hand.

Amanda's not here. There's nowhere to hide her and I doubt David and Jake took the time to plaster her body into a wall space. The walls look intact. Apart from the occasional picture hook and dirty line where the frames have pressed into the wallpaper, there's no sign anything has been disturbed since the day the place closed down.

I lead the way quickly down the staircase and back through to the pub kitchen, closing the doors behind me. Back outside, I take huge lungfuls of cold fresh air, remove the brick from the door and lock the pub. No one will be any the wiser. I look at Shaun, who still looks absolutely terrified. I smile at him, open my mouth to speak, but suddenly I freeze. A car engine. Shit.

'The torches,' I hiss and quickly we snap them both off, plunging ourselves into darkness. Shaun flattens himself against the door, his eyes wide with fear.

Fuck. Who the hell is it? Oh, don't tell me it's the police. I tilt my ear to the gate and listen. The engine is idling. I can hear faint music through an open window. Not the police. Who is it then? Young lovers trying to find somewhere to park up? It's too much of a risk attempting to slide out of the gate. We only need one of them to glance in the rear view mirror as we're leaving and we'll be seen. But we are wearing dark clothing.

I look at Shaun, whisper, 'At least they're on the right side of the fence.'

His eyes widen.

'We'll give them a few minutes, see if they piss off.'

The danger is if they've come up here for another reason. A spot of breaking and entering. Perhaps they're brave enough to climb the razor-sharp fences. Within a few minutes, they could breach the fence and get the biggest shock of their lives when they come face to face with us.

After a few moments, the cold starts to get the better of me and my teeth begin chattering. I clench my jaw shut. What are they doing? Fuck it. I can't wait any longer. I step towards the gate and Shaun emits a tiny noise of protest, which I ignore.

Carefully, I curl my fingers around the side of the gate, gently push it out, just a few inches. I might be able to peer around, see what they're doing…suddenly a girly shriek cuts through the air, making me jump and hastily close the gate. My heart starts thumping madly and my throat dries up.

I tilt my head again. Laughter. Oh, they *are* making out. They'll be far too preoccupied with each other to see us slip out. I look at Shaun.

'You go first.' He shakes his head vigorously. I take hold of his wrist, tug him away from the door. He implores me with a look. 'Keep close to the building. Move quick. Don't stop. I'll meet you at the car.'

I push open the gate just enough for him to squeeze through and, instantly, he flattens himself like a starfish against the wall and sidesteps away. My only problem now is the padlock. I must secure the gate.

I dig the padlock out of my pocket and push open the gate, slipping out. I flatten myself against the wood and hold my breath, not that they can hear it, and glance at the car. The courtesy light is on, lighting up the interior. From here, I can only see one head. The driver's as it rises a little past the headrest. Three guesses as to what his passenger is doing. I turn my upper body round and quickly slide the shackle through the metal loop on the gate and fix it into position. My throat is so dry. I need a bloody drink. Another quick glance at the car before I move. His passenger is coming up for air. I step away from the gate and, because I'm not watching where my feet go, my toe accidentally kicks over a stray beer bottle. Shit. Powerless, I watch it roll across the pavement towards the kerb which drops down into the disabled parking space. Don't, I think, but I'm already away when I hear it launch off the kerb and land with a loud noise.

If the occupants of the car hear it, they'll assume it was an animal. A fox or worse a rat. I hurry through the beer garden, around the loose fence post, and I go down the steps, taking one at time. In the dark, these slippery surfaces are treacherous and the last thing I want to do is break an ankle.

When I reach the bottom, I pause to look around. The path extends left and right as well as straight on. To my left, under the orange light of a lamppost, about thirty feet away, a figure stands and waits. I back off, step back into the darkness, hear a distant voice say, 'Come on, Daisy. We're not stopping at every lamppost.'

A dog steps into the light and the figure pulls the lead and they walk away.

I shake my head, run a palm over my forehead, and wipe the sweat onto my jeans before heading off again, back to the car.

I open the passenger door. Shaun has the heating on full blast and is swigging water from a huge bottle. He looks at me with wide eyes, lowers the bottle and offers it to me.

I close the door, take a huge swig, point at the rucksack. 'Side pocket,' I say. He unzips it and removes a bar of chocolate. He unwraps it, snaps two squares off and shoves them in his mouth.

'It was a couple indulging in oral sex,' I tell him, chucking my coat on the back seat and pulling the chocolate bar out of his hand. I break a square of chocolate off and pop it into my mouth. He looks puzzled. 'The car that turned up. Are you alright, Shaun?'

He nods unconvincingly. 'Sorry, Will,' he apologises shakily. 'I was so nervous. I kept expecting the police to turn up. I nearly tripped coming down the steps.' He holds his palm out. 'Think I've got a splinter off the handrail.'

'You did really well for your first ever breaking and entering.' I look at the time on the dashboard. Nearly midnight. 'Let's call it a night. Are you okay to drive?'

'Yeah, I am.'

'Okay.' I click the seatbelt on. 'Let's go. Nice and steady.'

He pulls away from the kerb, textbook style, like he's on his driving test. He heads back to the office where my car is.

'Look on the bright side,' I say. He glances at me. 'One pub down, only two to go.'

He groans. 'Only two, you say. I hope to God they've put her in one of them.'

'Me too,' I agree, 'because if they haven't, I've run out of ideas.'

Chapter 58

'The Window Cleaner told me, and I have no reason not to believe him, that the Lexington Exchange has *always* been alarmed.'

'Since the day it closed?'

I raise an eyebrow. 'Yes, Shaun, since the day it closed. Now, correct me if I'm wrong, and I rarely am, David isn't and Jake wasn't an alarm specialist.'

'That is correct…well, not to our knowledge. They…'

'Trust me on this. This means that they couldn't have hidden Amanda's body inside. The owner has gone to a lot of trouble and expense to safeguard the empty property. There could well be CCTV cameras inside and outside. *And* as you are playing a key part in this investigation, you're almost certainly going to get caught faster than you can say "Family business". Sorry, Shaun. I'm joking,' I say hurriedly when I see the flash of horror on his face.

'The owner might even regularly check up on the place, so they're bound to notice the addition of a corpse on the premises,' Shaun adds. 'You're right, Will, it's not worth the risk. We can't possibly get inside. I'm also glad I'm not an alarm specialist. You know,' he leans back in the chair, stretches his arms above his head, 'Lexington Exchange isn't the most ideal disposal site anyway. It's in a busy high street, on the end of a row, with another boozer next door and a car park behind. How would they be able to access the pub? Alarm or not. They'd be seen. No matter what time of the night they were there.'

'Yeah,' I say, 'that's what I thought, but I did the recce anyway. Good job I looked suspicious enough that the bloke came over.'

Shaun goes to speak but a yawn takes him by surprise and he cups a hand over his mouth. 'Oh, God, sorry. I slept crap.'

'It's the adrenalin,' I tell him. 'I slept shit too. At seven o'clock I was out running, trying to burn some of it off. I've been looking at The Jester.' I dig through the paperwork on the desk, pulling out various sheets and discarding them to the side. 'It's more remote than the others. It's just off junction 5 of the A5689. There's a small car park used by walkers on the other side of the road. From there is a path across a field which leads to some woods and lots of well-trodden paths overlooking the surrounding countryside. When the pub was open, it was an ideal spot for a post-walk pint and a ploughman's. I reckon, with some careful planning, which I've started, this is somewhere we should do in the daytime.'

Shaun's jaw drops. 'You're kidding? We'll be seen…'

'I don't think so. It's far riskier at night. The road is a back route to Lexy and still used by a lot of drivers trying to avoid the many junctions and hold ups on the A road. A car parked in that car park at night will almost certainly draw attention and we only need a passing police car to see it, and that will ruin our search. But in the day…we could just be on a woodland walk. It's our cover story.'

'You've done a recce, haven't you?'

'Yeah, this morning. I've found a way round the fencing. Through the hedge. It's a bit thorny and muddy, but we can take precautions. Maybe a change of footwear. Anyway, I've drawn a very rudimentary floor plan for you. It's based purely on memory.'

Shaun raises an eyebrow with interest that I know a pub so well that I can draw a picture of it. 'Been on a few dates there in the past,' I explain, thrusting a sheet of paper into his hand. Briefly, I explain the history and layout of The Jester. 'It dates back to Edwardian times and, interestingly, it is a listed building. Something about rare features inside. A fireplace or something, I don't know. As you can see,' I lean forward with interest. 'It's a large pub. Has four entrances: two on the front, one on the side and the service entrance at the rear. I've marked the layout accordingly. Our best way in is through the service entrance.'

'Is it alarmed?'

'It doesn't look to be from the front, but we'll have a better look when we're closer.'

Shaun studies the layout. 'There are a lot of rooms.' He traces a fingertip over the many lines. 'Romantic nooks, I think you'll find they're called. That square area in the centre is the bar and can be accessed on all sides. One half of the pub was mainly a dining area, the other mostly for drinkers only. Throw in some alcoves and hidden corners, and there was a pub that tried to cater for all. I think it appealed to David and Jake for two reasons: it's listed, which means it's protected. When it failed, as far as I can tell, there's been no interest in renovating it because of its protected status. It would cost an absolute fortune to do up. Its location is remote, and if it's not alarmed, that means it's easy to enter. I'm not saying she's inside, Shaun, but we have to check.'

He drops his gaze back to the layout. 'It's a big ask,' he points out.

'I can go alone if you prefer to sit it out. I won't think any the less of you.' I pause. 'Well, I might a bit, but not so that you'd notice.'

He looks up, frowns but chuckles. 'Of course, I'll come. It's a big place; it'll be quicker to search with two of us.'

'How about tomorrow?'

He nods. 'Yeah. I can't do the day after; I'm working.'

'Yeah? Me too.' He raises an eyebrow. 'My first shift at the pub.'

'You might regret taking this job, you know. Ben is a tyrant.'

'He can't be worse than—'

'Hi!' a female voice shouts down from the other end of the corridor.

I jump. Shit. Is that Bronwyn? A spear of dread, excitement, fear shoots through my chest and I push the seat back, leaping to my feet. It can't be her. There's no way she'd just turn up out of the blue as if nothing has happened.

Shaun takes his legs off the arm of the chair and sits up straight. I open the office door with no idea what I'm going to say to her. But it's only Nisha. Relief floods my chest.

A baby's car seat in the crook of her elbow weighs one side of her upper body down; there's a heavy looking bag on the other shoulder and an A4-sized envelope tucked into her armpit.

'Can I have a hand?' she pleads.

'Yeah, of course.' I take the car seat off her. The weight of it pulls my arm down painfully and, as I carry it through to the office, the hard plastic seat bangs repeatedly into the side of my leg. 'Christ, she weighs a ton,' I complain. 'What the bloody hell are you feeding her?'

'Kebab and chips,' Nisha jokes, trailing after me. 'She's skipped baby food and moved straight onto solids. She has the appetite of a T-Rex. Hi Shaun. How are you?'

'Hi Nisha. Fine, thanks. Is this little Anya?' he asks, getting up to peer at the sleeping baby.

'No. It's little Jasmin now.' Nisha shrugs. 'We changed our minds. But Jasmin *is* official; we registered her today, so there's no going back.' She casts her gaze over the desk at the propped-up tablet, the paperwork. 'How's the case going?' Nisha drops the bag onto the floor and balances the envelope on top. She takes the car seat from me and positions it safely on a chair, unclipping the belt. She removes a soft pink blanket tucked around Jasmin.

'It's making progress,' I explain, watching her neatly fold it. There's no need to throw a warning look at Shaun to keep his mouth shut. He knows Nisha would hit the roof and go through it if she knew what we have been doing.

'I'll go and look at that thing you sent me, Will,' Shaun says, picking up his notebook and the pub layout and backing out of the door. 'Would you like a drink, Nisha?'

'I'm fine, Shaun. Not long had a Costa.' She closes the door behind him and looks at me. 'Got time for a quick chat.'

'Yeah.'

Even though we're soon going to be partners, she still manages to put me on edge. It's the way she frowns at her desk with my messy work on it. The way she can change an atmosphere just by turning up unannounced. But then I am discussing illegal entry into a building. No wonder I feel nervous.

I spy the envelope lying on top of the baby bag. It bears my name. Oh. Is that the contract? Now is the time to back out, save myself twenty grand and a load of grief. This was something I lay awake last night thinking about. Round and round my head it went. Am I doing the right thing? Should I make such a big financial commitment going into business with Nisha? I will never be able to walk away from Lexington or this business. And then, like a meandering woodland path, my thoughts led me deeper and I started considering all aspects of my life: my living arrangements, my zero bank balance, my relationships. Will this business venture bring me happiness? Probably not. Perhaps this business partnership will be my lot. All I'm destined to have. One half of a business I'm pretty okay at. No home of my own, but it's okay at Mrs Penn's until she decides she's had her fill of lodgers. No girlfriend unless I try online dating and get lucky on the first date. Not much chance of that happening. Besides, I need a break from all that. This thing with Bronwyn has wrung me out. Maybe Michael is right. I am a fuck-up, unable to maintain relationships with women. I should make the most of being single if it's going to be my permanent relationship status.

'You're not having second thoughts, are you?' Nisha gently asks. She's sat in a comfy chair, cradling Jasmin, a baby's bottle tipped upside down and clamped in the baby's mouth. 'Have you spoken to Bronwyn about it? She must be all for it.'

I wonder if she knows what's happened, if she's fishing for information. I picture Bronwyn stumbling onto the pavement outside here crying and distraught, strangers eyeing her suspiciously and giving her a wide berth. She staggers back to her Merc, throws my present in the boot amongst the rest of her purchases and sits behind the wheel, desperate to pour her heart out to someone. But who? Not Michael or her mum. The obvious choice is Nisha; they've been friends for years.

'I haven't discussed it with her,' I reply.

'Oh…' she says, staring at me. 'I thought you would have done now that you're practically a couple. Any particular reason?'

She knows alright. Nisha has engineered this entire visit and is steering the conversation appropriately because she wants to take me to task over my treatment of Bronwyn. Bloody women ganging up on men.

I hesitate. 'Yes, because it's none of her business.'

Nisha frowns. 'What do you mean, Will? I thought you and she were—'

'Drop the pretence, Nisha. You know full well that Bronwyn and I are over.'

She sighs and gives me a long hard look of disgust. 'Bronwyn was in no fit state to drive. It's a miracle she didn't have an accident and that would have been on your conscience.' She points an accusing finger at me. 'She rang me from her flat. I could hardly get any sense out of her. How could you kick her out of the office, Will? Don't you—'

'I didn't kick her out of the office,' I object. 'I told her to leave.'

'Same thing.'

'The conversation wasn't going anywhere. I saw no reason to continue it—'

'That's so heartless of you, William. Do you have any idea of the difficult position Bronwyn's in? She's been trying to find the right time to finish with Michael. It isn't easy because he sorts out her workplace IT issues—'

'He *did*,' I correct. 'Currently he's suspended from work. Did she tell you that? Or did she only tell you her side of the story? Or maybe you only cherry-picked the bits you wanted to listen to i.e. the bad bits about me. And please don't forget to state how easy it's been for me since I've had no girlfriend to dump.'

'It's always easier for you men to dump women and move onto the next pretty face.'

I laugh without humour. 'That is a fucking horrible sexist comment to make. Men struggle with the break-up of relationships too. Why do you think the suicide rate is higher in men?'

'Are you blaming women for that?'

I shake my head. 'I'm just pointing out a statistic, that's all.'

'Are you struggling with the break-up of your relationship with Bronwyn? Or are you over her?'

I don't like her tone. I find her implication that I'm cold and uncaring frankly insulting. But her question makes me wonder if she will report my answer back to Bronwyn. I reply honestly because it is the truth and if she does contact Bronwyn after this conversation, it might spur her into action.

'No, I am not over Bronwyn. I was falling in love with her, which is why all this hurts. I just…' I pause trying to find the right words. Then I remember something. Evidence that Bronwyn betrayed me. She told Michael about three of my past relationships. Relationships that all ended badly.

'Michael knew about Justine, Gretchen and Claire,' I point out to Nisha once I've explained what exactly Michael said to me that day in the alley. 'That could only have come from Bronwyn. Why would she do that? Is she playing us against each other?'

Nisha stares at me and shakes her head slightly. 'Do you really believe that Bronwyn would do such a thing?'

'How else can you explain—?'

She interrupts. 'Easy. One day, perhaps months ago,' and she waves a hand to signify it's long in the past, 'he casually asks Bronwyn if you're married. Don't forget, he's a bloke. He's edgy about his new girlfriend having a male friend. Bronwyn says no, you were once engaged, but it didn't work out. He guesses that it was your fault. So for his next question, he asks if you have a girlfriend. Bron says no, you were seeing someone last summer for a short while but she left the area. As for Claire, he googles you and discovers that you investigated her disappearance. The trial was in all the local papers. Now, in Michael's tiny brain, men and woman cannot be just friends. He concludes that you were madly in love with Claire and the loss of her has utterly devastated you. Which it has. Easily explained I'd say. Wouldn't you?'

She smiles smugly at me and I silently conclude that yes, her explanation is feasible. I can absolutely picture that scenario. But stubbornly I can't tell her I agree. Him knowing about my relationships and mocking their failure stings like hell though.

Nisha tips the bottle upright, checking how much milk is left before reinserting the teat into Jasmin's mouth. I know she's planning her next move, her next comment to continue a pointless conversation. If Nisha doesn't mention my putting Michael under surveillance then I doubt she knows. I wonder why Bronwyn didn't tell her the lengths I'd gone to. Is she trying to protect me from a worse telling off?

'William, if you love Bronwyn, you should tell her,' she tells me in a condescending tone as if that's all it will take. 'It's pointless suffering in silence. How can you sort this out if you cut off all contact—'

'I haven't cut off all contact. I'm quite willing to talk to Bronwyn if she finishes with Michael.'

'You told her you were done with her,' Nisha accuses. 'You broke her heart, Will.'

I roll my eyes, my frustration starts to grow. 'I was angry, Nisha. It's obvious there's no point in me telling you things from my perspective, how messed around I felt. Your mind's made up. I'm the bad guy. Men always are in your world, aren't they?'

'Of course not, William. Don't be stupid.'

I shake my head and walk to the window. I move the voiles aside to look down into the high street. It's nearly lunchtime and, outside the bakery, a queue is forming. School kids, workmen, office staff. I wonder if Shaun will have the sense to join the queue and get us our lunch.

'For your information, I advised Bron to finish with Michael,' Nisha informs me in her newly adopted patronising tone. I say nothing. Does she think her advice will propel Bronwyn into doing something I've been pressuring her to do for ages? Does the same advice have more weight to it if a female friend suggests it? I won't hold my breath. The best thing Bronwyn could do is dump him over the phone.

'I told her to do it by phone.'

I turn from the window, the voile falling back into place, lift my chin with interest.

She continues. 'That's how I'd dump someone manipulative like him.'

'And has she done it?' I ask tentatively.

'I don't know,' she answers regretfully. 'I haven't heard from her. Her mobile's going to voicemail.'

He's probably talked her around into giving him another chance because he's suddenly developed a terminal illness. Preferably something nasty like Ebola.

'*You* should ring her too. She might answer your call.'

410

But why should I? Is it my turn now? Bronwyn's had hers, she made the first move. Now, it's mine, it's only fair. And what if she hasn't finished with him? What if I phone her and she's out with him and I'm interrupting them on a date? I don't think I could take the humiliation. I can almost hear her voice, whispering to Michael that, 'It's only Will. Can I ring you back?' Michael's laughter in the background will feel like a knife in the throat.

'No,' I tell Nisha firmly. 'It's completely up to Bronwyn to contact me. I'll talk to her, but only if she has something I want to hear.'

'For God's sake, William. How—'

'I'm not discussing it anymore.'

For several moments, she says nothing. I watch as she drops the empty bottle into the opened bag and starts rubbing Jasmin's back. She smiles lovingly at her daughter. 'Matt and I have decided to give Jasmin the middle name of Claire. I think Claire would've liked that.'

I picture Claire grinning with joy that her name is living on. 'Yeah, she would.'

'I've been thinking a lot about her these last few days. Mostly what she'd make of my life. The business, working with you, having another baby. I think she'd be thrilled.'

'Yeah. She would. She got a lot of enjoyment from her friends' happiness. I remember how over the moon she was when I got into the police. She even shed a tear when I got engaged. Despite the fact that she didn't care much for my fiancée. She wanted to be my best man. Which was weird.'

Nisha nods. She looks up, fixes me with a hard stare and asks, 'How thrilled do you think Claire would be if she could see the mess you're making of your own happiness, Will?'

I stare back, our eyes locked. Very clever, I think. It's not as if I haven't given any thought to that. And I know Claire wouldn't be impressed. But she wouldn't be chuffed if I let someone walk all over me either.

'You know what? I think I will give this contract a bit more thought.' I nod at the envelope. 'It might be a big mistake tying myself to this town and this business.'

'Oh. What else are you going to do?' Nisha asks, amused. 'Go travelling, move away and start again?'

'Well, they're beginning to sound more appealing alternatives.'

'Stop being a sulky, pigheaded bastard, William,' she sneers.

For the second time this week I open the office door with the intention of chucking someone out. 'If you don't mind, Nisha, I've got a case to close.'

She smiles with amusement and deliberately takes her time putting the baby back into the car seat, gathering her belongings. She taps the envelope with a fingertip. 'I'll leave that there. In case the travelling and fresh start don't appeal.'

I shepherd her down the corridor to the outer door and, through the doorway on my right, glimpse Shaun at his desk busily tapping away at the keyboard as if he's suddenly found some urgent typing. Rather suspiciously, he doesn't glance across at us and I wonder if he's been eavesdropping.

I hold the door open for her. 'Bye Nisha. And please stay out of my love life. I don't need you meddling in it.'

She turns, a smirk at the corner of her mouth, and rather sarcastically quips, 'And what love life would that be, William?'

Chapter 59

Five minutes late, Shaun's sporty Corsa enters the small car park, the tyres crunching on the loose stone. The inside of the vehicle is thumping from the loud music playing on his stereo. It's a miracle he doesn't have a hearing problem. But I suppose there's time to develop one.

Shaun raises a hand in acknowledgement and reverse parks next to the Mazda. I take a long swig of water and slide the plastic bottle back into my rucksack. There's no way I want to be without a drink. The last break-in gave me such a thirst. I glance through the window as Shaun busies himself behind the wheel, getting his stuff together. I know he's nervous. There's a few fiery pangs in my own stomach today, but in less than no time this search will be over, and we'll have either found Amanda or we'll be back to the drawing board. Already I feel this is another dead end. And God knows where we're going from here. Back to Ben's spread sheet, Jake's photos, or back to David? Without a shred of evidence, I know exactly what his response will be.

I get out of the car, swinging the bag onto my shoulder. The weather is mild but overcast. A gentle breeze ruffles my hair. Thankfully it didn't rain last night despite the forecast. The ditch should be less muddy.

Shaun smiles nervously, shifts awkwardly from foot to foot. 'Alright, Will?' he says.

'Yeah. You?'

'I'll be better when it's all over.'

We look at the three other cars parked up. All are empty. Perfect. The nearby road is silent.

I lead the way to the car park entrance, looking both ways across the road. To the left, the tarmac stretches away around a sweeping right-hand bend. To our right, it rises and disappears over the horizon. Nothing coming, not even in the distance. I stride quickly across the road, Shaun hurrying after me. I head straight for the metal fencing and the breach in the perimeter.

'This way,' I say, urging him to follow me quickly. We must get out of sight before we're seen by any passing cars.

The familiar metal panels completely block off the entrance, thwarting any attempt to fly-tip or park a vehicle. The last panel is at a slight angle, curving into the thorny hedge, making it impossible to get even so much as a moped through. Using my forearm, I push the sharp branches up and away, allowing Shaun to sneak through the gap. I squeeze through after him and we teeter on the sloping bank of the ditch. It's around two feet deep and there's a trickle of muddy water in the bottom. Brown leaves and rubbish line the banks of the ditch and float in the mud.

'It's wetter than I thought it'd be,' I say in a low voice. Carefully, I edge my feet down the solid dry ground and then step across the ditch, pushing my body forwards. Shaun follows suit and I hold my hand out just in case he needs it. We stand side by side, breathing hard, more from nerves than exertion.

I turn my head to the left. A vehicle. We freeze, lower our heads. Not that I have any fear we'll be seen. We're both wearing dark clothes and we're the right side of the hedge. The lorry thunders past and then it's silent again and we move on through another unforgiving prickly hedge which grabs at our clothes. We manage to startle a group of sparrows who quickly take to the air.

Away from the hedge, we find ourselves on pub property, on the edge of the access track which leads around to the back. I pause and look around. In the distance, heading down the road towards the pub is another lorry but the driver won't see us. Beyond the car park are field after field, all empty. A crow passes overhead, its dark wings stark against the colourless sky.

'Let's go,' I say. We cross the track, looking to our right where we might be seen if any walkers are returning and they happen to look directly at The Jester. But there's no one and we make it safely across. We climb the ranch fencing separating the track from the pub garden. The horizontal bars and the top of the fence posts have been colonised by slimy moss. I look across at the beer garden. Such a beautiful place back in its day. The lawn looks more like a meadow now. The grass is long and there are animal tracks criss-crossing through it, flattening it in several places.

In the centre of the overgrown grass is a tree with one of those wooden seats encircling its trunk. The branches have tiny little green leaves on them. Half of the seat has caved in. I remember sitting there with my ex-fiancée one summer's evening, planning our future and listening to a blackbird high up in the treetop singing his heart out.

The brick steps leading up to the patio are crumbling and the paving steps are broken and loose. More moss and weeds have gained a foothold in-between the slabs.

I smile sadly. Oh well, on with the show.

We cross the patio and I immediately scan the outside walls for any cameras and signs of an alarm, moving quickly across the sinking patio, around the rotting wooden bench/tables, the half barrels containing weeds now. The walls are bare. There's a security light above a door but, as it's daylight, it won't come on. Besides, if there isn't any alarm, what's the point of having electricity for a security light no-one can see unless they're at the rear of the property? The utilities will have been severed. Two rusty hanging basket hooks are screwed into the flaking grey painted brickwork. On the ground is a cone-shaped hanging basket; its woven material is unwinding. I carry on across the patio, past the boarded up windows.

Eventually the beer garden and patio come to an end, marked by waist-high ranch fencing which forms a perimeter to the grounds, keeping drinkers and diners out of staff only areas. A heavy-duty rusty padlock keeps the gate firmly closed but it's no deterrent for trespassers so I climb over, landing heavily on the paved area.

Under a painted black canopy, are double doors, painted in navy blue and this is our best way in. The service entrance.

I slide the rucksack off, have a quick swig of water and pull the Nitrile gloves on. Taking a tension wrench and a pick from the case, I kneel on the cold concrete and get to work unpicking the lock. The pins inside feel stiff. I anticipated that the lock might have been affected by the elements, which is why I bought a can of WD40. Shaun starts pacing, glancing nervously at me, fiddling with a dangling strap on his rucksack. It starts to irritate, putting me under unnecessary pressure. I blink hard and concentrate, feeling the pins resist the lift of the pick. My fingers start to cramp and I wonder if I should try another pick or maybe the rake when suddenly…a pin slides upwards and the others follow suit; the lock springs open.

'We're in,' I say triumphantly and put the tools quickly into the side pocket of the rucksack and get to my feet. My knees and ankles complain but I ignore the aching and take out my torch. I turn the door handle, bracing myself for the sudden noise of an alarm, and push open the right-hand door. Nothing. Eerie silence. I switch the torch on and aim the bright white light around my surroundings. It illuminates a wide square area with a low ceiling. The floor is tiled with dusty black tiles; cobwebs cling to a round glass light fitting and inside the frosted glass I see small specks. Are they insects?

I step forwards and Shaun shuts the door behind him. On the left-hand wall is another door, which opens into a cold cloakroom. Several brass pegs, minus any coats and bags, are screwed into the wall. Another door leads into a toilet and the tiniest hand basin. A sliver of dried orange soap lies in the indentation next to the cold water tap. A roll of shrivelled pink loo paper sits on the sill of the frosted glass window. I sniff the air. An unpleasant musty dampness. It evokes a memory of mildewy fabric. Must be something from my childhood. I dismiss it and move back into the corridor where Shaun waits.

'Cold, isn't it?' he remarks and I can see his teeth are chattering.

Coldness is creeping up my sleeves and down my neck, onto my bare skin and between the layers of my clothes. I shiver and move on. A door on the right leads to an empty room. A little brass sign screwed into the middle of the wood says: *Staff only.* A threadbare rug lies in the middle of the floor, its pattern faded by footfall and dust. Mouldy net curtains hang in the windows. A table, no chair, stands under the boarded-up window. Its top is bare, except for a biro, minus its lid. A four-drawer grey filing cabinet in one corner. I pull open the top drawer. It resists. Is it locked? She can't be inside, unless they dismembered her body and each drawer contains a segment. I abandon the search and back out of the room, continuing down the corridor towards a set of double doors. I open the right-hand one and step into the kitchen. I look around, impressed by its size and its extremely well-planned out area. To my right, through an arched doorway, is a side room, the length of the kitchen, but separated from it by a wall. A long line of doors leading to store cupboards and larders, individual catering fridges stand side-by-side like brushed-steel sentries, and more of the white-fronted doors with levers for handles. Freezers. Many of the fridges have notices attached to their doors, perhaps explaining to the kitchen staff what's stored in each one. At the end of the room, is another arched doorway leading back into the kitchen.

'You start in here,' I tell Shaun. 'I'll take the kitchen.'

He nods and begins. I walk inside and shine my torch around. The floor is composed of red stone tiles. Just beside my left foot, the tiles are sinking. I tap my toe on them and feel how loose they are. The grouting is crumbly. In the middle of the floor is a huge stainless steel island. Abandoned on its top, is a discarded once-white tea towel. Low-suspended lights hang down from the ceiling. Underneath the worktop are units with sliding doors. A couple are wide open and inside I see stacks of different sized white plates. The cupboards certainly look big enough to house a human body, if it was stuffed inside. I walk around the island, examining the other side, sliding across any closed doors. But there's no sign of human remains or blood inside. Well, I wouldn't have picked such an obvious hiding place either.

I continue my search starting with the left-hand wall. More units composed of scratched work surfaces and cupboards; sinks containing dirty dish sponges and washing up liquid bottles; dish racks; a food-stained griddle, a dirty fish slice lies on its front, the edge stuck in some food residue; an eight-ring stove; ovens. There's a horrible stale food smell in here. As if the smell of chargrilled steak, baking pastry and sizzling fish have become trapped inside the kitchen for years.

The floor underneath my boots feels tacky and gritty. I aim the white light of my torch down and see evidence of rodent activity. Little black droppings like shrivelled currants. I sniff the air. Smells like rodent piss. I remember Eddie had a hamster when he was 8. If he didn't clean it out often enough, it'd stink like this.

At the back of the kitchen is an alcove and another door. Looks promising. I grasp the lever and pull, but the hinges stick a bit so I yank harder and it opens with a protest. Oh. A larder. Metal racking. Catering-sized tins, the labels faded. A sack of rice on the floor, the corner of the plastic has been chewed off and little grains are scattered over the tiled floor. I walk through the larder to the end. Most of the shelves are empty. There's certainly no body. I leave, closing the door behind me, move onto the units, starting with the nearest and moving clockwise around the kitchen. I slide the doors across and peer inside. Pans with glass lids, frying pans of various sizes; chopping boards; sieves and colanders; other unknown items, things only a chef or kitchen hand could identify.

In the next cupboard, the light picks out a bulging black bin liner. Whatever it contains, it's big. The item has lifted the bin liner until it brushes the underside of the unit. I prod it with a finger. Something soft around something hard. Flesh and bone? Surely not after nearly seven years. There's no tell-tale human decaying smell. Unlikely to be human remains but I must look. I tug on the bin liner but it doesn't budge. I clamp the light between my knees so it shines inside the cupboard and grasp the plastic with both hands, pulling harder, but it's heavy and bulky and an unseen part of it is caught on the underside of the unit. I tug harder, my feet digging into the tiles. Still stuck and I have a vision of Amanda's fleshless elbow wedged inside.

417

I edge closer, readjust the light and pull again, exerting more force, the sort you might use in a tug-of-war, but it's too much because suddenly the item becomes unstuck and the object inside flies out at speed, making me yelp and jump back. The contents tip out like water cascading off a cliff, scattering tea towels and utensils everywhere. Wooden spoons, metal and silicone spatulas, ladles, graters surround my feet. A crumpled box sits in the mouth of the unit, one of its flaps wedged in the doorway.

My heart is thumping.

'Shit,' I say, looking at dozens and dozens of tools. Was someone going to steal them and changed their mind because the box was heavy and they feared getting caught?

'Will?' says Shaun nervously. 'Oh…you clumsy sod.' He helps me gather the utensils up, chucking them back into the bag and together we shove the whole lot back into the cupboard.

'I thought it might have been Amanda's bones,' I joke but he winces at my poor taste in humour.

I pull the bottle from my bag and taking a long swig, enjoying the feeling of cold water clearing the dust from my mouth and throat. We're done in here. There's nowhere else to look. I wait for Shaun by the double doors, which lead into the pub. I watch as he slides shut the last freezer door, but he doesn't step away immediately. He looks back down the row of fridges, frowning slightly.

'You alright?' I ask, holding out the water.

'Yeah,' he mutters vaguely, accepting the water and gulping it thirstily down.

'Let's go. I'm beginning to think this is going to be another fruitless search.'

I push the left hand door open and step into a wide short corridor. The floor is tiled with brown stone squares, the walls papered in a pretty white and green floral pattern. Through more double doors and we find ourselves in the pub.

I look up at the vaulted ceiling, made from arched lengths of wood. It's like something out of a church or the inside of a barrel, cut lengthways. This is the main dining room, containing the infamous fireplace at the end of the room, which doesn't look that special. Worth inspecting, just in case. It sounds like the sort of deposition site Jake would get a kick out of using. I walk across the wooden floor towards it, shining the torch across the walls and the sparse remaining furniture. Huge wooden tables, some minus chairs; the occasional threadbare rug, some oval, some rectangular, placed to break up the sea of wood. Huge cobwebs hang from the brass light fittings; they brush against my face and I wipe them away. There are a few framed pictures on the walls, and grimy marks where some once were. Thick dust covers all the surfaces and the air smells musty. I inspect the fireplace but there's no chimney, nowhere to shove a human body.

Shaun trails uselessly after me. I stop suddenly and turn to him.

'Find the cellar,' I instruct. 'It's an ideal hiding place.'

He nods, mutters, 'Okay,' and walks towards one of the many exits. I choose another, an arched doorway which leads to the bar. A square in the middle of another room. Smaller tables, minus chairs, are arranged on the floorspace. More brass light fittings; gold-framed countryside scenes on the walls; ornaments dot the tiled windowsills under boarded-up windows, animals, random jugs and drinking vessels. Pointless tack.

If I didn't know it used to be a bar, I might be forgiven for wondering what it might have once been. It's virtually unrecognisable now. There are no beer pumps, just marks and indentations in the wood where they once were. The shelves are empty of glasses, just an ice bucket and a pair of tongs remain. There are no full bottles of alcohol, but an empty bottle of champagne lying on its side in the porcelain sink. Perhaps the staff had one last drink together before they shut the place up. Draining the place dry. There's certainly no space to hide a body.

I continue with my search, locating the romantic nooks, which are all small, with no room to stuff a body. I meet Shaun by the front entrance. There's a smudge of dirt on his cheek and he looks dishevelled.

'Nothing in the cellar,' he tells me, with a shudder. 'Just the usual kegs, pipes and a rat. It was the size of a Jack Russell.'

'Bollocks,' I laugh. 'Everyone always says that. Have you checked the toilets?' And I nod at the three doors, little brass signs in the middle of the white-painted wood. *Women, men and disabled.*

'I've just checked the cellar, Will,' he complains. 'Can I not have a—?'

'The sooner it's done, the quicker we're out of here. Go on. I'll take this door.'

His shoulders sink but he hops to it, starting with the disabled toilet. My choice turns out to be a cleaner's cupboard, its only clue a mop, with a dried head, and a bucket, a dead spider inside. I remove the lock picking set from the rucksack and get to work unpicking the lock on the last door marked *private*.

Seconds later, Shaun appears confirming that the toilets are all empty. 'Even if she is here, how did they get in?' he asks. 'I was expecting to find a smashed window in the toilets, but nothing.'

'I wouldn't fancy squeezing a body through a tiny window,' I tell him. 'They'd have cut her to shreds. Blood everywhere. They must've got in the same way as us. It's easy enough to do...with practice.' I concentrate on the task in hand.

'That suggests her murder was planned well in advance.'

'Well, maybe from the day David laid her floor. We're in,' I announce, sliding the tools out of the lock and back into the case. I open the door to be faced with a flight of carpeted stairs. A porthole window is about halfway up. A vase containing a dusty dried flower arrangement on the sill.

The living quarters aren't anything special. The main bedroom contains a divan double bed with a stained mattress on top. There's nothing in the storage drawers. The wardrobe contains a couple of wire hangers, no clothing. The smaller bedroom contains a single bed; the mattress slightly more pristine. A bedside cabinet holds a dog-eared children's book in its drawer.

The bathroom is dirty. The toilet bowl is dry and piss-stained. A dead spider in the hand basin, a collection of dead flies in the shower tray. The shower curtain is covered in mould.

The kitchen is even worse. A dirty food-stained hob, a tarnished stainless steel sink. The fridge contains a plastic carton of milk but whatever is inside God only knows. I bet it absolutely reeks. I close the door firmly and turn with a sigh. Shaun is standing on the landing, looking up at the loft hatch. In his hand is a metal pole with a hook on the end.

I smile. 'Well, I'm damned sure, if I'd hidden my nagging selfish wife in the loft, then I'd take that,' and I jab a finger at the pole, 'with me.'

Shaun shrugs. 'I don't mind having a look. It *is* daylight and there is a pole. So there must be a ladder.' He inserts the end of the pole into the little hole in the hatch and turns it. We look up into the darkness.

'Oh. A loft ladder. Handy.' He inserts the end of the pole into the side of the folding ladder and slides the end out. It creaks noisily and I'm reminded of Hepworth spraining his ankle emerging out of Amanda's loft. Shaun ensures the ladder feet are flush to the floor before carefully climbing up, torch in his fist. He pokes his head and shoulders through the gap and turns on the torch.

'They defo have a rat problem,' he says, with a shudder. 'One's run across the floor. Horrible little…'

'Yeah. There's rat shit in the kitchen too. Environmental Health will have something to say about that.'

'There's nothing up here, Will. No human-shaped objects, or bin bags containing utensils either,' he jokes.

'Watch it, Hock, you're a long way up off the floor,' I warn jokingly.

Shaun climbs back down and we lift the ladder back inside, closing the hatch. He puts down the pole and we return to the pub.

'Where now?' Shaun asks. 'We've looked everywhere, haven't we?'

I shrug. 'She's not here. I'm beginning to think she is living the high life in the south of France under an assumed name. We've narrowed our murder suspects down, but where is the evidence that she's actually dead? There's nothing. And really, David getting his presumption of death order is no different than one day someone finding her body.'

'Poor Mrs Davies,' Shaun says sadly. 'I feel really mean charging her and failing to produce her daughter.'

'Yeah, me too, but we've both got to eat. Come on,' and I slap his arm, 'let's go.'

We retrace our steps back to the kitchen. I pause and look around in case I've missed something. I don't want something to suddenly occur to me at three o'clock in the morning. I've no intention of breaking in again. We've checked everywhere. Such a shame because The Jester, in one way, is perfect. It's a protected building, it's remote and vacant. I look up at the ceiling. No hatches. Shaun has stepped to my left and is gazing through the doorway at the line of upright fridges and the other doors. He's frowning.

'What is it?' I ask.

'Not sure.' He stands to the side of the first fridge and looks down the line of them, paying particular attention to the floor in front of each one. Then he walks past them like an army officer inspecting his troops. 'This one,' he says, stopping in front of fridge three, 'is out of alignment.'

I stand beside him. 'Didn't you look inside?'

'Well, I thought I did but you distracted me with that noisy bag of utensils. And you can see all the fridges look alike,' and he waves a hand down the lines.

This stainless steel fridge is around two metres tall and is on four wheels. The braking mechanism on the left-hand wheel is essentially a square of black plastic which is pressed down, setting its position between two more identical fridges, but on closer inspection, it's plain to see that it's a few centimetres forward of the others, the left-hand side is turned just slightly outwards.

'Hang on,' he says, his face lighting up. 'I saw something in one of the freezers which struck me as weird…let me just…' He hurries back down the line to a door with a lever, yanks on it and slides it across. He reaches inside and comes out holding up two square-shaped objects, like oven shelves but white.

He brings them closer and I reach out a hand. A couple of the plastic-coated corners have worn off exposing the metal underneath.

I look back at the fridge. 'Shit. These are fridge shelves.'

He nods. 'And what are they doing in a freezer? A freezer which contains proper metal racking.'

Shaun returns them to the freezer and we re-examine the fridge. The front of the fridge is covered in lots of bits of paper held on by fridge magnets. The sort of magnets you get on holiday: island-shaped ones saying *Ibiza* and *Sicily*, a square one of a tiger from a zoo, an Arsenal football club one. I reach out a hand…what's this? My fingers touch a dark blue line, roughly three centimetres in width which horizontally crosses the door, about shoulder height. It's like someone has drawn a line across it with a felt-tip marker. I touch it. Oh. It's material, smooth like the stuff made from seatbelts. The word comes to mind and I say, 'Webbing.'

'What?'

I try to slide a finger under it but it's tight against the fridge with absolutely no give in it, like it's been glued on. 'Give me a hand,' and I start to remove the notices and magnets, revealing what's underneath. Shaun helps and soon the floor is littered with paper and holiday souvenirs.

'It's a strap,' he says, puzzled. 'It goes around the side,' and he follows it with a finger.

422

'This side too.' My hand reaches around the side of the fridge as far as I can reach and I touch cold metal through the Nitrile glove. The buckle. 'It's a ratchet strap,' I tell Shaun. 'Used to tie cargo down for transportation, like on the back of a truck. I once saw a funeral director use one to—' I stop talking, look at Shaun.

'Why would someone use a ratchet strap on a fridge door?' he asks. 'Because the locking mechanism had bust and they needed to close the door to keep the food chilled.'

But my mind has wandered off to the scene in a local mortuary. I was there on behalf of the coroner to escort a body from one mortuary to one with a forensic suite. Whilst I waited for the funeral director who was parked outside to get his act together, I chatted to one of the mortuary staff, whose name I can't recall. But they were dealing with another undertaker and he was looping a worn blue strap, identical to this one, around a body lying on a wooden board. I watched him tighten it around the body bag. I'd never seen anything so undignified. From where I stood, I could see into the open fridge. The metal racking, similar to the ones we've seen in pub freezers, bodies lying on trays wrapped in sheets and white plastic, and there on the inside of the door: a big yellow button and a small warning notice. The exit if you're trapped inside.

This fridge has to have the exact same get-out-button. Not that many kitchen workers would end up trapped inside, but there's a first for everything. There's always the chance that someone might bundle you inside one, but they'd need to remove the racking first or you'd never fit, and how on earth do they stop you getting out?

Easy.

'Shaun,' I whisper and I can tell by his expression that he's suddenly overcome with nerves and feels slightly sick, because it's the exact same way I feel.

I don't even want to think of the terror Amanda must've felt when she was pushed screaming towards the open door. I hope to God she was dead before...but then why use the...? Of course...a fridge doesn't just keep things cold; it's air tight. And the small amount of air trapped inside would soon be used up, especially by someone in a panic.

I swallow hard and with a dry, croaky voice say, 'Shaun...I think we may have found her.'

Chapter 60

'First things first,' I say, sliding the rucksack onto the floor and unzipping it. 'We need to take photos.' I remove the camera I normally use for honey traps and put the strap over my head. No one can dare say I haven't thought of everything.

'You're going to photograph it?' Shaun says, horrified, putting a hand on my arm. 'Who for?'

'The police. Shaun, we *need* to take photos, to preserve the scene as much as possible. Mate,' I say, when he gives me another horrified glare, 'if Amanda is in this fridge, there's no way it's an accident. It's murder. Just opening the door means we're disturbing a crime scene.'

'Let's just phone the police. They can look,' he suggests urgently, pulling his mobile out of his back pocket.

'No,' I say sharply, putting a hand out. 'This is my case, *our* case. Don't you want to follow it through to the end?'

'What the bitter end?' he mocks. 'Being arrested and locked up, interviewed for hours and hours. No, fucking thank you. I do not.'

'Shaun, the police aren't going to suspect us. You were a mere teenager eight years ago and I was…doing whatever. The only thing we need to explain is what we were doing here—'

'Breaking and entering! That's what.'

I ignore that. 'Shaun, we're Private Investigators working on a MISPER case. A lead bought us here. We haven't damaged any property whilst obtaining entry…'

'I don't like this, Will,' he says, returning his phone to his pocket, even though I expressly told him a phone in a pocket has a tendency to fall out. 'What if she's in there?' He glances at the fridge door, his head turned away as if something from a horror film is going to leap out as soon as the strap is loosened.

'That's why I'm taking photos,' I explain, shining the torch onto the camera and adjusting the settings for the low light. 'If a pile of bones falls out, I want to capture it on film. Even though this is a digital camera and—'

'How can you make jokes at a time like this?' Shaun starts pacing the floor. The white light starts dancing around like a disco ball.

And then it occurs to me. What his problem might be? I ask, 'Are you squeamish?'

His blue eyes widen and he nods. 'I've never seen a dead body before. When my nan died a couple of years ago, Dad wouldn't let us see her at the Funeral Directors. She'd had a post-mortem and he thought she would look different.'

'They don't,' I tell him. 'Trust me. I've seen a few PMs in my time. Look, if you really don't want to be here, wait outside. I won't be long.'

But he shakes his head. 'I can't leave you to it. It's not fair. Like you said, it's *our* case.' He forces himself to smile but his nervousness is coming off him in waves. Beads of perspiration dot his forehead and his hands are shaking. I know from Isla, that she's always more concerned how male observers react to the sight of a dead body. Frequently it's them who have to leave the mortuary when the smell of the bowel hits them or the bone saw comes out. Women, she claims, have stronger stomachs.

'Do you want to take the photos?' I offer. 'I'll unstrap the door.'

He nods, slips the camera strap over his head and gets into position, giving me sufficient room to open the fridge.

With the toe of my boot, I flick up the brake and see how moveable the fridge is. Its wheels are sticky, probably coated in a variety of spilt and splashed food items, and it takes some force to move the structure further out of alignment and straighten it a little again. I reach down the side of the fridge, locate the release tab.

To the side of me, I hear the camera shutter making its distinctive noise as Shaun photographs me releasing the strap. Briefly I'm bathed in white brightness as the flash goes off. The strap loosens and slides down towards the floor. I pull it up from around the fridge and gather it up.

'In my rucksack, Shaun, is a large sealable plastic bag.'

He rummages inside and removes a rolled up plastic bag, the sort you store food in. He pulls it apart and helps me place the all-important ratchet part inside the bag to preserve any forensic evidence or fingerprints caught on the metal. The rest of the strap dangles outside the bag and we lay it on a kitchen worktop.

'You ready?' I say to him and he nods, swallowing hard, and getting back into position. The fridge lever is a horizontal chrome handle. I hook a couple of fingers behind it, rather than lay my palm across the top of it like the culprit might have, and pull it towards me.

There's a sucking noise as the door seal pulls away from the one around the frame, and then the smell hits me like a punch to the face: a combination of old cheese and ammonia - the telltale stench of human remains kept prisoner in an airtight chamber for nearly seven years.

The stench cloud envelopes us. Shaun swears, retches, but does a sterling job with the camera. Instinctively, I bring my forearm up to my nose, rest my right hand on my left shoulder and keep it there. It does little to filter the air.

'Fucking hell,' I whisper into the material and step back awkwardly, arm dropping back to my side. I'm best off just breathing it in, acclimatising myself to the smell. Shaun appears at my shoulder and I pull the door further open.

Together we look inside, we gasp as one, sucking in more foetid air.

The fridge is not empty.

A figure is slumped in the far right corner facing the door; knees up, toes pointing inwards. The head, I think, looks like it's been swathed in dirty yellow bandages like a mummy. I peer closer. It's a brittle substance like plaster of Paris and covers the forehead, eye sockets and cheekbones.

Clumps of long pale hair, not blonde but dirty and fluid-stained now, cling to the delicate scalp, as if the slightest brush against a surface would cause it to slough right off like a badly fitting wig. The skin around the lower half of the face and neck is leathery and tan-coloured, like a leather jacket from the late 1970's. Her dried lips are withered and hard, retracting back in a grimace, exposing her yellowing teeth.

'What's that white stuff, Will? Is it mould?' Shaun whispers.

'It's called adipocere, or corpse wax. It's derived from body fat,' I explain.

'It fucking stinks. Smells like a cheese counter.'

My eyes move down the figure for any kind of identifying mark. The airless environment has failed to completely dry the liquids, and the glistening pool on the bottom of the fridge, in which the figure sits, looks thick and gooey like syrup. The right arm is down by its side, but the left rests on the lap and on the wrinkled leathery ring finger, is a loose gold band, a diamond ring rests on a bony knuckle. The fingernails are long and dirty, the skin has mummified, retracting back to expose blackened nails like a witch's.

'She's married,' and I point to the rings. From the clothing, it's clear to see this is a female. Beige leather ankle boots; a long patterned skirt, its colour difficult to ascertain on account of

426

the heavy staining. Body fluids. Different colours. Autumnal. Like an artist's palette. Bile green, fatty yellow, dark red, shitty brown. She wears a short and fitted jacket, tweed I think, with a thin floaty scarf wrapped around the neck.

I remember from David's statement that he couldn't tell the police what his wife was wearing the day she disappeared. Unfamiliar with her clothes, he couldn't even guess what was missing from the wardrobe as he had nothing to do with her laundry, only his own. Would he recognise a description now? How will he react when he's told what's been found?

I step back, urge Shaun to take close-up pictures, and like a true SOCO, he gets in close, photographing the face, hands, feet, the pool of fluid. After a couple of minutes, he steps back, breathing deeply.

'Is it her?' he asks.

I step closer. The smell has dispersed but the inside of the fridge is pungent enough. 'Could be.'

The fact that she's dressed means that her clothes have soaked up a lot of the fluids caused by the decomposition. They're probably the only binding that's holding the mummified skin to her frame, keeping the putrefying organs inside.

'What are we going to do, Will?' Shaun whispers. 'Should we call the police?'

My gaze drifts downwards, from the willowy clumps of hair, the tasselled lilac scarf around her neck, her thin shoulders, bent up limbs. How tall would she be? I ask Shaun to hazard a guess.

He shrugs. 'I don't know, Will. She looks tall but that's maybe because she's thin.'

'In my bag,' I say, 'there's a tape measure. Hand it to me.'

He stares, horrified. 'You can't move her,' he protests. 'We're not supposed to be disturbing the—'

'I'm not going to. Please, Shaun.'

He fetches it and I pull a length of metal tape from the dispenser and, in a very rudimentary way, without touching her, I place the end at her heel and ask Shaun to add up the following numbers. Heel to ankle to knee to her thigh, length of torso, neck to top of skull.

'One hundred sixty five centimetres,' he answers.

'Five feet five. Same as Amanda.'

'What's that? There,' and he points into the fridge, his fingertip practically touching the material of her jacket. I peer closer, ignoring the waft of rottenness invading my nostrils. Poking out from beneath her lapel and the layer of clothing underneath, is a triangle of paper.

'Pocket where the tape measure was,' I instruct, 'is a pair of tweezers, pass them, will you?'

He rummages again through the bag, coming up with the goods. 'You've thought of everything, haven't you?' he says, impressed.

'I take this very seriously.' With the tweezers open and primed to grab, I step closer to the fridge until my toes touch the vent at the bottom and I reach deep inside. With all the steadiness of an experienced surgeon playing a game of *Operation,* I grasp the corner of the triangle securely, and gently but firmly ease it out. Is it a handkerchief folded into a triangle like men wear in the top pocket of the blazers?

I swivel around and Shaun aims his torch at it. Together we study it; I turn the object around. The one corner has a brown stain on it.

'It's paper,' I tell him. 'Folded up. Get me something to lay it on.'

Shaun rushes into the kitchen and starts yanking doors open and rooting noisily through the kitchen units for something suitable. Items drop to the floor making a horrific noise. Pan lids, baking trays, bread boards.

I hold the torch light up against it. It's been folded in half a couple of times but there's nothing written on either side. Why did she stuff it into her clothing? Is it important? Who keeps a piece of paper close to their chest, but between layers of clothing? Is it a love letter? From David? Or Martyn? Did she do this action because she realised there was no way out for her and she wanted to preserve it?

'Here,' Shaun calls, arranging a chopping board on the nearest kitchen surface. He takes another plastic sealable bag from my rucksack and slits the seams open with a penknife. He lays the plastic bag across the chopping board like a folded-out newspaper. I bring the paper over and lay it on the board, flipping it over. Shaun holds the torch close, aiming the white light on it. The two halves of the paper tent up, the crease neatly down the middle.

'See these lines,' Shaun says, and he points at them with a kebab skewer. 'It is clean,' he reassures me. Three faint lines across the paper indicate previous creases. This paper was once folded into thirds, but another hand has folded them into four equal-sized quarters.

Shaun props the torch up so its light points at the object and together we pin and unfold the paper, lying it on its back and exposing its words to our eyes. I stare at the document, the organisation in the top right-hand corner, the address on the left, an address I was only at recently. I read the name of the recipient, which doesn't come as a surprise, and yet it does, because why else would this poor deceased, murdered lady have *this* person's letter tucked in her clothes? It is no accident she has it and it is completely intentional that she has placed it where she has in her final moments. I can't think of a single "innocent" scenario why she would have this. Not one…but yes…the only one…and that indicates foul play.

'There's two sheets!' Shaun announces, excited. 'They're stuck together. Look,' and using the penknife blade, he parts the papers. I pull the top page away with the tweezers, lay it to the side where it immediately starts to fold back into its original position.

I read the second printed page. They're instructions. What to bring with you, how to cancel, parking charges, which back then were extortionate and now, are positively criminal.

As the bottom half of the first page continues its movement up and over, it exposes handwritten scribbles on the back of it. I flip it over with the tweezers like a steak in a frying pan, press the corners down and we silently read the black biro scrawling. Rude words, swear words, a name, shortened affectionately; some words are crossed out, replaced with similar words, cruder ones. And there, isolated from the structured doodlings, by a hand-drawn ring, is the chosen phrase. And underneath it, is a mobile number I recognise well because I've come across it before during this investigation. But why has the recipient of the letter written out a number they should know well, because they have dialled it probably every day?

Of course! Just how many of us can recite the phone numbers of our friends and family? It's the job of our mobiles to remember and store eleven-digit numbers.

There's only a few reasons why they would write this out. Either to give the number to someone else, to dial it from a different phone, or program into a new phone. Which is it?

But more importantly, why has Amanda kept this letter?

Shaun looks at me, confused and excited. 'I don't get it, Will. What does it mean? *Is* that Amanda? Have we found her?'

I nod sadly. 'I rather think we have, yes.' I stare at the papers, re-reading the words; gaze back at the open fridge, at my found person, no longer my MISPER. Poor Mrs Davies. But she knew in her heart of hearts that her daughter was dead. Will finding her be any consolation? But it can't end here. I refuse to hand all this over to the police, let them pick up where I was forced to leave off. And yet I can't take this evidence with me. I don't need another charge of perverting the course of justice. But without it, I have nothing to goad my suspects with.

Shaun retrieves the camera, adjusts a couple of dials and aims the lens at the paper. 'Can you flatten it?' he instructs bossily and I see what he's doing and get to work quickly. Using the tweezers, I pin the corners of the paper down so he can photograph the words. I flip the page over and he snaps a shot of the front page, bearing the recipient's name; the absolute proof of their involvement in Amanda's disappearance and murder. Shaun pulls apart two sealable bags, fresh from my rucksack, and we slide the pages inside, one in each, preserving any prints and forensic evidence.

'Nice work, Hock,' I praise and he smiles proudly, but it falls from his face as he gazes back at the fridge.

'She was alive when she was pushed inside, wasn't she? That's the reason for the strap. How long would it have taken her to die?'

'I'm sure there's a formula somewhere on Google that will answer that question fairly precisely, Shaun. Judging by the confined space, I'd estimate a couple of hours. Less if she was panicked and she almost certainly would be if she was conscious or woke up inside. Imagine waking up inside a coffin.'

Shaun shudders. 'I don't want to. Where do you suppose her handbag is? Inside there with her? Or do you think they hid it somewhere else?'

His comment reminds me of her missing diary. What I wouldn't give to have a flick through its pages. But if it's in there, someone else will find it.

'I'd say they had the perfect spot in there. Maybe she's sat on it. Right, we'll pack up our stuff and get out of here. Close the fridge door. We'll leave the notes and the strap on the work surface. There'll be some explaining to do later on but right now, we have a lead to follow.'

Shaun tidies up the mess he's left in the kitchen, shoving the trays and lids back inside the cupboards and firmly closing the doors. He neatly arranges the notes and the strap side-by-side on the unit.

I take a long swig of water, refreshing my throat and take one last look at Amanda Davies. As the oxygen ran out, all that was left was poisonous carbon dioxide to breathe in. And in such cramped conditions, with barely enough room to stand or sit, she must have screamed until her throat bled. What a truly horrible death. I wonder if the culprit or culprits thought of that when they bundled her inside and sealed her fate. Did they actually think about the suffering they would cause her, or did they just see the fridge as somewhere to hide her body? Did they wait out here until she stopped screaming and kicking? Or did they drive straight off to begin their fake alibis? Surely they didn't have time to wait until the fridge went quiet. Did they come back a couple of days later, a week maybe? Loosen the strap, check on their victim. Risky returning to the scene, but some do. Or were they absolutely confident that the fridge would do the job they couldn't do with their bare hands?

'Will,' Shaun says, snapping me out of my thoughts.

'Coming.' I follow Shaun back through the pub and outside where we close the door behind us and I securely lock it. We squeeze back through the hedge, over the ditch, pause whilst two people with a handful of dogs load them into the back of their people carrier and pull out of the car park. When we are back at the cars, I breathe deeply, drawing cold fresh air into my lungs. I can still smell the decay; it's clinging to the fine hairs in my nostrils. I need to make myself sneeze, blast the scent from within.

I unlock the Mazda, give Shaun his instructions. 'Go straight to the office, upload those pictures onto my iPad, print copies of the note and the photographs. I need to do something first. I won't be long. And for God's sake, make sure the kettle is on. We won't have much time before we need to head out again.'

'What are you going to do? Are you phoning the police? You're not waiting for them, are you?' he asks, his voice panicked. He chucks his rucksack onto the passenger seat, jumps in and turns the key.

'Not quite. Just go.' I close his door, watch him speed out of the car park, his tyres flicking up loose gravel.

I get behind the wheel of the Mazda, remove my mobile from inside my bag. No missed calls, no messages. I briefly think of Bronwyn. Wonder what she's doing now. Probably sat in a meeting, studying sales forecasts, or whatever else she does. I know one thing for sure, I bet she hasn't just found a dead body.

I scroll through my contacts, ring the number and wait. After four rings, a male voice answers. He sounds pissed off. No doubt he's sick and tired of hearing from me.

'Where are you?'

Evasively, he tells me. 'At work, where else would I be on a weekday morning?'

'What's your address?'

'Why?'

'Because I have some news for you, but I'm only going to give it to you face-to-face.'

He asks if it can wait until later, gives me yet another poor excuse as to why he won't grant me an audience. I don't tell him it's because I need to see his expression when I deliver the news.

'Fine,' I say haughtily. 'Have it your own way. Maybe you'll hear it from the police first... but I don't expect they'll give you the full facts...see you—'

'Wait! Okay.' With a noisy sigh, he gives me the address. I start the engine, pull away at speed. One more call left to make but that can wait until I'm back at the office for a pit stop.

Chapter 61

Back at the office, Shaun's tea is a drinkable temperature. I take mine into the toilet with me, balance the mug on the tiny hand basin whilst I change my clothes. I sniff the sleeve of my waterproof and pull a face. It's no wonder it stinks of decomposing bodies. The smell clings to fabric like glue. Which is why mortuary technicians wear scrubs. I stuff everything into a plastic carrier bag, tie the handles securely and leave it on the floor. I splash cold water on my face and stare at my reflection in the small mirror.

I can hardly believe that I've found her. That today I saw Amanda Davies. When I started this venture, I never really expected to find her. Dead or alive. And if I did manage to track her down, these weren't the circumstances I expected to locate her in. Homeless and shooting up in a derelict property, maybe. Or perhaps, a trace of her boarding a one-way flight to a faraway destination. Not stuffed inside a catering fridge in a listed public house.

I return to the office, leave my dirty cup in the sink and find Shaun at the printer, tapping his fingers against his thigh. The printer is whirring away, spewing warm sheets of paper with a handful of our chosen pictures on. He takes an empty file off the shelf and opens it up.

'I need to make one more phone call, mate, and then we'll be on our way,' I tell him.

He spins around from the printer. His expression is one of nervous excitement. I know there's no other place he'd rather be but he's terrified what might happen once I open that file and show those pictures.

'What's the plan? Where are we going?' he asks, carefully placing the pictures inside the file.

'Kelsall. We'll go in my car.' I walk down the corridor, mobile pressed to my ear as it rings out several times before it's answered.

A female voice, in a tone that suggests she's at work and isn't really supposed to be answering in work's time, says, 'Hello William.'

'Hi Sarge. How are you?'

'Stop calling me that,' she laughs. 'It's Yvette now and I'm fine. How are you?'

'I'm fine. Look, remember my MISPER? I've found her, but the thing is, she's dead. It's murder, Yvette. It's definitely murder.'

'Shit, William,' she hisses, lowering her voice. 'Have you phoned the police?'

'Yeah, I'm on the phone to them now.'

'I'm not police anymore. You know that.'

'Yvette, there's a very bloody good reason why I can't be there to meet them; I'm following a lead. I know what you're going to say, but spare me. You must know a good copper. One that'll go easy on a disgraced ex-cop.'

'Will, this really is out of order. You're supposed to stay at the scene of a crime, particularly murder…'

'I know that, but like you, I'm not police anymore. The scene is ultra secure. Please Sarge. For old time's sake.'

Silence. The go-ahead to continue. I give her the address, say "thank you" before urging Shaun to hurry up; we haven't got long.

*

Mistletoe Drive is in the middle of a housing development being built on the outskirts of Kelsall. It's in various stages of development, consisting of occupied dwellings, houses having soft furnishings fitted and those with just the foundations being laid. The houses are all detached, three or four bedrooms, with garages but nearly no front garden, just a patch of lawn and evergreen shrubs planted in a regimented line, acting as a border between neighbours.

I drive carefully through the streets, avoiding huge ridges of mud on the road, which bear impressions of tyre tracks from heavy-duty vehicles. Huge mounds of dug-up soil dot the landscape; men in hi-vis bibs and coats wander about carrying clipboards or mobiles; obligatory white vans are everywhere, partially blocking entrances and exits; pyramids of huge lengths of piping, stacks of bricks, bags of concrete sitting on newly-built paths, temporary car parks. And more metal fencing forming an impenetrable shield around the site.

'Mistletoe Drive,' Shaun announces, jabbing his finger at the passenger window glass. Black writing on a white signpost indicates the location.

I brake, turn hard left and steer around a group of workmen who have congregated on the junction to have a loud raucous chat. They turn their heads and eye the Mazda suspiciously and so they should; it's obvious none of the houses down here are occupied. And we're a long way from the show homes at the main entrance. Lawns are being laid, small shrubs are being planted and soft furnishings are being installed, including flooring.

David's van is parked half up the kerb with its rear doors open. David is sat inside the back, legs dangling outside the van with a sandwich in his hand. It reminds me that we're missing lunch. But I'm too hyper to eat.

At the sound of the approaching car, he looks up from his phone, lifts his feet up as if fearful of them becoming trapped by the Mazda when I pull up behind his van. Through the windscreen, I see him mouth something, a swear word no doubt judging by his annoyed expression. Getting his feet amputated by a car is going to be the least of his worries. We climb out of the Mazda, the file firmly in Shaun's hands.

'Afternoon David,' I call. 'Thanks for agreeing to see me.'

'Yeah, well, you didn't give me much choice.' He squashes the lid back on his lunchbox and jumps down, walking to the driver's side to chuck the plastic container inside before striding up the path to the front door of the house.

I march after him, Shaun following. 'Er, David, when I said I needed to talk to you, I really did mean face-to-face.'

'I'm working, Mr Bailey, in case you haven't noticed.' His voice echoes inside the hallway, reverberating off the bare walls and the concrete floor. He squats beside a huge roll of carpet wrapped in plastic and secured at various points with gaffer tape. I watch as he extracts a Stanley knife from a toolbox on the stairs and proceeds to slice through the tape.

'I'm working too. In case *you* hadn't noticed.'

He looks up from the floor, alerted by my forceful words. He sighs, slides the blade back inside the handle and stands, choosing to lean against the wall to hear my news.

'Are you alone in the house?'

He shakes his head. 'Two blokes upstairs painting the bedrooms. They've got the radio on so they won't hear. So, come on, get on with it. If this is about Jake, there's bugger all I can tell you.'

'I believe I've found Amanda,' I tell him.

His eyes widen and his folded arms loosen. He lifts himself off the wall. 'What?' he breathes. 'Are you sure? Where is she?' A frown creases across his forehead as the next most naturally occurring question presents itself. 'Is she alive?' He looks from me to Shaun, but neither of us immediately reply. Does he already know the answer? Is he faking his surprise? Is he

435

worried that his fail-safe deposition site wasn't good enough? Is he now wishing he and his accomplice had driven further afield?

'I'm afraid she's dead, David,' I say and he seems to lose some of his height. His knees bend slightly and he rests his shoulder back on the wall, his chin drops to his chest and his eyes stare at the floor.

'I knew she was…but part of me still hoped she was alive.' He brings a curled-up finger to his left eye, wipes the area underneath and when he looks up, he's tearful. 'Where did you… how did you find her? She wasn't in Lexington or the neighbouring area, was she? She caught a train out of the city, didn't she? Where did she go? North or south?'

I frown. What's he on about? Oh. He thinks that a mortuary has come forwarded with details of an unknown female they might have had for the last 8 years in one of their fridges.

'She's in Lexington, David. I suspect she was abducted from the train station before she got anywhere near the safety of her car; it's the only logical explanation. And from there she was transported, possibly knocked out but certainly not yet dead, to a secure location where she eventually died and her body kept hidden until roughly an hour ago.'

'You mean she was murdered?' David shakes his head. 'Who the hell would do that?'

'Have a think, David. During my investigation I found five people who had it in for your wife…'

'But you exonerated them! Hepworth, Lawrence Hayden—'

I cut him off. 'But not Jake.'

David laughs. 'Jake! Come off it. Not this again. Jake was not capable—'

'Or you,' I say, stepping closer. 'Both of you repeatedly lied to me. Refusing to explain the inconsistencies in your alibi and then suddenly,' and I wave a hand through the air like a magician casting a spell over a top hat, 'you remember the workmen at your house that day. All courtesy of Jake. I gave him the heads-up and I bet, no sooner than I walked out of his front door, he was straight onto the phone to you.'

'Bollocks,' David states.

'What was it?' I ask. 'What was the straw that finally broke the camel's back? Did Amanda renege on her promise to give you money for your brewing company? Did she discover you'd cheated on her? Who was it with? Holly? Some barmaid? An ex?'

'No!' he yells. 'No. I never cheated on Amanda; I loved her.'

436

'Right,' I scoff. 'Course you did. Did you and Jake plan it from the start? Perhaps from the day you laid her flooring. "Oh, here's a sex-starved woman in her thirties with lots of money and no life. What she needs is a handsome young man to—"'

'No,' he yells again. 'Holly and me only got together last year. We've kept it quiet out of respect for Jean.'

'Very decent of you,' I say sarcastically.

'Fuck you,' David shouts. 'I did not kill my wife.'

'Then where the hell were you the day she disappeared? And explain this. *If* you can.'

Shaun hands me the first sheet of paper. A copy of the letter we read in the kitchen. I hold it out to David who snatches it with a shaky hand and reads it. He looks up, confused. 'It's a letter from Lexington hospital to Jake.'

'I can see that. What's the date of the appointment?'

His gaze moves down the printed sentences, searching for the date. I watch as the significance of it dawns on him. 'Jake never denied he had an appointment the day Amanda went missing, but it was in the morning.'

'So what?' David demands, shoving the paper back at me and crushing it against my hand. 'So he had a hospital appointment on that day. It means nothing. Who cares?'

'You're right,' I agree. 'Who cares about an appointment letter from all those years ago, and I wouldn't normally. It's only important when you consider where I found it. Do you want to know where I found it, David?'

Above my head, I hear heavy feet clomping about, the sound of men laughing while they work. David shrugs. We debated, in the car as I drove over here, whether it was wise and not cruel to show David pictures of his wife in her current state. If he's innocent, it's not justified, but if he's guilty, then he should rightly see what's he done to her. After some persuasion, Shaun came round to my thinking and now he hands me the first photo of Amanda, face-down so David can't get a quick glimpse. If I'm wrong, I'll worry about the consequences later.

'I found it tucked into the clothing of your wife's decomposing body.'

David's mouth parts; I hand the picture of Amanda in glorious technicolour to him. He looks down at the glossy photo in his hands, blinks, brings it closer to his face, sucks air in sharply. His shoulder slams back into the wall, his left knee buckles from the sudden drop. But he

437

doesn't release the picture. His eyes fill with tears and he mashes his lips together, emitting a small squeaking noise as if his throat has constricted and that's the only noise it will let him make.

'How can you…show me this…? Oh, my God. Amanda…are you sure it's…?'

From my left, Shaun hands him another picture. Her skeletal hand showing her wedding and engagement rings. David accepts it, runs a trembling finger over the rings. 'Oh, God,' he gasps. He looks up, tears stream down his unshaven face, and nods. 'It's her. I couldn't afford a big diamond; Amanda paid for it. Where is she? Where did you find her? You have to believe me. I didn't kill her.'

More footsteps moving quickly towards us; I look up the stairs. One of the workmen, an overweight guy wearing a blue body warmer splattered with paint, is descending quickly. 'Need more paint,' he explains to us. 'What's going on? You alright, Dave?' he asks, but David buries his face into the wall and nods unconvincingly.

'You blokes shouldn't be in here,' he tells us. 'It's a construction site.'

'We're leaving in a few minutes,' I assure him.

He slides his jaw across thoughtfully, concludes it's none of his business, grabs two paint pots from the cupboard under the stairs, and clomps back upstairs.

'David, I'll tell you where she is, if you tell me where you really were that day,' I say. 'I know Jake was involved in her death. This letter, *his* letter, was on her person. You can see it on the photo. Just poking out from her jacket. It's conclusive proof that she encountered him that day.'

David presses his palm across his mouth. He thinks about it. After a few moments, he places the photos on the floor at his feet and slides his dark blue fleece off. Underneath he's wearing a dark grey t-shirt with a faded motif on the front. He holds out his right arm, rotates his thumb inwards until it points downwards, and indicates an area of his tattooed skin on the outer side of his forearm. Shaun and I peer closer. His sleeve is a work of art. A skull, complete with suture lines; a pocket watch and gold chain; a dagger. 'There. The red heart. That's where I was,' he explains, tapping it.

The bright red heart is two inches high and in its centre in swirly writing are the words: *Amanda, all my love forever*.

I look up, confused. How does this explain his whereabouts?

438

David relaxes his arm. 'I always meant to get her name tattooed on my arm, but I couldn't afford a registered tattooer. I have a mate,' he explains. 'His place was forced to close down, but he still had the gear. That's where I was. Having this done. And she never fucking saw it.' David clamps a hand back over his mouth, tears filling his eyes again.

I wait patiently for him to get a grip.

'You see why I couldn't say where I was, not without dropping my mate in it, and I wasn't going to do that. After I phoned the police and reported Amanda missing, I rang Jake and told him the police would ask where I was. I didn't know what to tell them. I was in a right fucking panic. It was Jake's idea to say we were together. He told me he was at home. It made sense.'

'You could have told me this,' I say. He looks up. 'I was only interested in finding your wife, not in illegal tattoo parlours.' He closes his eyes, nods in agreement. I'm not sure I believe him. I'll need to speak to his mate to confirm his new alibi, see what time they finished.

'Where was Jake?'

'At home. I just told you.'

But there's no-one who can vouch for him.

'What about this?' Shaun says and removes another sheet of paper from the file. He shows it me. Of course. The rude phrase. The one circled on the back of Jake's letter. This implicates David.

I say his name and he looks up. 'Does this phrase mean anything to you?'

He stares at the words incredulously, grabs the paper, tearing the corner of the sheet in the process. 'Shit. Where did you get this?'

I tell him.

'I don't understand…what's it doing on the back of Jake's letter?' He reads aloud some for the words. 'I don't get it. This phrase, the one circled, it was a text I got the night before Amanda disappeared. I deleted it. I was terrified she'd see it…she had a habit of…even though she promised never to snoop…'

'Who sent it to you?' I ask.

'I don't know. It was from an unknown number…'

'The content suggests the sender knows you. And intimately.'

He shakes his head. 'I thought it was a joke, sent by a mate.'

'Jake?' I suggest.

He shrugs. 'I asked him, but he said no. He was adamant, got arsey about it.'

'He either sent it from someone else's phone or perhaps he had two mobiles. And in his line of work, that's likely. It's his handwriting, I take it, and it's on his hospital letter. Conclusive proof of your mystery sender, David.'

'But why?' he demands. 'For what possible—'

'Do you really need me to answer that, David? Do you actually understand the depth of the hatred he had for your wife? He hated her as much as he loved you. And he had previous for meddling in your relationships. I wonder though…' I rub my chin with my finger. '…if he had someone in mind when he sent this. Someone to pin it on. Most likely suspect was an ex-girlfriend.' Someone to rope into his dastardly plan. An accomplice. With both of them having the same goal: to get David back into their lives.

David shakes his head. 'My last ex, the one before Amanda, moved away, got married herself. I can't see any of them doing this.'

'Who calls you Davey?' I ask. 'It's an affectionate shortened version of your name. Someone in your lifetime must've called you that. Think.'

'I have thought,' he protests in despair. 'How do you expect me to know *now* who it was? For fuck's sake.'

I look at Shaun, gesture for him to hand me another sheet with the words on and I read it aloud, '"I want you inside me again, Davey".'

I let the words sink in. He must know.

'It's definitely someone you've had sex with, a relationship even,' Shaun concludes. 'Someone obsessed with you, someone who knew that once she sent this, there was a chance Amanda would see it. Who fits that criteria? It has to be someone who regularly encountered you. They pined for you from a distance, perhaps occasionally getting too close for comfort. A girl who would risk everything on this message.'

I think. Not Holly. He never knew her before Amanda. Perhaps he would've chosen her instead. There were lots of women in Jake's pictures. Even Jake's sister picked one out, but she didn't know her name.

'What about your arm?' Shaun suggests. 'You have a tattoo of your wife's name. Who else's name have you got?'

440

Excellent point. I look at David. 'Well? You must know. It's your skin.'

Reluctantly, David inspects his arm. 'There are a couple,' he admits. 'On the skull, these black lines. There's one. AW. That's my last ex, the one who moved away.' He points to it. It's like calligraphy; without a break in its movement, the line swirls into the letters, a bit like a curly phone cable. His finger traces the thin line. 'And here...' His finger stops moving and he looks up. There's something in his eyes. A realisation. My heart quickens.

'Who is it?' I demand.

'It was years ago,' he says in a hollow voice as if he can scarcely believe it. 'I was only 21, she was nineteen. We were in—'

'Did Jake know her?'

David nods. 'We knew each other from school...'

'Who is she?'

And when he delivers the name, I wonder why it didn't occur to me sooner. The clues start fitting into place.

Chapter 62

We leave David to his grief and begin the twenty minute journey back to Lexy. It is just typical when you're in a rush that external factors conspire against you. Not that our suspect is going anywhere; she won't know we're coming. The A5689, the quickest route, is snarled up due to a truck shedding its load, so I take the back roads like everyone else.

'Why does half the county feel the need to go out in their lunch hour?' I demand. 'Why can't they stay at their desks?'

'I suppose it's the only chance some people get to go to the—'

'It's a rhetorical question, Shaun,' I snap. 'It doesn't require an answer.'

Ahead I see a gap in the oncoming traffic and flick the indicator up, pulling out behind the learner driver in the sporty hatchback. I put my foot down hard and we sweep past one, two, three cars before a lorry appears. putting an end to my fun. I tuck sharply behind a white van whose driver is thankfully practising the 60 mph speed limit.

'Bloody hell, Will,' Shaun gasps, gripping the armrest as he swings about in the seat. 'What's the rush?'

There is no rush, of course. It's not as if our suspect is likely to be out, and if she is, then we'll wait for her return. She won't have gone far: the off-licence, her new dealer, her parents. The police won't be onto her. Not unless they pay David a visit. He might tell them where we're headed. Shit. I press the accelerator down, pushing the Mazda closer to 65. The back of the van looms closer. But while the iron is hot, I want to strike. I want to throw this evidence in her face, shove the photo of a decomposing Amanda right before her eyes, show her what she and Jake have done, force her to think of her actions. Jake, of course. His blood is on her hands. Frankly, I'm surprised she was sober enough to do it. But why now? Why murder him now? What was the threat?

'I keep thinking about what Jenny told me,' Shaun says, staring out of the window at the blurry scenery. 'You know when Amanda humiliated David and told him to stop coming to the shop because he was "embarrassing me with your constant pestering". Tamsin went after him. And there's only one reason why she would risk doing that.'

'She was in love with him,' I say, indicating left and taking the second exit off the island at speed. I feel the Mazda tyres grip the sweeping corner and smile. God, I love this car. My dad would be so pleased to see me drive it like it's meant to be driven. 'Both Holly and Jenny must've felt awful for David, but to go after him is a sure sign of showing your feelings. That was probably Tamsin's tipping point. It must've been shock enough when he walked back into her life. But married to her boss, several years his senior. That would have dredged up all those long-buried feelings.' I know what that's like, I think. It's surprising the speed at which they return and the strength of them. It's like they've never really gone away. Just loitering beneath the surface: under your skin, in your heart and your head, poised for the slightest or the strongest reminder and then, like a torpedo strike, they breach your surface, detonating your feelings explosively.

That's what Bron did to me when we walked back into each other's lives. What she's still doing to me. I can't erase her. I don't want to. I want her back. Like Tamsin wanted David back.

She had to act. Had to tell him that she was there for him.

'Witnessing Amanda treat her beloved David like shit would have been too much for Tamsin to bear. And don't forget, it was around the time of their marriage that Tamsin's attitude nosedived and she started to have issues at work. I should've realised, should've put two and two together.'

'Did she mention him when you first met her?' Shaun asks.

'No. I remember she was very down about men, warned me that women can break hearts, but men will stamp them into the ground. I thought she was on about her ex. After all, he had left her with a child to raise.' I think. There was something else. What was it? Something about hair colour...oh, yes! 'She said she liked blond men but they didn't like her. I paid it no attention at the time.'

The road signs indicate a drop in the speed limit to 30 mph; I ease my foot up off the accelerator and the Mazda naturally slows. I head for Tamsin's flat. The lunchtime traffic in the centre of town is just as busy as the main roads but I make it unscathed to the block of flats and park in the nearest space to the entrance. We cut across the grass towards the communal door. I jab my finger on the bell, let it ring out for several seconds. I drum my fingers on the glass, waiting for her distorted voice to come out of the speaker, but nothing. I press the button again, try the door but it's locked.

'Fuck's sake,' I mutter. 'Typical.' I reach for the button again but Shaun swats my hand away and chooses another button.

'Hello?' asks a female voice from the speaker.

Shaun leans towards the panel. 'Yes, hello, love,' he says, putting on a much older man's voice. Has he been practising his accents? 'I'm from DHL. I have a parcel for flat 27C but the tenant isn't answering. Can you sign for it?'

'Yeah, no problem.' A loud buzzing noise comes from the door and I pull on the handle.

'Nice one, Hock,' I compliment, leading the way up the stairs, two steps at a time. The communal areas are still in a shit state. The air smells strongly of stale cigarette smoke and fried food. I march down the corridor, Shaun hurrying after me, to Tamsin's front door. Now I rein in my frustration, take a deep breath before politely knock twice on the battered wood. No point in alerting her to a problem. We wait. Silence. I knock again, louder, three times. I tilt my ear to the wood. Shaun opens his mouth to speak, but I hold up a finger to quieten him and he closes his jaw.

Music, turned down low. I knock the door again.

Shuffling in the hallway, tired feet in socks or slippers, barely enough strength to lift them. She's probably pissed or stoned. What a great interrogation this is going to be.

'Who is it?' the voice says from inside.

'Miss Archer, it's William Bailey. Can I have two minutes of your time, please?'

A two-second delay before she says, 'Hang on.' The shuffling moves away from the door and my internal siren starts ringing, but she can't possibly know why we're here. David wouldn't have phoned her. After all, she killed the two people closest to him. Surely he hasn't reciprocated her feelings.

She's unlocking the door. We step back, pasting neutral expressions on our faces.

She opens the door. Her hair is wet and is dripping on her yellow vest top, a grubby grey zip-up hoodie hangs loosely around her shoulders, the sleeves pulled over her hands. She wears black jeggings, a rip across the left knee and on her feet are pink ballet shoes, worn and dirty.

'Afternoon Tamsin,' I say. 'Sorry to interrupt you—'

'Checking up on me, are you? Making sure I took that brat to my parents. Well, I have. You can come in and see for yourself, if you like. Come on,' and she pushes the door open until it bangs onto the wall behind. She strides back into the dark flat, muttering about her parents' concern for the "little shit".

I glance at Shaun. I didn't think it'd be this easy. But it confirms that David hasn't phoned her; she really has no knowledge of why we're here.

'They accused me of not looking after him,' she continues in her whiny tone. 'Well, they'll see for themselves what an awkward shit he is.' She stops in the middle of the living room, which is still in an untidy state. The curtains are partially closed, there's an empty cheap vodka bottle lying on the floor; a half-full one is propped up against a squished cushion on the settee. An overflowing ashtray on the table, an empty foil takeaway, its cardboard top dirty face-down on the carpet.

Tamsin twirls around, sweeping an outstretched arm around the room. She nearly loses her balance, but steadies herself before she topples over. 'See?' she announces. 'He's not here. Wanna check the other rooms too?'

'No, thanks.'

She eyes me suspiciously. 'What you here for? If you've got more questions, I'd best get a drink. Talking makes me thirsty. Excuse me,' and she pushes past Shaun, sending him into the wall.

She starts banging cupboard doors, slamming drawers shut, muttering incoherently. I look around the room, not really expecting to find a blood-stained hammer but, in her permanently pissed state, she might have left it out. Apart from the multi-coloured scribblings on the walls, there's no sign of Ethan. No toys, colouring-in pencils, clothes.

'So, what do you want?' She appears in the doorway, shoulder against the wall, mug in her hand. She sips from it. 'I'll warn you; I'm not my best. Got a horrible headache,' and she waves the fingers of her other hand at her temple. 'I might be having a stroke,' she laughs.

'I've been speaking to David Bywater.' I watch her closely for a reaction. His name severs her laughter and she nearly loses her hold on the mug.

She gives a little shake of the head. 'I haven't seen him for years. Barely knew him—'

'Drop the act, Tamsin. I know you two were in a relationship.' She doesn't respond. 'Your initials are tattooed on his arm. David did extremely well keeping your relationship hidden

445

for all these years. I suppose, after concealing it from Amanda, it came second nature to continue the charade beyond her disappearance. Admitting it afterwards would make him look very suspect. And I have to say, I had him pegged as number one suspect. It appears that David really did love Amanda as much as he claimed. I've witnessed his grief. Although deep down he knew she was dead, the news has floored him.'

She frowns. 'What news?'

'Oh, sorry,' I say insincerely. 'Perhaps I should have started with that. We've found Amanda. Today. She's where you left her.'

She swallows hard, gives another little shake of the head as if she doesn't know what I mean. But it would have taken two people to move an unconscious Amanda. There's no way Jake could have done it on his own, not with his limitations.

'Jake decided on the deposition site. The Jester was perfect. A listed closed down building, unlikely to ever be renovated into something else. But let's not underestimate your part; it was just as important. After all, there's no way Amanda would've got in a vehicle with Jake; he needed you and I bet you didn't take much persuading.'

Just a hint of a triumphant smirk at the corner of her mean mouth. Tamsin alters her position, resting one foot on the other, leaning her hip on the wall.

'We debated the yarn you spun her.' I indicate Shaun and he continues.

'It had to concern David,' Shaun tells her. 'An injury that took him to A and E, and he asked you and Jake to pick Amanda up. She was so concerned that, without another thought, she innocently got into the car. Jake's car.'

'And that's where she found it: Jake's hospital letter. Chucked on the backseat or in the footwell. She reads it. She can't believe it. The handwritten words on the back. She instantly recognises the phrase because it's a text that was sent to David's phone the night before. "I want you inside me, Davey". That was your name for him, wasn't it?' I ask.

Still Tamsin says nothing. But the smirk grows across her lips.

'David confirmed it was. When he saw it, he thought it was you too. But for Amanda it was evidence that Jake was meddling in their marriage, taking advantage of her insecurities by pouring fuel on it. So she took the letter, hid it in her jacket to show David later, but she never made it to the hospital. She was knocked out, bundled into the catering fridge and sealed

446

inside by a ratchet strap. She suffocated, but the note was preserved. You should have checked her clothing.'

I look at Shaun and, from his bag, he extracts a glossy photo. He holds up the picture of Amanda to Tamsin. I watch her face change, expect to see a look of disgust but it doesn't appear. Her eyes sparkle as if with love, her smirk spreads across her lips until they're crescent-shaped like a clown's painted-on grin.

'She looks good,' Tamsin says and leans towards the photo, kisses the air above it, waggles her fingers at it. 'Hi Amanda, Looking good there, girl.' Tamsin grins at me. 'The years have been good to her, haven't they? I thought by now she'd have been a pool of goo or a pile of bones. But you can actually see Amanda in that face. Well, you wouldn't; you never met her before. I don't regret it,' she suddenly admits. 'I got a lot of pleasure from sealing her in that fridge. Jake too. The bullying bitch got exactly what she deserved.'

'For taking David from you?'

Tamsin shakes her head. 'For not appreciating who she'd married. David was…is wonderful. The only man I've ever loved. It was painful enough that they'd got married, but every time he popped into the salon to say hello to her, she'd put him down, humiliating him in front of us, her customers. He was devastated. I wanted him to know I was there any time for him. I needed him to see what the bitch was like. She was cruel, heartless, cold. Jake would tell me everything she did to Davey. It broke my heart over and over.'

'But he stayed with her,' I point out. 'David was determined to make his marriage work.'

'You did the only thing you could do,' Shaun tells her. 'And that was to remove Amanda. With her gone, David would need his friends for support, paving the way for you and Jake to step back into his life.'

'Except the only one to benefit from Amanda's disappearance,' I point out, 'was Jake. Not you.'

'No, not you,' Shaun agrees. 'David didn't want you. His brewing business took off and Jake went along for the ride. He got everything, and he wasn't going to share it with you.'

'You carried on with your lifestyle, drinking and shagging your way around Lexington to numb the pain and forget. Must've been the time Brett stepped into your life. And after that joyless chapter ending in an unwanted child, there was no way in the world David would

447

want you. He really had forgotten about you. Jake kept you close, just to see if you had any designs on David. Very clever of him.'

'Jake certainly knew how to use you, Tamsin,' Shaun continues. 'From the moment you abducted Amanda. Once you sealed her unconscious body in the fridge, he had to leave. He had an alibi to provide for David who was in a flap. But it was risky. What if Amanda got out? The story she could tell. He asked you to remain on sentry duty, just until it went silent in the fridge.'

Tamsin is grinning. She's loving this recap of the events, strolling down memory lane, reminiscing about the part she played in Amanda's death.

'Yeah, you're right. I stayed behind. But I volunteered to. I wanted to hear her final moments as she shouted and kicked and banged for help on the inside of the fridge door. As the air grew less and less, the kicks got slower, the shouting became pitiful whimpers. Can you imagine what that must've been like for her? I did. I still do.'

My eyes widen with horror as I watch and listen to this young woman who should be out there, enjoying life, not getting her kicks from reliving her part in a wickedly cruel murder. I wonder if her relationship with David had lasted, would she still have ended up like this?

'An hour and a half it took her to shut the fuck up,' Tamsin continues, seeing the disgust on our faces. 'I was starving when Jake came back for me. He took me to KFC.'

'Did you kill Jake?' I ask.

Tamsin alters her position but remains against the wall. She finishes whatever she's drinking but doesn't put the cup down, hooks her fingers through the handle. 'Yeah. I do regret that a bit. Occasionally, we'd get together...' Her face brightens as if something has occurred to her. 'Like the last time he was here. You remember? He stormed off because I joked that he was gay. Well, we'd reminisce about that day.' A dark cloud comes over her face. 'Yeah, that day. That did it for me. Admitting that he was behind me and Davey's break-up. If he hadn't interfered back then, I would be with the man I love. We'd be married and *I'd* have let the two of them do their brewing. Amanda wouldn't have happened, Ethan wouldn't have been born. It wouldn't have been fucked up like it is,' she shouts, raising her hand holding the mug. 'He got what he deserved. And it was fucking easy peasy. I made an appointment to go round his house, whinging like I always do that I needed something. He was sat in the chair, going through his stash. He was already half pissed. I hit him over the head and started the fire. I was back home within an hour. Ethan never even knew I'd gone out.' She laughs.

I resist the urge to shake my head. How can she alternate between anger and laughter?

'Are the police coming?' she asks.

Shaun glances at me. She spots the look. 'Oh. They're not. That's a shame. It feels good to get things off my chest, but one thing I decided from the start, was that I was never going to prison.'

Now I spot the mistake.

Her insistence on fetching a drink was a ruse so she could pen us in and put her nearer to the door. Shaun is two metres away from her, I'm further and there's a coffee table in the way.

Suddenly, she flings her arm back and throws the mug at my head. It sails in an arc through the air and with a yelp, I duck, landing on the narrow floor space between the settee and the table. The mug smashes into the wall behind me, splattering triangular fragments of porcelain onto the cushions and my back.

'Jesus—' I shout, looking up to see her yank something out of the back of her waistband.

Fuck. The hammer. My eyes widen and a warning cry gets stuck in my throat.

She swipes at Shaun. The heavy tool bends her wrist back but the attack is well-aimed. Shaun jumps back, slamming into the wall behind and putting his forearm up to protect his head, but the heavy ball part strikes his arm and he cries out in agony, dropping to the floor and clutching his arm to his chest with his uninjured hand. Tamsin chucks the hammer onto the floor. It thuds noisily and she races down the hallway, throwing the door open. It bangs into the wall and I jump to my feet, go to Shaun.

'Go after her!' he yells and I'm torn with wanting to help him, this lad I feel so responsible for, and going after the crazy bitch. 'I'm alright,' he assures me unconvincingly, but the pain on his pale face tells me otherwise.

I make my decision and run from the flat. After all, how far can she get in stupid shoes and no means of transport?

Chapter 63

My feet pound the concrete floor as I race down the corridor, past red door after red door, towards the stairwell. Quickly I realise that I'm definitely wearing the wrong footwear for running on a hard surface. Why didn't I wear my running shoes? Shockwaves pulsate up my lower leg bones and through my kneecaps. My right ankle threatens to give way from the lack of support. I reach the top of the stairwell, pause to look over the bannister and listen. I hear the faint slap-slap of feet receding down the stairs. She's getting away and once outside she can go in any direction, catch a bus even and though she might not get out of the town, she may well have an exit strategy. Hide low for a while, harboured by a sympathetic friend. After all, she was sober enough to arm herself with two weapons.

I thunder down the first flight of stairs. But coming towards me up the second flight of stairs is an overweight woman in her mid-fifties, her arms weighed down with bulging shopping bags. She's puffing noisily with exertion and, rather helpfully, has adopted the centre of the stairs, leaving no room either side of her.

'Shit,' I hiss, grabbing the handrail before I collide with her, and coming to a standstill on the landing. Quickly I wonder if I can squeeze past. Tamsin obviously did. But adding to the obstacle are two giggling little kids, around three years old, each with teddy bears. The kids have put their soft toys on the handrails, pretending they're all climbing the smooth slope upwards.

I muttering under my breath and all three look up. The kids gawp at me. No one makes a move to get out of the way.

'I need to get past,' I say urgently. 'This is an emergency.'

'Hold your horses,' she warns. 'Everyone's in a rush. Mind my grandkids.'

Below us, the outside door clangs shut. Tamsin's outside. Shit. It spurs me on and I go for it, stepping down onto the second flight and dancing to my right around the woman, brushing past a carrier bag. I lay a hand on the nearest child's head, keeping them still, whilst I step down and to the left, placing my hand on the other child's head, keeping him from moving. And then my route is clear and I leap the last three steps, stumble as I land and fling open the door so hard, the glass rattles in the frame. I run out onto the path, screeching to a halt and scanning the area.

To my left three young women with pushchairs are grouped together, chatting loudly and laughing. To my right, a man with a baseball cap, a dog poo bag in one hand and a leash in the other attached to the collar of a grey Staffordshire bull terrier, is stood stock still looking down at his mobile. Where the hell is she? Then I hear it: a car horn and a shout coming from the road and I hurry out of the building's shadow to see Tamsin running recklessly across a busy road, right into the traffic with no regard for her safety or the drivers. I contemplate going after her on foot but she has a head start. I need to catch up. I pull the car key out of my pocket and jump into the Mazda, pulling away with a judder of the tyres. At the junction I turn onto the main road, cutting in front of a bus, and receive a rebuke.

Immediately, I indicate left onto a residential street, heading in the same direction as Tamsin. Two long lines of grey-brick terraced houses face each other across the road, sandwiching parked cars which are close to the kerb. I keep it in second gear and, like a shark hunting for prey, the Mazda cruises slowly up the middle of the road. I look left and right, peering between the cars for movement, anything, a quickly ducked head, pink shoes poking out, but there's nothing. I reach a T-junction, look both ways. Left will loop back to the main road; I opt for right, speed up but scan both sides of the street, my head turning quickly, my neck beginning to ache. More houses, tiny bricked gardens, wheelie bins parked outside front windows. No sign of her.

My temper starts to rise again. Why didn't I anticipate what she was going to do? Why didn't I insist she take a seat? If she'd thrown the mug or swung the hammer from the other side of the coffee table, I could have used my foot to push the low piece of furniture into her shin. I'm supposed to lead by example. How can I expect Shaun to do the right thing if I can't? Shit. Shaun. Has he phoned the police? Is his arm broken? Fuck. The pain on his face. The panic he must've felt when she swung that hammer. If she'd struck him anywhere else: his head, chest, abdomen; the damage she'd have done. And for what? Where does she think she can escape to? Her parents, back home when she thinks the dust has settled and the police are not searching for a hammer-wielding maniac? Perhaps she wants to see David one last time, confess her crimes. Maybe she's deluded enough to think he will understand and forgive her.

I slam my hand on the steering wheel in frustration. Where the fuck is she? And just what do I think I'm going to do if I catch up with her?

She can't hope to run forever

At the end of the residential road, I look both ways…on my left: car driving away, further up a couple crossing the road; and right…what's that up ahead…a slim figure disappearing behind a skip parked in the road, garden waste spilling out of it. I yank the wheel hard right and accelerate, searching for any sign of her, but there's nothing. It's like she's vanished into thin air. I wonder if she dived into the skip, buried herself under twigs and grass cuttings and is waiting for me to pass with held breath.

Suddenly I brake hard and the Mazda stops; the seatbelt pulls tight across my chest. An alleyway between two houses. A simple cut-through for pedestrians to save them going to the end of the long street. Perfect for her. But not for me. I engage first gear and race to the end of the road, turning right onto an identical street, then right again in time to see her step off the kerb onto the road. Upon hearing the sound of an approaching vehicle, Tamsin hesitates in the middle of the quiet road, turns and looks right at me.

Her expression is one of fury. Her eyes are dark under untidy knitted brows and her thin mouth is snarling. Perhaps she thought I'd stay with my injured partner, didn't anticipate me giving chase.

I stare back, put my foot down, but she's off leaping onto the path and darting down another passageway like a rat up a drainpipe.

But I remember this area. These alleyways are evenly spaced out along these long streets, allowing for people to easily access other routes. Heading in this direction will bring Tamsin to Bridge Road, the main road which leads from Lexington Medical Practice to a large roundabout. Either side of Bridge Road, beyond the wide grass verges, are yet more houses. A veritable warren of residential streets, as if I haven't had enough of them. Bridge Road itself used to be a 50 mph speed limit, but several years ago a child was knocked off his bike and the locals campaigned to have the limit lowered to 40. Unfortunately, despite the warning signs, and because it's a nice straight road with a grass verge on one side, the rail track beyond the fence, and a path on the other side, there are no junctions. This allows drivers to put their foot down without fear of another vehicle pulling out in front of them. All I need to do is follow Tamsin, see what her intention is, then call the police and let them chase her all over the town. That's their job. I'm beginning to question if remaining with Amanda wasn't the best option after all. I'm not the police; I can't arrest Tamsin and she won't go quietly.

At the end of the road, I turn left, swinging the back end of the Mazda across the central white line, and speed up. I lean forward, close to the steering wheel, push the car to 30 mph, 35 and onwards. The traffic has died down, people have returned to work; I push on, I can afford to. I must get her in my sights. It's my fault she legged it. My fault she swung a hammer at Shaun. I must put it right.

At the island, I turn left and join the traffic on Bridge Road. In front of me is a large dirty white van with a rear step bar.

Through the passenger window is the grass verge, fencing and beyond that are the houses; through the driver's window is the path running parallel to the road. Further ahead is the footbridge which traverses the road, although people frequently prefer to risk crossing the road. A couple are walking a dog on an extendable lead. The animal is several metres away, sniffing the grass.

I look left and right, hunched over the steering wheel in an urgent position. My lower back starts to ache. About a third of the way down the road, when I am nearing the point where the right-hand path rises to become the start of the footbridge, a figure appears beyond the bridge heading in my direction. A woman in a hurry wearing a grey hoodie and black leggings, her face flushed, her head turning left and right as she surveys the traffic.

It's her.

It's Tamsin.

Which way is she going to go? Is she going to choose the safety of the footbridge? She might if she doesn't think I've followed her. Or will she dart across the road when there's a break in the traffic?

I watch her; she grows in size the closer I get. Suddenly, her head is still, her eyes looking in my direction, her body stiffening. She's seen me. She recognises the car.

She walks closer to the kerb, almost like a diver on the platform overlooking the swimming pool. She looks left and right. She's going to go for it. Dart across and disappear into the warren of houses and I won't be able execute a u-turn on a busy road. I'll have to continue down this mile-long road and turn back on myself at the island.

Then she steps back, as if deciding on a run up to get more speed. There aren't really any breaks in traffic. The time is nearing two o'clock. People are returning to their places of work.

.

Suddenly I see what her intention is. Her last words before she legged it from the flat come back to me. "I wasn't going to prison."

And it's true what people say, these things happen slowly in stages; you can see what's going to unfold but you're powerless to react, partly because you can't respond quickly enough and you can't believe it.

The van in front slows. Perhaps the traffic ahead is slowing as we approach the island or maybe he's concerned as to what her intention is.

However, the driver coming the other way in an equally-sized black van, isn't looking at Tamsin; he's chatting to his passenger, a man similarly dressed in a hi-vis clothing. He will pay the price for his lack of observation. And heavily too. He should have recalled the reason for the reduced speed limit. Perhaps it was before his time.

Suddenly, like a sprinter leaving the blocks on the B of the bang, Tamsin launches herself forward into the path of the black van, her face set in a determined grimace. The vehicle slams into her side-on, bending her body unnaturally like a backwards C over its front end, crushing her legs and pelvis around the bumper. And then, like the gaping jaws of an ambush predator, Tamsin's entire body is sucked under the front end, disappearing from view. I watch in horror, powerless and silent, as the van's undercarriage mows over her, churning her body up, tumbling limb over limb, snapping her back and flattening her.

All the vehicles bearing witness suddenly brake. The black van coming to a standstill several metres away; it spews a twisted bloody Tamsin out of its rear end. The white 4X4 behind is too close to stop safely and swerves erratically in an effort to avoid hitting the unidentified object. The large vehicle comes to a standstill across the central line.

The white van ahead of me screeches to a halt, wearing several inches of rubber from its tyres. Too late I realise that there's no way I can stop safely, a collision is inevitable. Panicked, I stamp down hard on the brake pedal, my hands grip the steering wheel as if that will help, like I can pull myself out of the manoeuvre like a pilot pulling a plane out of a dive. The rear van doors fill the entire windscreen, and I brace myself as the front of the Mazda crashes into the rear step bar, smashing the headlights and crumpling the long bonnet. The impact brings me to an abrupt hard stop, flinging me forwards into the steering wheel and back into the seat where I bite my tongue and taste blood.

I breathe in but my ribs hurt. I unclench the wheel, relax my arms to expand the capacity in my chest and take some slow deep breaths, drawing air through my nose. Through the slightly wound-down window, I'm aware of activity. Voices. One in particular taking charge. A man in his late fifties, the driver of the white van, striding over to the 4X4 and a woman seated behind the wheel screaming in horror. He talks to her through the driver's window. He has a comforting firm voice, and he tells her to get out and not look, to sit on the grass verge.

With trembling fingers, I fumble for the handle and open the door. Fresh air rushes in and I breathe hard. Air fills my lungs, livening up my senses. My legs feel like jelly but I swing my feet out of the footwell and onto the road.

A hand touches my shoulder, a concerned voice asking if I'm alright, advising that I should stay seated until help arrives, that I'm in shock. I look up into the face of a young black woman with kind eyes, wearing a pale blue tunic under a black cardigan.

I say something, but my fingers tighten on top of the door and I pull myself to my feet, wobbling slightly. Christ, my ribs hurt. I look at the wrecked Mazda, the crumpled bonnet, broken glass on the road. Shit. My dad's car. I want to cry, but how insensitive would that be, crying over a car and not a dead woman?

The woman takes my elbow, accompanies me to the scene. To my right I hear retching and look. The driver of the black van is throwing up. People are scattered everywhere, half out of their cars, some have poked their heads out of the windows and are rubber-necking, others are walking down the middle of the road or the safety of the grass. Those closest are offering assistance; others are on their phones calling for help.

The driver of the white van sees me approach, concern spreads across his face.

'I wouldn't…it's not good…there's nothing we can do for her…' he tells me, both hands up.

'He insisted,' the woman with me explains.

I don't remember speaking, but there's so much noise and chaos, perhaps I didn't hear my voice.

'Please,' I beg more loudly and he acquiesces, stepping aside, revealing the horrific scene.

Tamsin lies on the ground like a thrown-down rag doll. Clothes shredded, legs plaited, blood and viscera smeared across the road like jam on a slice of bread. And I'm reminded of a phrase often used at scenes like this. "Injuries incompatible with life".

Chapter 64

'What do you know about a diary?' Detective Chief Inspector Debra Harper asks me.

Across the table, my hand drops from my forehead and I stare at her, the question making my heart leap with excitement. The diary. Of course. Shaun and I suspected Amanda had it with her at all times. She knew Hepworth would be after it. 'You found it with Amanda? In the fridge?'

The female Detective Constable sitting beside Debra haughtily reminds me that they have yet to identify the remains found in the fridge.

I throw DC Grafton a withering look. She's in her early-thirties with frizzy ginger hair scraped back, within an inch of its life, into a stubby ponytail at the back of her neck. I'm guessing that, without the scrunchie keeping it down, it'd spring up into a halo of curls. To her credit, she glares back at me with hard brown eyes.

'Amanda Davies *is* the lady in the fridge, and ten quid says her name is scribbled in the inside cover of the diary.' I lean across the table to Debra. 'Have you managed to read any of it?'

'It's not in a very good state,' she informs me. 'The liquid from the decomposition has spoiled the pages but some of the sentences are legible. We should be able to clean it up.'

'I hope so.' Not least because of the promise I made to David. 'It's her teenage diary and documents her relationship with an older man. He groomed her and subsequently went on to abuse her. I had him pegged as a suspect in her disappearance,' I tell Debra, reaching for the plastic cup. Then I remember it's empty and withdraw my hand. All of this talking has given me an insatiable thirst and I'm starving. My blood sugar must be virtually zero. I haven't eaten since this morning.

'The name Marty appears often,' Debra says.

I nod. 'Yes. Martyn Hepworth—'

'The PE teacher?' gasps the DC.

'Taught at your school, did he?'

'He coached my sister.' The DC's face pales.

'Read the diary. I mention him quite substantially in my notebooks too. A very hostile witness and predatory paedophile. There are more victims. I talked to one. Hepworth has a way of silencing them without threatening them.'

'Is that conversation documented in your—' Debra begins.

'Notebooks, yes,' I confirm.

'Quite a treasure trove of information you've gathered,' the DC remarks in a belittling tone I don't like.

'It's my job,' I remind her, anger pricking my skin. What is it with her hostility? 'I don't have the memory of a super computer. Have you listened to a word I've said for the last…' I pause to check the time on my watch. Half seven. '…three hours? I've told you everything I can remember from the moment Jean Davies walked into my office and asked me to find her daughter to the moment Tamsin Archer committed suicide.'

'We don't know it was suicide,' the DC interrupts pointlessly.

I slam a palm on the tabletop, knocking the plastic cup over. 'It was suicide, alright?' I say loudly. 'I watched her pick her moment and step out in front of the van. It wasn't an accident. Suppose you're going to charge the poor van driver?'

'We can't discuss an ongoing…'

I interrupt. 'Yeah, yeah. I know how it works. I was a copper for long enough. Well, what's one more life ruined? Must be a dozen or more people whose lives are never going to be the same again.'

'They have closure now, Mr Bailey,' Debra says patiently. 'Thanks to you and your investigation.'

I nod weakly, but Jean, David and Oliver have Amanda's death to deal with now.

'The knowing is always better than the not knowing.'

'I know,' I say, thinking of Claire.

'No matter how hard the truth is to bear.' Debra turns to her subordinate. 'Stacey, get Mr Bailey another cup of tea.'

'What?' she snaps, voice bordering on argumentative.

Debra jerks her head back and regards her DC with contempt. 'Or do you consider yourself above making tea?'

'No, ma'am, but…'

'I don't want any more tea,' I say. 'But I would like to make a phone call. I want to see how Shaun is.'

'No problem.' Debra pushes her chair back. 'You too, DC Grafton. Let Mr Bailey have a few minutes alone.' She opens the door, ushers the scolded junior out, saying, 'You can make me a tea instead.'

Just before the door closes, she smiles at me. Debra Harper is Yvette's "trusted police officer" - the one I requested. After been given the all-clear from the Paramedic at the scene, the police bought me here and sat me in the interview room. Twenty-five minutes later, the door opened and a woman in her early fifties strode in. She had the air of leadership and experience. Five foot ten in her black ankle boots, dark trousers and a striped shirt which reminded me of candy floss. Her blonde hair had golden highlights in it and her blue eyes behind wireless frames regarded me with intrigue and interest.

So far, I've been impressed with her style of questioning. I only wish I'd had a superior like her when I was a copper. She's easy to respect because she listens, doesn't ask stupid questions and is objective. She trusts her instincts and is prepared to give a disgraced copper who has redeemed himself a chance. Obviously Yvette has vouched for me, and Debra trusts her friend.

I remove my mobile from my coat which is wrapped around the back of the chair, dial Shaun's number. He answers quickly. And his voice, when he says, 'Hi Will,' is such a comfort. He doesn't wait for a reply as he cheerily tells me that he has a fractured bone in his forearm but the painkillers have numbed the agony.

'You're high,' I state.

'Only a bit. Where are you?'

He has no idea what transpired after I left him. There's too much to tell him over the phone, and would he remember it?

'I'm at the police station—'

'Have they arrested you?'

'What for, Shaun?' I snap but remember he's high; he's making a joke. I'm tired, my patience is hanging by a thread. I breathe deeply, tell myself "not much longer and I'll be out of here". 'I'm helping them with their enquiries. Or rather, they'll finish what I started. I shouldn't be too much longer; I'm starving.'

'You'll be having a drive-thru McDonald's for tea then,' he laughs.

'Hardly. The Mazda's off the road.'

'What? How come?'

But I don't have the energy to explain that Tamsin is dead, the Mazda is probably beyond repair, and I'm stranded miles from home, tired, hungry and seriously pissed off. Shit. I bet the police won't give me a lift. Mum would but that'll mean explaining about the Mazda and I can't face that. Oh well.

'Do you need a lift? I can ask a mate to pick you up, or maybe my dad—'

'No,' I reply sharply. 'Not your dad. Jesus, Shaun, once he hears how you broke your arm, he'll be snapping mine in revenge.'

Shaun laughs loudly, promises to get me a lift.

The door opens and Debra returns, thankfully on her own.

'Better go,' I say to Shaun. 'We'll catch up properly tomorrow.' I end the call, smile as she sits opposite.

Maybe I should have said yes to the tea. I could have cheekily asked for a couple of biscuits. But they'd have made me more hungry. When I do eventually get home, I'll be too tired to eat. I might just fall into bed fully dressed but, after seeing Tamsin's body churned up by the van, I have a feeling that sleep will evade me for hours.

It might be better to return to the office. It's nearer. I could grab some chips and eat them whilst getting the case paperwork in order. I'll have to sort them over the weekend. I'm probably too wired to sleep and there isn't anything else that can take my mind off things.

Debra rests an arm across the empty chair beside her.

'Thanks for listening to me,' I tell her gratefully. 'I know you must've looked into my background. You know what I did...'

She nods. 'I also know *why* you did it. That you doggedly looked into your friend's disappearance. I remember the trial. I wish I had staff that are as dedicated and determined as you. We'd have a better clear-up rate. Look, William, can I call you...'

'Will, please.'

'Will.' She smiles. 'Yvette assured me that I can trust you and that is good enough for me. At the moment,' she stresses. 'I will need to go through your investigation with a fine-toothed comb.'

'I understand.'

'It had better be in order.' She raises a finger in warning and I just bet she knows how to haul a subordinate over the coals.

I smile. 'It will be.'

Her grin matches mine. 'Now get out of here. I'll see you nine o'clock Monday morning. There's nothing more to be done until we autopsy our lady in the fridge.'

And to know more about that, I'll be contacting Isla.

*

To add to my general fed-up-ness, dark clouds are hanging low turning the sky an ominous inky purple. Great, I think. I look back at the well-lit door to the police station, wonder if I can cadge a lift home from a copper heading my way. The wind whips up around my ears and I pull the zip further up my neck and step out onto the pavement, where the coldness quickly finds the breaches in my clothing: up my sleeves, across my scarf-less neck, my thin socks and shoes which are useless for walking great distances in. I have a blister on the back of my right heel.

I walk to the kerb, looking both ways, searching for a clue as to which direction is the best to head in. There's a few people milling about: at the bus shelter further down the road, the late-night pharmacy. To my right, a car approaches, its headlights on full beam. I look away from the white glare, mutter, 'Idiot,' and step back. An orange indicator light comes on and the vehicle pulls over to the kerb. I pull my mobile out, see that the battery is low. I change my mind; I can't face my mum. I'd have to explain that I've written off my dad's car. I can't face it.

'Fuck's sake,' I mutter. A drop of rain hits the back of my neck and I look up at the sky. I start to smile. 'Yeah. Bring it on. Why not fucking snow?'

'Will!' a voice calls and I look around. There's a bloke outside the police station wearing a woolly hat and pacing an area by the hedge, mobile clamped to his ear. I turn to the car. The passenger window is down and a figure is leaning over to the opening, calling my name again. Who the hell is that? I step closer and recognise the vehicle. Snow-white paintwork like a polar bear's coat, black roof, low-slung and sexy bodywork.

Bronwyn's Mercedes.

How the hell did she know I was here? Oh. Shaun. Of course. Motormouth, high on morphine. Is this his attempt at playing Cupid? And yet, my heart is thumping at the thought of her, at the prospect that she has finished with Michael.

'Will! Over here,' she calls as I walk over.

I reach the kerb, stoop to see inside the car and bloody hell it looks inviting. Comforting vanilla-scented heat escapes from the window, offering to warm my cold face. The raindrops get heavier, striking me across my shoulders like drumsticks. I shiver, shove my fists deeper in my pockets and inch closer, trying to soak up the heat, but already feel it vaporise as soon as it hits the cold.

Bronwyn has one hand on the steering wheel and leans across the passenger seat to smile at me.

'Hi Will,' she says. Her tone is slightly formal, cautious as if expecting a cold response.

'Hello Bronwyn,' I reply. Her nervousness gives me a strange feeling of confidence. I always knew the next time we encountered each other, I would gladly talk to her.

'I didn't know Shaun had your number,' I continue. 'I should give his detective skills more credit.'

She smiles in agreement. 'He phoned a little while ago, told me to get straight over here. All he said was that you were stranded and needed a lift home. I wasn't doing much. Just settling down in front of the telly with a cup of tea.'

'It's very kind of you to forfeit an evening to come to my rescue. I assume you're offering to be a taxi service?'

'I am, yes. It won't cost you a penny either.' She smiles and her hand on the steering wheel loosens its grip. She's relaxing, realising that I'm pleased to see her.

'It is my lucky day then,' I agree.

Her smile draws me closer. Her unzipped coat, over a black jumper, a thin silver scarf loose around her neck. My heart is pounding for the millionth time today and it suddenly feels pointless to deny that I'll turn down an offer of a lift, should she make one, and trudge home on foot instead. I have questions for her. One in particular. One that's been at the forefront of my mind since I kicked her out of my office.

From the drinks' holder, she plucks out a small bottle of water and hands it to me. 'Thought you'd be thirsty. Get in the car, Will, before all the warmth disappears.'

461

The offer excites me. I try the door handle but it's locked. I tell her, trying to keep the amusement out of my voice. She searches for a switch she has probably never noticed before. She's getting flustered.

My arm reaches through the open window, pointing at a switch on the dash, when she notices the same one and our fingertips graze mid-air. Her hand retracts as if she's touched something sharp, but her eyes hold my gaze, almost daring me to make a sarcastic remark. She flicks the switch and the locks spring up. I open the door, sit down and buckle up.

I find the one to close the window, flick it and the glass slides up, sealing us both inside. Our elbows nearly touch, her hand rests on the gearstick, inches from mine.

I smile at her, my heart leaping inside my chest at being this close to her again. I won't lie to myself that I don't want her. And I wonder if Nisha has told her that I'll talk to her if she's dumped Michael. Suddenly, that condition sounds so childishly dramatic that it feels embarrassing to have said it. What if she hasn't finished with Michael? What if he's still on the scene having persuaded her that this time things will be different? What if he's fine with her being friends with me? Where does that leave me? Can we go back to being friends? Do I want to? Isn't it best that I make a clean break?

'Will,' she says, her voice snappy.

I blink at her. What did she say?

'Where am I taking you?' she asks.

I resist the urge to make a smart-arse quip. I can't make any more of those until I know what's going on, why exactly she is here.

I tell her my address since she's never been there before and give her directions from the traffic lights. She engages first gear and pulls away. It'll take fifteen minutes at most to get home. I don't have long to find out what's going on with her.

I uncap the bottle, swig the cold water, which makes my empty stomach protest. I need to get home, get some food. The thought of returning to the office and organising my casework depresses me. I need a break from Amanda Davies.

Oh, shit, I think, with a heavy sinking feeling in my chest. And tomorrow I've got my first shift at the pub. Ben's going to be thrilled with me when I tell him that Shaun won't be turning up for work.

Bronwyn reaches for the stereo, turns the volume up from mute. A track is playing on *Heart 70s*. It's slightly too loud, preventing us from talking comfortably. Maybe she doesn't want to talk about us. Or she wants music on the short journey because, without it, the atmosphere is too awkward. It's my cue to stay quiet. I certainly don't want to talk about why I was at the police station without a car.

I consume half the water and risk a quick glance at her as she indicates left and exits the island. She's in deep concentration, her hands tight on the steering wheel. I settle back in the seat, stare out of the passenger window at the dark sky, the raindrops running diagonally across the glass.

If she has finished with Michael, that doesn't mean she wants me. She might've realised she's happier without any men in her life, that we bring nothing but hassle.

She could just be doing Shaun a favour. He isn't an easy lad to turn down. I've witnessed him pour on the charm; it oozes like warm honey. I smile at the thought of him, delighting whoever plasters his arm, telling them how he got injured by fending off a hammer-wielding maniac. I bet Hock won't be thrilled. I should expect a visit from him tomorrow, demanding to know why I put his son in danger. Something to look forward to, I suppose.

Bronwyn's voice slices across my clouds of thought. I frown at her. The music has been turned down.

'Sorry, Bron. I was miles away. What did you say?'

'I asked if you were hungry, Will. I can make you something. I went food shopping earlier.'

I ask what's on the menu and she runs through the options. 'Tomato soup and crusty bread, cheese on toast, fish finger sandwich?'

A childhood favourite. The image of it makes my stomach growl. Accepting her offer will buy me more time. 'Third option sounds good. Thank you.'

She changes lanes on the island without any warning and as the Merc exits, she stamps on the accelerator, flinging us both back in our seats.

I grab the door handle, feel my bruised ribs bend.

Suddenly she's in a rush.

Why?

463

Chapter 65

Bronwyn marches into the kitchen, switches the oven on and noisily slides a baking tray onto the middle shelf. I look for somewhere to hang my damp coat, but she whisks it out of my hand, offering to put it in the bathroom to dry.

'Take a seat in the living room if you want. I'll bring the tea through in a minute.' But as enticing as a comfy sofa sounds, in another room I won't be able to ascertain her relationship status, so I put the kettle on even though tea is the last thing I want. I line up the mugs and look around for any signs of *him* such as a pair of dirty wine glasses, a cardboard sleeve from a food dish which serves two people, but the kitchen is pristine. Bronwyn having already cleaned up from her own meal.

There's little point in looking around the rooms I can justify entering so I check my phone messages. None. I thought Shaun might have texted, offered some witticism at what he's organised. My battery is clinging to life. Just enough juice to make one last call before it dies. I slide it back into my front pocket.

'I'll have fruit tea, please, Will,' Bronwyn says, breezing into the kitchen where she removes a box of blackberry and apple teabags from the cupboard. I add one to my cup too and pour on the hot water.

Whilst I stir the tea, Bronwyn busies herself around me, removing the fish fingers from the freezer, slicing the loaf of crusty white bread, rummaging through the salad drawer for lettuce and tomatoes. I lean on a work surface out of her way, watching her multitask and realise, under the harsh white kitchen light, her hair is different. It's a lighter shade of blonde. She looks good.

'Your hair looks nice,' I say daringly. 'Suits you.'

She blushes, touches a lock. 'Thank you. My hairdresser suggested it was time for a change. You've had a haircut. I like it.'

'It was taking too long to do in a morning. Got more important things to do than stand in front of a mirror for hours.'

She turns back to the iceberg lettuce, slicing a chunk into shreds before dumping it into a colander and running it under the tap.

I finish the tea, slide the cup towards the sink. The atmosphere starts to feel awkward. The conversation, which wasn't great anyway, grinds to a halt. I'm sure I'm getting in her way, though she's too polite to say anything. I keep moving from one side of the kitchen to the other as she fetches items she needs.

I should sit in the living room. I should have accepted the lift only, said "no" to food. I'm only going to know if I ask the question, but then it'll look like I care, and if she's still with him, I'm going to feel an even bigger fool. Why are adults so childish, or it just me?

My mind races. I need to get on with it. How long do fish fingers take to cook? Twenty minutes, ten to eat, fifteen minutes journey home. Less than an hour to find out...

'How's work?' I ask, the question suddenly springing into my head. 'Any news about your job?'

She looks up from the cutlery drawer, fish slice in her hand, nods regretfully. 'Yes. They made an announcement yesterday. As I predicted they are making staff cuts. I was one of the lucky ones,' she says, but her tone doesn't signify she thinks of herself as fortunate. 'They've offered me a similar role to what I'm doing now, but it means moving to London.'

A pang of despondency hits me in the stomach. Is this her goodbye? This will be one to remember. "Here's your fish finger sarnie, Will, and have a nice life. Ta-ra."

Does she want a fresh start away from this town and me?

'Wow. London,' I say, trying to sound enthusiastic. 'Might be fun if you like city life...'

'I don't,' she replies. 'One city is much like another. From my experience anyway. I've accepted their generous redundancy package instead. It gives me time to work out what I want. I could even retrain.' She smiles. 'And do something completely different.' She noisily pulls a plate from the stack in the cupboard and turns to me. 'I've been thinking about my future.'

I nod encouragingly. Please, I urge silently. Please tell me that you've—

'I finished with Michael.'

My heart rises, buoyed by her news. Halfway there, but that doesn't mean she wants to replace him.

'You can do so much better, Bron. And how did he take it?'

I want to say "painfully" but that won't help her if he begged himself into a sobbing pathetic wreck. It means he won't go quietly.

'Not well. I chose not to say something that might aggravate him since I didn't know how he was going to react so I didn't tell him what you'd discovered. I stuck to my original plan, which is also the truth. That we were not compatible. He didn't and couldn't make me happy. He found that rather insulting. Such is his arrogance. He made the same old tired promises of changing his behaviour, even declaring that he loved me and had booked a romantic hotel for my birthday.' Bronwyn opens the oven door and reaches in to flip the fish fingers over. The noise of the fan muffles her words and I lean closer to hear. 'They're nearly done. Do you want tomato or tartare sauce, Will?'

'Neither, thanks. Just a dash of vinegar. A romantic trip, you say?' I say, keeping my voice casual. 'Do you think he might have been planning to propose?'

'I will never know. And I don't care. I put the phone down and haven't heard a peep since.'

Would he give up that easily? Most people would. Only the real weirdos would make a nuisance of themselves. I think about suggesting, just to be on the safe side, that a trip out of town, maybe to her parents, mightn't be a bad idea. But I don't want to alarm her. She does live on her own. I look up from the tiled floor, where I've been staring thoughtfully for several moments, to find Bronwyn watching me.

Her expression is serious. 'We need to talk too, William.'

William, is it? There are only a few situations where she uses my full name. Bad news or a telling-off being two of them.

I swallow hard, my throat suddenly dry. Dread fills my chest. This is what I wanted, to talk, but now I'm not sure I want to hear what she has to say. Am I going to be tossed onto the same pile of broken-hearted men as my adversary? Failed relationship number four. The shame of it.

I brace myself. I did always say that, one way or the other, I'd have closure.

I clear my throat before speaking. 'Okay. Fire away.' I offer her a big smile, try to hold it on my face. I can take this, I'm telling her. However hurtful and crushing it is, I refuse to break down.

'It's about the other day,' she begins, her voice now confident, 'in your office. I wasn't at all accepting of your findings. You went to a lot of trouble to show me the truth about Michael and I handled it badly. I'm an idiot. The very last thing I wanted was to fall out with you again. I'm so sorry.'

'It's not what I wanted either. It wasn't helpful kicking you out of the office. I could see you were upset. Suppose I was frustrated. Anyway,' I smile again. 'I only want you to be happy,

Bron. Without him, on your own, with someone else. I would've done the same for any friend.'

She puts the bottle of vinegar down. 'Friend?' she queries, tilting her head. 'Is that all I am to you now?'

Her question is a lifeline. A length of rope just out of my reach. If I stretch my arm, flex my fingers, can I grasp the end, pull her closer?

Suddenly her shining green eyes are the brightest colour in the kitchen; I am utterly focused on them, on reaching her.

'No, Bron, you'll never be just my friend.'

She steps closer still, pulling my heart all the way to the front of my chest wall. Her slim wrist is in reach. My desire to touch her threatens to overwhelm me. I feel giddy, like my feet are not planted on the floor.

'You mean the world to me,' I admit. My heart pounds on my ribs, demanding to be let out. 'I have missed you so much.'

'I've missed you too.' She smiles, but I can bear the distance no longer. I reach for her hand and pull her into my arms, savouring the thrill she gives me from my head down to my toes. I feel myself melt into her, smell the familiar scent of her hair, her perfumed skin. I desperately want her. It's torturous.

'William,' she whispers.

I look into her beautiful face. Her eyes are troubled, her smile is fading.

'I need to tell you something.'

'I need to as well.'

Those three little words, which mean so much, are on the tip of my tongue. Now is the time to tell her how I feel.

I lean towards her, my mouth brushing her lips, but a sharp beeping noise makes us jump. Bronwyn looks at the oven. The timer is on zero. The food is ready. She pulls away from me, grabbing the tea towel and whipping the baking tray out of the oven. As she neatly places the fish fingers onto the bread, she tells me we must talk after I've eaten.

'What's it about? Thank you,' I say, taking the plate from her. 'The other day?'

'Kind of. I want to tell you why I—'

I interrupt. 'This looks great.' I take a bite of one half of the sandwich and the hot fish burns my mouth; it tastes heavenly and my empty stomach rumbles with gratefulness. 'Can I go in the living room? I promise I won't make a mess.'

'Go ahead.'

Minutes later, I slide the empty plate onto the coffee table and relax back into the sofa. I could eat that again. I hope she bought cake. A slice of rich chocolate cake or a sugary jam donut would top it off. God, I'm tired. My back and head sink into the deep cushions and I feel the pull of sleep. I close my eyes, remember that Bronwyn wants to tell me something. It can wait a few minutes. Just need to…

I wake with a start, blinking with tired eyes. I look around, slightly disorientated. How long have I been asleep? I tug my mobile out of my pocket where it painfully digs into my groin. Only five minutes. I stand, clamping a hand on my achy back, and take the empty plate into the kitchen, calling Bronwyn's name, but there's no answer. I find a clue as to where she might be. The kitchen bin is minus its bag. I smile. Doing her least favourite household task. Back in the hall, the front door is on the latch, the outside light is on. How long does it take to drop a bag into a bin? Maybe she's chatting to a neighbour. I pour myself a glass of water and hear something. Footsteps on the gravel outside. I pull the horizontal slats of the kitchen blind down but there's no-one there. I finish the water and wander back into the hall, looking at the door. Bronwyn knows how to talk. I need to get home, get to bed before I keel over.

I open the front door. Chilly night air floods inside, around my feet, across my face. I shiver, shove my hands deep into my pockets, step outside and stop.

Voices.

I turn my head and listen.

An angry man. Is that him? Is it Michael?

Quickly, I walk down the side of the building, feet crunching on the gravel. Bronwyn's back is pressed against the wheelie bin, her head turned away from Michael who stands in an aggressive stance, feet apart, fists clenched. Seems he doesn't understand the meaning of "no".

'Answer me,' he demands. 'I have a right to know. Is there someone else?'

'Go home, Michael,' she argues. 'I've told you—'

'Oi,' I shout angrily. 'What the fuck do you want?'

Michael whips around, his face twisted angrily. He looks a mess. Unshaven, coat buttons undone. His hair looks in need of a wash and trim but I suppose, when you've been dumped and your job is hanging by a thread, personal grooming slips down your list of priorities.

'I should've known you'd be here,' he sneers. 'Always on hand, aren't you? Driving a wedge between us, poisoning her against me. I fucking warned you to stay away from my girlfriend. This is all your fault.' He jabs a finger at me.

'Yeah, yeah, whatever you reckon.' I peer over his shoulder at Bronwyn. 'Are you ok?' She nods, steps away from the bin, giving Michael a wide berth.

Michael glares at her, smirking nastily. 'This is really nice. The three of us together one last time. I did think I wouldn't have this chance but it's a gift finding you here, Bailey. If you want to take this treacherous bitch on, good luck to you.' He jerks a thumb at Bronwyn and she stops walking and glares at him. 'She's a skilful liar. She'll smile at you all lovey-dovey, whisper sweet nothings in your ear, and you won't see her hand round your back twisting that knife. Tell me, Bronwyn, are you going to tell precious William what you've done, or can I have the honour?'

What's he on about? I look at her, but she's glaring hatefully at Michael and it makes my blood run cold.

There *is* something. Shaun had his suspicions that Michael had something on her, preventing her from finishing with him. He even thought it might have something to do with me, but I had no idea what.

'I'd hate for your blossoming relationship to hit rocks on the first day,' Michael continues in an annoying sing-song tone. 'But it's always best to get betrayals out in the open. Start anew.' Betrayals? What is he on about? What's she done? Is this what she wanted to talk to me about? 'Bron,' I say, pleading with her to tell me before he does. 'What is it? Tell me.'

She takes a deep breath and looks at me. Her eyes are teary and she's biting her lip. There is a battle inside her. A need to confess but to brace herself against my reaction.

'Will, I did something foolish.' She pauses for a few moments to gather her courage and, when she speaks, her voice is full of conviction. 'Back in January, when you and I were lured to a car park by Phil Hock. I stayed in the car whilst you spoke to him outside.'

I nod. I remember. It was the day I punched his lights out.

'It was hot inside the Mazda because the heating had been on so I opened the window. I heard you both talking. About your time in prison.'

As usual Hock made his typical threats.

'A few days later, you and I went out for a meal.'

I nod encouragingly. When she walked out after I'd offended her, called her a poor substitute for Claire. Not my proudest moment but I was angry, suffering with grief.

'We had words. I was really upset and I shouldn't have done it. I have regretted it ever since. For so long I have wanted to come clean.' She takes a few moments to compose herself and launches into delivering the punchline. 'That night Michael picked me up; he asked what was wrong and I needed to tell someone...so I told him about the conversation you had with Hock, about hitting him, about your time in prison...doing jobs for Hock...for money...I'm so sorry, Will.'

Shit. Shaun was right. I should give that lad more credit. This was back in January. Has she carried this guilt for three months? Why the fuck didn't she tell me?

'Why didn't you—'

But Michael interrupts. He's grinning smugly.

'I must admit I was very wary of telling her anything personal about myself after that.'

The irony of it.

Bronwyn continues, jerking a thumb at Michael. 'He's found a Prison Officer who knows you. They're prepared to corroborate what you did for Hock, make a statement to the police, which would put you and Eddie back in prison. Every time I tried to finish with him,' she hesitates and glares at Michael, 'he'd threaten to tell you what I did. I had no choice but to put off finishing with him until I could work out what to do. I was terrified of losing you.'

I put a hand up to my forehead. Michael *was* blackmailing her. My disgraced past has caught up with me once more. It has dirtied and ruined something that started so well, that made me so happy. Am I ever going to rid myself of my past? Is it destined to always be there, lurking on the periphery, a niggling reminder? And I have dragged Bronwyn into it. She has paid the price for something I did. It has given her weeks of misery.

I should have pressed the matter with her, asked her outright, reassured her that it was okay if there was something, it didn't matter. But she stayed with him, put up with his lies and manipulation to save me and my brother.

470

A sharp noise cuts through my thoughts. Michael is clapping. The noise is loud in the night air.

'Very commendable, Bronwyn. I couldn't have put it better myself.'

I stare at him but it's Bronwyn who reacts more quickly. She rushes towards him, thrusting a finger in his face. He retreats until his back collides with the bin and it threatens to topple over.

'Since this is a night of revelation, why don't you confess your own lies, Michael?' she shouts. 'Go on. Why don't you admit that you've been lying to me for months? Telling disgusting sick lies about your brother, that he's ill with some unknown disease, when the truth is anything but. Tell us why you're really not at work. That you're suspended for making an inappropriate comment. And please, please don't leave out the revenge porn incident. We'd all love to hear about that.'

'What the fuck…' Michael looks at me then back at her, his face twisted with humiliation.

'I knew you were talking bullshit so I put you under surveillance,' I admit. 'I have photos and witness statements to corroborate it. It's an awful lot of dirt. Enough to bury you.'

'Yes, Michael,' Bronwyn continues. 'How would your family feel if they knew about this? Proud, happy, or would they disown you? If you don't leave me alone, I will tell them. I know Jamie's address.'

And then something else occurs to me. Something he probably hasn't considered. Something far more threatening. Use his weapon against him. 'Tell me, Michael,' I say, 'have you really been asking questions about Phil Hock?'

His eyes narrow. He has.

'I'm not sure that's wise.' I slide my mobile from my pocket. 'Let me show you something.' Quickly I scrawl through the news stories on our local paper's website. I hold the screen up to Michael.

Reluctantly he peers at it and shrugs. 'So what? It's just a house fire.'

'One that covered up a brutal murder. The victim was a drug dealer rumoured to have caused Hock some minor grief.' I slide the mobile away. Now Michael looks worried. 'The police *might* talk to Hock, but it'll be pinned on some other poor sod. Someone who can't protest. Which is why I'm concerned, if you've been bandying Hock's name about town, that he will get wind of it. He might already know.'

'I'm not scared of him,' Michael protests pathetically.

I smile with pity, say nothing. I look at Bronwyn. It looks like she has a lot more she wants to say. Weeks of frustration and stress have taken their toll, but why waste any more energy on this snivelling idiot? Let Hock have the final say. I have no doubt word will get round to him eventually. I say her name.

'Shall we go in? It's chilly out here.'

She nods, glares threateningly at Michael who noisily protests.

'You can't forgive her,' he shouts. 'You said you never—'

'Michael,' I say, holding out a hand, silencing him. 'There's only one thing I would never forgive Bronwyn for.'

Out of the corner of my eye, Bronwyn watches me.

I smile. 'Getting back with you.'

'She lied to you. She's a—'

Bronwyn pulls away from me, turns to him and screams, 'You're a disgusting sick creep. Fuck off, Michael.' She stomps back into the flat.

I watch her, feeling pride in my chest, my longing for her returns with a vengeance. I grin at Michael. 'Isn't she great?' I close the door, lock it and find her in the kitchen removing a bottle of brandy from the cupboard. She pours a generous amount into a glass.

Guess she won't be driving me home. Not that I want to leave here tonight.

She takes a big slug of the amber liquid, winces and coughs. She thrusts the glass at me. I take it, sip a little. Brandy isn't my favourite.

She holds a trembling hand out. 'Look at me; I'm shaking. I hate confrontations. My God, but he's had that coming for a very long time.'

'Yes, he has,' I agree, passing back the brandy and watching her gulp down more. Her limbs ease up and she leans back against the work surface. Her face relaxes and her eyes soften. A few moments later though, she looks troubled.

'Will,' she begins hesitantly. 'Can I ask? The Prison Officer…is there a chance, even a small one, that he might get you and Eddie in trouble with the police—'

'No, Bronwyn, there isn't. There is no proof. I was never caught. I didn't get extra time on my sentence. I suspect there isn't even a Prison Officer and why would they stick their neck out now? And for Michael? He doesn't strike me as someone anyone would want to help.' I

472

stop, sigh. 'The truth is, as much as we detest each other, Hock looks after his interests. And that includes me and my brother.'

'It's over then?' I nod and she smiles. 'Good. Because I never want to mention Michael again. That's what I wanted to tell you. There's nothing else. No more secrets. Wasn't there something you wanted to say to me too?'

'Yeah, two things. Number one, I'm going into business with Nisha. The money I made from working for Hock will buy me a partnership. Finally it will be 'Bailey and King Investigation Agency" on the door.'

'That's great, Will. Congratulations. And the second thing…?'

I pull the glass from her hand and slide it onto the work surface. Her smile brightens expectantly. I wrap an arm around her waist, press her to me. 'That was the best fish finger sandwich I've ever eaten.'

She blinks with bewilderment. 'Really? Well, you're welcome. I aim to please.'

My smile widens. I gaze deep into her eyes and kiss her gently, feel her respond. Her arms tighten around me, squeezing my ribs; I barely notice the pain.

'One more thing, Bron…'

'What's that?' she whispers.

'I love you.'

She grins. 'That's more like it, Will. I love you too.'

Epilogue

Shaun Hock switches the vehicle courtesy light on and examines the picture of a llama his sister drew on the plaster cast of his left forearm. She took the time to colour it in too and, against the white of the plaster, it looks like a tattoo. He smiles fondly despite the ache in his broken bone. He glances at the clock on his mobile, aware he's counting down the minutes until he can have his next dose of painkillers. He turns the light off and settles back in the seat. The streetlights are on, but his dad insisted on parking in the darkness, calling the lack of light an advantage, necessary under the circumstances.

His mind wanders back to earlier in the day. The near-frozen fear he had of illegally entering an empty property, spotting the fridge out of alignment, opening the door, seeing the rotting figure inside, taking the photos, capturing the events for the police investigation. He wouldn't change a single thing about today. Apart from the fractured arm. He remembers Will telling him about the knife wounds he sustained himself back in January, how this job comes with occupational hazards. Tempers, violence, denials. These are people's personal lives they deal with. Their freedom. Of course people will react to accusations, truthful or not.

Shaun didn't anticipate being on the end of a hammer though, but it's a lesson learnt. Expect the unexpected. Take safety measures. Isn't this what Will has been drilling into him since his very first day? Personal safety is paramount. Have an exit strategy. Or even better learn how to defend yourself.

Oh well, he thinks. It could have been worse and what's six weeks in plaster? He knows he's still a help to the agency and that's the most important thing to him now.

That and dealing with Michael Nicholls.

But for that he needs his father's help. And typical for his dad, he wasn't brimming with excitement at the thought of helping out an old adversary, even one his beloved son thinks the world of. But Shaun is persuasive, a trait he's got from his father. He surprises himself how much he can wrap his dad around his little finger, far more than his siblings can. He suspects it's because he's in line for taking over when Hock retires but Shaun has no interest in that. Being a private investigator is where his heart lies.

He glances across to the empty driver's seat. His dad has popped to the nearby Spar for a bottle of water and an iced coffee. Shaun is getting twitchy. If Michael suddenly appears on the street, Shaun won't be able to stop him on his own. With such an obvious injury, Michael will brush Shaun off, and if he gets wind of Hock, he could disappear back under the rock he only deserves to live under.

Shaun was loath to ask his dad for his help, but he could see no other solution. His dad has the power to nip this in the bud. It's risky. But there's no reason why Will should find out about it. Shaun swore Bronwyn and his dad to secrecy.

When Bronwyn phoned Will's mobile the day Will scolded Shaun for answering it, Shaun memorised her number, adding it to his own contacts' list, in case he ever needed it. He owes Will such a lot. This job, giving him a purpose, a direction, a career to aim for. Working in the pub is all well and good, but it's not interesting. He wonders how Will and Bronwyn are getting on, if they grabbed this opportunity Shaun handed them and made up. He hopes so. He replays the phone call he made to Bronwyn straight after he and Will ended theirs.

She'd hesitated, told Shaun that there was little chance of Will accepting a lift from her. Shaun told her what he'd overheard the day Nisha visited - that Will was in love with her, that he was as miserable as hell without her. And more importantly, that Will would almost certainly talk to her.

What could he do to help?

His charm worked and Bronwyn told Shaun about her dilemma.

He promised to sort it. All she had to do was get to Lexington police station straightaway to meet Will when he left and leave the rest to him.

The driver's door opens and Hock heaves his huge figure into the seat, hanging onto the top of the door frame for assistance. He passes the water and a chocolate bar to Shaun.

'You need to eat something if you're on painkillers,' his dad explains. 'Lines the stomach.'

Shaun unwraps the bar, taking a bite off the top. Flakes of chocolate fall down his front and he brushes them away with his hand. He watches his dad hook a finger through the ring pull of the can of iced cappuccino. It opens with a hiss and Hock takes a huge gulp, smacking his lips. He stares through the windscreen at an approaching figure.

'This him, son?' Hock nods at the glass.

It's Michael. His hands are buried deep in his pockets, shoulders hunched over in defeat. Shaun smirks. He's been sent packing by Will and Bronwyn. Now all his dad has to do is frighten him into obedience.

'Yes, that's him.'

Hock finishes the coffee and slides the empty can into the drinks' holder. 'The things I do for you.' Before he opens the door, he turns to Shaun. 'You're going to owe me for this. Big time.'

'Yes, Dad,' Shaun says. 'Whatever it costs. Within reason.'

Hock shakes his head and opens the door straight into Michael's path.

'Michael Nicholls? Can I have a word?' His dad's voice is friendly, with just a hint of a threat.

'Who the fuck are you?' comes the aggressive reply.

'Why don't you take a seat inside the vehicle? It's warm.'

'How about I don't?'

'I wasn't asking. Get in.'

Shaun turns in his seat to watch his dad manhandle a pitifully complaining Michael into the backseat, followed by Hock who forms a barricade across the exit. The door slams shut.

'This is nice,' Hock says, with a smile. 'Cosy. I like cosy chats. Just so you know, Michael, that door,' and his finger points at the other rear door, 'is locked too. Child locks. I got kids, you see. Got to keep them safe. This is my eldest son.' He gestures to Shaun who can't help but give Michael a little wave.

'Who are you?' Michael demands. 'What the fuck do you want?'

Hock smiles patiently. 'Several little chirpy birds have told me that you've been asking questions about me. Lots of questions about my involvement with the Bailey brothers, about which pies my fingers are in.' Hock lays a heavy arm along the top of the back seat, leans close to Michael. Shaun is amused to see Michael back away. Is it dawning on him whose car he's sat in, who he's talking to?

'You look confused, Michael. Oh, I see. You don't know who I am? Tell him who I am, son.'

Shaun smiles at Michael. When he asked his dad to interfere, he made him promise to let Shaun have a couple of lines, like an extra on a film set. He's been looking forward to this.

'This is Phillip Hock,' Shaun informs Michael.

Instantly Michael's eyes widen and he backs off towards the other door, his hand blatantly fumbling for the door handle.

'Ask me what you like,' Hock says welcomingly, holding his hands out as if to gather Michael up. 'And I'll answer as honestly as I can. And then, when we're done, you can

476

answer my questions.' He leans closer still, shoving his stubbled chin right up to Michael's paling face. 'All of them.'

Acknowledgements

This book is dedicated to my mum - Jennifer. Thank you for all the support and encouragement you've given all my life. It means such a lot to me.

I want to thank the following people for the huge amount of help I've had turning this novel into a Kindle book: Maria and Sarah for your methodical proofreading; Dr Liz Barlow for her expertise on burnt bodies; Mark Westbrook for the fantastic book cover; Tim for his photography skills and technical support; Lauren for her character names.

And finally to all the readers who have been extremely supportive and patient in their long wait for book four - this is also for you!

Other books in the William Bailey series: In Their Absence, The Wrongful Rights and A Bitter Resentment.

Disclaimer

This is a work of fiction. Names, characters, businesses, places, events and incidents are either the products of the author's imagination or used in a fictitious manner. Any resemblance to actual persons, living or dead, or actual events is purely coincidental.

Printed in Great Britain
by Amazon

71932772R10271